Magic
A Sociological Study

MAGIC

A Sociological Study

By

HUTTON WEBSTER

OCTAGON BOOKS

A division of Farrar, Straus and Giroux

New York   1973

Reprinted 1973
by special arrangement with Stanford University Press

OCTAGON BOOKS
A DIVISION OF FARRAR, STRAUS & GIROUX, INC.
19 Union Square West
New York, N. Y. 10003

Library of Congress Cataloging in Publication Data

Webster, Hutton, 1875-1955.
   Magic: a sociological study.

   Reprint of the ed. published by Stanford University Press, Stanford, Calif.

   Includes bibliographical references.
   1. Magic. I. Title.
BF1589.W4   1973   133.4   73-4250
ISBN 0-374-98318-6

Printed in USA by
Thomson-Shore,Inc.
Dexter, Michigan

TO

EDWARD ALSWORTH ROSS
INSPIRING TEACHER, ABIDING FRIEND

"In what depends on the known or the regular course of nature . . . . the mind trusts to itself; but in strange and uncommon situations it is the dupe of its own perplexity and, instead of relying on its prudence or courage, has recourse to divination, and a variety of observances, that, for being irrational, are always the more revered. Superstition, being founded in doubts and anxiety, is fostered by ignorance and mystery."—ADAM FERGUSON, *An Essay on the History of Human Society* (5th ed., 1782).

"Human power failing, superhuman power is called in; the mysterious and the invisible are believed to be present; and there grow up among the people those feelings of awe, and of helplessness, on which all superstition is based, and without which no superstition can exist."— HENRY THOMAS BUCKLE, *A History of Civilization in England* (1857–61).

PREFACE

MAGIC and taboo rank among the most important of those erroneous beliefs and futile practices which engage the interest of the philosophic student of mankind. The positive attitude of magic contrasts with the negative attitude of taboo. It is an act of magic when a Tongan chief, filled with *mana,* cures an inferior by touching the patient with his foot; it is a prescription of taboo when a Maori chief is forbidden to scratch his most sacred head, lest its sanctity be impaired or dissipated by being communicated to his less sacred fingers. It is an act of magic for a Samoan commoner to protect his plantation by a no-trespass sign showing this to be charged with *mana,* whereas the prohibition of trespass is a taboo whose sanction, or "sting in the tail," is the fear of a would-be thief that he will be blasted by the deadly potency inherent in the sign. Both magic and taboo thus rest fundamentally on the conception of impersonal occult power. Its beneficial influence may be utilized if proper precautions are taken by the operator; its injurious influence must be avoided by measures of isolation or insulation.

The significance of this conception was first set forth by John H. King in a two-volume work, *The Supernatural: Its Origin, Nature, and Evolution* (London and New York, 1892). His book, though well written, acutely reasoned, and supported by considerable evidence, seems to have made little or no impression on contemporary thought. In truth, the climate of opinion at the time was not favorable to its reception. The animistic (soul and ghost) theories, propounded by E. B. Tylor, Herbert Spencer, and their successors, then commanded the assent of most students of religious origins, while the phenomena of magic and taboo had only begun to receive attention at the hands of J. G. Frazer, himself an adherent of the animistic hypothesis. We search the writings of these students in vain for any realization of the part that has been played by "supernal" power—as King called it— in the formulation of magical beliefs and practices. The mystic "efficacy" of spells, curses, and blessings; the "luck" of charms and ritual hocus-pocus; and the "virtue" resident in the magician himself, his materials, and his instruments all continued to be regarded, never as impersonal qualities or properties, but always as the mode of activity of personal spiritual beings.

In a paper on "Pre-animistic Religion," read before the meeting of the British Association for the Advancement of Science in 1899 and published the following year in *Folk-Lore,* R. R. Marett of Oxford challenged the sufficiency of the current animistic theories and advanced, quite in ignorance of King's book, some of its leading arguments. In 1904 Marett published a second paper in *Folk-Lore* entitled "From Spell to Prayer," further elaborating his views. Independently of both King and Marett, two sociologists in France, Henri Hubert and Marcel Mauss, issued in 1904 their important essay, "Esquisse d'une théorie générale de la magie," in the seventh volume of the *Année Sociologique,* and made the conception of occult power in its impersonal aspect the basis of their treatment of magic. In Germany K. T. Preuss adopted Marett's views and elaborated them in a series of articles, "Der Ursprung der Religion und Kunst," appearing in *Globus* in 1904–1905. Once the academic ice had been broken, further contributions to the subject were soon made by E. S. Hartland in England, Nathan Söderblom in Sweden, A. O. Lovejoy in the United States, and by other writers. And the French anthropologist, Arnold van Gennep, suggested that the impersonalist theory of magic and taboo, as contrasted with the personalist theory of animism, might well be described as "dynamism."

King, followed by Marett, Hubert, and Mauss, and other writers, adopted the word *mana,* found in the Melanesian languages, to designate occult or "supernal" power regarded as impersonal. The word and its significance had been brought to the attention of European students by R. H. Codrington, long a missionary in Melanesia. But Codrington's own researches, supplemented by those of later investigators, show clearly that in this part of the Pacific area *mana* much more often has a personal aspect, originating with ghosts and spirits and from them acquired by men. What is true of the Melanesian conception holds true, also, of the conception in some other regions. It is now evident that by *mana* we must understand occult power in general, this being sometimes denotive of an impersonal quality or property and sometimes ascribed to a definite personality, a spiritual being. Consequently the distinction between magic and animism remains vague and ill-defined in the lower culture. It becomes sharply marked only with the growing personalization and humanization of spirits and gods. Furthermore, neither King nor those who came after him seem to have been justified in postulating the logical or the chronological priority of the impersonal aspect of occult power over its personal aspect. The evidence at our disposal warrants no conclusion that magic preceded animism or that animism preceded magic in development. For aught we know they arose and flourished together in "the dark backward and abysm of time."

This book embraces the whole subject of magic, but only as found among so-called preliterate peoples. To trace its history and enormous influence in the civilizations of antiquity and then onward through the medieval period to the civilizations of the modern age would be a task calling for the co-operation of a galaxy of scholars. My humbler task has been to set forth the chief principles of magic, and these are as well exemplified in rude communities as in those of higher type. Indeed, there is little or nothing in the magic of old Egypt, Babylonia, India, and China, of the Christian West and the Moslem East, which cannot be duplicated in savage Australia, Melanesia, Africa, and America. Magic is as thoroughly primitive as it is cosmopolitan.

Divination cannot be excluded from the content of magic, for the diviner works by the occult power belonging to himself or to his procedures and instruments. Without it he would work in vain. However, the various branches of divination are not treated here systematically, though omens, dreams, revelations in the ecstatic state, and prophetic inspiration receive due attention. As for the abstract relations between magic and religion, a subject on which much ink has been spilled, these are not discussed at all. They are not discussed because religion is a term defined at pleasure, whereas magic and animism are terms with an accepted signification. To say this is not to deny the obvious fact that every religious system, whether of low peoples or of high, is saturated with magic as well as with animism. The magic is always there, officially sanctioned or officially condemned.

The reader of this book will learn, it is hoped, that much which has been described as magic does not properly deserve that designation. Magical beliefs and practices are extensive enough, but there are many "superstitions" which lie outside it and remain unconnected with it. Such expressions as medicine man, shaman, spell, charm, and sorcery are also given a more exact delimitation than they have usually received, even in the writings of professional students. In social science as in natural science we must define as best we can and then keep to our definitions.

While I have written directly from the primary sources, I

would not disguise my indebtedness to those authorities who have preceded me in the study of magic. Some have been already mentioned, but there are others : A. E. Crawley, F. B. Jevons, Carveth Read, Edward Westermarck, Lucien Lévy-Bruhl, F. R. Lehmann, Wilhelm Schmidt, Gunnar Landtman, Rafael Karsten, Bronislaw Malinowski, J. H. Leuba, W. G. Sumner, A. G. Keller—to mention only a few. Even when I have disagreed with them I have learned from them.

HUTTON WEBSTER

PALO ALTO, CALIFORNIA
February 1948

CONTENTS

CHAPTER VII

PROFESSIONAL MAGICIANS 180

CHAPTER VIII

THE MAKING OF MAGICIANS 202

CHAPTER IX

THE POWERS OF MAGICIANS 237

CHAPTER X

THE FUNCTIONS OF MAGICIANS 279

CHAPTER XI

PUBLIC MAGIC 306

CHAPTER XII

CHAPTER XIII

CHAPTER XIV

CHAPTER XV

SAFEGUARDS AGAINST SORCERY 433

CHAPTER XVI

THE BELIEF IN MAGIC 474

CHAPTER XVII

THE ROLE OF MAGIC 497

Chapter I

OCCULT POWER

The contrast between what was ordinary and what was extraordinary in man's world must from the start have impressed his nascent mentality. Some objects, both animate and inanimate, were understandable. He recognized them by what they did to him; he knew them familiarly and made use of them. Human beings, animals, and "lifeless" things might also act in ways abnormal and inexplicable, thus manifesting a power not apparent to the senses nor yet legitimately inferable from sense impressions—an occult power. Whatever aroused man's attention, excited his interest, and did not fit into the routine of his thought, whatever filled him with wonder and provoked emotional reactions varying from simple fear and avoidance to awe and reverence, would reveal a potency mysterious in nature, marvelous in operation, and effective both to blast and to bless. With reference to the Tlingit Indians of southern Alaska a competent authority points out that their conception of "supernatural" energy must be carefully differentiated from that of natural energy. "It is true that the former is supposed to bring about results similar to the latter, but in the mind of the Tlingit the conceived difference between these two is as great as with us. A rock rolling down hill or an animal running is by no means a manifestation of supernatural energy, although if something peculiar be associated with these actions, something outside of the Indian's usual experience of such phenomena, they may be thought of as such. Although the Indian has, in this latter case, reasoned to an erroneous cause, the difference is none the less great."[1] This statement might well be generalized and made of universal application if in it we substitute for the term "supernatural" the term "occult," to designate whatever lies outside the range of plain understanding. The idea of the supernatural did not arise until man had envisaged a normal course of nature, broken, if at all, only by miraculous happenings. But such an idea was long foreign to the human mind, for which

1

no boundary existed between what could occur and what could not occur, between the possible and the impossible.

Many primitive peoples have isolated in thought the occult power that produces effects beyond man's ordinary capacity or experience and have indicated it by a definite name. Some primitive peoples, distinguishing between its good and bad aspects, employ for the one or the other a special designation.

Comparative study of the terms for occult power began with the word *mana,* as first discussed by R. H. Codrington in his classical work on the Melanesians. "The Melanesian mind is entirely possessed by the belief in a supernatural power or influence, called almost universally *mana.* This is what works to effect everything which is beyond the ordinary power of man, outside the common processes of nature; it is present in the atmosphere of life, attaches itself to persons and to things, and is manifested by results which can only be ascribed to its operation. When one has got it he can use it and direct it, but its force may break forth at some new point; the presence of it is obtained by proof. . . . . But this power, though itself impersonal, is always connected with some person who directs it; all spirits have it, ghosts generally, some men. If a stone is found to have a supernatural power, it is because a spirit has associated itself with it; a dead man's bone has with it *mana,* because the ghost is with the bone; a man may have so close a connection with a spirit or ghost that he has *mana* in himself also, and can so direct it as to effect what he desires; a charm is powerful because the name of a spirit or ghost expressed in the form of words brings into it the power which the ghost or spirit exercises through it." Elsewhere our authority states that no man has the *mana* power of his own. "All that he does is done by the aid of personal beings, ghosts, or spirits; he cannot be said, as a spirit can, to be *mana* himself, using the word to express a quality."[2]

This account of *mana,* as being "itself impersonal" and yet as ultimately derived from ghosts or spirits, seems to reflect the vagueness and fluidity of the conception in Melanesia as in other parts of the aboriginal world. Investigators since Codrington have stressed the spiritualistic character of *mana* in most of the area, except, perhaps, in the Banks Islands and the Torres Islands.[3]

It is an interesting and significant fact that the Australian aborigines, who in material culture rank among the lowest of mankind, not only recognize the existence of occult power but in some cases have a name for it. According to an early account of the western tribes (those near Perth), a magician possesses *boylya,* which he extrudes from his body and passes into the body of a person to be made ill. Another magician effects a cure by drawing out the *boylya* from the patient in the form of pieces of quartz. The natives keep these as "great curiosities."[4] According to another early account of the Perth aborigines the *boglia,* or magician, has in his stomach a quartz crystal (also called *boglia*) which is the embodiment of all his "extraordinary and occult power." After his death it passes into the stomach of his son. The magician can hurl a fragment of it invisibly at an enemy and injure or kill him even at a great distance. The natives believe that all deaths are thus caused by evil-minded magicians.[5]

The Wonkonguru of the Lake Eyre district describe by the word *kootchi* anything "uncanny," such as an unusual stone, an abnormal vegetable growth, or some deformity exhibited by a child at birth.[6] Among the southeastern tribes the malignant or destructive aspect of occult power receives a special name, such as the *mung* of the Wurunjerri (Victoria), the *gubburra* of the Yuin (New South Wales), and the *muparn* of the Yerkla-mining (South Australia).[7]

In the Kabi tribe of Queensland *manngur* as an adjective means "charmed" and *manngurugur* (the superlative form) means "life possessing," "life giving." These terms are applied to the tribal medicine man, the former to a doctor who cures or kills by means of the magical crystals inside him and the latter to one of higher degree who, in addition to crystals, has a magical rope for use in healing. Another word applied to a doctor is *muru muru,* "full of life."[8] Evidently *manngur* or *muru muru* expresses the "vitality" which fills the doctor and whereby he performs his feats.

The word *kunta,* as used by Queensland tribes of Cape York Peninsula, refers to "a force residing in all things sacred or dangerous to the profane." An incestuous marriage is *kunta;* the eating of human flesh is *kunta;* and *kunta* are the sacred stones associated with certain ancestral beings that are reverenced as culture heroes. In relation to objects of the hero cult the word is definitely personal; in other applications it is impersonal. The natives do not distinguish, however, the two senses.[9]

The Arunta term *arungquiltha* is "always associated at bottom with the possession of supernatural evil power." The term is applied indiscriminately to the evil influence or to the object in which it is resident, either temporarily or permanently. It is "sometimes regarded as personal and at other times as imper-

sonal."[10] A person suffering from a disease to which young people
are especially susceptible conveys *arungquiltha* to women, from
whom it is passed on to men having unlawful intercourse with
them. Any pointing bone or stick over which the proper spells
have been recited ("sung") is endowed with it. Certain stones
are charged with it. Spears which touch the stones carry it away
on their points and when thrown in the direction of an enemy
will produce an eruption of boils. A tree which marks the spot
where a blind man died contains this evil power; should the tree
be cut down all the men of the locality would become blind. If
anyone wishes to produce blindness in an enemy, he need only go
alone to the tree, rub it, and mutter his desire and an exhortation
to the *arungquiltha* to go forth and afflict the object of his hate.
The Magellanic clouds contain *arungquiltha*. Sometimes they
come down to earth and choke men and women when asleep.
Mushrooms and toadstools, which are believed to be meteorites,
also contain it; hence the natives, who are almost omnivorous,
never eat them. An eclipse of the sun is attributed to the presence
of *arungquiltha* in that luminary.[11] The *ittha* of the Kaitish corresponds to *arungquiltha,* as signifying evil power or an object
endowed with this power. Spencer and Gillen relate that after
much urging they got an old Kaitish man to show them how
pointing sticks were used in nefarious magic. When he had completed his demonstration his excitement, aided probably by a rush
of blood to the head, made him feel dizzy. He declared that the
ittha had affected him and that he felt, as he looked, very ill. He
was reassured when our authors explained to him that in their
medicine chest they had a plentiful supply of powerful magic that
would effectually counteract that in the pointing stick. On this
occasion there was no one into whom the old man wanted to project the evil influence in the instrument, so he naturally concluded
that it had entered himself.[12]

The native tribes of Central Australia have no special name for
good power, in contrast to bad, but the conception is embodied
in the Arunta word *churinga,* meaning "something sacred or
secret" and most frequently referring to the sacred stones and
sticks which are the equivalent of the bull-roarers of other tribes.
The term describes both an object and the quality possessed by
it. Thus it finds use "either as a substantive, when it implies a
sacred emblem, or as a qualifying term, when it implies sacred
or secret."[13]

The Murngin of the Northern Territory of Australia, have a

term *maraim*, which signifies, as nearly as it can be translated, sacred or taboo. It is used to describe anything tabooed to women and uninitiated boys, including totemic emblems, ceremonial grounds, certain names known only to the older men, and certain artistic designs. All things that are *maraim* are endowed with an "extra-mundane quality" called *dal*. The literal meaning of *dal* is "hard," "strong," but the word has reference to strength only in the sense of "ritually 'powerful'." Such things are hard or strong because "they have *mana* and possess spiritual power."[14]

In the western islands of Torres Straits the name for a magical formula is *unewen* (*wenewen*). This term, in its wider signification, seems to be "the equivalent of the *mana* of Oceania." It is employed to render "spiritual power" in the translation of the Gospels for native converts.[15] In the eastern islands of Torres Straits "when anything behaved in a remarkable or mysterious manner it could be regarded as a *zogo*." The term was generally used as a noun, but used adjectivally it is best translated as "sacred." A concrete object, rain, wind, a shrine, a form of words uttered in a rite, or the rite itself might be *zogo*. As a rule anything *zogo* was employed for beneficent purposes, for instance, a rain-making ceremony, but some *zogo* things had a malevolent application.[16]

The Marind, who live on the southeastern coast of Netherlands New Guinea (near Merauke), entertain a conception of *dema* described as being an exact parallel to that of *mana*. By *dema* the native understands now an impersonal and all-pervasive power attaching to everything unusual or rare, and now a personalized spiritual being from whom this power proceeds. The Dema (collectively) are ancestral ghosts, the forefathers of the various tribal groups. They appear to the magician in dreams, and with them he holds intercourse.[17] In the northeast of Netherlands New Guinea, south of Humboldt Bay, live the Stone Age Papuans known as Sentani. They use the word *uarpo* (*uarafo*) to designate an impersonal occult power which is both beneficial and harmful in its operation. Whatever has *uarpo* belongs to the mystical world, thus being set off from the world of ordinary and understandable things (*pujakara*). In most cases objects that have *uarpo* are taboo, and any unauthorized contact with them results disastrously for the person concerned. According to our authority it is often difficult to determine how far the natives separate this conception of impersonal occult power from the power exercised by spiritual beings, the Uarpo. These are not ancestral ghosts, as are the Dema of the Marind, but spirits of the earth, water, and air.[18]

We possess two accounts of the *imunu* conception among the Namau tribes of the Purari Delta, Papua. The first account, by a missionary who lived long among them, describes *imunu* as the "soul" of things. It has personality, but only as taking on the specific characteristics of its habitat. If in a man, it is human; if in a god, divine. It has attributes, can be kind or malign, can cause pain and suffer pain, can possess and be possessed. Though intangible, it manifests its presence as does the mind. It permeates everything that has life, yet it is not *rokoa*, "life," but *imunu*. The second account, by a government anthropologist, ascribes to *imunu* an adjectival instead of a substantive significance. It stands for a quality, or a complex of qualities, rather than a thing. The term is applied to many ceremonial objects such as masks, bull-roarers, hunting charms, old relics, grotesque carvings, and freaks of nature. "Such objects are queer or mysterious or secret; they are holy in the sense that they are unapproachable or untouchable; they have some kind of potency for good or evil, they are treasured with the utmost care; age seems to add to the *mana* of them. . . . . Anything which the native dreads for the harm it may do him, and fears because of its strangeness, and cajoles for its favors, and fondly treasures for its old associations, he will tell you is *imunu*."[19] From these statements it appears that by the Namau tribes the occult power which is *imunu* or has *imunu* can also be endowed with some measure of personality.

The Koita term *aina* bears the general signification of "sacred." It is used to indicate a contagious quality harmful to those in contact with it; thus a corpse or a homicide (until purified from bloodletting) is *aina*. The term corresponds to the Motu *helaga*, meaning "set apart, charged with virtue."[20]

By the Elema tribes the word for "heat" (*ahea*) has come to be used for "a potency above the ordinary." Instead of referring to the purely physical heat of fire or the sun, it now denotes that of the magician who is in a condition enabling him to do something beyond normal human capacity. Old men, bull-roarers, certain carved wooden plaques of great sanctity, and the magician's charms also possess *ahea*. It is especially found in the leaves and bark secretly used by him and in the ginger which he chews with the express purpose of making himself "hot." Things in which *ahea* resides "are charged with power, and those who handle them without authority may expect a shock; or they are fierce and liable to snap."[21] Similarly among the Mailu the sorcerer chews pepper leaf, cinnamon bark, or wild ginger root, and so acquires "heat" or "power" (*odaoda*) for the more deadly forms of his magic.[22] Among the Suau-Tawala the word *gigibori,* which means "hot" and "heat," also means "powerful" and "power." The word is applied to persons and things in which resides "something" capable of affecting other persons and things in a way that is not regarded as natural and normal.[23]

In Dobu, an island of the D'Entrecasteaux group to the southeast of New Guinea, this notion of "heat" is particularly associated with the black art. A miraculous fire issues from the pubes of a female witch, "and there is not a man who has not seen the fire flooding the night with light, or hovering to and fro in the air—and not slept for hours after, but huddled about the fire in fear of witchcraft and death in consequence of it." The body of such a woman is also unusually "hot." A sorcerer engaged in his nefarious practices believes that he must keep himself hot and parched; hence he drinks salt water, chews ginger, abstains from food for a time, and refrains from sexual intercourse with his wife or with anyone else. "He does not diffuse his heat." Chewed ginger also finds use in connection with incantations for healing, for warding off a squall at sea, and for making a canoe speedy and seaworthy. "The sight of a magician chewing ginger, spitting it on to the object charmed at intervals, and muttering his spell at the same time is a common one in Dobu."[24] In Rossel Island heat is always associated with magic; it is a necessary attribute of magical potency. Where the Melanesians would use *mana* or a similar term the Rossel people would employ the word for "hotness."[25]

The Trobrianders have the noun *megwa,* which describes the magical rites and spells employed by them. In a narrower sense it means the "force" or "virtue" of magic. The word can also be used as an adjective to describe anything of a magical character and as a verb referring to the performance of magic.[26]

By the Fijians the word *mana* is only applied to ghosts and spirits (*kalou*), to chiefs as representatives or incarnations of the *kalou,* and to medicines. Some medicines are still believed to be made effective through spiritual agency, and it is probable that originally all were so regarded.[27]

The term *mana* is or has been of universal occurrence in Polynesia. Indeed, both the word and the ideas which it denotes may be of Polynesian origin. Its occurrence in Melanesia is in regions that have been markedly affected by influences from the Pacific area. *Mana* is used either as a noun or as an adjective. In the Maori language it means authority, influence, prestige, supernatural power, "having qualities which ordinary persons or things do not possess," effectual, effective. Essentially similar meanings are found in the Samoan, Tahitian, Hawaiian, Tongan, and Marquesan languages.[28] Occult power, marvelous, wonder-working, and particularly associated with the gods and their human representatives, the chiefs and priests, is evidently the root-conception.[29]

Some equivalents or near equivalents of *mana* are discernible in the Indonesian area. The native word for "invisible power" in the Mentawei Islands is *kere* or *kerei*. The more *kerei* a man has, the more he can accomplish.[30] The Javanese term *kesakten* has a closely related meaning.[31] The Toba Batak of Sumatra have the conception of *tondi*, the power that keeps all living things alive and in lifeless things resides as a potential energy. Not all men are equally endowed with *tondi*. Chiefs, rich and highly placed people, those with many children, and magicians possess more *tondi* than common folk. It is divisible, and some of it can be transmitted from one person to another.[32] In Flores, besides the soul there is also said to be another "something" which men possess. It is their *manar*. A person who is lucky in his undertakings is thought to have received a special endowment of *manar*, making him exceptionally clever and cunning. Magicians have more of it than ordinary men. They get it from the herbs which they use. The "power" of *manar* is also found in animals, plants, trees, and even stones.[33] In Halmahera there is the conception of *gurumini*, described as a universal, all-pervading energy which is not bound to any single material object, but is found in all living things, in human beings most of all. It belongs to the newly born child and increases with advancing years. In extreme old age it becomes worn out and exhausted. *Gurumini* is not the soul but the power by which the soul can be manifested. The importance of a dead man in the other world depends upon the greater or less amount of this "life fluid" which he possessed while alive.[34]

By the Kayan of Borneo the word *bali* finds use on many occasions as a form of address. The being to whose name it is prefixed is always one "having special powers of the sort that we should call supernatural," and the prefix marks this possession of such powers. "It may be said to be an adjectival equivalent of the *mana* of the Melanesians or of the *wakanda* or *orenda* of North American tribes, words which seem to connote all power other than the purely mechanical." The word is used even more extensively by the Kenyah, who prefix it to the names of several of their gods. The Klemantan term, employed in the same way, is *vali*.[35] The name Petara, by which the Sea Dayak or Iban designate their chief divine being and his many anthropomorphic manifestations, also bears at times the vague sense of "supernatural." It will be applied, for instance, to white men: "They are Petara," say the natives. "Our superior knowledge and civilization are so far above their own level that we appear to them to partake of the supernatural."[36]

The word by which the Taiyal or Ataiyal of Formosa designate a ghost is *ottofu*. But sometimes, we learn, it seems to be used much as *mana* is used by other Pacific peoples. When a man is guided in all his actions by the ghost of some powerful ancestor he himself becomes imbued with more than human wisdom, strength, and power.[37]

The Ainu of Japan, that last remnant of a widespread prehistoric people, have a term *kamui*, which, while it refers to a supreme and creator God, also has reference to a multitude of spirits. When applied to good spirits, it expresses the quality of being beneficent and helpful to men; when applied to evil spirits, it indicates what is most to be dreaded. The term has a further application to human beings, as a title of respect, and even to animals and natural objects. These are not necessarily regarded as divine and worthy of worship.[38] Though the ordinary Japanese word for God, *kami*, is not certainly derived from Ainu *kamui*, it closely agrees with the latter term in signification. Motoöri, the great Shinto scholar, writing in the eighteenth century, declares that not only the various deities of heaven and earth and human beings such as the successive Mikados ("with reverence be it spoken"), but also birds, beasts, plants, trees, seas, mountains, "and all other things whatsoever which deserve to be dreaded and revered for the extraordinary and pre-eminent powers which they possess, are called *kami*. They need not be eminent for surpassing nobleness, goodness, or serviceableness alone. Malignant and uncanny beings are also called *kami* if only they are objects of general dread." When referring to natural objects it was not their spirits that was meant. "The word was applied directly to the seas or mountains themselves as being very awful things."[39]

The Malays of the Malay Peninsula apply the name *badi* to the "evil principle." A fairly exact English equivalent would be "mischief," as in the expression "It's got the mischief in it." The name refers to everything that has life, including even inert objects, for these too are considered animate. *Badi* issues from a tiger which one sees (because of the fascination which that beast has for its prey), from a poison-tree under which one passes, from the saliva of a mad dog, and from "the contagious principle of morbid matter." There are as many as one hundred and ninety-three of these mischiefs, though some people would reduce them to only one hundred and ninety. They correspond exactly in number to the jins or genii, who form an extensive class of godlings or spirits. While the jins may do good, which the *badi* never do, both are believed able to inflict infinite harm on mortals, and both dwell in hollows of the hills, patches of primeval forest, and other solitary places.[40] In Patani, Jalor, and other more civilized districts of the Malay Peninsula the *badi* are definite spirits, but in the Federated Malay States they appear as little more than evil influences "devoid of personality."[41]

The Peninsular Malays also have a term *kramat,* which means "sanctity," but is generally used adjectivally and is applied to men, animals, inanimate objects, and holy places. In the case of persons it implies "special sanctity and miraculous power." A little girl of Malacca, reputed to be *kramat,* used to be visited by pilgrims, who sought some benefit from her. They secured it by swallowing a small quantity of her saliva in a cup of water. *Kramat* animals generally have some physical peculiarity, such as a shrunken foot or stunted tusk; they are sometimes white (that is, albino individuals of a species which is not usually white) and thus marked out by the characteristic sacred color.[42] Finally, there is the word *daulat,* which refers to the surpassing holiness of the Malay rulers. "Not only is the king's person considered sacred, but the sanctity of his body is believed to communicate itself to his regalia, and to slay those who break the royal taboos. Thus it is firmly believed that anyone who seriously offends the royal person, who touches (even for a moment) or who imitates (even with the king's permission) the chief objects of the regalia, or who wrongfully makes use of any of the insignia or privileges of royalty, will be *kena daulat,* i.e., struck dead, by a quasi-electric discharge of that Divine Power which the Malays suppose to reside in the king's person."[43]

According to the thought of the Annamites all things in nature possess an "operative energy" called *tinh.* It is the light-giving capacity of the sun, the germinative virtue of the grain, the curative efficacy of a remedy—in short, the "essential principle" of all activity. The word *tinh* may also be used for "spirit," in the sense of personified power both good and evil.[44] The Moi of French Indo-China denote by the term *pi* all the "occult powers" whose intervention in human affairs is anticipated and feared. Our authority declares that it roughly denotes the idea of "supernatural action" and corresponds in meaning to the Melanesian *mana*.[45] The Bannar or Bahnar, a subdivision of the Moi, who designate a sorcerer by the word *deng,* likewise use it to describe the evil power which he wields. The word seems also to be used verbally in the sense of endowing objects with such power.[46]

Among the Karen of Burma the underlying principle of magic is called *pigho,* "that all-pervasive impersonal power which is so potent for good or ill." It may reside in certain persons who, by its aid, accomplish unusual tasks. When imparted by incantations and ceremonies to certain objects, it converts them into charms. The deities also possess *pigho* and so can do wonderful things. It is the Karen equivalent of *mana*.[47]

The Andaman Islanders, among the most primitive of peoples, have a term, *ot kimil,* which, while it means "hot" in the sense of the English word, also conveys a metaphorical meaning. Thus it is used in connection with illness (a sick person is "hot," his getting well is getting "coolness"); when speaking of stormy weather; to denote the condition of a youth or girl who is passing through or has recently passed through the initiation ceremonies, and to denote the ceremonies themselves; and to describe the condition of a person who has eaten certain articles of food containing a malefic quality. Various plants and animals, together with the bodies of dead men and their bones, are especially charged with "hotness." All contact with them is dangerous, but the danger can be avoided by ritual precautions. The Andamanese have not reached the point of giving a distinctive name to the occult power which, in some of its manifestations, they regard as a sort of heat, nor have they drawn any line between these as being either essentially good or essentially evil.[48]

In India, among both Hindus and Moslems, the conception of occult power is widely held. The Hindus call it *śakti* (*shakti*), "a creative dynamic force or power in everything visible and invisible; in things animate and inanimate." Its good effects are *barkat,* its bad are *aniṣṭ.* It is dangerous and cannot be lightly treated, "but from one point of view the whole of man's endeavors in magic and religious ritual are concentrated on getting control of this power." The Moslems call it *kudrat.* When it produces good its effects are *barkat* (the Hindu term), when evil, *harkat.*

The most common word used by Hindus as synonymous with
śakti is *dev*, or "god." Moslems use the word *tab*, or "heat," as
a synonym for *kudrat*.[49]

A similar, if cruder, conception of occult power is not unknown
to some of the aboriginal peoples of India. The Ho, a Munda-
speaking tribe of Chota Nagpur, call it *bonga*, "a very big power,"
vague and mysterious, which pervades all space. Itself formless,
it can assume any form. It destroys evils, stops epidemics, cures
diseases, produces the current in rivers, and gives venom to snakes
and strength to tigers. Its existence accounts for the evil eye, the
evil tongue, sorcery, and the activity of every maleficent and beneficent deity. Eventually it becomes identified with the object with
which it is associated, and so a mountain, a river, the sun becomes
a Bonga. So distinctly is this occult power conceived of that the
belief in particular spirits may be destroyed without affecting the
general belief in the presence and influence of *bonga*.[50] We learn,
further, that *bonga* is possessed by both inanimate and animate
objects to a greater or less extent, thus accounting for their respective qualities. In human beings the differences in power and
influence between them are explained by their differing endowments of *bonga*. A Ho will not take food from a stranger, will not
cook food along with members of other clans in the same kitchen,
will not use an oven already used by others. Such avoidances, instead of being based on a regard for ceremonial cleanliness, are
precautions to prevent contacts between people who have different
degrees of approachability "on account of their inherent power,
or *bonga*."[51] The Oraon of Chota Nagpur apply the adjective
bangi to a person supposed to have good luck in all his undertakings. The word further conveys the idea of a "mysterious
impersonal force" which is believed, for example, to give to the
leaves of a mango tree its power of fertilization, to prehistoric
stone celts ("thunder-stones") their power of curing certain diseases, to iron which has been exposed in the open during an eclipse
a power to ward off evil, and to charred bits of wood used in
burning a corpse a power to cure fever.[52]

The Malagasy term *hasina* means "supernatural power." Like
the Malay *daulat* it especially attaches to rulers. A clan chief, for
example, has very great *hasina* because he belongs to a family
known to possess it and also because various rites of consecration
have been performed by his parents and by magicians to endow
him with it. Like *daulat*, also, *hasina* is extremely contagious, so
much so that anyone affected by it, who cannot assimilate it, is

likely to fall ill and die. Hence a chief ought not to speak directly to his subjects but employ an immunized intermediary. Nobles and members of the royal family also possess *hasina,* though to a less extent than rulers. Commoners likewise have it in some degree, as well as certain animals, trees, and stones.[53] The native term for Deity used by the Tanala, a hill tribe of Madagascar, is *zanahary* (*za,* article, *nahary,* "creator"). As a noun it designates a powerful Being or class of Beings who have never been human. As an adjective it means "divine," "supernatural," or simply "extraordinary." It may even be used with little more emphasis than our "wonderful."[54] This adjectival use of the term would seem to be a close approximation to that of *mana* and cognate words describing what is mysterious or occult.

The Bantu-speaking peoples of South Africa, we learn on high authority, recognize the existence in the world of an "Energy or Potence," impersonal, intangible, everywhere present, immanent in all things but especially centered in certain conspicuous objects. In itself it has no moral character, but it can be turned to good use or bad according to the intent of the user. A man's dealings with this occult power consist very largely in getting it to work for his benefit and in avoiding whatever will bring him into harmful contact with it.[55] To much the same effect another authority tells us that the African's beliefs rest primarily on the concept of "an abstract Power or natural potency, formless as the ether, all-pervasive, and definitely never regarded anthropomorphically."[56]

For the Bathonga, above the gods whom the common people worship and call by name, there exists Heaven (Tilo), a conception which to the majority remains vague and ill-defined. In ordinary language *tilo* designates the blue sky. But if Heaven is a place, it is something more than a place. It is a power which acts and manifests itself in various ways, a power regarded as entirely impersonal. The natives "appear to think that Heaven regulates and presides over certain great cosmic phenomena to which men must, willingly or unwillingly, submit, more especially those of a sudden and unexpected nature . . . . above all, rain, storms, and, in human affairs, death, convulsions, and the birth of twins."[57]

The Bavenda of the Transvaal believe that every object, animate or inanimate, possesses a "kinetic power" for good or evil. The art of the magico-medical practitioner consists in directing this power into the desired channels.[58] The Ba-ila of Northern Rhodesia conceive of a force "neutral" in character, usually "quiescent," and in itself neither good nor bad. It can be tapped by those who have the secret of manipulation and so can be used for good or for ill. Objects in which it resides are dangerous to interfere with; hence they are taboo to ordinary people. The conception has no animistic basis, for such objects are not supposed to be possessed by a soul, ghost, or spirit. For this occult power our authorities found no special designation, though as a near approach to one they suggested the term *bwanga,* meaning "the contents" or "that which is contained in things," and applied to the medicines used by magicians.[59] Among the Balamba, another Rhodesian group of tribes, this term (in the form *ubwanga*) similarly refers to charms, medicines, actions, and even words which doctors and sorcerers employ in their operations. As among the Ba-ila, it is an "inherent potentiality" generally "automatic" in action, but usually subject to the control of those who know how to use it. There is also a synonymous expression, *ichyanga.*[60]

A term, *mulungu,* is widely found in the Bantu languages of East Africa. Among the Wayao of Nyasaland it denotes an inherent property or quality, as life and health inhere in the body. "It's *mulungu,*" exclaims a native, when shown anything beyond the range of his understanding. The missionaries have adopted the term as the designation of God, but the untaught native refuses to assign to it "any idea of being or personality." Yet such an idea is approached when he speaks of what Mulungu has done and is doing. Mulungu made the world, the animals, and man.[61] Among the Anyanja of Nyasaland, the generic name for God is Mulungu. This designation includes, not only the deity, but all that appertains to the spirit world. Whether in its principal sense the word conveys the idea of personality is uncertain, for it belongs to an impersonal class of nouns and always takes the concord of an impersonal class. When, however, the deity is referred to in respect of any of his attributes, for instance, as "the Creator" or as "the Almighty," there is no doubt that personality is attributed to him.[62] The Wabena of Tanganyika recognize the existence of an "impersonal ambivalent" force (*mulungu*) that pervades everything but may become associated with certain persons or things. This conception seems to be strongest with the more backward sections of the community. There is also a belief in Mulungu, a high god and creator, a belief usually associated with the more educated people who have had contact with Islam or Christianity or with both. But the two ideas are often inextricably mingled. A man in the same breath speaks of Mulungu as a person who will help him and of a medicine that is *mulungu.* In its impersonal aspect *mulungu,* the "summation of the supernatural," is said to be akin to *mana.*[63]

By the Masai the word Engai (Ngai) is used "either quite indefinitely and impersonally of remarkable natural phenomena (especially rain, the sky, and volcanoes), or else definitely and personally of supernatural beings." In the latter sense there are two deities, the Black God and the Red God, the one kindly but the other malevolent. Fortunately, the good god is near at hand and the bad god is far away, so the people do not find it necessary to engage in cruel methods of propitiation. To Engai as a distinct personality prayers for children, rain, and victory are addressed; as the natives say, Engai is one "who is prayed to and hears."[64] This belief in a high god and creator is also found among the Akamba of Kenya. They regard Mulungu or Engai as a spiritual being to whom prayers are occasionally addressed and sacrifices offered by the elders of the tribal shrines, representing the priestly class. For the common people, however, Mulungu is a very vague and indefinite conception.[65] Among the Akikuyu Engai also appears as a high god, who hears the prayers and receives the sacrifices of his worshipers. His name has been borrowed from the Masai.[66]

This evidence in regard to the Wayao, Anyanja, Wabena, Masai, Akamba, and Akikuyu of East Africa suggests strongly that among these peoples the definitely personal character assigned to the high god represents a development from an earlier and vaguer conception of occult power as impersonal. Our authorities expressly assign such a conception to the more backward and "untaught" natives. But, as has been shown, the two ideas are often inextricably mingled in their minds.

The Baganda of Uganda had a cult of the *lubale.* These were the ghosts of persons who in their lifetime gave evidence of the possession of "supernatural" powers and who manifested themselves after death in order to help their descendants by foretelling the future and by revealing to them "magical" means of obtaining wealth, fertility, and success in enterprises of all kinds. Certain natural objects, such as wells, large rocks, and trees, were believed to be associated with the *lubale* and were treated with respect. The trees could not be cut down, the water of the wells was used with special care, and not for all purposes, and offerings were placed by the wells and rocks. The Baganda had stories of the marvelous behavior of these objects and of their power to confer benefits upon people who dealt properly with them. But, in general, the connection of ancestral ghosts with natural objects was so vague that the phrase "to have a *lubale*" seems to have meant nothing more than "to be endowed with supernatural qualities."[67]

The Lango, a Nilotic tribe of Uganda, have a high god who rejoices in the name of Jok. He is known under a variety of titles, corresponding to his different manifestations and activities, but actually he is regarded as an indivisible entity permeating the entire world. So powerful is Jok that any proximity to him is dangerous, not necessarily because of his ill will, but because mortals cannot endure contact with the divine essence unless duly safeguarded; hence the avoidance of hills in which he may be immanent; hence, also, the evil consequences of building a village, even unwittingly, in the path which he is accustomed to travel. While Jok is now a full-fledged deity, with shrines and ministrants who divine his will, we also learn that "anything strikingly unusual or supernatural in character is commonly attributed to Jok and is said to be 'god-like'."[68] The conclusion would seem to be irresistible that Jok is no more than *mana* personified.

The Azande of the Anglo-Egyptian Sudan entertain a conception of *mbisimo*, the "soul" of a thing. It is an inherent power as mysterious to them as to us. They do not clearly understand how a sorcerer kills people, but declare that he sends the "soul of his witchcraft" to eat the soul of the flesh of a man. But in saying that witchcraft has a soul the native means little more than that "It does something" or, as we would say, "It is dynamic." If you ask him how it works, he replies, "It has a soul." If you then inquire how he knows it has a soul, he answers that he knows because it works. The word *mbisimo* thus describes and explains all action of a mystical order, whether that of sorcery, of the poison oracle, or of the drugs used to cure internal diseases.[69]

The *mian* of the Bari-speaking tribes is a "power or energy" contained in rivers, mountains, big trees, rocks, animals named after dead ancestors, old men, the husbands of puerperal women, sacred places, and certain stones used in rain-making magic.[70] The name of the Bongo high god is Loma. The term *loma* also denotes equally luck and ill luck. If a man falls sick he attributes his condition to *loma*. If he loses a wager, fails to win a game, returns from the hunt without trophies, or from war without booty, he is said to have had no *loma* (*loma, nya*), in the sense of having had no luck.[71]

The Bambute Pygmies, who live in the Ituri Forest of northeastern Belgian Congo, entertain a belief in a "magic power" known as *megbe*. People use it during their lifetime as a means of protection. After a man's death part of it goes with him to the grave. The other part is transferred to his eldest son. The son bends down and puts his mouth against that of his dying father, thus receiving it with the latter's final breath. *Megbe* is present in all things and in human beings. Its distribution is not always uniform, however, for a man may possess more or less of it.[72]

The Nkundu of the Belgian Congo designate by the term *elima* an "intangible, impersonal" power. Our authority calls it the "power of magic" and likens it to *mana*. It is everywhere, but some localities, such as parts of certain rivers, and some objects, such as certain great trees, contain it most intensively. If one passes a place where there is *elima,* it enters one's joints and causes pain. Old men, especially those who are influential and well known, also possess *elima*. Before dying they hand over their occult power to their successors, for it cannot be carried to the grave. The totem animal of a clan and the clan elder have *elima* specially concentrated in them; indeed, the Nkundu seem to believe that the clan elder derives his *elima* from the totem animal. Certain elders, because of their possession of *elima,* exercise almost unlimited authority. No one would dream of opposing them in any way for fear of being killed by magic. Some old men (not necessarily clan elders) claim to be able to utilize the mystic energy of *elima*. They confine it in charms and sell these to others. A native, when asked to explain the exact nature of this occult power, replied, "When you grab at an electric fish in the water you get a shock. Then you let the fish drop. *Elima* is just like the power the electric fish has to give you such a shock."[73] The Mangbattu (Monbuttu) use the word *kilima* for "anything they do not understand"— thunder, the rainbow, a shadow, a reflection in water. The word is also applied to the supreme being in which they "vaguely" believe.[74] Among the Ababua the term which designates the dynamic quality or qualities of every object is *dawa*.[75]

The Bangala (Boloki) describe as *likundu* the "occult power" supposed to be possessed and exercised by many people, with or without their knowledge. A person may be accused of having *likundu* if he or she is extraordinarily successful in hunting, fishing, skilled labor, or the accumulation of property. To excel all others is regarded as proof that a man used this power to his own advantage and thus deprived his neighbors of their rightful shares. Sometimes the accusation is brought playfully and is then merely equivalent to our expression "You are too clever." But when leveled seriously at a person he must disprove it (if possible) by undergoing successfully the poison ordeal for witchcraft or at least refrain from the reprobated activity. There is also a common belief that boys and girls "have plenty *likundu*."[76] To the same effect we are told that a man whose enterprises prosper, whose enemies ruin themselves or perish, who, in short, is always fortunate will be supposed to have very strong *likundu*.[77] We conclude from these statements that while the Bangala conceive of this power as bringing good luck to the owner they also think that its undue exercise injures the community. For them, therefore, a person with much *likundu* is a natural-born sorcerer or witch.

A conception very similar to that of *likundu* is entertained by the widespread Fang or Pangwe tribe in Gabun and the Cameroons. They call it *evu* (*ewu*). By them three classes of people are recognized. First, ordinary folk, who live peaceably with their neighbors and practice no nefarious arts. They possess no *evu*. Second, all outstanding and gifted persons such as witch doctors, cult leaders, chiefs, artists, and singers; they have enough *evu* to qualify for these professions and thus to lift themselves above the common herd. This sort of *evu* is called *wu-besi*. Third, wicked persons with much bad *evu* (*evu bojem*), which they use to injure and kill their neighbors.[78] It would appear from this account that by the Fang, *evu*, or occult power, when only slightly developed, is not regarded as socially harmful, rather as something which brings rich rewards to its possessor. But a man heavily endowed with *evu* is a sorcerer or witch.

The Bantu-speaking tribes of the Lower Congo basin have a term *nkissi* (*nkici*), meaning, specifically, the spirit, the power, the mystery "that is contained in medicines, in trees and herbs, and in the earth. Hence it has come to mean 'any mysterious power'."[79]

The term *njomm*, as used by the Ekoi of southern Nigeria, can with difficulty be defined, but it includes "all uncomprehended, mysterious forces of Nature. These vary in importance from elementals, so powerful as to hold almost the position of demigods, to the *mana* — to use a Melanesian term — of herb, stone, or metal."[80] By the Hausa, who entertain a pronounced belief in the evil eye, *k'wari*, or occult power, is regarded as projected from the eyes; indeed, *k'wari* means "the power to mesmerize." This word and another word, *k'afi*, "are the Hausa equivalent of, or approximation to, the Melanesian *mana*."[81]

The Yoruba of the Slave Coast express the idea of "supernatural and supersensuous power" by the term *ogun*. Wooden masks worn in the rites of the Oro secret society, the Oro stick, or bull-roarer, the magician's staff, and the words of a curse all possess *ogun*.[82] In Dahomey the conception of *vodun* applies to everything that surpasses human capacity and intelligence, everything "astonishing, out of the ordinary, terrible, prodigious," such as great whirlpools, the rainbow, big rivers and lakes, the ocean, thunder and lightning, tigers, boa constrictors, crocodiles, and smallpox. All these are endowed with "superhuman virtues" and are believed to be the abodes of "mysterious powers and spirits."[83] Among the Twi of the Gold Coast, Bohsum is the name applied to a class of family or local deities. The name also means the moon. It has further an adjectival meaning in the sense of "occult," "mysterious," or "sacred"; thus, *bohsum eppoh,* "the mysterious sea."[84]

The Kpelle of Liberia apply the word *sale,* meaning medicine, poison, magic, to every remarkable object of a beneficial or a harmful character. *Sale* also refers to the power contained in anything of this character. But the object and its indwelling power are not separated in thought; they form a unity.[85]

The Lobi of French West Africa recognize the existence of an evil force or energy called *kele*. It belongs to the "little" gods and perhaps to the ancestors and by them is communicated to sacred animals, plants, rocks, caverns, and streams, and also to certain persons—in particular, to twins. Magicians and priests make use of it. People who come into contact with anything or anybody possessing *kele* will sicken and die, unless they resort to expiatory sacrifices and purifications.[86] A somewhat similar conception of evil occult power is found among the Mandingo tribes, under the name of *gnama* (*n'ama*). It is specialized in wild and dangerous animals and in certain human beings, including the poor and disinherited, newly born children, and the aged. The bodies of suicides, of murdered persons, and of women dying in childbirth are full of *gnama* and it is conveyed by contact with them. It also affects people who have transgressed divine laws or have offended spiritual beings.[87]

The word *baraka,* which means "blessing," is used by the Berbers and Arabic-speaking peoples of Morocco to denote a "mysterious wonder-working force" regarded as a blessing from God. Our leading authority on the beliefs and rites of these peoples defines it as "holiness," also as "blessed magic virtue." He describes at length the various persons and things endowed with *baraka,* its miraculous manifestations, its beneficial but often dangerous aspects, and its sensitiveness to contact with polluting influences, especially those of a "supernatural" kind. The dangerous elements in *baraka* are in many cases personified in the shape of *jnūn* (*jinni*), which according to Moslem orthodoxy form a special race of spiritual beings created before Adam. The relations between saints and *jnūn* are often of a very intimate character, so much so that the borderline between them may be well-nigh obliterated. While the conception of *baraka* is closely connected with the religion of the Prophet, the various ideas and practices embodied in it are "often only a religious interpretation of a belief in mysterious forces infinitely older than Islam, which prevailed among the ancient Arabs and Berbers alike."[88] The impersonal force of evil the Moors call *bas*. Misfortunes ascribed to it can with difficulty be distinguished from those believed to be caused by the *jnūn,* who are mostly malignant in character; indeed, *bas* and *jnūn* are sometimes confounded in popular speech.[89]

While occult power for the Indians of South America "often seems to have a somewhat vague and impersonal character," in general the tendency to personify it and give it a spiritualistic interpretation is more pronounced than in some other parts of the aboriginal world. But whether an object "is thought actually to be the habitation of a spiritual being or only to possess an impersonal magical potency, is a wholly superfluous question to which the savage Indian himself probably, in most cases, could not give an exact answer. To him there is evidently no clear distinction between the Personal and the Impersonal."[90]

The Chané, an Arawak tribe in northern Argentina, and the Chiriguano, a Guaraní tribe in central Bolivia, designate "superhuman" power by the word *tunpa*. But these Indians also personalize the conception, for the Tunpa are certain dead persons who possess this power. With them the medicine men are in close association. The Tunpa also include many characters appearing in the tribal legends.[91] Some tribes of Matto Grosso, on the upper Guaporé River, are said to have a belief in an "invisible magic substance" that floats in the air and permeates altars, rattles, and other sacred objects. Magicians catch the mysterious stuff, knead it between their fingers, hold it against their chests, and give it to other persons, who make sucking noises as if swallowing it. All the participants in a ceremony receive some of the substance, which is regarded as especially beneficial to sick people. Even food acquires virtue "if filled with this *mana*," as is evidenced by the eagerness of the natives to have their magicians bless it. These

Indians seem also to believe in an evil principle regarded as an invisible substance.[92]

The Jivaro of eastern Ecuador recognize the existence of a force or quality called *tsarutama*. It is possessed by a large group of gods and spirits as well as by all the animals and plants that are mentioned in the Jivaro myth of their origin. It is also contained in impressive natural objects. These are usually personified, such as the river god and the rain god. Etsa, the sun, and Nantu, the moon, are full of this power, which influences everything that happens on earth. The chonta palm, much used by the Indians for making weapons, utensils, and even houses, also contains *tsarutama*. A lance made entirely of chonta wood will be more effective in fighting than one which is tipped with iron. *Tsarutama* is described as "impersonal magical power" and as being "more or less the equivalent" of *mana*.[93]

The Chorti Indians of Guatemala, whose religion represents a fusion of native and Catholic elements, entertain very definite conceptions of *aigres,* the substances which enter human bodies and cause pains and illness. There are several kinds of *aigres,* namely, those which are natural, those which are sent upon a victim by black magic, and those which are acquired by contact with ritually unclean persons and objects. People with the evil eye, pregnant and menstruating women, corpses, sorcerers, apparitions, and spirits of the dead all possess this third kind of *aigre* (called in Spanish *hijillo*) and infect others with it at close range. *Hijillo* is so murky and unclean as to be almost visible like a dirty vapor. It enters the body through any opening and saturates the clothes. But one may get it merely by looking at a person who has it, unless at a safe distance.[94]

The belief that some specific objects, natural phenomena, animals, and human beings, together with all spirits and gods, possess qualities or attributes which are naturally superior to those of men is universal among the North American Indians. A majority of the tribes, in addition to such belief, have also reached the conception of a power which is wonderful and capable of accomplishing extraordinary things, a power either helpful or harmful in its manifestations, and a power only "vaguely localized," if at all. It is often designated by a special name. The conception may even approach that of a supreme deity, "hardly anthropomorphic" in character.[95]

The Iroquoian tribes describe by the word *orenda* the inherent energy possessed and exerted in some characteristic degree by every object, inanimate and animate. They also use the term *otgon* or *otkon* to denote the malefic aspect of *orenda* in its relation to mankind. It even tends to displace *orenda* as a generic term, seemingly because "the malignant and destructive, rather than the benign, manifestations of this subsumed mystic potence produce the more lasting impressions on the mind." Under missionary influence *otkon*, an adjective, has become in a nominative form the common name for the Devil of Christian belief.[96]

Among the central Algonquian tribes the corresponding expression is *manito* (*manitu, manitou*). It may be applied to anything that exhibits wonder-working power. When used to denote a property of objects or a virtue in them, the word has inanimate gender; when the property is associated with objects, the gender becomes obscure and confused. As taken over into the vocabulary of the white man, *manito* has signified spirit, good, bad, or indifferent, and god or devil.[97] The Menomini *hawatuk* means, primarily, a god and thus applies to the sun, the thunderers, horned snakes, and the Supreme Being or Creator. The word has also come to denote the "supernatural power" imparted by one of those gods to a mortal being. As an adjective it qualifies anything animate or inanimate which is a seat of supernatural power granted by one of the beings possessing it.[98] Among the northern Algonquian tribes, Penobscot *ktahando* and Malecite and Passamaquoddy *ktahant* are cognate terms, rendered by the most careful interpreters as "great magic." Used adjectivally, they all refer to what is mysterious, powerful, miraculous, "enabling things to be done supernaturally."[99] The Micmac term *mundu*, "magic power," has lost its original significance in the minds of the modern Indians and has acquired the meaning of "devil" given to it by the missionaries who translated the Bible and other religious works into the Micmac language.[100] Among the Blackfoot (Siksika), an Algonquian confederacy of the northern plains, the term in use is *natoji*.[101]

With the Siouan tribes the word for occult power is *wakan* (*wakanda*), Omaha *wakonda,* meaning "mysterious, incomprehensible, in a peculiar state, which, from not being understood, it is dangerous to meddle with."[102] An equivalent term in use among the Omaha and Ponca is *xube* (*qube*), defined as meaning "sacred," "mysterious," or "occult."[103] The Crow term is *maxpe*. It does not designate "particular individualized supernatural beings," but conveys the idea that a person or object is possessed of "qualities transcending the ordinary." It describes an abstract notion to which concrete experiences are or are not assimilated.[104] The Hidatsa of North Dakota have the term *mahopa*. It may be applied to anything "of a very wonderful or sacred nature."[105]

The Pawnee, who belong to the Caddoan linguistic stock, differentiate the conception of occult power by the use of two terms, *waruxti* and *paruxti*. The former refers to what is mysterious or not readily comprehended in earthly affairs, for instance, sleight-of-hand performances by medicine men; the latter has reference to lightning and other wonderful phenomena of the heavens, which derive their origin from the gods.[106]

Expressions equivalent or nearly equivalent to *orenda, manito, wakanda,* and the like are employed by many other Indian tribes: *digin,* by the Navaho;[107] *dige,* by the Apache;[108] *hullo,* by the Chickasaw;[109] *poa,* by the Southern Paiute of Utah, a Shoshonean-speaking people;[110] *puha,* by the Paviotso or Northern Paiute of Nevada;[111] *tipni,* by the Yokuts of California;[112] *kaocal,* by the Pomo;[113] *matas,* by the Coast Yuki;[114] *tinihowi,* by the Achomawi;[115] *tamanous,* by the Twana and Klallam of Washington;[116] *naualak* (*nawalak*), by the Kwakiutl;[117] *sgana,* by the Haida;[118] and *yek,* by the Tlingit.[119]

Throughout the Eskimo area there is a belief that a mysterious power resides in the air and manifests itself in changes of the weather and other natural phenomena not understood. This power is Sila, the Air Spirit, sometimes described as masculine and sometimes as feminine. No cycle of myths accounts for the origin of Sila, nor is the Ruler of the Elements believed to have once been a human being who had actually lived on the earth at some definite time. The conception of Sila in its nonmaterial aspects resembles that of *mana,* yet does not correspond exactly to *mana,* since Sila is not merely a power or virtue but at times is endowed with some degree of personality. The conception would seem to be relatively old in Eskimo thought because of its wide currency and also because the personification of "supernatural force" in natural phenomena is elemental and presumably primitive.[120]

Primitive peoples, from the sun-baked deserts of Central Australia to the frozen wastes of Arctic America, are thus found to entertain a conception of occult power for which they have a definite name, most conveniently expressed by *mana*. We have seen that the conception may be imperfectly generalized. It will then be referred to by some locution such as "hardness" or "hotness," these words being used in a metaphorical sense. Where no designation of occult power is discoverable the inference must be that the native mind conceives of it only in one or other of its specific manifestations. Among the Bagobo of Mindanao, when a phenomenon out of the ordinary or difficult to explain has been observed, it is called by one of several names implying what we describe as occult. But the name used bears a meaning of its own and refers to the mystic potency of a particular person or thing.[121] Similarly, the Tanala of Madagascar have no name for the "impersonal magical power" which they seem to believe is concentrated in charms. While firmly convinced that the owners of charms are able to utilize this power, they formulate no ideas as to its source or nature or as to the exact way it is applied. The Tanala are unconscious of any need for such formulation. "In this they are quite comparable to persons in our own culture who believe in the efficacy of lucky coins, etc., without being able to explain the way they are efficacious."[122]

Occult power is commonly considered as neutral in character, but capable of being manipulated toward ends good or bad as these are recognized by a particular society. Nevertheless a differentiation between its beneficent and maleficent aspects is not seldom made, as in the Central Australian *churinga* and *arungquiltha,* Malay *kramat* and *badi,* Moorish *baraka* and *bas,* and Iroquoian *orenda* and *otkon.* When the beneficent aspects of *mana* are emphasized, the word often has an adjectival meaning of "sacred" or "holy."

Occult power is sometimes thought of as localized and confined to a limited range of objects which particularly impress the imagination and appear wonderful in aspect or activity. On the other hand, it is often regarded as ubiquitous and all-pervasive, a universal potency, a *mana* with every kind of mystic efficacy, a "voltage" capable of being "tapped" by adepts familiar with the requisite procedure. Some of the most primitive peoples, we have learned, are familiar with the latter conception. As developed by modern science, this has become the conception of force or energy behind all phenomena, both explicable and inexplicable.[123]

NOTES TO CHAPTER I

[1] J. R. Swanton, in *Twenty-sixth Annual Report of the Bureau of American Ethnoloy,* p. 451, note.

[2] R. H. Codrington, *The Melanesians* (Oxford, 1891), pp. 118–20, 191. See further H. I. Hogbin, in *Oceania,* VI (1935–36), 241–74; A. Capell, *ibid.,* IX (1938–39), 89–96. Codrington's first reference to the Melanesian conception of *mana* occurs in a letter to Professor Max Müller, quoted by the latter in his Hibbert Lectures for 1878 (*The Origin and Growth of Religion as Illustrated by the*

Religions of India, pp. 51 f.) : "There is a belief in a force altogether distinct from physical power, which acts in all kinds of ways for good and evil, and which it is of the greatest advantage to possess or control. . . . . This *mana* is not fixed in anything, and can be conveyed in almost anything; but spirits, whether disembodied souls or supernatural beings, have it, and can impart it; and it essentially belongs to personal beings to originate it, though it may act through the medium of water, or a stone, or a bone." See also Codrington's early article, "Religious Beliefs and Practices in Melanesia" (*Journal of the Anthropological Institute,* X [1881], 277 ff., 299, 301, 305, 309), where *mana* is defined as "supernatural power" and its operation is described.

Mana is the word used in the New Hebrides, the Banks Islands, and the Solomon Islands about Florida. In the Santa Cruz group a different word, *malete,* is found, but with the same meaning (R. H. Codrington, *op. cit.,* pp. 191, 197). In San Cristoval, one of the Solomons, the word is *mena* (C. E. Fox, *The Threshold of the Pacific* [London, 1924], p. 251). In Guadalcanal we find a corresponding term, *nanama,* and in Mala or Malaita the term *mamanaa* (H. I. Hogbin, in *Oceania,* VI [1935–36], 244, 259). In Ulawa the term *nanamanga* means "power" (W. G. Ivens, *Dictionary and Grammar of the Language of Sa'a and Ulawa, Solomon Islands* [Washington, D.C., 1918], p. 67). Among the Mono people, inhabiting three islands in Bougainville Strait, the term *kare,* which means "strength," "power," "force," approaches the idea of *mana* (G. C. Wheeler, in *Archiv für Religionswissenshaft,* XVII [1914], 90). In the Torres Islands magic is based on *mena* (W. J. Durrad, in *Oceania,* XI [1940–41], 186). In the island of Tikopia two terms, *mana* and *manu,* designate concrete results "which are more than those produced by ordinary efforts" (Raymond Firth, *We, the Tikopia* [London, 1936], pp. 333 f., 489). In the Loyalty Islands *men* or *man* is equivalent in meaning to *mana* (Maurice Leenhardt, *Notes d'ethnologie Néo-Calédonienne* [Paris, 1930], pp. 256 f., 260). The Lifu version of St. Mark's Gospel uses the word *mene* to render both Greek δύναμις, "power," "might," and ἐξουσία, "authority" (S. H. Ray, quoted in *Reports of the Cambridge Anthropological Expedition to Torres Straits,* V, 329). No term corresponding to *mana* has been recorded for New Caledonia, although a conception of occult power, essentially similar to that found elsewhere in the Melanesian area, seems to be entertained. See Fritz Sarasin, *Ethnologie der Neu-Caledonier und Loyalty Insulaner* (Munich, 1929), p. 282.

According to W. H. R. Rivers it is certain that the term *mana* (like *tapu* or *tambu,* "taboo") belongs to the culture of the immigrants into Melanesia and not to that of the aboriginal inhabitants of the islands (*The History of Melanesia Society* [Cambridge, 1914], II, 485). According to E. S. C. Handy the "pure" *mana* concept was Polynesian, and in Melanesia it was "adulterated" by amalgamation with ghost-cult elements ("Polynesian Religion," *Bernice P. Bishop Museum Bulletin,* No. 34, p. 27, note 3).

The origin of the term *mana* remains uncertain. Father Wilhelm Schmidt would derive it from the Indonesian *manang* (Malay *menang*), meaning "superior" or "victorious" force, whether occult or not (*Literarisches Zentralblatt,* LXVII [1916], coll. 1091 ff.). *Manang* in the language of the Dayaks of Borneo means as a noun a medicine man or woman and as a verb to have or use a magician.

³ Hocart declares that the word *mana* "is out and out spiritualistic" in meaning; it is almost, if not entirely, confined to the action of ghosts and spirits (A. M. Hocart in *Man,* XIV [1914], 100). With reference to San Cristoval Fox says that *mena* seems to be thought of as "an invisible spiritual substance in which objects may be immersed" (*op. cit.,* p. 251). According to Ivens, on the island of Mala (Malaita) in the Solomons the word *mamana* (*mamanaa*), which signifies to be powerful in some occult way, has a direct reference to the power of ghosts. There is no idea of a thing being magically powerful in itself (W. G.

Ivens, *The Island Builders of the Pacific* [London, 1930], p. 137). In Guadalcanal *nanama* is an attribute of all ghosts and spirits. A man's affairs are believed to prosper only by virtue of the *nanama* which they exert on his behalf. While in ordinary conversation people are likely to say of a successful man that he has *nanama*, this only means that the ghosts or spirits have advanced his interests (H. I. Hogbin, *loc. cit.*). To the Tikopians the only real source of *mana* or *manu* is in the spirit world. It is something derived from the gods or from the ancestors (Raymond Firth, *op. cit.*, p. 502). On the other hand, in some parts of the Melanesian area *mana* is declared to be occasionally regarded as wholly impersonal, without any reference to ghosts or spirits, e.g., a curiously shaped stone may contain *mana*, though no spiritual power is associated with it (Felix Speiser, *Ethnographische Materialien aus den Neuen Hebriden und den Banks-Inseln* [Berlin, 1923], pp. 343 f.).

[4] Sir George Grey, *Journals of Two Expeditions of Discovery in North-West and Western Australia* (London, 1841), II, 266, 337.

[5] D. Rudesindo Salvado, *Memorie storiche dell' Australia* (Rome, 1851), p. 299. According to still another early account, referring specifically to the Watchandi of Western Australia, the source of *boollia* is in the human body. Some magicians procure it by repeated rubbings of the right hand on the left arm; others get it by hard blows on the stomach. The "essence" thus collected is left in the operator's left hand, from which it is transmitted by frequent light tappings to another person, "the enchanter at the same time making a hissing sound much resembling that made by a galvanic battery in action." See Augustus Oldfield, in *Transactions of the Ethnological Society of London* (n.s., 1865), III, 235. In the southern parts of Western Australia the equivalent of *boollia* is called *moolgar* (*loc. cit.*).

[6] G. Horne and G. Aiston, *Savage Life in Central Australia* (London, 1924), p. 132. Among the Dieri, who are neighbors of the Wonkonguru, Kutchi is described as a "powerful and malignant being," who endows a medicine man with the ability to produce and to cure disease (A. W. Howitt, *The Native Tribes of South-East Australia* [London, 1904], p. 358; cf. R. B. Smyth, *The Aborigines of Victoria* [Melbourne, 1878], I, 457 f.). It would seem that in this tribe the conception of occult power is definitely personalized.

[7] A. W. Howitt, *op. cit.*, pp. 365, 372, 450.

[8] John Mathew, *Eaglehawk and Crow* (London, 1909), pp. 143, 192; *idem, Two Representative Tribes of Queensland* (London, 1900), pp. 172, 176, 236, 241, 243.

[9] D. F. Thomson, "The Hero Cult, Initiation, and Totemism on Cape York," *Journal of the Royal Anthropological Institute*, LXIII (1933), pp. 510 f. Our authority points out the close relationship of the *kunta* conception to the Melanesian *mana*.

[10] Sir Baldwin Spencer and F. J. Gillen, *The Native Tribes of Central Australia* (London, 1899), pp. 548, note 1, 566. According to our authorities the idea that an object has *arungquiltha* can sometimes be best expressed by saying that "it is possessed by an evil spirit." Thus a spear-thrower and spear, used in nefarious magic, contain *arungquiltha*, but in this case the evil power is regarded as an evil spirit resident in the weapon. To the men who are about to use it to mutilate and kill an enemy it speaks, saying, "Where is he?" Upon hearing the voice and a sound like a crash of thunder afterward they know that the spear has gone straight to the victim (p. 549).

[11] *Iidem*, pp. 412 (and note 1), 537, 550, 552, 566. According to the missionary Strehlow the word *arunkulta* is applied to bones and pieces of wood used as magical charms, the venom of snakes, and the poison of certain plants. It now also designates poisons, such as strychnine, with which the natives have become

familiar from intercourse with white settlers. Always it is that which quickly ends life—"evil power," "noxious power," (Carl Strehlow, *Die Aranda und Loritjastämme in Zentral-Australien* [Frankfurt am Main, 1907–20], II, 76, note 2).

[12] Spencer and Gillen, *The Northern Tribes of Central Australia* (London, 1904), pp. 464, note 1, 750; *iidem, Across Australia* (2d ed., London, 1912), II, 326 f.

[13] *Iidem, The Native Tribes of Central Australia,* pp. 139, note 1, 648. Strehlow (*op. cit.,* II, 81) spells the word *tjurunga.*

[14] W. L. Warner, *A Black Civilization* (New York, 1937), pp. 236, 264.

[15] A. C. Haddon and W. H. R. Rivers, in *Reports of the Cambridge Anthropological Expedition to Torres Straits,* V, 183, and note 3. The version of the Gospels used in Torres Straits was translated from the Samoan version, which, in turn, was directly rendered from the Greek. *Unewen* represents Samoan *mana* and the latter, Greek δύναμις "power," "might" (S. H. Ray, *ibid.,* V. 329).

[16] A. C. Haddon, *ibid.,* VI, 242 ff.; cf. I, 357. "There are some analogies between *zogo* and *mana*" (VI, 243, note 1).

[17] Paul Wirz, *Die Marind-anim von Holländisch-Süd-Neu-Guinea* (Hamburg, 1922–25), Vol. I, Pt. II, p. 6; Vol. II, Pt. III, p. 79.

[18] *Idem,* in *Tijdschrift voor Indische Taal-Land-en Volkenkunde,* LXIII (1923), 24 ff.; *idem,* "Beitrag zur Ethnologie der Sentanier (Holländisch Neuguinea)," in *Nova Guinea* (Leiden, 1924–34), XVI, 300 f.

[19] J. H. Holmes, *In Primitive New Guinea* (London, 1924), pp. 149 ff.; F. E. Williams, "The 'Paimara' Ceremony in the Purari Delta, Papua," *Journal of the Royal Anthropological Institute,* LIII (1923), 362 f.

[20] C. G. Seligman, *The Melanesians of British New Guinea* (Cambridge, 1910), pp. 101, note 2, 129 f., 130, note 1, 161, 169, 247. James Chalmers defines *helaga* as meaning "sacred" (*Pioneering in New Guinea* [2d ed., London, 1887], p. 164).

[21] F. E. Williams, *Drama of Orokolo* (Oxford, 1940), pp. 111 f.

[22] M. J. V. Saville, *In Unknown New Guinea* (London, 1926), p. 269.

[23] W. E. Armstrong, in *Territory of Papua. Anthropological Reports,* No. 1, p. 7. According to W. M. Strong the association of harmful magic with heat is widespread in the Territory (p. 3).

[24] R. E. Fortune, *Sorcerers of Dobu* (London, 1932), pp. 99, 295 f. The word *mana* appears in the Dobuan *bomana,* meaning a "sacred prohibition," or taboo, "to secure power of a magical nature" (p. 233, note 1).

[25] W. E. Armstrong, *Rossel Island* (Cambridge, 1928), pp. 172 f.

At Saa in Mala or Malaita (one of the Solomon Islands) all persons and things in which the "supernatural power" of *mana* resides are said to be *saka,* that is, "hot." Powerful ghosts are *saka,* so also are men who have knowledge of things supernatural. A person who knows a spell which is *saka* mutters it over water, thus making the water "hot" (R. H. Codrington, *op. cit.,* pp. 191 f.). *Saka* seems to be the same word as *'ako* ("hot") in the Lau language of North Mala, meaning "magically powerful." The noun *akoakolaa* is used to refer to the success of a man or to the effect of an incantation; it is the equivalent of our "hot stuff" (W. G. Ivens, *op. cit.,* p. 137).

We may compare the use by the Achinese of Sumatra and by the natives of the Malay Archipelago in general of the words "hot" and "heat" to express all the powers of evil, while ideas of happiness, peace, rest, and well-being are expressed by words signifying "coolness" (C. S. Hurgronje, *The Achehnese* [Leiden and London, 1906], I, 305). In India occult power in many forms is associated with heat, as the power of a divinity, a saint, or a bridegroom. A

Hindu deity of great potency is described as "very hot," "burning," or "having fire." Sindi Moslems believe that a man in communion with God becomes "hot." The curse of a saint is spoken of as his "fire." Ascetics by their penances acquire "heat." But heat is also associated with certain forms of impurity which result in the destruction of occult power (J. Abbott, *The Keys of Power* [London, 1932], pp. 5 f., 9). Among the Ewe of Togo the word for magic is *dzosàsa* (*dzo* meaning "fire" and *sa* "to bind"). For the Ewe fire is something wonderful (Jakob Spieth, *Die Ewe-Stämme* [Berlin, 1906], pp. 515 f.).

²⁶ Bronislaw Malinowski, *Argonauts of the Western Pacific* (London, 1922), p. 424. Cf. *idem, Coral Gardens and Their Magic* (New York, 1935), II, 146 f. Among the Trobrianders "the concept of magical force pervades their whole tribal life" (II, 66). "Every magical ceremony is, in its essence, a handling of *mana*. The nearest word for this concept is *megwa*" (II, 68).

²⁷ A. M. Hocart, in *Man*, XIV (1914), 98. As Hocart has shown, the early missionaries to Fiji completely mistook the meaning of *kalou* when they applied it to the natives' highest notion of a god ("On the Meaning of 'Kalou' and the Origin of Fijian Temples," *Journal of the Royal Anthropological Institute*, XLII [1912], 437–49). According to Thomas Williams, the term *kalou* is constantly in use "as a qualificative of anything great or marvelous," thus giving a probable root-meaning of wonder or astonishment. He adds that among the *kalou* monsters and abortions are aften included, "and the list, already countless, is capable of constant increase, every object that is specially fearful, or vicious, or injurious, or novel, being eligible for admission" (*Fiji and the Fijians* [3d ed., London, 1870], p. 183). Hocart holds that this application of *kalou* to objects exciting wonder or astonishment is simply a corollary of the conception of *kalou* as "the dead." Ghosts and spirits, being *mana*, can do marvelous things; therefore what seems marvelous is *kalou*. When muskets were dubbed "*kalou* bows," the natives really thought that spirits had made them or possessed them (*J.R.A.I.*, XLII, 446). The missionaries in Fiji use the word *mana* in a compound expression, *dhakadhaka-mana*, signifying "miracle," and it is also applied to the divine name of Jehovah (Wallace Deane, *Fijian Society* [London, 1921], p. 88). According to David Hazelwood *mana* as a noun means a wonder or a miracle; as an adjective it means effectual or efficient as a remedy (*A Fijian and English and an English and Fijian Dictionary* [2d ed., London, 1872], p. 76).

²⁸ Edward Tregear, *The Maori-Polynesian Comparative Dictionary* (Wellington, New Zealand, 1891), *s.v. mana*.

²⁹ See E. S. C. Handy, "Polynesian Religion," *Bernice P. Bishop Museum Bulletin*, No. 34, pp. 26–34; F. R. Lehmann, *Mana. Der Begriff des "ausserordentlich Wirkungsvollen" bei Südseevölkern* (2d ed., Leipzig, 1922), especially pp. 2–5; R. Thurnwald, "Neue Forschungen zum Mana-Begriff," *Archiv für Religionswissenschaft*, XXVII (1929), 93–112.

The Maori word *atua* (Tongan *otua*, Marquesan *etua*, Hawaiian *akua*), while generally translated as "god," is also applied to evil spirits, ancestral ghosts, diseases thought to be of spiritual origin, and malicious or quarrelsome persons. It further applies to "various phenomena not understood," as menstruation, and, in fact, to "almost anything that is disagreeable or viewed as being supernatural." See Elsdon Best, "The Lore of the Whare-Kohanga," *Journal of the Polynesian Society*, XIV (1905), 210; *idem, The Maori as He Was* (Wellington, New Zealand, 1934), p. 67. Ivens thinks that the common rendering of *atua* as "god" was due to the missionaries rather than to any radical idea of deity possessed by the word itself. See W. G. Ivens, "The Polynesian Word 'Atua.' Its Derivation and Use," *Man*, XXIV (1924), 114 ff., 133 ff., 146 ff.

Another Maori word, *tipua*, denoting something "uncanny or strange," is also sometimes rendered as "demon." Inanimate objects, such as rocks and trees, might for one reason or another be considered as *tipua*, and any "impious interference" with them always brought down punishment upon the offender. All objects of this character possessed "an indwelling spirit or power" (Elsdon Best, *The Maori as He Was*, p. 53).

³⁰ A. C. Kruijt, in *Tijdschrift voor Indische Taal-Land-en Volkenkunde,* LXII (1922), 126 f. A magician is called *si-kerei,* "one who has magical power" (E. M. Loeb, "Shaman and Seer," *American Anthropologist* [n.s., 1929], XXXI, 66).

³¹ J. Ph. Duyvendak, *Inleiding tot de ethnologie van de Indische Archipel* (Groningen-Batavia, 1935), p. 146.

³² Johannes Winkler, *Die Toba-Batak auf Sumatra in gesunden und kranken Tagen* (Stuttgart, 1925), pp. 2 f. See also Johannes Warneck, *Die Religion der Batak* (Göttingen, 1909), pp. 8 ff.

³³ Paul Arndt, *Mythologie, Religion, und Magie im Sikagebiet (östl. Mittel-flores)* (Emde, Flores, 1932), pp. 92 ff. *Manar,* our authority notices, seems to be connected with the Melanesian *mana* (p. 94).

³⁴ A. Hueting, "De Tobeloreezen in hun denken en doen," *Bijdragen tot de Taal-Land-en Volkenkunde van Nederlandsch Indië,* LXXVII (1921), 251 ff.

³⁵ Charles Hose and William McDougall, *The Pagan Tribes of Borneo* (London, 1912), II, 29, note 1.

³⁶ J. Perham, "Petara, or Sea Dyak Gods," *Journal of the Straits Branch of the Royal Asiatic Society,* No. 8 (1881), 135.

³⁷ Janet B. Montgomery McGovern, *Among the Head-Hunters of Formosa* (London, 1922), pp. 146 f.

³⁸ John Batchelor, *The Ainu and Their Folk-Lore* (London, 1901), pp. 581 f.; idem, "Ainus," Hastings' *Encyclopaedia of Religion and Ethics,* I, 239 f. According to B. H. Chamberlain, "God," "supernatural," "wonderful" are perhaps the nearest approximations to the meaning of *kamui* (*Transactions of the Asiatic Society of Japan,* XVI, 33).

³⁹ W. G. Aston, *Shinto* (London, 1905), pp. 8 f. Motoöri's statements in regard to the *kami* are repeated almost word for word by his celebrated pupil Hirata. See E. M. Satow, "The Revival of Pure Shiñ-tau," *Transactions of the Asiatic Society of Japan,* Vol. III, Pt. I (Appendix), pp. 42 f. (pp. 48 f. of the original edition).

⁴⁰ W. W. Skeat, *Malay Magic* (London, 1900), pp. 93 f., 427 f.

⁴¹ Nelson Annandale, in Annandale and Robinson, *Fasciculi Malayensis, Anthropology,* Part I (London, 1903), p. 100.

⁴² W. W. Skeat, *op. cit.,* pp. 673 f., quoting C. O. Blagden. According to another account, "the word *kramat,* as applied to a man or woman, may be roughly translated prophet or magician. It is difficult to convey the real idea, as Malays call a man *kramat* who is able to get whatever ·he wishes for, who is able to foretell events, and whose presence brings good fortune to all his surroundings" (Skeat, p. 61, note 2, quoting G. C. Bellamy). We are further told that the application of this word to many old trees, stones, and some elephants, crocodiles, and other animals, "which are believed to possess a supernatural character," points rather to an older conception than to the notion of the personal sanctity of a living or a dead man, i.e., Moslem saintship. See R. J. Wilkinson, *A Malay-English Dictionary* (Singapore, 1901–1903), II, 509, *s.v. kěramat* or *karâmat.*

⁴³ W. W. Skeat, *op. cit.,* pp. 23 f. In Malacca the regalia include a book of genealogy, a code of laws, and a few weapons; in Perak they are drums, pipes, flutes, a betel box, a sword, a scepter, and an umbrella. In Selangor the regalia consist of the royal instruments of music, together with a betel box, a tobacco box, a spittoon, an umbrella, and several swords and lances. On state occasions these

are carried in procession (pp. 24 ff.). Some remarkable instances of the dangerous sanctity of these objects are mentioned by our authority (pp. 41 f.).

[44] Paul Giran, *Magie et religion Annamites* (Paris, 1912), pp. 21 ff.

[45] Henry Baudesson, *Indo-China and Its Primitive People* (London, 1919), p. 103.

[46] J. P. Combes, in Dourisboure, *Les sauvages Ba-Hnars (Cochinchine Orientale)*, (Paris, 1873), pp. 428 f.

[47] H. M. Marshall, *The Karen People of Burma* (Columbus, Ohio, 1922), pp. 210, 267, 318. *Ohio State University Bulletin*, Vol. XXVI, No. 13.

[48] A. R. Radcliffe-Brown, *The Andaman Islanders* (Cambridge, 1933), pp. 266 ff., 305 ff., 404.

[49] J. Abbott, *The Keys of Power*, pp. 3 ff. In the Punjab *barkat* varies in potency according to the rank and dignity of a person and also with the special merits which he may have obtained by heredity or by his own efforts. See Audrey O'Brien, "The Mohammedan Saints of the Western Punjab," *Journal of the Royal Anthropological Institute*, XLI (1911), 515 f.

[50] D. N. Majumdar, *A Tribe in Transition* (London, 1937), pp. 133 f.

[51] *Idem*, "Bongaism," in *Essays Presented to Rai Bahadur Sarat Chandra Roy* (Lucknow, 1942), pp. 60–79. Our authority points out that while *bonga* power may condense itself and be identified with things in the native environment (bicycles and locomotives have become Bongas and an airplane a very great Bonga), still the conception always remains quite indefinite and borders on the impersonal. Questions as to the shape, size, and other characteristics of Bongas are usually evaded by the tribal priests because they know nothing about them (pp. 64 ff., 77). Perhaps it should be rather said, they do not speculate about them.

[52] S. C. Roy, *Oraon Religion and Customs* (Ranchi, India, 1928), pp. 110 f. What, asks Sir Herbert Risley, do these jungle folk really believe? In most cases "the indefinite something which they fear and attempt to propitiate is not a person at all in any sense of the word. . . . . The idea which lies at the root of their religion is that of power, or rather of many powers." They do not define closely the objects making for evil rather than for good in the world about them—the primeval forest, the crumbling hills, the rushing river, the tiger, the poisonous snake. Some sort of power is there, and that is enough for them. Whether it is associated with a spirit or an ancestral ghost, whether it is one power or many, they do not stop to inquire *(Census of India*, 1901, Vol. I, Pt. I, pp. 352 f.).

[53] Arnold van Gennep, *Tabou et totémisme à Madagascar* (Paris, 1904), pp. 17 f., 81 f., 115 f. The Malagasy have the word *andriamanitra*, which seems originally to have signified "divine" and under Christian influence to have taken on the sense of "God." According to the missionary, William Ellis, "Whatever is great, whatever exceeds the capacity of their understandings, they designate by the one convenient and comprehensive appellation, *andriamanitra*. Whatever is new and useful and extraordinary, is called god." The word is applied to silk, rice, money, thunder and lightning, earthquakes, the ancestors, a deceased sovereign, and also to a book, "from its wonderful capacity of speaking by merely looking at it" (*History of Madagascar* [London, 1838], I, 390 ff.). Andriamanitra, though now in almost universal use as the divine name, is said to be of relatively recent derivation. See H. M. Dubois, "L'idée de Dieu chez les anciens Malgaches," *Anthropos*, XXIV (1929), 281–311; XXIX (1934), 757–74.

[54] Ralph Linton, *The Tanala* (Chicago, 1933), p. 162. *Field Museum of Natural History, Anthropological Series*, Vol. XXII.

[55] E. W. Smith, *The Religion of the Lower Races as Illustrated by the African Bantu* (New York, 1923), pp. 9 f.

[56] J. H. Driberg, "The Secular Aspect of Ancestor Worship in Africa," *Supplement to the Journal of the Royal African Society*, No. 138 (1936), pp. 3 f.

[57] H. A. Junod, *The Life of a South African Tribe* (2d ed., London, 1927), II, 429 ff.

[58] H. A. Stayt, *The Bavenda* (London, 1931), p. 262.

[59] E. W. Smith and A. M. Dale, *The Ila-speaking Peoples of Northern Rhodesia* (London, 1920), II, 79–90. According to R. J. Moore *bwanga* is more closely translated as the "essence of substances," their "operative properties" ("'Bwanga' among the Bemba," *Bantu Studies*, XV [1941], 40). For the Babemba *bwanga* is an abstraction such as our terms "properties" and "efficacy" (p. 44).

[60] C. M. Doke, *The Lambas of Northern Rhodesia* (London, 1931), pp. 290 f., 300 ff. *Ubwanga* is also used synonymously with *uwulembe*, the poison which Balamba put on their arrows (p. 291).

[61] A. Hetherwick, "Some Animistic Beliefs among the Yaos of British Central Africa," *Journal of the Anthropological Institute*, XXXII (1902), 93 f.

[62] *Idem*, "Nyanjas," Hastings' *Encyclopaedia of Religion and Ethics*, IX, 419 f.

[63] A. T. Culwick and G. M. Culwick, *Ubena of the Rivers* (London, 1935), pp. 100 ff.

[64] Sir Charles Eliot, in A. C. Hollis, *The Masai* (Oxford, 1905), pp. xviii ff. The Masai conception of the deity "seems to be marvelously vague. I was Ngai. My lamp was Ngai. Ngai was in the steaming holes. His house was in the eternal snows of Kilimanjaro. In fact, whatever struck them as strange or incomprehensible, that they at once assumed had some connection with Ngai" (Joseph Thomson, *Through Masai Land* [London, 1885], p. 445). According to another statement Ngai ("the Unknown") embodies the Masai "apprehension of power beyond human faculties of coping with." Thunderstorms, rain, the telegraph, and a locomotive are all referred to as Ngai (S. L. Hinde and Hildegarde Hinde, *The Last of the Masai* [London, 1901], p. 99). M. Merker describes Ngai as an incorporeal being, a spirit all-powerful, all-knowing, omnipresent, and eternal (*Die Masai* [Berlin, 1904], p. 196).

[65] C. W. Hobley, *Bantu Beliefs and Magic* (London, 1922), p. 62. According to Charles Dundas, Mulungu and Engai among the Akamba "are merely collective words meant to denote the plurality of the spiritual world" (*Journal of the Royal Anthropological Institute*, XLIII [1913], 535). According to Gerhard Lindblom, while some facts seem to substantiate a conception of Mulungu as a personal being, other facts suggest the idea of "a vague and somewhat impersonal" Mulungu. His significance varies even within the same tribe (*The Akamba in British East Africa* [2d ed., Uppsala, 1920], p. 249).

[66] W. S. Routledge and Katherine Routledge, *With a Prehistoric People* (London, 1910), pp. 225 ff. According to another account the Akikuyu recognize three gods—two good and one bad—but all are called Ngai (H. R. Tate, in *Journal of the Anthropological Institute*, XXXIV [1904], 263).

[67] Lucy P. Mair, *An African People in the Twentieth Century* (London, 1934), pp. 229 f., 234 f.

[68] J. H. Driberg, *The Lango* (London, 1923), pp. 216 ff., 224, 241, note 1. Among the Dinka, Jok comprises a host of ancestral ghosts, especially those of long dead and powerful persons. Among the Shilluk, Juok is a high god, for the most part otiose (p. 216, note 1). Among the Lotuko, Ajok is likewise a high god, but this word may also designate a spirit, good or bad, a pestilence, a misfortune,

and "anything marvelous" (L. Molinaro, "Appunti cerca gli usi, costumi, e idee religiose dei Lotuko dell'Uganda," *Anthropos*, XXXV–XXXVI [1940-41], 179).

[69] E. E. Evans-Pritchard, *Witchcraft, Oracles, and Magic among the Azande* (Oxford, 1937), pp. 33, 35, 82, 320 f., 463, 505 f. The Azande, declares Mgr. Lagae, believe that every natural object is endowed with a hidden virtue or specific property, good or evil, which he can utilize to his advantage. Happy the man who is able to discover this quality in things when others are ignorant of it (C. R. Lagae, *Les Azande ou Niam-Niam* [Brussels, 1926], p. 143).

[70] C. G. Seligman and Brenda Z. Seligman, *Pagan Tribes of the Nilotic Sudan* (London, 1932), p. 275, note 1, quoting G. O. Whitehead. According to the Seligmans *mian* is associated with the ghosts of the dead; in fact, *juokon* ("spirits") is a synonym of *mian*. This "dynamic potency," as our authors call it, is also contained in lightning. The Bari medicine man possesses *mian,* because of his intercourse with and control of the ghosts (pp. 251, 302).

[71] Georg Schweinfurth, *The Heart of Africa* (3d ed., London, 1878), I, 144.

[72] Paul Schebesta, *Revisiting My Pygmy Hosts* (London, 1936), pp. 187, 200.

[73] *Idem, My Pygmy and Negro Hosts* (London, 1936), pp. 263 ff. It appears from this account that while the clan elders are naturallly endowed with *elima* because of their relationship to the totems, all other people must acquire it. A man devoid of it is incapable of procreation (p. 263).

[74] Guy Burrows, *The Land of the Pigmies* (London, 1898), p. 100.

[75] A. de Calonne-Beaufaict, in *Le mouvement sociologique international,* 10ᵉ année (1909), 384.

[76] J. H. Weeks, "Stories and Other Notes from the Upper Congo," *Folk-Lore,* XII (1901), 186 f.; cf. *idem, Among Congo Cannibals* (London, 1913), p. 315.

[77] Cyrille van Overbergh, *Les Bangala (État Ind. du Congo)* (Brussels, 1907), p. 263, citing Lieutenant Coquilhat.

[78] Günter Tessmann, *Die Pangwe* (Berlin, 1913), II, 127 ff.

[79] R. E. Dennett, *The Folk-Lore of the Fjort* (London, 1898), pp. 131, 135. The terms *bu-nissi* and *mkissi-nssi* (the former probably the older) seem to be the equivalent of Dennett's *nkissi* and to convey the same conception of mysterious power. See E. Pechuël-Loesche, *Volkskunde von Loango* (Stuttgart, 1907), pp. 276 f. Among the Ovimbundu the term *cikola,* "sacred," which they apply to the idols and charms of a witch doctor, also means "powerful." See G. A. Dorsey, "The 'Ocimbanda,' or Witch Doctor of the Ovimbundu of Portuguese Southwest Africa," *Journal of American Folk-Lore,* XII (1899), 184.

[80] P. A. Talbot, *In the Shadow of the Bush* (London, 1912), p. 49.

[81] C. K. Meek, "The Meaning of the Cowrie; the Evil Eye in Nigeria," *Man,* XLI (1941), 48.

[82] S. S. Farrow, *Faith, Fancies, and Fetich, or Yoruba Paganism* (London, 1926), pp. 118 f.

[83] G. Kiti, "Le fétichisme au Dahomey," *La reconnaissance Africaine,* II (1926), 2 f., quoting a Christianized native. According to M. J. Herskovits a native translates the term *vodun* by the word "god." He quotes a lay informant who, when asked the nature of *vodun,* replied, "One does not know what it is. It is a power. . . . . It is the power, the 'force' that goes about in the temple" (*Dahomey* [New York, 1938], II, 170, 172).

[84] Sir A. B. Ellis, *The Tshi-speaking Peoples of the Gold Coast of West Africa* (London, 1887), pp. 18 f.

[85] Diedrich Westermann, *Die Kpelle* (Göttingen, 1921), pp. 201 f.

[86] Henri Labouret, *Les tribus du rameau Lobi* (Paris, 1931), pp. 437 ff.

[87] *Ibid.,* pp. 497–502. See also Labouret, *Les Manding et leur langue* (Paris, 1934), pp. 121 ff., referring specifically to the Bambara. According to another authority *n'ama* is rather to be considered as an evil force, energy, or power possessed, not only by certain animals and human beings, but by every living thing. It causes sickness, suffering, and death. See J. Henry, *L'âme d'un peuple Africain; les Bambara* (Münster in Westfalen, 1910), p. 27.

[88] Edward Westermarck, *Ritual and Belief in Morocco* (London, 1926), I, 35–261. Among the Berbers of the Rif *baraka* is usually confined to the supposed descendants of the Prophet. It is dependent on their possession of a "magical emanation" supposedly transmitted to them from Mohammed. A man having it can predict the future, perform miracles, heal or destroy by his touch or by employing some object which has been in contact with his body, such as a part of his clothing, a piece of bread, or an egg which he has kissed (C. S. Coon, in *Harvard African Studies* [Cambridge, Mass., 1931], IX, 157).

[89] Edward Westermarck, *op. cit.,* I, 387 f.

[90] Rafael Karsten, *The Civilization of the South American Indians* (London, 1926), pp. 155, 375.

[91] Erland Nordenskiöld, *Indianerleben* (Leipzig, 1912), pp. 251, 257 f., 260.

[92] Alfred Métraux, in *Bulletin of the Bureau of American Ethnology,* No. 134, p. 150.

[93] M. W. Stirling, "Jivaro Shamanism," *Proceedings of the American Philosophical Society,* LXXII (1933), 137 f.; *idem,* "Historical and Ethnographical Material on the Jivaro Indians," *Bulletin of the Bureau of American Ethnology,* No. 117, pp. 115 f.

[94] Charles Wisdom, *The Chorti Indians of Guatemala* (Chicago, 1940), pp. 317 f., 326 ff.

[95] Franz Boas, "Religion," *Handbook of American Indians,* Part II, p. 366. In Indian languages a word is usually found "comprehending all manifestations of the unseen world, yet conveying no sense of personal unity. It has been rendered spirit, demon, God, devil, mystery, magic, but commonly and rather absurdly by the English and French, 'medicine'." In addition to *manito, oki,* and similar terms among North American tribes, there are the Aztec *teotl,* the Quechua *huaca,* and the Maya *ku.* "They all express in its most general form the idea of the supernatural." See D. G. Brinton, *The Myths of the New World* (3d ed., Philadelphia, 1896), p. 62. The same idea seems to have been expressed by the word *zemi,* as used by the Taino, the extinct aborigines of the Greater Antilles. *Zemi,* "meaning originally magic power, came to be applied to all supernatural beings and their symbolic representations." In several Arawak dialects the word for tobacco is *tchemi,* evidently referring to its magic power (*zemi*). See J. W. Fewkes, in *Twenty-fifth Annual Report of the Bureau of American Ethnology,* p. 54.

[96] J. N. B. Hewitt, "'Orenda' and a Definition of Religion," *American Anthropologist* (n.s., 1902), IV, 33–46; *idem,* "Orenda," *Handbook of American Indians,* Part II, pp. 147 f.; *idem,* "Otkon," p. 164. *Orenda* is a Huron word. A Jesuit Father, Paul Ragueneau, in his *Relation* of 1647–48, declares that most things "that seem at all unnatural or extraordinary to our Hurons are easily accepted in their minds as *oky,*" i.e., as possessing occult power (*Jesuit Relations and Allied Documents* [Cleveland, 1896–1901], XXXIII, 211). According to a still earlier account the name for spirit in Huron is *oki.* See F. G. Sagard, *Le grand voyage du pays des Hurons* (Paris, 1865), pp. 160 ff. Sagard's travels were originally published in 1632. If we are to believe Captain John Smith, the Powhatan Indians of Virginia definitely personified Oke as their chief god. His image, "evil-favoredly carved," was set up in the temples. See *Travels and Works of Captain John Smith,* edited by E. Arber (Edinburgh, 1910), I, 75.

[97] William Jones, "The Algonkin 'Manitou,'" *Journal of American Folk-Lore*, XVIII (1905), 183–90 (with reference to the Sauk, Fox, and Kickapoo Indians); A. F. Chamberlain, "Manito," *Handbook of American Indians*, Part I, pp. 800 f.

[98] Alanson Skinner, "The Menomini Word 'Häwätûk,'" *Journal of American Folk-Lore*, XXVIII (1915), 258 ff.

[99] F. G. Speck, "Penobscot Shamanism," *Memoirs of the American Anthropological Association*, No. 28 (Vol. VI, Pt. 4), p. 240 and note 1.

[100] Frederick Johnson, "Notes on Micmac Shamanism," *Primitive Man*, XVI (1943), 58 f.

[101] Clark Wissler, "Ceremonial Bundles of the Blackfoot Indians," *Anthropological Papers of the American Museum of Natural History*, VII, 103. According to Blackfoot speculation a power (*natoji* or sun power), most closely associated with the sun but pervading the entire world, can manifest itself through any object, animate or inanimate. Such a manifestation is by speech rather than by action. In every narrative relating to *natoji* it is stated or implied that at the moment of speaking the object becomes for the time being "as a person." The power communicates with mankind through dreams (*loc. cit.*).

[102] The Rev. W. J. Cleveland, in S. R. Riggs, *A Dakota-English Dictionary* (Washington, D.C., 1890), pp. 507 f. *Contributions to North American Ethnology*, Vol. VII. Our informant adds that *wakan* seems to be the only word for "holy," "sacred," but among the wilder Indians there is the feeling that if the Bible, the church, and the missionary are *wakan* they are to be avoided, "not as being bad or dangerous, but as *wakan*" (*loc. cit.*).

On Omaha *wakonda* see Alice C. Fletcher and Francis La Flesche, in *Twenty-seventh Annual Report of the Bureau of American Ethnology*, pp. 597–99; Miss Fletcher, "Wakonda," *Handbook of American Indians*, Part II, pp. 897 f. Among the Oto the concept of *wakonda* has been personalized under Christian influence, so that today they think of Wakonda as the Great Spirit, or God (William Whitman, *The Oto* [New York, 1937], p. 84).

Among the Winnebago the term *wakan* is exactly equivalent to our word "sacred," while *wakandja*, which is identical with the Omaha word *wakonda*, refers to an individualized spirit, in this case, the thunderbird. It would seem that among these Indians, owing to the marked development of deities and cosmogonic myths, "sacred" objects are interpreted "as being either some manifestation of a spirit, some transformation which he had assumed, or as inhabited by a spirit" (Paul Radin, in *Thirty-seventh Annual Report of the Bureau of American Ethnology*, pp. 282 f.). Elsewhere our authority points out that *wakandja*, as used by the Winnebago, always referred to "definite spirits, not necessarily definite in shape," and that the same was true of the term *manito*, as used by the Ojibwa (Chippewa), an Algonquian tribe. "If at a vapor bath the steam is regarded as *wakanda* or *manito*, it is because it is a spirit transformed into steam for the time being; if an arrow is possessed of specific virtues, it is because a spirit has either transformed himself into the arrow or because he is temporarily dwelling in it; and, finally, if tobacco is offered to a peculiarly shaped object, it is because either this object belongs to a spirit or a spirit is residing in it" ("Religion of the North American Indians," *Journal of American Folk-Lore*, XXVII [1914], 349). What we have in the case of these Indians is, clearly enough, a pronounced trend toward personalization, resulting in the emergence of distinctly animistic conceptions.

[103] Fletcher and La Flesche, in *Twenty-seventh Annual Report of the Bureau of American Ethnology*, p. 486. Cf. J. O. Dorsey, "A Study of Siouan Cults," *Eleventh Annual Report*, p. 367.

[104] R. H. Lowie, "The Religion of the Crow Indians," *Anthropological Papers of the American Museum of Natural History*, XXV, 315 ff.

[105] Washington Matthews, *Ethnography and Philology of the Hidatsa Indians* (Washington, D.C., 1877), pp. 47 f. *Department of the Interior, U.S. Geological and Geographical Survey, Miscellaneous Publications*, No. 7.

[106] G. A. Dorsey, *Traditions of the Skidi Pawnee* (Boston, 1904), pp. 330 f.

[107] Washington Matthews, *Navaho Legends* (New York, 1897), p. 37. The word means "sacred, divine, mysterious, or holy." It does not seem to be used with an application to anything evil. The word *digini* refers to holy people, gods, or divinities.

[108] Grenville Goodwin, "White Mountain Apache Religion," *American Anthropologist* (n.s., 1938), XL, 28. The word means "holy, supernatural, or supernatural power." The original source of this power, exhibited in awe-inspiring and unexplainable phenomena, is the supreme deity.

[109] F. G. Speck, "Notes on Chickasaw Ethnology and Folk-Lore," *Journal of American Folk-Lore*, XX (1907), 57 and note 1. The word means "mystery," "supernatural agency." A girl's first menstrual experience is called *hulabe*.

[110] Edward Sapir, *Southern Paiute Dictionary* (Boston, 1931), p. 622. *Proceedings of the American Academy of Arts and Sciences*, Vol. LXV, No. 3.

[111] W. Z. Park, *Shamanism in Western North America* (Evanston, 1938), pp. 15, 20. *Northwestern University Studies in the Social Sciences*, No. 2. The White Knife Shoshoni of Nevada call "supernatural" power *buha*. Everybody must have a minimum amount of *buha* in order to live at all—it is the life-principle—but some people possess much more of it than others (J. S. Harris, in Ralph Linton [editor], *Acculturation in Seven American Indian Tribes* [New York, 1940], pp. 56 f.). These Shoshoni also have a special name, *dijibo*, for the "power for evil" (p. 62).

[112] A. L. Kroeber, *Handbook of the Indians of California* (Washington, D.C., 1925), pp. 512 f. The term is the "obvious equivalent" of *mana, orenda, wakanda,* and *manito*. It is used "to denote spirits, supernatural or monstrous beings of any sort, men who possess spiritual or magical power, and, if indications are not deceiving, the essence or power or quality itself."

[113] E. M. Loeb, "Pomo Folkways," *University of California Publications in American Archaeology and Ethnology*, XIX, 306 f. The Pomo conception of *kaocal* bears no reference to spiritual beings; it relates to human beings who possess *kaocal* and transmit it. When a man gave to a maternal nephew or to a son his position and dignity in the tribe he also gave the boy his store of *kaocal*. Its bestowal took place gradually, from the time the child was very young until the period of initiation at puberty. The *kaocal* was transmitted partly by prayer and partly by rubbing the recipient's body—the arms to make him an expert shot, the legs to make him a good runner and dancer. Bows and arrows were rubbed with pepperwood leaves in order to give them *kaocal*. If a man was always successful, he was said to have *kaocal*, and the same was true of a bow and arrow (*loc. cit.*).

[114] E. W. Gifford, in *Anthropos*, XXXIV (1939), 368. *Matas* is said to be the "equivalent" of *mana*.

[115] Jaime de Angulo, "La psychologie religieuse des Achumawi," *ibid.*, XXIII (1928), 154 and note 12, 160. The word *tinihowi* is the nominative form of a verb of which the root—*how*—signifies "*sacré*, mysterious, extraordinary, supernatural, powerful." By this term the Indian refers to a force regarded as diffuse and immanent in all things and yet at the same time possessed by a particular being, a tutelary spirit.

[116] Myron Eells, in *Annual Report of the Smithsonian Institution for 1887,*

Part I, p. 672. The noun, *tamanous,* in the Chinook jargon, refers to any spiritual being, good or bad, more powerful than man. As an adjective *tamanous* "is used to describe any stick, stone, or similar article in which spirits are at times supposed to dwell, and also any man, as a medicine man, who is supposed to have more than ordinary power with these spirits; hence we often hear of *tamanous* sticks and *tamanous* men. It is likewise a verb, and to *tamanous* is to perform the incantations necessary to influence these spirits" (*loc. cit.*). Similarly the Quinault use the jargon word *tomanawus* as meaning tutelary spirit, or even "power," in a sense "almost equivalent to *mana* or impersonal, unpersonified power" (R. L. Olson, *The Quinault Indians* [Seattle, 1936], p. 120, note 46).

[117] Franz Boas, "Religious Terminology of the Kwakiutl," in *Race, Language, and Culture* (New York, 1940), pp. 612 f. *Naualak* is defined as "supernatural power" (*idem,* in *Thirty-fifth Annual Report of the Bureau of American Ethnology,* Part II, p. 1416).

[118] J. R. Swanton, in *Memoirs of the American Museum of Natural History,* VIII, 13. *Sgana,* a word which Swanton's interpreters rendered by "power," also means "supernatural being" (p. 38).

[119] *Idem,* in *Twenty-sixth Annual Report of the Bureau of American Ethnology,* p. 451, note. *Yek,* or "supernatural power," impresses the Tlingit "as a vast immensity, one in kind and impersonal," but taking on "a personal, and it might be said a human personal form" whenever it manifests itself to men. The term is therefore used to describe the innumerable spirits with which the Tlingit invest the world.

[120] E. M. Weyer, *The Eskimos, Their Environment and Folkways* (New Haven, 1932), pp. 389 ff. With reference particularly to the Eskimo of West Greenland Kai Birket-Smith declares that *sila* means "mystic power," but is also translated as "weather," "world," or "understanding." Its primary sense seems to be "that which is outside everywhere," the mystic power permeating all existence and in itself neither good nor bad but dangerous to those who do not know how to handle it. The conception is comparable to the Iroquoian *orenda* and the Melanesian *mana* (*Meddeleleser om Grønland,* LXVI [1924], 433).

[121] Laura W. Benedict, *A Study of Bagobo Ceremonial, Magic, and Myth* (New York, 1916), pp. 203 f. *Annals of the New York Academy of Sciences,* Vol. XXV.

[122] Ralph Linton, *op. cit.,* p. 218.

[123] The religious systems of antiquity contain terms equivalent, or nearly equivalent, to *mana.* Such a term was the Egyptian *hīke,* conveying the idea of the "mysterious efficacy" resident in certain words and actions and then by extension describing all "magical arts" which required special marvelous knowledge to perform. See A. H. Gardiner, in *Proceedings of the Society of Biblical Archaeology,* XXXVII (1915), 253; XXXVIII (1916), 52; T. E. Peet, in *Cambridge Ancient History,* I, 354, II, 199 ff. The notion of *mana* also inheres in the Semitic (Hebrew) term *'ēl* ("god, God, divine power"), which seems originally to have referred to what was strange or uncanny and hence magically operative. See Karl Beth, "El und Neter," *Zeitschrift fur die alttestamentliche Wissenschaft,* XXXVI (1916), 129 ff., 153. In India the term *brahmă* (neuter) meant the magical power of a rite or spoken formula, as in the *Rig-Veda,* and then the "holy power" evoked by chants and sacrifices. In some of the Upanishads and the *Mahabharata* the impersonal *brahmă* becomes a personal Brahmā (masculine), the Supreme God. Buddhist *ṛddhi* (Pali *iddhi*) is translated as the "wondrous gift" or power which some men acquire by pious works, penance, the recitation of certain formulas, and especially by contemplation. In Greece the conception of *mana* is expressed by the word *dynamis* (δύναμις), "power," especially miraculous power, as in the New Testament (Mark V, 30, and many other

passages). Another word, *exousia* (ἐξουσία), often appears there, designating "authority" or "freedom" to use the force expressed by *dynamis*. Christianity also employed the term *charis* (χάρις) in the sense of the divine "grace" freely granted to believers. *Charisma* (χάρισμα), plural *charismata*, describes this "gift of grace." Here the *mana* power is regarded exclusively under its good and noble aspect. The Latin word corresponding most closely to *mana* is *numen*, not in its developed sense of the power of the gods or of deity, but in the earlier, vaguer sense of mysterious and therefore dangerous power, hardly personal at all, *Numen inest, numen adest.*

Chapter II

MAGIC AND ANIMISM

Occult power, when conceived of as impersonal, pertains as a quality or property to certain objects, on the basis of man's experience with them and their attributes. Being impersonal, it can be brought under man's control. If manipulated by the right operator, in the right way, and at the right time, it will produce a wished-for effect, unless nullified by another and stronger operator, human or nonhuman.

Occult power, when conceived of as personal, attaches to spiritual beings, who are volitional agents. The denizens of the unseen world form a motley company: ghosts of the dead, or disembodied souls; spirits, good and bad, who never had a human embodiment; and gods of low or high degree. Their number is legion, they are omnipresent, and in their several ways they are constantly interposing for weal or woe in human affairs. Sometimes man attempts to compel them to do his bidding; more often he takes a humble, petitionary attitude toward them and seeks by prayer and sacrifice an abundance of good things in this life and the next; always he tries to conciliate them when angered and to avoid entirely those spiritual beings who are never thought of as benevolent but are feared as hostile and malignant. It is impossible to imagine ghosts, spirits, and gods without emotions, desires, a certain amount of intelligence, and bodily shape—in short, without some measure of human personality. The personalizing tendency becomes stronger with advancing culture and reaches its height in the great polytheistic religions of antiquity.

There is, then, a fundamental distinction between a power exhibiting uniform invariable tendencies, which man can utilize for his own purposes, and a power manifested capriciously toward man by spiritual beings, whose capriciousness increases with their growing personalization. Clear and definite though the distinction be for us, it remains vague and fluid for primitive thought. When an object is regarded as inactive, any particular quality or property which it possesses will necessarily assume an impersonal character.

38

When, on the other hand, the emphasis is on the object as acting, the quality or property in question will be attached to a personal being. Primitive thought passes without difficulty from the one formulation to the other, so that an "influence" is readily magnified into a "spirit" and a "spirit" is as readily attenuated into an "influence." In this twilight zone magic, which is always effectual of itself (*ex opere operato*), and animism, which always involves the intervention of spiritual beings, merge insensibly into each other. Whether the impersonal or the personal manifestations of occult power receive the more attention will depend entirely on the relative prevalence in one or the other society of the magical or the animistic interpretation of the phenomenal world. As has been pointed out, with particular reference to the rude Oraon of Chota Nagpur, "soul, spirit, energy, and power are generally convertible terms in the primitive vocabulary."[1]

Spiritual beings are often credited with a knowledge of magic. They hand it down to men and sometimes use it in their relations with men.

It is a general belief among the southeastern tribes of Australia that "song-charms against magic" are communicated by the ancestral ghosts to people in their sleep.[2] In New South Wales Baiame, an idealized headman and incipient high god, is called by one of the tribes the "mightiest and most famous" of magic workers.[3] Central Australian medicine men, when not initiated by old practitioners, derive their occult powers from the *iruntarinia*. These are, in reality, doubles of the tribal ancestors, who lived in the far-distant Alcheringa time and possessed a natural knowledge of magic. They themselves practice it. If a plentiful supply of witchetty grubs, emus, or other items of the tribal dietary should appear without the performance by the natives of certain magical ceremonies (the *intichiuma*), it is said that well-disposed *iruntarinia* have celebrated them.[4] The power of magicians among the Murngin of Northern Territory comes to them directly from the ghosts of the dead.[5] In the mythology of the Kimberley tribes of Western Australia Kaleru, the most sacred of the totemic ancestors, figures as the maker of rivers, rain, spirit children, and marriage laws. "He is the source of magical power not only in the past but also in the present."[6]

The folk tales of the western islanders of Torres Straits represent Kwoiam, the warrior hero, as employing magical formulas and objects for assistance in various ways.[7] The weather magic of the Marind in Netherlands New Guinea comes from Jawima, the

Rainmaker and Thunderer. When a great drought had blasted all vegetation and the people were in dire straits, he first produced for them the healing showers. One of his sons is the west monsoon, which brings rain and stormy seas; the other son is the east monsoon.[8] The procedure followed by a Keraki magician is supposed to follow the model set up aforetime by Kambel the Originator or by his son, Wambuwamba.[9]

Among the myths of the Trobrianders are those relating to the spirits who taught men certain practices of nefarious magic. The magical art, for these islanders, was never invented. "In olden days, when mythical things happened, magic came from underground, or was given to a man by some non-human being, or was handed on to descendants by the original ancestress." The very essence of magic is the impossibility of its being originated by man, its complete resistance to any change in it by him. "It has existed ever since the beginning of things; it creates, but it is never created; it modifies, but must never be modified."[10] In Rossel Island a god, called Ye, appears in animal form as a huge fish hawk. He is one of the few exceptions to the general rule that the principal gods are embodied in snakes. Unlike them, also, he possesses a wicked nature. Once Ye had an incestuous relationship with his sister. A little dog near by laughed at the sight, whereupon Ye converted the dog's speech into an unintelligible bark, which would not spread the news of his shameful act. He afterward killed his sister by sorcery. She was the first to die as the result of its practice. To Ye is attributed the origin of sorcery, "the most evil thing in the world."[11]

The coast dwellers of the Gazelle Peninsula, New Britain, ascribe sickness and other ills to ghosts and evil spirits. Spells nullifying their machinations are revealed by spirits well disposed toward mankind.[12] The spells of the Solomon Islanders came to them from their ancestors, who learned them in dreams from forefathers still more remote.[13]

A Maori myth deals with Tu-matauenga, a child of Heaven and Earth and one of the first generation of gods. He devoured his four brothers and converted them into food. For each article of food he assigned a fitting incantation that it might be abundant and easily procured. Another myth relates how the god Rongo-takawiu shaped the hero Whakatau out of the apron which a woman, Apakura, wore in front as a covering, gave him life, and then taught him "magic and the use of enchantments of every kind."[14] The Maori personified witchcraft (*makutu*). The wicked goddess Makutu dwelt with Miru, another goddess equally wicked, in the dread underworld. Thither came Rongomai, a celebrated demigod and ancestor of the Maori. He learned from Makutu and Miru charms and spells and the art of witchcraft, together with ritual songs, dances, and games. One of his companions was caught by Miru, who claimed the man as payment for the knowledge imparted, but Rongomai and the rest of his bold band got away safely and returned to the bright world of the living.[15] According to another Maori belief witchcraft was especially associated with Whiro, described as one of the most active and pernicious of the departmental gods. He represented both evil and death. He and his satellites were always trying to destroy both living men and the souls of the dead in the underworld. All magic of the black variety was connected with Whiro and was believed to have originated in his abode. From Whiro sorcerers drew their power.[16]

The deified legendary founder of the Japanese Empire, Jimmu Tenno, is said to have first taught the use of magical formulas, while to the gods Ohonamochi and Sukunabikona is ascribed the origin of other forms of magic.[17]

According to a story current among the Land Dayak there was a time, long, long ago, when the people lived in great distress. They knew no remedies for illness nor how to preserve their rice fields from blight and animal pests. Then Tupa Jing looked down from heaven and saw their plight and pitied them. He rescued a poor sick woman, whose husband was about to burn her alive, in accordance with the custom of dealing with those who seemed hopelessly ill, took her up to his sky dwelling, and instructed her in all magical mysteries. Upon returning to earth she taught the people everything she had learned, and so they became familiar with the healing art and the proper magic for their crops.[18] By the Lushai of Assam an acquaintance with sorcery is attributed to the creator god Pathian. From him his daughter learned it, and she in turn imparted it to Vahrika, another mythological figure, as a ransom for her life. From Vahrika the knowledge and practice of black magic passed through other intermediaries to mankind.[19] The Maria Gond of Bastar say that the first person in the world to practice sorcery was Nandraj Guru and that from him all the gods and the Dead acquired the art. It happened once upon a time that a Maria, while digging roots in the jungle, came upon the Guru teaching the disciples and went there secretly every day to listen to what was said. At length the Guru discovered his presence and had him eat, unwittingly, the liver of his own son, thus giving him knowledge of evil and death. He became the first sorcerer, and from him men learned how to injure and kill their enemies.[20]

The divining doctor in South Africa (a very important functionary) is a specialist who diagnoses the "real" cause of a disease. In the Sotho tribes he follows set rules which are learned from other diviners and often makes no claim to any special endowment from the ancestral ghosts. But in the Bathonga, Xosa, Zulu, Swazi, and related tribes the majority of practitioners claim to be directly guided and controlled in all their activities by the ancestors.[21]

The magician among the Lango, a Nilotic tribe of Uganda, derives his unusual powers of clairvoyance, hypnotism, and ventriloquism from the high god Jok, either directly or through an ancestral ghost. These powers not only make him very impressionable to the personality of Jok but also give him "a kind of directing influence" over that deity. By the use of substitutes, scapegoats, and magical tricks he is even able on occasion to exert an influence superior to that of Jok himself.[22] The Shilluk medicine man, who practices magic for the good of the people, has received his powers either directly from the high god Juok or through the ancestors as intermediaries.[23]

Mbori, the Supreme Being of the Azande, created the world and everything in the world, including magical objects and oracles. But the connection between these and Mbori is very remote. If you ask a native where a medicine came from he will reply that the people always possessed it or that it originated with another people from whom it was borrowed. Only when you press him to produce an ultimate origin will he mention Mbori. However, the Azande possess a few myths accounting for magical objects or vouching for their efficacy in past times. A story of this sort tells how, long ago, the magician Rakpo, a primitive Moses, went forth with his chief to battle against invaders. On the return the army found itself with the enemy in the rear and a wide river in front. Then Rakpo, who could do many wonderful things, took some medicine from his horn and threw it into the river, so that the waters parted and left a stretch of dry land. The army crossed over safely, but when the enemy pursued into the river, the waters "shook and caught them and flowed over them and slew them so that they all perished."[24]

The Nkundu of the Belgian Congo say that since Dzakomba

created everything, he created magic. It is divine. It comes from God.[25] Similarly the Bakongo attribute to Nzambi, the supreme being and first cause of all things, the origin of charms. These he gave to the ancestors. They may indulge in magical activity and be themselves dominated by the magic employed by their living descendants.[26]

For the Bafia of Cameroons all magic was originated by Mubei, their tribal progenitor. He it was who devised the first magical instrumentalities.[27] The Ekoi of southern Nigeria recognize the existence of two deities, Obassi Osaw, the sky god, and Obassi Nsi, the earth god. Witchcraft (*ojje*) is supposed to be derived from the former, while all good magic comes from the latter. Sometimes the people pray to Obassi Nsi to destroy witchcraft, for they believe that it cannot withstand his might.[28] The Yoruba believe that Ifa divination was taught to human beings by the gods themselves. Furthermore, Ifa, the god from whom this divinatory system takes its name, controls those elements of the procedure which we, in our ignorance, would ascribe to chance.[29]

Magic (*gbo*) in Dahomey comes from Mawu, "the generic symbol of deity," as its ultimate source, but mediately from Legba, her youngest child. Certain other divine beings also know magic and, when called upon to perform cures, make use of it. This is testified by the aphorism, "Without *gbo* the gods cannot cure." From them magic was transmitted to mankind.[30] In Togo the people say that the supreme deity made good magic when he made men. He gave it to them for help in all their concerns. Since the deity dwells far removed from earthly affairs they cannot seek after him and find him, but the magicians are always available in his place.[31]

The Arecuna, a Carib tribe of southeastern Venezuela, ascribe the origin of magic to a mythical *piai,* or medicine man, who met five runaway children in the forest. He instructed them in magical arts and gave them tobacco and other medicines, not for themselves alone but for all doctors who should come after them.[32] The Arawak of British Guiana have a culture hero, Arawanili, who was initiated into the mysteries of magic by a river spirit. Arawanili used it to combat the activity of the malignant creatures causing sickness and death among men. He thus became "the founder of that system which has since prevailed among all the Indian tribes."[33] The Cayapa of Ecuador regard their spirits as very powerful magicians for both good and ill and think that by their aid men are enabled to practice the magical art.[34] The ancient Mexicans believed that their magical rites had been taught them by two divinities, Oxomoco and Cipactonal.[35]

In the Navaho myth of origins we are told that First Man and First Woman, during a visit to a mountain where the gods dwelt, learned the "awful secrets" of witchcraft.[36] The Zuñi origin myth tells how two witches accompanied the Indians on the way from the underworld to the surface of the earth and the bright sunlight. "Now why did you come out?" they were asked. "You ought not to come out. Have you something useful?" And they answered, "Yes, we are to be with you people because this world is small. Soon this world will be full of people and as the world grows smaller and smaller (i.e., more crowded) we shall kill some of the people."[37] According to the Hopi myth witches are descendants of Spider Woman, who has a prominent part in the accounts of the beginnings of human life on the earth. Originally all people lived in crowded quarters underground. Many of them fell into evil ways. So the chiefs led their good subjects to the surface and left the malefactors beneath it, all save Spider Woman and several other witches, who managed to get out with the others. Not long after this happened Spider Woman or one of her wicked followers brought about the first death. Since then the Hopi have considered witchcraft to be the most common cause of death.[38]

In the mythology of the Tlingit of southern Alaska Yehl (Jelch), the Raven, has a prominent role. He was the creator of men and their benefactor, but he also taught them the art of sorcery during his life on the earth.[39]

All the incantations of the Siberian Koriak were bequeathed to them by the Creator, who wanted to aid their struggle against disease-inflicting spirits. He and his wife constantly appear as acting personages in the incantations.[40] The Buriat call by the name of "smiths" those spirits, both good and bad, from whom occult powers are derived by men. Such spirits, it is thought, first taught men the smith's craft as well as the art of magic.[41]

The intervention of spiritual beings is often sought by placatory means to give efficacy or an additional efficacy to a rite which in form is magical. They are addressed by the magician in persuasive or conciliatory language and perhaps are provided with appropriate offerings. In a few cases such procedures seem to be regarded as really superfluous; the magical rite is assumed to be effective without them.

In a time of severe drought the Dieri of South Australia, "crying out in loud voices the impoverished state of the country and the half-starved condition of the tribe," beg the ghosts of their remote predecessors, the sky-dwelling Mura-Mura, for power to make a heavy rainfall. Then they go through an elaborate performance to generate rain in the dark clouds. Two medicine men, supposed to have received a special inspiration from the Mura-Mura, are bled, and the blood is made to flow on their comrades. At the same time they throw up handfuls of down, some of which adheres to the bodies of the other men, while the rest floats in the air. "The blood is to symbolize the rain, and the down, the clouds." Meanwhile large stones are carried away by the medicine men and placed high up in the tallest tree to be found. The stones represent real clouds mounting upward in the sky and presaging rain. Finally the other men of the tribe, young and old, surround a hut which has been erected for the occasion, butt at it with their heads, and force their way through, repeating the process until the hut is wrecked. "The piercing of the hut with their heads symbolizes the piercing of the clouds, and the fall of the hut symbolizes that of the rain." If after these ceremonies the rain fails to come, the Dieri believe that the Mura-Mura are angry with them; should there be no rain for weeks or months thereafter they suppose that some other tribe has "stopped their power." In rainy seasons, when the downpour has been too heavy, the Dieri also supplicate the Mura-Mura to hold back the discharge from the heavens. Old men have been seen in a state of frenzy, believing that by their ceremonies they had brought on an oversupply of rain.[42]

In the Warramunga tribe of Central Australia there are elaborate ceremonies concerned with the Wollunqua, a mythical snake so gigantic that were it to stand up on its tail its head would reach deep into the heavens. It lives now in a certain large water hole remote from men, but the natives are fearful that sometime it may come out of its hiding place and destroy them. The ceremonies, in scope and nature, are precisely similar to those connected with totemic animals, and the Wollunqua itself is a dominant totem, the great Father of all snakes. But the performers have no idea of securing the increase of the Wollunqua, as with the other totemic ceremonies; it would seem, rather, that they wish to conciliate this dreaded creature. The Wollunqua is said to be pleased when the ceremonies are carried out and displeased when they are omitted. Our authorities describe them as being "a primitive form" of propitiation, the only ones of the sort with which they have come into contact. At the same time an element of coercion is not absent, for the ceremonies are believed to control, to a certain extent, the activity of the Wollunqua.[43]

In rain making as practiced by the Keraki, a Papuan tribe, the operator imitates the actions which he believes that Wambu-wamba, the heavenly rain maker, must perform before rain can come. At the same time he calls upon this mythological being, in a form of speech "which we can hardly refuse to designate as prayer" to send the rain.[44] Among the Orokaiva the ghosts of the dead are appealed to, not only in magic performed for public ends, but also in that of the nefarious and disreputable sort.[45] Similarly among the Mailu all the magical formulas include an appeal to an ancestral ghost, particularly the ghost of some recently deceased ancestor such as the father or grandfather of the man reciting the spell.[46] A Kiwai magician occasionally appeals to two sky beings, Delboa and Sura, to send down rain. When doing so, he takes water in his mouth and blows it upward.[47] The Kai, a mountain-dwelling tribe in what was formerly German New Guinea, constantly invoke the help of the ghosts, both those of the recent dead and those of men and women who for eminent achievements in their lives are long remembered after death. Thus to make rain the Kai pronounce a spell over a stone, at the same time calling upon two ghostly heroes to drive away Jondimi, the woman who holds up the rain. When in answer to this mingled spell and prayer enough rain has fallen, the people stop the downpour by spreading hot ashes over the stone or by putting it in a wood fire. In this case there is no animistic invocation; the magic alone suffices.[48] By the Yabob, who occupy two small islands off the southeastern coast of New Guinea, spirits are regularly invoked and offerings made to them in magical rituals to bring rain, create sunshine, and secure a calm sea for sailors.[49]

The Trobianders, who associate ancestral ghosts with certain magical performances, ask them to accept food offerings and make the magic successful. At some ceremonies these ghosts are supposed to be present, and, if anything goes wrong, they will "become angry," so the people say. In general, they act as advisers and helpers who see to it that everything is done in accordance with the traditional procedure. The ancestors also appear in dreams and tell a magician what to do. He does not command them directly; they are never his instruments.[50] The Dobuans, on the contrary, control a "pantheon of demons" by means of spells. Not all spiritual beings are thus subject, however, to the magician's will. Some can act independently. When, for instance, the rain is delayed after the recital of a rain spell, spirits that have not been called upon in the spell will be credited with frustrating the magic. "So the face of the ritualist is saved in time of trouble."[51] In the northern islands of the D'Entrecasteaux group a distinction is frequently made between sorcery which requires an address to a spirit to be effective and sorcery without such an invocation. Each kind has its own name.[52]

A magician of New Britain (Gazelle Peninsula) relies for occult power on the spirits from whom he received his spells or on the forefathers who practiced magic before him and handed down to him their spells. In his operations, therefore, he will call on the spirit or ghost concerned or at least will silently presume the assistance of the one or the other.[53] The natives of New Ireland, in order to detect a person who has killed someone by sorcery, get another magician to recite a spell over the hair of the victim. At the same time the magician calls upon the ghosts of his clan relatives for assistance. They find the guilty party and cause worms to enter his stomach and come out in his feces. Everyone will then know who is the culprit. A few spells, used mainly by fisher folk, also contain invocations addressed to the ghosts of clan ancestors. Thus, when a new line and hook are first used, four dead men, who were clan relatives of the magician, are asked to help look out for fish. After the catch has been made, half of a fish and half of a taro are burned on hot stones, and the ghosts are called upon to come and eat what is set before them. It is thought "in some vague way" that the ghosts enjoy the repast, even though the food has been entirely consumed by the fire, and that their assistance will be secured for the next fishing. Ghosts can cause some people to become insane. A war spell, used by the villagers of Lesu, contains an invocation to a dead father to make their enemies go mad and deliver themselves into the hands of the attacking warriors.[54]

In the northern Solomons (Bougainville and Buka) a person who thinks that he has angered the ghosts uses magic to protect himself against their vengeance. A friendly ghost is helpful, however. To ensure good fishing its name will be breathed over a magical mixture which is rubbed on a fishline.[55] In Guadalcanal a Haumbata man, wishing to kill an enemy on the land, goes to a sacred place belonging to a certain spiritual being (a bird associated with the exogamous group to which the man belongs) and calls on it for the *mana* necessary to fulfill his dark design. To it he offers various kinds of food, as well as tobacco. Should a Haumbata man desire to do away with an enemy on the sea, he makes offerings to a certain shark, and this mythic creature, if pleased to accept the sacrifice, will break up the enemy's canoe and devour its unlucky occupant. Similarly, a Kindapalei man sacrifices to his sacred snake in order to obtain *mana* from it.[56] In the southern Solomons (Mala or Malaita and Ulawa) the power of a spell resides in the formal invocation of ghosts with which it concludes. Thus for black magic the operator takes some object such as an areca nut belonging to the man to be bewitched, mutters some words over it, throws it upon the altar of a ghost, and burns it. In most cases the object is also breathed upon to endow it with mystic virtue. Before reciting the spell the operator bids the ghost in a most respectful manner to work through the medium of the abstracted nut. Spells with a similar invocation of ghosts are used for control of the weather, success in fishing, and recovery from sickness. All divinatory practices likewise involve an appeal to the ghost that is named in the spell.[57]

When there is continual sunshine and the yams are withering, the natives of the Santa Cruz Islands give money and food to the ghost supposed to control the rain. These offerings are accompanied by an appeal to the ghost not to withold the desired downpour. At the same time the magician in charge of the rite goes into the ghost house and pours water over the ghost post there, "that it may rain." If, on the other hand, sunshine is desired, the magician will not wash his face for a long time nor will he work lest he perspire, "for he thinks that if his body be wet it will rain."[58] Some form of spiritual agency is always concerned in the magic of the Banks Islands. Certain stones or other objects believed to contain *mana* are used, and this *mana* is definitely associated with the presence of a spirit (ghost). It seems to be considered, however, that a spiritual being has no power to resist a human operator or to withold the magical effect desired.[59] In the island of Malekula, one of the New Hebrides, people use a single word to denote practices which involve an invocation to the ghosts or spirits and those which lack it.[60] In some parts of New Caledonia to procure rain the people offer large quantities of food to the ancestors. Prayers are also addressed to them by the officiating magician. Before the skulls of the ancestors stand a number of pots full of water, and in each pot is placed a sacred stone more or less like a skull in shape. In order to hasten the approach of the rain clouds the magician climbs a tree and waves a branch in their direction.[61]

In the island of Ontong Java the due performance of a rite requires that certain leaves shall be collected beforehand. While the operator recites a formula he holds them close to his mouth so that they may be charged with the occult power that issues from the breath. All the formulas in use have the form of petitions to the ancestors. Despite this fact the rite is regarded as an "infallible means" of securing what the operator wants.[62]

The Toradya of central Celebes do not irrigate their fields and consequently depend wholly on the rainfall at the proper time to bring in their rice crops. When rain is needed the people go to a neighboring stream and splash or squirt water through bamboo tubes on each other, or they will smite the water with their hands. The people also hang water snails on a tree, telling these creatures that there they must remain until the rain comes. Then the snails begin to weep and the gods, in compassion for them, send the desired showers. Sometimes, when the land was blistered by drought, the Toradya would visit the grave of a celebrated chief, drench it with water, and say, "O grandfather have pity on us; when thou wilt, give us rain that this year we may eat." The grave is kept water-soaked until the rain comes.[63] The Ifugao of Luzon have a form of sorcery in which the sorcerer calls to a feast the ancestral ghosts of some man whose death he desires to encompass, together with many evil spirits and deities. He bribes them to bring to him the soul of the intended victim, incarnated as a bluebottle fly, a dragon fly, or a bee. When one of the insects comes to drink of the rice wine set out before them, it is caught and put into a bamboo joint tightly corked. The enemy, being thus deprived of his soul, dies. This sorcery cannot be practiced with success unless the operator knows the names of the ancestral ghosts whose services he would employ.[64]

While planting *padi* (rice) a Bornean woman waves her charm over the field and at the same time addresses the seed: "May you have a good stem and a good top, let all parts of you grow in harmony." Then she exhorts the pests: "O rats, run down the river, don't trouble us; O sparrows and noxious insects, go feed on the *padi* of the people down river." But if the pests are very persistent, the woman may kill a fowl and scatter its blood over the growing crop, while she charges the pests to disappear and calls on the god of harvests to drive them out.[65] Among the Kenyah the most important bird of omen is the whiteheaded carrion hawk, Bali Flaki, who acts as a messenger and intermediary between the people and the supreme being. A man who intends to injure another makes a rough wooden image of his enemy, retires to a quiet spot, and waits until a carrion hawk appears in the sky. He smears the image with the blood of a fowl and, as he does so, says, "Put fat in his mouth." This is an appeal addressed to the hawk and means "Let his head be taken." The natives are head-hunters, who put fat into the mouth of every head they take. Then he strikes at the breast of the image with a small wooden spear and throws it into a pool of water reddened with red earth; finally he takes it out and buries it in the ground. If the hawk flies away in the proper direction (to the left), he knows that he will prevail over his enemy, but if it goes to right he knows that his enemy is too strong for him.[66]

The Garo of Assam, when there has been a long-continued drought, perform a simple ceremony to end it. The male members of a village repair to a large rock in the neighborhood. Each man holds a gourd filled with water. The priest, having first implored the god for mercy on his people, sacrifices a goat and smears its blood upon the rock. Then everybody pours the contents of the gourds over the priest, until he is thoroughly drenched. All this is done to the accompaniment of drum beating and the blowing of wind instruments. Should the rainfall be excessive, it is possible for the Garo to obtain sunshine merely by lighting fires around the rocks, at the same time offering up a goat or a fowl to the god.[67]

The Toda of the Nilgiri Hills always accompany an act of sorcery by an invocation to divine beings to give it efficacy. The names of four most important deities are so mentioned, "and it seems quite clear that the sorcerer believes that he is effecting his purpose through the power of the gods."[68] When rain is badly needed the Oraon of Chota Nagpur perform the following ceremony: On the morning of the appointed day the women of the village, with the wife of the village priest at their head, proceed to a tank or spring where each one (after ablution) fills her pitcher with water. Then they go to a sacred fig tree and pour the water over the foot of the tree, saying as they do so, "May rain fall on earth like this." The wife of the village priest also paints the trunk of the tree with vermilion diluted in oil. Finally, after the women have left the spot, the village priest offers a sacrifice of a red cock to the god Baranda. The Oraon are firmly persuaded that rain is now bound to come in a day or two; they even say that a heavy shower is likely to overtake the women on the way home from the sacred tree.[69]

A Basuto magician makes rain by stirring a concoction of herbs and roots with a reed. At the same time he calls upon the ghosts of his ancestors to move the supreme being. "It may be," declares our missionary informant, "that, being a good judge of the weather, like most intelligent natives, he used to occupy himself in this manner just when rain was probable; it may have been pure coincidence; or, again, that the Almighty did indeed hear and answer the prayers of this untaught old heathen."[70] Among the Babemba of Northern Rhodesia the magician, after procuring his medicine, must call on the name of Lesa, the high god, "without whom the magic is believed not to work."[71] When the Ba-ila are suffering from a prolonged drought, the people repair, first of all, to a diviner. He consults his oracles and perhaps announces that a certain ancestral ghost has sent the visitation and that an offering should be made to it for relief. But if he declares that a ghost is not responsible, then the people go to a prophet or prophetess. He or she orders them to pray to Leza (Lesa) and at the same time to conduct a rain ceremony. The rain maker takes a pot, puts in it water and the roots of a certain tree, and with a small forked stick stirs the liquid and makes it froth. He throws the froth in all directions, in order to collect the clouds. Then another kind of medicine is burnt. It produces a dense smoke, supposed to have some connection with clouds. The ashes are placed in a pot of water so that the water becomes very black—another reference to black clouds. Once more the rain maker twirls his stick in the mixture, and the movement will bring up the clouds just as the wind does. All this time the people are singing and invoking the praise-names of their high god. "Come to us with a continued rain, O Leza fall!"[72]

In Nyasaland, when rain does not come, the people say, "Look at this, the rain keeps refusing to fall from above; come, let us try to propitiate the rain spirit, and perhaps the rain may come." So they make beer from maize. Then some of it is poured into a pot buried in the ground, and the man in charge of the ceremony says, "Master, you have hardened your heart toward us, what would you have us do? We must perish indeed. Give your children the rains; there is the beer we have given you." Everyone then drinks a little of the beer that remains. When they have finished they take up branches of trees and begin to sing and dance. Upon returning to the village they find that an old woman has drawn water in readiness and put it in the doorways. The people dip their branches in it and wave them aloft, scattering the drops. "And then they see the rain come in heavy storm clouds."[73]

The magic of the Wanyamwezi of Tanganyika is performed with the assistance of the ghosts.[74] With reference to the Masai it is said that the power of a magician lies not in himself but in his ability to approach Ngai, the high god, "who works through him and imparts magical virtue to various objects."[75] A similar statement is made with reference to the Akikuyu.[76] If a protracted drought threatens the Nandi with famine, the old men lead a black sheep to the river and push it into the water. Then they take beer and milk into their mouths and spurt it out in the direction of the rising sun. When the animal scrambles out of the water and shakes itself, the old men sing a short prayer addressed to the Deity. Give us rain, they say; we are suffering even as women in labor.[77]

The chief rain maker among the Bari of the Anglo-Egyptian Sudan begins operations by first oiling his magical stones and crystals. Next he manipulates certain iron rods by means of which the storm clouds can be drawn in any desired direction. Then in low tones he utters a prayer to his "father" Lugar: "Oh, my father, send the rain! Send the rain! Send the rain! You were in your day a mighty rain maker. . . . . Now you are dead, and I am left to make rain in your stead. Oh, send the rain! Send the rain!"[78]

The Bangala of the Upper Congo think that heavy storms and other terrifying natural phenomena, when occurring about the time a person dies or is being buried, have been caused by the deceased. Hence if a storm threatens to break during a funeral the people call upon the beloved child of the deceased to stop it. He takes a lighted ember from the hearth, waves it toward the horizon where the storm is brewing, and says, "Father, let us have fine weather during your funeral ceremonies." This done, the boy must not drink water or put his feet in water for one day. Rain would fall at once if he failed to observe the prohibitions.[79]

Among the Angas of northern Nigeria rain making is one of the duties incumbent on the Sarkin Tsafi, the religious head of a village, who also serves in some cases as the civil chief as well. Every village has a special rain hut in which a sacred pot of water is kept during the rainy season. If no rain falls or if it is delayed unduly, the people assemble outside the hut. The Sarkin Tsafi enters it, sacrifices a pullet, and pours the blood around the base of the pot. He says, "Water, thou seest that our farms are all dried up. We beseech thee to come down upon our crops." Then, taking a mouthful of water from the pot, he squirts it about him in a shower. If the rain does not follow quickly, the officiant must have been in an improper state of mind. Some angry words that had passed between him and a member of his family or of the community must have caused discordant thoughts. To purge himself of them he offers up a goat at the central shrine. All is now well. Rain is sure to fall.[80]

The Huichol, a tribe in the Mexican state of Jalisco, think that a magician cannot work sorcery unless one of the principal gods, having been invoked by him, lends assistance.[81] To the Tarahumara, animals are by no means inferior creatures; they understand magic and may help the people in rain making. All their characteristic songs and calls in spring the Tarahumara regard as appeals to the deities for rain.[82] The Lillooet of British Columbia believe that the coyote and the hare have power over the cold weather, the mountain goat over snow, and the beaver over rain. When for any reason they want a change of the weather they burn the skin of the animal concerned and then pray to it.[83]

Pressure may be brought upon spiritual beings to secure their intervention and give efficacy or an additional efficacy to a rite of magic. A Peninsular Malay, after modeling a waxen image of his enemy and burying it, addresses Prophet Tap and says, "Do you assist in killing him or making him sick: if you do not make him sick, if you do not kill him, you shall be a rebel against God. . . . . Do you grant my prayer and petition this very day that has appeared."[84] In this rite a magical act is combined with a request for help and a threat in case of noncompliance.

A sorcerer among the Kuraver, a predatory tribe or caste of southern India, first makes an image of the enemy whom he desires to injure or kill. Then he recites a spell. His god, having been duly addressed by name, is told where the enemy resides and what must be done to ruin the latter's crops or, perhaps, bring him to an untimely end. A limit in days or hours is even set for this fell work to be accomplished. The god is threatened with punishment should he fail to execute the allotted task. "If you do not descend I shall come and put a thorn through your nose, and you will

find it difficult to breathe. If you do not help me in my desperate
plight I shall cut you in pieces, hang your limbs on the branches
of a tree, and the twigs will bear the weight of your arms, legs,
and bones. Come at noon precisely; catch my enemy, and bring
him to the grave. . . . . Bring him! Bring him! If not I will
cut your shoulder on the right and on the left, and will grip you
by the throat till you are dead, dead, dead."[85]

The distinction between purely magical observances and such
magico-animistic observances as have been described relates to
the mental attitude of the operator, and this may vary between
different rites or when the same rite is carried out on different
occasions. Sometimes he will have no commerce with spiritual
beings, preferring to rely for success upon his own occult power
and that of his spells and charms. At other times their intervention
is considered as in some degree necessary, if his magic is to accomplish
its declared purpose. Whether he resorts to placatory or to
coercive measures in dealings with them will depend chiefly on
how powerful he considers them to be. A ghost, spirit, or god
with much *mana* is likely to be treated in a friendly fashion and
asked to grant the desired blessing; one with little *mana* is as
likely to be the recipient of insults and blows for failure to confer it. In neither case, however, does the operator have any assurance in advance that his desires will be satisfied. A spiritual
being, though in general well-disposed, may be temporarily dis-
gruntled and out-of-sorts and hence not inclined to act as re-
quested; another spiritual being, the reverse of good-humored and
kindly, may be unmoved by coercion or threats of coercion. For
ghosts, spirits, and gods are human-like personalities, with wills
and passions of their own and generally capricious in their attitude
toward mankind.

There is, however, a third and very extensive class of magico-
animistic observances in which spiritual beings are definitely regarded as under the operator's control. He sends them forth
into men's bodies to cause or cure disease, to kill or save from
death. He drives them from their embodiment in men and trans-
fers them, willy-nilly, to an animate or inanimate scapegoat. As
a necromancer he summons ghosts from the underworld to give
oracles or discover hidden things; as a seer he requires spirits to
make revelations of good or evil fortune. Furthermore, the widespread belief that spiritual beings are really dependent on man
accounts for what may be called augmenting rites intended not
so much to constrain them as to renew their energies and rein-

force their powers. Finally, it should be noticed how prayers, sacrifices, and other animistic rites, when long continued and formalized, may come to have for the suppliant a constraining or an augmenting effect upon their objects. In all these observances the capriciousness of ghosts, spirits, and gods approaches the vanishing point. They are no less subservient to the magician than are men and women, the brute creation, and everything in the realm of nature. They must fulfill his desires, even as the genii summoned when Aladdin's lamp was rubbed.

Magic may now be defined. As a belief, it is the recognition of the existence of occult power, impersonal or only vaguely personal, mystically dangerous and not lightly to be approached, but capable of being channeled, controlled, and directed by man. As a practice, magic is the utilization of this power for public or private ends, which are good or bad, orthodox or heterodox, licit or illicit, according to the estimate placed upon them by a particular society at a particular time. Magical rites, with reference to their purpose, are classified as divinatory, productive, or aversive in character. The magician discovers or foretells what is otherwise hidden in time or in space from human eyes; he influences and manipulates the objects and phenomena of nature and all animate creatures so that they may satisfy actual or assumed human needs; and, finally, he combats, neutralizes, and remedies the onslaught of the evils, real or imaginary, afflicting mankind. The range of magic is thus almost as wide as the life of man. All things under heaven, and even the inhabitants of heaven, become subject to its sway.

NOTES TO CHAPTER II

[1] S. C. Roy, "Magic and Witchcraft on the Chota-Nagpur Plateau," *Journal of the Royal Anthropological Institute,* XLIV (1914), 324. With reference to the California Indians we are told that "a native who has learned the significance of our phrases 'essence,' 'pervading quality,' 'intangible diffused power,' will of his own accord give these definitions for his own concept; but at other times he will as blithely render it by 'spirit' in the sense of something limited, personal, and spatial" (A. L. Kroeber, *Handbook of the Indians of California* [Washington D.C., 1925], p. 513). In South America, declares Rafael Karsten, "the savage Indian at one moment conceives the supernatural as a more or less personal spirit or demon; the next moment, again, as an impersonal *mana*" (*The Civilization of the South American Indians* [London, 1926], p. 505; cf. 375).

[2] A. W. Howitt, *The Native Tribes of South-East Australia* (London, 1904), p. 89. The Kurnai, Wurunjerri, and other tribes believed that certain spirits injured people who came near their haunts. They cast objects of "evil magic" into the bodies of trespassers, thus causing lameness. Such objects were only

visible to medicine men, who, therefore, were alone able to extract them in the form of stones, bones, or other things (pp. 355 f.).

3 Mrs. K. L. Parker, *Australian Legendary Tales; Folklore of the Noongah-burrahs* (London, 1896), p. 97. Byamee, "the mighty *wirreenun*," is said to live forever. But no one may look upon his face, for death would follow the sight of this old man. So he dwells alone in a thick scrub on a mountain ridge (p. 105).

4 Sir Baldwin Spencer and F. J. Gillen, *The Native Tribes of Central Australia* (London, 1899), pp. 519 ff.; *iidem, The Northern Tribes of Central Australia* (London, 1904), p. 480. The *iruntarinia*, though in general kindly, can be very cruel to people who offend them. For instance, one of them may place a barbed pointing stick in a man's body and by pulling on the string attached to it cause him intense pain. Only a very skillful doctor can remove this invisible stick (*Native Tribes*, p. 541).

5 W. L. Warner, *A Black Civilization* (New York, 1937), pp. 228 f., 237.

6 Phyllis M. Kaberry, *Aboriginal Woman, Sacred and Profane* (London, 1939), p. 201.

7 A. C. Haddon, in *Reports of the Cambridge Anthropological Expedition to Torres Straits*, V, 329.

8 Paul Wirz, *Die Marind-anim von Holländisch-Süd-Neu-Guinea* (Hamburg, 1922–25), Vol. I, Pt. II, pp. 99 f.; Vol. II, Pt. III, pp. 74 f.

9 F. E. Williams, *Papuans of the Trans-Fly* (Oxford, 1936), p. 324.

10 Bronislaw Malinowski, *Argonauts of the Western Pacific* (London, 1922), pp. 397 f.

11 W. E. Armstrong, *Rossel Island* (Cambridge, 1928), p. 132.

12 J. Meier, "Die Zauberei bei den Küstenbewohnern der Gazelle-Halbin-seln, Neupommern, Südsee," *Anthropos*, VIII (1913), 3.

13 H. I. Hogbin, *Experiments in Civilization* (London, 1939), p. 119, with reference to the island of Mala (Malaita).

14 Sir George Grey, *Polynesian Mythology and Ancient Traditional History of the New Zealand Race* (2d ed., Auckland, 1885), pp. 7 f., 72 f. Maui, the great Maori hero, captured the sun in a noose and, using an enchanted weapon, gave that luminary such a severe wound that, ever since it has gone slowly and feebly on its course, instead of rushing across the heavens and burning up the world. By his spells and the use of an enchanted fishhook Maui also drew up dry land (New Zealand) from the bottom of the sea (pp. 21 ff., 34). A story of the lassoing of the sun by Maui is also told in Samoa and Mangaia. See Edward Tregear, *The Maori-Polynesian Comparative Dictionary* (Wellington, New Zealand, 1891), pp. 234 f.

15 *Ibid.*, pp. 200, 243 f.

16 Elsdon Best, *The Maori* (Wellington, New Zealand, 1924), I, 235, 323, 328, 330. *Memoirs of the Polynesian Society*, Vol. V. In the Hawaiian Islands one of the oldest schools of sorcery was said to have been established by the goddess Pahulu. The island of Molokai was its especial seat. The sorcerers who flourished there had more *mana* than those in other islands (Martha Beckwith, *Hawaiian Mythology* [New Haven, 1940], pp. 107 f.

17 W. G. Aston, "Japanese Magic," *Folk-Lore*, XXIII (1912), 187 f.

18 H. L. Roth, *The Natives of Sarawak and British North Borneo* (London, 1896), I, 309 f., quoting William Chalmers.

19 J. Shakespear, *The Lushei Kuki Clans* (London, 1912), pp. 109 f.

20 Verrier Elwin, *Maria Murder and Suicide* (Bombay, 1943), pp. 60 f.

21 Mrs. A. W. Hoernlé, "Magic and Medicine," in I. Schapera (editor), *The Bantu-speaking Tribes of South Africa* (London, 1937), p. 230.

22 J. H. Driberg, *The Lango* (London, 1923), pp. 236 f.

23 Wilhelm Hofmayr, *Die Schilluk* (Mödling bei Wien, 1925), p. 209. According to another account the medicine man's power is due to possession by the ghosts of the early Shilluk kings. Only three of these kings are said thus to become immanent in living magicians. See C. G. Seligman and Brenda Z. Seligman, *Pagan Tribes of the Nilotic Sudan* (London, 1932), p. 100.

24 E. E. Evans-Pritchard, *Witchcraft, Oracles, and Magic among the Azande* (Oxford, 1937), pp. 197, 441.

25 Paul Schebesta, *My Pygmy and Negro Hosts* (London, 1936), p. 263.

26 J. Van Wing, "Bakongo Magic," *Journal of the Royal Anthropological Institute,* LXXI (1941), 85.

27 Günter Tessmann, *Die Bafia und die Kultur der mittelkamerun-Bantu* (Stuttgart, 1934), p. 190.

28 P. A. Talbot, *In the Shadow of the Bush* (London, 1912), pp. 13, 191.

29 W. R. Bascom, "The Sanctions of Ifa Divination," *Journal of the Royal Anthropological Institute,* LXXI (1941), 44.

30 M. J. Herskovits, *Dahomey* (New York, 1938), II, 256, 259.

31 Jakob Spieth, *Die Religion der Eweer in Süd-Togo* (Göttingen, 1911), p. 252.

32 Theodor Koch-Grünberg, *Vom Roroima zum Orinoco* (Berlin, 1917–28), II, 63 ff.

33 W. H. Brett, *The Indian Tribes of Guiana* (London, 1868), p. 401.

34 S. A. Barrett, *The Cayapa Indians of Ecuador* (New York, 1925), Part II, p. 348. *Indian Notes and Monographs,* No. 40.

35 H. Beuchat, *Manuel d'archéologie Américaine* (Paris, 1912), pp. 331 f., with a representation of the two divinities after the *Codex Borbonicus.*

36 Washington Matthews, *Navaho Legends* (New York, 1897), p. 70. First Man and his eight companions lived in the fourth of the twelve underworlds. They were the first witches "and the cause of sickness and fatal diseases" (The Franciscan Fathers, *An Ethnologic Dictionary of the Navaho Language* [St. Michaels, Arizona, 1910], p. 348).

37 Elsie C. Parsons, "The Origin Myth of Zuñi," *Journal of American Folk-Lore,* XXXVI (1923), 137.

38 H. R. Voth, *The Traditions of the Hopi* (Chicago, 1905), pp. 10 ff. *Field Columbian Museum, Anthropological Series,* Vol. VIII; Mischa Titiev, "Notes on Hopi Witchcraft," *Papers of the Michigan Academy of Science, Arts, and Letters,* XXVIII (1942), 549 and note 1.

39 Aurel Krause, *Die Tlinkit-Indianer* (Jena, 1885), p. 292.

40 W. Jochelson, in *Memoirs of the American Museum of Natural History,* X, 59.

41 Marie A. Czaplicka, *Aboriginal Siberia* (Oxford, 1914), p. 285.

42 A. W. Howitt, *op. cit.,* pp. 394–96, on the authority of Samuel Gason. According to Erhard Eylmann, who lived long with the Dieri, the name Mura-Mura, meaning "very holy," applies to the good spirits of the tribe. The highest of these spirits ranks as the creator of men, animals, and plants (*Die Eingeborenen der Kolonie Südaustralien* [Berlin, 1908], p. 184 and note 2).

43 Sir Baldwin Spencer and F. J. Gillen, *The Northern Tribes of Central Australia,* pp. 226 ff., 248.

44 F. E. Williams, *Papuans of the Trans-Fly,* p. 324.

[45] *Idem, Orokaiva Magic* (London, 1928), p. 208.

[46] Bronislaw Malinowski, in *Transactions of the Royal Society of South Australia*, XXXIX (1915), 661.

[47] Gunnar Landtman, *The Kiwai Papuans of British New Guinea* (London, 1927), p. 61.

[48] C. Keysser, in R. Neuhauss, *Deutsch Neu-Guinea* (Berlin, 1911), III, 153 f. Similarly among the Bukaua, requests are sometimes addressed by magicians to the ancestors (Stefan Lehner, *ibid.*, III, 448).

[49] Albert Aufinger, "Wetterzauber auf den Yabob-Inseln in Neuguinea," *Anthropos*, XXXIV (1939), 277 ff.

[50] Bronislaw Malinowski, *Argonauts of the Western Pacific*, pp. 422 f. Cf. *idem, The Sexual Life of Savages in North-Western Melanesia* (New York, 1929), p. 389; *idem, Coral Gardens and Their Magic* (New York, 1935). I, 65, 95 f., 287, 468.

[51] R. F. Fortune, *Sorcerers of Dobu* (London, 1932), pp. 99, 143. Though the words of spells are words of power, these must be used with due consideration for the spirits involved. Our authority found no spell where the magician says, "Come on yams, now grow, and be snappy about it." The yams, as personal beings, are not to be domineered over (p. 130; cf. 120).

[52] D. Jenness and A. Ballantyne, *The Northern D'Entrecasteaux* (Oxford, 1920), pp. 141 f.

[53] J. Meier, in *Anthropos*, VIII (1913), 8 f.

[54] Hortense Powdermaker, *Life in Lesu* (New York, 1933), pp. 304 and note 1, 339 f., 343.

[55] Beatrice Blackwood, *Both Sides of Buka Passage* (Oxford, 1935), pp. 471 f. In San Cristoval everything to which a native imparts *mena* (*mana*) is breathed upon. The breath is the life; the soul, "if it can be conceived at all," is the breath (C. E. Fox, *The Threshold of the Pacific* [London, 1924], pp. 251 f.).

[56] W. H. R. Rivers, *The History of Melanesian Society* (Cambridge, 1914), I, 243 f. In Guadalcanal, sacrifices are constantly made to the spirits to obtain their good will and with it their *nanama* (*mana*). Spirits to whom these obligations are not discharged are likely not only to withhold the power desired, but, if severely displeased, to send illness and disaster (H. I. Hogbin, "Mana," *Oceania*, VI [1935–36], 245).

[57] W. G. Ivens, *Melanesians of the South-East Solomon Islands* (London, 1927), pp. 278, 324, 351 f. In the little islands of Owa Raha and Owa Riki, which are included in the Solomons, every spell is directed to a particular ancestral ghost. Since the ghosts react to different formulas the number of these and of the associated practices is legion (H. A. Bernatzik, *Owa Raha* [Wien, 1936], p. 257).

[58] W. O'Ferrall, "Native Stories from Santa Cruz and Reef Islands," *Journal of the Anthropological Institute*, XXXIV (1904), p. 225.

[59] W. H. R. Rivers, *op. cit.*, II, 406.

[60] A. B. Deacon, *Malekula, a Vanishing People in the New Hebrides* (London, 1934), p. 663.

[61] Lambert, *Mœurs et superstitions des Néo-Calédoniens* (Nouméa, 1900), pp. 297 f. According to Father Lambert the New Caledonians have a great variety of magical stones, the use of which is determined by their various shapes and appearances. One stone causes a famine, one drives people mad, one brings rain, one produces a drought, one helps fishermen, one makes yams grow, one blights coconut palms, and so forth. It would seem that all the magic performed

with these stones is accompanied by invocations to the ancestral ghosts (pp. 292 ff.).

[62] H. I. Hogbin, "Mana," *Oceania*, VI (1935–36), 269. In Ontong Java there is no name for the "supernatural power" supposed to be possessed by ghosts (*loc. cit.*).

[63] N. Adriani and A. C. Kruijt, *De Bare'e-sprekende Toradja's van Midden-Celebes* (Batavia, 1912–14), II, 258 f.

[64] R. F. Barton, "Ifugao Law," *University of California Publications in American Archaeology and Ethnology*, XV, 70.

[65] Charles Hose and William McDougall, *The Pagan Tribes of Borneo* (London, 1912), I, 110.

[66] *Ibid.*, II, 56. The Klemantan rite is essentially the same, though more elaborate (II, 117 ff.).

[67] A. Playfair, *The Garos* (London, 1909), pp. 88 f.

[68] W. H. R. Rivers, *The Todas* (London, 1906), p. 450.

[69] S. C. Roy, "Magic and Witchcraft on the Chota-Nagpur Plateau," *Journal of the Royal Anthropological Institute*, XLIV (1914), 330.

[70] D. F. Ellenberger, *History of the Basuto, Ancient and Modern* (London, 1912), p. 93.

[71] Audrey I. Richards, in *Bantu Studies*, IX (1935), 249.

[72] E. W. Smith and A. M. Dale, *The Ila-speaking Peoples of Northern Rhodesia* (London, 1920), II, 208 f.

[73] R. S. Rattray, *Some Folk-Lore Stories and Songs in Chinyanja* (London, 1907), pp. 118 f.

[74] F. Bösch, *Les Banyamwezi* (Münster in Westfalen, 1930), p. 169.

[75] Joseph Thomson, *Through Masai Land* (London, 1885), pp. 444 f.

[76] W. S. Routledge and Katherine Routledge, *With a Prehistoric People* (London, 1910), p. 227.

[77] A. C. Hollis, *The Nandi* (Oxford, 1909), p. 48.

[78] F. Spire, "Rain Making in Central Africa," *Journal of the African Society*, No. 17 (1905), 17.

[79] J. H. Weeks, in *Journal of the Royal Anthropological Institute*, XL (1910), 383; idem, *Among Congo Cannibals* (London, 1913), p. 281.

[80] C. K. Meek, *The Northern Tribes of Nigeria* (London, 1925), I, 245; II, 64 f.

[81] Carl Lumholtz, *Unknown Mexico* (London, 1903), II, 238.

[82] *Ibid.*, I, 331.

[83] James Teit, in *Memoirs of the American Museum of Natural History*, IV, 281.

[84] W. W. Skeat, *Malay Magic* (London, 1900), p. 571.

[85] W. J. Hatch, *The Land Pirates of India* (London, 1928), pp. 49 f.

CHAPTER III

PROCEDURES AND TECHNIQUES
OF MAGIC

For primitive thought the qualities of objects are substantial entities, both separable and transmissible. The transmission occurs most often by bodily contact—a touch, the absorption of food and drink, or sexual intercourse. Contact can be established in other ways, as by a look, a gesture, or a spoken word. Even the mere proximity (real or assumed) of one object to another may result in the transmission of qualities. This "substantializing tendency," as it has been called, applies to all qualities, whether physical or psychological.

In some Central Australian tribes men suffering from headache will wear women's head rings, usually those of their wives. The pain passes into the rings, which are then thrown away into the bush. The Luritja sometimes kill a healthy child and feed its flesh to a younger child who is weak and sickly. Young men among the Larakia admire the chirping of a large grasshopper, and they eat this insect in order to acquire its musical talent. The natives of the Marshall Islands are persuaded that if a man eats a breadfruit which has fallen from a tree and burst he will himself fall from a tree and burst in like manner. Among the Tinguian of Luzon one often sees, on the summit of a high hill, a pile of stones beside the trail. They have been placed there during many years. Each traveler, as he ascends a steep slope, picks up a stone and carries it to the pile on top. As he does so, he leaves all weariness behind him and continues his journey fresh and strong. A Basuto wears on his chest an insect which lives long, in spite of the mutilation of its legs, and thus expects to obtain its remarkable vitality. The Azande of the Anglo-Egyptian Sudan apply hailstones to the chests of children so that their hearts may be cool when they grow up. The Bellacoola of British Columbia rub a baby girl with the warm limbs of a freshly killed beaver, so that the child may become a busy worker like that industrious animal. In Morocco even the death to which a person is exposed can be passed to an animal by slaughtering it. There is no blessing, the people say, on a family which does not own animals, because they protect the family from sickness and death.

The qualities of objects are also considered to reside in their detachable parts or appurtenances and to be likewise capable of transmission. Whatever belongs to the whole man belongs as well to everything associated with him—not only his bodily members, hair, teeth, nails, blood, secretions, and excretions, but also his voice, shadow, reflection, footprint, and name, together with his food, clothing, tools, weapons, and other possessions. It is the same with the *disjecta membra* of animals and things inanimate. This notion of an "extended personality" confuses an ideal relationship with an actual relationship, a connection in thought with a connection in fact. But for immature minds whatever can be imagined can be accepted as veritably real.

In one of the islands of Torres Straits the sweat of a renowned warrior was drunk by young men. They also ate mixed with their food the scrapings from his finger nails, which had become saturated with human blood. These practices made them "strong and like stone; no afraid." Some Papuan tribes believe that if a man's food is stolen and given to a young dog, the great annoyance felt by the owner of the food passes into the animal, which will then grow up very fierce and courageous in attacking wild pigs. It is said that among the Sea Dayak of Borneo the gift of a tiger's tooth to a chief will make him a friend for life. He would not dare to fail the giver or turn false to him, for fear of being devoured by the tiger. The Klemantan, another Bornean tribe, try to make an enemy's boat heavier and so retard its progress by tieing a quartz pebble under one of the benches. Some Malays of the Peninsula consider the "desert goat" to be the most surefooted of all animals. Should it fall from a cliff it immediately licks itself whole. Accordingly, its tongue is carried as an amulet against falling and also as a sure cure for wounds caused by falling, when rubbed on the part affected. Among the Lhota Naga, if anything connected with a person, such as a cloth or a knife, is sold, the seller retains a thread from the cloth or scrapes a tiny shaving off the handle of the knife. Were he to sell the whole of an object almost a part of himself, the buyer would posses some of his personality and might be able to do him harm. When Europeans expostulated with the Swazi concerning the atrocities practiced by one of their rulers, they admitted that these were indeed shameful. But he was not really blameworthy, for as a child he had been fed on the hearts of lions so that he might become fierce and cruel. The Bathonga think that a lion's larynx, burnt and reduced to ashes, will impart to the xylophone the tremendous volume of sound emitted by the king of beasts. The beak of the stilt-walker, when similarly treated, will give to the instrument the strange and appealing cry of this bird. To secure these results the ashes must be mixed with fat and rubbed on the xylophone. For the Ga of the Gold Coast a man's washing sponge contains so much of his personality that he may be injured or killed by an enemy who performs black magic over it. Some Amazonian Indians never shoot a poisonous snake with a poisoned arrow from a blowpipe. The poison of the snake would neutralize that on the arrow; it would even neutralize whatever poison was in the hunter's possession at the time. By the Barama River Caribs the larynx bones of the "howling baboon" are charred, pulverized, mixed with water, and drunk as an infusion to cure coughs and infection of the throat. Among the Creek Indians it was customary for a warrior to drink out of a human skull, in order to imbibe "the good qualities it formerly contained." Among the Northern Saulteaux a man who finds a bear's winter den during the summer and desires to slay the animal the following winter will take a bullet from his pouch, warn it not to tell anyone, and lay it in the den, "expecting it to guard his prize until he returns." Young men among the Tinne of southern Alaska procure the old trousers of a good runner, since by wearing them they will acquire the speediness of their former owner. Mothers also beg for these garments and out of them make pantaloons for their boys. Polar Eskimo, to secure long life and fortitude for themselves, sew to their clothing bits of an old hearth stone which has shown its enduring qualities by resistance to the fire.

The ideas and practices under consideration are further illustrated by the time-honored doctrine of *similia similibus curantur*. The natives of Nias, an island to the west of Sumatra, think that the swelling caused by contact with a ground snake will be relieved if the swollen part is rubbed with ashes of the reptile's burnt tail. The Toradya of Celebes preserve the teeth of mad dogs. When a person has been bitten by such an animal, scrapings from one of the teeth, mixed with water and curcuma, are applied to the wound. The Malays regard the spines of a certain fish as poisonous, but believe that its brain, if applied to the wound, will act as a complete antidote to the poisonous principle. A Zulu about to cross a river infested by crocodiles will chew some of a crocodile's excrement and scatter it over his person as a protective measure. Some East Africans, when passing through a region where lions and leopards abound, provide themselves with the claws, teeth, lips, and whiskers of these animals and hang them around their heads. An elephant hunter wears the tip of an elephant's trunk. By some West Africans the blood and pieces of the heart of a slain enemy are consumed by all the warriors who have never killed a man before. If they did not do so, their vigor and courage would be secretly wasted by the haunting spirit of the slain man. Among the Kagoro of northern Nigeria, when a person has been injured by a sword or a spear and the wound does not heal, the weapon, if obtainable, is washed in water. The sufferer drinks the water, his wound closes up, and recovery follows.

The qualities of objects are readily associated with their "souls." The soul, as the common vital principle, pervades the living body and all the members. Particles of it, conceived of materially, are distilled from it and are passed over to anything with which the living body or the members come into contact or proximity. Various Papuan tribes, who have a belief in the soul (the "thing within" which leaves the body at death and becomes a ghost), believe also that to it attaches what is described as its "strength." They try, therefore, to increase their own "strength" by acquiring that of animals, plants, and inanimate objects, for all these are endowed with souls. For the Kai, in what was formerly German New Guinea, the qualities of a man's soul are attached not only to all parts of the body, such as his hair, nails, and saliva, but also to his shadow, reflection, and personal name, even to his voice, the glance of his eyes, his actions, and his possessions. Hence their intense fear of the black magic that can be wrought by a sorcerer who obtains any separable part of a man or anything belonging to him. At death the qualities of the soul perish with the body, but the soul itself continues to exist as a ghost. The Gende, another Papuan tribe, believe so firmly in "life matter" or "soul substance" that they will not use firewood upon which women have stepped, because woman's soul substance, being inferior to man's, would affect the latter injuriously. For the same reason they will take from the hands of women only such articles of food as have a shell or a thick skin, for instance, nuts, but no thin-skinned vegetables. The protective covering must always be removed before the food is eaten. Conceptions of soul substance prevail widely in Indonesia.[1] For the Malays of the Peninsula all magic may be said to consist of the methods by which *semangat*—equivalent to soul substance—is "influenced, captured, subdued, or in some way made subject to the will of the magician."[2] In South America we are told that the Indians regard shadows reflected on the water, photographs, and other images as being the souls of the persons represented, just as locks of hair and nail parings "are supposed to contain the soul of the person to whom they have belonged."[3] In these instances, as in many others like them, a marked development of animistic thinking has led to the identification of impersonal qualities with the soul of their owner. It is significant that such notions are most elaborated in Indonesia and South America, where we have seen that a definite conception of *mana* in its impersonal aspect, while not unknown, is rare.

Innumerable observances thus find an explanation in ideas relating to the qualities of wholes or of parts and to the transmission of qualities. Cannibalism, head-hunting, animal and human sacrifice, the use of animal and human relics, transference of evils to a scapegoat, ceremonies of purification by means of water, fire, and various disinfectants, confession of sins, blood brotherhood, and the wearing of ornaments, together with a great variety of prescriptions and prohibitions in regard to alimentation, are largely accounted for by such ideas.

All these observances assume the existence between phenomena of relations and affinities which wider knowledge of causation has shown to be nonexistent. Nevertheless, they accord, or seemingly accord, with man's ordinary experience: hot things burn; cold things freeze; food nourishes and strengthens but sometimes poisons; diseases spread by infection among men, animals, and plants; children resemble their parents. It is said that the Tinne are fully aware that fresh meat or fresh fish will be rapidly tainted if placed close to some meat already tainted; that dough will be soured by admixture of yeast or of already fermented dough; and that a recently smoked moose skin will impart its color to another skin of paler hue if the latter is pressed against it for a few hours.[4] What wonder if these Indians should conclude that *all* qualities are capable of transmission!

There is nothing magical in the ideas and practices that have been described, nothing secret or esoteric or mysterious about them. They are familiar to everyone; anyone can be concerned with them. They do not depend for their efficacy on the occult power which belongs to the magician, his acts, his words, and the things employed by him and which enters as the essential element into his art. To notice qualities in objects and endeavor to acquire them (or avoid them) is a procedure, not of magic, but of common sense.[5]

But occult power is itself regarded as a quality of some objects or of their detachable parts or appurtenances. Men and women possess it, men more fully, as a rule, than women; the old more fully than the young; the healthy more fully than the weak and ailing; and the members of a superior class more fully than commoners. Some people possess it to an exceptional degree: professional magicians, by birth, inheritance, or initiation; chiefs and public functionaries so often regarded as "sacred"; strangers, who are regularly credited with a mysterious nature making them carriers of both good and evil; persons whose physical or mental characteristics distinguish them from their fellows, such as those with bodily malformations or with marked psychopathic tendencies; and all persons in a temporary or permanent condition of ritual uncleanness, especially menstruous, pregnant, and parturient women. It attaches to the dead and to all the living related to or concerned with the dead. It belongs to certain animals, the wild rather than the domesticated, as being the less familiar and the more fearful. It belongs to certain plants of a poisonous nature, to those used as narcotics and intoxicants, and to those employed for medicinal purposes. It clings to certain gestures; to the words of a spell; to blessings and curses; to personal names, especially those of the dead, of chiefs and kings, and of spirits and gods; to myths and legends, which must not be recited lightly or represented in an unbecoming way; to certain places; to periods of time, particularly lucky and unlucky days; to sacred or symbolic numbers and colors; and to ritual actions of every sort. It is found in material objects used as charms or "medicines" and in instruments of divination. It is also contained in the weapons of warfare and in those for hunting and fishing. Finally, its presence is revealed in all the phenomena of nature which impress the imagination as being either "awful" or awesome. What the Romans, a magic-ridden people, called *monstra* and *portenta* embraces for the primitive-minded everything unusual, abnormal, and extraordinary, whether animate or inanimate.

From these sources occult power radiates through space, as do electromagnetic waves, and affects for good or ill whatever comes within its range. In the territory of the Urabunna tribe of Central Australia there are two stones marking the spot where a remote ancestor of the tribe and two women perished as the result of breaking the marriage law. To approach the spot is to incur sudden death, though very old men can do so safely. Sometimes they will go near it and throw bushes on the stones so as to keep down their baneful emanation. The natives of North Australia, it is said, associate anything which they do not understand with evil occult power. When they first came across the track of a cart they thought that it was the path along which this mysterious and dreaded force was being conducted. If they had to cross the path they jumped over it as high in the air as they could so as to avoid all contact with it. Among the Mailu, a Papuan tribe, evil occult power may be conveyed to a certain tree by means of a rite and a spell. If anyone passes the tree so that the wind blows from it to him or if its shadow falls on him, or even on his shadow, he will get sick and die. A Solomon Islander, possessor of the evil eye, injures a man by a mere glance. A Tongan chief heals a follower by an application of his "sacred" foot or hand to the sufferer's body. A Maori father transmits his *mana* to his son by having the latter bite the great toe of his left foot. After this delicate operation both father and son must fast for eight days. A Fijian, by striking a certain stone which possesses an uncanny influence over the wind, can produce a light breeze, and by breaking off a piece of the stone can raise a violent storm. A Zulu, suspicious of his wife's fidelity, obtains medicine from a doctor and takes it internally. By cohabiting with his wife he conveys to her the seeds of a certain disease. Should a lover now have intercourse with her he would get the disease, though all the time the wife does not suffer from it.

The use of detachable parts and appurtenances finds frequent illustration in so-called exuvial magic, as when an Australian blackfellow makes his deadly "pointing bone" out of the fibula of a corpse, so that it gains the potency associated with a ghost, or when a Melanesian, having secured the hair, footprints, or feces of an enemy, proceeds to bewitch him. Exuvial magic is also employed for beneficent ends, as by some East African peoples, who bring good fortune to a person or protect him from evil by spitting copiously in his face. Almost always an operator must work over his materials with spells and charms before his magic becomes potent to bless a friend or blast a foe.

Occult power, when not regarded as inherent in an object or its detachable parts or appurtenances, can be imputed to it if in appearance, activity, or some other respect it resembles another object whose nature is known and familiar. The perception of similarity between objects is fundamental to human thought; our intellectual life largely depends on it; but in magic its application is illegitimate. The magician fails to discriminate the categories of likeness and identity, so that for him things, acts, or processes that are alike are the same, and the one may be substituted for the other. Almost any analogy, however slight or far-fetched, however superficial or fanciful, will suffice to establish the necessary resemblance. To the range of such analogical processes no limits can be assigned. It is a maxim of magic that feigned things are accepted for true—*ficta pro veris accipi.* What is said of the Melanesians in this respect has a general application. "A man comes by chance upon a stone which takes his fancy; its shape is singular, it is like something, it is certainly not a common stone, there must be *mana* in it. So he argues with himself, and he puts it to the proof; he lays it at the root of a tree to the fruit of which it has a certain resemblance, or he buries it in the ground when he plants his garden; an abundant crop on the tree or in the garden shows that he is right, the stone is *mana,* has that power in it. Having that power it is a vehicle to convey *mana* to other stones."[6]

The magic of some primitive peoples relies to a very great extent upon this process of imputation. With reference to the Bathonga of South Africa we are told by a sympathetic and understanding missionary that "the native mind is extremely quick at perceiving a similarity between the most heterogeneous objects or phenomena, and immediately establishes a causal relation between them. . . . . *Color* acts on color; black sheep and black smoke produce a black cloud full of rain. *Form* produces a similar form; a necklace of maize grains round the neck of a smallpox patient produces an eruption of small, transparent postules, which are not dangerous, in place of the large, thick, deadly ones. *Disintegration* produces disintegration; the chewing of a bean ensures the melting of the iron ore in the kiln. *A certain state of mind* produces a similar condition in living beings, and even in material phenomena; the continence of little children ensures control over the flame of the furnace, whilst the passion of married people accelerates disease and increases the fury of wild beasts."[7]

Symbolic rites of the Zuñi of New Mexico include the placing on every altar of water from a sacred spring, "that the springs may always be full"; the sprinkling of water to induce rainfall; the blowing of smoke and the mixing of bowls of yucca seeds to produce clouds; the rolling of the thunderstones; the planting of seeds in the floor of new houses as a fertility rite; the placing on winter solstice altars of ears of corn for plentiful crops and of clay images of peaches, domestic animals, jewelry, and even money to secure the increase of these objects; the presentation of dolls to pregnant women for safe delivery; the use of bear paws in medicine ceremonies "to call the bear"; and, finally, the whole practice of masking, in order to compel the presence of spiritual beings in their other bodies as rain.[8]

The efficacy ascribed to charms by the Arapaho Indians is "invariably" dependent on symbolism. A nut with some resemblance to a skull keeps off ghosts. Pebbles resembling teeth are kept so that the owner may live to an age when his teeth fall out. An iron chain or ring, being hard and indestructible, insures good health. Triggers worn on a necklace cause the guns of the enemy to misfire. Light blue beads, whose color resembles that of smoke, make fighters invisible. Beads in the shape of a spider's web render the wearer, like the web, impervious to missiles and at the same time ensure the trapping of the enemy, just as insects are caught in it. Even when the virtue of an object is due to some abnormality such as its rarity, curious shape, or mysterious origin (as in the case of pebbles found inside animals), symbolism is never absent, though it may be really superadded and a secondary feature.[9]

The transmission of imputed occult power is variously accomplished. A Papuan woman, pregnant and anxious for a male child, conceals a mangrove stamen (which looks like a penis) under her skirt. Boys in the Solomon Islands chew the long tap-root of a certain plant. The longer the root chewed by them the longer their hair will grow. Burglars in Java spread earth from a grave in a house which they intend to rob. By doing so they cause the inmates to sleep as soundly as the dead. A Babemba magician makes a charm by taking part of the brains or heart of a rabbit (proverbially a cunning creature) and mixes this with the root of a certain plant which sends out runners and establishes itself firmly in all directions. A traveler who carries with him this invaluable talisman is assured of a safe journey. The Cuna Indians, who live on the Isthmus of Panama, say that to become skillful in weaving baskets you must first place cleverly made birds' nests in your bath. When planting mandeoca it is desirable to pull a fat woman by the leg; doing so will cause the roots of the plant to grow thick and sturdy. The Papago Indians of Arizona make an intoxicating liquor from the fruit of the giant cactus. The fig-like fruit ripens just at the end of the dry season, and its juice is therefore thought

to be a prototype of the coming rain. In order to bring this blessing, every man must drink his fill of the liquor, drink to saturation,
in fact, even as the rain-soaked earth. A Cherokee doctor puts into
a decoction intended as a vermifuge some of the red fleshy stalks
of the common purslane, because these resemble the worms to be
expelled from the patient. He will also insert a sharp flint so as to
communicate cutting qualities to the medicine and enable it to
slice the worms into pieces.

The transmission may be purely verbal, by means of spells.
Yoruba warriors, at the outset of an expedition repeat the statement, "Right through is the cutting of the swordfish." By thus
identifying themselves with that fearsome creature they ensure
their success in battle, because the swordfish is supposed to cut
in two all its enemies in the sea. To prevent frostbite a Cherokee
Indian, about to start out on a cold morning, rubs his feet in the
ashes of the fire and then sings a song of four verses by which
he acquires in turn the cold-defying powers of the wolf, deer, fox,
and opossum. These four animals, it is said, are never frost-
bitten. After reciting each verse he imitates the cry and characteristic movements of the animal referred to. Among the Chukchi
of northeastern Siberia a jealous wife describes her rival as a
piece of carrion—"old carrion inflated with rottenness"—and her
husband as a big and very hungry bear. The bear eats the carrion,
vomits it, and says, "I do not want it." At the same time the wife
calls herself a young beaver that has just shed its hair. The husband then looks upon her fondly, turns away from his former
attachment, and goes back to his first love.

The transmission may be by manual acts imitating or prefigur-
ing in miniature a desired outcome. When the Havasupai, an Arizona tribe, want rain they lay a notched stick flat on an inverted
basket and then rub it with another stick. The grating sound thus
produced is said to resemble the croaking of a frog, a creature
associated with water. By whistling through rushes the Shoshoni
make the clouds gather and the rain descend. In this case the
whistling obviously symbolizes the rushing winds which herald the
approach of a storm. If buffalo were scarce the Shoshoni would
cut out the sinew of a buffalo they had killed and, having blackened
their fingers with charcoal, would cover the sinew with black dots.
Then they placed it on the ground and built a fire over it so that
the two ends, as these dried in the heat, would gradually approach
each other, even as buffalo come together from opposite directions.
This done, they felt sure of finding game a few days later. When

the Crow Indians wanted buffalo to appear a game magician took a buffalo skull and set it down with its nose toward the camp. When enough of the animals had been killed he reversed the skull.

Manual acts of this symbolic character affect people and things at a distance, perhaps even afar off, by reason of the intimate relationship presumed to be set up between them and the magician. A Bornean wife, while her husband is on the warpath, takes care to cook and scatter popcorn on the verandah each morning so that his movements will be agile. She will wear a sword, day and night, so that he may be always thinking of his weapons. Among the Bathonga, while a man is hunting the hippopotamus, his principal wife must shut herself up in the hut. By keeping within its circular walls she confines the animal within the circle formed by the hunters' canoes on the river and so prevents its escape. The wife of a Kwakiutl hunter, besides eating little and keeping as quiet as possible, is careful to walk slowly. By being slow in her movements the animals will be likewise and hence easy for her husband to catch. A seal hunter's wife lies down on her bed and covers herself with a new mat, so that the seal will be asleep when her husband comes upon it.

What may be called iconic magic makes use of effigies, models, or other representations of anything to be affected magically. The image sometimes bears only a distant resemblance to the object for which it stands, perhaps no resemblance. All the same it typifies the object, for that is the magician's will, and serves, therefore, as something upon which he can vent his emotions, whether of affection or of envy and hatred. In the Loyalty Islands a woman whose husband or son is on the warpath takes a piece of coral, representing the absent warrior, and with her right hand moves it up and down to indicate his movements in the fight. With her left hand she brushes away imaginary obstacles to his progress. Among the Wachagga of Mount Kilimanjaro, if a youth died without undergoing circumcision, the rite had to be performed in a symbolic manner so that he might join the tribal ancestors and be married in their ghostly realm. For this purpose a banana blossom was used to represent the youth and its tip was duly operated on. In the case of a girl who had died without being incised, an operation was performed on a banana fruit. The banana was then put in a miniature hut representing the hut where the girl would have been confined until her recovery from incision. To multiply his domestic animals a Cora Indian of Mexico models them in wax or clay or carves them from tuff and places them in a cave in the mountain. Mountains, by the Cora, are considered to be the source of all riches. For every cow, dog, or hen he wants he must provide a corresponding image. Among the Thompson Indians of British Columbia the wife of a gambler takes an elongated stone, or oftener a stone hammer, and suspends it by a string above her husband's pillows. If she knows that he is meeting no success as a gamester she turns the stone rapidly around, "thereby reversing his luck."

In the more elaborate forms of magic, especially of the black variety, these several methods of transmission are often combined. Among the Murngin of the Northern Territory of Australia a sorcerer paints an image of his intended victim on a stone, with the head, arms, fingers, legs, and scrotum representing a man. The nose, ears, foot, and penis are those of a kangaroo. During the painting he talks to the image, saying, "You will kill So-and-So," and pronounces the man's name. A fire is built under the stone, which becomes so heated that it finally cracks with a popping noise. Then the operator knows that the soul of the man, though ever so far away, will scream in pain. The man's body swells up, his nose runs with blood, his elbows and nails split, his fingers slough off, and his skin and testes crack. He will walk around for a year or so before he dies. He perished of leprosy, in fact, but his relatives always feel that they should seek vengeance because an enemy in another clan must have caused the disease.[10]

In the western islands of Torres Straits the vine called *kuman* breaks up in dry weather into segments which often bear a close resemblance to some of the long bones of the human skeleton. A sorcerer collects the segments and to each one gives the name of some part of the intended victim's body. Then he crouches down like a fish eagle and, imitating the way in which the bird tears flesh off bones, throws the segments behind him. If he leaves the spot without turning around to look at the segments his enemy will die. However, if he picks them up and puts medicine on them his enemy will recover.[11]

In Wogeo, one of the Schouten Islands off the northern coast of New Guinea, a spell in common use for the protection of betel palms produces gangosa in a thief. This is a particularly loathsome skin disease, which often results in the loss of the entire nose. The spell begins with an address to the mythical personage supposed to have used it first. Then the fish hawk is asked to "eat the face of him who steals." Reference is also made to biting centipedes and black ants and to the sting ray. Mention of the bird finds an explanation in the fact that the gangosa sore really does look as if some bird or other creature had been tearing away the victim's flesh. Centipedes, ants, and the sting ray are mentioned because of their painful bites. While the spell is being recited the magician has to imitate the motions of a fish hawk tearing its prey. So deadly is this spell that the owner of the palm trees will not venture to gather his nuts without first performing another rite to render the magic ineffective.[12]

In Motlav, one of the Banks Islands, a form of black magic is performed by means of the fragments of a man's food, his nail parings, or his excrement. For example, the sorcerer will roast a yam, break it in two, and give half of it to his enemy. Apparently he eats the other half himself, but by sleight-of-hand he substitutes for this the half of another yam. Once in possession of his enemy's food-leaving he must recite potent spells over it and also use certain substances with a special reputation for *mana*. The victim dies when all these things are done. If the final rite is not performed, he lives on indefinitely, though in an enfeebled condition. The entire process lasts at least seven months, and the victim does not begin to suffer any ill effects until the magic has been operative for three months.[13]

The Malays of the Peninsula practice various forms of black magic by means of wax figures representing their victims. One method is to take parings of the nails, hair, eyebrows, saliva, and other separable parts of the person you would attack and make them up into his likeness with wax from a deserted bees' comb. Scorch the figure slowly by holding it over a lamp every night for seven nights, and say, "It is not wax that I am scorching, it is the liver, heart, and spleen of So-and-So that I scorch." After the seventh time burn the figure, and your enemy will die. A more elaborate method is to make the image like a corpse and to pierce with the sharp twig of a palm that part of it which you would affect in the victim. Piercing the eye makes him blind; piercing the head, breast, the waist makes him sick. If you wish to cause his death, the image must be transfixed from the head downward right through to the buttocks. Then you wrap the image in a shroud, pray over it as if you were praying over the dead, and bury it in the middle of the path that leads to the victim's abode, so that he may be sure to step over it.[14]

A Montagnais magician went through the following performance designed to kill a foreign sorcerer one hundred leagues away: First he prepared his charms, which were placed in a leather receptacle. Then he took two sharply pointed stakes and drove them with all his might into the ground, inclining them toward the place where he believed his enemy was and saying, "Here is his head." Next he descended into a deep ditch and there struck one of the stakes heavy blows with a sword and a poniard, at the same time holding his bundle of charms. Finally he emerged from the ditch, threw down before the spectators his weapons covered with blood, and declared that the foreign sorcerer, now fatally wounded, would soon die.[15]

When material objects, verbal expressions, or manual acts are employed analogically, they make clearer and more emphatic just what is wanted by the magician. If he wants rain he says "Rain!" and at the same time spurts out water and simulates a downpour. Before starting out on a hunt he pricks himself with an arrow so as to draw blood, as from a wounded animal, or goes through a series of contortions representing its struggles when trapped. To secure an abundant yield from his garden he and his wife cohabit within its precincts.[16] Much symbolism found in hunting dances, rain ceremonials, and the like is to be interpreted as "sign language," as being merely indicative or suggestive of a desired outcome rather than directly causative of it. To set an example encourages imitation, and this procedure, so effective with human beings, may be considered equally effective in dealings with the animal world and the impersonal forces of nature. But words or actions intended to show what was to be done would, by constant repetition, often come to be regarded as potent in themselves and so would acquire a magical character. Even spiritual beings may be thought of as responsive to this sort of magic.

Among the Arunta of Central Australia every local totemic group has its own *intichiuma* ceremony, whose purpose is the multiplication of the plant or animal after which the group is named. In the *intichiuma* of the witchetty grub group the performers go to a certain cave where there is a large block of quartzite representing the adult grub. About it are small rounded stones representing its eggs. The headman begins to sing and taps the block with a wooden trough used by women for carrying food. All the other men tap the block with twigs they have plucked from gum trees and chant songs, the burden of which is an invitation to the animal to lay eggs. The headman then takes up one of the small stones and with it strikes each man on the stomach, saying, "You have eaten much food." A similar ceremony, with chanted invitations to the animal to come from all directions and lay eggs, is repeated by the side of a large rock at whose base another stone, representing the adult grub, is supposed to be imbedded.[17]

In the garden magic of the Kiwai Papuans certain objects are employed to "teach" the yams, sweet potatoes, coconuts, and sugar cane how to grow. When yams are planted the roots of a few of them may be rubbed with a mixture composed of the slime of certain amphibians, earth and water from their holes, certain sweet-smelling herbs, some coconut oil, a feather of a bird of paradise, and a cassowary's sinew; to these objects a small piece of stone is added. The amphibians, which burrow their way out of the ground and jump about, show the yam shoots how to grow through the earth and spread over the garden. The slime makes the tubers smooth and without disfiguring knobs. The bird of paradise and the cassowary, which are thought to swallow their food whole and to cause many plants to spring up by dropping the seeds with their excrements, teach the yams how to spring up everywhere. The stone teaches them how to become big and strong.[18]

A Dobuan who wishes the growing vine to produce thick foliage calls to its attention various thick foliaged trees and shrubs. When he would have the tuber grow large he refers it to the mound raised by a species of shellfish. Does he want the yam to grow knobby he speaks of being hunched up with cold. All these remarks are made "delicately," for vines, tubers, and yams must be handled with care, must be shown what to do, not ordered to do it.[19] Similarly in New Ireland a native expresses a wish that his taro may become tall just as the *tsuri* leaf does; that it may wax fat like a certain fish; and that it may grow quickly even as a certain well-known weed. To make a dog an expert hunter it is likened to a shark, and the wish is expressed that the dog will run around in the bush catching wild pigs just as the shark roams the ocean seeking its prey. If a man wants to fatten his domestic pig he wishes that it will become as big as a certain tree which grows to an enormous size.[20]

A magician in New Caledonia, who would make sunshine, climbs a high mountain exposed to the first rays of the morning sun. At the precise moment when the sun rises from the sea he kindles a fire by burning a bundle of charms suspended over a flat stone. The charms include some coral, three species of plants—always three—two locks of hair from a living child of his family, and two teeth or, better still, an entire jawbone from the skull of an ancestor. As the smoke curls up, he rubs the altar stone with dry coral and invokes his ancestors, saying, "Sun! I do this that you may be hot and eat up all the clouds in the sky." The same ceremony is repeated at sunset.[21] The magician's words thus explain the significance of his symbolic act: as the fire seems to consume the smoke which rises from it so the sun is to "eat up" the clouds.

A Maori spell often takes the form of an affirmation presenting an analogy to the event to be enacted or the situation desired by the operator. Thus a formula to give speed and grace to a canoe may refer to the swiftness of a bird on the wing or the lightness of a gull floating on the water. Or it may mention the names of woods noted for their buoyancy.[22]

In the Kei Islands, to the southwest of New Guinea, the women whose men folk have departed on a foray, bring out fruits and stones, anoint them, and place them on a board. Then they implore their lords, the sun and moon, to let the bullets rebound from their loved ones, even as raindrops rebound from the fruits and stones which have been smeared with oil.[23]

Among some of the Tibeto-Burman tribes of Assam it is usual in a time of drought to kill a fish and scatter bits of its body on the village dam. Then the people inform their deities that the fish are all perishing for lack of water. Another method of attracting the attention of the rain gods is found in Manipur. The people drag their boats along the mud of the moat and the rajah, whose great racing boat heads the solemn procession, then asks the spiritual powers for rain.[24]

When the Oraon of Chota Nagpur celebrate one of their festivals every householder puts a live crab upon the hearth. As the crab crackles in the heat, the women exclaim, "May our lentils and pulse burst their pods like this." As the creature stiffens its legs and brings them together, presenting the appearance of a cluster of pods, the women say, "May the pods of our lentils and pulse come out as thick and full as this."[25]

The magic of modern Japan includes many practices seemingly intended for the guidance of spiritual beings, so that they may exercise their powers in the direction desired by the operator who seeks their aid. The legend is told of a hermit who wished to erect a temple "to the god who might be fittest to ensure the salvation of the human race." Two deities who manifested themselves were rejected as being not fierce enough and strong enough for the accomplishment of the great business in hand. Then the hermit stood for seven days "with glaring eyes and clenched fists, so that the gods might better understand the nature of his requirements," until at last there appeared before him a being "pale with concentrated rage" and clearly adequate for his needs. In certain mountainous districts, when there is a drought, some of the men go forth on a "praying for rain" expedition. They climb the highest accessible peak, where the most powerful of the deities whom they wish to invoke resides. Then they build a bonfire before the shrine on the top, fire off guns, shout, and roll boulders down the slopes, in order to represent the storm which they desire. Our authority for these and similar practices does not attempt to decide whether they may have been purely magical at the start and later adapted to the belief in spiritual beings or whether they represent a degradation of animistic conceptions.[26]

In the black magic of the Japanese there are some practices which contain no suggestion of the activity of a spiritual being. When, for example, an image is used to represent the person to be injured, the effect produced on the image is assumed to be reproduced directly on the victim. But there are other *majinai,* as these practices are known, in which, while an image is employed, it seems to have served originally for the guidance of an outraged and angered spirit or deity. In one form of love magic an offended woman goes at night to the sacred tree of a shrine near her home and, having stated her purpose and the number of times she intends to come, drives a nail through an image and affixes it to the tree. She then pays the specified number of visits, on each occasion driving a nail through the image and into the tree. After the requisite number of nails have been inserted, blood will issue from the tree if the victim is to die. Our authority interprets this practice as designed to anger the indwelling spirit of the tree and thus to call it forth to seek vengeance in the direction indicated by the wounds on the image of the victim.[27]

The Akikuyu of Kenya secretly resort to a smith for the most potent and destructive curses. "May the members of this family have their skulls crushed as I crush the iron with my hammer! May their bowels be seized by hyenas as I seize the iron with my tongs! May their blood spurt from their veins as the sparks fly from beneath my hammer! May their hearts freeze from cold as I cool this iron in the water." Such curses operate effectively though the persons to be influenced may be a hundred miles away.[28]

The Azande of the Anglo-Egyptian Sudan, to promote the growth of melons, make use of a certain kind of tall grass (*bingba*) which grows luxuriantly on cultivated land. A man throws the grass like a dart and transfixes the broad leaves of his melons. Before doing so he says, "You are melons, you be very fruitful like *bingba* with much fruit." Likewise, when he pricks the stalks of bananas with crocodiles' teeth he says, "Teeth of crocodile are you, I prick bananas with them, may bananas be prolific like crocodiles' teeth."[29]

The Peruvian Indians, on the eve of a war expedition, were accustomed to starve certain black sheep for several days and then to kill them, saying, as they did so, "As the hearts of these beasts are weakened, so let our enemies be weakened."[30]

The Mandan Indians, a Siouan tribe, held a mask dance when no buffalo had been seen for some time near a village. The dance never failed to attract the animals, for it was kept going incessantly until they appeared. Every dancer carried a bow or spear and wore the head and horns of a buffalo, to which were attached a strip of the skin and the long tail. "When one becomes fatigued of the exercise, he signifies it by bending quite forward and sinking his body towards the ground; when another draws a bow upon him and hits him with a blunt arrow, and he falls like a buffalo— is seized by the bystanders, who drag him out of the ring by the heels, brandishing their knives about him; and having gone through the motions of skinning and cutting him up, they let him off, and his place is at once supplied by another, who dances into the ring with his mask on; and by this taking of places the scene is easily kept up night and day, until the desired effect has been produced, that of 'making buffalo come'."[31]

A magical rite normally involves a manual act, a verbal expression (spell or incantation), and the use of some material, inanimate object (charm or "medicine") possessing occult power either original with it or ascribed to it. No one of the three elements can be considered primary and the others derivative, since a system of magic may emphasize consistently either the manual act, the spell, or the charm. It is likewise obvious that when they are combined in a particular rite any one of them may assume the greatest importance in the mind of the operator. All three are capable of extensive development. Simple manual acts pass into elaborate ceremonials; brief spells become lengthy formulas; charms accumulate in vast number and amazing diversity. The art of magic tends to be ever more complicated, more esoteric, until its practice is limited to a professional body of wonder workers.

Properly performed, a magical rite has an efficacy which is superadded to that of its component parts. The magician must choose an auspicious occasion and the right place. Perhaps he must repeat his performance, or part of it, several times, according to the mystic or symbolic character so often attributed to certain numbers.[32] He must also be himself qualified as an officiant, often by the observance of food and sexual taboos, by preliminary ablutions, and by wearing a special and appropriate costume.[33] Under such conditions he carries out his acts, recites his spells, and manipulates his charms. Any mistake or omission in the proceedings or any interruption by an unauthorized person will be held to invalidate the rite and nullify the magic, perhaps with disastrous results to himself and others. Magical observances are thus set apart from those of ordinary life. They take place in an atmosphere of the abnormal, which imparts to them a special dynamic character. When in a time of drought the Bagobo of Mindanao wash their pigs and goats, their pots and pans, or when, to stop a downpour, the Kaingáng of Brazil boil rain water until it all evaporates, these things, it must be assumed, are done decorously and even solemnly. They are performed in accordance with time-honored methods, and to the accompaniment, it may be, of songs, dances, and other ritual acts. It does not follow that a Bagobo will create rain every time he washes a pig, nor does it follow that a Kaingáng woman stops the rain every time she boils water for cooking.

It is true, indeed, that in any community the significance attached to a magical rite will depend very much on whether it is performed by an amateur or by a professional. As a rule, everyone knows a few simple spells or possesses a few rude charms which he feels himself qualified to use without more ado whenever necessary. For magic affecting the welfare of the social group or of its more prominent members the services of a regular operator are commonly required, and these involve on his part a much more elaborate preparation. Between different communities, again, wide differences may prevail in respect to the setting of the rite, the sequence of its several parts, and the special condition of the officiant. The systematic magic of the Trobrianders, that concerned, for instance, with the building of a canoe, a fishing expedition, or the making and harvesting of a garden, must be scrupulously carried out. To the native mind the magical rite is quite as indispensable for the success of the enterprise as is the practical activity which it accompanies.[34] On the other hand, among the Azande a magical rite is not a formalized affair. There may be quite extensive variations in what is done and said and in the sequence of actions and words. The entire performance is far less rigidly defined than it is in the Melanesian area.[35]

There are also magical procedures whose efficacy depends little or not at all on manual acts, the recital of spells, and the use of charms. In the opinion of many primitive peoples the human will can be projected mentally in a given direction and bring about the results desired by the operator. Imperative willing, intense concentration of the mind, autosuggestion (which is far more common and more easily produced among primitives than among ourselves) can suffice, when combined with a strong emotional drive, to create the faith that moves mountains.

In northern Queensland "a black will earnestly yearn for some particular fruit, etc., to come into season, and will send one of the larger species of spider to bring it——and it will come. The coastal aborigines especially and firmly believe in this method of satisfying any particular craving."[36] In Central Australia a Kaitish woman, desiring to injure a person, first blows on her fingers and then jerks her hands up and down in the direction of the intended victim. She takes good care, of course, that no one sees what she is doing. The poor man gradually wastes away into a mere skeleton.[37] Among the Buccaneer Islanders of northwestern Australia, if it was desired to injure someone in another tribe, men would leave the camp and proceed to a secluded sandy spot. Here they made a depression in the sand and placed thereon the rude figure of a man. "By concentrating their thoughts on the one they desire to harm, and by singing a weird song, the mischief is wrought. The subject of their animosity will develop a high fever and will probably die within a day or two."[38]

If an Orokaiva has two wives the less-favored one will sometimes practice *gose,* the "evil wish," against him. For instance, should he return from the hunt with game and give it all to his favorite spouse, the fury of the scorned woman finds satisfaction in her saying to herself, "Very well, next time he hunts he will waste his time." Should the bigamist return empty-handed, he is likely to suspect one or the other of his wives of having wished ill luck upon him. The Orokaiva also believe that an evil wish may be transmitted by a look. Your enemy need only cast a malicious glance at you when you are starting out to hunt to spoil your chances for the day. That is why it is advisable, if you are going to hunt by yourself, to sneak out of the village quietly and unobserved.[39]

When an Elema man goes a-wooing he sometimes impersonates

the moon, whom the myths describe as peculiarly attractive to women. For this purpose he makes use of the moon's secret name Marai. He does not whisper to himself, "Marai, help me to win this woman," but he thinks, without even whispering, "I am Marai himself, and I will get her."[40]

The people of Tikopia, an island which forms an outpost of Polynesian culture, believe that it is quite possible for barrenness to be caused in a normal married couple by a person's ill will. Sometimes, for instance, a rejected lover will send his personal deity (atua) to bring about a succession of miscarriages by the woman.[41] The Maori distinguished by a special name (hoa) the exertion of the human will to affect something at a distance. The words uttered by the operator acted merely as the vehicle connecting his will power with the object in question. A person generally resorted to this practice for the purpose of injuring a person, but he might also do so for his own benefit, as when a warrior would make use of it to hasten his flight from the foe.[42]

In the Nicobar Islands it is believed that some people are able to cause a person's death "merely by thinking of it." A man who dreams that an ill-wisher is thus trying to make an end of him flees at once to another island. The culprit, if found, is fastened to a tree and left to starve to death.[43]

Among the natives of southeastern Madagascar the term vurike forms practically the equivalent of black magic, for it applies to all secret spells and charms devised for malefic purposes. Their efficacy is proportionate to the will of the person employing them, and when properly made they secure just the result desired. The most terrible of all vurike are those which produce their effect at a distance, by a mere look or gesture in a given direction. The eye or the finger then acts as swiftly and as surely as would a lightning flash. Among these Malagasy there is not a single malady or epidemic, accident or catastrophe, which is not attributed to the operation of vurike.[44]

The Bergdama, a Negro people of South Africa, are persuaded that a dying man who has had a quarrel and has not been reconciled to his enemy cannot have a peaceful end. So they try to find the enemy and bring him to the deathbed. No verbal reconcilation occurs, but the visitor moistens his hand with his saliva and passes it over the chest and back of the sufferer. His influence will be still more potent if he spits some of his urine upon the patient. Should the antagonist fail to come in person he will send a garment on which there are traces of his perspiration. The garment, when donned by the patient, produces at once the desired effect, and he draws his final breath with no more difficulty. A person appealed to for help in this way never refuses.[45]

The Bakgatla of the Bechuanaland Protectorate describe by the word *boloi* ("bewitching with the mouth") the action whereby a man injures another by hating him. This *boloi* takes two forms. In the first form a man threatens an enemy with some evil, or expresses a desire that it may befall him, or indicates a hostile attitude by pointing the index finger at him. Even though no words accompany the gesture you know that evil is being called down upon your head, and when some sickness, accident, or other misfortune happens to you the evil-minded man will be held responsible. In the second form of *boloi* the offended person simply broods over a grievance without uttering any words or performing any act. His revengeful feeling, his "bitter heart," suffices to inflict the harm desired. This *boloi* is attributed only to one's seniors, not to one's juniors. The underlying idea is that a man against whom it is directed has failed to show proper respect to his senior relatives. The sickness caused by it can be cured by washing the patient's body, but the washing should be performed by the person supposed to have done the mischief. It he refuses to act, on the ground of nonresponsibility, a magician may himself wash the patient. His treatment, however, is not regarded as equally effective for a cure. The ancestors are called upon to help in the curative process. Sometimes this kind of *boloi* is believed to be due to the anger of a deceased person. In such a case it can be removed by a propitiatory sacrifice of an ox or a goat at the grave of the offended ancestor. Remedial measures are not always effective. So many people perish as the result of this practice that, as a native declared, "there is no peace in the tribe."[46] According to a summary account, applying to all the Bechuana tribes, it is thought that the anger of a living father, grandfather, uncle, or older brother, as well as that of dead relatives, may be physically injurious to those upon whom it has been directed. Children are most susceptible to its malign influence. Should a child become ill soon after a family quarrel the diviner is likely to announce that the illness has been caused by one of the father's elders, either of his family or of his clan. No cure can be found until the elder, having been duly pacified, washes the child with medicine and recites a formula over it.[47]

The Ba-ila of Northern Rhodesia think that suppressed anger sometimes exerts a destructive power. A grumbler who is not satisfied with the amount of eland's meat handed to him, but who fails to voice his displeasure, will cause wens and goiter to appear in his child or in a relative.[48]

The Wakonde of Nyasaland and Tanganyika strictly forbid the name of a brother to be spoken in anger, for to do so might cause his death. The spirits hear angry words and, assuming that there is justification for them, send a disease or engineer an accident which kills the person named. A daughter who despises her father may be punished with barrenness if the angry parent so desires. Once a daughter incensed her parent to such a degree that he called upon his ancestors to destroy her. She became ill the same day and died the next. The friends or relatives of an absent person, having no news of him for some time, may give way to their grief or vexation, and the emotion they feel causes illness in the absent one. A diviner tells him why he is ill and directs him as a cure to drink the infusion of a certain plant and to recite a formula ("Let the words of these people fall back on them").[49] The Sandawe of Tanganyika believe that if a person is very angry someone in the neighborhood will die. This idea is so strongly entertained that after a dispute or an insulting word a fowl is killed and its blood is spread about to appease the vengeance of the ancestors. Our missionary authority tells of a catechist who had an altercation with his wife and got very angry with her. A traveler, passing through the village, overheard his words. The man became ill before he reached home and died there a few hours later. When the diviner found out what had happened he assessed the catechist three cows and three goats as damages for the man's life.[50]

Among the Dinka of the Anglo-Egyptian Sudan a "powerful" man may make people ill without seeing them "by desiring it in his heart." For the sickness thus produced there is no cure.[51] The Acholi suppose that anyone's ill-will or envy brings misfortune upon whomsoever it falls. To counteract it an infected person must be "blessed." This is accomplished by laving him with water from a bowl into which every villager has expectorated. Then the man will be lucky again.[52]

The Bangala of the Upper Congo, together with many other African peoples, require a person accused of sorcery to prove his innocence by undergoing the poison ordeal. If he refuses to do so he is regarded as guilty. Sometimes an over-sensitive person, really innocent, will not swallow the deadly drink, in the belief that, after all, he may be the sorcerer whose identy is sought. For what constitutes guilt? Simply a strong desire that someone might die; "and how often in their uncontrollable anger have they wished for one another's death."[53]

For the Ga people of the Gold Coast, the practice of witchcraft does not involve the use of spells, medicines, or rites. Its evil influence "is simply projected at will from the mind of the witch."[54]

When a Lengua Indian expresses a desire for rain or for a cool south wind, his neighbors, if they do not want a change in the weather, protest strongly and implore him not to persist in his desire.[55] Among the Chorti Indians of Guatemala the aid of a professional sorcerer is not required for sending a curse. Anyone can send sickness or death to an enemy, his family, or his domestic animals "if he wishes such misfortune often enough." He usually goes to a secluded spot and utters his malediction in a loud voice. It is then brought to the victim by the wind gods.[56] The Tarahumara, a Mexican tribe, ascribe sickness and even death to the "mere looks or thoughts" which some persons can direct upon people who have offended them. The first idea of a sick man is: Whose anger have I aroused against me? What have I taken that I should have left alone and what have I kept that I should have given? Then the poor fellow, accompanied by his wife, goes about the village and tries to find the person who has bewitched him. If he succeeds in doing so and can pacify the bewitcher, he will recover.[57]

The Zuñi think that ordinary people can bewitch by an envious thought, though in the pueblo of Laguna only the envy of medicine men is supposed to be thus magically powerful.[58] The Hopi, during a drought, are urged not to think that rain will fail to fall. "Throw away your bad things; just let the rain come." But it is known that some evil-minded people actually wish it *not* to rain and even insult the clouds. Persons suspected of doing so may be seized and tortured to make them confess what they have done and to tell how their machinations can be frustrated.[59] A Navaho ought never express a wish that someone should die, for this might actually result in the death of the person referred to. "No one knows how powerful spoken words are, or how far they travel." Furthermore, the ghost of the murdered man would discover the identity of the ill-wisher and inflict some dire punishment upon him, perhaps insanity or a fatal illness.[60]

An important force at the disposal of a Naskapi Indian is the "power of thought." One of its manifestations is the wish. Many tales are told of hunters, conjurors, and legendary heroes who solely by wishing attained their desires. One method is that of silent communion, in which a person concentrates his mind upon the object to be secured and waits for his Great Man (his soul as a guiding agency) to make it a reality for him. The wishing process is stimulated if the wisher sings, drums, shakes a rattle, or contemplates the designs in beadwork, embroidery, and other decorations.[61]

Among the Omaha will power might be used to a person's injury. Members of a society or of an honorary chieftainship sometimes exercised the "directive energy" which pertained to them to punish a disturber of the peace within the tribe or a person offensive to the chiefs. They fixed their minds on the offender and placed upon him the consequences of his actions, so that he was excluded from all helpful relations with men and animals. This form of excommunication was greatly feared. It frequently resulted in the death of the victim.[62]

Among the Ponca, when a man was to be punished, all the chiefs met and smoked a ceremonial pipe. Then each chief put his mind on the offender, as the leader took the pipe to clean it. He poured some of the tobacco ashes on the ground and said, "This shall rankle in the calves of the man's legs." Then he twirled the cleaning stick in the pipe, took out more ashes, put them on the ground, and said, "This shall be for the base of the sinews, and he shall start with pain" (in the back). Again he twirled the cleaning stick, put more ashes on the ground, and said, "This is for the spine, at the base of the head." A fourth and final time he twirled the cleaning stick in the pipe, poured out more ashes, and said, "This is for the crown of his head." The man died soon after.[63]

A Winnebago ceremony, known as "concentrating one's mind," was performed by a hunter before he started out for bear or deer. It assured the capture of the game. For the religiously inclined Indian the efficacy of any ceremony depended upon mental concentration, whether it applied to the spirits, to the details of the ritual, or to the precise end held in view. All other thoughts ought to be rigidly excluded. Very frequently failure on the warpath or nonsuccess of a rite was attributed to insufficient emphasis on this preliminary concentration.[64]

In the magic of some California tribes direct willing forms a large element. This is particularly true of the Yurok, in the extreme northern part of the state. For them to express a wish with sufficient intensity and frequency is a potent means of realizing it. Thus a man at night or when alone will keep calling out, "I want to be rich" or "I wish *dentalia*" (shell money), perhaps weeping at the same time. Such statements do not seem to be addressed to any particular or named spirits.[65] When a Shasta man was murdered, his friends and relatives went about praying that the murderer might be injured in an accident or might die. Members of his family were generally included in the prayers. These supplications were often supposed to produce the desired result.[66] In Hupa magic "evil wishes" are powerful.[67]

Among the coastal tribes of British Columbia, "if one Indian is vexed with another, the most effectual way of showing his displeasure, next to killing him, is to say to him (what would be in English), 'By-and-by you will die.' Not infrequently the poor victim thus marked becomes so terrified that the prediction is verified. When this is the case, the friends of the deceased say that they have no doubt about the cause, and therefore (if they are able to meet the contest which may ensue) the prognosticator, on the first opportunity, is shot for his passionate language."[68]

The Yukaghir of northeastern Siberia believe that the supply of game animals can be cut short by the hostile thoughts or incantations of an ill-wisher from another community. They will make every effort to conciliate a guest or chance visitor and will provide him with the lion's share of the products of the chase.[69]

It may be plausibly conjectured that many magical procedures and techniques, particularly those of the nefarious sort, originated in such wishful thinking as has been described. When gestures and words appeared these at first must have been more or less spontaneous, translating desire into action and thus relieving the overcharged emotions of the magician. But with constant repetition and passage from one officiant to another manual acts would become stereotyped and invariable, while verbal expressions would develop into set, conventional formulas. The magical rite came to be practiced as a matter of custom, and the way was opened for the creation of a system of magic ever more elaborate and complicated.

NOTES TO CHAPTER III

[1] See A. C. Kruijt, *Het animisme in den Indischen Archipel* (The Hague, 1906), *passim*. E. M. Loeb properly points out that the marked development of the idea of soul substance in Indonesia seems to have relegated the *mana* idea to the background (*Sumatra, Its History and People* [Vienna, 1935], p. 78).

[2] W. W. Skeat, *Malay Magic* (London, 1900), p. 580.

[3] Rafael Karsten, *The Civilization of the South American Indians* (London, 1926), p. 201, note 2.

[4] Julius Jetté, "On the Superstitions of the Ten'a Indians," *Anthropos*, VI (1911), 258 f.

[5] The qualities of wholes or of parts are often supposed to be transmitted from one object to another because of a sympathetic relationship which exists between them. By those Australian tribes which practice the evulsion of teeth as an initiatory ordeal for boys, an intimate association is believed to continue between a lad and his extracted teeth. Among some of the tribes of New South Wales the tooth was placed under the bark of a tree near water. If the bark grew over the tooth, or if the tooth fell into the water, no evil could befall the lad, but if it was exposed and was overrun by ants, he would suffer from a disease of the mouth. The Yerkla-mining, a tribe of South Australia, think that if anyone but a medicine man touches the flint knife with which a boy has been incised the boy will become very ill. If a Melanesian has been wounded by an arrow and the arrow, or a part of it, has been secured, it will be kept in a damp place or in cool leaves; then the inflammation will be slight and soon subside. But if the man who inflicted the wound secures the arrow he puts it into the fire. Moreover, he keeps his bowstring taut and occasionally pulls it, thus causing tension of the nerves and spasms of tetanus in the victim.

The sympathetic relationship may be set up arbitrarily. A Papuan woman, pregnant but not wanting a child, slashes the skin of a cucumber and then cuts herself about the midriff; the cucumber rots and she has a miscarriage. A warrior in Nyasaland slits open the abdomen of a slain enemy to prevent it from swelling. Should he fail to do so, his own abdomen would swell like that of the corpse when putrefaction sets in.

The sympathetic relationship between near of kin or members of the same community gives rise to various prescriptions which do not involve the transmission of qualities. When the Kiwai Papuans are on the warpath, the few old women who are associated with the men's clubhouse must keep fires burning in it, in order that it may be "warm"; otherwise the warriors would be certain to meet with defeat. The whole village also keeps silent while the warriors are away, lest the enemy be forewarned and take to flight. In Sea Dayak villages, during the absence of the men on a foray, the roofing of the communal house is opened before dawn every day, so that they may not lie too long asleep and fall into the hands of their enemies. The Wagogo of Tanyanyika believe that a wife's unfaithfulness makes her husband unsuccessful in the hunt. Among the Canelos Indians of Ecuador the nearest relatives of a sick man put themselves on a diet, because incautious eating on their part would aggravate his illness. Prescriptions of such a character are matched by corresponding prohibitions. These include many pregnancy and puerperal observances, most cases of couvade, or "male childbed," certain rules of abstinence followed by hunters, fishers, and warriors when absent from home and by relatives and friends whom they have left behind, various dietary regulations, many name avoidances, and avoidance customs generally.

[6] R. H. Codrington, *The Melanesians* (Oxford, 1891), p. 119. In the Banks Islands a piece of water-worn coral often bears a surprising resemblance to a breadfruit. "A man who should find one of these would try its powers by laying it at the root of a tree of his own, and a good crop would prove its connection with a spirit good for breadfruit. The happy owner would then for a consideration take stones of less marked character from other men, and let them lie near his, till the *mana* in his stone should be imparted to theirs" (p. 183).

[7] H. A. Junod, *The Life of a South African Tribe* (2d ed., London, 1927), II, 369.

[8] Ruth L. Bunzel, "Introduction to Zuñi Ceremonialism," *Forty-seventh*

Annual Report of the Bureau of American Ethnology, pp. 491 f. It has been pointed out how strong, pervasive, and influential is the "dramaturgic tendency" of the Zuñi. They believe that the phenomena of nature can be controlled and made to act by men "if symbolically they do first what they wish the elements to do, according to the ways in which, as taught by their mystic lore, they suppose these things were done or made to be done by the ancestral gods of creation time." This dramaturgic tendency can be studied in the moods in which the Indians do some of the ordinary things of life. Thus they think that because a stone often struck wears away faster than when first struck it is therefore helpful in overcoming its obduracy to strike it by a preliminary ritualistic striking, whereupon it will act as though actually worked over, and will be less liable to breakage (F. H. Cushing, "Zuñi Creation Myths," *Thirteenth Annual Report of the Bureau of Ethnology*, p. 374).

[9] A. L. Kroeber, in *Bulletin of the American Museum of Natural History*, XVIII, 452 f.

[10] W. L. Warner, *A Black Civilization* (New York, 1937), pp. 206 f.

[11] A. C. Haddon, in *Reports of the Cambridge Anthropological Expedition to Torres Straits*, V, 325.

[12] H. I. Hogbin, "Sorcery and Administration," *Oceania*, VI, (1935–36), 5 f.

[13] W. H. R. Rivers, *The History of Melanesian Society* (Cambridge, 1914), I, 161 ff.

[14] W. W. Skeat, *op. cit.*, pp. 570 ff.

[15] Paul le Jeune's *Relation* of 1634, pp. 75 f. *The Jesuit Relations and Allied Documents* (Cleveland, 1896–1901), VI, 197, 199.

[16] Among the Kiwai husband and wife engage in sexual intercourse just before setting out the first yams. The husband's semen is then applied to the roots of the plants as a powerful medicine (Gunnar Landtman, *The Kiwai Papuans of British New Guinea* [London, 1927], p. 77). In some parts of Java, when the rice plant is about to bloom, married couples go to their fields by night and there have intercourse (G. A. Wilken, "Het animisme bij de volken van den Indischen Archipel," in *Verspreide Geschriften* [The Hague, 1912], III, 41). The Jakun of Malaya have annual feast days when they sing and dance, drink heavily of freshly brewed liquors, and engage in "what can only be called their 'game of exchanging wives'." The whole performance is regarded as exerting some sort of productive influence upon the sources of the food supply (W. W. Skeat and C. O. Blagden, *Pagan Races of the Malay Peninsula* [London, 1906], II, 121). Among the Tangkhul of Manipur, before the rice is sown and when it is reaped, "the severity of their ordinary morality is broken by a night of unbridled license." (T. C. Hodson, in *Journal of the Anthropological Institute*, XXXI [1901], 307). When the Oraon of Chota Nagpur are about to begin sowing their fields, they observe for several days the Sarhul festival. The older people get drunk to their hearts' content, while the young men and women sing, dance, and make merry without any restraint except their sense of decency. As our authority suggests, the saturnalian aspects of this festival seem to be associated with the idea of ensuring the fruitfulness of the fields (S. C. Roy, *The Oraons of Chota Nagpur* [Ranchi, India, 1915], p. 149). The Pipiles of Central America, when about to plant cacao, required the tillers of the soil to keep apart from their wives for four days, "in order that on the night before planting they might indulge their passions to the fullest extent." Certain persons, it is said, were appointed to perform the sexual act at the very moment when the first seeds were deposited in the ground (H. H. Bancroft, *The Native Races of the Pacific States of North America* [New York, 1875–76], II, 719 f., III, 507).

[17] Sir Baldwin Spencer and F. J. Gillen, *The Native Tribes of Central Australia* (London, 1899), pp. 170 ff.

[18] Gunnar Landtman, *op. cit.*, pp. 77 f. See also pp. 88, 96, 105. When a dog has killed a wild pig the hunter cuts off one ear of the animal and lets the dog eat it. This is considered as a sort of medicine for the dog, "teaching him to act in the same way next time" (p. 118). A sorcerer who would do harm to men out on the reef harpooning dugong procures a piece of wood from an old hut erected over a grave and lays it down on the beach close to the water. With a fragile reed or piece of bamboo he pretends to spear the wood. The reed or bamboo splits at once under the pressure, and this splitting "teaches" the shafts or heads of the men's harpoons to break (p. 137).

[19] R. F. Fortune, *Sorcerers of Dobu* (London, 1932), p. 130.

[20] Hortense Powdermaker, *Life in Lesu* (New York, 1933), pp. 301, 303.

[21] Lambert, *Mœurs et superstitions des Néo-Calédoniens* (Nouméa, 1900), pp. 193 f.; Glaumont, in *Revue d'ethnographie*, VII (1888–89), 116.

[22] Raymond Firth, *Primitive Economics of the New Zealand Maori* (London, 1929), p. 260.

[23] C. M. Pleyte, in *Tijdschrift van het Nederlandsch Aardrijkskundig Genootschap* (n.s., 1893), X, 805.

[24] T. C. Hodson, "The 'Genna' amongst the Tribes of Assam," *Journal of the Anthropological Institute*, XXXVI (1906), 96.

[25] S. C. Roy, *op. cit.*, pp. 330 f.

[26] W. L. Hildburgh, "The Directing of Conscious Agents in Some Japanese 'Imitative' Magical Practices," *Man*, XVII (1917), 4f.

[27] *Idem*, "Notes on Some Japanese Magical Methods for Injuring Persons," *Man*, XV (1915), 117 f.

[28] C. Cagnolo, *The Akikuyu* (Nyeri, Kenya, 1933), p. 188.

[29] E. E. Evans-Pritchard, *Witchcraft, Oracles, and Magic among the Azande* (Oxford, 1937), pp. 449 f.

[30] Joseph de Acosta, *The Natural and Moral History of the Indies* (London, 1880), II, 342. This ceremony is also mentioned by Bernabé Cobo (*Historia del nuevo mundo* [Seville, 1895], IV, 82).

[31] George Catlin, *Letters and Notes on the Manners, Customs, and Condition of the North American Indians* (2d ed., New York, 1842), Letter No. 18. The Mandan also held a dance every year in spring, to ensure the procreation of buffaloes. The performers wore the entire skins of the animals, complete with horns, hoof, and tail, and assumed a horizontal position in order to imitate their movements with fidelity. The central feature of this ceremony was the simulated leap of the buffalo bull on the buffalo cow, a proceeding which was carried out four times, "to the great amusement and satisfaction of the lookers-on" (George Catlin, *op. cit.*, Letter No. 22). During the celebration of this dance by the Hidatsa, a tribe akin to the Mandan, the younger men ceremonially offered the use of their wives to the older men, and the offer was generally accepted. No doubt its purpose was to promote magically the multiplication of buffaloes. See Edwin James, *An Account of an Expedition from Pittsburgh to the Rocky Mountains* (London, 1823), in R. G. Thwaites (editor), *Early Western Travels*, Vol. XV, pp. 129 f.; Maximilian, Prince of Wied, *Travels in the Interior of North America* (London, 1843), in *Early Western Travels*, Vol. XXIII, p. 334.

[32] In the Small Islands of the New Hebrides the number four and its multiple eight seem to convey the idea of "completion" or "perfection." In nearly every magical performance either four leaves or other objects are used, or else all or part of the action is completed four times, or else the spell, itself usually consisting of four parts, is recited four times in succession (John Layard, *Stone Men of Malekula* [London, 1942], pp. 644 ff.). Among the Akikuyu of Kenya

seven is the most unlucky of all numbers in divination as practiced by the medicine men (W. S. Routledge and Katherine Routledge, *With a Prehistoric People* [London, 1910], p. 274). The Cherokee Indians accompanied the planting and cultivation of corn, their principal food crop, with much ceremony. Seven grains of corn, the sacred number, were put into each hill, and these were not afterward thinned out. After the last working of the field the medicine man and his assistant (generally the owner of the field) raised there a small inclosure, entered it, and sat down on the ground with lowered heads. While the assistant kept perfect silence, the medicine man, with rattle in hand, sang songs of invocation to the corn spirit. This ritual was repeated on four successive nights, after which no one went to the field for seven nights. Then the officiant entered it. If all the sacred regulations had been properly observed, he found young ears upon the corn stalks (James Mooney, "Myths of the Cherokee," *Nineteenth Annual Report of the Bureau of American Ethnology*, Part I, p. 423). For the Blackfoot seven was the perfect number. They called the Pleiades by a word meaning "the seven perfect ones." In the purification of a medicine man a hole in the form of a triangle was dug in the ground, seven heated stones were thrown into it, and cold water was poured over the stones for a vapor bath. While thus bathing invocation was made to the Pleiades for assistance in curing various diseases (Jean L'Heureux, in *Journal of the Anthropological Institute*, XV [1886], 302 f.). Nine is a symbolic number among the Goldi and other Tungusic tribes. A shaman and his assistants dance nine circles or a number of circles that is a multiple of nine (I. A. Lopatin, in *Anthropos*, XXXV–XXXVI [1940–41], 354, note 4).

[33] The partial or complete nudity of an officiant is sometimes regarded as an essential condition for the performance of magical rites. In Rossel Island a woman can practice sorcery "by her own intrinsic power," if she takes off her petticoats (W. E. Armstrong, *Rossel Island* [Cambridge, 1928], p. 175). For the Maori the organs of generation were deeply imbued with *mana;* hence, when a man repeated a spell he would place his hand on his genitals in order to give additional power to his words (Elsdon Best, in *Journal of the Polynesian Society*, XIV [1905], 208). In India, among both Hindus and aboriginal tribes, nudity is very common, for example, in rites for stopping rain, dispersing hailstorms, driving fleas out of a village, and curing paralysis in cattle. It is also found in some forms of black magic. See William Crooke, "Nudity in India in Custom and Ritual," *Journal of the Royal Anthropological Institute*, XLIX (1919), 237–51. In Morocco, where witchcraft is supposed to be rife on New Year's Eve, there are women who on this night strip themselves and secretly take water from a neighbor's spring in order to use it in malefic arts. Among the Tsul, when rain is wanted, women go to a retired place where they cannot be seen by men and, completely naked, play a certain game of ball with wooden ladles. The game itself has a magical effect, but its virtue is emphasized by the nakedness of the players. Among the Ait Warain two or four naked women play a kind of hockey with sticks to bring rain (Edward Westermarck, *Ritual and Belief in Morocco* [London, 1926], II, 170, 268 f., 271). Among the Chukchi the sexual organs have a part in some forms of magic. Malignant spells acquire "additional force" through their use. A black shaman who would devise an especially powerful spell, strips himself naked and goes outside some night when there is moonlight. Then he calls out, saying, "O Moon! I show you my private parts. Take compassion on my angry thoughts. I have no secrets from you. Help me on such and such a man." While uttering these words the shaman tries to weep, in order to work on the moon's feelings. He also makes peculiar movements of his mouth, as if catching and munching something. These signalize his desire to catch and eat up the intended victim (W. Bogoras, in *Memoirs of the American Museum of Natural History*, XI, 448 f.). In these instances the organs of generation are clearly regarded as the seat of occult power. It possesses a prophylactic virtue against evils and can also be used positively to add

efficacy to a rite of magic. The prevalence of phallic motives in amulets, pictures, and certain indecent gestures often has a similar explanation. The common belief that witches, when engaged in their nefarious practices, go about naked is also connected with the same train of ideas.

[34] Bronislaw Malinowski, *Argonauts of the Western Pacific* (London, 1922), pp. 413 f.

[35] E. E. Evans-Pritchard, *op. cit.,* p .449.

[36] W. E. Roth, *North Queensland Ethnography Bulletin,* No. 5, p. 27.

[37] Sir Baldwin Spencer and F. J. Gillen, *The Northern Tribes of Central Australia* (London, 1904), p. 464.

[38] W. H. Bird, in *Anthropos,* VI (1911), 177.

[39] F. E. Williams, *Orokaiva Magic* (London, 1928), p. 180.

[40] *Idem,* in *Oceania,* III (1932–33), 164.

[41] Raymond Firth, *We, the Tikopia* (London, 1936), pp. 487 f.

[42] S. P. Smith, "The 'Tohunga'-Maori," *Transactions and Proceedings of the New Zealand Institute,* XXXII (1899), 263. According to an early missionary among the Maori, the power of bewitching could be exerted by anyone, "a simple wish often being sufficient." When the natives accepted Christianity they were very careful to ask a blessing on their food to prevent the ill wishes of enemies from affecting it (Richard Taylor, *Te Ika A Maui* [2d ed., London, 1870], pp. 203 f.). We are also told that "a person is supposed to be bewitched by smoking from the pipe of an ill-wisher, lying in his hut, putting on his dress, drinking from the same calabash, eating together from the same basket, paddling in the same canoe, and even bathing in the same river" (J. S. Polack, *Manners and Customs of the New Zealanders* [London, 1840], I, 280; cf. I, 236, 263). "Evil wishes," conveyed by the eye, could cause a child's death or the serious illness of an adult (I, 269). A native woman, who had known of a case of "willing to death," declared that if the victim learned that he had been thus bewitched he would consult a *tohunga* (magician), who was able not only to save him but also to cause the death of the ill-wisher. But if he remained ignorant of the designs upon his life, he rarely survived two days and frequently expired at the appointed time. See Frances Del Mar, *A Year among the Maoris* (London, 1924), p. 86.

[43] P. Barbe, in *Journal of the Asiatic Society of Bengal,* XV (1846), 351 f.

[44] Gustave Julien, in *Revue d'ethnographie et des traditions populaires,* VIII (1927), 5.

[45] Heinrich Vedder, *Die Bergdama* (Hamburg, 1923), I, 128 f.

[46] I. Schapera, "Oral Sorcery among the Natives of Bechuanaland," in *Essays Presented to C. G. Seligman* (London, 1934), pp. 296 ff.

[47] W. C. Willoughby, *The Soul of the Bantu* (Garden City, N.Y., 1928), p. 194, note 1.

[48] E. W. Smith and A. M. Dale, *The Ila-speaking Peoples of Northern Rhodesia* (London, 1920), I, 241.

[49] D. R. MacKenzie, *The Spirit-ridden Konde* (London, 1925), pp. 268 f., 277.

[50] Martin van de Kimmerade, in *Anthropos,* XXXI (1936), 412.

[51] C. G. Seligman and Brenda Z. Seligman, *Pagan Tribes of the Nilotic Sudan* (London, 1932), p. 194.

[52] E. T. N. Grove, "Customs of the Acholi," *Sudan Notes and Records,* II (1919), 175.

[53] J. H. Weeks, *Among Congo Cannibals* (London, 1913), p. 191; cf. p. 293.

[54] Margaret J. Field, *Religion and Medicine of the Ga People* (Oxford, 1937), p. 135.

55 W. B. Grubb, *An Unknown People in an Unknown Land* (4th ed., London, 1914), p. 138.

56 Charles Wisdom, *The Chorti Indians of Guatemala* (Chicago, 1940), p. 333.

57 Carl Lumholtz, *Unknown Mexico* (London, 1903), I, 315 f.

58 Elsie C. Parsons, "Witchcraft among the Pueblos: Indian or Spanish?" *Man*, XXVII (1927), 107 f.

59 Barbara W. Aitken, as reported in *Conger's international des sciences anthropologiques et ethnologiques, Compte-rendu de la première session* (London, 1934), p. 294. The Hopi on one occasion attributed a continued drought to the "discordant thoughts and speeches" of certain Oraibi chiefs and elders (Elsie C. Parsons [editor], *Hopi Journal of Alexander M. Stephen* [New York, 1936], p. 437, note 1).

60 Mrs. F. J. Newcomb, *Navajo Omens and Taboos* (Santa Fe, New Mexico, 1940), p. 79.

61 F. G. Speck, *Naskapi, the Savage Hunters of the Labrador Peninsula* (Norman, Oklahoma, 1935), p. 184.

62 Alice C. Fletcher and Francis La Flesche, in *Twenty-seventh Annual Report of the Bureau of American Ethnology*, pp. 216, 497, 583 f. We are also told that upon the occasion of a race an Omaha may bend his thought and will upon the contestant whom he favors, in the belief that this "sending his mind" will help his friend or relative to win (Alice C. Fletcher, "Notes on Certain Beliefs Concerning Will Power among the Siouan Tribes," *Science* [n.s., 1897], V, 332).

63 Alice C. Fletcher and Frances La Flesche, in *Twenty-seventh Annual Report of the Bureau of American Ethnology*, p. 48.

64 Paul Radin, in *Thirty-seventh Annual Report of the Bureau of American Ethnology*, pp. 111, 255, 278, 370 f. Cf. *idem*, "Religion of the North American Indians," *Journal of American Folk-Lore*, XXVII (1914), 367, (Winnebago and Ojibwa).

65 A. L. Kroeber, *Handbook of the Indians of California* (Washington, D.C., 1925), p. 41.

66 R. B. Dixon, in *Bulletin of the American Museum of Natural History*, XVII, 453.

67 P. E. Goddard, "Life and Culture of the Hupa," *University of California Publications in American Archaeology and Ethnology*, I, 88.

68 R. C. Mayne, *Four Years in British Columbia and Vancouver Island* (London, 1862), p. 292, quoting the Rev. Mr. Duncan.

69 W. Jochelson, in *Memoirs of the American Museum of Natural History*, XIII, 125.

Chapter IV

THE MAGICAL WORD: SPELLS

The utilization of occult power, whether by an amateur or a professional, as a rule requires a vocal expression of the operator's will, that is, a spell or incantation. If there is power in wishes, threats, or commands unuttered, how much greater must be the power of words which affirm or describe what the magician wants to come to pass. Speech has definiteness in contrast to more or less hazy thought; it wings its way to its destination; it carries the wish home. The magician's verbal reference to a desired result becomes for him an instrument producing it. Oral rites of magic thus stand on the same ground as manual rites. Both represent, figuratively and symbolically, the one in language and the other in action, a wished-for outcome.

The significance which the primitive mind attributes to words may be traced by the speculative student back to those earlier ages when speech, man's first and greatest intellectual creation, disclosed to him a whole new world. Verbal language, we may well believe, was the primary element of culture and, once formed, became the chief means of cultural transmission until supplemented by writing, the "divine art," as Plato called it. What wonder that words should seem to be instinct with magical power, that in them should reside mysterious potencies!

Rudimentary spells are little more than spontaneous ejaculations, though always tending, with constant usage, to harden into conventional formulas. A spell used by the Kurnai of Victoria against evil magic was the simple expression of a wish—"Never shall sharp *barn* catch me"—repeated in a monotonous chant. A Kurnai doctor, by means of a song of three words, could stop the furious winds which prevented the natives from climbing tall trees in the western forest. It bade the west wind be bound or tied. He sang a similar modest but effective ditty to cause the western gales to rise. When they came the people gave him presents so that he would send them away.[1] The Southern Massim have a folk tale containing a spell to open a cave—"O rock, be cleft!" and, to shut a cave, "O rock, be closed!"[2] An Orokaiva who would drive off the rain shouts "Cease rain!" utters a long-drawn inarticulate cry, and sweeps back the clouds with a wave of his arm. A pig hunter whispers, "Come hither, come hither!" as he waits in the garden by moonlight. A boy, visiting his bird traps and finding one of them collapsed, says "Kill, kill!" and hopes to come upon a dead bird under the wreckage. The planter of taro exclaims "Taro, sit tight!" (i.e., take root) or "Taro arise!"[3] In the Solomon Islands the spells used in fishing sometimes are direct commands: "Come, bonito, come plenty, come to my village!" "Garfish, garfish, come and take hold of my line!" Or a command may be given to the fishing apparatus to do its work: "Catch them, catch them!" said to the bonito hook. Or, again, the spell may be a simple statement that what is required will or has come to pass: "You and I spit on the taro, now it is large."[4]

In black magic, as practiced by the Bavenda of the Transvaal, a spell is always uttered exhorting the enemy to fall ill, go mad, or suffer death, as may be desired. A magic powder and fat are put into an antelope's horn, which is then blown like a whistle, while such words as "O you," living at so-and-so, "die, die, die!" are interpolated between blasts of the horn.[5] In the old days, when Bechuana warriors assembled for an attack on enemy territory, there came to them a woman, who carried a winnowing fan. This she shook violently, at the same time keeping her eyes shut and crying, "The army is not seen!" A doctor then sprinkled medicine over the spears, repeating, meanwhile, the same formula.[6] When the Bakongo of the Lower Congo set their traps to catch rodents, they mumble, "Eh, that the *mbende* (a much appreciated rodent) may come and bite at the bait!" In the same way they mention severally the different species of rodents they wish to entrap. They continue, "Eh! May the *niengi* (a noncomestible animal) not venture to approach; if he tries to, may his teeth become thorns!" And, in the same way, they mention all those other rodents which they consider undesirable for eating. To the sparrows which the bird catcher hopes to ensnare by means of birdlime, he softly chants, "Eh! Sparrows, see the termites (bait)! Eh! I catch hordes of sparrows, which eat my termites."[7]

Instead of uttering a wish, threat, or command, or using expressions which assert that the desired result has already occurred, the operator may resort to verbal impersonation. Among the Kutubu, a Papuan tribe, a gardener when putting out his cuttings mutters, "This is not sugar cane; it is *kaveraro*" (a useless kind of cane which grows abundantly). He thus expresses a hope that his sugar cane will flourish even as *kaveraro*. Similarly, when he plants sweet potato he calls it a species of wild vine and wishes it to grow as strongly. Again, a spell employed in hunting may identify the hunter with a bird of prey; a hawk, for example. Here the symbol represents success in a predatory expedition.[8] Sulka warriors in New Britain, when approaching hostile territory, refer to their enemies as "rotten tree trunks," a designation which causes the limbs of the foe to be slow of movement.[9] A Maori likens a stone which lies by the kitchen hearth to his enemy's brain and declares "how very sweet" this would be if he ate it.[10] A Peninsular Malay, engaged in deer hunting, often addresses the animals as if they were human beings. After entering the jungle he recites a spell: "It is not I who am huntsman, it is Pawang Sidi ('wizard' Sidi) that is huntsman. It is not I whose dogs these are, it is Pawang Sakti (the 'magic wizard') whose dogs these are."[11] An elephant hunter among the Akamba, upon first catching sight of his quarry, will say, "Yonder is a stone." The hunter wishes that the elephant, like a stone, will remain motionless so that it can be shot.[12] Among the Lummi of Washington, a deer hunter who knows *suin* (magic) makes use of impersonation to bring him good luck. As if addressing someone acquainted with his plans, he names the places where he intends to hunt and then adds, "I suppose our grandchild is wandering along the shores about this time. Her limbs are strong and she trusts in them to escape us, but let them become numb when we see her." When the hunter approaches his quarry it seems not to notice him, and he easily shoots it. A fisherman experienced in *suin* says to his hook, "How nice it will be when the halibut will try to find his way to you. I suppose he is waiting for us to come." He then calls the halibut by its secret name. The fish hears the magical words, straightway bites the hook, and gets caught.[13]

The efficacy of a spell depends in large measure upon its mysteriousness, hence it is often couched in cryptic or archaic language incomprehensible to the laity and, perhaps, to the magician himself. Unintelligibility may be deliberately sought when spells are composed by professional practitioners, to whom the elaboration of magical formulas and procedures is of supreme interest; again, it may be the result of an unconscious degeneration, when words which were once meaningful are repeated over and over, perhaps without much regard to their application to the matter in hand.

Quite apart from these considerations it is obvious that expressions and formulas handed down orally from one generation to another, must in process of time suffer innumerable changes, because of faulty human memory, and that the alterations which take place will usually make for unintelligibility rather than the reverse. Primitive peoples may assert and believe that their magic, like the faith once delivered to the saints, is the same yesterday, today, and forever, but the contrary is true.

Among the Unmatjera, a tribe of Central Australia, the words used to "sing" evil magic into a pointing stick, in order that the victim may sicken and die, convey no meaning to the operator.[14] Many spells used by the Gende of New Guinea are very old and no longer understood by the magicians themselves.[15] The chants recited in the Duk-Duk mysteries of New Britain are in an unknown tongue.[16] In New Ireland many spells are in an ancient and now obsolete language.[17] With reference to those used in Yap, one of the Carolines, we are told that it is impossible to extract a literal meaning from them, for they are not in the modern Yap language nor in that of the people of any neighboring island.[18] In Minahassa, a district of Celebes, the language of the so-called priests is frequently incomprehensible to the people, "owing to the use of many words which are now no longer spoken."[19] Sea Dayak spells are said to be unintelligible. No native has the least idea what they mean.[20] Magicians among the Kayan (Bahau) use a special older speech—"spirit speech."[21] Cherokee Indian spells contain many archaic and figurative expressions often understood only by the medicine men and sometimes not even by them.[22] Magicians among the Sioux or Dakota purposely make their speech unintelligible to the laity by employing words taken from other Indian languages, by introducing descriptive names of things, and by giving new significations to words in common use.[23] In the Ojibwa ritual of the Midewiwin the phraseology is largely in an archaic language. Members of the society delight to make use of it during the ceremonies, "not only to impress their hearers but to elevate themselves as well."[24] The special language used for songs and incantations by Eskimo shamans contains many words with a symbolic significance and others of an archaic form. The incomprehensibility of "magic words" makes them all the more potent.[25] Of about forty incantations collected by an investigator among the Chukchi only one was found to be quite meaningless, but all the others contained obsolete words.[26]

Whether intelligible or unintelligible, whether a straightforward, coherent statement or a string of nonsense syllables, a spell gains in efficacy by its mode of utterance. It is often whispered or mumbled or spoken so rapidly that it cannot be understood. Especially will this be the case when spells are private property, not to be heard by people without right to them. There is also the notion that unauthorized persons who listened to them might be gravely injured by their occult power. When practicing the black art, an Arunta "in muttered tones hisses out" his spells or sings "low chants" addressed to an evil spirit resident in his magical implement.[27] In the western islands of Torres Straits a magical formula, expressing a wish or command, is muttered or spoken rapidly in a low voice.[28] A Kai magician always speaks in whispers.[29] In Dobu Island, which belongs to the D'Entrecasteaux group, spells are spoken in a "sing-song undertone." People who own them take the utmost care to prevent being overheard and usually resort to a remote part of the bush for their recital. Spells are the most private of private property, but there is always danger of their being stolen and used by an unprivileged person.[30] In New Ireland spells are always recited almost inaudibly and as a rule with much abbreviation or mutilation of the words.[31] Cherokee medicine men take the utmost care that their formulas shall not become known to outsiders or to their rivals in the magical profession. Hence the words of a formula are uttered in such a low tone that they cannot be understood even by the person for whose benefit they are recited.[32] By the Polar Eskimo all magical formulas must be spoken "softly and with lowered voice," and every word must be repeated.[33] The Chukchi shaman pronounces his incantation in an "inaudible whisper." Should even a stone hear the mysterious words it would deprive the owner of their possession and acquire them for itself. After finishing a recital the shaman spits at his left side in order to fasten the incantation to the object addressed.[34]

The efficacy of a spell is likewise dependent upon its correct repetition. Even minor variations of wording may be disastrous. A Trobriand spell has to be memorized with absolute accuracy. Any change in the wording, unauthorized curtailment, or wrong method of recital is considered to diminish or nullify its power. As the spell is acquired, word for word, it sinks down into the abdomen and there takes residence. "When the magician recites it the action of the throat, which is the seat of the human mind or intelligence, imparts the virtue to the breath of the reciter. This virtue is then transmitted in the act of recital directly to the objects charmed or to the substances which will be afterwards applied to the objects charmed."[35] Before beginning to acquire a spell of black magic a Dobuan performs a rite to empty his stomach (the seat of memory) of blood and water. He thus puts it into a receptive condition to hold the magical words. Once the pupil has memorized the spell, the teacher places it in some object and brings the latter into contact with the pupil's body. If he has learned it word-perfect, he cannot be injured by this attempt at infection, for his magic is equal in power to that used against him. If, however, he fails to retain a firm memory of the spell his magic will be inferior in power and he will contract the disease which the spell is supposed to produce. "Some youths are afraid of learning sorcery, but the great majority realize that it should be done, and face the ordeal bravely."[36] A Maori *karakia* had to be uttered without the slightest mistake, for the omission of a single word from it or the insertion of one not originally there made the spell of no avail. A mistake reacted on the *tohunga* himself and, in the case of very sacred spells, might even cause his death. Some *karakia* were recited in a peculiar voice, more or less like intoning, with the words flowing on in an even and rapid stream interrupted only by the necessity of the magician's taking breath. The words of other spells required recitation without a break if they were to be efficacious. For these a relay of reciters was provided, each one to intone the words as soon as his predecessor's breath gave out.[37] Should a Singhalese magician make even a slight mistake during the performance of a "serious" ceremony, that is, one in which he was summoning malignant and powerful devils, they would immediately attack him and perhaps kill him. For this reason the spells (mantras) employed were memorized and not read from a book, because it was easier to make a mistake in reading than in reciting.[38] A Navaho who makes a mistake in learning or in practicing the Night Chant, a great ceremony of healing, will become paralyzed.[39] With the Zuñi Indians every word, every gesture, every bit of the regalia of a ritual performance has magical compulsiveness. "Hence the great perturbation in Zuñi if a dancer appears wearing a feather from the shoulders instead of the breast of the eagle, if a single gesture before an altar is omitted, or if the words of a prayer are inverted."[40]

Occasionally, however, some latitude is allowed the reciter of a spell. Among the natives of the Polynesian island of Tikopia a magician will often withdraw phrases from his formula and insert others, in the hope that it may thereby be made more successful.[41] With the Azande important magical rites are normally accompanied by the operator's directions to his medicines, telling them what he wants them to do, but his words have no power in themselves and do not assume the character of set formulas. Of course, people who use the same medicines for the same purposes will tend to use the same language toward them, so that there is naturally much uniformity in these so-called spells.[42]

"Magical songs," which must be described as spells, figure largely in accounts of the magic, both white and black, used by the aborigines of Australia. In the neighboring islands of Torres Straits practically every magical act is performed to the accompaniment of some wish or command, expressed vocally, or of a spoken formula.[43]

Few set or conventional spells seem to be known to the Orokaiva of New Guinea, who depend, rather, upon the employment of magical substances, or charms. However, the use of a charm is not invariable, for some forms of magic can be worked by ejaculations and gestures alone.[44] For the Mountain Arapesh, another Papuan tribe, magic consists primarily in the use of spells, though magical herbs are also employed. The spells are pairs of names and repetitive verbal statements. The Arapesh have no explanation to offer for their potency. They work automatically and powerfully because that is their nature. It is very dangerous to tamper with them. Even the rightful owner or the members of his family may be injured by incautious handling of this magical machinery. The owner is likely to fall ill if he carelessly recites a spell near food and then eats the food. His wife and children may become sick because he has placed a spell, in the form of a curse, on the fence of his garden.[45] Among the Bukaua a spell accompanies practically every magical act.[46]

In the Trobriand Islands, while there is a special word (*yopa*) for a spell, yet the natives often use the term *megwa,* which means magic, or the occult power of magic, to describe a spell. For the Trobrianders the main creative force of a magical rite resides in the words which accompany it. In many cases the spell alone, if directly breathed upon its object, suffices to produce the effect desired. If magical substances also find a place in the rite, their purpose is only to intensify the power of the spell. No rites are ever performed without appropriate spells.[47] In Dobu a magical performance often requires the use of certain charms (leaves, roots, and fluids), which have power in their own right. For their greatest efficacy they need, however, to be accompanied by spells. Particular families own such spells, and a man can seldom buy one unless he is related to the family possessing it.[48] In the northern D'Entrecasteaux Islands spells are seldom used alone, though they form an indispensable part of all magic, whether white or black.[49]

In New Ireland the success of a magical performance depends chiefly upon the spell which accompanies it, and sometimes this alone is employed by the operator.[50] In divination, as practiced by the Solomon Islanders, the real power is thought to lie in the spell. Divinatory objects, such as a bow, a spear, firesticks, or a leaf of dracaena, are no more than accessories.[51] At Mala (Malaita) in the Solomons the word akaloa means both magic and spell.[52] Among the Maori, also, the word karakia, meaning an uttered formula, is in use as a generic term for magic.[53] Ask any old native what produces a magical effect, and he will tell you it is the karakia itself, the form of words employed.[54]

Among the Barundi, a Bantu-speaking people of Ruanda-Urundi (Belgian Congo), a magician imbues his implements with evil power by means of his spells and his evocation of spirits. Until he does so they are quite useless for the purposes of the black art.[55]

The spells used by Cherokee medicine men covered almost every aspect of Indian life, for they dealt with hunting, fishing, the crops, warfare, medicine, love-making and love-keeping, witchcraft, sports, and the protection of the individual against dangers and misfortunes. A candidate for the magical art had to cultivate a long memory, for no formula was recited by his instructor more than once. If he failed to remember it after the first hearing he was considered unworthy to be accounted a medicine man. The difficulty of keeping many spells in mind was partly removed by the fact that all of them were constructed on regular principles, with constant repetition of the same set of words.[56]

Among the Greenland Eskimo all charms require the application of spells to make them work.[57] The spells of the Ammassalik Eskimo on the east coast of Greenland are very old and as a rule are handed down from one generation to another by sale. The natives do not conceive of any spirits in connection with them. It is only the words themselves, they say, that have "power." Spells have greatest efficacy when used for the first time, and little by little decline in strength. Hence they must not be recited except when the owner is in grave danger or when being transferred

from one person to another.[58] An Iglulik Eskimo once induced
an old woman to part with a few "magic words" which had come
down in her family "right from the time of the first human being."
In return he provided her with food and clothing for the rest of
her life.[59]

By some Siberian tribes incantations are held in great esteem.
These find employment on almost every occasion. A Chukchi
driving reindeer will use an incantation to shorten his journey.
A hungry person, eating from the same dish with others, will try
by an incantation to make the motions of his rivals slower than
his own. Women apply an incantation to their sinew-thread to
strengthen it. In short, there is scarcely an action so trifling as to
lack its magical formula. Chukchi charms derive much of their
power from the words spoken over them. Hence ancient charms,
over which many magical formulas have been pronounced in a
succession of years, are exceedingly powerful.[60] The Koriak likewise believe that an incantation increases the efficacy of a charm
and makes it more permanent. Almost every Koriak family includes some women, generally an elderly person, who is familiar
with magical formulas. In many cases the woman acquires such
a reputation for using these that she becomes a rival of the professional shaman. She keeps them secret, for, if commonly known,
they would lose their power. When she sells one she promises the
buyer never to use it again herself or to divulge it to anyone else.
Selling a magical formula to a foreigner is regarded as a sin.[61]

Elsewhere far less reliance may be placed on the spoken word
as an element of a magical rite. In the Banks Islands magical
power seems to reside in an object, rather than in the spells accompanying its use. Consequently a person who steals a stone
possessing *mana* may be able to carry out the rite successfully
even though he is ignorant of the spell that goes with the stone.[62]
The Tanala of Madagascar have scarcely any belief in the efficacy
of spells. Practically all their magical procedures are associated
with some material substance which for them is the source of the
power exercised. Even in the manufacture of charms spoken
formulas are rarely used and, if used, are considered of little
importance.[63] Spells used by the Lovedu of the Transvaal have
no fixed phraseology; they merely tell the medicine what to do
and the name of the person to be affected. Very often the medicine is thought to be as efficacious without the spell as with it.[64]
Among the Pondo of Pondoland, the medicine that is used assumes the chief place in both white and black magic; the spell is

of secondary importance. At the most it merely expresses the operator's wish for the success of his performance and, in the case of sorcery, includes the mention of his enemy's name. Verbal accuracy in the repetition of the spell is not necessary.[65] The various forms of magic found among the Bakgatla of the Bechuanaland Proctectorate rely for efficacy chiefly on the use of material substances. The rite itself is occasionally important, and so may be the spell. But in love magic and in certain forms of agricultural magic, for instance, no spell is used. All that matters is the correct application of the proper charms.[66]

For the Azande the virtue of a magical rite resides principally in the medicines employed. If they are operated correctly and the requisite taboos are observed by the magician, they must obey his will and do as they are bid. Our authority saw a native tying magical creepers round his garden. He told the medicine to break anyone who came to spoil the plants, then twisted a length of creeper and repeated, "Break, break, break!" He then tied it to sticks thrust in the ground to support it and as he did so said again, "Break, break, break!" This performance was repeated with each length of creeper. Most injunctions of the character described are spoken in a normal, matter-of-fact voice. However, when the medicines are regarded as very dangerous and when the task assigned to them is one of great social importance, for instance, vengeance magic, they are carefully instructed as to their specific duties. The Azande do not always address their medicines. For example, if these are administered as antidotes or counter-medicines in a long rite canceling the effects of vengeance magic, not a word may be spoken to them. The native explains that in such a case the medicines have nothing to do, hence there is no need of instructing them.[67]

The language of a spell is naturally correlated with the rite of which it forms a part, whether this be blessing or cursing, exorcism of evil spirits and of evil influences in general, or the production of some effect for good or ill upon the outside world. Very important is the use of names in spells, for in primitive thought name and thing named are one and the same. A man's name is as much himself as are his bodily members. One who utters it can use it in black magic against him or upon his soul, which is so frequently identified with his name.

The formal recital of personal names to secure control over their owners appears as a constant feature of magical procedures. For the Maori a blow given by proxy amounted to the same thing as one actually inflicted on an enemy. To injure him you struck the ground a succession of blows, and as you did so you named one after another various parts of his body. When a new stockade was being erected in war time, some of the largest posts would be named after the chiefs of a hostile tribe and then the people would fire at the posts, "by way of expressing the deadly nature of the feud."[68] In South Africa the natives have a simple but effective way of dealing with a boy given to petty theft. Medicines are put into a pot of boiling water and his name is shouted out, not once but many times, until they feel sure that it has penetrated deeply into the decoction. Then the pot is covered up and placed at one side for several days. At the end of this time the boy, who is utterly ignorant of the liberties taken with his name, will be quite cured of his thievish propensity.[69] The Ewe of the Slave Coast, to procure the death of an enemy, wrap palm leaves and strips of calico around a stump and adorn it with a string of cowrie shells. Then they pound the top of the stump with a stone and pronounce the name of the person whose destruction is desired. This is done, we are told, not simply with the purpose of informing the stump (or its "animating principle") who is the person to be destroyed. The people believe that by uttering his name his personality is in some way transferred to the figure which represents him.[70]

An elaborate variety of oral magic appears in the recital of stories relating to the fulfillment of a wish and often introducing by name some character well known in myth or legend. The entire narrative may be thought to exert an occult influence, or this may be concentrated in the words of power which it contains, whether the sublime *Fiat lux!* of Genesis or the "Open, Sesame!" of the *Arabian Nights*.

These narrative spells, as they have been called, are found among various tribes in what was formerly German New Guinea. Their recital is supposed to procure an abundant harvest of yams, taro, bananas, and sugar cane, on which the natives chiefly depend for food. Thus among the Kai "tales of long ago" are recited only during the planting season, obviously with the idea that by reviving the memory of the mythical beings, to whom the origin of agriculture is ascribed, the welfare of the crops will be promoted. At the end of every story the narrator names the different kinds of yams and adds, "Shoots (for the new planting) and fruits (to eat) in abundance!"[71] The Yabim, a neighboring tribe, have a story of a certain man who labored in his taro field and complained that he had no shoots for planting. Then two doves, which had devoured much taro, perched on a tree in the field and vomited up all the taro. Thus the man got so many shoots that he even had some to sell to his neighbors. When the taro will not bud the Yabim describe how an eel, caught at ebb-tide on the seashore, seemed to be in its last gasp. But with flood-tide the creature came to life again and plunged into deep water. This story is recited over the twigs of a certain tree, while the magician strikes the ground with them. The taro is now sure to bud.[72]

In the Trobriand Islands, after the soil has been cleared, the crops planted, and the fences put up, there is little garden work to be done for a time. It is the season of the northeasterly monsoons, and the natives are often kept indoors or near their houses by bad weather. Then they relieve the tedium of the hours by telling each other interminable stories, mainly ribald in character. Every speaker must wind up his narrative with a set formula, rhythmically intoned. It describes how the yams are breaking forth in clusters, and how the story teller is cooking taro pudding, which So-and-So (an important person present) will eat. This composition makes the yam plants mature as a staple food crop.[73]

In Bougainville most magical formulas begin with a word such as "strength" or "vitality," and then comes a list of all the deceased magicians who in the past performed the rite successfully. The operator does not call on them for assistance; he merely states that they were successful and that he, therefore, is following in their footsteps.[74]

The Ifugao of northern Luzon have literally hundreds of myths that are recited on ritual occasions for their magical effect. In general, the myths refer to critical events in the past which were confronted and happily surmounted by the gods or heroes. Reciting them "renews the forces that formerly brought about the desirable outcome."[75]

The spells of the Taulipáng, a Carib tribe of Venezuela and Brazilian Guiana, can be used by ordinary folk as well as by a professional magician. Almost every event in the lives of these Indians calls for their recital. Most of them are introduced by a short mythical narrative in which helpful animals or plants or the powers of nature (wind, rain, thunder and lightning) play a role.[76] Among the Cuna Indians every spell recited for the cure of sickness must be preceded by a narrative describing the origin of the remedy used, otherwise this is not efficacious.[77]

Among the Indians of northwestern California there is a

special development of spoken formulas regarded as magically potent. Each one is little more than a mythical narrative, and practically every important myth is either in whole or in part also a formula. "Not only purification from death and other defilement, but luck in hunting and fishing, and success in felling trees and making baskets, in the acquisition of wealth, in short, in the proper achievement of every human wish, were thought to be accomplished by the proper knowledge and recitation of these myth-formulas."[78]

The magic songs or stories of the Iglulik Eskimo are fragments of old narratives handed down from earlier generations. They can be bought or communicated as a legacy by a dying person, but they would lose their power if heard by anyone not the rightful owner. Reference is constantly made to the wonderful power of certain words contained in the stories. These words are invariably absent, however, for the person who once knew them kept them for his own use. The stories are recited to children, so that they may learn how mighty a power lies concealed in words. The best-known narrative (told throughout Greenland) tells of an old grandmother who, in order to find food for her grandchild, changed herself into a young man by means of magic words.[79]

The Koriak have a tale of the Supreme Being, or Universe, who sent a heavy rain on earth from the vulva of his wife. Big Raven and his son transformed themselves into ravens, flew up to heaven, and by a trick stopped the downpour. This myth must not be recited during fine weather, but only when there is rain or a snowstorm.[80]

Blessings and curses, as a means of communicating good and bad fortune, are purely magical, if their efficacy is held to depend upon the operator's occult power and that of the words he utters. They assume a magico-animistic character when a spiritual being is asked to enforce them or, at least, to give them an added efficacy. The use of such helpful and harmful words, especially of the latter, is widespread among primitive peoples.[81]

The natives of Eddystone Island, one of the Solomons, describe by the word *maulu* the practices which we would differentiate as cursing, oath-swearing, and speaking words of abuse. *Maulu,* as a curse, is employed to bar a road ("The man who walks there let him walk in the defecating place"); to protect a house against intrusion ("Let him eat excrements, the man who enters the house"); to guard against stealing ("Let him who stole from me defecate on his basket"); to stop a fight ("The evil curse, you two do not wrestle") ; and by a father to prevent his daughter from marrying a suitor unwelcome to him. If a person disregards one of these imprecations he is liable to a fine; if he does not pay up the curser and the cursed have a fight the next time they meet.[82] In the Banks Islands a curse may take the form of a wish for evil to befall someone, with a mental if not a verbal reference to a spiritual being. There is also a milder form of cursing, analogous to a practice found among ourselves. A person's troublesome or impertinent remark will be countered by saying to him, "You are a dead man's bone" or by pointing to a certain tree and using a formula which means not much more than "You be hanged!" thereon.[83] In the Loyalty Islands (Lifu) imprecation finds such common use for causing sickness that one form of the verb meaning "to be sick" now signifies "to be cursed."[84]

The Samoans constantly resorted to imprecations to frighten thieves and prevent stealing. When a man visited his plantations and discovered that some bananas had been stolen, he would shout at the top of his voice two or three times, "May fire blast the eyes of the person who has stolen my bananas! May fire burn down his eyes and the eyes of his god too!" This terrible cry rang throughout the adjacent plantations and made the thief tremble. A Samoan priest had a large wooden bowl, which he called *lipi* ("sudden death"). It represented the cuttlefish god Fe'e. In a case of stealing, the injured party brought gifts to the priest and asked him to curse the thief. The priest and some members of his family then sat down around the bowl representing the god and prayed for speedy vengeance on the guilty man. The latter, if he became ill, would be carried on a litter to the priest's house and would confess his misdeeds. His friends made many presents to the priest and begged him to pray over the death bowl that the curse might be withdrawn.[85] In the Hawaiian Islands a priest could also discover a thief. For this purpose the priest made a fire by the friction of sticks and threw into it the kernels of three nuts, at the same time uttering an anathema "to kill the fellow." The same ceremony would be repeated with other nuts unless the thief appeared and made restitution (which generally happened). If he proved obdurate, he soon lost strength and died, knowing full well that he had been "prayed to death."[86]

The curses in use in the Tonga Islands were very numerous. Most of them, we are told, consisted of wishes or commands that the person cursed would eat or otherwise maltreat his relatives or his gods: "Bake your grandfather till his skin turns to cracknel, and gnaw his skull for your share!" "Go, and ravish your own sister!" "Dig up your father by moonlight, and make soup of his bones!" To produce the desired effect a number of such curses, sometimes as many as thirty or forty, had to be repeated consecutively, in a firm voice, and with real malevolence. Even so they would be futile if the curser was lower in rank than the man he cursed.[87]

Among the Maori a curse was generally an expressed wish that the indignity of being cooked should be the lot of the person insulted: "May your head be cooked!" Another form consisted of such statements as, "Your skull is my calabash," "My fork is of your bone." An old man was at work in a plantation during a shower of rain. The sun came out and made the moisture rise in a cloud from his body. A lad (of another tribe) standing by remarked innocently, "The steam from the old man's head is like the steam from the oven." These words were considered a curse, and a bloody war ensued between the two tribes. A chief, jealous of the fame of the great leader Te Rauparaha, said of him, "His head shall be beaten with a fern-root pounder." War followed the insult, as on another occasion when it was reported to the redoubtable Te Rauparaha that a man had cursed him by declaring, "I will rip open his stomach with a barracouta tooth." To liken a man to an animal or an inferior was also a curse. If, when hair had been cut from the head of some person of consequence and had not been removed to the sacred enclosure, a person should say, "How disgusting to leave it about; whose is it?" that would have been a curse on the owner of the hair. Sometimes the curser would name some part of his opponent's body or limbs and at the same time would strike the ground, thus bestowing a blow by proxy.[88]

Curses in the Luang-Sermata Islands threaten some undescribed misfortune: "Evil shall devour you!" Or they enter into particulars and express a wish that you be blasted by thunder, struck by lightning, consumed by the sun, or transfixed by the *serui* fish.[89] The Sea Dayak of Borneo have a summary way of dealing with an inveterate liar. One who has been deceived by him takes a stick and throws it down at a frequented place, saying in the presence of witnesses, "Let anyone who does not add to this liar's heap suffer from pains in the head!" Then the bystanders do likewise and all others who pass by the spot, lest the pains described come upon them. In this way the heap sometimes attains the size of a small haystack and, being known by the name of the liar, causes him great shame.[90]

A Toda sorcerer commonly employs spells to cause an enemy to fall ill or meet some misfortune. A man who learns from a diviner that he is suffering from the effects of such a spell then seeks out the sorcerer and promises him gifts to remove it. If there is a reconciliation, the sorcerer rests his foot on the man's head and recites a counter spell in the form of a blessing.[91]

The Zulu word *unesisila* means "You have dirt" or "are dirty," that is to say, you have done or said something, or a person has said or done something to you, "which has bespattered you with metaphorical dirt—in the Scriptural sense, has defiled you." The worse possible curse that can be addressed to a woman is to declare that she does or will bear children to her father-in-law. She is very much upset, in consequence, for to this relative she pays the greatest respect. Fortunately, the terrible effects of the imprecation can be removed. If an ox or cow belonging to the person who spoke the evil words is killed and its flesh is eaten by old women or little children (but by none of marriageable age), the slain animal absorbs the *insila,* the defilement, leaving the woman clean.[92]

A pronounced development of the curse occurs in eastern equatorial Africa. The worst remark that can be addressed to a Nandi man is, "May a blade eat thee!" meaning, may you die after perjuring yourself, and to a Nandi woman is, "Mayest thou die of impossible labor!"[93] The Masai, when cursing, spit copiously. If a curser spits in his enemy's eyes, blindness will follow.[94]

Cursing among the Akamba seems to be confined to the family circle, in which it is used by a parent against a refractory child. A father who has failed by gentle means or chastisement to master a disobedient son puts a curse upon him, and if this is not removed he will die before long. He soon gives in, begs to be released from the curse, and seeks, instead, the paternal blessing. A mother may similarly punish a son if he fails to perform the tasks she sets him, but spends his time dancing and lounging about with other young men. For a more serious transgression on the son's part, for example, stealing her milk or one of her cows, a mother inflicts a very terrible curse. She washes her loincloth, throws out the water violently, so that it splashes in all directions, and says, "May you splash thus, as I have given you birth with this my *kino!*" (the name of the female pudenda). Youths and young girls will also lay a curse on one of their number who has become unpopular by refusing to conform to their group standards or practices. A girl thus cursed is ostracized by all her associates. Her position quickly becomes unbearable, especially as her parents are also given the cold shoulder, and she is soon forced to abandon an attitude of defiance. The curse is removed by four youths and four maidens, who spit ceremonially on her. What makes this imprecation so dreadful is the belief that a girl subject to it can never bear children.[95]

The Bakongo believe that parents and grandparents possess a "vital influence" by means of which their curses are able to affect magically (*loka*) a child or grandchild who proves refractory and refuses to obey commands. The child thus cursed is pursued by misfortune everywhere, in the hunting field as well as in the market place, until at length he returns, begs on his knees for forgiveness, makes propitiatory offerings, and gets the curse removed. The power of *loka* may also be exercised by a maternal uncle who for any reason disapproves of the marriage of a nephew or a niece. His curse results in the wife's unfruitfulness or in the birth of premature children. Our missionary authority, who has known personally "a great number" of well-authenticated cases of sterility following a curse, asks if the phenomenon is to be attributed to autosuggestion.[96]

The curse of dying persons, soon to become members of the spirit world and the revered ancestors of the community, is particularly impressive. Among the Akikuyu, for instance, a man about to die may lay a curse upon a certain plot of land belonging to him, so that it shall not pass out of the family. An inheritor who sold it would meet with a speedy death. Our authority makes the interesting suggestion that in this case (which is one of many) an origin of entail and of testamentary dispositions in general may be detected. Sometimes a father on his deathbed will curse a worthless son to the effect that he shall neither grow rich nor have wives.[97] The Wachagga of Mount Kilimanjaro believe in the "piling up of cursings," so that a curse may affect not only an individual but also result in injury or death to the social group to which he belongs by blood. Characteristic of this belief is the curse attributed to a certain chief who was cursed by a woman he had caused to be strangled. He died the same day, but not before uttering the terrible imprecation, "After my death may the girls be without hips and may the fat humps of the cattle disappear from the world!"[98]

A peculiar form of the curse is employed by the Anuak of the

Anglo-Egyptian Sudan when a person has been greviously wronged. This *atshini,* as it is called, does not operate until after the death of the curser. Old people of both sexes resort to it. In the first form of an *atshini* the wrongdoer dies at once from some unknown cause or he may meet his end as the result of an accident or be killed by a wild animal. For the second and milder form the wrongdoer develops painful ulcers. Proper treatment by a medicine man may remove the effects of an *atshini,* but medical help is not always accessible, especially when the victim is away from home. The practice "would seem to have a distinctly restraining influence on injustice."[99]

Some African peoples are persuaded that it is possible for a person to burden another with a curse without wishing to do so. The Wanyamwezi of Tanganyika regard any slight but merited reprimand as the equivalent of a curse.[100] The Emberre and other tribes of Kenya think that words not spoken seriously can nevertheless acquire a dangerous potency and become an effectual curse. Parents who abuse their children, even in a fit of momentary irritation, may find that they have brought misfortune on them, and a doctor must be called in to remove the evil thus caused.[101] A teacher in a missionary school of Gabun once reproached a senior pupil, saying, "You will always have a bad character." Years later the former schoolboy came to the teacher and complained that the curse thus laid on him had made him an unhappy man, without courage or energy to improve himself. When the missionary explained to him that the remark was not a curse but only a statement uttered in momentary anger, he became quite happy and believed that he could now start life afresh.[102] Among the Yoruba any prediction of evil to come or even a friendly warning against some untoward event arouses great fear. Such words are regarded as a curse. They possess *ogun,* or occult power, which goes forth with them to bring about what is prognosticated.[103]

An oath forms essentially a conditional self-curse, whereby a person subjects himself to some evil if what he says is not true. Its effectiveness bears no relation whatever to his intent, for one who swears falsely in ignorance usually calls down upon his head the same penalty as that to which the willful perjurer is exposed. Various methods are adapted to charge an oath with occult power. In general, these are intended to establish contact between the oath-swearer and some object, animate or inanimate, whose qualities will infect him and punish him automatically if he lies.

An Eddystone Islander, accusing another of theft and meeting with a denial of the charge, will say, "Swear, you who have stolen the matches." To which the accused answers, "I have not taken them, skull house in Nduli" (or "skull house in Mbiru"). If he refuses to take such an oath he stands convicted.[104] A native of Samoa, disputing with another, will say to him, "Touch your eyes, if what you say is true" (i.e., may you be struck with blindness if you are lying). Or the doubter would say to him, "Who will eat you? Say the name of your god." Or the person whose word was doubted might take a stick and dig a hole in the ground, an action which meant "May I be buried immediately if what I say is not true." If a Samoan chief, upon inquiry into a case of theft, could not discover the culprit, he would compel all the suspected parties to swear to their innocence. A tuft of grass was placed on the stone which represented the village god, and then each one laid his hand on this sacred object and swore, "If I stole the thing may I speedily die." The grass on the stone constituted "a silent additional imprecation" that the culprit's wife and children might also perish and that grass might grow over the family domicile.[105]

A Sumatran oath, which introduces the element of intent, runs as follows: "If what I now declare, namely . . . . is truly and really so, may I be freed and clear from my oath; if what I assert is wittingly false, may my oath be the cause of my destruction."[106] A Peninsular Malay, who swears an oath of fidelity or alliance, drinks water in which daggers, spears, or bullets have been dipped and says, "If I turn traitor may I be eaten up by this dagger" (or spear or bullet).[107]

A Sema Naga, in a dispute concerning the ownership of land, takes an oath on a bit of the earth, which he swallows. It is supposed to choke him if he swears falsely. Or he may swear on his own flesh, sometimes only biting a finger, sometimes swallowing a little of it. A man accused of murder (and undoubtedly guilty) has been seen to chop off the end of his forefinger and swallow it to add force to his assertion of innocence. An oath taken on a tiger's tooth is popular with perjurers, for tigers are now becoming so scarce in the Naga country that no one is afraid of being carried off if he bites the tooth on a false oath. There are oaths of such weight, however, that both guilty and innocent people hesitate to take them. One of these is on the water of a certain river. No one who swore falsely by that stream could ever cross it again or even enter it, for he would certainly be drowned, nor could he ever eat fish from it during his whole life, for he would certainly die if he did. The oath on a village spring is another serious matter, since a perjurer would perish if he ever drank of its water. An oath by cutting iron is very powerful. If a man performs this act and then swears falsely, members of his clan will die without apparent cause. "Such is the power of the metal when treated disrespectfully." Among the Angami Naga there is a general belief that a perjurer will suffer death or at least some grave misfortune.[108]

If a Nandi is accused of a falsehood he will pluck a few blades of grass or pick up a little earth and say, "May this grass (or earth) eat me." However, one cannot depend on such an assertion. The form of oath binding on all men consists in striking a spear with a club or stepping over a spear, preferably one which has killed a man, and saying, "May the blade eat me." Women are bound to speak the truth if they step over a woman's belt and say, "May this belt eat me."[109]

On the Gold Coast of West Africa there is a very powerful oath sworn by the life of the king and meaning, "May he, the king, die, if my cause be not avenged or substantiated."[110]

In Morocco conditional curses may be directed, not against the curser himself, but against somebody else. This is the case with the rite called *l'ar*. It involves the sacrifice, for example, of an animal, which serves as the vehicle for the transference of a conditional curse upon a person in order to compel him to grant a request. Spirits (*jnūn*) and dead saints are also frequent objects of the rite, thus affording an instructive instance of the magical compulsion of spiritual beings.[111]

We have seen that a magical act is often combined with a petition or prayer. Even the lowliest savage has learned to pray, though with him fear and not reverence usually is uppermost. In some instances the prayer seems to be an afterthought, making assurance doubly sure, adding to the effectiveness of the magic but yet not an indispensable adjunct to it. We have seen, also, that the language of a spell cannot always be separated from that of a prayer, since in both there may be personification and the use of a vocative. It is often a nice matter to distinguish between them. Everything depends, in truth, on the extent to which the object of the address is personified and endowed with human-like feelings and will. If the spiritual being is supposed always to grant a request or obey a command, then the speaker's words act automatically and constitute a spell. If, on the other hand, the spiritual being retains some freedom of action and may or may not accede to the speaker's words, then these will take the form of a supplication or entreaty, that is, of a prayer.

Spells and prayers are found side by side in primitive society. There seems to be no reason for the assumption of a genetic relation between them. It is true enough that prayers which must be recited over and over again, with verbal accuracy and the right intonation, tend to become "petrified" into traditional formulas, and to acquire magical potency from their mere repetition. What began as an intelligible appeal ends as a rigmarole. It is equally true that a spell addressed to a spiritual being needs only the addition of a simple "Please," perhaps only a change of tone on the speaker's part, to make it a prayer. One who knew intimately the Australian aborigines has remarked that if we really understood and appreciated their mental attitude, "we should find more in their so-called incantations of the nature of invocations. When a man invokes aid on the eve of a battle, or in his hour of danger and need; when a woman croons over her baby an incantation to keep him honest and true, and that he shall be spared in danger, surely these croonings are of the nature of prayers born of the same elementary frame of mind as our more elaborate litany."[112]

Many spells of the Trobriand Islanders begin with a long enumeration of the *baloma,* or ancestral ghosts, which at one time wielded this kind of magic. Such references to the *baloma* must not be omitted, for to tamper with a magical formula is to destroy its efficacy. The lists in question are found in the rites relating to gardens, fishing, and the weather, but not in those for war or love-making. It is not easy to decide whether the names recited in the formulas constitute real prayers, appealing to the ghosts to facilitate the magical operation, or whether they represent mere items of tradition, hallowed by age and full of occult power just because of their antiquity. It is likely, thinks our authority, that both the petitionary and compulsive attitudes are present in the native mind. But there seems to be no idea of the *baloma* as the agents through which the magician works and without whom his activity would be in vain. The Trobriander merely feels and sometimes expresses his feeling that a benevolent attitude of the *baloma* is very favorable to the activities of gardening and fishing and that if angered they would affect these activities injuriously. In some vague way they participate in the rites, and it is a good thing to keep on the right side of them.[113]

It is very difficult, if not impossible, to find in any Melanesian language a word which means "prayer," as we understand it, "so closely does the notion of efficacy cling to the form employed." Thus in San Cristoval, one of the Solomon Islands, the ancestral ghosts are called upon for help in warfare, for relief from sickness, and for good crops, but the formula used conveys the notion of a spell rather than that of a prayer; it is handed down from father to son or is taught for a consideration. In the Banks Islands a *tataro* is strictly an invocation of the dead and as such is a prayer, but in the New Hebrides the same term will be applied to a spell used, for example, in a storm at sea, a spell that works by the occult power residing in the words and in the names of the spirits mentioned.[114]

The *karakia* of the Maori were addressed to the gods or the ancestral ghosts, but their mere recital compelled these spiritual beings to do the will of the reciter. "The Maori, in his heathen state, never undertook any work, whether hunting, fishing, planting, or war, without first uttering a *karakia*; he would not even take a journey without repeating a spell to secure his safety; still he could not be said to pray, for, properly speaking, they had no such thing as prayer. . . . . As the kingdom of heaven suffers violence, and the violent take it by storm, so the heathen Maori sought, by spells and incantations, to compel the gods to yield to their wishes; they added sacrifices and offerings at the same time, to appease as it were their anger, for being thus constrained to do what they wished them."[115]

The formulas employed by the Peninsular Malays are described as often being a mixture of spell and prayer. Numerous spirits are invoked in them so that the particular spirit whose help is wanted or whose malevolence is to be balked will not escape mention.[116]

Of the words addressed by Vedda magicians to the ancestral ghosts some are straightforward appeals for their help or recitations describing their exploits when in this earthly life. Other addresses to the ghosts have the nature of spells. It is probable that many of these are the remains of old Singhalese spells which have been taken over by the Vedda and in the course of time have become so mangled and out of place as to be incomprehensible.[117]

A clear case of the degeneration of a prayer into a magical formula is afforded by the Toda of the Nilgiri Hills. There is no doubt that they pray in their ordinary concerns, as well as in the dairy ritual, where the aid of the gods is invoked to protect the sacred buffaloes. A prayer of this ritual is always uttered "in the throat," so that the words cannot be distinguished by anyone hearing them. It consists of two parts: a preliminary list of names of objects of reverence, followed by the word *idith,* "for the sake of"; and a petition to avert evils from the buffaloes or to bring blessings on them. The first part is now regarded as more important than the second; the latter, indeed, will be abbreviated or even omitted from the recitation. This alteration in the relative importance of the two parts of the prayer needs to go little further to produce a situation in which the dairyman recites only the names, "and an anthropologist visiting the Todas at this stage would find them using formulas which would not be recognizable as prayers."[118]

Prayer, for the Zuñi, "is not a spontaneous outpouring of the heart. It is rather the repetition of a fixed formula." Not only must a prayer be repeated verbatim to be effectual, but it must have been acquired from someone who had the right to it, and it must be paid for. Otherwise, declare the Zuñi, "maybe you can say it but it won't mean anything, or maybe you'll forget it when the time comes to say it." There is feeling that in teaching prayers —"giving them away"—the teacher loses some of his power over them. A man who will repeat readily enough a long, difficult prayer that he learned out of curiosity, or as an investment when the present owner dies, will refuse to recite some simple little prayer, for instance, for offering corn meal to the sun, which everyone knows, but which nevertheless "belongs" to him in a way that the other does not. This attitude helps to explain why Christian missionaries make no converts among the Zuñi. "They throw away their religion as if it weren't worth anything and expect us to believe it." Such conduct seems to these Indians not only ludicrous but irreverent.[119]

Such, then, is the role of helpful and harmful words in magic, whether they find use alone or contain a reference to spiritual beings. With the development and enlargement of animistic conceptions spiritual beings no longer appear as mere tools in the operator's hands, but take an ever more active part and become for their worshiper the sole source of good and bad fortune. Spells depending on the human will for efficacy will be replaced by prayers which seek to move the divine will; even the blessing, the curse, and the oath come to require the interposition of the deity. This evolutionary movement can be followed in the civilizations of antiquity and from them as it passed into the medieval and the modern age.

NOTES TO CHAPTER IV

[1] A. W. Howitt, *The Native Tribes of South-East Australia* (London, 1904), pp. 377, 397 f. The Kurnai *barn* is a magical rite to bring about a man's death. It requires the use of pointed sticks, which are thrown at the intended victim, and the chanting of the *barn* "song."

[2] C. G. Seligman, *The Melanesians of British New Guinea* (Cambridge, 1910), pp. 399 f.

[3] F. E. Williams, *Orokaiva Magic* (London, 1928), pp. 174 f., 180 f.

[4] Beatrice Blackwood, *Both Sides of Buka Passage* (Oxford, 1935), p. 478 (Bougainville and Buka).

[5] H. A. Stayt, *The Bavenda* (London, 1931), pp. 277 f.

[6] W. C. Willoughby, "Notes on the Totemism of the Becwana," *Journal of the Anthropological Institute*, XXXV (1905), 304.

[7] J. Van Wing, "Bakongo Magic," *ibid.*, LXXI (1941), 85 f.

[8] F. E. Williams in *Oceania*, XI (1941), 376 ff.

[9] R. Parkinson, *Dreissig Jahre in der Südsee* (Stuttgart, 1907), p. 198.

[10] Richard Taylor, *Te Ika A Maui* (2d ed., London, 1870), p. 208.

[11] W. W. Skeat, *Malay Magic* (London, 1902), pp. 171, 175.

[12] Gerhard Lindblom, *The Akamba in British East Africa* (2d ed., Uppsala, 1920), p. 290.

[13] B. J. Stern, *The Lummi Indians of Northwest Washington* (New York, 1934), pp. 84 f.

[14] Sir Baldwin Spencer and F. J. Gillen, *The Northern Tribes of Central Australia* (London, 1904), p. 460.

[15] Heinrich Aufenanger and Georg Höltker, *Die Gende in Zentralneuguinea* (Wien-Mödling, 1940), p. 142.

[16] William Churchill, "The Duk-Duk Ceremonies," *Popular Science Monthly*, XXXVIII (1890–91), 242.

[17] Hortense Powdermaker, *Life in Lesu* (New York, 1933), p. 302.

[18] W. H. Furness III, *The Island of Stone Money* (Philadelphia, 1910), pp. 77 f.

[19] S. J. Hickson, *A Naturalist in North Celebes* (London, 1889), p. 259.

[20] H. L. Roth, *The Natives of Sarawak and British North Borneo* (London, 1896), I, 269.

[21] A. W. Nieuwenhuis, *Quer durch Borneo* (Leiden, 1904–1907), I, 111.

[22] James Mooney, "Sacred Formulas of the Cherokees," *Seventh Annual Report of the Bureau of Ethnology*, p. 343.

[23] S. R. Riggs, *Grammar and Dictionary of the Dakota Language* (Washington, D.C., 1852), p. xvii. *Smithsonian Contributions to Knowledge*, Vol. IV.

[24] W. J. Hoffman in *Fourteenth Annual Report of the Bureau of Ethnology*, Part I, p. 61.

[25] William Thalbitzer, "Les magiciens Esquimaux," *Journal de la Société des Américanistes*, (n.s., 1930), XXII, 75 f. (Greenland) ; Franz Boas, in *Sixth Annual Report of the Bureau of Ethnology*, p. 594 (Central Eskimo) ; E. M. Hawkes, *The Life of the Copper Eskimos* (Ottawa, 1922), p. 187 ; Knud Rasmussen, *The Netsilik Eskimos* (Copenhagen, 1931), p. 278. *Report of the Fifth Thule Expedition*, Vol. VIII, Nos. 1–2.

[26] W. Bogoras, in *Memoirs of the American Museum of Natural History*, XI, 473.

27 Sir Baldwin Spencer and F. J. Gillen, *The Native Tribes of Central Australia* (London, 1899), pp. 534, 550.

28 A. C. Haddon, in *Reports of the Cambridge Anthropological Expedition to Torres Straits*, V, 329.

29 C. Keysser, "Aus dem Leben der Kaileute," in R. Neuhauss, *Deutsch Neu-Guinea* (Berlin, 1911), III, 113.

30 R. F. Fortune, *Sorcerers of Dobu* (London, 1932), p. 96. In the Trobriands, on the other hand, spells are chanted aloud, for in these islands the right of possession is socially acknowledged and not infringed by an unprivileged overhearer (p. 107).

31 Hortense Powdermaker, *op. cit.*, p. 333, note 1; Gerhard Peekel, *Religion und Zauberei auf dem mittleren Neu-Mecklenburg, Bismarck Archipel, Südsee* (Münster in Westfalen, 1910), p. 84.

32 James Mooney, "Sacred Formulas of the Cherokees," *Seventh Annual Report of the Bureau of Ethnology*, p. 310.

33 Knud Rasmussen, *The People of the Polar North* (London, 1908), p. 45.

34 W. Bogoras, in *Memoirs of the American Museum of Natural History,* XI, 472.

35 Bronislaw Malinowski, *Coral Gardens and Their Magic* (New York, 1935), I, 445. In Mala (Malaita), one of the Solomon Islands, a man's magic is supposed to be stored up in his chest, the seat of memory. When, therefore, he uses magic he must breathe hard, or sometimes spit, in order to make sure that it will come forth in all its strength (H. I. Hogbin, *Experiments in Civilization* [London, 1939], p. 118). In Malekula, one of the New Hebrides, the sorcerer begins operations by breathing deeply. When he can hold his breath for one or two minutes, he performs his magical act. At the very end he mutters an imprecation, which is the final shot of the rite and releases, as it were, his concentrated emotion (A. B. Deacon, *Malekula, a Vanishing People in the New Hebrides* [London, 1934], pp. 687 f.).

36 R. F. Fortune, *op. cit.*, p. 148.

37 S. P. Smith, "'The 'Tohunga'-Maori," *Transactions and Proceedings of the New Zealand Institute*, XXXII (1899), pp. 262, 265. See also Elsdon Best, "Maori Religion and Mythology," *Dominion Museum Bulletin*, No. 10, pp. 196 f.

38 W. L. Hildburgh, "Notes on Sinhalese Magic," *Journal of the Royal Anthropological Institute*, XXXVIII (1908), 156.

39 Gladys A. Reichard, *Social Life of the Navajo Indians* (New York, 1928), p. 145.

40 Ruth L. Bunzel, "Introduction to Zuñi Ceremonialism," *Forty-seventh Annual Report of the Bureau of American Ethnology*, p. 492.

41 Raymond Firth, *Primitive Polynesian Economy* (London, 1939), p. 185.

42 E. E. Evans-Pritchard, *Witchcraft, Oracles, and Magic among the Azande* (Oxford, 1937), pp. 450 f.

43 A. C. Haddon, in *Reports of the Cambridge Anthropological Expedition to Torres Straits*, V, 183 and note 3, 329 (western islands).

44 F. E. Williams, *op. cit.*, pp. 173 f., 181.

45 Margaret Mead, in *Anthropological Papers of the American Museum of Natural History*, XXXVII, 343. With the Arapesh a new spell is sometimes the result of dreaming. Two or three words of the dream furnish clues upon which the spell is built up and assigned to a special purpose (p. 343, note 6).

46 S. Lehner, in R. Neuhauss, *op. cit.*, III, 448.

47 Bronislaw Malinowski, *Argonauts of the Western Pacific* (London, 1922),

pp. 403, 408, 424, 427. Cf. *idem, Coral Gardens and Their Magic*, I, 445. A Trobriander never builds a house on piles, because doing so would greatly facilitate the sorcerer's operations. He could burn a magical substance, over which a spell has been recited, below the platform of such a house, and the smoke would enter the nostrils of its inmates and make them ill. According to native ideas occult power is most readily absorbed and consequently is most effective when snuffed up by a person (*idem, The Sexual Life of Savages in North-Western Melanesia* [New York, 1929], p. 449).

48 R. F. Fortune, *op. cit.*, p. 96.

49 D. Jenness and A. Ballantyne, *The Northern D'Entrecasteaux* (Oxford, 1920), p. 134. These islanders have a certain spell, called *awabutu*, which, used alone, will slay a man. The sorcerer walks along the path to meet his enemy and softly sings the spell. When the two men have met they gossip for a moment and then each goes on his way. The victim, following the fatal path, soon falls ill; seldom does he live more than two days after being bewitched. An *awabutu* is powerful enough to kill two men at the same time, but if more than two walk along the path together it is harmless (pp. 143 f.).

50 Hortense Powdermaker, *op. cit.*, pp. 298 f.

51 W. G. Ivens, *Melanesians of the South-East Solomon Islands* (London, 1927), pp. 345, 351.

52 H. I. Hogbin, *op. cit.*, p. 119.

53 Raymond Firth, *Primitive Economics of the New Zealand Maori* (London, 1929), p. 259.

54 S. P. Smith, "The 'Tohunga'-Maori," *Transactions and Proceedings of the New Zealand Institute*, XXXII (1899), 265.

55 J. M. M. van der Burgt, *Un grand peuple de l'Afrique équatoriale* (Bois le Duc, 1904), p. 55.

56 James Mooney, "Sacred Formulas of the Cherokees," *Seventh Annual Report of the Bureau of Ethnology*, pp. 307 ff. Mooney in 1887–88 obtained about six hundred formulas on the Cherokee reservation in North Carolina. The original manuscripts containing them had been written by the medicine men of the tribe for their own use. These formulas were handed down orally from a remote period, until the invention of the Cherokee syllabary by Sequoyah in 1821 made it possible to commit them to writing. See further James Mooney and F. M. Olbrechts, "The Swimmer Manuscript. Cherokee Sacred Formulas and Medicinal Prescriptions," *Bulletin of the Bureau of American Ethnology*, No. 99.

57 Henry Rink, *Tales and Traditions of the Eskimo* (Edinburgh, 1875), p. 53.

58 Gustav Holm, in *Meddelelser om Grønland*, XXXIX (1914), 87 f. It is believed by the Navaho that a magical formula should not be used too often, for each use wears out its power (Gladys A. Reichard, *op. cit.*, p. 147).

59 Knud Rasmussen, *Intellectual Culture of the Hudson Bay Eskimos* (Copenhagen, 1930), p. 165. *Report of the Fifth Thule Expedition*, Vol. VII, No. 1.

60 W. Bogoras, in *Memoirs of the American Museum of Natural History*, XI, 470 f.

61 W. Jochelson, *ibid.*, X, 59 f.

62 W. H. R. Rivers, *The History of Melanesian Society* (Cambridge, 1914), I, 156 f.

63 Ralph Linton, *The Tanala* (Chicago, 1933), p. 217. *Field Museum of Natural History, Anthropological Series*, Vol. XXII.

64 Mrs. Eileen J. Krige and J. D. Krige, *The Realm of a Rain Queen* (London, 1943), p. 253.

118 MAGIC: A SOCIOLOGICAL STUDY

65 Monica Hunter, *Reaction to Conquest* (London, 1936), p. 306.

66 I. Schapera, "Oral Sorcery among the Natives of Bechuanaland," in *Essays Presented to C. G. Seligman* (London, 1934), pp. 295 f. Our authority witnessed a number of magical rites which were performed in absolute silence. Apparently it is only when the operator does not feel sure of his medicines that he reinforces them with a spell. A leading magician of the tribe once remarked, "My medicines are good enough; I don't need words to strengthen them" (*idem*, "Herding Rites of the Bechuanaland Bakxatla," *American Anthropologist*, XXXVI [*n.s.*, 1934], 583).

67 E. E. Evans-Pritchard, *op. cit.*, pp. 451 ff.

68 Edward Shortland, *The Southern Districts of New Zealand* (London, 1851), p. 26.

69 Dudley Kidd, *Savage Childhood* (London, 1906), p. 73.

70 Sir A. B. Ellis, *The Ewe-speaking Peoples of the Slave Coast of West Africa* (London, 1890), pp. 95, 98.

71 C. Keysser, "Aus dem Leben der Kaileute," in R. Neuhauss, *op. cit.*, III, 125 f., 161. Similar stories are told by the Bukaua, but in this case they always end with a prayer to the ancestral ghosts for a good harvest. As the story-teller utters the prayer he looks toward the house where the young shoots for planting or the ripened fruits are kept (S. Lehner, *ibid.*, III, 478 f.).

72 H. Zahn, in R. Neuhauss, *op. cit.*, III, 333.

73 Bronislaw Malinowski, *Coral Gardens and Their Magic*, II, 156 f.

74 D. L. Oliver, "The 'Homomorun' Concepts of Southern Bougainville; a Study in Comparative Religion," *Studies in the Anthropology of Oceania and Asia. Dixon Memorial Volume* (Cambridge, Mass., 1943), p. 54, note 12. *Papers of the Peabody Museum of American Archaeology and Ethnology*, Vol. XX.

75 R. F. Barton, *Philippine Pagans* (London, 1938), pp. 14 f. Our authority mentions one ritual occasion—a mock headfeast—when about forty-five myths were thus recited.

76 Theodor Koch-Grünberg, "Zaubersprüche der Taulipáng-Indianer," *Archiv für Anthropologie*, XLI (1914), 371.

77 Erland Nordenskiöld, "La conception de l'âme chez les Indiens Cuna de l'Isthme de Panama," *Journal de la Société des Américanistes de Paris* (n.s., 1932), XXIV, 6.

78 A. L. Kroeber, "The Religion of the Indians of California," *University of California Publications in American Archaeology and Ethnology*, IV, 344; *idem*, "California," Hastings' *Encyclopaedia of Religion and Ethics*, III, 142.

79 Knud Rasmussen, *Intellectual Culture of the Hudson Bay Eskimos* (Copenhagen, 1930), pp. 157 f. *Report of the Fifth Thule Expedition*, Vol. III, No. 1.

80 W. Jochelson, in *Memoirs of the American Museum of Natural History*, X, 142 f.

81 The curses of magicians are especially potent. By the Maori the "anathema" of a *tohunga* was regarded as a "thunderbolt" that no enemy could escape (J. S. Polock, *Manners and Customs of the New Zealanders* [London, 1840], I, 248 f.). Among the Jaluo or Nilotic Kavirondo the magician by his curse causes an illness which is cured only if he can be induced to recall the fatal words (Max Weiss, *Die Völkerstämme im norden Deutsch-Ostafrikas* [Berlin, 1910], pp. 236 f.). No Amhara under any circumstances would slay either a magician or a priest, from a dread of his dying curse (W. C. Harris, *The Highlands of Aethiopia* [2d ed., London, 1844], III, 50).

82 A. M. Hocart, "Medicine and Witchcraft in Eddystone of the Solomons," *Journal of the Royal Anthropological Institute*, LV (1925), 262 f.

[83] R. H. Codrington, *The Melanesians* (Oxford, 1891), p. 217.

[84] S. H. Ray, in *Journal of the Royal Anthropological Institute,* XLVII (1917), 297.

[85] George Turner, *Samoa* (London, 1884), pp. 30 ff., 184.

[86] J. J. Jarves, *History of the Hawaiian Islands* (3d ed., Honolulu, 1847), pp. 24 f. Cf. C. S. Stewart, *Journal of a Residence in the Sandwich Islands during the Years 1823, 1824, and 1825* (London, 1828), pp. 264 f.

[87] John Martin, *An Account of the Natives of the Tonga Islands . . . . from the Extensive Communications of Mr. William Mariner* (3d ed., Edinburgh, 1827), I, 237, note; II, 190 f.

[88] Edward Tregear, *The Maori Race* (Wanganui, New Zealand, 1904), pp. 204 ff. "To bid you go and cook your father would be a great curse, but to tell a person to go and cook his great grandfather would be far worse, because it included every individual who had sprung from him" (Richard Taylor, *op. cit.,* [2d ed.], p. 208). For an example of a Maori counter curse see Edward Shortland, *Maori Religion and Mythology* (London, 1882), p. 33.

[89] J. G. F. Riedel, *De sluik-en kroesharige rassen tusschen Selebes en Sumatra* (The Hague, 1886), p. 317.

[90] Charles Hose and William McDougall, *The Pagan Tribes of Borneo* (London, 1912), II, 123. Even an undeserved curse is considered a terrible thing. To curse a person for no reason at all is an offense punishable by a fine (E. H. Gomes, *Seventeen Years among the Sea Dyaks of Borneo* [London, 1911], p. 64). For examples of the very effective curses against thieves see *ibid.,* pp. 64 ff.

[91] W. H. R. Rivers, *The Todas* (London, 1906), pp. 256, 260. The Toda have a ceremony for anticipating evil which might befall the sacred cattle. Two dairy priests pour a mixture of milk and clarified butter into the hands of the assistant in the dairy, and he rubs it over his head and entire body. The priests then recite a curse calling upon wild beasts to catch the assistant and carry him off. This curse is no sooner uttered than it is removed by the recitation of a formula of blessing. Our authority conjectures that by the curse the assistant becomes responsible for any ritual offense committed against the dairy, and that its prompt removal is intended to avoid the misfortunes which would descend upon him were this not done (pp. 138 ff.).

[92] David Leslie, *Among the Zulus and Amatongas* (2d ed., Edinburgh, 1875), pp. 169 f., 174.

[93] A. C. Hollis, *The Nandi* (Oxford, 1909), p. 85. A Nandi father who ritually strikes his son with his fur mantle has, in effect, cursed him. The curse is supposed to be fatal, unless the son obtains forgiveness (Sir H. H. Johnston, *The Uganda Protectorate* [2d ed., London, 1904], II, 879).

[94] S. L. Hinde and Hildegarde Hinde, *The Last of the Masai* (London, 1901), p. 48.

[95] Gerhard Lindblom, *op. cit.,* (2d ed.), pp. 182 ff.

[96] J. Van Wing, "Bakongo Magic," *Journal of the Royal Anthropological Institute,* LXXI (1941), 90 ff.

[97] C. W. Hobley, *Bantu Beliefs and Magic* (London, 1922), pp. 145 f.

[98] Bruno Gutmann, *Das Recht der Dschagga* (Munich, 1926), p. 514.

[99] C. R. K. Bacon, in *Sudan Notes and Records,* V (1922), 127 ff.

[100] F. Bösch, *Les Banyamwezi* (Münster in Westfalen, 1930), p. 246.

[101] G. St. J. Orde Browne, *The Vanishing Tribes of Kenya* (London, 1925), p. 203.

[102] Albert Schweitzer, *African Notebook* (New York, 1939), pp. 63 f.

[103] S. S. Farrow, *Faith, Fancies, and Fetich, or Yoruba Paganism* (London, 1926), p. 119.

[104] A. M. Hocart, "Medicine and Witchcraft in Eddystone of the Solomons," *Journal of the Royal Anthropological Institute*, LV (1925), 263.

[105] George Turner, *op. cit.*, pp. 183 ff.

[106] William Marsden, *The History of Sumatra* (3d ed., London, 1811), p. 240. For Batak oaths see Johannes Warneck, *Die Religion der Batak* (Göttingen, 1909), 39 ff.

[107] W. W. Skeat, *op cit.*, p. 525, note 2.

[108] J. H. Hutton, *The Sema Nagas* (London, 1921), pp. 164 ff.; *idem, The Angami Nagas* (London, 1921), p. 144. See further J. Butler, in *Journal of the Asiatic Society of Bengal* XLIV, I (1875), 316.

[109] A. C. Hollis, *op. cit.*, p. 85.

[110] A. Clark, "On the Judicial Oaths Used on the Gold Coast," *Journal of the Anthropological Institute*, XXIX (1899), 311.

[111] Edward Westermarck, *Ritual and Belief in Morocco* (London, 1926), I, 518 ff., 551.

[112] Mrs. K. L. Parker, *The Euahlayi Tribe* (London, 1905), pp. 79 f.

[113] Bronislaw Malinowski, " 'Baloma'; the Spirits of the Dead in the Trobriand Islands," *Journal of the Royal Anthropological Institute*, XLVI (1916), 384-402.

[114] R. H. Codrington, *op. cit.*, pp. 145 ff. In Mala (Malaita) at the end of a spell there is a tag which seemingly transforms it into a prayer to the ghosts that are there named. They are asked to exert their occult power, or *mana*. In spite of this appeal to the dead ancestors, the natives imagine that the magic of the words is the effective agency in bringing about the desired result. Excuses given for failure of the formula are its faulty recitation or the counter magic of an enemy, but never the anger of the ghosts. These are coerced, rather than implored, to exert themselves for man's benefit (Hogbin, *op. cit.*, pp. 119 f.).

[115] Richard Taylor, *op. cit.* (2d ed.), pp. 180 f. To the same effect we have the statement of a later investigator, who declares that there was really no element of supplication in a *karakia*. The Maori gods would despise a person who abased himself before them, but they were ready at all times to do their duty toward mankind if compelled thereto by one who possessed the requisite *mana*. (W. E. Gudgeon, "The 'Tohunga' Maori," *Journal of the Polynesian Society*, XVI [1907], 64). *Karakia* formed the personal property of a *tohunga* and his disciples, and in many cases were known only to them. Their magical efficacy depended very much on the personal *mana* of the reciter (Gudgeon, *loc. cit.*). According to Elsdon Best true invocations, or direct appeals to the gods, were very rare and, when found, were mostly in the higher type of ritual pertaining to matters of the utmost importance ("Maori Religion and Mythology," *Dominion Museum Bulletin*, No. 10, pp. 192 f.).

[116] Sir R. O. Winstedt, *Shaman, Saiva, and Sufi. A Study in the Evolution of Malay Magic* (London, 1925), p. 56.

[117] C. G. Seligman and Brenda Z. Seligman, *The Veddas* (Cambridge, 1911), p. 133.

[118] W. H. R. Rivers, *The Todas*, pp. 214 ff., 229 f. Elsewhere this authority remarks that the dairy utterances, "which were probably at one time definite prayers calling on the gods for help and protection, are now on their way to become barren and meaningless formulae" (p. 453).

[119] Ruth L. Bunzel, "Introduction to Zuñi Ceremonialism," *Forty-seventh Annual Report of the Bureau of American Ethnology*, pp. 493 f.

CHAPTER V

THE MAGICAL OBJECT: CHARMS

A MATERIAL, inanimate object or collection of objects, supposed to possess occult power inherent in it or imputed to it, is a charm or "medicine." If small and portable, it will often be worn on the person, carried about, or preserved. But anything, irrespective of its size, can serve as a magic container. Most charms are privately owned; some belong to a family or social group; some have no owners.

A distinction is often drawn between talismanic charms to bring good fortune and amuletic charms for protection against real or imagined evil. However, a charm may be employed now in the one way and now in the other, or it may combine positive and negative qualities. Many charms never serve either as talismans or as amulets. On the other hand, innumerable objects, which are used in some way to acquire their qualities, rank as talismans or amulets but not as charms, since no occult power is attributed to them.

Any object which attracts attention by reason of its uniqueness, rarity, curious appearance, or mysterious properties, or because of unusual circumstances connected with its discovery and employment, is likely to be endowed with occult power. If its possession seems to have brought success to the owner it will be kept, as being "lucky," while a similar object that has been used unsuccessfully will sooner or later be discarded. The Lhota Naga treasure certain stones as bringers of good luck. These *oha* are smooth, water-worn objects, which vary in size from that of a man's head to that of a walnut and rest on the ground in little nests they have made for themselves. "Anyone finding such a stone brings it home, and then notices whether his family increases quickly, or he has good crops, or is particularly successful in trade. He thus finds out what particular form of good luck is attached to the stone in question." The larger *oha* are communal possessions, and on them the prosperity of the whole village depends.[1] The *bina*, or charms, of the Guiana Indians consist chiefly of plants, and these

121

with very few exceptions are different varieties of caladium. Each variety is a charm for help in taking a particular species of game. The plants grow spontaneously in old fields, from which the more valued kinds are carefully removed and cultivated in the immediate neighborhood of the settlement. As a rule, women are supposed not to handle or even to see them. The leaves of the plants in most cases bear a real or fancied resemblance to the animal for which they are reputed to have an affinity. Thus the bush-hog charm has a leaf representing that animal's scent gland; the charm for deer shows a deer's horns; and the charm for armadillo typifies its small projecting ears. The special efficacy of each charm was originally discovered, say the natives, by a simple process of experimentation. Trial was made by the hunter of one plant after another. If he came upon a tiger or a snake the plant in his possession was immediately discarded; if, however, he met with a scrub-turkey or similar game he kept the plant for future use—and so on for each animal or bird of economic value.[2] Such coincidental experiences have doubtless played a large part in charm making; certainly they have done much to confirm a belief in the efficacy of charms as well as of spells and manual acts.

The choice of particular charms is sometimes the result of a dream or of a vision. A form of black magic much practiced by the Kurnai of Victoria consists in the use of a rounded black pebble called a *bulk*. When placed in the fresh excreta of the intended victim it injures his intestines, and he dies. A *bulk* is revealed by the ghosts to a man when asleep.[3] Among the Koita, a Papuan tribe, the ghosts will tell a person in a dream where a charm is to be found and for what it is to be used.[4] The charms of the Kayan of Borneo are generally acquired in the first instance through indications afforded by dreams. A man dreams that something valuable is to be given him. If, on waking, his eye falls upon a quartz crystal or any other object more or less peculiar, he hangs it over his sleeping place. When he goes to bed he addresses it, saying that he wants a favorable dream; if this comes to him the object serves henceforth as a charm, but if his dream is inauspicious the object is rejected.[5] Among the Mikir of Assam charms are either discovered by chance in river, field, or jungle, or a man dreams where they are to be found.[6]

The North American Indians have their medicine sacks, bags, or bundles, these being collections of miscellaneous charms kept in wrappings when not in use. They are regarded as direct gifts of the spiritual powers that rule the world. Some bundles are associated with the tribe as a whole or with its clans and secret societies, while others are private property acquired as the result of a dream, vision, or adventure.[7]

Sometimes charms reveal themselves to certain people by a particular sign or action. A Salinan Indian in central California dreams of some object which is to be his charm and, on awakening, finds it in his hand.[8] A Chukchi once stumbled against a stone and nearly sprained his ankle; this was evidence that the stone wanted to become his charm. Another man, while sleeping on the tundra, found a charm under his pillow.[9]

What objects shall serve as charms is necessarily determined by accidents of local supply and the particular requirements of their users; hence their innumerable forms. While many objects are employed as "specifics," being regarded as efficacious in some more or less special way, others incorporate undifferentiated occult power and have several, perhaps many, applications. Salt, with its preservative qualities; quartz pebbles which, when struck, give out a bright spark; flint, intimately associated with lightning; magnetic iron, with its attractive power; and such narcotic and stimulant plants as tobacco and peyote among the American Indians— these are but a few examples of the latter class of objects. All possess to a marked degree the element of mysteriousness characterizing what is magical.

The use of quartz pebbles (crystals) as charms is widespread. In Australia medicine men of the southeastern tribes generally possess them and exhibit them to the novices during the initiation ceremonies. A young man after being initiated said to Mr. Howitt, "When I was a little boy I did not believe all I heard about the Joias, but when I saw the Gommeras at the Kuringal bringing them up from their insides, I believed it all." The tribal elders at the Kuringal which Howitt witnessed were much troubled when one of the youths whom they had initiated fell sick. They feared that the novice's extracted teeth had been placed in Howitt's bag, which contained some of the marvelous crystals, and that the evil power in these objects, by entering the teeth, had injured the boy to whom the teeth had once belonged.[10] The Kabi and Wakka of Queensland say that crystals, which convey extraordinary vitality upon their possessor, are bestowed by certain male spirits haunting mineral springs. A doctor who has lots of them inside him is known as a *kundir bonggam,* meaning "pebbles many."[11] The Arunta and their neighbors call the crystals *atnongara.* A doctor keeps them in his body and produces them at will. By projecting them into a patient's body he is able to combat the evil influences at work therein; they may be described as "antitoxins." As long as the doctor retains the *atnongara* he is capable of functioning as a healer, but if for any reason he loses them his remedial power disappears for good.[12]

Nearly everyone in Dobu Island possesses volcanic crystals. They are used only by a diviner, who gazes into them, and by a magician who knows the proper spell for projecting them into a victim or for ejecting them from him. Their insertion or removal is to us a trick, but actually the magician does not so consider it. To him the presence of the crystals in his hand after he is supposed to have sent them forth or after he has supposedly withdrawn them is "immaterial." This manner of thinking cannot be reconciled, of course, with our more prosaic attitude toward the performance.[13]

A magician among the Semang, the rude Negrito tribes of Malaya, cures sickness by means of a crystal. This he makes or else obtains from the Chinoi, the little beings who dwell in the heavens or in flowers. By looking into it he sees the disease afflicting the patient and then can prescribe the appropriate remedy. The magician keeps the crystal in his chest and brings it up, when required, by striking himself there with his fist.[14]

Among the Kobéua of northwest Brazil little white stones (*dupa*), of a magical nature, are inserted in the head of a candidate for the office of medicine man.[15] The Jivaro of eastern Ecuador ascribe great occult power to crystals. The magician always professes to have acquired them in a dream. They are used, particularly, as remedies against chills and other afflictions. One of the stones is put into a gourd containing tobacco juice; a spell is uttered over the concoction, and this is then drunk.[16] An Iroquois medicine man might possess within himself a "live" crystal, which he produced from his mouth or nose. When placed in a bowl of water it made visible the apparition of a person who had practiced witchcraft upon another. By applying it to the body of the bewitched individual hairs, straws, leaves, pebbles, and other small objects could be drawn out.[17]

In addition to quartz pebbles or crystals other stones often serve as charms. Among the Angami Naga stones of peculiar shape or appearance or of large size "readily become objects of awe."[18] The Sema Naga venerate any queerly shaped stone, but they most prize a water-worn black stone approximately spherical in shape and with a thin white stratum dividing it. Such an object gives success in war to the village fortunate enough to possess it.[19] The Karen of Burma, especially the wilder tribes, hold some stones in great reverence. They are generally private property, though in some villages there are stones "so sacred and powerful that none but certain of the wisest elders dare look on them." Such objects are generally pieces of rock-crystal or curiously stratified rock. "Anything that strikes the poor ignorant Karen as uncommon is regarded as necessarily possessing occult powers."[20] Among the Zuñi Indians of New Mexico the objects most valued to give success in the hunt are natural rock concretions resembling the game animals, together with those in which the evident original resemblance to the animals has been heightened by artificial means. It is assumed, at least by the priests, that they are either actual petrifactions of the animals or were such originally. They are "exhorted," by means of prayers and ceremonies, to bring good luck to the hunter, and sacrifices are offered to them.[21] They must be regarded, therefore, as the abodes of personal beings, but it seems obvious that they have been spiritualized under priestly influence.

Animal relics, especially bones, form a large class of charms. The Bagobo of Mindanao credit a number of animals with "mysterious qualities" and hence assign a special virtue to certain parts of their bodies, such as the hair of the flying lemur and the liver and foot of the crow.[22] The Banda of Ubangi-Shari, French Equatorial Africa, believe that a panther's beard, when put in beer, kills him who drinks the beer.[23] When Creek Indians went forth on a raid after scalps the leader or the medicine man had charge of a bundle of magical objects. Among the potent charms in this bundle were parts of the horns of a certain mythical snake which had been captured and killed by the people after destroying many of them for generations. The horns, it was believed, would prevent the warriors from being wounded.[24] By the Lillooet of British Columbia certain parts of animals were called "mysterious" and might be eaten only by old men. Other people who ate them fell sick. Hunters cut out these parts, pierced them with a stick, ·and placed them on the branch of a tree.[25] In these instances and many others like them relics are not worn or used in any way to acquire the well-known qualities of a given animal—its speediness, endurance, courage, or ferocity. The choice of the charm is dictated solely by the desire to obtain the occult power ascribed to the animal and believed to be resident in the bones or other bodily parts.

Human relics are very commonly treasured as charms. The Tasmanians believed that a bone from the skull or the arms of a deceased relative, when sewn up in a piece of skin and worn around the neck, preserved the wearer from sickness and premature death.[26] In the Buandik tribe of South Australia it was thought that human hair, spun into yarn, daubed with ocher and grease, and wound around a wooden pole, would turn aside lightning.[27] The aborigines of Victoria used as a hunting charm some fat or skin or piece of bone of a dead man.[28] In Queensland the fat from about the kidneys of a dead man was sometimes carried by hunters as a charm to bring good fortune.[29] Among the Arunta and other Central Australian tribes the hair of a dead man is cut off, made into a girdle, and given to his eldest son, or, failing him, to a younger brother. This girdle has great power. It confers upon its possessor all the warlike skill of the dead man, especially ensuring his accuracy of aim while at the same time destroying that of an adversary.[30] Among the Murngin of Arnhem Land, Northern Territory, the heart's blood of a man whose soul has been stolen by a "black" magician is carefully preserved. It often turns up as a kind of resin, supposed to be the hardened blood. It gives "a little extra power" in fighting, hunting, or fishing. A "white" magician sometimes places it in his bag to add to the latter's potency. Such blood (or resin) acquires still more *mana* by passing through the hands of a number of people. It is frequently traded in among the Murngin from distant regions to the south of the tribe.[31] In New Britain it was customary for the leg bones and arm bones of an enemy who had been killed and eaten to be placed on the butt end of a spear. A fighter who carried a spear thus equipped could not be wounded by any relatives or friends of the dead man.[32] By the Andamanese human bones are esteemed as a means of driving away the evil spirits causing sickness. They also burn yellow ocher so that it turns red like blood and use this as a powder or mixed with fat as a paint. Applied to the throat and chest it cures coughs, colds, and sore throat; applied to the ear it is equally efficacious to stop earache.[33] The Pomo of northern California considered that the bones of human beings possessed *kaocal*, or occult power, by their very nature, whereas whalebones lacked *kaocal* until this had been induced into them by an initiate of the tribal secret society. Only members of the society were allowed to gather the bones of the dead and to use these for doctoring.[34] The Koniag of Kodiak Island, Alaska, secreted the mummies of former successful whalers in caves and carried them in the canoe when on an expedition to catch whales. The Nootka of Vancouver Island had the same práctice. The Quinault Indians of Washington are also said to have used the bones of a male ancestor as a whaling charm.[35]

Thus the same train of ideas which has led to the use of animal relics as charms accounts for the use of human relics. The occult power of a dead person abides with his remains, which can be employed, therefore, in magical rites. As we shall learn, the corpse-eating sometimes actually practiced by magicians or prospective magicians must be explained along similar lines. The same explanation applies to the necrophagous practices so often attributed to witches, along with their other dark and obscene rites.

It is possible, by one device or another, to increase the efficacy of charms. Their manipulation for this purpose offers the magician ample opportunities for the exercise of ingenuity and duplicity. An Orokaiva sorcerer, having made a magical concoction to injure a man, rams it into a piece of bamboo, stops it with beeswax or a plug of leaves, and suspends it over a fire. As the heat increases with the brightening of the fire, so will the discomfort of the victim increase with it. The sorcerer, after preparing his charm, may also sit on it in order to squash it the more effectively, or he may bury it under a heavy stone which will exert the pressure suiting the mood of the torturer. This procedure seems to find an explanation in the feelings of weakness or lassitude which are common symptoms of tropical illness and which the sorcerer aims to produce in the unhappy object of his attentions.[36] A garden magician of the Keraki, another Papuan people, constantly uses some kind of stimulant, or what he regards as a stimulant, to infuse extra "pep" into the charm or to give an additional "kick" to his procedure. Because chewing ginger root or a species of astringent bark makes him feel hot, he adds these to the magical mixture or else chews and spits them on the object with which he is dealing.[37] Among the Tanala, a hill tribe of Madagascar, a person usually acquires the benefit of a charm if he wears it or keeps it in his house. For a few charms, however, inoculation is necessary. When a man purchases a charm for skill in curing fractures an incision is made in his right hand and a little of the medicine is rubbed in. A hunter who obtains a charm to make a blow gun deadly must have his lip split and some of the medicine inserted in the cut.[38] Among the Ba-ila, if a man wants very special luck, he will procure from a witch doctor a charm called *musamba* and "under the doctor's instructions he commits incest with his sister or daughter before starting on his undertaking. That is a very powerful stimulus to the talisman."[39] Among the tribes of Gabun all magic of great importance requires for its effectiveness the sacrifice of human life. The magician often orders an applicant for a charm to kill a near relative and declares that if the murder is not accomplished the applicant himself will die. "What a number of people used to be murdered in this country because hunters wanted a powerful ju-ju for their elephant hunting!"[40]

Being magically powerful, a charm is preserved with care and kept from contaminating influences. Any taboos or other prohibitions attached to it must be observed, lest its efficacy be impaired or destroyed.

The Singhalese are careful not to go near charms when attending a funeral, nor when sleeping near women in their menses, nor when engaged in sexual intercourse. The virtue of the charms would be destroyed by such contact with the impure and polluting and, once lost, could not be renewed.[41]

By the Pondo of Pondoland any form of ritual impurity (*umlaza*) is supposed to destroy the value of the plants used as medicines. A person with *umlaza* who touches a medicine makes it useless; hence a menstruating woman will get someone else to gather the necessary plants. A woman ritually unclean never enters the hut where the chief's medicines are kept. Should she disregard these taboos and others like them her flow would never cease.[42] Some Basuto medicines, if used carelessly or without observance of the taboos connected with them, may do harm. Thus a medicine for mending fractured limbs is likely to break limbs instead, should it be left lying around or be improperly applied. The very powerful medicine to protect the cattle kraal can cause the cows to abort and a woman to have painful menstruation should she enter the kraal when the cattle are there.[43] Almost invariably the Ba-ila charms have prohibitions associated with them. Some of these are easily understandable on the principle of analogy. For instance, eating the ground pea is forbidden to people who possess charms to prevent rain from falling. These peas are hard, and when poured into a pot they make a rattling sound like distant thunder; rain follows thunder, thus the result would be to "kill" the charm. But other prohibitions are less capable of explanation. Why should a man with *wombidi* medicine not allow another to carry a pot behind his back? And when he is in a hut and a pot is passed in, why must he not take hold of it but only shove it across the ground? Perhaps, as our authorities suggest, the only reason for such rules is to "impress appropriate thoughts" on a person's mind.[44]

By the Yoruba "immorality" is believed to exert a destructive influence on charms. Hence a medical man usually has an isolation room where he keeps his stock-in-trade. Only children may enter this room.[45] The Ga people of the Gold Coast make much use of medicines prepared for them by professional magicians. A medicine is regarded as the abode, at any rate intermittently, of a spiritual being (*wong*). But the object itself is often spoken of as a *wong* and the owner as its father or controller. A *wong* usually has no name. It will act for anyone, provided the owner has observed the proper ceremonies when acquiring it and is careful to observe any taboos attached to its use. "There is an automatic quality about a *wong*—press the right button and the machine works for you wherever you are." Various forms of uncleanness spoil a medicine. For example, no medicine will retain its power if taken to a latrine. A man who has a protective medicine to make him proof against murder can be murdered in such a place. For this reason magicians, chiefs, and other people likely to have enemies, who usually possess protective medicines, do not enter public latrines. The most dangerous taboos for an ordinary person to break are those attached to his medicines, whether a healing one owned by a physician, a hunting one to bring success in the chase, or a trading one to safeguard against thieves. Usually the more valuable the services performed by a medicine the more exacting are the conditions attached to it. The breaking of the taboos not only spoils its efficacy but also usually results in the illness and death of the owner.[46] While these Ga medicines are said to be possessed by spiritual beings, the animistic attitude toward them would seem to be very lightly held. Perhaps it is in process of dissolution.

The medicine bundles of the Sauk and Fox Indians must always be treated with great respect. They are never opened except for good reason and are never allowed to touch the ground. There is a very strict rule against women touching them or approaching them when open. No menstruating woman should come near them even when closed, for she would spoil their power and would herself bleed to death.[47] Among the Blackfoot most men own some kind of bundle, however small. An owner must care for it properly and never shirk the ritual burdens connected with it. By its possession and proper care he confidently expects to enjoy long life, health, and happiness. Even an ex-owner is believed to participate, as long as he lives, in this insurance against misfortunes of every sort. It is said that though a Blackfoot may have fallen a victim to utter poverty, he will still be judged wealthy and resourceful if many important bundles have passed through his hands.[48]

With reference to the Iglulik Eskimo we are told that it is not enough that a charm should have occult power; the owner, also, must possess such power. Sometimes a man finds himself very unlucky in hunting and so becomes an object of scorn to his fellows. The reason is that his charms are worthless, for he had received them from a person who lacked any ability to enter into communication with the unseen world. On the other hand, a man may lose a charm and yet retain its virtue, for this can be conveyed to the finder only if he gives something to the former owner of the charm.[49]

Charms may be so dangerous that only the owner dares touch them or even come near them. Sometimes they have no owners, but are avoided by everybody. The Wonkonguru of South Australia believe that certain objects bring misfortune to those who use them. Our authority tells of finding a large boomerang down a rabbit burrow. The aboriginals at once recognized it as being old and "very bad poison." One who fought with it always got hurt. "If a man who did not know its strength wielded it, he would only get hurt a little bit, but if it was used by anyone that knew its history and used it in bravado, the man would be killed in the fight. It must not be destroyed, but could be lost. It had been lost scores of times, but it was always turning up again."[50] To touch a Kurnai *bulk* (magical pebble) is thought to be highly injurious for anyone but its possessor. Women and girls are terrified if an attempt is made to place one of these objects in their hands.[51]

Some Koita charm stones are so highly charged with occult power that " it is not considered safe for them to be touched with the hand, even by the man who is about to bring their power into play."[52] Sorcerers among the Roro-speaking tribes obtain from a black snake a stone which kills instantly any person touched by it. It can be made innocuous if dropped into a bowl of salt water, which immediately hisses and bubbles as though boiling. When no more bubbles arise the stone is "dead." No layman would willingly touch or look at a sorcerer's magical stones, and any contact with them, even when not expected to produce death, is avoided as unlucky.[53]

A sorcerer of Malekula (in the New Hebrides) manipulates his charm materials with two sticks, not unlike chopsticks. Should he touch the materials with his fingers the power in them would affect him as well as his intended victim. Similarly, when trying to cause death by "poisoning," he is careful not to absorb any of the "poison" himself; hence during the operation he keeps his mouth shut.[54]

Among the Maori, people of ignoble birth or unskilled in magic were warned never to look upon any "enchanted object" for fear of losing their sight or their eyes. The story is told of a sorcerer who possessed a magical wooden head so powerful that it killed anyone who came within a certain distance of it. A brave warrior, renowned for skill in magic, determined to rid the country of the pest. By means of his charms and spells he enlisted the aid of thousands of spirits benevolently disposed toward mankind. After a battle royal between them and the malignant spirits guarding the head the latter were defeated and the sorcerer was put to death.[55]

Among the Kenyah of Borneo each household has a bundle of charms hanging over the principal hearth beside the human heads and constituting the most precious possession of the whole household or village. No one, not even the chief, willingly touches the bundle. When transferring it to a new house, some old man is specially told off for the duty, since he who touches it is in danger of death. "Its function seems to be to bring luck or prosperity of all kinds to the house; without it nothing would prosper, especially in warfare."[56]

By the Akamba it is considered dangerous for a layman to touch any objects employed by a medicine man in his magical arts. He himself will never sell his divinatory apparatus or dispose of it in any way.[57] Among the Ovimbundu of Angola the witch doctor's charms are regarded as "powerful" or "sacred." Common people dare not touch them. For a white man to touch them would be a sacrilegious act.[58]

If the demand for charms outruns the available supply of natural objects a professional magician is always prepared to make them, for a consideration, of course. The more powerful they are the more expensive they are likely to be. Charms are often made by means of spells, thus transferring to material objects the occult power held to reside in words and formulas. They may be models or representations of things already used in magic. Or, again, they may be composed of various magical ingredients. The stranger, the more abhorrent, and the more difficult to obtain they are, the greater is their potency; they sometimes recall the witches' brew in *Macbeth.*

Analogies, perhaps of an elaborate character, may determine what ingredients of a charm shall be selected by the magician. Among the Bavenda of the Transvaal a traveler wears around his neck a small piece of wood as an amulet. It is taken from the bough of a tree overhanging a difficult climb in a well-frequented path. Every wayfarer grasps the bough as he mounts upward, and by doing so inordinately increases its power of rendering assistance; it thus becomes an obvious source from which a charm can be obtained. Conversely, a charm to injure a traveler is made from a root growing in a well-frequented path, because it is in a spot where almost every passer-by knocks his toe against it.[59] Among the Jukun of northern Nigeria a charm to facilitate concealment contains leaves from any plant growing on an ant heap (because ants work unseen), some fat of a goat of uniform color (because uniformity of color lessens the possibility of detection), a piece of wood from a certain tree whose fruit resembles the human eye, and mucous which sweat flies deposit in the eyes of men (thus interfering with their vision). These ingredients are wrapped up in the rags of a blind person, and the bundle is then enclosed in a cow's or a goat's fetus (a fetus is blind). If you tie this bundle round your waist you can walk unseen through the midst of enemies or past your guards, for they will be stricken with temporary blindness.[60]

Many primitive peoples have material inanimate objects, or collections of such objects, associated with a spiritual being. These *sacra* must be approached with due caution and treated with becoming reverence. Stringent taboos protect them from being seen or touched by uninitiated or unclean persons; conversely, their revelation to those entitled to enter within the holy of holies often forms the culminating feature of a solemn ceremony. Such objects are properly described as charms, since they incorporate impersonal occult power which is discharged automatically by contact with them or in their proximity.

The Arunta *churinga* include, besides wooden bull-roarers, bits of polished stone in a great variety of forms. Many *churinga* are connected with the mythical ancestors of the tribe, who wandered over the tribal territory and finally descended into the earth at the places where their *churinga* are now deposited for safekeeping. Each one contains the attributes of its spirit owner and imparts to the man carrying it about courage and accuracy of aim as a fighter. So firm is this latter belief that if two men are fighting and one of them knows the other to carry a *churinga*, he will certainly lose heart and suffer defeat. When a man is ill he scrapes his *churinga*, mixes the dust with water, and drinks it. The potion is "very strengthening." A ceremony called "softening the *churinga*," which consists in rubbing them with red ocher, indicates that they are regarded as much more than pieces of wood or stone. Being intimately associated with the ancestors, each one has " 'feelings' just as human beings have," and these can be soothed by rubbing in the same way as the feelings of living men. In the Kaitish tribe the performance of certain ceremonies, in the course of which the *churinga* are handled by an old man, renders him so full of their occult power that he becomes for a time taboo.[61]

It is the rule among the Australian aborigines that women and children must never be shown the bull-roarer. Its peculiar humming or whirring sound, when rapidly swung, is supposed by them to be the voice of the spirit or god who founded and still supervises the tribal ceremonies. Thus in the Urabunna tribe of Central Australia a boy at initiation is told that on no account may he allow a woman or a child to see the mystic stick, "or else he and his mother and sisters will tumble down as dead as stones."[62]

The bull-roarer is commonly used in Australia and New Guinea to bring rain, promote the growth of vegetation, and provide for the increase of food animals. The Dieri think that after a youth has passed through a very secret rite of initiation he becomes inspired by the Mura-Mura who presides over it. He then has the power to secure a good supply of snakes and other reptiles by whirling a bull-roarer round his head when out in search of game.[63] By the Larakia bull-roarers are supposed to be full of occult power. They must be rubbed over the bodies of old men before they can be handled with safety by initiated youths. The latter are allowed to carry them about as a means of catching fish and game.[64] In the western islands of Torres Straits bull-roarers are swung to make the gardens grow.[65] On Kiwai Island, in the Papuan Gulf, whirling of the bull-roarer insures a good crop of yams, sweet potatoes, and bananas.[66] The Yabim believe that by whirling bull-roarers and at the same time calling out the names of the ancestral ghosts they can procure an especially good yield of their gardens.[67]

The Keraki, who live in southwestern Papua, endow a bull-roarer with hidden and dangerous qualities, which may be transmitted from a man who owns and wields it to his wife. Before and after using it he must refrain from sexual relations with her. She would become ill as the result of such intercourse while the influence of the bull-roarer still affected her husband.[68] By the Koko, another Papuan tribe, extreme care is taken to prevent the bull-roarers from being broken while in use. Should a bull-roarer break and a chip strike anyone, that person, when he goes hunting or fighting, would be wounded by a boar's tusk or by an enemy's spear, as the case may be, and in the very place where the chip struck him.[69]

In the D'Entrecasteaux Islands an ancient pot was regarded as the greatest ruler of the winds, the rain, and the sunshine. Some people said that it had never been made by human hands; others declared that it had been brought from a distant district by its owner, a headman. He kept it out of sight in a hut within his hamlet. "Only on one special occasion might this hut be entered or the people see the pot, otherwise mighty earthquakes would shake the land, and floods and tempests devastate it, followed by famine and the death of many people. But at one yearly ceremony a few were privileged to behold it, for then its owner carried it in procession, and the train of natives followed after, crouching low towards the ground. In fear and trembling they brought it food, still crouching low, and hurriedly retired again." Its owner long levied tribute by means of this sovereign pot.[70]

In Malekula, one of the New Hebrides, the tall tapering hats or masks worn by members of a secret society possess extreme sacredness. The methods of making and decorating them are revealed only to initiates. It is a terrible accident for a mask to fall to the ground. In former days the luckless man who had such an accident while dancing was put to death. A man who stepped across part of a mask suffered the same fate. A dog, pig, or other animal which touches one is killed.[71]

Some of the Fijian tribes revere the ivory teeth of the sperm whale. A subtle "aura" seems to emanate from them, "breathing of mystery." Those most sacred are kept in special baskets and are seldom seen except by the few who know of their existence. No worship is paid to them, but they serve as venerated mascots and embody the tribal "luck."[72]

The Samoans paid reverence to sacred stones. In one island the shrine of the god Turia was a very smooth stone, which was kept in a sacred grove. The priest carefully weeded the ground about it and covered it with branches, so that the god might keep warm. "No one dared to touch this stone, lest a poisonous and deadly influence of some kind should at once radiate from it to the transgressor."[73]

Certain bells, namely those which seem never to have had tongues, are the most sacred of the Toda sacred objects. Nearly all receive offerings of milk, curds, or buttermilk during the dairy ceremonial. There is much reason to believe that their present sanctity has come about gradually by a process of transference from the sanctity of the bell-cows or buffaloes to the bells which they carried.[74] Ceremonial arrows are important in the cults of the Vedda. The "more sophisticated" natives, who believe in the periodical uncleanness of women (a belief borrowed from the Singhalese), are careful to avoid contamination of these sacred objects. This is generally accomplished by keeping them in a cave or in the roof thatch.[75]

The Akikuyu of Kenya possess a magical object known as *kithathi*. It is a curiously striped piece of reddish burnt clay, roughly tubular in shape and with four holes along the edge. This object is so powerful that it must never be touched by human hands or carried into a house, lest some disaster befall the inmates. It is kept buried in the bush at some distance from the village and is only removed when used to detect criminals. A person accused of witchcraft makes contact with it by inserting twigs in the holes and then protests his innocence of the charge. If he dies within three months his guilt is manifest. Until this period has expired he must keep away from the plantation and his wife, for he is supposed to be charged with the deadly influence of the *kithathi*.[76]

The Wanyika possess a great drum made out of the hollowed section of a tree trunk. This drum is so sacred that when it is brought out all uninitiated persons must hide, for should they see it they would surely die.[77] One of the Baganda clans had charge of a drum which was brought to court and beaten when the king wished to announce to his people the end of a period of mourning "The drum was sacrosanct; for example, if a slave disliked his master, and escaped to the drum-shrine, he became the servant of the drum, and could not be removed. So, too, if any person had been condemned to death and was able to escape to the shrine, he might remain there in safety, he was the slave of the drum. Should any cow, goat, or sheep stray there, it became the property of the drum, and could not be taken away or killed; it might roam about as it liked, in the future it was a sacred animal."[78]

The sacred trumpets, used by the Uaupés of Brazil to produce the *jurupari* (forest-spirit) music are never shown to women. When their music is heard the women must retire to the woods. Death would be the penalty for even an accidental sight of these objects, "and it is said that fathers have been the executioners of their own daughters, and husbands of their wives, when such has been the case."[79] The Yahuna, a tribe of southeastern Colombia, say that if women and small children saw these sacred instruments the former would die at once and the latter would eat earth, become sick, and then die.[80]

Among the Zuñi of New Mexico sacred objects are taboo to people who do not "belong" to them. No one would dare to touch those most sacred except the head of the priesthood which has them in charge, and no one but he and his female counterpart would enter the room where they are kept. The same is true, also, of the masks and altars of the secret societies. Prayer sticks and ceremonial garments are handled with great respect, and no more than necessary.[81] In former days, when the Hopi clans lived apart, each clan possessed sacred objects, the *wimi,* which were associated with the clan ancestors (katcinas) and were endowed with mysterious qualities. After the formation of the united Hopi community the priestly fraternities received the custody of the *wimi,* but they continued to be owned by the original clans.[82]

The Cherokee, the Creeks, and many Plains Indians had sacred objects of tribal veneration; for example, the "flat pipe" of the Arapaho and the great shell of the Omaha. Such an object formed a true palladium, upon whose continued safe possession the prosperity of the tribe depended. It was guarded by a priest and was seldom or never shown except on certain great occasions. Like the Hebrew Ark of the Covenant it was sometimes carried into battle to insure victory. According to a common belief, the presence of so powerful an object would be enervating or positively dangerous to people in its vicinity unless they were fortified by a ceremonial tonic. "For this reason every great 'medicine' is usually kept apart in a hut or *tipi* built for the purpose, very much as we are accustomed to store explosives at some distance from the dwelling or business house."[83]

Many primitive peoples, again, have material, inanimate objects whose occult power is due to their possession, temporarily or permanently, by spiritual beings. Such objects are fetishes. The indwelling spirit of a fetish is not its soul or vital essence, but a spirit which voluntarily or by man's compulsion has been attracted to the object and become embodied in it. While fetishes, as a rule, are privately owned, some belong to a clan, village, or other social group. The owner of a fetish treats it as he treats persons, propitiating, cajoling, or coercing it as circumstances require. Fetishism has reached an elaborate development in West Africa, where it was first encountered and described. But fetishes are found the world over.

A fetish, whose activity depends on the will of the spiritual being within it, must be distinguished from a charm, which has no will of its own but acts automatically. Yet to draw a dividing line between the two classes of objects may be as difficult as sometimes to separate a prayer from a spell. A fetish is selected for the same reasons which lead to the choice of a charm; like a charm it works to bring good fortune or avert ill fortune of every sort; and like a charm it may be either a natural or a manufactured object. The distinction between them depends solely on the degree to which they are personified. The personifying process, applied to what were formerly Zuñi charms, has converted them into fetishes, the recipients of ceremonies intended to induce their capricious indwelling spirits to become subservient to man's desires. On the other hand, in the case of the Ga medicines, their spirits seem to be regarded more or less as mechanical agencies working for anyone who presses "the right button." These are but illustrations of the twin processes of personalization and depersonalization, always operative.[84]

Some primitive peoples are greatly devoted to the use of charms, especially as talismans or amulets worn on the person. Thus among the Ba-ila of Northern Rhodesia almost every native wears one or more charms around his neck or on his arm or head. It is impossible to exaggerate the part which these *misamo* play in the life of the people. "Their use constitutes a system of insurance against the ills and calamities of life. Instead of paying an insurance premium as we do . . . . the Ba-ila invest in powerful charms, which in their belief will keep them from violence, robbery, etc., etc.; and if not altogether from death at least will postpone it, and enable them to determine their mode of life beyond the grave."[85] Among the Akikuyu few men and women are without a half a dozen charms sealed up in a sheep's horn and attached to the waist band.[86] The Wataita, another tribe of Kenya, exhibit absolute faith in the efficacy of the charms obtained from their magicians. A native, in this lion-infested region, will blow the lion medicine to the four points of the compass and then will lie down in the open and go peacefully to sleep even in the midst of a man-eater's district. If a man is attacked by a lion, the brute makes sure that he does not live to become an unbeliever; if he survives, it is of course clear that he owes his immunity to the lion medicine.[87] Of the Baganda we are told that almost every ailment known to the medicine men might be treated with some kind of charm. When the patient had been cured by its use, it was not cast aside but was decorated and worn as an ornament, being thus ready for instant use upon any return of the old symptoms.[88] In West Africa "charms are made for every occupation and desire in life—loving, hating, buying, selling, fishing, planting, traveling, hunting. . . . . A new-born child starts with a health-knot tied round the wrist, neck, or loins, and throughout the rest of its life its collection of charms goes on increasing." However, this collection does not attain inconvenient dimensions, since charms that do not work will be discarded.[89] Among the Fang or Pangwe of Gabun, whose fear of black magic is so pronounced, one finds, wherever one looks, the medicines to nullify it—"in the huts, on the village square, in the assembly house, on the paths, even in the jungle, everywhere, everywhere."[90] Charms hold an important place in the everyday life of the American aborigines, both south and north. There is also evidence of their regular use by the Mexicans, Maya, and Peruvians, in spite of the fact that the magical practices of these Indians were largely swept away after the Spanish conquest. Eskimo charms are innumerable. Among the Polar Eskimo, women rarely possess them since women spend the greater part of their time in the settlements and so do not face the dangers to which their nomadic husbands are constantly exposed.[91] Among the Siberian Chukchi some persons put no trust in charms. One man said to a Russian inquirer, "I do not wear anything upon my body because I am convinced that protection by such small objects must be a mere delusion." A professional magician went further and declared that nothing created by man has any power, for all power resides in the deity who created man.[92] But such skepticism is indeed rare.

NOTES TO CHAPTER V

[1] J. P. Mills, *The Lhota Nagas* (London, 1922), pp. 166 f.

[2] W. E. Roth, "An Inquiry into the Animism and Folk-Lore of the Guiana Indians," *Thirtieth Annual Report of the Bureau of American Ethnology*, pp. 281 ff.

3 A. W. Howitt, *The Native Tribes of South-East Australia* (London 1904), p. 378.

4 C. G. Seligman, *The Melanesians of British New Guinea* (Cambridge, 1910), pp. 173 f. We are told of an old magician who dug up what the natives regarded as a most powerful charm to produce rain and abundant crops and sold it to a missionary. A spirit put two more charms on the magician's chest as he lay asleep and ordered him to bury them (H. H. Romilly, *From My Verandah in New Guinea* [London, 1889], pp. 176 f.).

5 Charles Hose and William McDougall, *The Pagan Tribes of Borneo* (London, 1910), I, 110; II, 125. Cf. J. Perham, "Manangism in Borneo," *Journal of the Straits Branch of the Royal Asiatic Society*, No. 19 (1887), p. 89 (Sea Dayak).

6 Edward Stack, *The Mikirs* (London, 1908), p. 30.

7 See, in general, George Catlin, *Letters and Notes on the Manners, Customs, and Condition of the North American Indians* (2d ed., New York, 1842), Letter No. 6; H. R. Schoolcraft, *Oneóta, or Characteristics of the Red Race of America* (New York, 1845), p. 456; Francis Parkman, *The Jesuits in North America* (Boston, 1867), p. lxxi.

8 J. A. Mason, in *University of California Publications in American Archaeology and Ethnology*, X, 185.

9 W. Bogoras, in *Memoirs of the American Museum of Natural History*, XI, 339.

10 A. W. Howitt, *op. cit.*, pp. 523, 533, 535, 560, 562.

11 John Mathew, *Two Representative Tribes of Queensland* (London, 1910), pp. 170 f.; *idem, Eaglehawk and Crow* (London, 1899), p. 143.

12 Sir Baldwin Spencer and F. J. Gillen, *The Native Tribes of Central Australia* (London, 1899), pp. 481, 525, 531.

13 R. F. Fortune, *Sorcerers of Dobu* (London, 1932), p. 298.

14 I. H. N. Evans, *The Negritos of Malaya* (Cambridge, 1937), pp. 206 f. According to Father Paul Schebesta possession of one of these magical stones is necessary for a man who would become a *hala*, or magician (*Among the Forest Dwarfs of Malaya* [London, 1929], p. 193).

15 Theodor Koch-Grünberg, *Zwei Jahre unter den Indianern* (Berlin, 1910), II, 155.

16 Rafael Karsten, in *Boletín de la Academia Nacional de Historia* (Quito, 1921–22), III, 143; IV, 317.

17 Mrs. Erminnie A. Smith, "Myths of the Iroquois," *Second Annual Report of the Bureau of Ethnology*, pp. 68 f.

18 J. H. Hutton, *The Angami Nagas* (London, 1921), p. 407.

19 *Idem, The Sema Nagas* (London, 1921), pp. 174 f.

20 C. J. F. S. Forbes, *British Burma and Its People* (London, 1878), p. 295.

21 F. H. Cushing, "Zuñi Fetiches," *Second Annual Report of the Bureau of Ethnology*, pp. 9–45.

22 Laura W. Benedict, *A Study of Bagobo Ceremonial, Magic, and Myth* (New York, 1916), p. 217. *Annals of the New York Academy of Sciences*, Vol. XXV.

23 Daigre, in *Anthropos*, XXVII (1932), 180.

24 F. G. Speck, in *Memoirs of the American Anthropological Association*, No. 8 (Vol. II, Pt. 2), p. 118.

25 James Teit, in *Memoirs of the American Museum of Natural History*, IV, 280.

²⁶ James Barnard, in *Report of the Second Meeting of the Australasian Association for the Advancement of Science* (1890), p. 605. Cf. James Bonwick, *Daily Life and Origin of the Tasmanians* (London, 1870), p. 89.

²⁷ Mrs. James Smith, *The Booandik Tribe of South Australian Aborigines* (Adelaide, 1880), p. 30.

²⁸ R. H. Mathews, *Ethnological Notes on the Aboriginal Tribes of New South Wales and Victoria* (Sydney, 1905), p. 55.

²⁹ Carl Lumholtz, *Among Cannibals* (New York, 1899), p. 272.

³⁰ Sir Baldwin Spencer and F. J. Gillen, *The Native Tribes of Central Australia* (London, 1899), pp. 538 f.; *iidem, The Northern Tribes of Central Australia* (London, 1904), p. 477.

³¹ W. L. Warner, *A Black Civilization* (New York, 1937), p. 237.

³² Wilfred Powell, *Wanderings in a Wild Country* (London, 1883), p. 92.

³³ A. R. Radcliffe-Brown, *The Andaman Islanders* (Cambridge, 1933), p. 179.

³⁴ E. M. Loeb, "Pomo Folkways," *University of California Publications in American Archaeology and Ethnology,* XIX, 307.

³⁵ Margaret Lantis, "The Alaskan Whale Cult and Its Affinities," *American Anthropologist* (n.s., 1938), XL, 443, 451.

³⁶ F. E. Williams, *Orokaiva Magic* (London, 1928), p. 183.

³⁷ *Idem, Papuans of the Trans-Fly* (Oxford, 1936), p. 316.

³⁸ Ralph Linton, *The Tanala* (Chicago, 1933), p. 222. *Field Museum of Natural History, Anthropological Series,* Vol. XXII.

³⁹ E. W. Smith and A. M. Dale, *The Ila-speaking Peoples of Northern Rhodesia* (London, 1920), I, 261.

⁴⁰ Albert Schweitzer, *African Notebook* (New York, 1939), p. 66. Cf. Günter Tessmann, *Die Pangwe* (Berlin, 1913), II, 134.

⁴¹ W. L. Hildburgh, "Notes on Sinhalese Magic," *Journal of the Royal Anthropological Institute,* XXXVIII (1908), 195.

⁴² Monica Hunter, *Reaction to Conquest* (London, 1936), p. 46.

⁴³ E. H. Ashton, "Medicine, Magic, and Sorcery among the Southern Sotho," *University of Cape Town, Communications from the School of African Studies* (n.s., 1943), No. 10, p. 5.

⁴⁴ E. W. Smith and E. M. Dale, *op. cit.,* I, 255.

⁴⁵ A. G. Agisafe, *The Laws and Customs of the Yoruba People* (London, 1924), p. 46.

⁴⁶ Margaret J. Field, *Religion and Medicine of the Ga People* (Oxford, 1937), pp. 111 f., 118 f. Not only are the taboos attached to a medicine exacting, but they also involve a stern moral code. "The holder of the medicine must refrain from adultery, stealing, trying to harm others, abusing others, or quarreling. If others try to pick a quarrel he must turn the other cheek, but if unjustly attacked he may fight heartily, knowing that his medicine will fight with him. Medicines of this kind, with their great rewards and great demands, are naturally avoided by people who have not courage and character."

⁴⁷ M. R. Harrington, *Sacred Bundles of the Sac and Fox Indians* (Philadelphia, 1914), p. 159. *University of Pennsylvania, Anthropological Publications of the University Museum,* Vol. IV, No. 2.

⁴⁸ Clark Wissler, "Ceremonial Bundles of the Blackfoot Indians," *Anthropological Papers of the American Museum of Natural History,* VII, 276. The contents of the medicine bundle are kept a profound secret. No one but the owner knows what is in it, and he alone may touch it. "Other Indians would

be afraid to meddle with it" (E. F. Wilson, in *Report of the Fifty-Seventh Meeting of the British Association for the Advancement of Science* [1887], p. 187, quoting a Blackfoot chief).

49 Knud Rasmussen, *Intellectual Culture of the Hudson Bay Eskimos* (Copenhagen, 1930), pp. 150 ff. *Report of the Fifth Thule Expedition*, Vol. VII, No. 1.

50 G. Horne and G. Aiston, *Savage Life in Central Australia* (London, 1924), p. 77.

51 A. W. Howitt, *op. cit.*, p. 378.

52 C. G. Seligman, *op. cit.*, pp. 174 f.

53 *Idem*, pp. 282 ff. See also James Chalmers, *Pioneering in New Guinea* (2d ed., London, 1887), p. 316.

54 A. B. Deacon, *Malekula, a Vanishing People in the New Hebrides* (London, 1934), pp. 666 f.

55 J. W. Stack, in *Report of the Third Meeting of the Australasian Association for the Advancement of Science* (1891), p. 384.

56 Charles Hose and William McDougall, *op. cit.*, II, 124 f.

57 Gerhard Lindblom, *The Akamba in British East Africa* (2d ed., Uppsala, 1920), p. 262.

58 G. A. Dorsey, "The Ocimbanda or Witch-Doctor of the Ovimbundu of Portuguese Southwest Africa," *Journal of American Folk-Lore*, XII (1899), 184.

59 H. A. Stayt, *The Bavenda* (London, 1931), p. 262.

60 C. K. Meek, *A Sudanese Kingdom* (London, 1931), p. 303.

61 Spencer and Gillen, *The Native Tribes of Central Australia*, pp. 130 ff., 135 and note 1; *iidem, The Northern Tribes of Central Australia*, pp. 265, note 1, 293. Among the Worora of northwestern Australia an old man, very feeble, had his vigor restored by first exposing him to the smoke of grass fires and by rubbing him all over with bull-roarers (J. R. B. Love, *Stone-Age Bushmen of To-Day* [London, 1936], p. 203).

62 Spencer and Gillen, *Northern Tribes*, p. 498. With the Arunta the exclusion of women from ceremonies in which the bull-roarer is employed is not absolute. Bull-roarers are actually whirled close to women while certain rites are in progress, and during a performance of the Emu totemic group women see the bull-roarers clearly, though at some distance away. We cannot help feeling, declare our authorities, that perhaps the women "know a little more than they are given credit for" (*iidem, The Arunta* [London, 1927], I, 100, note 1).

63 A. W. Howitt, *op. cit.*, p. 660.

64 Sir Baldwin Spencer, *The Native Tribes of the Northern Territory of Australia* (London, 1914), p. 212.

65 A. C. Haddon, in *Reports of the Cambridge Anthropological Expedition to Torres Straits*, V, 346 f.

66 *Ibid.*, V, 218.

67 H. Zahn, in R. Neuhauss, *Deutsch Neu-Guinea* (Berlin, 1911), III, 333. The use of the bull-roarer in agricultural operations is found in North America, as among the Zuñi and Hopi Indians (J. W. Fewkes, in *Journal of American Ethnology and Archaeology*, I [1891], 15, 23, note 1) and the Apache (J. G. Bourke, in *Ninth Annual Report of the Bureau of Ethnology*, pp. 476 f.). Among the northern Algonquian tribes it was customary to swing bull-roarers after the first thaw of late winter. By doing so they caused the cold winds to return and form a crust on the snow so that travel by snowshoes and transport by toboggans would be less laborious (J. M. Cooper, in *Proceedings of the Twenty-third International Congress of Americanists* [New York, 1928], p. 515).

[68] F. E. Williams, *Papuans of the Trans-Fly*, p. 183.

[69] E. W. P. Chinnery and W. N. Beaver, "Notes on the Initiation Ceremonies of the Koko, Papua," *Journal of the Royal Anthropological Institute*, XLV (1915), 71.

[70] D. Jenness and A. Ballantyne, *The Northern D'Entrecasteaux* (Oxford, 1920), pp. 129 ff.

[71] A. B. Deacon, *op. cit.*, p. 440.

[72] A. B. Brewster, *The Hill Tribes of Fiji* (London, 1922), pp. 22 ff.

[73] George Turner, *Samoa* (London, 1884), p. 62.

[74] W. H. R. Rivers, *The Todas* (London, 1906), pp. 424 ff.

[75] C. G. Seligman and Brenda Z. Seligman, *The Veddas* (Cambridge, 1911), pp. 137 ff.

[76] C. W. Hobley, *Ethnology of A-Kamba and Other East African Tribes* (Cambridge, 1910), pp. 139 ff. See also W. S. Routledge and Katherine Routledge, *With a Prehistoric People* (London, 1910), pp. 273 ff.

[77] Charles New, *Life, Wanderings, and Labours in Eastern Africa* (London, 1873), pp. 112 f. According to another account only the elders of both sexes may look on this drum (Sir R. F. Burton, *Zanzibar* [London, 1872], II, 91).

[78] John Roscoe, *The Baganda* (London, 1911), p. 167.

[79] A. R. Wallace, *A Narrative of Travels on the Amazon and Rio Negro* (London, 1853), pp. 348 f.; cf. p. 501.

[80] Theodor Koch-Grünberg, *Zwei Jahre unter den Indianer* (Berlin, 1910), II, 293.

[81] Ruth L. Bunzel, "Introduction to Zuñi Ceremonialism," *Forty-seventh Annual Report of the Bureau of American Ethnology*, p. 502.

[82] J. W. Fewkes, "The Owakülti Altar at Sichomovi Pueblo," *American Anthropologist* (n.s., 1901), III, 211 f.

[83] James Mooney, "Palladium," *Handbook of American Indians*, Part II, pp. 193 f.

[84] Charms (including medicines) are often treated as if they had some measure of life and personality, but not, apparently, as being the abodes of spiritual powers. In the western islands of Torres Straits the natives had small wooden images in human shape. These *madub* were placed in the gardens. It was believed that at night they became animated and went around the gardens swinging bull-roarers, dancing, and singing to make the plants grow (A. C. Haddon, in *Reports of the Cambridge Anthropological Expedition to Torres Straits*, V, 345 f.). An Ao Naga keeps luckstones in a little basket. "If only one is obtained it will soon find a mate, it is believed, in some mysterious way known only to itself, and there will be two in the basket where there was only one before. These two breed until there may be quite a large family. If neglected, the stones will fly away" (J. F. Mills, *The Ao Nagas* [London, 1926], p. 290). The Tanala of Madagascar believe that the strength of a charm increases with its age. Some charms are so strong that they become animate and even move and speak (Ralph Linton, *op. cit.*, p. 218). Among the Babemba of South Africa the various methods of divination in vogue would appear to our eyes as nothing more than ways of tossing-up or appealing to chance. But for native thought the methods are ways of asking the medicines which have the property of acting in a particular and known fashion to do so if the answer to the diviner's questions is positive, or to refrain from doing so if it is negative. Thus the efficacy of any divinatory method is held to be entirely dependent on the nature of the medicines employed (R. J. Moore, " 'Bwanga' among the Babemba," *Africa*, XIII [1940], 233). In Ruanda-Urundi, Belgian Congo, when divination is practiced by means

of knucklebones, these are believed to listen attentively to the operator and answer correctly "like men." The operator merely interprets what they have to tell. So when balls of butter are used he addresses them and begs them to whiten, to become absolutely white, and thus give a favorable sign. It is always supposed that the butter hears his supplication and changes in color as desired (A. Arnoux, "La divination au Ruanda," *Anthropos*, XII–XIII [1917–18], 18, 51). The virtue of an Azande medicine is sometimes spoken of as its "soul" and is believed to rise in steam and smoke when being cooked. Therefore people place their faces in the steam so that the virtue or soul may enter into them. When a man makes vengeance magic and it kills a witch, they say that the "soul of the medicine" has gone out to seek its victim. So also the poison oracle has a soul, which accounts for its ability to see what human beings cannot see. (E. E. Evans-Pritchard, *Witchcraft, Oracles, and Magic among the Azande* [Oxford, 1937], pp. 36, 463, 465). A Bakongo native, in order to "wake up" a bundle of charms, first beats it with a stick and then puts it on the ground in the midst of several small heaps of gunpowder. These are exploded, and the bundle is held over the smoke. A whistle is also blown vigorously. Thus the charms become alert to perform their allotted functions (J. H. Weeks, *Among the Primitive Bakongo* [London, 1914], p. 235). Among the Northern Shoshoni a man obtains occult power by sleeping at night on the mountain side. Next morning he rises and looks for roots. Having found them, he addresses the sun, saying, "Look, I take this medicine." He brings the roots home, ties them up in a buckskin bag, and wears the bag about his body. In the night the medicine speaks to him and counsels him (R. H. Lowie, in *Anthropological Papers of the American Museum of Natural History*, II, 223 f.). For the Eskimo of East Greenland an animal amulet is more than a mere representation of the animal in question. "The amulet is alive because it has been made during the recitation of a charm or spell, when the dominating qualities of the animal or the part of the body have been invoked; the power of these qualities is at any rate potentially in the amulet." For native thought there is evidently little difference between using an animal or the representation of an animal as an amulet; it has the same power in both cases. When the amulet is a knife or some other implement these Eskimo believe that suddenly in the hour of danger it "begins to grow and effects the killing itself or covers the pursued person" (William Thalbitzer, "Ethnographical Collections from East Greenland," *Middelelser om Grønland*, XXXIX [1914], 630 f.).

[85] E. W. Smith and A. M. Dale, *op. cit.*, I, 252. Our authorities point out that *misamo* act on the dead as well as on the living. A man may procure a charm enabling him, after death, to become a lion, an eagle, or an anthill. Or, if evil-minded, he may be transformed by means of a charm into a vengeful, destructive ghost, "one who goes killing and smiling." His victims fall suddenly dead. In such distressing circumstances the only thing to be done is to procure a potent medicine and doctor the ghost into a state of desuetude (I, 264).

[86] W. S. Routledge and Katherine Routledge, *op. cit.*, p. 269.

[87] J. H. Patterson, *The Man-Eaters of Tsavo and Other East African Adventures* (London, 1907), pp. 126 f.

[88] John Roscoe, *op. cit.*, pp. 330 f.

[89] Mary H. Kingsley, *Travels in West Africa* (London, 1897), p. 448. Cf. R. H. Nassau, *Fetichism in West Africa* (New York, 1904), p. 85.

[90] Günter Tessmann, *op. cit.*, II, 140.

[91] Knud Rasmussen, *The People of the Polar North* (London, 1908), p. 139.

[92] W. Bogoras, in *Memoirs of the American Museum of Natural History*, XI, 347.

CHAPTER VI

MAGICIANS

CERTAIN physical peculiarities, distinguishing a man from his fellows, may indicate his possession of natural qualifications for the exercise of magic. An old "doctor" among the Tasmanians owed his position to the fact that he suffered fits of spasmodic contraction of the muscles of the breast, a malady which greatly impressed the aboriginals. He was cunning enough, we are told, to take full advantage of the effect which this mysterious affliction produced.[1] In New Caledonia the consideration in which a magician is held will be much increased if he has a deformed or stunted body, extra fingers, red eyes, or some other physical defect of a striking character.[2] The Samoans thought that hunchbacks and other persons with some physical malformation were endowed with the gift of divination. When grown to manhood, hunchbacks frequently became priests.[3] By the Ovambo tribes of South Africa misshapen persons, and hermaphrodites in particular, are suspected of sorcery.[4] By the Lovedu of the Transvaal a person with an "unpleasant face" is often regarded as a witch, though no specific acts of black magic may have been definitely attributed to him.[5] Among the Akikuyu of Kenya a native ordinarily acquires occult power by inheritance from his father. But anyone born with some deformity, for instance, with crooked toes, will be marked out as a magician.[6] Both the Akikuyu and the Akamba consider that children born feet first are destined to be unlucky throughout life. When a male child, thus afflicted, grows up and marries, his wife will soon die; when a female child is married, her husband will not live long. A child cutting its upper incisor teeth first is likewise very unlucky. It must not eat the first fruits, nor may it admire a growing crop, for in that case the crop would never reach maturity. This evil influence can to a great extent be mitigated if, when the first of the milk teeth drops out, the father of the child cohabits with the mother.[7] The Azande likewise believe that people who as children cut their upper teeth first exert an unlucky influence upon the crops of their neighbors. At

144

sowing time it is usual to protect the crops against these possessors of bad teeth. Special medicines are also used to injure them if they partake of the first fruits of the harvest. The Azande also say that a man who has bad teeth can spoil anything new. If he admires and fingers your fine new stool or bowl or pot it will surely crack. A man may do this without malice and perhaps without intent, but he is responsible none the less, since he knows of his evil influence and ought to avoid handling new utensils. Hence he has only himself to blame if he suffers from the protective magic of his neighbors.[8] Typically, though not always, the Shilluk sorcerer is a monorchid. Men with double undescended testicles or with unusually small glands also tend to be regarded as natural-born dealers in black magic. The malignity attending such a condition is so fully recognized that a child thus marked out is often killed at birth. Its death can be accomplished only by putting it into a specially woven basket and then drowning it. Were this not done the child—such is its power—would surely survive.[9] The Warega of the Belgian Congo consider that a child who cuts the upper teeth first brings evil to the entire community. An isolated house is immediately prepared for his reception, and there he must always live. When grown up he mingles with the villagers, though continually subject to abuse and insult. A woman who consents to marry him shares his fate. The *dino*, as he is called, may not touch grain prepared for planting, lest the harvest be lost. Nor may he eat bananas from a plantation in full bearing; otherwise the fruit would rot.[10] In the region of the Lower Congo albinos are usually considered to be sacred and their persons as inviolable. They may be elevated to the priesthood.[11] The Fang or Pangwe of Gabun believe that the power of witchcraft resides in old women or deformed men. Children who have been "specially indoctrinated" by such persons also possess this power.[12] In southern Nigeria barren women or those past the age of childbearing are most often supposed to be witches.[13] By the Ijaw any lame or deformed person, especially if a woman, runs a risk of being suspected of witchcraft.[14] In Togo some of the Ewe believe that a child born with teeth or one who cuts the upper teeth before the lower will grow up to be powerful in evil magic. Such a child used to be drowned or sold into slavery.[15] Among the Ojibwa Indians persons that are deformed and ill-looking gain a reputation for witchcraft, though they may make no pretensions to the magical art.[16] The Tinne of Alaska say that people with deformities singling them out of a crowd must be naturally predisposed to the office of magician. A cross-eyed or crippled man or a sterile woman is more likely than a physically normal person to be chosen for the profession.[17] A medicine man of the Point Barrow Eskimo was considered to be a very good doctor and exorciser, "by virtue of his paper thinness." He could get into places which larger men were unable to penetrate; hence an evil spirit had a hard time in concealing itself from him.[18]

The attainment of extreme old age (rare in primitive society) will sometimes suffice to mark out a person as possessing exceptional occult power. A very old man among the Lovedu is likely to gain a reputation for witchcraft. He has lived so long, the people say, because he has bartered the lives of younger relatives for his own.[19] The Ba-ila are very reluctant to kill an old person even though, tired of life, he begs to be released from earthly ties. For in the course of long years he may have accumulated many charms which would injure, perhaps fatally, anyone who harmed him.[20] The Akikuyu frequently ascribe an evil occult influence to old women, especially those who are blind, toothless, or decrepit.[21] In the Bongo tribe of the Anglo-Egyptian Sudan old people of both sexes, but especially old women, are readily suspected of sorcery. Whenever any vigorous man in the prime of life dies suddenly, they are held responsible; he could not have perished, the people think, unless he had been a victim of black magic. So the supposed sorcerers are killed off, with the result that few of the Bongo live to be very old.[22] When several young men in an Ibibio family die one after another, suspicion is likely to fall on a very aged person who has been drawing out "the strength of their young limbs and the breath of their nostrils" to keep himself alive. He will be killed.[23] By the Chorotí of the Bolivian Gran Chaco old men are supposed to be endowed with especially strong powers of magic, and for this reason they are not allowed to die a natural death. When weak and sickly the people kill them and burn their bodies, together with all their possessions. The Chorotí say that were an old man permitted to end his days in peace he would, after death, become an evil spirit and kill everybody. His premature violent death prevents such a transformation.[24]

People who have undergone some unusual experience or have survived accidents normally fatal in character, are supposed to be natural-born magicians. A black-fellow belonging to a tribe in Victoria once sat upon the wrong end of the limb of a gum tree which he was cutting. When it fell to the ground, he fell with it but got up unhurt. His apparent invulnerability resulted in his prompt recognition as a magic worker.[25] Among the Bannar of French Indo-China a person who becomes feverish and ill after eating frogs, mice, or other articles of food entirely harmless to ordinary folk is clearly marked out for the magical profession. He (or she) then repairs to a regular practitioner for a formal initiation into it.[26] The Andamanese believe that a sick man who becomes unconscious and seemingly dies, but afterward revives, acquires the nature and occult power of a spirit.[27] Among the Barundi a man generally inherits the magical art from his father. But anyone who has had some momentous experience, particularly an unexpected deliverance from grave danger and death, can become a magician.[28] Among the Bororó of Brazil the man who can hold out longest in their bouts of drinking palm wine is adjudged worthiest to officiate in a magical capacity.[29] It is said that the Moxo (Mojo) of northern Bolivia designated for the office of magician and priest only those persons who had been attacked and wounded by a jaguar, an animal worshiped by these Indians.[30] A precisely contrary opinion was entertained by the Itonama Indians, who also worshiped the jaguar. When a man during a long journey had not been attacked by this animal he was appointed a priest, "because he was considered to be favored by God." Such a person acted as a healer; he also had to know the names of all the jaguars in his territory.[31] The Aymará of Peru distinguished a special class of magicians whose "grace and virtue" were derived from thunder. A person who had recovered from a shock of lightning would proclaim "how the thunder had revealed to him the art of curing by herbs and how to give replies to those who consulted him."[32] An Apache woman became a magician because she escaped from a lightning stroke and also from the clutches of a mountain lion.[33] A Pima was chosen for the magical office because he recovered from a rattlesnake bite.[34] It is a common belief of the Zuñi that people who recover after being struck or shocked by lightning are qualified to become magicians. Such people must first be properly doctored. They drink some rain water which fell during the storm and eat some black beetle and salt.[35] One of the best-known of the Hopi medicine men became a curer after he was struck by lightning and later dreamed that the cloud deities had thus imbued him with some of their power.[36] In British Columbia an Indian who recovers from a fit in which he remained unconscious and motionless so long that he was thought to have died is deemed competent to be a healer. It is believed that while seemingly dead he had received "supernatural power" for dealing with diseases and had shown an ability to resist the effects of "bad medicine" or the attack of an evil spirit.[37]

Twins (and triplets), being abnormal, are often regarded as highly dangerous to the community, and in many parts of the world they are put to death immediately after birth. Not infrequently their mothers meet the same fate. Some peoples take precisely the opposite attitude toward twins, deeming them bearers of good fortune rather than of evil, and treating them with respect and even reverence. Such twins, it is believed, have marvelous powers. They can produce rain or drought, a heavy wind or a great calm; because of their prolific virtue they can multiply food animals and plants; they also make successful diviners. Their parents, particularly the mother, may share these powers with them. In short, twins are born magicians and are naturally marked out for a professional career, sometimes only in childhood but in other cases also during adult life.

Taboos affecting twins are occasionally found in Australia and widely in the Pacific area, but no magical functions seem to be ascribed to them. In Ceylon a sprained limb can be cured if the mother of twins secretly tramples the limb in the evening for two days.[38] The Hindus of the Central Provinces in India believe that a twin can save the crops from rain and hail if only he will paint the right buttock black and the left buttock some other color and will then go and stand in the direction of the storm.[39]

In Africa twins often act as magicians. The Zulu think that twins are scarcely human and that their birth is something entirely outside the ordinary course of nature. They are so clever that grown-up people bring their quarrels to a twin child for settlement and consult him almost as though he were a diviner. Being fearless and wild, a twin in wartime was placed right in front of the attacking army. All the goats belonging to a twin are supposed to have young in couples. Twins can foretell the weather. People who want rain will go to a twin and say, "Tell me, do you feel ill today?" If he replies that he feels quite well they know it will not rain.[40] On the other hand, the Bathonga very generally look upon the arrival of two or three babies at the same time as a great misfortune, a defilement which can only be removed by special rites of purification. They are now allowed to live, but in former days the feebler of the two was strangled or left to die of starvation. The intimate relation of the mother and her offspring to Heaven, or the sky, is clearly seen in the rain customs. The day following the birth of twins is a rest day. Nobody tills the ground, in fear that to do so would prevent the rain from falling. To end a drought people put a mother of twins into a hole and on her pour water up to her breasts. This will produce a rainfall. The graves of twins are watered, in order to get rain. Twins are buried in damp places; if it happens that their bodies lie in dry ground these are exhumed in a time of drought. When lightning threatens a village the people say to a twin, "Help us! You are a Child of Heaven! You can therefore cope with Heaven; it will hear you when you speak." So the child prays to Heaven to go and roar far away. When the thunderstorm has passed, the child is thanked. The child's mother can help in the same way. When caterpillars swarm in the bean fields, the people about Delagoa Bay pick them off the bean stalks and then have a twin girl throw them into a neighboring lake. In the minds of the natives the appearance of the pests is mysteriously connected with Heaven; hence the "water cure" for their depredations.[41] The Bomvana believe that twins can drive away hail. A hut inhabited by them is safe from lightning.[42] In Northern Rhodesia, when a pigeon cote is erected, the natives get a woman who has borne twins to drive the first stakes. This is done, they say, in order that the pigeons may multiply.[43]

The Baganda regarded the birth of twins as due to the direct intervention of the god Mukasa. Any sickness which befell them was looked upon as the result of the god's anger, which might extend to the whole clan. Twins always took Mukasa's name and came under his special protection. He also favored their parents and through them dispensed blessings wherever the father and mother went on ceremonial visits. People who were thus honored "thought that, not only they themselves would be blessed and given children, but that their herds and crops also would be multiplied."[44] Among the Basoga, when a woman bears twins, the people to whose clan she belongs do not sow any seed until the children have been brought to the field to witness the sowing. The field planted is then said to be the field of the twins. The mother of twins, who has thus given proof of her fecundity, must always sow her seed before any other member of her clan.[45] Among the Bateso, a Nilotic tribe of Uganda, the birth of twins is a welcome event. It is followed by ceremonial visits of the father to members of his own and of his wife's clans. From them he receives presents of food and animals for the feast to be held when the twins are formally presented to the clans. Should no hospitality be offered to him when making the round of visits, the father does not enter the house but passes on elsewhere. "This is regarded by its occupants as a loss, because the blessing of increase which rests upon the father of twins is not communicated to the inhospitable family."[46] The Lango, another Nilotic tribe of Uganda, think that twins bring good luck, not only for the family and clan of the parents, but also for the whole village. The same auspicious character attaches to triplets.[47]

The Igarra of southern Nigeria believe that twins are able to prognosticate with regard to the offspring of a pregnant woman, but they can exert this divinatory power only when young. Twins are never poisoned, for no poison would have any ill effect upon them.[48] By the Yoruba no phenomenon is invested with greater importance or with deeper mystery than that of twin births. Twins are "almost credited" with extrahuman powers, and the influence of their birth is exerted even upon single children that may be born after them.[49] There is a general belief in northern Togo that twins are the offspring of mischief-loving dwarfs. They retain their occult nature until the arrival of puberty, when they assume their proper human characteristics and lose to a certain extent the magical powers with which their fairy fathers had endowed them.[50] The Negroes of Sherbro Island, Sierra Leone, resort to twin children for dealing with various complaints. Women, particularly, seek their aid in cases of pregnancy or absence of pregnancy. Potent medicines are administered by them in "twin houses" set up for the purpose in the bush.[51] The Kpelle of Liberia think that twins possess from birth an abnormal influence and hence can do wonders, even surpassing those performed by medicine men. Twins enjoy an exceptional position, being treated with respect not unmixed with fear, and many gifts are made to them to gain their good will.[52] The Manja of French Equatorial Africa believe that twins exercise a mysterious control over snakes and scorpions. A person stung by a scorpion can at once be healed if the first finger of a twin is placed on the wound. Twins themselves never fear snake bite or scorpion sting. With the help of their animal intermediaries twins can hurl curses or kill parents who mistreat them.[53]

Similar ideas as to the magical powers of twins find expression among the North American Indians. The Hopi believe that twins can cure urinary or digestive complaints, but only when young.[54] In Laguna Pueblo it is thought that if twins are crossed in their wishes they will do some harm to the person who has vexed them.

When twelve years old they are made to drink water mixed with dirt and urine; then they lose their ability to inflict evil.[55]

Some of the southeastern tribes, including the Natchez and Cherokee, considered that the younger of twins was likely to make a good prophet. Triplets made still better prophets.[56] The Iroquois believe that twins can foretell future events and do other remarkable things, but they lose their powers if a menstruating woman prepares their food.[57]

Among the British Columbia tribes twins assume great prominence. The Thompson Indians call them "grizzly-bear children" or "hairy feet," because a pregnant woman is generally made aware of their approaching birth by the repeated appearance of the grizzly bear in her dreams. Twins are supposed to be under the protection of this animal and to be endowed by it with special powers, such as the ability to create good or bad weather. The birth of twins brings about an immediate change of the weather.[58] The Shuswap endow twins with power over the elements, especially over rain and snow. "If a twin bathed in a lake or stream, it would rain."[59] The Bellacoola hold the salmon responsible for the birth of twins. In former days many twins could assume the salmon form at will; they could also understand the speech of fish, birds, and land animals.[60] Kwakiutl twins can bring a wished-for snowfall, rain, or good weather. Their magical powers are also exerted by their parents. A mother (or father) of twins, sitting in a boat, performs a simple ceremony to cause a wind at sea. If the route is southward, she turns her face to the north and moves her hands around to the south, saying, as she does so, "I call you, Northwest Wind!" The movement and the words are repeated three times. Then she adds, "Paddle away from the Northwest Wind!" The mother of twins is also able to dissipate a fog.[61] By the Nootka twins are regarded as somehow related to salmon. Their birth prognosticates a good salmon year. Should the fish fail to come in large numbers, the twins will soon die. They are never allowed to catch salmon and may not eat or even handle these when freshly caught. Twins are able to make fair or foul weather by painting their faces black and then washing them; they can even do so merely by shaking their heads.[62]

The belief that it is possible to cast a baleful look upon a man or his possessions exists in full vigor among many peoples of the lower culture and, with no essential variation, among the primitive-minded in civilized lands. The origin of the belief must surely be sought in the expressiveness of the human glance, which seems to concentrate the whole potentiality of a person and makes him all the more potent if his eyes are in any way remarkable, for instance, by being crossed, or squinting, or differently colored, or with double pupils. But any physical peculiarity, whether of beauty or of ugliness, may suffice as evidence of the possession of the evil eye. This dread power is sometimes supposed to be exerted voluntarily, in which case its injurious effects may be intensified by gestures or speech. More commonly it works involuntarily or even without the knowledge of its possessor.

The belief under consideration seems to be absent, or nearly so, from Australia.[63] It is found in New Guinea. There are Orokaiva sorcerers who need only fix an eye on an intended victim to make him fall sick.[64] The belief is also found in the Melanesian Islands. In Eddystone Island, one of the Solomons, a *njiama,* a man with the evil eye, causes a throat disease, hemorrhage, and rapid death. He is said to eat a person's insides. Sometimes he attacks animals. His murderous influence is fitful, being dependent upon the spirit of a deceased *njiama.* This spirit roams about the bush and consumes the throats of men, causing them to vomit blood. A person who would act as a *njiama* first goes into a trance and converses with his familiar spirit. He then feels tired and sleepy, has a headache and fever, and rolls his eyeballs in a way that strikes terror to beholders. His powers are marvelous. He can change into a fish if he wants to bathe or into a bird if he would fly away; with a look he kills fish, brings down coconuts, and fells trees; he can even eat dynamite as another person would eat sugar, but otherwise his diet is quite normal. In former days he would have been clubbed to death; now the natives must tolerate his depredations.[65] The natives of the New Hebrides think that the evil eye penetrates most readily through the openings of the body, in particular, the genitals. For that reason men are very careful to keep the penis and women the vulva well covered.[66] In Ambryn Island a man with a "fish" eye, an eye opaque and white like that of a boiled fish, is feared as a dangerous fellow.[67]

In Samoa a certain "high priest and prophet" was greatly feared. "If he looked at a coconut tree it died, and if he glanced at a breadfruit tree it withered away."[68] A Maori sorcerer could blast shrubs and trees by looking at them; he could even strike people dead by his fatal glance.[69]

An Italian traveler in northern New Guinea was asked by some Alfuro (aborigines of Celebes and the Moluccas) to leave their village as soon as possible. "Our sons began to die," they said to him, "so soon as you came and looked at them. Five died in three days. It is you who have killed them with your eyes. Depart, or all the rest will perish."[70] In Amboina certain people, by anointing their eyes daily with various ingredients, can increase their sharpness of vision and acquire a "warm eye." They are greatly feared because by concentration of look they can make anyone ill and change good food into poison.[71] The Ifugao, a non-Christian tribe of northern Luzon, believe that certain persons have an evil "cut" of the eye, which brings misfortune or sickness on whomsoever or whatsoever they see. The injury may be effected intentionally or unintentionally. In the latter case no punishment is inflicted on the perpetrator. This affliction can be cured if its possessor offers a sacrifice of the proper sort.[72]

Among the Shans of Burma people with a reputation for the possession of the evil eye are shunned by their neighbors and often expelled from the village.[73] In Malabar, where fear of the evil eye is prevalent, people tell of fine buildings that have fallen down and ripe fruits and grain crops that have withered all because of being "overlooked" by someone with the fatal gift.[74] The aborigines of Chota Nagpur think that not only some human beings but also some animals possess the evil eye and by a glance can cause disease and death. The Oraon and Munda wear iron rings and arm bands which have been previously exposed to the air during an eclipse of the sun. With these charms they can oppose to the evil eye of witches and the evil attentions of ghosts and spirits a resistance as strong as that of the eclipse-hardened iron.[75] The Toda have a well-defined belief in the evil eye, which is called by them "if looking anxiously." One of its commonest effects is indigestion, hence no one wants to be seen eating. A person suffering from the effects of the evil eye can be cured by a magical specialist, who puts salt and a certain kind of thorn into a fire and recites an incantation in the presence of the patient. The magician may also practice "absent treatment" if he is unable to visit the sick man. In this case he puts the salt on the ground, strokes it with the thorn, and recites the necessary incantation. The salt is then sent to the sufferer, by whom it is eaten. All this must be done three times for the treatment to be efficacious.[76]

The Ba-ila of Northern Rhodesia believe that there is "something baneful" in the direct glance. A person who stares fixedly at another is supposed to be planning, or actually causing, some evil to befall him; such a person is called "hard-eyed."[77] A Masai suspected of producing sickness in men or animals by the evil eye must not be seen in the neighborhood of the village kraal. Everybody avoids him. He lives in his own enclosure. Should he visit a strange settlement he would probably be killed.[78] The Suk also compel the possessor of the evil eye to live by himself. Children must not see him and adults, as a protective measure, spit when passing him by. It is believed that if he looks at an ox he can bring about the death of the owner's child.[79] According to Nandi belief such a person can cause children and calves to fall sick and pregnant women and cows to abort. Spitting is a protective measure with the Nandi, as with the Suk, but it must be done by the possessor of the evil eye upon the approach of a person or an animal that might be harmed by contact with him.[80]

Similar ideas are entertained by the Akikuyu and the Akamba.[81] The Wachagga of Mount Kilimanjaro attribute the possession of the evil eye to strangers and also to their own people, especially those who are old and whose eyelids are inflamed.[82] According to the belief of the Jaluo or Nilotic Kavirondo a glance of the evil eye can make a well man sick. It can even kill a man who is ill or an unborn child.[83]

The belief in the evil eye seems to be universal among Nilotic peoples of the Anglo-Egyptian Sudan.[84] The Bari-speaking tribes believe that monorchids are the most dangerous possessors of this power.[85] The Shilluk think that the evil eye is possessed by old women, widows left childless, homely men, and men who through their own fault have made a failure of their lives. All these persons, it is held, are consumed by envy of their more fortunate fellows.[86] According to another account of the Shilluk belief the power of the evil eye can be inherited. It is also acquired suddenly by some people. They do not know how it comes. While those who have it cannot always be distinguished from normal individuals, one with eyes in which the whites are small and the irises are large in proportion and very dark is pretty likely to possess the power. Unfortunately some who have it are not so marked, and some who are so marked lack it. A man endowed with the evil eye is aware of the fact. The evil eye operates when its possessor looks fixedly at an intended victim. He is usually in an envious or jealous mood or is angry at the time, so that his pernicious influence really emanates from his whole personality, not from his eye alone. The bewitched person says that the eye has gone into him. For relief he seeks out a medicine man, who heats a nail and with it blinds a sheep. This procedure not only cures the patient but also typifies what will happen to the person who cast the baleful glance. If the latter's eyes do not become inflamed forthwith it is obvious that the treatment has not been successful.[87]

The Bomitaba of the Belgian Congo, while recognizing that a person may sometimes die naturally after a long illness, do not admit the same explanation of a sudden death. The deceased has come to his end either by the action of a spirit or of a living enemy. In the former case nothing can be done. In the latter case it is necessary to find someone who cast an evil eye with mortal effects upon the victim. A person thus accused must undergo the poison ordeal to establish his innocence or else, admitting his guilt, flee the village.[88] In northern Nigeria, where the evil eye is very much feared, the food of chiefs and priests is often prepared and eaten in secret, as a precaution against the malicious glance of sorcerers. The Nigerian custom, by which chiefs used to speak from behind curtains, is explained by some natives as a precaution against the evil eye of their subjects, though some would say that it was to protect subjects from that of the chief. The Hausa have a proverb, "The eye is poison."[89]

By the Rwala Bedouin of northern Arabia a man who lacks both upper eyeteeth or who has blue eyes is carefully avoided as the possessor of the evil eye. Such a man is sometimes strong enough to bring down a bird from the air by his mere glance.[90]

Instances of the belief under consideration seem to be rare in aboriginal America, thus affording a marked contrast to its prevalence in the Old World. It is said to be entertained by the Araucanians of southern Chile.[91] The Indians of Nicaragua supposed that certain people had a deadly look, which was especially dangerous to children.[92] All sorcerers among the Chorti of Guatemala possess the evil eye and infect others with it out of mere spite or jealousy.[93] A similar conception is found among the Cuicatec, a tribe in the Mexican state of Oaxaca.[94] Belief in the evil eye is familiar to the Navaho Indians, especially among women of the tribe.[95] There was once a Cheyenne medicine man who could kill persons by his mere glance. He had to use great caution, consequently, to keep from injuring his friends.[96] A Shuswap magician can kill a person merely by looking at him.[97] The Tsetsaut of British Columbia have a legend of a man who married his sister. This act of incest apparently conferred upon him the power of killing everything by a glance. One day he killed every member of his tribe. After this murderous exploit he traveled all over the world and left many signs of his presence, such as remarkable rocks.[98] We are told of the fate of an Eskimo sorcerer in Greenland, who suffered death according to the "old customs." He was first harpooned and eviscerated, then a flap was let down from his forehead "to cover his eyes and prevent his seeing again." He had, it would seem, the evil eye.[99]

The evil tongue may be a natural endowment of certain persons, as much so, in fact, as the evil eye. If an Ifugao, afflicted with the "blasting word," goes into a neighbor's house and, seeing a sow with a litter of pigs, remarks, "That's a fine litter of pigs you have!" the animals are sure to die. Yet the possessor of this power might be without intent to do injury, might be even ignorant that he had this fatal power.[100] By the Malays of the Peninsula an evil influence is believed to affect children who are taken notice of by people kindly disposed toward them. It is unlucky, for instance, to remark on the fatness or healthiness of a baby.[101] The Toda suppose that various misfortunes will happen to a man if a person remarks on how well he is looking or how well he is dressed. Bad luck also results from declaring that a man's buffalo gives much milk; the animal will probably kick her calf or will suffer in some way soon after the words have been spoken. The ill effects of such unseemly statements can be removed, however, by appropriate treatment and the recital of incantations.[102]

Among the Akikuyu, if you audibly admire a neighbor's cow and shortly afterward it falls sick, and if this misfortune happens several times, so that people can compare notes, you are likely to be credited with the possession of the evil tongue. A medicine man cannot remove the affliction which the culprit has caused; only the latter can do so and then only in the morning before he eats any food. Should such an ill-wisher admire a pregnant woman she will have a miscarriage. If she is not pregnant his expressed admiration will cause her breasts to become highly inflamed. He must then rub a little of his saliva on them to remove the swelling. Should he admire some object, a spear for instance, it will soon afterward be broken; if his admiration is for the leather-covered sheath of a sword, it will probably be gnawed by rats and spoilt. The possession of this fatal gift is looked upon as an unavoidable misfortune; consequently if death or loss occurs by its exercise the person to whom it is attributable cannot be sued for compensation before the council of elders. In time the Akikuyu get to know the people who have it. When one of them enters a village he will be asked in a friendly way to spit ceremonially on all the children to prevent any injury happening to them from his visit. A father who possesses the power can preserve his children against its action either from himself or from any other person by shutting his eyes and then ceremonially spitting into the mouth of each child.[103] Among the Akamba, if a person possessing the evil tongue sees an object and says, "This is good," or words to that effect, it is sure to be destroyed. A living creature so referred to is doomed to perish. He who has the power in question can ward off its influence by spitting on the object or person affected. There is an entire clan of which every member has both the evil eye and the evil tongue. The clansfolk are often sought out to cure burns and bruises by spitting on the wound.[104]

The Hausa immediately resent any expression of admiration. The praising of a woman's beauty by any man except her husband is a serious injury. The proper reply to complimentary remarks, however sincerely made, is, "I don't care, do you hear?"[105]

Mental peculiarities may distinguish the magician from his fellows. He discloses hypnotic power over himself or over others, evinces a capacity for ecstatic experiences, or is subject to hysteria, convulsive actions, and epileptic seizures, ending, perhaps, in some form of permanent insanity. Hence he is often endowed with the special knowledge and special powers required for a healer, wonder-worker, diviner, and prophet.

The people of Niue or Savage Island looked upon a magician as god-inspired. Anyone liable to epileptic fits or a victim of temporary insanity was marked out for the magical profession. This tended to be confined, therefore, to certain families which were "afflicted with a high degree of mental instability." In the old days fakers seem to have been unknown, nor were delusions fostered by artificial means.[106] In Samoa epileptics became diviners.[107] Of some Indonesian peoples, including the Batak of Sumatra, it is said that by preference they select weak or sickly persons for the office of magician.[108] Among the Subanun of Mindanao the magician of marked success is usually a neurasthenic and eccentric person. He is often recognized by his neighbors as "verging upon insanity." However, their respect for him and confidence in him are not thereby lessened. It is perfectly reasonable, they think, that a man of power in spiritual things, one who can have visions, hear the voice of supernatural beings, and at times be possessed by a spirit, should be weak in the practical concerns of daily life.[109]

The magician among the Sema Naga is essentially a seer, a dreamer, a clairvoyant. "Second sight he no doubt often has in some degree or other, and since it is an intermittent gift, he must simulate it when absent, for the sake of his reputation, and descend to deception just as a European medium does." He is in a measure possessed and has fits "somewhat resembling epilepsy."[110] An anthropologist, working among the Andaman Islanders, met a man seemingly "subject to epileptic fits." He was regarded by the natives as a great magician.[111]

Most Akamba magicians evince at times such shyness and nervousness that a European observer would pronounce them to be mentally deficient. The natives certainly regard them as imbeciles in ordinary matters. "The more proficient they are in their art the less sane are they held to be."[112] Among the Lotuko a person is usually marked out to become a magician if he has some physical peculiarity, for instance, a humped back or a limping gait, or gives signs, real or fictitious, of madness. He separates himself from human society and goes to live in the forest for several months before taking up the duties of his profession.[113]

By the Bachwa Pygmies of the Belgian Congo, epileptics and albinos are regarded as being more powerful magically than normal people. Our authority on these Pygmies met an epileptic boy, "little more than a child," who was declared to be the most formidable magician in the district. Everybody exhibited much aversion to meeting him.[114] The Nkundu believe that epileptics possess tremendous occult power, or *elima*. [115] By the Bangala of the Upper Congo "half-daft persons" and those who had recovered from insanity were regarded with much fear. They were often spoken of as being powerful magicians.[116]

By the Ibo of southern Nigeria certain persons are said to possess *agwu*. They sit very quietly and preferably alone; they act "childishly" and point to objects while calling them by name; occasionally they may be seen trembling at the knees or gnashing their teeth; they are also believed to be sexually impotent. Inherited *agwu*, that for which an ancestral spirit is responsible, can never be cured, though a doctor is able to afford some temporary relief to a patient afflicted with it. *Agwu* may also be acquired voluntarily, since a person with this mental disease is supposed to possess desirable occult power. All doctors, for example, obtain it in order to perform the duties of their profession, and persons who dance or wrestle professionally and need great physical strength likewise desire to be endowed with it. Initiation into certain secret societies, controlled by the spirits who cause *agwu*, is the regular means of acquiring it. Such acquisition is only temporary, however, and the power thus gained may sometimes be "spoiled" or neutralized by certain ceremonies. The Ibo carefully distinguish this type of abnormal behavior from *ala,* which is a condition of permanent lunacy.[117]

The Patagonian Indians are said to choose their magicians from children who have the St. Vitus dance. According to another account of these Indians a boy or a girl, "if what we should call odd," is considered by them to be naturally marked out for the magical office.[118] Among the Araucanians the magician, "through his training, mode of life, and natural temperament, is generally a person of a highly strung, nervous disposition, to whom the faculty of throwing himself into a cataleptic or hypnotic trance is a second nature."[119] Some Lengua magicians appear able to hypnotize themselves by sitting in a strained position for hours and fixing their gaze upon some distant object. While in this state they are believed to see visions and to send out their souls from their bodies.[120] The Karayá of eastern Brazil believe that nervous people and epileptics are peculiarly qualified for the magical profession.[121] Among the Guiana tribes the office of magician seems to be hereditary and to pass from a father to his eldest son. We are told, however, that if there should be no son to succeed his father the members of the magical fraternity choose and train some other boy for the profession, "one with an epileptic tendency being preferred."[122] Curers and other "wise men" among the Chorti Indians of Guatemala exhibit a slight strain of insanity. This peculiarity the people consider to be natural and proper for those who engage in occult pursuits.[123]

An Apache youth may enter the magical profession if he can convince his friends that he possesses an "intense personality."[124] Among the Achomawi Indians of northern California almost all the medicine men seem to be of a highly neurotic temperament. They are persons who feel themselves impelled by an inner urge, which they cannot resist, to become magicians.[125] Candidates for the magical office among the Haida are chosen by the whole body of magicians. A youth exhibiting "psychic gifts" is generally selected.[126] In eastern Greenland only dreamers, visionaries, and people of an hysterical disposition become magicians.[127]

Among the Koriak of Siberia those who rank as magicians are usually "nervous young men subject to hysterical fits." Their wild paroxysms alternate with a condition of complete exhaustion, when they will lie motionless for two or three days, neither eating nor drinking. Finally they retire to the wilderness and there endure privations, in order to prepare themselves for their profession. The Chukchi magicians with whom a Russian anthropologist had intercourse were as a rule "extremely excitable, almost hysterical, and not a few of them were half-crazy. Their cunning in the use of deceit in their art closely resembled the cunning of a lunatic." Among the Giliak of Sakhalin Island magicians are nearly always persons who suffer from hysteria in one form or another.[128]

There are still other persons and groups of persons with inherent occult power for good or ill. For instance, in southeastern Australia, where each tribe consists of two exogamous intermarrying classes (moieties), an occult influence is ascribed to members of one class which is injurious to those of the other. Thus among the Wurunjerri of Victoria, when people of the two classes were camped at the same fire, a man would not touch a stick belonging to a man of the opposite class, lest his fingers should swell. If this happened, he went to a magician, who drew out the evil which had thus lodged in his hand.[129] Among the Arunta of Central Australia a man is careful not to let certain relatives by marriage see what he is eating lest they project their "smell" into the food and spoil it. Should he eat an animal which has been killed by one of these relatives its meat would disagree with him and he would become very ill.[130] Among the Anula the magical profession is hereditary in the members of the Falling-star totemic group, who are especially associated with unfriendly spirits living in the sky. The Anula magician is a sorcerer rather than a doctor, since he can hurt but cannot heal.[131] In Mer, one of the eastern islands of Torres Straits, all the inhabitants belonged, or could belong, to one or other of the two sections of the community. The Zagareb section alone had the power of making rain and of performing certain kinds of private magic, while the Beizam le section enjoyed the exclusive privilege of practicing certain kinds of divination.[132] In Mabuiag, one of the western islands of Torres Straits, members of the Dog clan were supposed to have great sympathy with dogs, to understand their habits better than other men, and to exercise a special control over them.[133] Among the Trobrianders certain magical rites and spells are confined to a special subclan. Though transmitted in the female line, they are usually carried out by men alone. This exclusive magic forms one of the most valued possessions of the subclan.[134]

There are persons among the Keraki of the Morehead District, Papua, who can cause their blood to pass from them into people with whom they come into contact. The transmission is particularly liable to happen when they are overheated by exertion. A man with this uncanny power will, if he feels hot, warn his friends not to sit too close to him until he cools down. The power is quite profitable to those who possess it, for they alone can cure the ailments which it causes. Some natives profess their inability to control the transmissive process, but others acknowledge that they acquire it by swallowing certain large ants and chewing secret medicines.[135]

In the island of Mala (Malaita) in the Solomons, the inland people are supposed to have much more *mana* than dwellers on the coast. The "prayers" uttered by them to the ghosts for help in battle, for the cure of sickness, and for abundant crops are especially efficacious. They are so "hot" (*saka*) that when one of them visits a coastal community he dares not spread out his fingers as if pointing, for to point the finger at anybody is equivalent to shooting him with a charm. The person so indicated would be in danger of death. If he spat on a person the latter would die at once.[136] In the Banks Islands some men possess a mysterious potency "which the natives find it difficult to explain." This is their *uqa*. Suppose you sleep in a strange man's habitual sleeping place during his absence and afterward become ill, you know then that the *uqa* of the stranger is responsible for your trouble. Suppose, again, that you leave an associate and go elsewhere to sleep, still you will be followed and struck by the *uqa* of the man you have left. You rise in the morning feeling weak and languid; if you were unwell before now you will be worse. Although there is no witchcraft in all this a person must pay money to the injured party for what his *uqa* has done and by "an act of his will" take off the malignant influence.[137] In Aurora, one of the New Hebrides, a man who wished to catch octopus (*wirita*) would take with him one of the members of the Octopus family to stand on the beach and cry out, "So-and-So wants *wirita*"; then plenty would be taken.[138]

Among the Sea Dayak there are men who can exert "a peculiar magic influence" by which they nullify bad omens. Their faculty is most usefully employed. When a family has received a warning of this sort, something grown on the family farm—a bit of Indian corn, a little mustard, or a few cucumber shoots—is taken to one of the gifted men. He quietly eats it raw and thus appropriates to himself the evil omen. In him it becomes innocuous.[139] With these Dayak the treatment of the sick is not confined to a professional *manang,* or magician. Sometimes a man, "supposed to be lucky," will be called in as a practitioner. He chews a hot and stimulating mixture of betel and pepper leaf and then squirts his saliva over the affected part of the patient's body, meanwhile rubbing it gently with his fingers. This treatment is believed to be most efficacious.[140] The Land Dayak of Sarawak attributed magical power over the rice crop to their English rajah, James Brooke. When he visited a tribe, they would bring to him some of the *padi* seed which was to be sown the next season, so that he might fertilize it by shaking over it the women's necklaces. When he entered a village the women bathed his feet, first in water, then in coconut milk, and lastly in water again. All this water was preserved so that it might be distributed on the farms. Tribes too far off for the rajah's visits would send to him a small piece of cloth and a little gold or silver, and when these objects had been affected with his fertilizing power they would be buried in the rice fields.[141]

In earlier times the Karen of Burma used to drive orphan children from the village and compel them to live by themselves. These unfortunates were credited with the possession of occult powers, probably because a child who managed to survive in the jungle was assumed to be supernaturally protected.[142] The Lakher, a hill tribe of Assam, credit certain persons with the ability to send their souls into other people's bodies and cause a severe stomachache which may result in death. Such an *ahmuo,* as he is called, is always of an envious disposition and anxious to acquire his neighbor's possessions.[143] Among the Angami Naga some persons of both sexes can produce illness in men and animals and bring about other misfortunes as well. Their "occult powers" are exercised not only voluntarily but also involuntarily, "by virtue of an evil influence emanating from them at the waning of the moon."[144] Each village of the Lhota Naga formerly had two chief priests (*puthi*), who took the leading part in all ritual proceedings. Nowadays there is often only one priest in a village. The position is not attractive because of the belief that any verbal mistakes committed by the officiant in the ceremonies will call down upon him divine displeasure. A person chosen to serve as a *puthi* must be one who has never met with certain misfortunes or accidents— must never have been wounded by a wild animal or an enemy, or have been injured by falling from a tree or a rock, or have burnt himself. The welfare of the village is bound up with that of its *puthi*; were he unlucky the village itself would meet with disaster.[145]

Among the Kharia of Chota Nagpur there are persons endowed with a special good luck (*sae*) as respects the rice. A possessor of *sae* is sure to thresh out a much larger proportion of rice grains, with a much smaller proportion of chaff, than any of his neighbors. Unfortunately, some persons can take away a man's *sae* by merely looking at his threshed rice. Those suspected of this wicked practice are not allowed to enter a threshing floor.[146] Certain clans of the Birhor, another jungle tribe of Chota Nagpur, possess specific occult powers, differing according to the region from which the clan ancestors originally came. There are two clans, for instance, whose members can control the weather. If a high wind is coming on, a man of either of these clans has merely to pour a jug of water in front of the tribal encampment and bid the storm turn aside, whereupon it will immediately take a different direction. Again, there is a clan whose members can control the monsoon winds and rain. These will always abate their force when they approach a settlement of the clan in question.[147] Among the Gond, an aboriginal people of Central India, certain persons profess to be able to call tigers from the jungle, to seize them by the ears, and to control their voracity by whispering to them a command not to come near the villages.[148] Toda sorcerers are said to belong only to certain families from which they inherit their dread power of evil-doing.[149]

In the Punjab certain persons, entire families, and even all the inhabitants of certain villages are credited with the power of curing diseases, wounds, sores, and swellings. Their "virtue" has descended to them from some eminent ancestor or has been communicated by some friendly saint or fakir. Contact with one of these gifted persons, without the aid of spells, medicines, or ceremonies, suffices to produce a cure. The healing contact is established by a touch of hand or foot or big toe. It is equally efficacious to eat food cooked by the healer, to drink water from his hand, to be breathed upon or spat upon by him, or to be rubbed by him with earth or ashes. These beliefs are shared by Hindus and Moslems, peasants and vagrants; they are irrespective of race, caste, or creed.[150] A firstborn son in the Punjab can stop a hailstorm by cutting a hailstone with a knife. He can stay a dust storm by standing naked in front of it. He is particularly susceptible to lightning, and for this reason he is not allowed to go outdoors on a rainy day. Snakes become torpid in his presence.[151] Moslems believe that firstborn children can arrest storms by stripping themselves naked and standing on their heads. These remarkable children are also able to stop a rain which may have poured down continuously for days by simply making a cloth candle and burning it.[152]

It is believed by the Ba-ila that certain persons possess *chesha,* a lucky hand for sowing. Consequently their services are in general demand by cultivators of the soil.[153] Members of the Anjilo clan, a division of the Akikuyu, have hyenas as their "obedient slaves." The clansmen can employ their power over these animals most usefully, for instance, to keep them away from the cattle kraal.[154] Members of the Eithaga clan are able to make or withhold the rain. In the latter case they take care not to let the fields of a smith suffer, for though magicians themselves they fear the more potent magic of the workers in iron.[155] Among the Kipsigis, a branch of the Nandi-speaking peoples, the elders of the Toiybi clan are the rain makers. The special relation of this clan to rain is indicated by its secondary totem, the lightning.[156]

The tribes of the Anglo-Egyptian Sudan believe fervently in the good luck or bad luck attaching to certain people. "Thus, if a crop does well one year, the success is often put down to the good luck of the man who planted the ground and the boy who threw the seeds; and the next year these two are hunted for and usually receive a higher wage in order to induce them to help again. If a new man comes to a village, and the rains are bad that year, the failure is debited to the stranger."[157]

Many heathen tribes of northern Nigeria ascribe particular powers of magic to certain families. Among the Waja one family in a village may have the ability to control the weather, another to drive away locusts, and another to deal with rats. The family especially honored by the community has the secrets of a good harvest, and no one may proceed with reaping until its head gives the word to do so. Among the Berom some persons are supposed to possess special powers of preventing a rainfall. Such persons rank as witches, and when the rains are delayed the tribal elders meet to probe into the matter and discover the offender.[158]

Special powers of magic were associated with certain totemic groups of the Omaha Indians. The Bird subclan, when blackbirds devoured the corn, undertook to stop their depredations by chewing some grains of corn and spitting these out over the fields. Members of the Reptile clan dealt effectively with worms which infested the corn. They pounded up some of them with a little corn, made soup of the mixture, and ate it. When the Turtle subclan wished to dissipate a fog they drew the figure of a turtle on the ground and placed upon it small pieces of a red breech-cloth, together with some tobacco. The Wind People, by flapping their blankets, could start a breeze to drive away mosquitoes.[159]

The Klallam of Washington credited the people of a certain village (Elkwa) with a mysterious power over all the other Indians. By merely talking in low tones about a person, who might be as far as fifty miles away, they could summon him and he came. If they talked ill and wished to do evil to anyone thus distant, his eyes were made to whirl "and the evil wish came to pass." They secured this mysterious and dreaded power by washing their hands in the black water which always filled basins in certain rocks far up in the mountains. It was magical (*tamanous*) water.[160]

To early man the processes of iron working must have seemed indeed mysterious, so that both smelting and forging would naturally be invested with an occult character. This attitude would be strengthened by the fact that the art of metallurgy is so often practiced by outsiders, men of strange speech and habits, who keep the secrets of their craft strictly to themselves and form a guild or caste apart. No doubt the various superstitions that from time immemorial have gathered about iron because of its novelty when first introduced, and perhaps because of its observed magnetic power, contributed to the mystery surrounding metallurgy. Iron objects, it is well known, avert the evil eye and serve as amulets against witches, ghosts, demons, and malign influences generally. Such objects also find use as talismans.[161]

By many African peoples smiths are regarded as wonder workers. They may be honored for their possession of occult power, but at the same time they will be greatly dreaded as possible sorcerers. Sometimes smiths serve as medicine men or as priests. The "iron doctor" among the Ba-ila is a most important personage, for without his magic it would be impossible to extract the iron from the ore. Before smelting operations begin, two children, a boy and a girl, are brought from the village and put into the kiln. The doctor gives each a bean, which they are to crack in their mouths. The bean, when cracked, makes a noise, and the men hearing it raise a loud shout. The noise is associated with that of the fire in the kiln and is supposed to conduce to proper smelting.[162] When this operation begins, the doctor spits out upon the ore in the kiln the drugs which he has chewed. The packing of the kiln is done almost entirely by the doctor, who also adds certain medicines, including a piece of an elephant's hide and some feathers of a guinea fowl. They are used because the fire makes loud sounds like those of the animal and the bird and therefore will promote the process of combustion. The fire is taboo and must not be called "fire" but "the fierce one." By being complimented in this way it will burn better.[163]

Among the Akikuyu of Kenya a member of the guild of smiths can place a spell on a patch of forest to prevent anyone from destroying it. If sugar cane is stolen from a garden or goats are stolen out of a village by night, the owner goes to a smith, taking with him the iron necklace or bracelet of a deceased person. The smith heats it in his fire and then severs it with a chisel, saying, "May the thief be cut as I cut this iron!" Or he may take a sword, heat it, and then quench it in water, saying, "May the body of the thief cool as this iron does!" Both spells are equally effective. The culprit will get a terrible cough, become very thin, and gradually fade away. The ordinary native is too afraid of the magic of smiths to steal anything from one of them. In former times smiths were supposed to bewitch people against whom they bore a grudge; they could also afflict an entire village by their sorcery. Even a medicine man has no power over a smith.[164]

The Somali fear the smith not only as a magician but also as an ally of evil spirits. Consequently every effort is made not to antagonize him.[165] No Nandi dares steal anything from a smith, for the owner of the stolen article will heat his furnace and, while blowing his bellows, will curse the thief and surely cause the latter's death.[166] By the Wachagga of Mount Kilimanjaro the smith is regarded with awe as being the maker of deadly weapons, one who has the marvelous power of uniting iron with iron. Since metallurgy is practiced only by certain clans and families, more or less isolated from the tribal life, he is also feared as a worker in things strange and foreign and hence is readily endowed with a magical personality.[167] Among the Lango the manufacture of "rain spears," used in rain making, is confined to smiths of a certain clan. These smiths also make a spear with barbs intended to resemble locusts' wings. It is employed to avert a swarming of the insects.[168] Among the Bari, smiths possess occult powers, and iron plays a large part in warding off and curing sickness.[169] The Bakongo regard the forge of a blacksmith as sacred and they never steal from it. If anyone did so he would contract a severe form of hernia; if anyone was bold enough to sit on the anvil his legs would become swollen.[170] Among the Fang of Gabun the blacksmith of a group of villages is also, as a rule, its medicine man or "priest."[171] By the Tiv of Benue Province, Nigeria, the smithy and every article connected with it are considered to be imbued with occult power. A person who possesses or wears any tool of a smith is amply protected against a witch trying to injure him. The witch would be annihilated by a thunderbolt. Many Tiv chiefs, though not smiths, are careful to keep on hand a complete set of their tools.[172] Teda smiths are credited with the ability to prepare magic potions and with other black arts.[173] By the Bambara of the French Sudan the smiths, who form a class apart, are regarded as possessors of "supernatural" power and as being in constant intercourse with the spirits. Smiths are rich, for anything they want must be given to them.[174] Smiths among the Tuareg tribes hold a high social position. They rank as both physicians and magicians.[175] In Abyssinia smiths are supposed to be sorcerers, with the power of turning themselves into hyenas. "Few people will molest or offend a blacksmith."[176]

Among the Siberian tribes the smith's craft usually passes from father to son. In the ninth generation the smith becomes, automatically, a magician, able to cure diseases and make predictions. His inherited power goes on increasing with the number of ancestors who have been smiths. Spirits are afraid, above all, of the clink of iron and the noise of the bellows. The Yakut have a saying, "Smiths and shamans come out of one nest." They also say, "The wife of a shaman is to be respected; the wife of a smith is worthy of honor."[177] According to the belief of the Buriat, blacksmiths attend black shamans and aid them in the practice of sorcery. The smith makes out of iron a model of the intended victim and then smashes it with his hammer. The man whom the model represented will shortly die.[178]

Inherent occult power likewise belongs to persons regarded as "unclean." Women during pregnancy, at confinement, after confinement, and at menstruation; boys and girls at puberty; newly married couples; widows, widowers, and mourners generally; manslayers; those who have anything to do with the dead (undertakers and gravediggers); and strangers are all in a state of ritual pollution until they have undergone a ceremony of purification. So evil is the influence which they radiate that it has been found necessary to invest them with stringent taboos, not only for their own protection, but for that of the community as well.[179] Inherent occult power also attaches to "sacred" chiefs and other public functionaries, who are surrounded by taboos intended, on the one hand, to safeguard their followers and, on the other hand, to prevent the dispersion of their sacredness by contact with what is common or "profane." The regulations affecting them will be redoubled when the sacred person is held responsible for the growth of the crops, the increase of animals hunted or domesticated, rainfall, and the general well-being of his people. We shall meet many illustrations of the idea that these divine chiefs and kings can control for weal or woe the course of nature.

NOTES TO CHAPTER VI

[1] James Backhouse, *A Narrative of a Visit to the Australian Colonies* (London, 1843), p. 103. The author spent nearly six years in Tasmania, from 1832 to 1838.

[2] Fritz Sarasin, *Ethnologie der Neu-Caledonier und Loyalty-Insulaner* (Munich, 1929), p. 291. A chief of the Belep group, near New Caledonia, was considered a very powerful sorcerer because he possessed an extra finger on both hands (Viellard and Deplanche, in *Revue maritime et coloniale*, VI [1862], 78).

[3] S. Ella, in *Report of the Fourth Meeting of the Australasian Association for the Advancement of Science* (1892), pp. 622 and note, 638.

[4] Hans Schinz, *Deutsch-Südwest-Afrika* (Oldenburg, 1891), p. 314.

[5] Mrs. Eileen J. Krige and J. D. Krige, *The Realm of a Rain Queen* (London, 1943), p. 269.

[6] P. Cayzac, "La religion des Kikuyu (Afrique Orientale)," *Anthropos,* V (1910), 311.

[7] C. W. Hobley, *Bantu Beliefs and Magic* (London, 1922), pp. 158 ff.

[8] E. E. Evans-Pritchard, *Witchcraft, Oracles, and Magic among the Azande* (Oxford, 1937), pp. 57 ff.

[9] C. G. Seligman and Brenda Z. Seligman, *Pagan Tribes of the Nilotic Sudan* (London, 1932), p. 99. A Shilluk father who does not kill a monorchid child is held responsible for all the evil done by it when grown up. (D. S. Oyler, in *Sudan Notes and Records* II [1919], 130).

[10] C. Delhaise, *Les Warega (Congo Belge),* (Brussels, 1909), p. 154.

[11] J. L. Wilson, *Western Africa* (London, 1856), p. 311; W. Winwood Reade, *Savage Africa* (New York, 1864), p. 413. In Senegambia, where occult power is also attributed to albinos, they are regarded as sorcerers and are killed without compunction (Cornelio Doelter, *Über die Kapverden nach dem Rio Grande und Futah-Djallon* [2d ed., Leipzig, 1888], p. 182).

[12] R. M. Connolly, "Social Life in Fanti-land," *Journal of the Anthropological Institute,* XXVI (1897), 150.

[13] P. A. Talbot, *The Peoples of Southern Nigeria* (London, 1926), II, 208.

[14] *Idem, Tribes of the Niger Delta* (London, 1932), p. 109.

[15] Franz Wolf, in *Anthropos,* VII (1912), 86.

[16] Peter Jones, *History of the Ojebway Indians* (London, 1861), pp. 145 f. Our authority (a full-blooded Ojibwa) adds that all persons esteemed witches are, as a rule "remarkably wicked, of a ragged appearance and forbidding countenance" (*loc. cit.*).

[17] Julius Jetté, "On the Medicine Men of the Ten'a," *Journal of the Royal Anthropological Institute,* XXXVII (1907), 165.

[18] Middleton Smith, "Superstitions of the Eskimo," in Rudolf Kersting (editor), *The White World* (New York, 1902), p. 126.

[19] Mrs. Eileen J. Krige and J. D. Krige, *op. cit.,* p. 269.

[20] E. W. Smith and A. M. Dale, *The Ila-speaking Peoples of Northern Rhodesia* (London, 1920), I, 416 f.

[21] C. W. Hobley, *op. cit.*, p. 195.

[22] Georg Schweinfurth, *The Heart of Africa* (3d ed., London, 1878), I, 145.

[23] P. A. Talbot, *Life in Southern Nigeria* (London, 1923), p. 145.

[24] Rafael Karsten, *The Civilization of the South American Indians* (London, 1926), p. 481, note 1.

[25] R. B. Smyth, *The Aborigines of Victoria* (Melbourne, 1878), I, 465.

[26] Guerlach, in *Les missions Catholiques*, XIX (1887), 514.

[27] A. R. Radcliffe-Brown, *The Andaman Islanders* (Cambridge, 1933), pp. 176 f. The author met a man who was said to have died and been restored to mortal existence no less than three times. Another man during a serious illness lay unconscious for twelve hours, so that his friends thought that he was dead (p. 177).

[28] Hans Meyer, *Die Barundi* (Leipzig, 1916), p. 130.

[29] Karl von den Steinen, *Unter den Naturvölkern Zentral-Brasiliens* (Berlin, 1894), p. 491.

[30] Robert Southey, *History of Brazil* (London, 1817–19), III, 202. Cf. Alcide d'Orbigny, *L'homme américain de l'Amérique méridionale* (Paris, 1839), II, 235. We are also told that a Moxo who had suffered an accident depriving him momentarily of his senses became a magician. He then underwent a year of severe abstinence. At the end of this time the juice of certain pungent herbs was infused into his eyes, to purge his "mortal sight." (See Alfred Métraux, in *Bulletin of the Bureau of American Ethnology*, No. 134, pp. 76 f.

[31] T. J. Hutchinson, in *Transactions of the Ethnological Society of London* (n.s., 1865), III, 323.

[32] C. R. Markham, *Narratives of the Rites and Laws of the Yncas* (London, 1873), p. 14, citing Cristóbal de Molina.

[33]. J. G. Bourke, "The Medicine-Men of the Apache," *Ninth Annual Report of the Bureau of Ethnology*, p. 456.

[34] Frank Russell, in *Twenty-sixth Annual Report of the Bureau of American Ethnology*, p. 257.

[35] Elsie C. Parsons, "A Few Zuñi Death Beliefs and Practices," *American Anthropologist* (n.s., 1916), XVIII, 249.

[36] Mischa Titiev, "Notes on Hopi Witchcraft," *Papers of the Michigan Academy of Science, Arts, and Letters*, XXVIII (1942), 552.

[37] R. C. Mayne, *Four Years in British Columbia and Vancouver Island* (London, 1862), p. 289, quoting the Rev. Mr. Duncan.

[38] A. A. Perera, "Glimpses of Singhalese Social Life," *The Indian Antiquary*, XXXIII (1904), 57.

[39] M. N. Venketswami, "Superstitions among Hindus in the Central Provinces," *ibid.*, XXVIII (1899), 111.

[40] Dudley Kidd, *Savage Childhood* (London, 1906), pp. 45 ff. The author's account of Zulu beliefs relating to twins was obtained from a chief's son, a twin.

[41] H. A. Junod, *The Life of a South African Tribe* (2d ed., London, 1927), II, 433–42. The Bavenda of the northern Transvaal, who kill both twins, place the bodies in one pot and bury it in a damp place by the side of a river. If this is not done, it is feared that there will be a drought (H. A. Stayt, *The Bavenda* [London, 1931], pp. 91, 310).

[42] P. A. W. Cook, *Social Organization and Ceremonial Institutions of the Bomvana* (Cape Town and Johannesburg, 1931), p. 103.

[43] Cullen Gouldsbury and Hubert Shean, *The Great Plateau of Northern Rhodesia* (London, 1911), pp. 307 f. "There is a native woman I know who has had twins three times, and she is in great demand for laying the foundations of pigeon and chicken houses, goat and sheep pens, and even a cattle kraal" (Dugald Campbell, *In the Heart of Bantuland* [London, 1922], p. 155).

[44] John Roscoe, *The Baganda* (London, 1911), pp. 64-73.

[45] *Idem, The Northern Bantu* (Cambridge, 1915), p. 235.

[46] *Ibid.*, p. 265.

[47] J. H. Driberg, *The Lango* (London, 1923), pp. 142 ff.

[48] A. G. Leonard, *The Lower Niger and Its Tribes* (London, 1906), p. 463.

[49] Samuel Johnson, *The History of the Yorubas* (London, 1921), p. 80.

[50] A. W. Cardinall, *Tales Told in Togoland* (London, 1931), pp. 85 f.

[51] T. J. Alldridge, *The Sherbro and Its Hinterland* (London, 1901), pp. 149 ff.

[52] Diedrich Westermann, *Die Kpelle* (Göttingen, 1921), pp. 68, 212, 355. Twins are magic children throughout Liberia. Parents never chastise them. Anyone who struck them on the hand would soon die. Their help is sought in cases of illness, hence nearly all become doctors (J. Büttikofer, *Reisebilder aus Liberia* [Leiden, 1890], II, 317).

[53] A. M. Vergiat, *Mœurs et coutumes des Manjas* (Paris, 1937), pp. 48 ff. The Bambara believe that a scorpion will not hurt twins, but that it will sting anyone whom they hold a grudge (Joseph Henry, *L'âme d'un peuple Africain. Les Bambara* [Münster in Westphalen, 1910], p. 98). Hausa twins are supposed to be able to pick up scorpions without injury, "but I have seen others do it who were not twins" (A. J. N. Tremearne, *Hausa Superstitions and Customs* [London, 1913], p. 94).

[54] Elsie C. Parsons, *Pueblo Indian Religion* (Chicago, 1939), II, 1055, note.

[55] Franz Boas, in *Publications of the American Ethnological Society*, Vol. VIII, Pt. I, p. 298.

[56] J. R. Swanton, in *Forty-second Annual Report of the Bureau of American Ethnology*, p. 615. Among the Cherokee, children destined by their parents to become sorcerers are usually twins. For twenty-four days after birth they must be fed, not their mother's milk, but the liquid portion of corn hominy, and they must be kept rigidly excluded from all visitors. Such twin children are marvelously endowed: they can fly through the air, dive underground, and walk on the sunrays. They can assume all human and animal shapes conceivable. A boy twin is a most successful hunter, and a girl twin is expert in all woman's work. When they are grown up they are most pernicious persons, able to make you dejected, lovesick, ill, or even in a dying condition merely by thinking of you in one of these states. "Whatever they think happens." The only way of protecting the community from their depredations is to work magic against them during the period of their seclusion. This cannot be done with success later, for at the end of the twenty-four days they have the full power of sorcerers. See James Mooney and F. M. Olbrechts, in *Bulletin of the Bureau of American Ethnology*, No. 99, pp. 130 ff.

[57] F. W. Waugh, *Iroquois Foods and Food Preparation* (Ottawa, 1916), p. 59. *Geological Survey Memoir*, No. 86.

[58] James Teit, in *Memoirs of the American Museum of Natural History*, II, 310 f., 374. The Lillooet believe that twins are the real offspring of grizzly bears. Many of these Indians say that twins are grizzly bears in human form and that when a twin dies his soul goes back to them and becomes one of them (James Teit, *ibid.*, IV, 263).

[59] James Teit, *ibid.*, IV, 586 f.

60 Erna Gunther, "A Further Analysis of the First Salmon Ceremony," *University of Washington Publications in Anthropology*, II, 171.

61 Franz Boas, in *Thirty-fifth Annual Report of the Bureau of American Ethnology*, Part I, pp. 631 ff. The twins were considered the children of salmon or transformed salmon. They were not allowed, when young, to go near the water lest they should return to the fish form (*idem*, in *Report of the Fifty-ninth Meeting of the British Association for the Advancement of Science* [1889], p. 847).

62 *Idem*, in *Report of the Sixtieth Meeting of the British Association for the Advancement of Science* (1890), pp. 59 f. By the Songish of Vancouver Island twins were supposed to possess "supernatural powers" at their birth. They were at once taken to the woods and washed in a pond in order to give them a normal personality (p. 574).

63 It is said that Tasmanian magicians could destroy "numbers" by means of the evil eye (James Bonwick, *Daily Life and Origin of the Tasmanians* [London, 1870], p. 177). The Kurnai of Victoria believed that the white man could do marvelous things by a mere glance, such as suddenly drawing together the two banks of a river or instantly flashing death to a beholder (A. W. Howitt and Lorimer Fison, *Kamilaroi and Kurnai* [Melbourne, 1880], pp. 248 f.).

64 F. E. Williams, Orokaiva Magic (Oxford, 1930), p. 180, and note 1.

65 A. M. Hocart, "Medicine and Witchcraft in Eddystone of the Solomons," *Journal of the Royal Anthropological Institute*, LV (1925), 231 f.

66 Felix Speiser, *Ethnographische Materialien aus den Neuen Hebriden und den Banks-Inseln* (Berlin, 1923), pp. 368 f.

In the New Hebrides men wrap the penis (but not the testicles) in many yards of calico or some other material, thus making a bundle as much as two feet long and needing to be supported from the waist band. (B. T. Somerville, in *Journal of the Anthropological Institute*, XXIII [1894], 368). It seems probable that a magical purpose accounts for the sole article of clothing worn by the Tapiro pygmies of Netherlands New Guinea. This is a large case, made of a gourd and enclosing the penis. It sometimes measures over fifteen inches in length (or more than a fourth of the pygmy's height). The natives are extremely unwilling to expose themselves without this protection. See A. F. R. Wollaston, *Pygmies and Papuans* [London, 1912], pp. 161 f., 198 f. Penis envelopes, worn not only as a natural protection but also to keep off "supernatural evils," are found among many Brazilian tribes. See Rafael Karsten, *op. cit.*, pp. 150 f.

67 Robert Lamb, *Saints and Savages* (Edinburgh, 1905), p. 273.

68 George Turner, *Samoa* (London, 1884), p. 23.

69 J. W. Stack, in *Report of the Third Meeting of the Australasian Association for the Advancement of Science* (1891), p. 384. We are told of a celebrated sorcerer, living on the Waikato River, that his shadow could blast trees not protected against it, while if it fell on men paddling on the river they stiffened and died. Hence they gave up traveling by canoes as long as he lived. No one dared kill him (A. S. Thomson, *The Story of New Zealand* [London, 1859], I, 118).

70 L. M. d'Albertis, *New Guinea* (London, 1880), I, 53.

71 J. G. F. Riedel, *De sluik-en-kroesharige rassen tusschen Selebes en Papua* (The Hague, 1886), p. 61.

72 R. F. Barton, "Ifugao Law," *University of California Publications in American Archaeology and Ethnology*, XV, 70.

73 Mrs. Leslie Milne, *Shans at Home* (London, 1910), p. 194.

74 Edgar Thurston, *Ethnographic Notes in Southern India* (Madras, 1907), p. 255, quoting S. A. Iyer. On the belief in the evil eye in northern India see

William Crooke, *Religion and Folklore of Northern India* (London, 1926), pp. 276–307. See also J. Abbott, *The Keys of Power* (London, 1932), pp. 116–48.

[75] S. C. Roy, *The Oraons of Chota Nagpur* (Ranchi, India, 1915), pp. 332, 341. To divert the evil eye of spirits or of socerers a cultivator sets up a wooden pole in the center of his field. On the pole he hangs upside down an earthen vessel with its bottom painted black and white. These colors attract the evil eye and thus keep it from blasting the crops (p. 344).

[76] W. H. R. Rivers, *The Todas* (London, 1906), pp. 263 ff.

[77] E. W. Smith and A. M. Dale, *op. cit.*, I, 224.

[78] M. Merker, *Die Masai* (Berlin, 1904), p. 203.

[79] M. W. H. Beech, *The Suk* (Oxford, 1911), p. 25.

[80] A. C. Hollis, *The Nandi* (Oxford, 1909), p. 90. Among the Kipsigis, a branch of the Nandi-speaking peoples, the power of the evil eye is hereditary and may belong to either sex. It is usually manifested by a woman of a very jealous disposition. She cannot see anyone who is healthy or prosperous without wanting to cast a spell on him (J. G. Peristiany, *The Social Institutions of the Kipsigis* [London, 1939], p. 226).

[81] C. W. Hobley, *op. cit.*, p. 177; Charles Dundas, "History of Kitui," *Journal of the Royal Anthropological Institute*, XLIII (1913), 534.

[82] O. F. Raum, *Chaga Childhood* (London, 1940), p. 111, note 1.

[83] G. A. S. Northcote, in *Journal of the Royal Anthropological Institute*, XXXVII (1907), 64.

[84] C. G. Seligman and Brenda Z. Seligman, *op. cit.*, pp. 99 f. (Shilluk), 112 (Anuak), 128 f. (Acholi), 193 f. (Dinka), 251 (Bari), 486 (Moro).

[85] *Idem*, in *Journal of the Royal Anthropological Institute*, LVIII (1928), 437.

[86] Wilhelm Hofmayr, *Die Schilluk* (Mödling bei Wien, 1925), p. 221.

[87] D. S. Oyler, "The Shilluk's Belief in the Evil Eye. The Evil Medicine Men," *Sudan Notes and Records*, II (1919), 123 ff.

[88] E. Darré, in *Revue d'ethnographie et des traditions populaires*, III (1922), 320 f.

[89] C. K. Meek, "The Meaning of the Cowrie; the Evil Eye in Nigeria," *Man*, XLI (1941), 48.

[90] Alois Musil, *The Manners and Customs of the Rwalla Bedouins* (New York, 1928), pp. 408 f. On the evil eye in Morocco and North Africa generally see Edward Westermarck, *Ritual and Belief in Morocco* (London, 1926), I, 414–78. In this part of the Arab world it is difficult to distinguish between dread of the evil eye and fear of the *jnūn* (*jinni*), or spirits. The misfortunes caused by the evil eye and by spirits are largely the same, and so are the charms for protective or aversive purposes (I, 388 f.).

[91] E. R. Smith, *The Araucanians* (New York, 1855), p. 230.

[92] E. G. Squier, "Observations on the Archaeology and Ethnology of Nicaragua," *Transactions of the American Ethnological Society*, Vol. III, Pt. I (1853), p. 142; H. Beuchat, *Manuel d'archéologie Américaine* (Paris, 1912), p. 401 (Niquirans).

[93] Charles Wisdom, *The Chorti Indians of Guatemala* (Chicago, 1940), pp. 326 f.

[94] J. B. Johnson, *The Elements of Mazatec Witchcraft* (Göteborg, Sweden, 1939), p. 138. *Ethnological Studies*, No. 9.

[95] William Morgan, *Human Wolves among the Navaho* (New Haven, 1936), p. 39. *Yale Publications in Anthropology*, No. 11.

[96] G. B. Grinnell, *The Cheyenne Indians* (New Haven, 1923), II, 145.

[97] James Teit, in *Memoirs of the American Museum of Natural History*, IV, 616.

[98] Franz Boas, in *Report of the Sixty-fifth Meeting of the British Association for the Advancement of Science* (1895), p. 565.

[99] Elisha Kent Kane, *Arctic Explorations* (Philadelphia, 1856), II, 127.

[100] R. F. Barton, "Ifugao Law," *University of California Publications in American Archaeology and Ethnology*, XV, 70.

[101] W. E. Maxwell, "Folk-Lore of the Malays," *Journal of the Straits Branch of the Royal Asiatic Society*, No. 7 (1881), pp. 27 f.

[102] W. H. R. Rivers, *op. cit.*, pp. 263 ff.

[103] C. W. Hobley, *op. cit.*, pp. 177 f.

[104] Charles Dundas, "History of Kitui," *Journal of the Royal Anthropological Institute*, XLIII (1913), 534.

[105] A. J. N. Tremearne, *Hausa Superstitions and Customs*, p. 161; idem, *The Ban of the Bori* (London, 1914), p. 174.

[106] E. M. Loeb, "The Shaman of Niue," *American Anthropologist* (n.s., 1924), XXVI, 395.

[107] S. Ella, in *Report of the Fourth Meeting of the Australasian Association for the Advancement of Science* (1892), p. 638.

[108] G. A. Wilken, "Het shamanisme bij de volken van den Indischen Archipel," in *Verspreide Geschriften* (The Hague, 1912), III, 376.

[109] E. B. Christie, *The Subanuns of Sindangan Bay* (Manila, 1909), p. 71. *Philippine Bureau of Science, Division of Ethnology Publications*, Vol. VI, Pt. I.

[110] J. H. Hutton, *The Sema Nagas* (London, 1921), p. 247.

[111] A. R. Radcliffe-Brown, *op. cit.*, p. 177. According to E. H. Man epileptic fits are not considered "in a superstitious light" by the Andamanese (*On the Aboriginal Inhabitants of the Andaman Islands* [London, 1932], p. 15; idem, in *Journal of the Anthropological Institute*, XII [1883], 83).

[112] Charles Dundas, "History of Kitui," *Journal of the Royal Anthropological Institute*, XLIII (1913), 533 f. The Akamba choose boys of a neurotic temperament for the magical profession (Gerhard Lindblom, *The Akamba in British East Africa* [2d ed., Uppsala, 1920], p. 254).

[113] L. Molinaro, "Appunti cerca gli usi, costumi, e idee religiose dei Lotuko dell'Uganda," *Anthropos*, XXXV–XXXVI (1940–41), 199.

[114] Paul Schebesta, *My Pygmy and Negro Hosts* (London, 1936), p. 240.

[115] *Ibid.*, p. 263.

[116] J. H. Weeks, in *Journal of the Royal Anthropological Institute*, XXXIX (1909), 130.

[117] H. A. Wieschoff, "Concepts of Abnormality among the Ibo of Nigeria," *Journal of the American Oriental Society*, LXIII (1943), 262 ff.

[118] Thomas Falkner, *A Description of Patagonia* (Hereford, 1774), p. 117; G. C. Musters, *At Home with the Patagonians* (2d ed., London, 1873), p. 191.

[119] R. E. Latcham, in *Journal of the Royal Anthropological Institute*, XXXIX (1909), 346. Cf. J. Nippgen, "La religion, les superstitions, la magie, et la sorcellerie des Araucaniens," *Ethnographie* (n.s., 1914), No. 4, p. 61.

[120] W. B. Grubb, *An Unknown People in an Unknown Land* (4th ed., London, 1914), p. 146.

[121] P. Ehrenreich, *Beiträge zur Völkerkunde Brasiliens* (Berlin, 1891), p. 33.

[122] Sir E. F. im Thurn, *Among the Indians of Guiana* (London, 1883), p. 334.

[123] Charles Wisdom, *op. cit.*, p. 346. Our authority points out that since

174   MAGIC: A SOCIOLOGICAL STUDY

mental and emotional peculiarities suggest that their possessor is a possible sorcerer the community attitude toward him may convince him that he really is a sorcerer. This is most likely to happen if he is markedly antisocial and given to doing strange things which the people neither understand nor approve (pp. 334 f.).

124 J. G. Bourke, "The Medicine-Man of the Apache," *Ninth Annual Report of the Bureau of Ethnology*, pp. 452 f. Many magicians are old and in their dotage, yet the Apache, who have great reverence for "feeble-minded and crazy" people, believe everything they say, and credit them with extraordinary powers (A. B. Reagan, in *Anthropological Papers of the American Museum of Natural History*, XXXI, 306).

125 Jaime de Angulo, "La psychologie religieuse des Achumawi," *Anthropos*, XXIII (1928), 582.

126 Charles Harrison, *Ancient Warriors of the North Pacific* (London, 1925), p. 99.

127 William Thalbitzer, "Les magiciens Esquimaux," *Journal de la Société des Américanistes de Paris* (n.s., 1930), XXII, 77.

128 W. Jochelson, in *Memoirs of the American Museum of Natural History*, X, 47; W. Bogoras, *ibid.*, XI, 415; Leo (L. J.) Sternberg, "Die Religion der Giljaken," *Archiv für Religionswissenschaft*, VIII (1904–1905), 462 ff.

129 A. W. Howitt, *The Native Tribes of South-East Australia* (London, 1904), p. 401. In the Wakelbura tribe of Queensland a magician, when acting in a professional capacity, used only objects of the same class as himself. The Wakelbura thought of everything in nature as attached to one or other of the two classes into which the tribe was divided (pp. 113, 399).

130 Sir Baldwin Spencer and F. J. Gillen, *The Native Tribes of Central Australia* (London, 1899), p. 469.

131 *Iidem, The Northern Tribes of Central Australia* (London, 1904), pp. 488 f. The sorcery of the Anula magicians consists solely in the use of the pointing bone to kill people. Their association with falling stars is probably to be explained by the belief of another tribe, the Wotjobaluk of Victoria, who, when they see a falling star, think that it is falling with the heart of a man who has been "boned" by a sorcerer (Howitt, *op. cit.*, p. 369).

132 W. H. R. Rivers, in *Reports of the Cambridge Anthropological Expedition to Torres Straits*, VI, 175.

133 A. C. Haddon, in *Journal of the Anthropological Institute*, XIX (1890), 325, 393.

134 Bronislaw Malinowski, *The Sexual Life of Savages in North-West Melanesia* (New York, 1929), pp. 41, 48.

135 F. E. Williams, *Papuans of the Trans-Fly* (Oxford, 1936), pp. 350 f.

136 R. H. Codrington, "Religious Beliefs and Practices in Melanesia," *Journal of the Anthropological Institute*, X (1881), 301 f.; *idem, The Melanesians* (Oxford, 1891), p. 192.

137 R. H. Codrington, *op. cit.*, pp. 222 f.

138 *Ibid.*, p. 26.

139 J. Perham, "Sea Dyak Religion," *Journal of the Straits Branch of the Royal Asiatic Society*, No. 10 (1882), 232. An omen is frequently regarded, not only as prognostic of good or bad luck, but also as a cause of the foreshadowed event; in such a case an evil omen can sometimes be manipulated so as to nullify its malefic effect or turn it to a beneficial end. A Maori who met a lizard in his path would kill it, spit on it, and then burn the pieces in order to avert the evil omen (Elsdon Best, *The Maori* [Wellington, New Zealand, 1924], I, 275). When

the Borneans, paddling down the river, hear the note of a hawk on the wrong side they feel sure this betokens some imminent disaster. At once they turn the boat about, pull to the bank, and light a fire. "By turning round they put the hawk on the right side, and being satisfied in their own minds they proceed on their journey as before" (A. C. Haddon, *Head-Hunters, Black, White and Brown* [London, 1901], p. 387). Among some of the tribes of Manipur, if a man on a journey meets a mole, he tries to kill the unlucky animal (T. C. Hodson, *The Native Tribes of Manipur* [London, 1911], p. 132). Among the Kuraver, a predatory tribe or caste of southern India, if a person gives up his journey because of certain signs observed on the way, and then sees the same signs while he is coming back, "the ill omens become good omens, and it is safe for him to return and carry out his purpose and commit his crime" (W. J. Hatch, *The Land Pirates of India* [London, 1928], p. 99). The Tanala of Madagascar believe that the future is determined by fate, yet they repose the utmost faith in the efficacy of charms. Even when the course of events has been determined by divination, "the future can nearly always be modified by the proper magic" (Ralph Linton, *The Tanala* [Chicago, 1933], pp. 217 f.). The Bakgatla regard the behavior of cattle in certain instances as ominous of ill fortune. If a cow lies down, curls its tail, and then beats it on the ground continuously, this "forebodes evil." Unless the animal is caught and quickly killed the owner or one of his relatives will die. It is another bad omen when a cow drinks its own urine or bellows like a bull, but here, again, killing the animal averts the threatened danger (I. Schapera, "Herding Rites of the Bechuanaland Bakxatla," *American Anthropologist* [n.s., 1934], XXXVI, 581). Among the Akikuyu it is unlucky for a woman to sleep with her leather blanket inside out, but the consequences of doing so may be avoided if she spits on the ground (a lucky action) and turns the garment the right way. The Akikuyu have an idea that a child born feet first and regarded, therefore, as a bearer of bad fortune, should never step over a person lying on the ground. If he does so, he must at once step back over the recumbent figure before him (C. W. Hobley, *op. cit.*, pp. 117, 158). The Bangala of the Upper Congo consider that the repetition rather than the reversal of an unlucky action is the appropriate procedure to avoid its injurious effect. For them to kick a person is equivalent to cursing him. When this has been done accidentally, the offender must turn around and slightly kick again the person touched, who otherwise would certainly meet with some misfortune (J. H. Weeks, *Among Congo Cannibals* [London, 1913], p. 300). The Timne of Sierra Leone believe that if a "spider" (probably a beetle is meant) beats its "drum" in a man's ear one of his relatives will die. The "drumming" is regarded, not as simply ominous, but as itself bringing about the death. In this case no sacrifice or other propitiatory measure avails to avert a fatal result: the omen cannot be manipulated (N. W. Thomas, *Anthropological Report on Sierra Leone*, Part I [London, 1916], p. 71). A Cherokee Indian, who has dreamed of being bitten by a snake, will be treated in the same way as if he had actually been bitten. Otherwise the place supposed to be affected would swell and ulcerate in the usual manner, though years might pass before this happened (James Mooney, "Sacred Formulas of the Cherokees," *Seventh Annual Report of the Bureau of Ethnology*, p. 352). Omens among the Tinne of southern Alaska "imply an obscure idea of causality, inasmuch as the omen is taken not as merely foreboding what is going to happen, but as being in some manner instrumental in bringing it about." Hence the belief of these Indians that the avoidance of the omen averts the calamity which it threatens. As our missionary authority observes, the same attitude toward omens is displayed by "superstitious whites" (Julius Jetté, "On the Superstitions of the Ten'a Indians," *Anthropos*, VI [1911], 241). Among the pagan Ifugao of northern Luzon favorable omens have the primary purpose of controlling the future; the forecast of the future is secondary. "Thus, the bird omen primarily causes the game to be speared, or causes the enemy to be beheaded, or causes a slave-selling or trading trip to be successful, and is only secondarily a prediction." Hence, as our authority points out, the divinatory rites are "a kind of magic." See R. F. Barton, "The Religion of the Ifugaos," *Memoirs of the American Anthropological Association*, No. 65, p. 206.

140 J. Perham, "Manangism in Borneo," *Journal of the Straits Branch of the Royal Asiatic Society*, No. 19 (1887), p. 87.

141 Hugh Low, *Sarawak* (London, 1848), pp. 259 f.

142 H. M. Marshall, *The Karen People of Burma* (Columbus, Ohio, 1922), pp. 269 f. *Ohio State University Bulletin*, Vol. XXVI, No. 13. Among the Yualayai of New South Wales, Baiame, the high god, will listen to the cry of an orphan child for rain. The child has only to run out of doors when clouds are overhead, look at the sky, and call out, "Water come down. Water come down." If there has been too much rain, the "last possible child" of a woman can stop it by burning *midjeer,* a certain kind of wood (Mrs. K. L. Parker, *The Euahlayi Tribe* [London, 1905], p. 8).

143 N. E. Parry, *The Lakhers* (London, 1932), pp. 462 f.

144 J. H. Hutton, *The Angami Nagas* (London, 1921), p. 243. In Khonoma, described as a typical Angami village, a ceremony to stop rain must be performed by a man who has had no children. All that is necessary is for him to take a dish of water outdoors and boil the water until it evaporates. Then he must say, "Let the days be fine like this," and no rain will fall for seven years. In Kohima village rain-making ceremonies are performed only by a dozen or so families belonging to the *putsa* ("kindred") of a certain clan (p. 236).

145 J. P. Mills, *The Lhota Nagas* (London, 1922), pp. 121 f.

146 S. C. Roy and R. C. Roy, *The Kharias* (Ranchi, India, 1937), II, 408 f.

147 S. C. Roy, *The Birhors* (Ranchi, India, 1925), pp. 108 f.

148 Stephen Hislop, in R. Temple (editor), *Papers Relating to the Aboriginal Tribes of the Central Provinces* (Nagpore, India, 1866), p. 19.

149 W. H. R. Rivers, *op. cit.,* p. 256.

150 Charlotte S. Burne, "Occult Powers of Healing in the Panjab," *Folk-Lore*, XXI (1910), 313–34. The notes on folk medicine in this paper were collected for H. A. Rose by Indian correspondents. We are told that in a Moslem family possessing *barkat* (beneficent occult power) there is a constant struggle as to its inheritance. The eldest son tries to maintain the principle of primogeniture, whereas the younger brethren argue that *barkat* is inherited by all alike, and that they also are saints, competent to cure diseases as was their father, and entitled to share equally in the profits of this lucrative profession. See Audrey O'Brien, "The Mohammedan Saints of the Western Punjab," *Journal of the Royal Anthropological Institute,* XLI (1911), 512.

151 A. J. Rose, in *Folk-Lore,* XIII (1902), 278.

152 *Panjab Notes and Queries,* I (1883–84), 14, 53.

153 E. W. Smith and A. M. Dale, *op. cit.,* I, 139.

154 P. Cayzac, "Witchcraft in Kikuyu," *Man,* XII (1912), 128.

155 C. W. Hobley, *op. cit.,* pp. 165, 178.

156 J. G. Peristiany, *op. cit.,* pp. 228 f. When a heavy thunderstorm occurs it is the duty of the Thunder clan (Toiyoi) to seize an ax, rub it in the ashes of a fire, and then throw it outside the hut, exclaiming at the same time, "Thunder, be silent in our town" (A. C. Hollis, *op. cit.,* pp. 9, 99).

157 H. C. Jackson, "Seed-time and Harvest," *Sudan Notes and Records,* II (1919), 6 f.

158 C. K. Meek, *The Northern Tribes of Nigeria* (London, 1925), II, 41 f., 67 f.

[159] J. O. Dorsey, "Omaha Sociology," *Third Annual Report of the Bureau of Ethnology,* 238 f., 240 f., 248; *idem,* "A Study of Siouan Cults," *Eleventh Annual Report of the Bureau of Ethnology,* p. 410.

[160] Myron Eells, in *Annual Report of the Smithsonian Institution for 1887,* p. 673.

[161] On the use of iron as a charm see W. W. Skeat, *Malay Magic* (London, 1900), pp. 274, 338, 398 (an iron nail protects a new-born child and the rice soul from the powers of evil; a pair of scissors, symbolizing iron, when laid on the breast of a corpse, will scare malignant spirits and keep them at a distance); W. L. Hildburgh, "Notes on Sinhalese Magic," *Journal of the Royal Anthropological Institute,* XXXVIII (1908), 151 (iron abhorred by devils); Edgar Thurston, *Ethnographic Notes in Southern India,* p. 341 (women after childbirth keep a knife or some other iron object in their room and carry it about with them when they go out; people who pass by burning grounds or other haunted places carry a knife or an iron rod); Verrier Elwin, *The Agaria* (Calcutta, 1942), pp. 133, 158 (babies are touched with a red-hot sickle; nails of "virgin iron"—the iron extracted from a new furnace used for the first time— are driven into the doors of houses); Sir H. H. Johnston, in *Journal of the Anthropological Institute,* XV (1886), 8 (a pregnant woman among the Wataveta wears a deep fringe of tiny iron chains hanging over her eyes); Sir A. B. Ellis, *The Yoruba-speaking Peoples of the Slave Coast of West Africa* (London, 1894), p. 113 (iron rings and bells attached to the ankles of a child and iron rings round its neck by their jingling keep away the evil spirits that cause a fatal illness in the young); Arthur Leared, *Morocco and the Moors* (2d ed., London, 1891), p. 269 (an iron knife or dagger under a sick man's pillow protects him against demons).

[162] The choice of a little boy and a little girl to crack the beans would seem to be dictated by their ignorance of sexual matters. The innocence or "coolness" of the children prevents the flame in the kiln from being too fierce and spoiling the whole operation. See H. A. Junod, *op. cit.,* II, 359, note 1. Among the Bathonga a married person must not set fire to the furnace in which the potter (a woman) fires her pots. A married person is "hot" and would cause the fire to become uncontrollable, thus cracking all the pots (II, 358 f.).

[163] E. W. Smith and A. M. Dale, *op. cit.,* I, 203 ff.

[164] C. W. Hobley, *op. cit.,* 167 ff.

[165] G. A. Haggenmacher, in *Petermann's Geographischen Mittheilungen, Ergänzungsheft* No. 47, p. 26.

[166] A. C. Hollis, *op. cit.,* p. 37. In like manner no one dares steal from a potter (a woman), for the next time she heated her wares she would say, "Burst like a pot, and may thy house become red," and the person so cursed would die (p. 36).

[167] Bruno Gutmann, "Der Schmied und seine Kunst im animistischen Denken," *Zeitschrift für Ethnologie,* XLIV (1912), 82 f.

[168] J. H. Driberg, *op. cit.,* pp. 248 f.

[169] C. G. Seligman and Brenda Z. Seligman, *op. cit.,* p. 257.

[170] J. H. Weeks, *Among the Primitive Bakongo* (London, 1914), p. 240.

[171] O. Lenz, *Skizzen aus Westafrika* (Berlin, 1878), pp. 85, 184. Cf. A. Bastian, *Ein Besuch in San Salvador* (Bremen, 1859), p. 161; *idem, Die deutsche Expedition an der Loango-Küste* (Jena, 1874–75), II, 217.

[172] R. C. Abraham, *The Tiv People* (Lagos, Nigeria, 1933), p. 139.

[173] Gustav Nachtigal, *Sahara und Sudan* (Berlin, 1879), I, 443.

174 Gabriel Gravier, *Voyage à Ségou, 1878–1879* (Paris, 1887), pp. 152 f., 448;
Charles Monteil, *Les Bambara du Ségou et du Kaarta* (Paris, 1923), p. 143.

175 Ferdinand Goldstein, in *Globus*, XCII (1907), 187.

176 Mansfield Parkyns, *Life in Abyssinia* (2d ed., London, 1868), pp. 300 f.
Cf. Sir R. F. Burton, *First Footsteps in East Africa* (London, 1856), p. 33, note.

177 W. G. Sumner, "The Yakuts. Abridged from the Russian of Sieroshevski," *Journal of the Anthropological Institute*, XXXI (1900), 104.

178 N. Melnikow, in *Globus*, LXXV (1899), 133.

179 Though "unclean" and hence subjected to rigorous taboos, a pregnant
woman sometimes uses her occult power beneficently. The natives of Nias, an
island to the west of Sumatra, consider it very desirable for fruit trees to be
planted by a pregnant woman because of the fertilizing influence which proceeds
from her (J. P. Kleiweg de Zwaan, *Die Heilkunde der Niasser* [The Hague,
1913], p. 171). The Menangkabau of Sumatra require a woman far advanced
in pregnancy to partake of a feast in a rice barn, obviously because her condition
will help the rice to be fruitful and multiply (J. L. van der Toorn, in *Bijdragen
tot de Taal-Land-en Volkenkunde van Nederlandsch-Indië*, XXXIX [1890], 67).
The Nicobarese think themselves lucky to get a pregnant woman and her husband
to plant seed in the gardens (Sir R. C. Temple, in *Census of India, 1901*, III,
206). Wherever she goes and into whatever house she enters she brings good
luck (W. Svoboda, in *Internationales Archiv für Ethnographie*, V [1892], 193 f.).
Among the Zulu she sometimes grinds corn, which is subsequently burnt among
the half-grown crops in order to fertilize them (Dudley Kidd, *op. cit.*, p. 291).
Among the Coast Yuki of northern California a pregnant woman normally gives
her husband good luck for deer hunting. However, if he meets no success as a
hunter, he will not be allowed to continue, for fear that he spoil the hunting for
everybody (E. W. Gifford, in *Anthropos*, XXXIV [1939], 368). In Greenland
an Eskimo woman in childbed and for sometime thereafter can lay a storm. All
she has to do is to go outdoors, fill her mouth with air, and, coming back into
the house, blow it out again. If she catches rain drops in her mouth there will
be dry weather (Hans Egede, *A Description of Greenland* [2d ed., London,
1818], p. 196, note).

The magical power of menstruous women and menstrual blood is likewise
sometimes regarded, not as maleficent, but as beneficent. The Mountain Arapesh,
a Papuan tribe, believe that a man who sees a *marsalai*, a "supernatural" being
usually embodied in some water creature, will die unless he can get the help of a
woman in her courses. "She either gives him a drink of water in which leaves
stained with menstrual blood have been soaked or she massages his chest or
beats him upon the chest with her closed fist, while he holds aloft his right hand,
the hand which he uses in hunting, to keep 'the power of getting food for children'" (Margaret Mead, in *Anthropological Papers of the American Museum
of Natural History*, XXXVII, 345). In this ceremony the potency of the woman
will exorcise the evil influence possessing the man, but since contact with her is
dangerous it must not be allowed to affect his prowess as a hunter. The procedure described can also be used successfully when a man fears that black
magic has been worked upon him. Another prophylactic measure, doubtless
equally efficacious, is to drink a potion in which leaves, covered with menstrual
blood, have been steeped (*ibid.*, p. 422). The Ainu of Japan consider menstrual
blood to possess a talismanic property, so much so that a man who sees a drop
of it on the floor will wipe it up and rub it over his chest. He will even ask a
menstruous woman to give him a piece of her protective cloth (B. Pilsudski, in
Anthropos, V [1910], 774). The Nama or Namaqua, a Hottentot tribe, take
pains to lead a girl, when menstruating for the first time, round the village.
She touches all the rams in the folds and the milk vessels in the houses (Sir J. E.
Alexander, *Expedition of Discovery into the Interior of Africa* [London, 1838],

I, 169). The Herero also consider that the mysterious influence of a menstruous woman is positively beneficial to cattle. Hence every morning the milk of all the cows is brought to her so that she may consecrate it by touching it with her lips (Hans Schinz, *op. cit.,* p. 167; J. Irle, *Die Herero* [Gütersloh, 1906], p. 94). The Ba-ila of Northern Rhodesia believe that tsetse flies can be driven away if menstruating women will go where the flies are, sit down, and allow themselves to be bitten (E. W. Smith and A. M. Dale, *op. cit.,* II, 27). Among the Bavenda of the Transvaal, before a wife is restored to normal life after her confinement, she is visited ceremonially by her husband, who proceeds to rub on the palms of his hands and the soles of his feet a powder made from menstrual blood. The wife then presents him with a bracelet. If this purificatory rite is not performed, the husband willl be attacked by a shivering disease from which he will not recover (H. A. Stayt, *op. cit.,* p. 88). The Barundi, an East African tribe, instead of secluding a girl at puberty, lead her all over the house and have her touch everything, so that she may bless the objects with which she comes into contact (Oscar Baumann, *Durch Massailand zur Nilquelle* [Berlin, 1894], p. 221). Among the Lillooet of British Columbia, if in winter time the ground was too soft and muddy and the people desired frost, they got a pubescent girl to walk around constantly. Very soon, or within a day or two at the furthest, the ground would freeze and harden. Among the Shuswap one way of obtaining mild weather in winter time was to have a pubescent girl light a fire and heat some stones. When these were nearly red-hot she took them with tongs and threw them into the snow, at the same time uttering a prayer that the weather would become mild and melt the snow "in the manner these stones had done" (James Teit, in *Memoirs of the American Museum of Natural History,* IV, 290, 601). For the Tinne of Alaska menstrual blood has health-preserving and curative properties, because it embodies the principle of life. Hence a mother who has lost several children will require a surviving child to wear a harness made out of a woman's drawers soiled with her blood. Rags thus soiled are steeped in a basin of water, and the liquid will then be used to bathe young children or will be administered to them as an internal remedy. A mother never uses blood which she could obtain from herself, but always gets the soiled rags from another woman. The idea seems to be that her own child has already received from her all the vital power she could impart, so that for the treatment it is necessary to procure an additional store of vitality from someone else (Julius Jetté, "On the Superstitions of the Ten'a Indians," *Anthropos,* VI [1911], pp. 257, 703).

CHAPTER VII

PROFESSIONAL MAGICIANS

THE professional magician may be a medicine man, one who employs material objects (charms or "medicines") endued naturally or by himself with occult power.[1] He also makes use of spells and ritual actions which give effect to his medicines or, at least, add to their potency. For the successful practice of the magical art he often depends upon friendly ghosts or spirits—"helpers"—to whom he owes his special endowments, with whom he is in constant communication, and from whom he regularly receives aid and comfort. The medicine man is the only type of magician in Australia and among the great majority of American Indian tribes, both North and South. He is likewise found, but less commonly, among other primitive peoples in New Guinea, the islands of the Pacific, and Africa.

The professional magician may also be a shaman, temporarily or permanently "possessed" by a spiritual being, who speaks by his mouth and under whose influence he acts.[2] By one means or another the shaman throws himself into a state of hypnosis, a condition of dissociation, in which he has visions that seem to him to be real, enjoys second sight, reveals the future and hidden things, and performs feats that are impossible for ordinary persons in the workaday world. The shaman is the prevailing type of magician in Melanesia, Polynesia, Micronesia, Indonesia, Malaysia, southern India (Dravidians), Africa, and northern Asia, as well as among the Eskimo. His figure also appears among some American Indian tribes.[3]

Typically, medicine men do not exhibit a psychopathic personality. Thus in respect to those of the Arunta and Kaitish tribes in Central Australia we learn that they are "characteristically the reverse of nervous or excitable in temperament"; they are, at the same time, "more highly gifted with imagination than others." Hence they persuade themselves and then their fellows that in dreams they have seen and held converse with the ancestral ghosts.[4] The Ona medicine men of Tierra del Fuego are described as being "spiritually sound," not abnormal psychically.[5] We have seen, however, that a pronounced neurotic character is by no means unusual even among Indian medicine men and, it may be added, this is often strengthened by their use of drugs and in other ways.[6] Just as typically the Siberian shaman is an unadapted person, ill fitted for practical life, more or less introvert, easily excited, given to hallucinations—in short, morbid and hysterical. Yet it is said that the Tungus shaman, who uses artificial methods of falling into a trance and of maintaining it during his performance, must have a sound body and a good nervous system. Otherwise psychical maladies would interfere with his ability to produce an ecstatic condition.[7] Thus we find that medicine men may sometimes exhibit all the mental instability associated with shamans and that shamans may sometimes be as healthy-minded as medicine men.

Not their differing mental endowments but the absence or presence of possession marks off the two great classes of professional magicians, one from the other. It is true that there may be difficulty in determining the reality of this phenomenon. When the magician goes into a trance state, with loss of consciousness, trembling limbs, and other accompaniments seemingly of dissociation, we cannot always be sure that he thinks of himself or is thought of by others as having been actually possessed by a spirit or only as spiritually enlightened. "Come ancestors and make things clear to us!" declares a Tembu diviner in South Africa, as he passes into a trance. But the diviner is not said to be possessed by ancestors. The same ambiguity as to the existence of possession has been noticed among other primitive peoples. Nevertheless, the distinction between medicine men and shamans is fundamental, whether they practice magic which is socially approved or as sorcerers engage in the black art.

The distinction between magicians and priests is equally fundamental. The magician relies upon the exercise of his occult power alone or enlists the aid of spirits subordinate to his will; the priest ordinarily professes humility toward them and adopts the posture and procedure of a suppliant. The one acts in his own name and by his own authority; the other serves as the official representative of the community in its relations with spiritual beings, and often in some sense as a mediator between it and the gods. The performances of the one are, as a rule, simple and confined to narrow circles; whereas public ceremonies of a more or less elaborate character, especially sacrificial rites, come under the direction of the other. The role of the one usually reflects his direct personal experience with the unseen world, while the position of the other depends rather upon the learning and experience acquired by a long apprenticeship. With the development of animism, the recognition of full-fledged gods, and the institution of a complicated ritual of sacrifice and prayer, the dividing line between the magical and priestly offices becomes ever more definite. The magician will be relegated to a minor role, perhaps as faith healer, rain maker, prophet, or interpreter of omens. If magic has become disreputable, an art practiced only in holes and corners, the magician and all his works will be cast into outer darkness.

Among some very rude peoples and others not so rude the functions of magic worker and cult leader are still combined in one person, as originally must have been always the case before the rise of priesthoods. In Australia and New Guinea the medicine man, besides acting as a doctor and at times as a sorcerer, has charge of ritual performances in behalf of the whole group.[8] With reference to the Melanesians generally we are told that "wizards, doctors, weather-mongers, prophets, diviners, dreamers" all work by the power of *mana* and that knowledge of this power is handed down from father to son or from uncle to sister's son "in the same way as is the knowledge of the rites and methods of sacrifice and prayer; and very often the same man who knows the sacrifice knows also the making of the weather, and of charms for many purposes besides."[9] In every village of the Solomon Islands there is one person who leads in "prayers" before the people go out to fish or fight, to plant or harvest the crops; blesses the canoes; heals the sick; and searches out people suspected of practicing sorcery against their neighbors.[10] In the Fiji Islands some magicians, but not all, acted as priests.[11] The ranks of the official priesthood in Tahiti included professional sorcerers (*tahutahu*) of high degree. They were supposed to exercise their malefic arts against the enemies of the community both in it and outside it.[12] Among the Maori the village *tohunga*, essentially a magic worker, controlled or performed all ceremonial acts which were considered important.[13] In Celebes, among the Minahassa and Bugi, the offices of shaman and priest are united.[14] In Nias the magician is also the sacrificer.[15] Among the Kayan of Borneo the *dajung* discharges the duties of both magician and priest, and the same thing is true of other Dayak tribes.[16] Among the Lushai of Assam the *puithiam* ("great knowers") have charge of the sacrifices, but their only training for this priestly rite consists in memorizing the spells which must be uttered by a sacrificer.[17] In northern India, among its more primitive forest peoples, one cannot draw the line between the magician and the priest.[18] Bavenda medicine men perform all sacrificial rites except those carried out once a year at the beginning of the harvest season.[19] Among the Akikuyu they offer the sacrifices and make the prayers when tribal ceremonies are performed.[20] Among the Akamba, on the other hand, while a medicine man usually decides when the time has come to sacrifice to the ancestral ghosts, whose mouthpiece he is, he does not officiate at the sacrifice itself. This is performed by certain old men and women, who thus serve in a priestly capacity.[21] The exercise of magical and priestly functions by the same person is reported of other African peoples, including the Mashona of Southern Rhodesia, the Wagogo of Tanganyika, the Shilluk, and the Fang.[22] In North America magical and priestly functions are sometimes combined, as with the Eskimo and on the Northwest coast (Haida, Tlingit). Among the more advanced tribes of the Eastern plains (Pawnee, Ojibwa) and in the Southwest (Navaho, Apache, Pueblo Indians), magicians are clearly distinguished from priests, though the latter, besides conducting the tribal ritual and preserving the sacred myths, may also cure disease, dispel witchcraft, and bring plentiful supplies of rain. In the Maya-Aztec, Chibcha, and Inca cultural areas there was an organized priesthood, while the class of magicians remained unorganized and in some cases itinerant. Among the more primitive Indians of South America each tribal group usually contains one person who performs all magical and priestly duties.[23] Among the Siberian tribes the shamans take part in public festivals, prayers, and sacrifices. Usually they serve in a subordinate capacity, and there are many ritual performances at which their participation is not essential.[24]

The possession and exercise of occult power is seldom an exclusive privilege of medicine men and shamans, though they possess it more completely and exercise it more constantly than do laymen. In the lower stages of culture every adult person commonly believes that he can work some forms of magic; if he is skeptical of his own ability, he entertains no doubt of his neighbor's competence in this field. Of magical acts which do not require expert aid some are very simple in character. In a magic-ridden community, however, even the acts which ordinary persons can perform, if only they know what to do and have a strong desire to do it, may sometimes be carried out with a considerable degree of elaboration.

The aborigines of Tasmania, now extinct, are said to have had no professional magicians.[25] In northern Queensland it is hard to distinguish between regular practitioners and "quacks," that is, between the recognized magicians and other men, equally sharp-witted, who arrogate to themselves similar powers of working magic.[26] Among the Arunta, Ilpirra, and other tribes of Central Australia any man may have recourse to sorcery, but only medicine men can counteract it. Certain very old practitioners are endowed with the power of bewitching whole groups of people, a power not possessed by other magicians.[27] In the Murngin tribe of the Northern Territory, it is not necessary to be a professional magician in order to make rain. "Anyone can do it, providing he follows the correct procedure."[28]

Among the Elema of the Papuan Gulf, just as every man is his own carpenter, so for the most part he is his own magician. He has magic for fishing, planting, wooing women, and other pursuits. Naturally he keeps it to himself, lest neighbors discover the secret of his success.[29] The Orokaiva have no name for a person who makes white magic but only for him who practices magic of the illicit and antisocial sort. Every man knows and uses white magic, "whether he recognizes it as such or whether it appears to him as common sense."[30] Among the Kiwai Papuans, though every man is his own magician, there is often a marked specialization of magical power. For instance, a person may be able to raise the wind but cannot lay it, while another can summon rain but is unable to stop it.[31] The Koita and Roro-speaking tribes possess much magic which is employed by laymen, in addition to that wielded by "departmental experts."[32] With regard to the Tamo of Astrolabe Bay we are told that any old man can be a magician, but, of course, some men enjoy more reputation than others.[33] In the D'Entrecasteaux Islands no man denies knowledge of white magic. He is proud of what he knows and always anxious to learn more.[34] The Melanesians have no order of magicians any more than an order of priests. Almost every man of consideration possesses some knowledge of secret or occult practices, just as he knows how to approach some ghosts or spirits. The qualification, "of consideration," calls attention to the fact that common folk, not being of account in life, are equally nobodies after death; neither alive nor dead do they have the *mana* which enables them to work magic.[35] While this statement is broadly true, it would appear that in most of the islands any evilly disposed person can make "poison" (black magic) if he or she is familiar with the proper methods. In the New Hebrides, for instance, there is no adult member of the community unacquainted with some form of magic which he performs on occasion, either for his own benefit or for that of others.[36]

Among the Maori the exercise of magical power was not confined to the *tohunga*. There were spells, however, which only those experts employed.[37]

In the island of Flores everyone can use some forms of magic, though only the regular practitioners do so to a great extent.[38] Professional magicians are said to be unknown among the Igorot of northern Luzon; "everyone helps himself."[39]

In the Andaman Islands, while the professional magician has most knowledge of the occult properties of objects, every man and woman knows something about them and by their means treats illness, prevents bad weather, and performs other marvelous acts.[40]

The office of magician is not hereditary among the Babemba of Northern Rhodesia. Old people normally have magical functions by virtue of their position as heads of families.[41] Akamba magic is not a monopoly of professional operators. Most hunters, for instance, know how to concoct the medicine for snaring game.[42] All Azande magic is individually owned. "Princes acquire medicines to attract dependents; women acquire medicines for feminine pursuits; youths acquire medicines for youthful activities; the habitual hunter acquires hunting medicines, the smith medicines for his forge, the consulter of the rubbing-board oracle medicines for his oracle." A man may get someone who owns a medicine to use it on his behalf, or he may obtain actual ownership of a medicine and himself employ it. It thus comes about that every native, except small children, whether old or young, whether man or woman, is to a certain extent a magician. At one time or other in his life an Azande will be sure to use a medicine.[43]

Sorcery, among the Patagonian Indians, is not exclusively practiced by medicine men. Anyone may be suspected of indulging in it.[44] The Araucanians have professional medicine men, but magical functions are not exercised by them alone.[45] Among the Apinayé, a Brazilian tribe, any "half-way adult" person, if evilly disposed, is believed capable of causing illness by witchcraft.[46] Rain magic is very commonly practiced by the Karayá of eastern Brazil. Almost everyone has some knowledge of the art and can improvise the necessary apparatus for producing moisture when the need arises.[47]

Any Apache, man or woman, is a "potential recipient" of occult power.[48] The Navaho say that all people have power for good and power for evil "in some measure," but there are people who have "a good deal."[49] Among the Arapaho the great majority of adult men receive "supernatural" communications and the accompanying power. Consequently a distinct profession of magician hardly exists in this tribe.[50] Since dreamed power is essential for any important public duty among the Yuma the medicine man is not set off sharply from the rest of the community. He may at the same time be a singer, an orator, or a chief. Sorcery is generally practiced by professionals, but sometimes ordinary people bewitch; "they suddenly get the power."[51] The difference between the power of a Yokuts-Mono medicine man and that of a nonprofessional may be described as being of quantity rather than of quality. The spiritual world was accessible to everyone through dream experiences; any person might try to establish contact with it; some persons had more ability to do so than others, and these were the magicians.[52] Of the Southern Maidu it is said that there was nothing which most magicians did which an ordinary man could not do, provided he knew about the various medicines and observed the proper restrictions and prohibitions.[53] In addition to the professional medicine men among the Klallam of Washington, there were always many laymen who had "just a little" occult power.[54] Among the Haida of Queen Charlotte Islands anyone might practice sorcery if he possessed himself of the proper formulas.[55] Among the Tinne Indians of Canada "ordinary mortals" practiced witchcraft.[56] Among the Eskimo of the Mackenzie River "all phenomena are controlled by spirits, and these spirits are controlled by formulae, or charms, which are mainly in possession of the medicine men, although certain simple charms may be owned and used by anyone."[57]

The exclusion of women from priestly activities and, indeed, from all that pertains to sacred rites, symbols, and myths prevails generally in the lower culture. Being ritually unclean, women would defile sacred things. Sometimes, too, it is thought that they themselves might be injured by contact with the occult power resident in what is sacred. As compared with men, they are less able to resist and overcome a dangerous influence which may be harmful as well as helpful, which may kill as well as cure. The disabilities of women in regard to the practice of magic are far less usual; in many cases these are nonexistent.

Instances of women acting as magicians among the southeastern tribes of Australia seem to be very rare.[58] In northern Queensland, though a woman dares not handle or even look upon the pointing-bone, which is used to kill at a distance, she knows and sometimes practices the "trick" of removing by mouth or hand the objects supposed to be inserted by sorcerers in the body of a sick person. She may be a doctor's wife, but even so she is not allowed to join in the secret consultations of the medical practitioners.[59] Among the Arunta and other Central tribes women seldom become doctors. However, certain forms of nefarious magic, pertaining to the sexual organs, are exercised by them. Syphilis in men is very frequently attributed to their machinations. In the Kaitish tribe this sort of magic is used by a wife to punish a man who had unlawful intercourse with her without her consent. A woman may also cause by magic the illness or death of one of her own sex.[60] Among the tribes in the Kimberley Division of Western Australia women by magic can inflict illness on their enemies; its effects, however, are never mortal. They are familiar with the general form of the sorcery rite but not with the songs, which the men alone know.[61]

The Keraki, a tribe of southwestern Papua, have no female practitioners of the various branches of magic such as rain making, divination, doctoring, and sorcery.[62] Among the Gende, women seldom practice the magical art of healing.[63] The Kiwai, however, do not debar women from the exercise of either white or black magic.[64] Among the Mailu every grown-up man has a special magic to make his coconuts and bananas thrive and his fishing ventures successful. It is private property and inalienable. A father transmits it to his son and a husband initiates his wife into its mysteries. Women never inherit magic from their fathers except when there are no male children in a family.[65] By the Suau-Tawala people women are regarded as more capable of magic than men. Any exceptional knowledge or dexterity which a man may exhibit is always attributed to his special initiation by a female magician.[66] Among the Marind of Netherlands New Guinea a woman may enter the magical profession after receiving the necessary instruction from a recognized practitioner.[67]

In the Dobu Island, one of the D'Entrecasteaux group, old women possess the spells which control the winds for rain making, produce hurricanes, and bring these to an end. They keep this superior magic closely to themselves and thus decide whether or not their husbands shall embark safely upon the seas and visit strange ports. Dobuan women also have spells for witchcraft, spells which enable them to fly by night, to kill, to dance upon the graves of their former victims, to disinter the bodies of the slain, and in spirit to feast upon them. The neighboring Trobriand women do not exercise this malignant art; consequently Dobuan men feel themselves safer in the Trobriands than at home. The women of Dobu also have a monopoly of that form of sorcery which produces illness and death by abstracting the victim's soul.[68]

Women in New Britain may obtain spells and charms and use them in the same way as men. Such magical power as women exercise is due to "their reputation as witches who might do harm."[69] It would seem, however, that most magicians are men, as is certainly the case in the Gazelle Peninsula. Here, as elsewhere in the Melanesian area, women cannot belong to the secret societies, which have an intimate connection with the art of magic.[70] In New Ireland both men and women are magicians, though the former predominate.[71] In the islands of Mala (Malaita) and Ulawa, which belong to the Solomons group, the ghosts of women are not regarded as magically powerful, or "hot" (saka), but as magically weak, or "cold" (waa).[72] In the Banks Islands women work healing magic but not magic of the hurtful sort.[73] In the New Hebrides women, as well as men, have controlling spirits which visit them in their sleep and reveal magical secrets to them.[74]

Among the Maori a woman sometimes acted as a tohunga, but apparently she was not allowed to practice the higher branches of the magical profession.[75]

In Celebes old women act as diviners, reading omens from the cries of birds and from the condition of pigs' livers. Women who practice as doctors are not allowed to marry.[76] In Halmahera, the largest of the northern Moluccas, "most of the shamans are women."[77] Among the Batak of Sumatra female magicians are far more numerous than those of the male sex, and in several districts the magicians are always women.[78] On the other hand, men are more commonly magicians than women in the Mentawei Islands.[79] Among the Bagobo of Mindanao and the Tinguian of Luzon the "mediums" or shamans are generally middle-aged or old women.[80] The Negritos of Zambales allow women to be doctors.[81] Among the Kayan of Borneo there are more female magicians than male.[82]

Among some of the Bannar (Bahnar) tribes of French Indo-China women alone are believed to possess the occult power, or *deng,* by virtue of which they act as magicians, but in other tribes only the men have this power.[83] Certain specially favored persons, supposed to be endowed with "supernatural powers," are magicians among the Andamanese. They may be of either sex, though it is more usual for men to become distinguished in this way than for women.[84] Similarly in the Nicobar Islands "female professors" of the magical art, both white and black, are much less numerous than male practitioners.[85] Toda women may not divine or engage in sorcery, but apparently are not debarred from healing functions.[86]

Among the Tanala of Madagascar men are the more numerous practitioners, but some of the most famous *ombiasy* are of the female sex.[87]

In Africa the profession of magician is very often open to women. The magicians of the Bushmen are of either sex.[88] Zulu doctors are mostly married women.[89] Among the Bavenda a man usually inherits knowledge of magic from his father and a woman from her mother. A woman without a daughter may teach her son. Occasionally a normal heir is deprived of his birthright because of a revelation received from the ancestral spirits in a dream.[90] Among the Akamba female magicians are rare.[91] The Jaluo (Nilotic Kavirondo) "seemingly" have no professional medicine men; the only doctors are women.[92] Among the Lango the most competent and renowned magicians have always been women.[93] Most magic is a male prerogative among the Azande. This is partly because so many medicines are associated with the activities of the men. It is also due to the feeling that magic confers a power best kept in men's hands. In so far as women need protection against sorcery they may rely upon the aid of their husbands. They are expected to use only those medicines which are associated with purely feminine pursuits, such as salt-making and beer-brewing, and with childbirth, menstruation, and lactation.[94] There are some male magicians among the Barundi of Ruanda-Urundi (Belgian Congo), but the majority are women, particularly old women.[95] Women occasionally practice the magical art among the Fang of Gabun.[96] Among the Yoruba of the Slave Coast female sorcerers are more common than male sorcerers.[97] This is true, also, of the tribes of southern Nigeria.[98] Among the Nupe, a mixed Moslem-pagan tribe of northern Nigeria, the power of men in practicing the black art is declared to be much weaker than that of women, and the activities of male sorcerers do not call forth an elaborate organization to combat them as is the case with female sorcerers.[99] Among the Ekiti, also, "wizards are by no means as powerful as witches."[100] Female sorcerers are more numerous than their male counterparts among the Bambara and other Sudanese.[101]

There are female magicians among the Ona (Selknam) and the Yahgan (Yámana) of Tierra del Fuego, but they do not enjoy anything like the influence of male practitioners.[102] Among the Abipones of Paraguay the magicians are of both sexes, though "female jugglers," declares our missionary informant, "abound to such a degree that they almost outnumber the gnats of Egypt."[103] While the office of magician may be held by an Araucanian woman, instances of the sort are rare.[104] The Apinayé of Brazil have no female magicians.[105] These are found, however, in other Brazilian tribes.[106] The Arhuaco-speaking Indians of Colombia are without female magicians.[107] Among the Guiana tribes the *piai*, or magician, is occasionally a woman.[108] In ancient Mexico there were both male and female doctors. The former attended men only and the latter, women.[109]

Women acted as magicians among many Indian tribes of North America. In the Southwest they practiced chiefly as midwives and herbalists. The methods of some of them were said to be "quite rational and effectual."[110] The Pima had three orders of magicians. As many women as men belonged to the order of Examining Physicians, who treated disease by magical methods. The second order was that of the Makai (magicians), who had power over the crops, the weather, and warfare. Only one or two women were ever admitted to it. The third order included both men and women. They employed simple empiric remedies for the cure of ailments. Though not highly esteemed, as compared with the other practitioners, they were the true physicians of the tribe.[111] The Havasupai, a Yuman-speaking tribe of Arizona, do not allow a woman to practice magic.[112] There are many medicine women among the Chiricahua Apache.[113] A Cheyenne cannot become a doctor by himself. When he receives the "power" of doctoring, his wife—who is afterward his assistant—must also be taught and be initiated into certain secrets. Should his wife be unwilling to serve in a medical capacity, he must find another women to work with him.[114] A Blackfoot woman helps out her husband in treating the sick.[115] Female magicians among the Paviotso of Nevada are highly respected and are on an equal footing with their male colleagues, though it would seem that men have always been the outstanding practitioners.[116] Among the Pomo of northern California only men receive a call to enter the magical profession, whereas among the Shastika and Klamath Indians the magicians are most often women.[117] Yurok magicians are almost all women.[118] Among the Klallam of Washington women sometimes practiced magic, but they never attained the position held by men.[119] This was the situation, also, among the Shuswap of British Columbia.[120] Tinne medicine men exceed medicine women in the proportions of about five to one. Both sexes are equally admissible, however, to the magical profession.[121]

In the Eskimo area shamanism is predominantly a masculine profession, though female practitioners are by no means unknown. They are found among the Aleuts.[122] Among the Mackenzie River Eskimo some women enjoy an especially high esteem as magicians.[123] The Eskimo of Baffin Land open the profession of magician to both men and women, but only those people with some special qualification, such as the ability to throw themselves into "a perfectly genuine trance," attain the highest dignity.[124] In Greenland the *angakok* might be either a man or a woman.[125]

According to some students only feminine shamanism formerly existed in Siberia, a view which perhaps finds substantiation in traditions among several tribes that the shamanistic gift was first bestowed on women.[126] At the present day, while female shamans are met with, they have nothing like the prestige and power enjoyed by their male counterparts.[127]

It appears from the foregoing evidence that while women almost never serve as magicians in Australia and rarely in the Melanesian and Polynesian areas, their exclusion elsewhere from the magical profession is not common. In Indonesia, Africa, and America female magicians sometimes outnumber their male competitors in a community, though they are seldom the only professional practitioners. On the whole, however, the tendency seems to be to relegate to women such practices as soothsaying, the interpretation of dreams and omens, and the cure of disease by means of simple remedies, and to reserve to men the higher branches of the magical art.

Medicine men and shamans sometimes wear women's dress and act like women. Their abnormality indicates that they are specially endowed with occult power and most effective when they have thus undergone an assumed change of sex. Transvestitism does not seem to have any necessary connection with homosexual practices, though these are frequently found in communities when the custom under consideration is prevalent.

A *manang bali*, among the Sea Dayak of Borneo, is a magician wearing a woman's costume. He has put it on, he will tell you, in obedience to a supernatural command conveyed three times in dreams. If he disregarded the command he would die. Before being permitted to assume female attire he is sexually disabled. People treat him as a woman, and he engages in feminine pursuits. His magical services are in much request and well recompensed. The prospect of inheriting his wealth is enough to induce a man to marry him, in spite of the ridicule of the tribesmen. The "husband's" position is by no means enviable, for the "wife" manifests much jealousy of him and punishes every little infidelity with a fine. The *manang bali*, being a person of great consequence, frequently becomes the chief of a village and acts as a peacemaker in the community. The number and variety of his cures, coupled with the generous use of his wealth, make him a popular figure.[128] In Rambree Island, which lies off the Arakan coast of Burma, a magician sometimes adopts female dress, becomes the "wife" of a colleague, and then acquires a woman as a second wife for the "husband." With this woman both men cohabit. Every respectable native, we are told, looks upon a transvestite "with disgust and honor," a statement implying that, though reprobated as a man, his occult powers are held in high esteem.[129]

Magicians among the Bateso, a Nilotic tribe of Uganda, often dress as women and wear feminine ornaments.[130] A Bangala magician, in a rite to detect a witch, dresses as a woman.[131]

Among the Patagonians male magicians are chosen for their office when they are children, and "a preference is always shown to those who at that early time of life discover an effeminate disposition." Such persons are obliged to dress as women and are not allowed to marry.[132] There are transvestites, who are also homosexuals (*hueye*), among the Araucanian magicians. They wear a skin apron, as a sign of their calling, and women's ornaments. Their hair is long and uncombed. Though formerly much respected, many Indians now despise them.[133]

With reference to the Illinois, a confederation of Algonquian tribes, and the Sioux or Dakota of the Upper Mississippi, we learn from Father Marquette that among these Indians some men assume female dress for life, never marry, do all that is done by women, yet go to war, assist at "juggleries" and dances (singing but not dancing), and attend councils. Nothing is decided without their advice. Because of their extraordinary way of living they are regarded as "manitous," or supernatural beings, and hence are treated as persons of consequence.[134] Transvestites are found among the Arapaho, as also among the Cheyenne, Ute, and many other Plains tribes. They possess "miraculous power," being able, for instance, to make an intoxicating drink from rain water. Their power comes to them from birds and other animals.[135]

Among the Yurok Indians of northern California transvestitism was fairly common. A man usually manifested the first symptoms of his proclivities by beginning to weave baskets; soon he donned female garb and pounded acorns. All *wergern*, as these persons were called, seem to have officiated as magicians.[136] Among the Takelma of Oregon, who allowed both men and women to become magicians, transvestitism seems to have been at least an occasional phenomenon. We are told of an Indian "with man's voice and female attire" who was credited with strong occult powers.[137]

Transvestites enjoyed great consideration among the Koniag of Kodiak Island, Alaska. Most of them were magicians.[138] The Eskimo of Baffin Land and Hudson Bay have a story of an *angakok* who turned himself into a woman and became a very powerful magician. A man saw him rubbing the skin of his face so that it came off and made him look like a woman; the man dropped dead at the sight. Another man, who had not been a successful hunter, married him. When the couple went out hunting the transformed shaman, with his bow and arrows, killed many caribou. In course of time he bore a child.[139]

Among the Chukchi, besides normal shamans, there are special or transformed shamans who pass as women. The assumption of this office is much dreaded by youthful adepts, and some of them prefer death to obeying the call of the spirits. A "soft man" enters upon his profession by several stages. First he personates a woman only in the manner of braiding and arranging his hair. Next comes the adoption of female dress. Finally, he gives up all the pursuits of men, throwing away the rifle and lance, the lasso of the reindeer herdsman, and the harpoon of the seal hunter, and takes to the needle and skin scraper. His body alters, if not in outward appearance, at least in its faculties and forces, and his mental characteristics become more and more those of a woman. The transformation goes so far that he often is taken as a wife by another man, with whom he leads a regular married life. He is supposed to excel in every branch of his profession, including ventriloquism. Ordinary people dread him greatly and even an untransformed shaman avoids having a contest with him. Among his helpful spirits he has a supreme protective spirit, who plays the part of a supernatural husband and head of the family. It is noteworthy that Chukchi women rarely assume the male character.[140]

The legends of the Koriak contain accounts of male and female shamans who changed their sex in obedience to the commands of the spirits. Such persons were reputed to be very powerful.[141] A transformed shaman among the Yakut arranges his hair like a woman and braids it; during a performance he lets the hair down. On his apron are sown two iron circles representing breasts. He wears ordinarily a girl's dress made of the skin of a foal. He may not lie on the right side of a horse-skin; this side is regularly forbidden to women. During the first three days after a confinement, when men are not allowed to be near the woman lying-in, he has access to her house.[142]

It has been pointed out that the idea of "election" lies at the root of the belief in the occult power of a Siberian shaman. This power comes to him from the assistant spirits who are ever at his disposal. But they are not his voluntary servants; their duties have been imposed upon them by a supreme spirit who rules over them and who out of sexual love has chosen someone for the shamanistic profession. If the spirit is of the male sex, he visits the conjugal bed at night and becomes the regular spouse of his earthly lover; if of the female sex, she seeks a male companion. Thus the sex of the shaman's supreme protective spirit depends on the shaman's sex, for they are "like husband and wife." This sexual motive in shamanism has been found among many Siberian tribes in which homosexuality is unknown or else very rare and condemned by public opinion. Among the Chukchi, however, the shaman and the spirit are of the same sex. Homosexuality, being quite usual with the Chukchi, is naturally assumed to prevail also in the spiritual world.[143]

NOTES TO CHAPTER VII

[1] "The fur traders in this country," writes Catlin, "are nearly all French; and in their language a doctor or physician is called '*Médecin.*' The Indian country is full of doctors; and as they are all magicians, and skilled, or profess to be skilled, in many mysteries, the word '*médecin*' has become habitually applied to everything mysterious or unaccountable; and the English and Americans, who are also trading and passing through this country, have easily and familiarly

adopted the same word, with a slight alteration, conveying the same meaning; and to be a little more explicit, they have denominated these personages 'medicine men,' which means something more than merely a doctor or physician. These physicians . . . . are all supposed to deal more or less in mysteries and charms, which are aids and handmaids in their practice" (George Catlin, *Letters and Notes on the Manners, Customs, and Condition of the North American Indians* [2d ed., New York, 1842], Letter No. 6).

² "Shaman," meaning one who is "excited," "exalted," was derived by Russian explorers of Siberia in the seventeenth century from the Tungus form *saman*. The term seems to be of native coinage. It is also current as a borrowed term among the Buriat and Yakut. See Berthold Laufer, "Origin of the Word 'Shaman'," *American Anthropologist* (n.s., 1917), XIX, 361–71. Other names for the shaman are Buriat and Mongol *bo* (*boe*), Yakut *ojun* (*oyum*), Ostiak *senin*, Semoyed *tadebei*, and Altai Tatar *kam*.

³ Instances of true possession and of its accompaniment, genuine shamanism, have been reported among the Bororó of Brazil, Jivaro of Ecuador, Arecuna of Venezuela, Yuma of Arizona, Haida of Queen Charlotte Islands, British Columbia, and Tlingit of southern Alaska. Other instances, as yet unreported, are probably to be found among the South American Indians.

⁴ Sir Baldwin Spencer and F. J. Gillen, *The Native Tribes of Central Australia* (London, 1899), p. 278 and note 1; *iidem, The Northern Tribes of Central Australia* (London, 1904), p. 451. Cf. W. L. Warner, *A Black Civilization* (New York, 1937), p. 210 (Murngin of Arnhem Land, Northern Territory).

⁵ Martin Gusinde, *Die Feuerland Indianer* (Mödling bei Wien, 1931–37), I, 735.

⁶ The plants which the American Indians used to bring on an ecstatic condition include tobacco, coca, yerba mate, various daturas, especially *Datura meteloides* and *Datura stramonium* (Jimson weed), and peyote, a small spineless cactus indigenous to the lower valley of the Rio Grande. See W. E. Safford, "Narcotic Plants and Stimulants of the Ancient Americans," *Annual Report of the Smithsonian Institution for 1916*, pp. 387–424. See also Ruth Shonle, "Peyote, the Giver of Visions," *American Anthropologist* (n.s., 1925), XXVII, 53–75. By the Tarahumara of Chihuahua, northern Mexico, datura is considered a bad plant and contrary in nature to peyote, a good plant. It can be safely touched only by medicine men endowed with the mystic virtue of peyote (W. C. Bennett and R. M. Zingg, *The Tarahumara* [Chicago, 1935], p. 138).

⁷ S. M. Shirokogoroff, "General Theory of Shamanism among the Tungus," *Journal of the North China Branch of the Royal Asiatic Society*, LIV (1923), 247.

⁸ A. P. Elkin, *The Australian Aborigines* (Sydney, 1938), p. 215; Bernhard Hagen, *Unter den Papua's* (Wiesbaden, 1899), 276.

⁹ R. H. Codrington, *The Melanesians* (Oxford, 1891), p. 192; cf. p. 127.

¹⁰ A. I. Hopkins, *In the Isles of King Solomon* (London, 1928), p. 206.

¹¹ Thomas Williams, *Fiji and the Fijians* (3d ed., London, 1870), p. 209.

¹² Teuira Henry, "Ancient Tahiti," *Bernice P. Bishop Museum Bulletin*, No. 48, pp. 205 f.

¹³ Elsdon Best, "Maori Religion and Mythology," *Dominion Museum Bulletin*, No. 10, pp. 163, 193. Cf. Edward Tregear, *The Maori-Polynesian Comparative Dictionary* (Wellington, New Zealand, 1891), *s.v. tohunga*.

¹⁴ A. C. Kruijt, *Het animisme in den Indischen Archipel* (The Hague, 1906), pp. 450 ff.

¹⁵ E. M. Loeb, *Sumatra, Its History and People* (Vienna, 1935), p. 155.

[16] A. W. Nieuwenhuis, *Quer durch Borneo* (Leiden, 1904–1907), I, 110.

[17] J. Shakespear, *The Lushei Kuki Clans* (London, 1912), p. 80.

[18] William Crooke, *Natives of Northern India* (London, 1907), p. 247.

[19] E. Gottschling, in *Journal of the Anthropological Institute,* XXXV (1905), 379.

[20] C. Cagnolo, *The Akikuyu* (Nyeri, Kenya, 1933), p. 135; P. Cayzac, "La religion des Kikuyu (Afrique Orientale)," *Anthropos,* V (1910), 313.

[21] Gerhard Lindblom, *The Akamba in British East Africa* (2d ed., Uppsala, 1920), p. 257.

[22] Charles Bullock, *The Mashona* (Cape Town and Johannesburg, 1928), pp. 140 f.; Heinrich Claus, *Die Wagogo* (Leipzig, 1911), p. 42; Diedrich Westermann, *The Shilluk People* (Philadelphia and Berlin, 1912), p. xliv; Oskar Lenz, *Skizzen aus Westafrika* (Berlin, 1878), p. 87.

[23] J. R. Swanton, "Shamans and Priests," *Handbook of American Indians,* Part II, pp. 522 f.; Clark Wissler, *The American Indian* (2d ed., New York, 1922), pp. 199–204. See also R. B. Dixon, "Some Aspects of the American Shaman," *Journal of American Folk-Lore,* XXI (1908), 1–12.

[24] V. M. Mikhailovskii (Mikhailowski), "Shamanism in Siberia and European Russia," *Journal of the Anthropological Institute,* XXIV (1895), 91; Marie A. Czaplicka, *Aboriginal Siberia* (Oxford, 1914), pp. 191 ff.

[25] H. L. Roth, *The Aborigines of Tasmania* (2d ed., London, 1899), p. 65. According to one statement, quoted by Roth, no native was presumed to be more qualified than another to effect a cure; according to another statement, some natives practiced more than others and hence were called doctors by the English colonists.

[26] W. E. Roth, *North Queensland Ethnography Bulletin,* No. 5, p. 31.

[27] Sir Baldwin Spencer and F. J. Gillen, *The Native Tribes of Central Australia,* pp. 530, 533.

[28] W. L. Warner, *op. cit.,* p. 218.

[29] F. E. Williams, *Drama of Orokolo* (Oxford, 1940), p. 100.

[30] *Idem, Orokaiva Magic* (Oxford, 1928), pp. 209, 223.

[31] Gunnar Landtman, *The Kiwai Papuans of British New Guinea* (London, 1927), p. 298.

[32] C. G. Seligman, *The Melanesians of British New Guinea* (Cambridge, 1910), pp. 171, 280 f.

[33] Bernhard Hagen, *op. cit.,* p. 268.

[34] D. Jenness and A. Ballantyne, *The Northern D'Entrecasteaux* (Oxford, 1920), p. 133.

[35] R. H. Codrington, *op. cit.,* pp. 125, 192, 253 f., 258.

[36] John Layard, *Stone Men of Malekula* (London, 1942), p. 629, with particular reference to Vao, one of the Small Islands of the New Hebrides.

[37] Richard Taylor, *Te Ika A Maui* (2d ed., London, 1870), p. 204; S. P. Smith, "The 'Tohunga'-Maori," *Transactions and Proceedings of the New Zealand Institute,* XXXIII (1899), p. 261.

[38] Paul Arndt, *Mythologie, Religion, und Magie im Sikagebiet (östl. Mittelflores)* (Ende, Flores, 1932), p. 290.

[39] Fedor Jagor, *Travels in the Philippines* (London, 1875), p. 211.

[40] A. R. Radcliffe-Brown, *The Andaman Islanders* (Cambridge, 1933), pp. 179, 306.

[41] J. H. W. Sheane, "Some Aspects of the Awemba Religious and Super-

stitious Observances," *Journal of the Anthropological Institute*, XXXVI (1906), 155.

⁴² Charles Dundas, *ibid.*, XLIII (1913), 528.

⁴³ E. E. Evans-Pritchard, *Witchcraft, Oracles, and Magic among the Azande* (Oxford, 1937), pp. 428 ff.

⁴⁴ G. C. Musters, *At Home with the Patagonians* (2d ed., London, 1873), p. 191.

⁴⁵ E. R. Smith, *The Araucanians* (New York, 1855), p. 238.

⁴⁶ Curt Nimuendajú, *The Apinayé* (Washington, D.C., 1939), p. 147. *Catholic University of America, Anthropological Series*, No. 8.

⁴⁷ Fritz Krause, *In den Wildnissen Brasiliens* (Leipzig, 1911), p. 333.

⁴⁸ M. E. Opler, "The Concept of Supernatural Power among the Chiracahua and Mescalero Apaches," *American Anthropologist* (n.s., 1935), XXXVII, 67, 70.

⁴⁹ Gladys A. Reichard, *Social Life of the Navajo Indians* (New York, 1928), p. 148.

⁵⁰ A. L. Kroeber, in *Bulletin of the American Museum of Natural History*, XVIII, 419. The power thus received by a man might be fatal to his family, whose members die, one by one (p. 436). Similarly among the Azande it is believed that the acquisition of powerful magic may cause a death in the family of the newly made magician (E. E. Evans-Pritchard, *op. cit.*, p. 207, note 1).

⁵¹ C. D. Forde, in *University of California Publications in American Archaeology and Ethnology*, XXVIII, 181 f., 194.

⁵² Ann H. Gayton, *ibid.*, XXIV, 389, 413.

⁵³ R. L. Beals, *ibid.*, XXXI, 386.

⁵⁴ Erna Gunther, in *University of Washington Publications in Anthropology*, I, 296.

⁵⁵ J. R. Swanton, in *Memoirs of the American Museum of Natural History*, VIII, 41.

⁵⁶ A. G. Morice, in *Annual Archaeological Report for 1905* (Toronto, 1906), p. 208.

⁵⁷ Vilhjalmur Stefansson, *My Life with the Eskimo* (New York, 1913), p. 391. Cf. Knud Rasmussen, *The People of the Polar North* (London, 1908), p. 126.

⁵⁸ According to James Dawson, a witch in Victoria always appeared in the form of an old woman. He cites the case of a powerful witch of the Kolor tribe (*Australian Aborigines* [Melbourne, 1881], pp. 52 ff.).

⁵⁹ W. E. Roth, *Ethnological Studies among the North-West-Central Queensland Aborigines* (Brisbane, 1897), p. 158.

⁶⁰ Spencer and Gillen, *Native Tribes*, pp. 526, 547 f.; *iidem, Northern Tribes*, pp. 464 f.

⁶¹ Phyllis M. Kaberry, *Aboriginal Woman, Sacred and Profane* (London, 1939), pp. 212 f.

⁶² F. E. Williams, *Papuans of the Trans-Fly* (Oxford, 1936), p. 149.

⁶³ Heinrich Aufenanger and Georg Höltker, *Die Gende in Zentralneuguinea* (Wien-Mödling, 1940), p. 136.

⁶⁴ E. B. Riley, *Among Papuan Headhunters* (London, 1925), p. 27.

⁶⁵ Bronislaw Malinowski, in *Transactions of the Royal Society of South Australia*, XXXIX (1915), 655 f.

⁶⁶ W. E. Armstrong, in *Territory of Papua, Anthropological Reports,* No. 1, p. 8.

⁶⁷ Paul Wirz, *Die Marind-anim von Holländisch-Süd-Neu-Guinea* (Hamburg, 1922–25), Vol. II, Pt. III, p. 67.

⁶⁸ R. F. Fortune, *Sorcerers of Dobu* (London, 1932), pp. 74, 150, 213 f.

⁶⁹ George Brown, *Melanesians and Polynesians* (London, 1910), p. 200.

⁷⁰ Joseph Meier, "Die Zauberei bei den Küstenbewohnern der Gazelle-Halbinseln, Neupommern, Südsee," *Anthropos,* VIII (1913), 5.

⁷¹ Hortense Powdermaker, *Life in Lesu* (New York, 1933), pp. 297 f. In the village of Lesu there are thirteen magicians, only two being women. One of them knows erotic magic and the other medical spells (*loc. cit.*).

⁷² W. G. Ivens, *Melanesians of the South-East Solomon Islands* (London, 1927), p. 181. In the little islands of Owa Raha and Owa Riki magicians are always of the male sex (H. A. Bernatzik, *Owa Raha* [Wien, 1936], p. 250).

⁷³ R. H. Codrington, *op. cit.,* p. 198 f.

⁷⁴ T. W. Leggatt, in *Report of the Fourth Meeting of the Australasian Association for the Advancement of Science* (1892), p. 707, with special reference to the island of Malekula.

⁷⁵ Elsdon Best, "Maori Religion and Mythology," *Dominion Museum Bulletin,* No. 10, pp. 163, 170.

⁷⁶ J. G. F. Riedel, in *Bijdragen tot de Taal-Land-en Volkenkunde van Nederlandsch-Indië,* XXXV (1886), 83. Among the Toradya there are generally more female practitioners than men. See A. C. Kruijt (Kruyt), *De West-Toradjas op Midden-Celebes* (Amsterdam, 1938), II, 503.

⁷⁷ *Idem, Het animisme in den Indischen Archipel,* p. 454.

⁷⁸ Bernhard Hagen, "Beiträge zur Kenntniss der Battareligion," *Tijdschrift voor Indische Taal-Land-en Volkenkunde,* XXVIII (1882), 538.

⁷⁹ E. M. Loeb, "Shaman and Seer," *American Anthropologist* (n.s., 1929), XXXI, 66, 79.

⁸⁰ Fay-Cooper Cole, *The Wild Tribes of Davao District, Mindanao* (Chicago, 1913), pp. 62, 97; *idem, The Tinguian* (Chicago, 1922), p. 301. *Field Museum of Natural History, Anthropological Series,* Vols. XII, No. 2, XIV, No. 2.

⁸¹ W. A. Reed, *Negritos of Zambales* (Manila, 1904), pp. 65 f. *Department of the Interior, Ethnological Survey Publications,* Vol. II, Pt. I.

⁸² A. W. Nieuwenhuis, *op. cit.,* I, 110.

⁸³ J. B. Combes, in Dourisboure, *Les sauvages Ba-Hnars (Cochinchine Orientale)* (Paris, 1873), pp. 429 f.

⁸⁴ A. R. Radcliffe-Brown, *op. cit.,* p. 176. According to another account magicians ("dreamers") are invariably of the male sex (E. H. Man, *On the Aboriginal Inhabitants of the Andaman Islands* [London, 1932], p. 28; *idem,* in *Journal of the Anthropological Institute,* XII [1883], 96 f.).

⁸⁵ George Whitehead, *In the Nicobar Islands* (London, 1924), p. 149.

⁸⁶ W. H. R. Rivers, *The Todas* (London, 1906), p. 266.

⁸⁷ Ralph Linton, *The Tanala* (Chicago, 1933), p. 199. *Field Museum of Natural History, Anthropological Series,* Vol. XXII.

⁸⁸ I. Schapera, *The Khoisan Peoples of South Africa* (London, 1930), p. 196.

⁸⁹ A. T. Bryant, "The Zulu Cult of the Dead," *Man,* XVII (1917), 142.

⁹⁰ H. A. Stayt, *The Bavenda* (London, 1931), p. 264.

⁹¹ Gerhard Lindblom, *op. cit.* (2d ed.), p. 257.

[92] Sir H. H. Johnston, *The Uganda Protectorate* (2d ed., London, 1904), II, 750.

[93] J. H. Driberg, *The Lango* (London, 1923), p. 234.

[94] E. E. Evans-Pritchard, *op. cit.*, pp. 427 f.

[95] J. M. M. Van der Burgt, *Un grand peuple de l'Afrique équatoriale* (Bois le Duc, 1904), p. 55.

[96] Oskar Lenz, *op. cit.*, p. 87.

[97] Sir A. B. Ellis, *The Yoruba-speaking Peoples of the Slave Coast of West Africa* (London, 1894), p. 117.

[98] P. A. Talbot, *The Peoples of Southern Nigeria* (London, 1926), II, 200.

[99] S. F. Nadel, "Witchcraft and Anti-Witchcraft in Nupe Society," *Africa*, VIII (1935), 424.

[100] O. Temple, *Notes on the Tribes, Provinces, Emirates, and States of the Northern Provinces of Nigeria* (2d ed., Lagos, Nigeria, 1922), p. 103.

[101] Louis Tauxier, *La religion Bambara* (Paris, 1927), p. 44.

[102] Martin Gusinde, *op. cit.*, I, 733; II, 1386.

[103] Martin Dobrizhoffer, *An Account of the Abipones* (London, 1822), II, 67, 86 f.

[104] E. R. Smith, *op. cit.*, pp. 238 f. Cf. R. E. Latcham, in *Journal of the Royal Anthropological Institute*, XXXIX (1909), 352.

[105] Curt Nimuendajú, *op. cit.*, p. 142.

[106] C. F. P. von Martius, *Beiträge zur Ethnographie und Sprachenkunde Amerika's zumal Brasiliens* (Leipzig, 1867), I, 78 f.; P. Ehrenreich, *Beiträge zur Völkerkunde Brasiliens* (Berlin, 1891), p. 33 (Karayá); Alfred Métraux, *La religion des Tupinamba* (Paris, 1928), p. 83 (Indian tribes now extinct).

[107] Gustaf Bolinder, *Die Indianer der tropischen Schneegebirge* (Stuttgart, 1925), p. 127.

[108] W. E. Roth, "An Inquiry into the Animism and Folk-Lore of the Guiana Indians," *Thirtieth Annual Report of the Bureau of American Ethnology*, p. 334.

[109] Gerónimo de Mendieta, *Historia ecclesiastica Indiana* (Mexico City, 1870), p. 136.

[110] Aleš Hrdlička, "Physiological and Medical Observations among the Indians of Southwestern United States and Northern Mexico," *Bulletin of the Bureau of American Ethnology*, No. 34, p. 224.

[111] Frank Russell, in *Twenty-sixth Annual Report of the Bureau of American Ethnology*, pp. 256 f.

[112] Leslie Spier, in *Anthropological Papers of the American Museum of Natural History*, XXIX, 277. Whether women were ever magicians among the Maricopa is doubtful (*idem, Yuman Tribes of the Gila River* [Chicago, 1933], p. 238).

[113] M. E. Opler, *An Apache Life-Way* (Chicago, 1941), p. 201.

[114] G. B. Grinnell, *The Cheyenne Indians* (New Haven, 1923), II, 128 f.

[115] William McClintock, *The Old North Trail* (London, 1910), pp. 248 ff.

[116] W. Z. Park, *Shamanism in Western North America* (Evanston, 1938), p. 21. *Northwestern University Studies in the Social Sciences*, No. 2.

[117] Stephen Powers, *Tribes of California* (Washington, D.C., 1877), pp. 152, 246. *Contributions to North American Ethnology*, Vol. III.

[118] A. L. Kroeber, "The Religion of the Indians of California," *University of California Publications in American Archaeology and Ethnology*, IV, 347.

[119] Erna Gunther, in *University of Washington Publications in Anthropology*, I, 298.

[120] James Teit, in *Memoirs of the American Museum of Natural History*, IV, 613.

[121] Julius Jetté, "On the Medicine-Men of the Ten'a," *Journal of the Royal Anthropological Institute*, XXXVII (1907), 162.

[122] Aleš Hrdlička, *The Aleutian and Commander Islands and Their Inhabitants* (Philadelphia, 1945), p. 152, citing I. Veniaminov.

[123] Vilhjalmur Stefansson, *op. cit.*, p. 392.

[124] J. W. Bilby, *Among Unknown Eskimo* (London, 1923), pp. 196, 199.

[125] Henry Rink, *Tales and Traditions of the Eskimo* (Edinburgh, 1875), p. 58.

[126] Marie A. Czaplicka, *op. cit.*, pp. 243 f. In Mongolian myths the goddesses were shamans and the bestowers of the shamanistic gift on mankind (p. 244, note 1). Nearly all the Neo-Siberian tribes have a common name for the female shaman, while each tribe has a special name for the male shaman. This is true of the Yakut, Buriat, Tungus, Mongols, Tatars, Altaians, Kirgiz, and Samoyed (p. 244, note 2).

[127] Uno Holmberg, *The Mythology of All Races* (Vol. IV), *Finno-Ugric, Siberian* (Boston, 1927), p. 499; Åke Ohlmarks, *Studien zum Problem des Schamanismus* (Lund and Copenhagen, 1939), p. 354.

[128] H. L. Roth, *The Natives of Sarawak and British North Borneo* (London, 1896), I, 270 f., quoting Brooke Low. The *manang bali* does not go to war with the men. He sees little of his "husband," who is generally a widower with a family to support (Hugh Low, *Sarawak* [London, 1848], pp. 175 f.). A young man does not become a *manang bali*. Usually an old or childless man, without other means of support, adopts the profession in order to gain a living. Before doing so he must prepare a feast and sacrifice pigs lest the tribe suffer some evil as the result of his action (E. H. Gomes, *Seventeen Years among the Sea Dyaks of Borneo* [London, 1911], pp. 179 ff.). There is reason to believe that in former times all Sea Dayak magicians, upon initiation, assumed female attire for the rest of their lives, but the practice is now rare, at least in the coastal districts. See J. Perham, "Manangism in Borneo," *Journal of the Straits Branch of the Royal Asiatic Society*, No. 19 (1887), 102. See also A. Hardeland, *Dajacksch-deutsches Wörterbuch* (Amsterdam, 1859), pp. 53 f.; William Howell and D. J. S. Bailey, *A Sea-Dyak Dictionary* (Singapore, 1900), p. 99.

[129] William Foley, in *Journal of the Asiatic Society of Bengal*, IV (1835), 199, note.

[130] A. L. Kitching, *On the Backwaters of the Nile* (London, 1912), p. 239.

[131] J. H. Weeks, in *Journal of the Royal Anthropological Institute*, XL (1910), 388.

[132] Thomas Falkner, *A Description of Patagonia* (Hereford, 1774), p. 117. Cf. T. J. Hutchinson, in *Transactions of the Ethnological Society of London* (n.s., 1869), VII, 323 (Puelche).

[133] R. E. Latcham, in *Journal of the Royal Anthropological Institute*, XXXIX (1909), 351, 353. Cf. J. Nippgen, "La religion, les superstitions, la magie, et la sorcellerie des Araucaniens," *L'Ethnographie* (n.s., 1914), No. 4, p. 67. See further, Alfred Métraux, "Le shamanisme Araucan," *Revista del Instituto de Antropología de la Universidad National de Tucumán*, II, 309–62.

[134] *Récit des voyages et des découvertes du P. Jacques Marquette*, p. 248; J. G. Shea, *Discovery and Exploration of the Mississippi Valley* (2d ed., Albany, 1903), pp. 36 f.

135 A. L. Kroeber, in *Bulletin of the American Museum of Natural History,* XVIII, 19.

136 *Idem, Handbook of the Indians of California* (Washington, D.C., 1925), p. 46.

137 Edward Sapir, "Religious Ideas of the Takelma Indians of Southwestern Oregon," *Journal of American Folk-Lore,* XX (1907), 41, note 1, on the authority of Mrs. Frances Johnson, a full-blooded Takelma.

138 H. J. Holmberg, in *Acta Societatis Scientiarum Fennicæ,* IV (1856), 400 f., quoting a Russian authority. We are also told of Koniag transvestites that their residence in anyone's house was considered as "fortunate" (Urey Lisiansky, *A Voyage Round the World* [London, 1814], p. 199).

139 Franz Boas, in *Bulletin of the American Museum of Natural History,* XV, 325 f.

140 W. Bogoras, in *Memoirs of the American Museum of Natural History,* XI, 448 ff.

141 W. Jochelson, *ibid.,* X, 52 f. Among the Koriak of today Jochelson found no instances of transvestitism.

142 Marie A. Czaplicka, *op. cit.,* p. 199, referring to a Russian authority, V. F. Troshchanski. There is a popular belief among the Yakut that a shaman of more than ordinary power can bear children like a woman. They even give birth to various animals and birds. (W. G. Sumner, "The Yakuts. Abridged from the Russian of Sieroshevski," *Journal of the Anthropological Institute,* XXXI [1901], 103 f.).

143 Leo (L. J.) Sternberg, "Divine Election in Primitive Religion," *Congrès International des Américanistes, Compte-Rendu de la XXIe Session,* Deuxième Partie (Göteborg, Sweden, 1924), pp. 472 ff.

Chapter VIII

THE MAKING OF MAGICIANS

THE "call" to the profession of a medicine man often comes involuntarily, as the result of a dream, a vision, or some other sensory experience which is regarded as a visitation by spirits. In other cases, as among many North American Indians, the would-be magician retires from human society and practices various austerities, in order to become susceptible to spiritual influence. The call, however it comes, is compelling, for those who receive it seldom make "the great refusal."[1]

A medicine man among the southeastern tribes of Australia was generally supposed to be made by the ancestral ghosts or by a high god (Daramulun, Baiame, Bunjil). The Wotjobaluk of Victoria believed that a "supernatural being," said to live in hollows of the ground, met a man in the bush, opened his side, and inserted in it quartz crystals and other magical objects. From that time on he could, as the natives said, "pull things out of himself and others." Among the Mukjarawaint a youth who could see his mother's ghost sitting by her grave was marked out to be a medicine man. The Kurnai thought that the ancestral ghosts either visited a sleeper and communicated to him protective or harmful chants and knowledge, or else they completed his knowledge elsewhere. Among the Yuin of New South Wales medicine men obtained in dreams magical songs against sickness and other ills. They received their powers from Daramulun, and a very great medicine man could even get Daramulun to slay his enemies for him.[2]

In northern Queensland a man who would learn the art of using the pointing bone goes out of the camp for three or four days, "practically starves himself," and gets "more or less 'cranky.' " When in that condition he sees Malkari, a nature spirit, who is pleased to make him a doctor by inserting small flints, bones, or other objects in his body. Other Queensland doctors acquire their powers from Karnmari, a nature spirit in the form of a water snake, and still others, by sitting beside a grave,

202

obtain them from a ghost.³ Among the Kabi and Wakka of Queensland a man's power in the occult art was proportioned to his vitality, and the amount of that which he possessed depended upon the number of quartz crystals inside him and the quantity of fur rope (*yurru*) which he carried with him. He obtained *yurru* from Dhakkan, the rainbow, the great possessor of vitality. This creature, a combination of fish and snake, lived in the deepest waterholes. When visible as a rainbow he was supposed to be passing from one waterhole to another. Though at times tricky and malignant, he could do a good turn to a man already possessed of some magical faculty. While a magician lay in a deep sleep on the brink of a waterhole, Dhakkan dragged him down into the depths and presented him with *yurru*, in exchange for a number of crystals which he took from the man. Then he brought the magician once more to the surface and deposited him safely on the bank. Upon waking up, the man was now a doctor of the highest degree and so "full of life" that he could make thunder and lightning, fly through the air, vanish underground, and do other marvelous things.⁴

The Arunta and Ilpirra tribes of Central Australia recognize a distinction between magicians made by the ancestral ghosts (*iruntarinia*) and those initiated by other magicians. The latter class has less repute than the former. When a man feels that he is capable of entering the magical profession he goes away from the camp and directs his steps to a certain cave, which is supposed to be occupied by the *iruntarinia*. He does not venture to enter the cave, lest they snatch him up and take him away forever, but he lies down and goes to sleep. At break of day one of the *iruntarinia* comes to the mouth of the cave and, finding the man asleep, throws at him an invisible lance. It pierces the neck from behind, passes through the tongue, making a large hole, and then comes out by the mouth. The man's tongue remains throughout life with this hole in it, as the outward sign of the spiritual visitation. "In some way, of course, the novice must make it himself, but naturally no one will ever admit the fact; indeed it is not impossible that, in course of time, the man really comes to believe that it was not done by himself." The ghost throws a second lance, kills the man, and carries him into the depths of the cave, an Arunta Paradise, where the *iruntarinia* live in perpetual sunshine and among streams of running water. Here he receives a new set of internal organs and also a supply of magical stones. He is then led back to the camp by the ghost, who is invisible except to a few highly gifted magicians and also to the dogs. For several days the man presents a strange appearance and acts in a queer manner. One morning it is noticed that he has painted with powdered charcoal and fat a broad band across the bridge of his nose. Everyone now knows that a new magician has been graduated. However, he must not engage in practice for about a year. If during this time the hole in his tongue closes up, as it sometimes does, then he considers that his power had departed, and he will abandon the magical profession. During the period of probation he cultivates the acquaintance of his professional brothers and learns their secrets. These consist principally in the ability to hide about the person and to produce at will quartz pebbles and little sticks. Of hardly less importance than such sleight-of-hand is "the power of looking preternaturally solemn, as if he were the possessor of knowledge quite hidden from ordinary men."[5]

In the Mentawei Islands a man (or a woman) becomes a magician in one of three ways. He may have a vision, which comes voluntarily or involuntarily, and enables him to secure the aid of ghosts and spirits. Henceforth he can see them and converse with them; he has "seeing eyes and hearing ears." He may be bodily abducted by the spirits and from them obtain his power directly. Most commonly, however, a person receives a summons to be a magician as the result of sickness, dreaming, or temporary insanity. He will then be visited by a professional magician who announces that the spirits wish him to acquire the necessary power. He agrees to accept the spiritual invitation and enters on a course of instruction to fit him for his duties. In the island of Nias a vision is sought for. A young man will retire to the jungle and remain there for several days in order to get into contact with the spirits. Magicians alone can talk to the spirits and see the souls of sick people in the form of glowworms.[6]

In the Andaman Islands a person can become a magician by dying and coming back to life. When he dies, he naturally acquires the peculiar powers and qualities of a spirit, and these he retains if he returns to a mundane existence. Again, a man wandering alone in the jungle may be suddenly confronted by the spirits. They will kill him if he shows fear, but if he puts on a bold front they will keep him for a time and then let him go. Such an experience makes him a full-fledged magician. Finally, the same position may be attained by a man who has intercourse with the spirits in his dreams. It is noteworthy, however, that dream revelations are considered less significant than those which come from direct communication with the spirits.[7] In Car Nicobar a sickly person is called upon to become a magician. His condition has been caused by the ghosts of departed relatives and friends, who thus indicate their desire that he enter upon the magical profession. He knows that he must hold intercourse with them either as a live magician or as himself a ghost; naturally he chooses the former alternative. Nevertheless magicians often relinquish their unwelcome office as soon as they feel themselves again restored to health.[8]

The Tembu and Fingo of Tembuland, Cape Colony, believe in the existence of the River People, half fish and half human in form, with heads of long flowing hair. These mermen and mermaids live in kraals deep down under the streams. They are very wise and very powerful in magic. A man who would become a doctor and diviner will resort to them in order to learn their secrets. When he returns after several days' absence, laden with the medicinal roots and herbs which the River People have given to him, he is not questioned about his experience, for were this revealed they would call him back and kill him. But the people know that he has visited them, for now he can heal the sick, peer into the future, read the thoughts of others, prepare love charms, and combat witches.[9]

A medicine man of the Akikuyu, a Kenya tribe, is supposed to be called to his vocation by God (Ngai). He dreams constantly, has visions of people coming to him and leading a goat for sacrifice, and receives revelations of events that presently occur, such as the murder of a man or the death of a goat. Sooner or later he tells his wife and friends about these experiences, and then it is at once understood that Ngai has indeed marked him out for the magical profession. Should he resist the call the angry deity would cause his children to die or the people of his village to become ill. According to another account, Ngai appears to a person in a dream and asks him to become a magician. The next day he informs the villagers of what has happened and retires, "seemingly insane," into the woods, where he holds communion with Ngai all night long. Then he returns home and makes a public announcement of his divine call.[10]

The Apinayé, a Brazilian tribe, generally regard intercourse with ghosts as uncanny and something to be avoided as far as possible. On the other hand, magicians are introduced to the unseen world by their deceased close kinsfolk and move about in it at will. Thus they become intermediaries between the dead and the ghost-dreading tribesmen and acquire much useful knowledge of medicine. A ghost first appears to a prospective magician in a dream. If the ghosts fail to come to a practitioner, he or his shade will visit them in order to get their advice on difficult problems of medical treatment. This he does by smoking a great deal of tobacco until he begins to groan and tremble and finally collapses. His assistant lays him out and he lies prone on the ground while his soul is away from his body. To bring the soul back the assistant blows tobacco smoke on his own hands and places them on the magician's, thereby reviving him. This invaluable gift of sending one's soul to the realm of the dead is not possessed by all magicians.[11] Among the Kaingáng, another Brazilian tribe, a tutelary spirit comes to a man as the result of an accidental encounter with it. Sometimes the spirit will be "pointed out" to him by a magician who has himself been seeing it for a long time.[12]

No matter how eager an Apache may be to acquire occult power and with it the ability to perform the ceremonies by which diseases are cured, lost objects restored, childless women blessed with offspring, and all the difficulties of life successfully overcome, it can never be sought directly. Occult power comes to man as a gift from the Giver-of-Life, its ultimate source, but through certain agencies—lightning, the sun, various animals and plants. While these are the most common media, almost everything may be a conductor of the power.[13] No one knows in advance what kind of power may be offered to him or when or where it may be offered. "Something" speaks to a man, perhaps at night in a dream, perhaps during the day when he is alone in his camp or with a crowd. In any case the experience is for him only. If people are present when he has it they will not see the vision or hear the words spoken. For example, Bear may appear to a man and offer him power to cure "bear sickness." This is a malady marked by deformity. It occurs when a person is frightened or attacked by a bear, or has unknowingly crossed a bear's tracks, or has touched the animal's fur, or has entered its den. A man may accept or reject the power thus offered. If he accepts it, he receives directions for conducting a ceremony and learns the necessary songs and prayers. An Apache may in this way receive several ceremonies and become "loaded up with powers."[14]

The parents of a Lenape boy were very anxious that he should acquire spiritual aid. When about twelve years of age he was driven into the wilderness to fast there and shift for himself. It was hoped that a *manito* might take pity on the child and grant him some beneficent power that would be his throughout life. When a man had several sons he might take them into the forest and build there a rude shelter, where they remained for some time. The boys were not allowed to eat during the day, but just before sunrise every morning each one was given a medicine which made him vomit. He then ate a little piece of meat. This period of abstinence and privation might last as long as twelve days. When it ended some of the children had received such power from a kindly *manito* that they could rise into the air or go down into the ground. Other children were able to prophesy events several years in the future.[15]

Among the Micmac, an Algonquian tribe of Nova Scotia, occult power is sometimes imparted by the "little people" as a gift to a man who has won their friendship. An Indian hoping to be thus favored goes into the woods and builds there a camp large enough to shelter two persons. At his meals he is careful to set apart an equal share for the anticipated visitor. Upon his return to camp one day he finds his food already cooked and soon after observes a faint and shadowy form floating in front of the wigwam. He sees it more and more clearly until at length it is as visible as that of any mortal. Then the spirit becomes the man's friend and presents him with the wished-for power.[16]

An Arapaho Indian, more often an adult than a lad at puberty, goes out to some high hill or mountain peak and fasts for several days, in the hope and expectation of having a vision. If his quest is successful, there appears to him a spirit, in the form of a person, from whom he receives instruction. As the spirit vanishes, it is seen to assume the form of an animal. The peculiar powers of the animal will henceforth be acquired by the visionary. Parts of it are often used by him as medicine or charms, and in many cases its skin will be made into his medicine bag. Certain restrictions are generally imposed by the spirit upon the seeker after power. For instance, he may be told not to eat the heart or kidney or head of any animal and be threatened with some dire evil if he ever disobeys the injunction. Moreover, the future magician must be serious, high-minded, and not actuated only by desire for gain. Otherwise his newly acquired power would react on him for evil. It may happen that this power is bad for the recipient's family. The spirit did not tell him so, but the members of the family die off, one after another, finally leaving him alone. If a man knows that such will be the result of his accepting the power he ought to refuse it. The great majority of middle-aged men among the

Arapaho have had at least one successful experience of this sort and have thus been magically endowed.[17]

A Gros Ventre Indian, seeking spiritual aid, may wander about until he finds snakes in a hole. He then cuts off some of his flesh and feeds it to them; he may even give them an ear or a little finger. The voluntary sacrifice is effective. A snake says, "I pity this man. I will give him power and make him strong." So the snake enters the man's mouth and proceeds thence into his body. He has now become unkillable. A similar experience with bears would confer upon him invulnerability.[18]

A Blackfoot suppliant for occult power proceeds to a wild and remote spot, such as a hilltop, accompanied by an assistant. There a pole is set up and a rope is fastened to it. The assistant, having first prayed to the spirits of air, earth, and water that the suppliant be blessed and enjoy success in all his undertakings, drives pins through the flesh of the suppliant's breast and attaches them to the rope by strands of sinew. He is then left alone. All day long he must walk back and forth on the sunward side of the pole, crying aloud to the spirits for help, and fixing his eyes on the sun. He tries by convulsive jerks on the rope to tear the pins from his body. Neither food nor drink passes his mouth that day. In the evening the assistant returns and cuts his flesh to free him from the rope. He spends the night on the hilltop. In his sleep a wolf appears and tells him that his prayers have not been in vain. He shall be cunning like the wolf and able to outwit his enemies. Henceforth he must wear some hair of a wolf in a bundle fixed to his neck, and his quiver and bow case must be of wolfskin.[19]

Among the Shasta Indians of northern California a man enters the profession of magician as the result of a dream or a series of dreams. Often he dreams that he is on the edge of a precipice or on the top of a high tree and is about to fall, when suddenly he awakes. Another time he dreams that he is on the bank of a river and is about to tumble in. Such experiences are a sign that the person to whom they occur must become a doctor. At once he begins to exercise care in eating, to restrict his diet to vegetables, and to avoid the smell of meat or fat cooking. After the dreams have continued for some time one day he falls over in a swoon ("dies") and in this state sees an Axeki (Pain). An Axeki is a tiny, human-like creature, carrying a bow and arrow. The spirit talks to the man and sings to him. He must answer and repeat the song. Should he fail to do so the spirit kills him. But if he fulfills the requirements the Axeki offers to be his friend and gives him occult power in the shape of a small needle-like object resembling an icicle. This is a "pain." Henceforth he keeps it in his body, though he may produce it at will and shoot it into anyone who has made him angry. He can also extract such a "pain" from a person whom another doctor or, it may be, an Axeki has shot.[20] Female magicians among the Shasta are much more common than their male counterparts. A woman exhibits her capacity for the profession by falling into a trance, during which she remains rigid and hardly breathing for several hours. While in this state she sees a spirit and learns the spirit's song. Her moans as she emerges from the trance are interpreted as a repetition of the song and a recital of the spirit's name. When she utters the name, blood oozes from her mouth. The woman is subject to further cataleptic seizures while performing her initiation dances. Upon one of these occasions she receives the power of the spirit into her body. The bystanders must catch her before she falls into the trance, for otherwise the power would kill her, but if she survives she has it henceforth in her body in the shape of a "pain."[21]

The Quinault Indians have a story of a young man who went out into the woods seeking occult power. This came to him after he had bathed every day for a month and had met a strange, two-headed creature. Then he said to himself, "I am going to the mountains to find out how strong a power I have." He saw a deer, and as he looked at it the animal burst open and fell dead. Smoke arose from the spot. He had "poisoned" it. Similar experiences followed with a band of elk and with other animals. Finally, after a year, his power grew less and game no longer died at his glance. He then returned home.[22]

Some Lillooet medicine men have the ghosts of the dead as tutelary spirits. These are obtained by sleeping in burial grounds at intervals extending over several years. Magicians with such ghostly helpers are considered to be exceptionally powerful.[23] A Bellacoola magician is initiated by a special deity who lives in the woods. He carries a wooden wand which he swings and thereby produces a singing noise. When he jumps into the water it boils; when a woman meets him she begins to menstruate; when a man encounters him the man's nose starts to bleed. This deity initiates a youth by touching his chest with the wand and by painting his face with a rainbow design. The youth then falls down in a faint. Upon recovering he begins to sing a song, of which both the tune and the words have been given to him by the spirit.[24]

Tsimshian medicine men acquire their occult power from various kinds of spiritual beings. All but the very strongest novices, into whom the power enters, faint dead away. Vomiting of blood is also a sign that the power has been received.[25]

Among the Kutchin, a group of Athapascan tribes in northwestern Canada and Alaska, a magician acquires his power through dreams. These first come to him when he is not more than six or seven years of age. The child goes into the forest and begins to practice conjuring. He pulls small spruce trees out of the ground without breaking the tender roots and then puts the trees back in place so expertly as to leave no sign of their disturbance. As his dreams continue, he acquires more and more power and expects that eventually he will have the dream experience in which an animal appears to him and promises to aid him.[26] Among the Tahltan Indians, a branch of the Tinne, a would-be medicine man ranged the wilderness to find a pregnant moose, caribou, sheep, goat, or porcupine. If successful in his search, he followed the animal to be present at the birth of its young. These he wiped with some twigs and then switched the animal's legs to make it rise. He killed neither the mother nor the offspring, for he believed that occult power came to him from his presence at the birth.[27]

The call to the profession of a shaman comes as the result of possession by a spiritual being. Possession may be involuntary when the subject is a neurotic; sometimes it attends or follows a siege of illness, generally of a mental character. In other cases it is produced by prolonged dancing and other rhythmic movements, by various austerities such as fasting and flagellation, and by drug taking. The candidate, if susceptible, becomes hysterical, perhaps falls into a condition of ecstasy or trance, foams at the mouth, raves, and in other ways gives evidence that he has indeed been possessed by a spirit and that in his future career as a shaman he can reproduce by the same means these abnormal mental states.

No instances of possession have been recorded among the aborigines of Australia. It has been found in New Guinea. The natives of Windessi, in the Dutch part of the island, believe that a man, or sometimes a woman, can be inspired by the ghost of a former tribesman, and thus receive occult power for treating the sick. The seizure takes place during the funeral ceremonies, when the friends of the deceased are sitting about his corpse and lamenting his departure to the world of shades. Suddenly the prospective magician begins to shiver and utter monotonous sounds; then he falls into an ecstatic state; and when he shakes convulsively the ghost is supposed to have entered him. Before setting up in the magical profession the man undergoes initiatory rites in the forest, calls himself a lunatic, and on returning home acts as if he were half-crazed.[28]

The Melanesians, it is said, cannot distinguish between the possession which causes madness and that which prophesies, "and a man may pretend to be mad that he may get the reputation of being a prophet." In the Solomon Islands such a person will speak with the voice of someone recently deceased; he calls himself, and is addressed by others by the name of the dead man who speaks through him. Further evidence of ghost-possession is afforded by his eating fire, lifting enormous weights, and foretelling things to come. In the Banks Islands possessing spirits were the familiars only of people who knew them, and these were often women. A man who wished to be known to such a spirit (*nopitu*) gave money to a woman whose familiar it was, and then it would come to him. Henceforth he would call himself Nopitu, or rather, speaking of himself, would say, not "I," but "we two," meaning the *nopitu* in him and himself. Many wonders he performed by the power and in the name of the possessing spirit, not the least being the production from his person of unlimited quantities of shell-money—bags full—so new that it had not yet been strung.[29]

Among the Subanun of Mindanao it is often the case that an adolescent youth, during a long period of sickness and depression, will decide to become a magician. Thus one man, who suffered from a fever, heard a *divata* calling him. It told him that it was his friend and would be his familiar spirit. Upon recovery, he went to a practitioner of magic, entered into a kind of discipleship, and learned the secrets of the magical art. When acting as a medium a magician goes into a trance-like state and the spirit speaks through him. He may also speak in his own proper voice to the spirit and receive from it an audible reply.[30]

Among the Malanau, a division of the Klemantan of Sarawak, a woman (more rarely a man) who becomes insane or very ill is believed to be possessed by a "devil." She is urged to enter the medical profession, for as a doctor she can cure herself and at the same time can cast out devils from other sick people. Before being accepted by the people and by the spirits in the role of exorciser she must pass eleven nights in a condition of artificial hysteria. It does not follow, however, that even then she can tell whether an evil spirit has ceased to possess a sick person. One old woman, who had worked at the profession for fifteen years, admitted that, if a devil went into herself she could turn it out, but only a more powerful person than herself could expel it from someone else.[31]

The great majority of Zulu diviners are "clearly persons of the neurotic type." Their magical powers have been thrust upon them by the spirits. Since the exercise of such powers involves physical and mental discomfort nobody desires of his own accord to officiate as a magician. The person chosen by the spirits becomes afflicted with some strange disease which proves to be beyond the ability of the native doctors to cure. The disease is usually of a mental character, though it may turn out to be a kidney or lung complaint. At any rate it is believed to have been sent by a departed ancestor. The patient's relatives take him to a diviner of repute for a consultation. If spirit-possession is deemed the cause of the trouble, the sufferer is at once handed over to another diviner for initiation into the magical art. His novitiate may last from a few months to two years.[32]

The ghosts which possess the Bathonga and produce the disease described by the natives as the "madness of the gods," are not the ghosts of their ancestors but those of strangers, particularly of the Zulu. The process of exorcism is complicated, requiring as many as four principal rites. When these have been completed and the possessing spirit has been duly appeased and expelled, the patient enters upon his convalescence. This lasts for an entire year. The period is also one of apprenticeship, for he will now become himself an exorcist if his magical powers are sufficiently developed. The experiences which exorcised persons have gone through and their regular participation in the exorcism of others generally injure their minds; they have something wild about them and appear not to be in their right senses. This nervous instability may pass away. On the other hand, their abnormal mentality often seems to be intensified, so that they reveal special gifts of second sight, divination, prophecy, and wonder working.[33]

An Ovimbundu boy or girl who becomes a magician must have a neurotic temperament, "a spirit in the head," as the natives say. When a child is sick, a doctor visits him, tells him that he is wanted by the spirit, and that he must enter the magical profession. There does not seem to be any practice of intensifying a novice's natural psychosis by seclusion, starvation, beating, or any other ordeal.[34]

A Jivaro Indian who became a magician went through a course of training which lasted a lunar month. To his instructor he paid a high fee in food, clothing, and ornaments. For the first ten days both master and pupil ate nothing, but took various narcotic drugs, including a liquid infusion of tobacco, which was snuffed up the nose. As the result of their fast and drug-taking they became very light headed. Finally a spirit, Pasuca, appeared to them, in the form of a bold warrior. As soon as the spirit was seen the master began to massage the pupil's body with vigorous strokes. During this operation the pupil became unconscious. When he recovered, his body was sore from head to foot, sure evidence that Pasuca had "taken possession" of him. For the last twenty days of the course the pupil learned the methods of combating the spiritual agencies responsible for various diseases.[35]

The Haida shaman was chosen by a spiritual being as the medium through which to make its influence felt in the world. When so possessed, the shaman's own identity disappeared; for the time being he dressed like the spirit, acted like it, and used its words. If the spiritual being came from the Tlingit country the shaman had to speak Tlingit, though in his uninspired moments he remained totally ignorant of that language. After thus becoming the mouthpiece of a spirit the shaman ceased to be called by his own name and took that of his spiritual mentor. A similar belief in possession also prevailed among the Tlingit, but whereas the Haida shaman personated only one spirit at a time each Tlingit shaman had, in addition to the principal spirit possessing him, a number of subsidiary spirits which were supposed to strengthen his faculties. These minor and supporting spirits were depicted, along with the principal spirit, on the shaman's mask. Those around the eyes increased his power of sight and so enabled him to discover hostile spirits; those around the mouth increased his power of smell; those around the jaws kept them firm at all times, and so forth.[36]

The *angakok* of the Greenland Eskimo has acquired a special capacity for intercourse with the spirit world. He can see the spirits, converse with them, and enlist their aid in human affairs, thus acting as a mediator between them and ordinary mortals. To summon his spirits he needs only to know and utter their names. But this is after he has established a relationship with them, for on the first occasion the spirits visit him of their own accord or else he comes upon them unexpectedly when alone in the wilderness. With the spirits he holds converse in a mystic language, which seems to be much the same for all magicians. Presumably every practitioner learns a great part of it by listening to the colloquies of his professional brethren with the spirits whom they have summoned. The use of this language contributes in a high degree to the impressiveness of a magical performance.[37] It is also possible for a prospective *angakok* to get a revelation by an old tomb. He dies and becomes reduced to a skeleton. Then the inhabitants of the tomb appear to him and initiate him. Other spirits, also, issue from the underworld, tell him their names, and proclaim themselves his allies, upon whom he can call as often as he likes.[38]

Among the Siberian tribes the profession of shaman is not usually sought or entered willingly. On the contrary, the obligations which it imposes are regarded as a heavy burden, to which a person submits as being unescapable. Sometime in early youth, at a period coinciding with sexual maturity, the future shaman falls into hysterical fits, has fainting spells, and suffers hallucinations, all these often lasting for many weeks. Then, suddenly, a spirit appears to him, orders him to become a shaman, and offers to help him on his difficult way. At first he hangs back, but finally the threats and the promises of the spirit overcome his reluctance and he enters into an understanding with his guide. His fits now subside and he recovers his mental poise. The spirit who has so wonderously cured him will give him power to cure others. So for a time or forever the spirit possesses the chosen one, speaks through the latter's voice, and suggests to him everything done during a shamanistic performance. The shaman, in turn, obeys his spiritual guide implicitly. The supreme protective spirit also puts at the shaman's disposal assistant spirits, and it is really they who expel diseases and inspire the shaman with answers to questions put to him by his clients. Without their aid he would be unable to operate. Their duties are laid upon them by the supreme spirit, who rules over them and has ordered them to obey the shaman's will.[39]

No Koriak becomes a shaman of his own free will. The spirits take possession of anyone they choose and force him to obey them. Finally, they appear to him in visible form, endow him with power, and instruct him in shamanistic arts. The Yukaghir give to hysteria a name which means "possessed by evil spirits." The disease is particularly found in "nervously strained" youths who are inclined to become shamans. A patient's fit is preceded by loss of appetite, headache, apathy, and indifference to his surroundings, a condition which may last for several days. Suddenly he begins to sing, at first in a low tone, then loudly, meanwhile waving his arms and swinging his body. In his song he complains of the spirits that strangle him and threaten him with death if he does not enter upon the shaman's career. Sometimes, apparently, it is the possessing spirit that sings. This performance is followed by cramps, spasmodic bodily contractions, or an attack of epilepsy. The possessing spirit is then exorcised by the attendant shamans.[40]

It appears from the foregoing cases that a man's entrance upon the magical profession is commonly supposed to be due to the interposition of some friendly spiritual being (perhaps a ghost), who becomes henceforth his "helper" and "familiar," accompanying him, giving him knowledge of hidden things, enabling him to perform wonderful feats, and, where shamanism is found, possessing him and speaking oracularly through him. The relationship between the spiritual being and the magician varies from that of a benefactor to his protegé to that of a servant to his master, but always it is of an intimate character.[41] These spirits seldom receive prayer and sacrifice; they are not regularly worshiped. They are so little personalized that they appear as merely arbitrary agencies, mechanical factors, as it were, in producing the effects ascribed to them. They always remain at the magician's beck and call, so long, indeed, as he continues to be a master of his art and does not neglect its duties and responsibilities. Such tutelaries are often represented in animal form; as in Australia and North America. The "bush soul" of West Africa and the *nagual* of Central America and Mexico provide other instances of the same sort.[42]

Both the medicine man and the shaman may acquire their special powers by inheritance or, more rarely, by purchase or by gift. In the Tongaranka tribe of New South Wales an eldest son succeeds to his father, but only practices upon the latter's death.[43] A Murngin usually teaches his son the secrets of sorcery, saying to him, "You do this way and that way, and by and by, after I die, you can do this too." The novice must associate with his father in a murder or two before he can secure sufficient power to be considered a full-fledged sorcerer. His *mana* comes to him from the *mana* of the person whom he has killed or helped to kill.[44]

The beneficent magic of "departmental experts" among the Roro-speaking tribes of Papua is handed down by tradition. An expert usually trains one of his sons or one of his sister's. Sorcery is also hereditary. A well-known sorcerer explained that since his father had practiced it naturally the "power" involved passed to him.[45] Many magical formulas of the Trobriand Islanders are connected with particular localities and are hereditary in the female line from maternal uncle to nephew. Magic for the growth of the gardens, to bring rain, and to overcome enemies in war belongs to this class. Some formulas, not locally circumscribed, may be transmitted from father to son and even, at a fair price, from stranger to stranger. Magic for treating sickness, for initiating a man into certain crafts, for making love, for avoiding insect bites, and for removing the bad effects of incest is included in this second class.[46]

Among the Manus of the Admiralty Islands magical procedures are usually secrets which a father passes on to his son. They are also purchasable by outsiders.[47] In Eddystone Island, one of the Solomons, a sorcerer's power descends to his (or her) children, though they may be very young at the time of the parent's death.[48] In Mota, one of the Banks Islands, beneficent magic to bring rain and make the gardens fertile is the property of certain men. They have usually inherited their magical objects and rites from the maternal uncle and only exceptionally from the father.[49]

The special knowledge and arts of a Maori *tohunga* might be handed down from father to son, but the profession was not necessarily hereditary. Whether or not the son followed in the paternal footsteps depended on his personal inclinations and abilities.[50]

Among the natives of Yap, which belongs to the Caroline group, the office of a petty magician usually descends from father to son. If the father has no son, or if the son shows no desire to assume the office, the magician may impart his secret spells and rites to a kinsman or a close friend, who will succeed to them upon his death. The new magician takes care to preserve the skull of his predecessor, in order to acquire the latter's occult powers.[51] In the Palau Islands knowledge of the different kinds of magic is a secret jealously preserved by certain people. Only when about to die do they transmit it to their sons or nearest relatives.[52]

Among the Negritos of Zambales, Philippine Islands, the magical profession seems to be hereditary in most cases. However, anyone who belongs to a family of magicians or who has met success as a doctor can set up as a practitioner.[53] The office of magician is very often hereditary among the Land Dayak of Borneo.[54] This is also true of the Peninsular Malays and of the Negritos.[55] With the latter it is usually necessary for the son of a deceased *poyang*, should he desire to exercise his father's magical powers, to be inspired by the latter's soul. For this purpose the corpse of the dead man is carefully watched by friends and relatives for six days and nights, during which time the soul of the deceased transmigrates into a tiger. On the seventh day the son must watch near the corpse alone. Before long he sees the tiger, apparently about to make a fatal spring upon him. If he keeps cool and betrays not the slightest symptom of alarm, the seeming tiger will disappear. The forms of two beautiful women then present themselves to him, as he lies in a deep trance. These become henceforth his familiar spirits. Should the heir of the *poyang* fail to observe this ceremonial his father's soul, it is believed, will pass forever into the tiger's body and his magical powers will be permanently lost.[56]

The Bathonga doctor generally bequeaths his knowledge of the healing art to his son or to a uterine nephew who feels an urge to enter upon a professional career. This being the case, the doctors differ very greatly as regards competence. There are some "really clever" men whose fathers and grandfathers had practiced before them and had transmitted to them the valuable legacy of their experience.[57] The position of medicine man is not generally hereditary with the Akamba, but it seems to be easy for several members of the same family to enter the magical profession.[58] Among the Karamoja tribes of eastern Uganda the office of magician is hereditary in the male line.[59] A Shilluk medicine man usually designates as his successor a son who seems to possess occult power. A daughter may be chosen if she is indicated as its possessor.[60]

Certain members of the magical profession among the Barundi have the power to make rain. Before dying a father confides to a son or some other member of his family the secrets of the art, together with the necessary formulas.[61] A Bangala magician teaches his son all his "tricks." He will also teach (for a large fee) any youth in whose family there has been a magician. A candidate without this background is told that he must first kill by witchcraft all the members of his family, as offerings to the spirit of that branch of the profession to which he aspires. Of course, no man would be callous enough to commit all these murders, even were the prospective victims willing to be sacrificed. The result is that the secrets of the profession are confined to a few insiders.[62]

Among the Kwotto of Nigeria a magician transmits his power

to a successor by heredity, by voluntary gift, or by sale. The recipient is first taught the secret composition of charms and the necessary procedure for their manipulation. As long as the teacher lives his permission must be secured before the charms can be used, and suitable presents must be made to him as a sort of royalty payment. After the teacher's death the pupil keeps up regular sacrifices at his grave. Charms thus obtained are valueless to an outsider. It would not be worthwhile to steal them or counterfeit them, because a person who did so would lack the magical power required for their operation.[63]

The hereditary or virtually hereditary nature of the magician's office is reported for many Indian tribes in both South America and North America. Among the Witoto and Boro of the Upper Amazon the eldest son, "if efficient," succeeds to his father's practice. A medicine man often has with him a boy, who may be his son, actual or adopted, and who is, preferably, a child with an epileptic tendency.[64] Among the Yecuaná of Venezuela a father teaches a son, or a near relative takes charge of his tuition. Boys become magicians at an early age.[65] A Warrau *piai* teaches his eldest son the secrets of the profession. If he does not have sons he chooses a friend to succeed him.[66] A Tarahumara must always be instructed in the mysteries of magic. Dreaming, alone, does not qualify a person for its practice. A magician takes as pupils his own children or those of his brothers. Other pupils, not blood-relations, will seldom be taught all he knows. He may also transfer his knowledge to outsiders for a sufficient consideration.[67]

Pima Examining Physicians may be medicine men or medicine women. Entrance to the order is gained chiefly by inheritance.[68] Among the Apache almost every adult person is, in a way, a magician, since he is a potential recipient of occult power and the custodian of ceremonies which, as one native expressed it, afford him "help for everything against which he has to contend." Besides being acquired by a dream or some other experience, these ceremonies can be transmitted, usually from an elder to a youth, but the transfer must be made in accordance with the wishes of the "supernatural" agent granting the power in question. When ceremonies pass outside the family circle, a fee is always exacted by the original owner and teacher.[69]

With reference to the Northern Maidu of California we learn that the office of magician is almost always hereditary. Should a man have several children all would become magicians after his death. His tutelary spirits are also inherited, but they are very angry when their owner dies and someone else takes them over. They must be pacified with offerings, songs, and dances repeated many times, perhaps for several winters. Only when this has been done does the new magician dare to begin his practice.[70]

The Kwakiutl of British Columbia have many myths relating to spirits that are in constant contact with the Indians. Every young man, having first prepared himself by fasting and purificatory washings, tries to find a spiritual protector of this sort. It does not appear to him in dreams or visions, but is inherited from his clan ancestor, who originally acquired it. He authenticates his reception by the spirit by giving a dance in which he personates it and wears its mask and ornaments. The dance is thus a dramatic representation of the myth relating to the acquisition of the hereditary spirit. At the same time the dancer gives public notice that he is now endowed with the magical gifts once made to his clan ancestor. These gifts include a harpoon, whose possession insures success in sea-otter fishing; the death-bringer, which, when pointed against enemies, kills them; the water of life, which resuscitates the dead; the burning fire, which, when directed toward any object, consumes it; and a special dance, a special song, and certain cries that are peculiar to the spirit. A man in the possession of these gifts becomes *naualak* ("supernatural"), a designation which is also applied to the spirit itself.[71]

The office of a Haida shaman was usually hereditary, passing from the maternal uncle to a nephew. Before a shaman died he revealed his spirits to his successor, who might start with a rather feeble spirit and gradually acquire stronger and stronger spiritual guides.[72] Among the Tlingit of southern Alaska it is customary for a man to transmit to a son or grandson his shamanistic powers, together with the masks, trumpets, and insignia of his profession.[73]

It is the general opinion among the Mackenzie River Eskimo that of those spirits which can become familiars and tutelaries every one is in the service of some shaman. Hence, when a young man wants to enter the shamanistic profession, he must secure a spirit from a person who is already a shaman or else obtain one that has been freed by the death of its owner. Ordinarily a shaman possesses about half a dozen of these spiritual helpers, and when engaged in some professional activity, such as searching for a hidden article, he will summon them and send them out, one after another, to find it. Now if a shaman is old and decrepit or is simply "hard up," he may be willing to sell a spirit to some ambitious youth who can afford to pay for a possession so valuable perhaps as much as a canoe, twenty deer skins, two bags of seal oil, and a greenstone labret. The purchase price is not repaid should the young man, having summoned the spirit, find it recalcitrant and unwilling to appear to its new owner. When he has once publicly paid for a spirit he will seldom admit that it refused to associate with him, for then he could never officiate as a shaman, and, moreover, would lose social standing by reason of the contretemps. He pretends, therefore, that he has received the spirit and goes into as good an imitation of a trance as he can manage. If he succeeds in his undertaking, a cure, for instance, his reputation is made. If he fails, nothing is lost, "for it is as easy for an Eskimo to explain the failure of a shamanistic performance as it is for us to explain why a prayer is not answered."[74]

In all the Siberian tribes the shamanistic office seems to be hereditary whenever a descendant of a shaman shows a mental predisposition for this strenuous calling. If not bestowed by hereditary right, the office can be assumed only by someone whom the spirits have clearly chosen for their service.[75] Among the Alaren Buriat only people having in the male or female line ancestors who were shamans can enter the profession. If no adult is available a child that gives evidence of spirit possession, for instance, by weeping incontinently and starting up suddenly when asleep, is chosen and carefully trained to be a shaman. He may begin to practice when not more than thirteen years old.[76] Among the Chukchi the shamanistic call may come to mature people as the result of some great misfortune or during a serious and protracted illness. Then the subject, having no other resource, turns to the spirits for help. The shaman Niron received the shamanistic call during his search for a herd of reindeer that had run away in a thick fog. There was also the case of Katek, who had been carried away on an ice floe. In his desperation he made ready to kill himself when the head of a walrus appeared above the water and sang, "O Katek, do not kill yourself! You shall again see the mountains of Unisak and the little Kuwakak, your elder son." Katek returned home safely and made a sacrifice to the head of the walrus. From that time he was a shaman very famous among his people.[77]

A man may have had revelations through dreams or visions which persuade him and his associates that he has indeed been selected by the spirits to be a magician; he may have received occult power as the result of possession by spirits; or he may have inherited his power, purchased it, or obtained it as a gift. Yet the instances are few where he enters upon the duties of an exacting profession without a course of self-training or, more commonly, an initiation by the established masters of magic. His novitiate presents certain features repeated endlessly throughout the aboriginal world. The neophyte is secluded and thus separated from the activities of ordinary life; submits to fasting, loss of sleep, and other privations or to ordeals of a painful and perhaps repulsive character; observes severe restrictions and taboos; receives instruction in everything pertaining to his future career; and, finally, having been provided with the materials of his art, is admitted to practice by a ceremony of graduation or consecration.[78]

This formal preparation of medicine men and shamans resembles in its main features the ritual of initiation whereby young men at puberty or thereabouts are introduced to their duties and responsibilities as members of the community. Isolation and seclusion, ordeal and purification, are features common to both sets of rites. The likeness between the two often extends to details, such as the simulated death and rebirth of the novices and their acquisition of a new name and a new language in keeping with their changed state. Such resemblances are not fortuitous. It is the fundamental purpose of all these rites to place their recipients *en rapport* with occult power.

A Yualayai boy who has been chosen by the old medicine men to follow their profession is taken at night to a burial ground. He is tied down, fires are lighted all around him, and then he is left alone. That night the boy, if "shaky in his nerves, has rather a bad time." A spirit comes and turns him over. A big star falls close to him and from it emerges an iguana, his totem animal. Next a snake, the hereditary enemy of the iguana, approaches and, in spite of the boy's struggles to free himself, crawls over him and licks him. The snake goes away, leaving the boy "as one paralyzed." A huge figure, which has appeared on the scene, drives a yam stick into the novice's head and pulls it out through his back. In the hole thus made is placed a stone, a lump of crystal, by means of which magicians perform their feats. The spirits of the dead make their appearance and dance a corroboree, chant songs dealing with the medical art, and tell the novice how in the future he can enlist their aid. The spirits silently and mysteriously fade from sight, morning breaks, and the old medicine men release their prisoner. For several nights thereafter he is tied down again, visited by the ghosts, and given further instruction. His ordeal has now ended, but for the next two months he is not allowed to return to the camp. Several years pass before he may practice as a conjuror and healer.[79]

In the Arunta and Ilpirra tribes a youth who desires to be initiated by the medicine men is conducted by them to a secluded spot, required to stand up with his hands clasped behind his head, and told that whatever happens he must observe strict silence. Having withdrawn from their bodies a number of small clear crystals, they press these so firmly against his head and trunk that blood flows from the scoring and scratching. To be sure that the magical influence of the stones has really entered the candidate the operation is repeated three times on the first day and again on the two days following. An incision about half an inch long is also made in his tongue with a crystal. Water containing the stones is given him to drink and native tobacco containing them to chew. After these proceedings the candidate's body is smeared with grease and painted with special designs. The newly made magician is required to remain at the men's camp for a month, keep silent until the wound in his tongue has healed, and be very abstemious in his diet. At night he must sleep with a fire between him and his wife, so that the spirits will know that he is keeping away from women. Should he fail to do so, the spirits would cause his power to leave him and he could never officiate as a medicine man.[80]

Warramunga magicians, instead of projecting crystals into a candidate's body, insert through a hole in his septum a mass of tightly wound fur string. The deepest mystery attaches to this innocent-looking object, which was made by the snakes in the Alcheringa, the dream time when lived the mythic ancestors of the tribe. It is full of occult power and is the magician's emblem of his profession. During the initiatory period a candidate does not eat or drink, nor is he allowed a moment's rest. He must walk about until he becomes thoroughly exhausted and so stupefied that he is quite ready to believe that the officiating magicians have removed his internal organs and have provided him with a new set. In this tribe the food restrictions incumbent on newly made doctors continue to be observed by them until they reach old age. Any infringement of the restrictions would subject a man to the loss of his healing power and would also result in a severe, perhaps fatal, illness. Furthermore, a doctor whose hair has not turned gray must bring the forbidden articles of food to the old practitioners, under penalty, again, of becoming very ill. In fact, they can kill him with impunity if he fails to comply with this rule.[81]

In the western islands of Torres Straits the profession of magician seems to have been open to all men, but few cared to undergo the rigorous initiation required. A candidate was taken into the bush by his instructor, an old man, and forced to eat the decomposing flesh of a human corpse, that of a shark or of some other biting fish, and certain fruits and plants which made his eyes red, his skin itchy, and his "inside bad." He became very ill and half-frantic in consequence. Sometimes a candidate showed the white feather and gave up the whole business; sometimes he ruined his health and even died during the initiatory training. The ordeals lasted about a month, after which the would-be magician received instruction for three years in all the mysteries of his craft.[82]

A prospective magician among the Marind of Netherlands New Guinea eats nothing but fried bananas for a period of from five to seven days. Meanwhile his instructor prepares a magical potion, consisting chiefly of the juices of a corpse. This is drunk repeatedly and in considerable quantities by the novice. Sometimes he becomes unconscious as the result of the dosing; sometimes he raves like a madman. Corpse juice is also dripped into his nose and eyes. Thereby he is endowed with the ability to do things impossible for ordinary mortals and to see things which the ghosts, but not men, can see.[83]

In New Zealand the Whare Kura ("House of Learning"), also called the Whare Wananaga, was an organization of the Maori priest-magicians. Their esoteric knowledge of ritual, mythology, and magic, both white and black, was communicated only to a few young men carefully selected as worthy to receive it. During the period of training the pupils lived in some secluded spot away from the village or in a special house set apart for the purpose. No one not engaged either in teaching or learning was allowed to be present. Besides receiving instruction in the tribal lore and traditions, the pupils were practiced in sleight-of-hand, ventriloquism, and other branches of the magical art. Graduation was a public exhibition at which they displayed their proficiency.[84] It is said that very few students in the "House of Learning" completed the required course. A young man had to be very gifted, indeed, to retain and assimilate the vast stock of history, songs, spells, and genealogical information with which a *tohunga* was expected to be familiar.[85]

Among the Sea Dayak the initiation of a *manang* is carried out by three or four established practitioners, who assemble at the aspirant's house. The young man lies on a mat, with a pillow under his head and a blanket covering his body. Several bushels of rice are heaped upon him. His eyelids are pierced with two fish-hooks, which give him the power to see souls and diagnose diseases. A coconut is split in two with a chopper to signify that henceforth he has ceased to be an ordinary man and is now a *manang*. Then the magicians raise him to his feet and lead him round and round, meanwhile waving blossoms of the areca palm over his head. Finally the young man falls down in a swoon and is again covered with the blanket. Each one of the attending magicians now contributes some of his medicines, so that the neophyte may have the necessary equipment with which to begin his practice. The proceedings end with a feast and a sacrifice.[86]

In each Vedda community there is one person, the shaman, who has the power and knowledge to deal with the ghosts. If well treated, they will show loving kindness to their survivors and only if neglected will they fail to give assistance or become actively hostile. The shaman becomes possessed at times by a ghost, which speaks through his mouth in hoarse and guttural accents. He trains his successor, usually taking as a pupil his son or his sister's son. Among some of the Vedda master and pupil live in a special hut, from which women, being considered unclean, are excluded. The youth learns the invocations by which the ghosts are addressed and how to approach them with food offerings. It is carefully explained to them that they must not enter the pupil or hurt him while he is learning the principles and methods of his profession. No one, however well trained, is accounted the official shaman of a community during his teacher's lifetime, although, with the latter's consent, he may perform ceremonies and be subject to ghost-possession.[87]

Among the Baiga, an aboriginal tribe of the Central Provinces of India, the chief feature of initiation is a rite whereby a disciple absorbs physically a portion of the master's occult power. The master may take some liquor in his mouth, spit it into a leaf-cup, and then give it to the disciple to drink. Or the latter may drink his blood. Sometimes the master makes a cake from his excreta and requires this to be eaten.[88]

Among the Bavenda of the Transvaal a person who desires to become a medicine man will approach a master of good reputation and ask to be taken as his apprentice. The master, if agreeable to the request, throws his dice and consults his spirits, in order to learn whether the applicant meets their favor. If the dice decide in the negative, the request is refused. During the man's apprenticeship his earnings belong to the master, who also receives a substantial present when the period of tuition has ended. This usually lasts for two or three years, but long after it is over the budding practitioner continues to consult his teacher in difficult cases. The pupil learns all about the different trees and animals, acquires knowledge of the various medicines, and becomes practiced in magical treatments. The master also provides him with samples of all his powders and medicaments and explains their composition. These are mostly collected in the area inhabited by the Bavenda. Some of them cannot be obtained there, but must be procured from distant regions. Obviously the collection of an extensive dispensary is a matter of great difficulty, requiring patience and real acquaintance with the flora and fauna of the country.[89]

The Wachagga, like many other African peoples, treat the practice of sorcery as a crime punishable with death. Those who engage in it do so secretly and always at great personal risk. Sometimes, however, it is occasionally taken up in obedience to a sign from the ancestors; sometimes a witch mother, getting old, will instruct her daughter in the art. In the latter case she makes her daughter swear an oath never to tell what is revealed to her. And the mother continues: "My child, bear up! Even if you are burned with fire, hold out! Even if you are slashed with knives, do not yield! Even if you are stoned, do not abandon your secret!" Then the mother presents her with the materials of the magic art—a skull placed in a beer trough in the attic, the hand of a child preserved there in a pot, and the dried-up arm of a person long dead.[90]

The Bakongo of the Lower Congo have many classes or orders of magicians, the most powerful and wealthy being that of the witch doctors. These functionaries, as their name indicates, are engaged to discover witchcraft and ferret out its practitioners. The profession requires not only cunning but fearlessness as well, for the life of one who engages in it is often threatened by those whom he accuses of the black art. Every doctor has an assistant. "When the time comes for the assistant to receive full power, his master puts his fetish in the center of a circle, and his drum near to his pupil. He beats on his drum, shakes his rattle, and tries to drive his fetish power into his assistant. If the pupil sits stolidly, taking no notice of the drum-beating and rattle-shaking, the master says his assistant is not fit to be a witch doctor; but if the pupil sways to and fro to the rhythm of the beaten drum, jumps about like a madman, and does all kinds of stupid things— as they suppose under the influence of the fetish power that has entered him—he is now pronounced a fully initiated witch doctor, being now possessed by the fetish power of his master."[91]

Among the Calabar Negroes a boy who can see spirits, an *ebumtup,* is taught "how to howl in a professional way, and, by watching his professor, picks up his bedside manner. If he can acquire a showy way of having imitation epileptic fits, so much the better. . . . . You must know the dispositions, the financial position, little scandals, etc., of the inhabitants of the whole district, for these things are of undoubted use in divination and the finding of witches, and in addition you must be able skillfully to dispense charms. . . . . Then some day your professor and instructor dies, his own professional power eats him, or he tackles a disease-causing spirit that is one too many for him, and on you descend his paraphernalia and his practice."[92]

The apprenticeship of a Guiana *piai,* or magician, "was very far from being the proverbial bed of roses. Among other tests he had for many months to practice self-denial and submit under a stinted diet to the prohibition of what were to him accustomed luxuries. He had to satisfy his teacher in his knowledge of the instincts and habits of animals, in the properties of plants, and the seasons for flowering and bearing, for the *piai* man was often consulted as to when and where game was to be found and he was more than often correct in his surmises. He also had to know of the grouping of the stars into constellations, and the legends connected not only with them, but with his own tribe. He had likewise to be conversant with the media for the invocation of the spirits, as chants and recitatives, and also to be able to imitate animal and human voices. He had to submit to a chance of death by drinking a decoction of tobacco in repeated and increasing doses, and to have his eyes washed with an infusion of *hiari* leaves; he slowly recovered, with a confused mind, believing that in his trance, the effect of narcotics and a distempered mind, he was admitted into the company of the spirits, that he conversed with them, and was by themselves consecrated to the office of *piai.*"[93] Among the Barama River Caribs a newly made medicine man was subject to many restrictions for three months following his initiation. He might not have sexual intercourse, eat fish or meat, allow smoke or flames to touch him, or get into the steam coming off a cooking pot. If he did any of the forbidden acts, the spirits which had come to live with him would be offended.[94]

Among the Pima Indians the magical profession was commonly handed down from father to son, and those who entered it by inheritance were held in higher esteem than persons who became magicians as the result of dreams and visions. An aspirant had first to acquire the necessary power. The medicine man made him assume a position on all fours and then threw four sticks at him. If he fell to the ground, he was "shot" with the power. Then the instructor coughed up white balls, the size of mistletoe berries, and rubbed them into the breast of the youth. Four or five balls were thus administered, though sometimes the power began to work when only one or two balls had been used. The instructor would also teach the novice, receiving as fee a horse, some calico cloth, or other remuneration. During the initiatory period the novice might not go near a woman's menstrual lodge, nor might he practice until two or more years had elapsed.[95]

A young man who wished to become a shaman among the Haida had to seclude himself in the forest and eat very little food and that only at sunset. An instructor visited him regularly and made him fully acquainted with all the herbs used in the practice of medicine. During weeks of hardship, fasting, and solitude his body became emaciated and his mind somewhat deranged, so that he could see spirits and understand strange and "supernatural" things. In the old days the novice on his return to the village had to partake of human flesh, that of a witch, but later the shamans and chiefs in council decreed that it would suffice for him to bite a piece out of the flesh of the first person he met on the way home. Owing to European influence a dog was substituted for the human victim. The animal received great honor, because a shaman had partaken of a part of its body. If the associated shamans approved of the aspirant and he paid them the usual fees they admitted him into their fraternity.[96]

Among the Greenland Eskimo a boy who has been chosen by the magicians to follow their profession begins his secret novitiate when only seven or eight years old. It may last as long as twelve years. As a rule every budding *angakok* has several paid teachers, who instruct him in the various branches of the magical art.[97] A would-be shaman among the Iglulik Eskimo first makes a very valuable gift to the person under whom he desires to study. He may have two instructors, each of whom requires a present. His course of tuition is not long, sometimes not more than five days. Upon graduation he is required to abstain for an entire year from the marrow, breast, entrails, head, and tongue of animals. Whatever meat he does eat must be raw, clean flesh. Women during this year of probation submit to additional restrictions, the most important being the prohibition of any needlework.[98]

Among the Chukchi a person who has received the call to shamanship loses all interest in ordinary affairs, ceases to work or to talk to people, eats but little, and sleeps a great deal. He may live for a time in the wilderness and hold communion there with the spirits that are to be his familiars, or he may seclude himself in an inner room during the process of acquiring what the Chukchi call "shamanistic power." In addition he usually receives some tuition from an old shaman. This includes singing, dancing, drum-beating, ventriloquism, and other tricks of the profession. There may also be a transfer of occult power from the instructor to his pupil. A Chukchi shaman blows on the eyes or into the mouth of the pupil, or, having first stabbed himself with a knife, plunges it, still reeking with his "source of life," into the novice's body.[99] Among the Tungus, children who are to become shamans are taught by older practitioners the various forms and ceremonies. They also learn about the medical properties of plants and how to forecast the weather by watching the behavior and migrations of animals across the steppes.[100]

A formal ceremony of consecration completes the initiatory training and admits the youth to his office. Among the Yakut an old practitioner takes the candidate to a hill or an open field, clothes him in the shaman's costume, and gives him the tambourine and drumstick that are the symbols of his profession. He is placed between nine chaste youths and nine chaste maidens and required to promise that he will be faithful to his possessing spirit. Then the old shaman, having killed a sacrificial animal, sprinkles the candidate's clothes with its blood, after which the spectators proceed to feast on its flesh. The consecratory ritual among the Buriat is still more elaborate.[101]

It appears from these representative cases that the initiatory ordeals to which novices must submit are most severe and terrifying in the Australian area and South America. In North America the acquisition of occult power is often a matter of the aspirant's voluntary quest for an experience putting him in touch with the spirits, and in such cases the preliminary fasting, torture, and privations which he endures are self-inflicted. He is a suppliant before the spirits, and these must be propitiated. Among the Siberian peoples, as we have learned, a man does not usually become a shaman of his own free will but is called to the profession by the spirits. He must indeed submit to austerities, but these are undergone, not in reality, but in a dream or a vision. Once he has accepted the call to shamanship the spirits come to him and endow him with the necessary power. Ordeals as an initiatory feature do not seem to be stressed in the African area, where the emphasis is rather upon the necessity of a long and careful preparation for the magician's profession. On the other hand, every quarter of the aboriginal world affords instructive examples of the efforts made by the officiating magicians to transfer to a neophyte some portion of their power, without which he would work in vain.

NOTES TO CHAPTER VIII

[1] Among the North American Indians the two methods of acquiring occult power by medicine men have different distributions. In the western section of the Southwest, in the southern Great Basin, and in California as far north as the Maidu and Wailapi area the power comes involuntarily. The quest for it is found on the southern Northwest coast, in the Plateau region from the Apache in the south to the Tahltan in the north, in the Plains region, and throughout eastern North America. In northern California, southern Oregon, and the northern Great Basin both methods occur. See Leslie Spier, in *University of California Publications in American Archaeology and Ethnology*, XXX, 249 ff., with a map.

[2] A. W. Howitt, *The Native Tribes of South-East Australia* (London, 1904), pp. 404 f., 408, 436 f., 543. Cf. R. B. Smith, *The Aborigines of Victoria* (Melbourne, 1878), I, 462.

[3] W. E. Roth, *Ethnological Studies among the North-West-Central Queensland Aborigines* (Brisbane, 1897), p. 153; idem, *North Queensland Ethnography Bulletin*, No. 5, pp. 29 f. Malkari or Mulkari is described as the spirit or "supernatural power" that makes everything which the natives cannot otherwise account for.

[4] John Mathew, *Eaglehawk and Crow* (London, 1899), pp. 143, 146; idem, *Two Representative Tribes of Queensland* (London, 1910), pp. 171 ff. This myth of the acquisition of a fur rope from the rainbow is widespread in Queensland and other parts of Australia (W. Robertson, *Coo-ee Tales* [Sydney, 1928], p. 74).

[5] Sir Baldwin Spencer and F. J. Gillen, *The Native Tribes of Central Australia* (London, 1899), pp. 522 ff. On initiation by ancestral ghosts among the Unmatjira, Warramunga, Binbinga, and Mara see iidem, *The Northern Tribes of Central Australia* (London, 1904), pp. 480 ff.

[6] E. M. Loeb, "Shaman and Seer," *American Anthropologist*, XXXI (1929), 64, 66 ff.

[7] A. R. Radcliffe-Brown, *The Andaman Islanders* (Cambridge, 1933), pp. 176 f., 301 f. According to another account the position of a magician ("dreamer") is generally attained by a person who relates an extraordinary dream, the details of which are borne out subsequently by some unforeseen event such as a sudden death by accident. See E. H. Man, *On the Aboriginal Inhabitants of the Andaman Islands* (London, 1932), pp. 28 f.; *idem*, in *Journal of the Anthropological Institute*, XII (1883), 96 f.

[8] George Whitehead, *In the Nicobar Islands* (London, 1924), pp. 149 ff.

[9] B. J. F. Laubscher, *Sex, Custom, and Psychopathology* (London, 1937), pp. 1 f.

[10] W. S. Routledge and Katherine Routledge, *With a Prehistoric People* (London, 1910), p. 251; J. W. W. Crawford, "The Kikuyu Medicine Man," *Man*, IX (1909), 53.

[11] Curt Nimuendajú, *The Apinayé* (Washington, D.C., 1939), pp. 142 ff. *The Catholic University of America, Anthropological Series*, No. 8. The Apinayé consider that venomous snakes, their worst enemy, are the magician's special friends. Every would-be practitioner of the magical art is supposed to be bitten by such a snake and to be able to overcome the effects of its poison. Then the snakes lie in wait for him in order to converse with him (p. 148).

[12] Jules Henry, *Jungle People. A Kaingáng Tribe of the Highlands of Brazil* (New York, 1941), p. 74.

[13] Our authority knew of a man who claimed to receive occult power from his own "anal flatulence." He used it in games of chance (M. E. Opler, *An Apache Life-Way* [Chicago, 1941], p. 206).

[14] *Idem*, "The Concept of Supernatural Power among the Chiracahua and Mescalero Apache," *American Anthropologist* (n.s., 1935), XXXVII, 65-70. "Supernatural" power, declares our authority, is in the widest sense the animating principle, the life-force of the universe. Again and again medicine men have terminated a discussion as to the authenticity of this power by exclaiming, "It is alive! It speaks to me!" (*An Apache Life-Way*, p. 205.)

[15] M. R. Harrington, *Religion and Ceremonies of the Lenape* (New York, 1921), pp. 63 f. *Indian Notes and Monographs*, No. 19.

[16] Stansbury Hagar, "Micmac Magic and Medicine," *Journal of American Folk-Lore*, IX (1896), 170 ff.

[17] A. L. Kroeber, in *Bulletin of the American Museum of Natural History*, XVIII, 418 f., 435 f., 450. While the vision forms the most characteristic method of securing occult power among the Arapaho this is also sometimes sold or given by a man to a son or a nephew. Sometimes, again, animals and spirits may visit people without solicitation and offer to confer power upon them (450 f.).

[18] *Idem*, "Gros Ventre Myths and Tales," *Anthropological Papers of the American Museum of Natural History*, I, 122.

[19] G. B. Grinnell, *When Buffalo Ran* (New Haven, 1920), pp. 79 f. (an Indian's autobiographical account).

[20] R. B. Dixon, in *Bulletin of the American Museum of Natural History*, XVII, 471 f.

[21] *Ibid.*, XVII, 472 ff.

[22] R. L. Olson, *The Quinault Indians* (Seattle, 1936), p. 152. *University of Washington Publications in Anthropology*, Vol. VI, No. 1.

[23] James Teit, in *Memoirs of the American Museum of Natural History*, IV, 287.

[24] Franz Boas, "The Mythology of the Bella Coola Indians," *Memoirs of the American Museum of Natural History*, II, 42. The "wand" referred to seems to be the well-known bull-roarer.

[25] *Idem*, "Tsimshian Mythology," *Thirty-first Annual Report of the Bureau of American Ethnology*, pp. 332, 473 f.

[26] Cornelius Osgood, *Contributions to the Ethnography of the Kutchin* (New Haven, 1936), p. 156. *Yale University Publications in Anthropology*, No. 14.

[27] G. T. Emmons, *The Tahltan Indians* (Philadelphia, 1911), p. 112. *The University Museum, Anthropological Publications*, Vol. IV, No. 1.

[28] J. L. D. van der Roest, in *Tijdscrift voor Indische Taal-Land-en Volkenkunde*, XL (1898), 164 ff.

[29] R. H. Codrington, *The Melanesians* (Oxford, 1891), pp. 153 f., 218 f.

[30] E. B. Christie, *The Subanuns of Sindangan Bay* (Manila, 1909), pp. 71 f. *Bureau of Science, Division of Ethnology Publications*, Vol. VI, Pt. I.

[31] Charles Hose and William McDougall, *The Pagan Tribes of Borneo* (London, 1912), II, 130 f. Cf. Charles Hose, *Natural Man. A Record from Borneo* (London, 1926), p. 244.

[32] A. T. Bryant, "The Zulu Cult of the Dead," *Man*, XVII (1917), 141 ff. Cf. Henry Callaway, *The Religious System of the Amazulu* (London, 1870), pp. 259 ff.

[33] H. A. Junod, *The Life of a South African Tribe* (2d ed., London, 1927), II, 479 ff. A woman of the author's acquaintance had remarkable subliminal faculties. She could even discover witches! Once she met at night several men. One of them was leading his own wife, whom he intended to eat. The woman instantly recognized them as witches and said to them, "No use eating her. Her meat is bitter sour." Terrified, they fled and confessed their guilt the next morning (II, 500).

[34] W. D. Hambly, *The Ovimbundu of Angola* (Chicago, 1934), p. 273. *Field Museum of Natural History, Anthropological Series*, Vol. XXI, No. 2.

[35] M. W. Stirling, "Jivaro Shamanism," *Proceedings of the American Philosophical Society*, LXXII (1933), 140 f.; *idem*, "Historical and Ethnographical Material on the Jivaro Indians," *Bulletin of the Bureau of American Ethnology*, No. 117, pp. 117 f.

[36] J. R. Swanton, in *Memoirs of the American Museum of Natural History*, VIII, 38; *idem*, "Social Condition, Beliefs, and Linguistic Relationship of the Tlingit Indians," *Twenty-sixth Annual Report of the Bureau of American Ethnology*, pp. 463 f. Among the Shuswap of British Columbia a powerful magician always has more than one spirit at his command (Franz Boas, in *Report of the Sixtieth Meeting of the British Association for the Advancement of Science* [1890], pp. 645 f.). Among the Alaskan Eskimo the more spirits the shaman subjects to his will the stronger his magic (E. W. Nelson, in *Eighteenth Annual Report of the Bureau of American Ethnology*, Part I, p. 428). In eastern Greenland the spirits of an *angakok* number from ten to fifteen (William Thalbitzer, "Les magiciens Esquimaux," *Journal de la Société des Américanistes de Paris* [n.s., 1930], XXII, 79). The conception of the shaman's assistant spirits who, in turn, are ruled over by the shaman's supreme protective spirit, is widespread in Siberia. It has been found among Mongolian tribes (Yakut and Buriat), Altai-Turkish tribes (Teleut and Urankhai), the Palaeo-Asiatic peoples in the extreme northeast of Asia (Yukaghir, Chukchi, Koriak), and the Goldi of the Amur. See Leo (L. J.) Sternberg, "Divine Election in Primitive Religion," *Congrès International des Américanistes, Compte-Rendu de la XXIe Session*, Deuxième Partie (Göteborg, Sweden, 1924), pp. 472 ff.

[37] William Thalbitzer, "The Heathen Priests of East Greenland," *Verhandlungen des XVI Internationalen Amerikanisten-Kongresses,* Erste Hälfte (Wien, 1908), pp. 448, 454 ff. Thalbitzer points out that the relation between an *angakok* and his assisting spirits seems to be "a purely mechanical mastership" rather than "a mystical alliance." When the future magician arrives at the stage of his training when he obtains spirits they appear before him for service (p. 454).

[38] *Idem,* "Les magiciens Esquimaux," *Journal de la Société des Américanistes de Paris* (n.s., 1930), XXII, 78. Cf. Fridtjof Nansen, *Eskimo Life* (2d ed., London, 1894), pp. 281 f.

[39] Leo (L. F.) Sternberg, "Divine Election in Primitive Religion," *Congrès International des Américanistes, Compte-Rendu de la XXIe Session,* Deuxième Partie (Göteborg, Sweden, 1924), pp. 473 ff. A Giliak of Sakhalin said to Sternberg that he had been ill for two months, lying motionless and unconscious. "I should have died, had I not become a shaman" (*idem,* "Die Religion der Gilyaken," *Archiv für Religionswissenschaft,* VIII [1904–1905], 467 f.). All the Buriat shamans with whom Sandschejew had intercourse told him that they had adopted the shamanistic profession "most unwillingly" (Garma Sandschejew, "Weltanschauung und Schamanismus der Alaren-Burjaten," *Anthropos,* XXIII [1928], 977). Stadling was told by a young Samoyed shaman that possession by a spirit involves a severe mental crisis. It begins, as a rule, "with a feeling of deep anguish and trembling," followed by a state of trance in which the soul leaves its earthly tabernacle and enters the upper world of spirits. See J. Stadling, "Shamanism," *Contemporary Review,* LXXIX (1901), 95.

[40] W. Jochelson, in *Memoirs of the American Museum of Natural History,* X, 47; XIII, 31 f.

[41] The Yualayai of New South Wales believe that any injury to a magician's animal familiar (*yunbeai*) hurts him also (Mrs. K. L. Parker, The *Euahlayi Tribe* [London, 1915], pp. 20 ff.). In the Banks Islands there is a definite identification of personality between a man and his *tamaniu.* The injury or death of the one necessarily involves the illness or death of the other (W. H. R. Rivers, *The History of Melanesian Society* [Cambridge, 1914], I, 154 ff.). The Shuswap of British Columbia think that a man will die if his tutelary spirit (commonly an animal) is destroyed or if it is imprisoned and he cannot get it back (James Teit, in *Memoirs of the American Museum of Natural History,* IV, 612 f.).

[42] On tutelary spirits among the North American Indians see Sir J. G. Frazer, *Totemism and Exogamy* (London, 1910), III, 370–456. See further Ruth F. Benedict, "The Concept of the Guardian Spirit in North America," *Memoirs of the American Anthropological Association,* No. 29.

[43] A. W. Howitt, *op. cit.,* p. 404.

[44] W. L. Warner, *A Black Civilization* (New York, 1937), pp. 197 f.

[45] C. G. Seligman, *The Melanesians of British New Guinea* (Cambridge, 1910), pp. 279, 281.

[46] Bronislaw Malinowski, " 'Baloma': the Spirits of the Dead in the Trobriand Islands," *Journal of the Royal Anthropological Institute,* XLVI (1916), 388 f.

[47] R. Parkinson, *Dreissig Jahre in der Südsee* (Stuttgart, 1907), p. 402.

[48] A. M. Hocart, "Medicine and Witchcraft in Eddystone of the Solomons," *Journal of the Royal Anthropological Institute,* LV (1925), 229.

[49] W. H. R. Rivers, *op. cit.,* I, 156.

[50] Elsdon Best, "Maori Religion and Mythology," *Dominion Museum Bulletin,* No. 10, p. 166.

[51] S. Walleser, "Religiöse Auschauungen und Gebräuche der Bewohner von Jap (Deutsche Südsee)," *Anthropos*, VIII (1913), 1061.

[52] J. [S.] Kubary, in Adolf Bastian, *Allerlei aus Volks-und Menschenkunde* (Berlin, 1888), I, 47.

[53] W. A. Reed, *Negritos of Zambales* (Manila, 1904), p. 66. Department of the Interior, Ethnological Survey Publications, Vol. II, Pt. I.

[54] H. L. Roth, *The Natives of Sarawak and British North Borneo* (London, 1896), I, 260, quoting William Chalmers. Among the Sea Dayak, while the office of *manang* does not necessarily descend from father to son, it is usually confined to a particular family (*idem*, in *Journal of the Anthropological Institute*, XXI [1892], 115, quoting Brooke Low).

[55] W. W. Skeat, *Malay Magic* (London, 1900), pp. 57, 60; I. H. N. Evans, *Studies in Religion, Folk-Lore, and Custom in British North Borneo and the Malay Peninsula* (Cambridge, 1923), p. 159; Rudolf Martin, *Die Inlandstämme der malayischen Halbinsel* (Jena, 1905), p. 959.

[56] T. J. Newbold, *Political and Statistical Account of the British Settlements in the Straits of Malacca* (London, 1839), II, 388.

[57] H. A. Junod, *op. cit.*, (2d ed.), II, 452 f.

[58] Gerhard Lindblom, *The Akamba in British East Africa* (2d ed., Uppsala, 1920), p. 256.

[59] E. J. Wayland, in *Journal of the Royal Anthropological Institute*, LXI (1931), 206.

[60] D. S. Oyler, "The Shilluk's Belief in the Good Medicine Man," *Sudan Notes and Records*, III (1920), 110.

[61] J. M. M. Van der Burgt, *Un grand peuple de l'Afrique équatoriale* (Bois le Duc, 1904), p. 101.

[62] J. H. Weeks, *Among Congo Cannibals* (London, 1913), pp. 276 f.

[63] J. R. Wilson-Haffenden, *The Red Men of Nigeria* (London, 1930), pp. 190 f.

[64] Thomas Whiffen, *The North-West Amazons* (New York, 1915), p. 181 and note 1.

[65] Theodor Koch-Grünberg, *Vom Roroima zum Orinoco* (Berlin, 1917–28), III, 380.

[66] Richard Schomburgk, *Reisen in Britisch-Guiana* (Leipzig, 1847–48), I, 172.

[67] W. C. Bennett and R. M. Zingg, *The Tarahumara,* (Chicago, 1935), pp. 255 f.

[68] Frank Russell, in *Twenty-sixth Annual Report of the Bureau of American Ethnology*, p. 256.

[69] M. E. Opler, "The Concept of Supernatural Power among the Chiracahua and Mescalero Apache," *American Anthropologist* (n.s., 1935), XXXVII, 68 f.

[70] R. B. Dixon, "Some Shamans of Northern California," *Journal of American Folk-Lore*, XVII (1904), 25 f. If the children of a magician did not take up the magical profession, usually after his death, they too would die (*idem*, in *Bulletin of the American Museum of Natural History*, XVII, 274).

[71] Franz Boas, "The Social Organization and the Secret Societies of the Kwakiutl Indians," *Report of the U.S. National Museum for 1895*, pp. 393 ff.

[72] J. R. Swanton, in *Memoirs of the American Museum of Natural History*, VIII, 38. Sometimes a future shaman might be indicated by certain omens at his birth (Charles Harrison, *Ancient Warriors of the North Pacific* [London, 1925],

p. 99). With the Siberian Chukchi omens, such as meeting a particular animal or finding a stone or a shell of a peculiar form, are sometimes considered as indicative of a man's predisposition for the shamanistic profession (W. Bogoras, in *Memoirs of the American Museum of Natural History*, XI, 418).

[73] Aurel Krause, *Die Tlinkit-Indianer* (Jena, 1885), p. 284.

[74] Vilhjalmur Stefansson, *My Life with the Eskimo* (New York, 1913), pp. 392 ff. Among the Copper Eskimo a familiar spirit may be acquired by purchase from a shaman, but all that the latter can impart is his goodwill and a knowledge of how to approach and summon the spirit. It is still necessary for the purchaser to go out to some lonely place and try to meet the spirit, which may or may not put in an appearance. See Diamond Jenness, *The Life of the Copper Eskimos* (Ottawa, 1922), p. 191. *Report of the Canadian Arctic Expedition, 1913–18,* Vol. XII.

[75] V. M. Mikhailovskii (Mikhailowski), "Shamanism in Siberia and European Russia," *Journal of Anthropological Institute,* XXIV (1895), 85. However, an Ostiak shaman occasionally sells his familiar spirit. "After receiving payment, he divides his hair into tresses and fixes the time when the spirit is to pass to his new master. The spirit, having changed owners, makes his new possessor suffer; if the new shaman does not feel these effects, it is a sign that he is not becoming proficient in his office" (Marie A. Czaplicka, *Aboriginal Siberia* [Oxford, 1914], pp. 177 f., citing a Russian authority, P. I. Tretyakoff).

[76] Garma Sandschejew, "Weltanschauung und Schamanismus der Alaren-Burjaten," *Anthropos,* XXIII (1928), 977 f. The author is a descendant in the eighth generation of a famous shaman and himself received instruction in the shamanistic art.

[77] W. Bogoras, in *Memoirs of the American Museum of Natural History,* XI, 421 ff.

[78] See, in general, H. Hubert and M. Mauss, "L'origine des pouvoirs magiques dans les sociétés Australiennes," in *Mélanges d'histoire des religions* (Paris, 1909), pp. 172–78; W. Bogoras, "The Shamanistic Call and the Period of Initiation in Northern Asia and Northern America," *Proceedings of the Twenty-third International Congress of Americanists* (New York, 1928), pp. 443 f.

[79] Mrs. K. L. Parker, *op. cit.,* pp. 25 ff.

[80] Spencer and Gillen, *The Native Tribes of Central Australia,* pp. 526 ff.

[81] Iidem, *The Northern Tribes of Central Australia,* pp. 484 ff.

[82] A. C. Haddon and C. G. Seligman, in *Reports of the Cambridge Anthropological Expedition to Torres Straits,* V, 323. According to an early account of the South Australian tribes a would-be medicine man, in order to acquire "magic influence," at one time had to eat the flesh of young children and at another time that of an old person (E. J. Eyre, *Journals of Expeditions of Discovery into Central Australia* [London, 1845], II, 255, 359). The Wiimbaio of New South Wales required a candidate for the magical profession to chew the powdered bones of a corpse. He also had to carry about with him the humerus of a disinterred body and to keep gnawing it. These ordeals reduced a man to "a state of frenzy," so that he behaved like a maniac (A. W. Howitt, *op. cit.,* p. 404).

[83] Paul Wirz, *Die Marind-anim von Holländisch-Süd-Neu-Guinea* (Hamburg, 1922–25), Vol. II, Pt. III, pp. 66 f.

[84] Elsdon Best, "Spiritual Concepts of the Maori," *Journal of the Polynesian Society,* IX (1900), 176; idem, "The Maori School of Learning," *Dominion Museum Monographs,* No. 6, pp. 6 ff. When a *tohunga* had taught his pupil

and destined successor all his magical lore he would, if about to die, tell the pupil to bite some part of his body, just as the breath of life was passing from him. This act had the effect of transmitting the *mana* and knowledge of the dying man to the pupil (*idem, The Maori* [Wellington, New Zealand, 1924], I, 245. *Memoirs of the Polynesian Society*, Vol. V).

85 W. E. Gudgeon, "The 'Tohunga'-Maori," *Journal of the Polynesian Society*, XVI (1907), 65.

86 Leo Nyuak, "Religious Rites and Customs of the Iban or Dyaks of Sarawak," *Anthropos*, I (1906), 173. The author, a Christianized native, wrote originally in the Dayak language. According to another account there are three grades or degrees which may be attained by a candidate for the magical profession upon payment of the requisite fees and after undergoing initiation. As the final act of conferring the third and highest degree the candidate lies flat on the floor and the officiating magicians proceed to walk over him and trample him. By so doing they impart to him the occult power which they possess. See E. H. Gomes, *Seventeen Years among the Sea Dyaks of Borneo* (London, 1911), pp. 177 ff. See also J. Perham, "Manangism in Borneo," *Journal of the Straits Branch of the Royal Asiatic Society*, No. 19 (1887), p. 101.

87 C. G. Seligman and Brenda J. Seligman, *The Veddas* (Cambridge, 1911), pp. 125 ff.

88 Verrier Elwin, *The Baiga* (London, 1839), p. 343.

89 H. A. Stayt, *The Bavenda* (London, 1931), pp. 264 f.

90 O. F. Raum, *Chaga Childhood* (London, 1940), p. 369.

91 J. H. Weeks, *Among the Primitive Bakongo* (London, 1914), pp. 214 ff. In this quotation "fetish power" is equivalent to occult power.

92 Mary H. Kingsley, *West African Studies* (1st ed., London, 1899), p. 214.

93 W. E. Roth, "An Inquiry into the Animism and Folk-Lore of the Guiana Indians," *Thirtieth Annual Report of the Bureau of American Ethnology*, p. 338. According to W. H. Brett, when a novice by fasting and drinking tobacco water has been reduced to a condition of extreme sickness and weakness, "his death is loudly proclaimed and his countrymen called to witness his state" (*The Indian Tribes of Guiana* [London, 1868], p. 362). Among the Tupinamba, a group of closely related tribes (now extinct) of the Tupian stock, a novice could acquire the occult power of a magician if the latter blew tobacco smoke upon him. These Indians accorded to tobacco many virtues. Users of it had clear minds; it also kept them sprightly and joyous (Alfred Métraux, *La religion des Tupinamba* [Paris, 1927], pp. 88 f.).

94 John Gillin, *The Barama River Caribs of British Guiana* (Cambridge, Mass., 1936), p. 172. *Papers of the Peabody Museum of American Archaeology and Ethnology*, Vol. XIV, No. 2.

95 Frank Russell, in *Twenty-sixth Annual Report of the Bureau of American Ethnology*, pp. 257 f.

96 Charles Harrison, *op. cit.*, pp. 99 ff. Among the Kwakiutl, novices who take the *hamatsa* degree in a secret society become possessed by a violent desire to eat human flesh. In the old days they used to kill and eat slaves. They also devour corpses. See Franz Boas, "The Social Organization and the Secret Societies of the Kwakiutl Indians," *Report of the U.S. National Museum for 1895*, pp. 437 ff.

97 William Thalbitzer, "The Heathen Priests of East Greenland," *Verhandlungen des XVI Internationalen Amerikanisten-Kongresses*, Erste Hälfte (Wien 1910), pp. 452 ff. Among the Ipurina of western Brazil the preparation for the

magical profession usually begins in boyhood (P. Ehrenreich, *Beiträge zur Völkerkunde Brasiliens* [Berlin, 1891], p. 68). Among the Panama Indians it was customary to take boys from ten to twelve years old for training as future magicians (H. H. Bancroft, *The Native Races of the Pacific States of North America* [New York, 1875–76], I, 777).

⁹⁸ Knud Rasmussen, *Intellectual Culture of the Hudson Bay Eskimos* (Copenhagen, 1930), pp. 111 ff. *Report of the Fifth Thule Expedition*, Vol. VII, No. 1.

⁹⁹ W. Bogoras, in *Memoirs of the American Museum of Natural History*, XI, 425.

¹⁰⁰ Ludwick Niemojowski, *Siberian Pictures* (London, 1883), I, 13. Among the Reindeer Tungus some untrained persons who claim to be shamans only exercise their supposed powers when intoxicated. See Miss E. L. Lindgren, in *Journal of the Royal Central Asian Society*, XXII (1935), 222.

¹⁰¹ V. M. Mikhailovskii (Mikhailowski), "Shamanism in Siberia and European Russia," *Journal of the Anthropological Institute*, XXIV (1895), 86 ff. See also V. Klementz, "Buriats," Hastings' *Encyclopaedia of Religion and Ethics*, III, 15 f.

Chapter IX

THE POWERS OF MAGICIANS

Occult power, so carefully imparted to a medicine man or a shaman and by him preserved so jealously, can be lost if he proves to be unworthy of its retention or comes into contact with what is inimical to it. His power is likewise dissipated if he violates any restrictions laid upon him at the time of initiation or during the period of probation following his entrance upon his profession. Negative regulations of this character are rigorous taboos, which may carry an additional automatic penalty in the shape of sickness or some other evil. It is not uncommon, furthermore, for a magician to be subject to taboos throughout life or during his professional career. Often, also, special regulations must be observed by him when at work, if his power is not to be nullified and his magic to be of no avail. Thus the magician, at least the ideal magician, keeps himself unspotted from the world.

A former Kurnai doctor once could "pull things out of people" by means of his quartz crystals, but he became a drunkard and lost the crystals. From that time, as he explained, he had "never been able to do anything."[1] In the Yualayai tribe of New South Wales an old woman, supposed to have the power of calling up spirits, did not drink any sort of liquid which would heat her internally. If she did so, she could never again communicate with her spiritual advisers and helpers.[2] An Arunta medicine man must abstain from eating certain articles of food, such as fat and warm meat, and from inhaling the smoke of burning bones. Nor may he go near a nest of "bulldog" ants, because, if bitten by one of them, he would be permanently deprived of his powers. The loud barking of the camp dogs will sometimes cause his magical stones "to take flight." Among the Arunta every now and then you will meet an erstwhile doctor who tells you that his stones have gone away from him. In the Kaitish and Unmatjera tribes medicine men are careful not to eat too much fat or allow a big ant to sting them. They also avoid drinking anything hot. A doctor living near a European station was completely deprived of his powers through inadvertently taking a drink of hot tea. A Warramunga doctor lost his powers because, during a fight, he struck with a boomerang a doctor much older than himself.[3] Certain kinds of yams, considered to be "hot," are forbidden to a Kakadu who is being made into a medicine man.[4] A magician of the Murngin (in the Northern Territory of Australia) is subject to but one rigid taboo: he cannot submerge himself in salt water without losing his curative power. Contact with salt water, it seems, is fatal to his familiar spirits. The sad tale is told of an excellent doctor, with a large practice, who once ventured out on the ocean. He was standing up in a canoe when another canoe came along and hit it. Our doctor fell overboard and sank beneath the waves, carrying with him the spirits that had perched upon his head and shoulders. So he lost them forever and with them all his power as a healer. "If I had fallen down in fresh water," he said, "it would not have hurt those doctor children of mine."[5] Among the Bibbulmun of southwestern Australia the medicine men, once pillars of orthodoxy and upholders of tribal custom, took to the white man's drink and, as a result, could no longer perform their duties.[6]

Some of these prohibitions are understandable. The avoidance of fiery liquors and of hot and stinging things would seem to be explained by the belief that the magician is himself in a state of permanent "hotness" which would be neutralized by contact with anything possessing excessive heat.

The Orokaiva, a Papuan tribe, conduct rites for the placation of ancestral ghosts believed to control the growth of the taro plant, the staple food of the natives. The taro "experts," who have charge of the rites, must undergo a period of probation and observe certain food taboos. There is also a prohibition of bathing. Running water would carry off and dissipate the *mana* of the expert and thus render his operations futile. Novices in training are allowed, however, to wash themselves in still, swampy water. It sometimes happens that a Taro man will resign his onerous office because he cannot resist the temptation of forbidden foods (a fat eel, for instance) or because he can no longer forego the pleasure of a midday swim.[7] A Bukaua rain maker, after performing his magic, refrains from betel chewing and all kinds of work. He must rub black earth into his hair, dotting it also on his forehead and nose, and bathe in the sea at dawn. While bathing he extends his hands over the water and calls on the rain. If he observes all these negative and positive prescriptions, it is believed that his efforts will ultimately be rewarded by a big downpour.[8]

Of the food restrictions observed by a magician in the Trobriand Islands some depend on the contents of the spell which he recites. Thus, if red fish are mentioned by him, he must not eat them; if a certain dog is referred to, it must not be heard howling while he eats. In other cases the particular article of food which he seeks to affect by his operation is forbidden to him, as in fishing magic and garden magic. Still other restrictions relate to the performance of the magical act. The rain magician has to paint himself black and remain unwashed and unkempt while bringing about a downpour. The shark magician is required to keep his house open, to remove his pubic leaf, and to sit with his legs apart, "so that the shark's mouth might remain gaping."[9] In the D'Entrecasteaux Islands nearly every hamlet has its professional "singer," who knows the proper spell for yams and perhaps for other food plants as well. At the time of planting and for six months thereafter the singer sleeps apart from his wife. Not until the yams are ripe for harvest is the restriction removed. Certain choice articles of food are likewise forbidden him until the crop has been gathered. Should he fail to observe any taboo the yams would be sure to wither.[10] In Dobu Island the rain maker, besides keeping scrupulously clean by frequent bathing in the sea, must be shaven all over, both head and body. Even a little dirt on him would be inimical to rain.[11] In the Yabob or Yomba Islands, a small group lying off the coast of what was formerly German New Guinea, the success of the rain maker's magic is absolutely dependent upon his observance of certain restrictions until the rain comes. He must not drink water (though he may partake of coconut milk), eat anything cooked with water, or engage in sexual intercourse. The sun magician, who would compel that luminary to shine forth and warm the earth, observes the same regulations, but in his case they last for two months after the desired result has been attained.[12]

A sorcerer in the New Hebrides, before engaging in his nefarious art, must not have sexual intercourse and must not even approach a woman lest he "smell" her. Nor may he eat things short or round in shape, for these are connected with the female sex. Six or seven varieties of yams and breadfruit are thus interdicted. Furthermore, he avoids all contact with water and things connected with water, and for a few days takes no liquid at all. He eats nothing which lives in or belongs to the sea. Any moist food is likewise prohibited. In short, he must keep as dry as possible. Unless these negative rules are observed his magic will not be efficacious; indeed there is grave danger that it will bounce back and injure him instead of his intended victim. The length of time that a sorcerer will observe taboos depends partly on the degree of potency which he wishes to give to his magic and partly on the intensity of his wrath or desire for revenge. For a matter of no great importance he may be satisfied with abstentions lasting only a month or so, but if he has vowed undying vengeance they will remain in force perhaps as long as two years. In general, his food taboos last longer than those which prohibit his indulgence in sexual intercourse.[13]

A Maori seer who disregarded a rule of *tapu* (taboo) at once lost his power of second sight and became spiritually blind, that is, "he would be unable to see the portents and signs by means of which the gods warn man of dangers that threaten him, and enable him to peer into the future."[14]

In Yap, one of the Caroline Islands, magicians are numerous and influential. They observe certain taboos. The magician who pronounces incantations over the people must abstain from eating fish for three, five, or nine days, according to the importance of his rite. Sometimes he may not go near his wife. He may not eat food cooked by a woman or a child. However, an old woman, past the age of childbearing, is allowed to cultivate his garden for him and take its produce to his house. The war magician must never eat anything that grows in a hostile district. This prohibition is still observed, although wars have long been things of the past.[15]

A Hottentot magician never touches cold water and never washes from one year to another. His power resides, as it were, in the dirt which clings to his body. Touching water would lessen his power, while complete immersion would result in its disappearance. There was once a witch doctor who had engaged in evil practices. By the chief's order the culprit was ducked in a pond, and when his head bobbed out above the water, down he was plunged again. This treatment proved to be successful, for he lost all his magical potency.[16] Zulu diviners often fast, sometimes for several days at a time, and as a result become ecstatic and have visions. The natives put no faith in a fat diviner. "The continually stuffed body cannot see secret things," they say.[17]

The head magician (Ol-oiboni) of the Masai lives on milk, honey, and goats' livers; if he ate any other food he could no longer divine the future and devise potent charms. Nor may he pluck out his beard, a proceeding which would entail similar disastrous consequences.[18] Nandi rain makers, when engaged in practice, may not wash their hands or drink water or have sexual intercourse. They are also forbidden to sleep on the hide of an ox that has been recently slaughtered.[19] Among the Wachagga the doctor's power is diminished by sexual intercourse, eating mutton, drinking water except from a vessel, and taking something from a person who holds something else in his hand. More understandable is the belief that his power will also be sadly lessened if one of his patients succumbs under his ministrations.[20]

Among the Baya of French Equatorial Africa the magician does not eat antelope meat or fresh fish. Nor may he engage in sexual intercourse by day. He is supposed to die of the first malady that attacks him, a notion that does not contribute to the attractiveness of the magical profession for an aspiring youth.[21] Male sorcerers among the Nupe, a tribe of northern Nigeria, must not eat out of a cracked calabash. The prohibition endures for their lifetime, and its violation is followed by the permanent "escape" of their occult power.[22]

In some tribes of the Guaraní Indians of Paraguay female magicians are said to have been bound to chastity. If, nevertheless, they engaged in sexual intercourse they no longer "obtained credit."[23] The Jivaro magician, who during his preparatory training has been narrowly limited in his diet, must ever after avoid many common articles of food. He cannot eat the deer, armadillo, peccary, wild pig, tapir, cholo monkey, and manatee, in addition to certain birds, fish, and vegetables. All these foods possess *tsarutama*, or occult power. Should he eat any of them the power would enter him and "neutralize" his efforts to deal with the spirits.[24] A Warrau magician does not eat any foreign article of food. To do so would result in the loss of his power; the food "spoiled his mouth" for uttering spells.[25] Among the Huichol, a Mexican tribe, a man who wants to be a healer must be faithful to his wife for five years. It is an onerous restriction, but failure to observe it means that he will become ill and lose the power of curing.[26]

The possibility of a loss, temporary or permanent, of a magician's powers is entertained by many Indian tribes of North America. In the Pueblo area a practitioner's abilities suffer a gradual decadence as he grows older, but they can be revived to full strength if he rubs his back against a certain sacred stone.[27]

The Southern Ute of Colorado are persuaded that a doctor's curative power may become so weakened by being employed for many years that it retaliates by striking at its possessor. Should he ward off the attack, it strikes at his younger relatives, particularly children. Hence the Ute feel that a power which shows signs of weakening should no longer be used by a doctor. In any case it is always rested, if not abandoned, when he loses a patient.[28] A Yuma doctor, when engaged in practice, must fast, bathe at sunrise, and refrain from intercourse with his wife. If she is menstruating, he cannot cure.[29] A Paviotso medicine man could lose his powers through contact with menstrual blood.[30] He could also lose them in many other ways. Careless treatment of his paraphernalia or flouting of the instructions given to him by the spirits would deprive him of the ability to cure disease. The ill-considered or malicious acts of others might have the same result.[31] A Chemehuevi doctor might be unable to practice if he accused someone unjustly of sorcery. But a "good" doctor seldom suffered an impairment of his curative ability except in old age. When that happened, he soon died, for he had "nothing to live for."[32]

A Lillooet ex-magician declared that he no longer possessed abnormal gifts, partly because he had given up "exercising" himself after his conversion to Christianity, but more particularly because his wife, whom he married when a widow, had been careless about performing the customary purificatory ceremonies after her former husband's decease. She had also married him only a few months later, which was likewise contrary to the mortuary regulations. And so her "bad medicine" had robbed him of his mystery powers.[33] A Tinne doctor would never venture to heal in the presence of a Christian priest.[34] The familiar spirits of a Copper Eskimo shaman attach themselves to him voluntarily. If he breaks the food prohibitions imposed by them, they leave him at once, and he loses all his shamanistic powers.[35]

It is entirely permissible for a Chukchi shaman to abandon his profession after practicing it for several years. His spirits are not incensed if he does so. A Russian inquirer met several natives who asserted that they had now given up most of their exercises because of illness, old age, or an obvious decrease of their power. It is probable, thinks our authority, that in most cases they had simply recovered from the nervous condition which had originally predisposed them for a shamanistic career. So long, however, as the shaman feels himself inspired he must practice and cannot hide his power. Otherwise it will manifest itself by a bloody sweat or a fit similar to epilepsy.[36] Among the Koriak, female shamans suffer a temporary or permanent deprivation of their powers if they give birth to children. This is true, also, of many other Siberian tribes.[37]

Instances are not uncommon of magicians, both professional and nonprofessional, doing something very much out of the ordinary to acquire an extra dose of occult power for the business in hand. Among the Queensland tribes of Cape York Peninsula the eating of human flesh is regarded as a terrible thing; it is *kunta-kunta*, which means hard, strong, dangerous, that is, magically powerful. "By means of the appropriate ritual the danger may not only be averted, but it may even become a source of power, making a man specially brave, and giving special prowess in hunting."[38] In the western islands of Torres Straits magicians made a practice of eating anything disgusting or revolting when they were about to perform a special act of sorcery. They would eat the flesh of corpses or mix the juice of corpses with their food, thus becoming "wild." In this condition they cared for no one, not even their wives and children, and if angered by a person would not hesitate to murder him.[39] A Keraki magician can make himself invisible by eating human corpses.[40] In the Banks Islands a man or a woman can gain a power like that of vampires by stealing and eating a morsel of a corpse. The ghost of the dead man then becomes a close friend of the eater and will afflict anyone against whom he (or she) bears a grudge.[41] As we shall see later, corpse eating is very commonly attributed to witches, who thereby acquire and nourish their nefarious powers.

The deliberate commission of incest, though an act which excites universal abhorrence in primitive society, has sometimes been a recognized means of acquiring or increasing magical potency. Among the Antambahoaka of Madagascar, hunters, fishers, and warriors, before setting out on an expedition, have sexual relations with their sisters or nearest female relatives.[42] Among the Bathonga a hippopotamus hunter will have sexual relations with a daughter in order to be successful in his efforts. "This incestuous act, which is strongly taboo in ordinary life, has made him into a 'murderer': he has killed something at home; he has acquired the courage necessary for doing great things on the river!"[43] The Mashona think that the commission of incest is a cure for the bite of certain deadly snakes.[44] The Balamba, while abominating incest, consider that its commission may bring good luck to an elephant hunter about to go in quest of ivory.[45] Among the Babemba a sorcerer starts his career by performing some outrageous act, such as sexual intercourse with a daughter.[46] By the Ba-ila, incest under certain conditions, as when a man desires some good fortune, is not only permitted, but enjoined.[47] The Anyanja, a tribe of Nyasaland, believe that a man who has intercourse with his sister or his mother is thereby rendered bullet-proof.[48] Anyanja witches, it is said, often try to increase their nefarious power by committing incest.[49]

Among the Netsilik Eskimo, incest seems to be very rare and is strongly condemned. Nevertheless they believe that under certain circumstances it may convey exceptional power in magic. We are told of a man who had sexual relations with his mother and in consequence became a very great shaman, famous in all the villages.[50]

Primitive credulity sets no limits to the magician's ability as a wonder worker. In southeastern Australia the medicine man climbs heavenward by means of a cord which he throws up or which is let down to him from above, or by a thread issuing from his mouth. The thread is delicate as a spider's web, but strong enough to bear him aloft.[51] Some magicians in the Gazelle Peninsula, New Britain, can produce earthquakes.[52] A magician in the Banks Islands (Mota) knows a rite by which human life can be prolonged, and this knowledge he will sell to anyone desirous of longevity for the modest sum of five fathoms of shell money.[53] The Maori *tohunga* is a necromancer, able to summon the dead from Hades and make them converse with their living friends.[54] In the Marshall Islands a would-be magician who lies on his back for hours at a time and sticks out his tongue to the sun will absorb the influence of the solar rays. After he has devoted several weeks to this practice his tongue gains the power of sending out similar rays upon men, animals, and lifeless things.[55] Certain magicians of Yap, one of the Carolines, could, if they would, force the sun to alter its course in the heavens or to crash down on the earth. They could, if they would, swamp the entire island under the ocean or bring about a great pestilence. All these mighty deeds require only a very modest magical apparatus—the spine of a sting ray, a certain dead lizard, some sea water poured into a hole —for their accomplishment.[56] A Malay magician, by burning incense and reciting a spell, can walk on water without sinking in beyond his ankles.[57] In the Lovedu tribe of the Transvaal sorcerers are reputed able to send lightning to strike their enemies. A male sorcerer can change a woman's sex. He threatens to do so in order to frighten a girl into marrying him or to compel a wife who has run away to return to him.[58] A witch among the Bathonga reveals himself if he points with the index finger to someone. The person so indicated is sure to suffer misfortune sooner or later.[59] Among the Akikuyu a magician sometimes goes away for several days "to where he sees God." Upon returning to this mundane sphere no one asks him what God said to him—"they would be afraid."[60] Medicine men in some Brazilian tribes can destroy dogs or game and make fish leave a river.[61] Cuna medicine men and medicine women could call down thunder and lightning, produce floods, topple trees in the forest, send storms or abate them, and even prevent earthquakes from destroying a village.[62] The Apache think that mountains and rivers, even the sun and moon, were brought into existence by their medicine men.[63] Some Papago medicine men get their power from the sun. They are able to "take the light of the sun and throw it into the night." The strange illumination thus produced is stronger than daylight, and by it they can see objects many miles away.[64] A Zuñi Indian who remains continent for four years may secure the power to cause an earthquake.[65] The medicine men of Isleta Pueblo, New Mexico, are able to summon thunder and lightning and to direct these phenomena at will.[66] One of the characteristic feats of Passamaquoddy magicians was walking on hard ground and sinking at every step up to the ankles or the knees.[67] Crow medicine men possess an extraordinary faculty of recuperation. One of them is said to have aged, died, and come back to life three times, before finally quitting the scene of his earthly labors.[68] Maidu magicians can walk through fire unharmed.[69] The Klamath Indian magician is a clairvoyant. When the warriors are about to set out on an expedition, he dances in front of them in order to discover those who will be wounded in the fight; "he sees them bleeding."[70] Among the Thompson Indians of British Columbia magicians could shoot their enemies with their tutelary spirits. The victims fell sick at once and complained of headache.[71] Some medicine men among the Takulli (Carrier) Indians were able to bring rain or sunshine. In a dry summer a man with this power could cause a downpour merely by washing his body in a creek.[72] An Eyak medicine man has or may have five or more familiar spirits, by whose aid he can be carried all around the world in a few minutes.[73] The Netsilik Eskimo credit their shamans with the ability to crumple up the frozen sea or turn pack ice into flat ice.[74] Among the Iglulik Eskimo a shaman has a mysterious light which he feels inside his head and by means of which he can see in the dark, both literally and metaphorically speaking. Nothing is hidden from him; not only can he see things far away, but he can also read the future and discover the secrets of the human heart.[75] A very powerful *angakok* among the Eskimo of Baffin Land and Hudson Bay, by blowing on the face of a dead man, can restore him to life. A story is told of a man who wished to become a shaman. The *angakok* said that he must first die: "That is the best way of becoming an *angakok*." So he died, and the people covered him with stones and left him in the ground for three nights. But the great *angakok* revived his frozen body and initiated him into the shamanistic profession.[76]

One of the powers most commonly ascribed to a magician is that of shape-changing—in particular, the assumption of an animal form. It is usually practiced by sorcerers, in order to help them more successfully to carry out their fell designs, but it is not confined to them and may also be employed by practitioners of white magic. The animal selected for embodiment is any member of the species—any lion, tiger, snake, or crocodile. For primitive thought there is nothing surprising or absurd in such metamorphosis. Men and animals are "intimately interchangeable," and a magician would naturally desire to acquire in this way the qualities of creatures so often regarded as mightier or cleverer than human beings. The transformation is sometimes said to be effected when the magician sends his "soul" or a double or a replica of himself into the body of the animal, which then acts under his direction. In other cases no duplication of personality seems to be imagined. The magician and the animal are really one, though in outward semblance they remain distinct and apart. The primitive finds it not at all difficult to hold two absolutely contradictory beliefs at the same time.[77]

In the Yualayai tribe of New South Wales some persons, chiefly magicians or men intended to be such, receive from their brothers in the magical art a *yunbeai*. This animal familiar is of great assistance to a man because he has the power to take its shape; for example, if a magician who had a bird as his *yunbeai* was in danger of being wounded or killed, he could change himself into that bird and fly away. He must never eat his animal familiar or he would die, and any injury to it hurts him also.[78] In Lepers' Island, which belongs to the New Hebrides, sorcerers are credited with the power of changing their shape. The friends of a sick man are always afraid lest the person who caused the sickness should come in some form, as that of a blow fly, and strike the patient. They sit by him, therefore, use counter spells to protect him, and carefully drive away all flies. A sorcerer can also turn into a shark and eat an enemy or someone whom he has been hired to destroy. In Aurora and Pentecost, magicians assume the form of eagles and owls, as well as of sharks.[79] Maori magicians and "magic-possessing" chiefs could assume various animal forms.[80]

The Malays of Java, Sumatra, and the Malay Peninsula believe firmly in the reality of animal metamorphosis. To them the existence of were-tigers is a fact, and the assurances of Europeans that such fearful creatures do not, and never did, haunt the wilds excite derision and well-merited contempt. In Java not only are there people able to become tigers at will, but some magicians, by donning a yellow *sarong* (Malay skirt) with black stripes and by repeating certain spells, can turn human beings into tigers.[81] The Semang, a Negrito group of the Peninsula, think that not only can magicians turn themselves into tigers during their lifetime, but that after death their souls often enter tigers and other wild beasts. When these animal embodiments have died the souls proceed to their own paradise.[82] In northern India the familiar animals of the sorcerer, in whose shape he or she often appears, are the tiger and the cat.[83] An Oraon witch sends out her soul into a black cat, which roams about in a house where someone is lying ill. The sick person soon dies. It is very difficult to catch one of these creatures, but if you succeed in doing so and injure it in any way, the identical injury will be inflicted on the witch herself.[84]

The Bushmen thought that sorcerers could appear as birds or jackals.[85] A sorcerer of the Balamba will accost a man on the road and ask him if he is traveling by himself or if others are near at hand. Should the man be alone the sorcerer retires behind an ant hill, changes into a lion, and pursues his victim, whom he kills and eats. The sorcerer then resumes the human form and proceeds on his way.[86] By the Babemba, sorcerers are supposed to change into lions and other wild beasts. These creatures hunt at night and devour their prey in company.[87] Wanyamwezi sorcerers can turn themselves temporarily into lions and leopards. They do so in obedience to orders of the chief. People killed by these animals are invariably supposed to be victims of such transformed sorcerers.[88] There are sorcerers in Sennar, a province of the Anglo-Egyptian Sudan, who turn themselves into hyenas, in order to roam about at night, howling and gorging themselves on carrion. By day they return to their human bodies.[89] In the Lower Congo region people living near a river where crocodiles take a heavy toll of human lives believe that a sorcerer can assume the crocodile form. In districts where crocodiles are less feared the sorcerer is supposed to become a leopard.[90] For the Ekoi of southern Nigeria magic shape-changing is an everyday occurrence. "The bird which flies in at your open door in the sunshine, the bat which circles round your house at twilight, the small bush beasts which cross your path while hunting—all may be familiars of witch or wizard, and even the latter themselves, disguised to do you hurt."[91] Among the Ibo tribes the belief is general that sorcerers can and do change themselves into any kind of bird or animal, "and it is not by any means an unusual occurrence to come across persons who have seen the metamorphosis take place before their very eyes."[92] The Bullom and Timne of Sierra Leone suppose that the depredations of wild animals, as when a crocodile seizes a child or a leopard carries off a goat, are not really committed by them but by witches which have assumed their forms.[93]

By the American Indians magicians are very generally credited with the ability to transform themselves into animals. The Abipon *keebet,* when so changed, is invisible and cannot be killed.[94] The Araucanians are persuaded that a fox or a puma, prowling around the hut at night, is a witch woman who has come to see what she can steal. They drive the animal away but do it no bodily harm, for fear of reprisals.[95] Medicine men in Brazil, after they have narcotized themselves with tobacco, can assume any animal shape they desire and go anywhere while so transformed.[96] An Ipurina magician in animal form is not visible to ordinary people, but another magician can recognize him.[97] Similarly, among the Apinayé, he may assume the form of a bird and visit foreign villages, where, however, the resident magicians sometimes detect him in spite of his disguise.[98] The Witoto, Boro, and related tribes of the Upper Amazon believe that when a medicine man dies he returns to earth as a jaguar. Even during his lifetime he may assume this animal form in order to kill and eat other wild creatures of the jungle. Every medicine man has a jaguar skin, which he uses to effect his transformation. He keeps it hidden, lest someone steal it and gain the power of becoming a jaguar.[99] By the Canelos Indians of Ecuador professional medicine men and aged persons in general, who are mostly credited with the art of sorcery, are believed to be able to transform themselves into jaguars after death and even during their lifetime.[100] The Quechua and Aymará of Peru and Bolivia suppose that the skin, claws, and teeth of a sorcerer who has been changed into a jaguar possess a marvelous power, and that its fat provides an infallible remedy against rheumatic pains and other ailments.[101] If a Tarahumara harms a powerful sorcerer the latter, after death, enters into a mountain lion, jaguar, or bear, lies in wait for the man, and kills him.[102]

The Navaho believe that men and women, disguised in the skins of wolves and mountain lions, go about practicing witchcraft.[103] Every Penobscot medicine man had his "helper," which seems to have been an animal's body into which he could transform himself at will. The helper could be sent to fight or to work for its master, who remained inert while it was away on an expedition. Any injury done to it in an encounter was transferred to its human owner, and if it was killed the owner died instantly. He never partook of its flesh when killed by another man. The helper really functioned as a part of the owner himself. A medicine man usually has only one helper, but a very powerful practitioner might have as many as seven of these assistants.[104] The Iroquois believed that a sorcerer could assume, at will, the shape of a beast, bird, or reptile and, having executed his nefarious purpose, could return to his human form.[105] An Ojibwa magician will appear at times in the guise of an animal, in order to injure a person for whose destruction he has received a fee. He may be seen at night flying rapidly along in the shape of a ball of fire or of a pair of fiery sparks like the eyes of some monstrous beast.[106] "Bear doctors" in California were magicians who had received their power from bears, particularly grizzly bears, and took the form of these animals to revenge themselves upon their enemies. They were generally regarded as invulnerable or at least as able to return to life after being killed. The ferocity and tenacity of life of the grizzly evidently impressed the imagination of the Indians.[107]

According to the belief of the Copper Eskimo, who live in the vicinity of Coronation Gulf, a magician will often change his form and assume that of his animal familiar, or will at least acquire some of its characteristics. This metamorphosis may occur only when he is alone, but sometimes it takes place in the presence of spectators. There was once a magician who could change into a polar bear. He would bend down to the floor of the dance house, with his hands resting on the ground. Slowly his hands became the feet of the animal, then his arms became its legs, and finally his whole body and head would assume the shape of the bear. In this state he visited the neighborhood, saying to the children in each house as he entered, "Stand up against the wall beside the door and then I shall not eat you." The Eskimo have numberless stories of such transformations and never question their truth.[108]

A Chukchi shaman, seeking revenge on an enemy, first transforms him into a reindeer. Then the shaman becomes a wolf and in that guise quickly disposes of him.[109]

We have seen how an ordinary man can sometimes produce a magical effect by the exercise of his will alone. That of the professional magician has still greater potency, even though unaccompanied by any appeal to spiritual agencies and unsupported by any reliance on spells, charms, or ritual acts.

If a medicine man in the western islands of Torres Straits threw a stone into the air, naming the person for whom it was intended, the projectile accomplished its purpose just as effectively as if it had hit him.[110] By "ill-wishing" a sorcerer in the Solomon Islands can bring sickness upon an obnoxious person or cause the latter's death.[111] The will power of a candidate for the office of a Maori *tohunga* was carefully tested. After completing his preliminary instruction he had to grasp a smooth, hard stone, repeat a special *karakia*, or spell, and then shiver the stone into fragments without injury to his hand. If he passed this test, then he tried to kill a bird or a dog by simply willing its death. The creature always died if the pupil was really proficient in his art. Finally, he had to will to death some near relative—an uncle, aunt, brother, or sister, but never a father or mother or one of his own children. It is an interesting fact that while the Maori's strongest passion was the desire for revenge, such an exhibition of the magician's fatal power over human beings did not lead to retaliation.[112] An anthropologist, working among the Toda of the Nilgiri Hills, was told by two natives that "a sorcerer, by merely thinking of the effect he wished to produce, could produce the effect, and that it was not necessary for him to use any magical formula or practice any special rites."[113] Nandi magicians "can kill people by mere will power and at a distance of many miles."[114]

Similar beliefs in the will power of magicians are entertained by some American Indians. Medicine men and medicine women of the Itonama can heal sick people without actually visiting them, though their patients may be many days' journey away.[115] There are Cuna medicine men who, "merely by concentrating," can clear broad forest lands.[116] Most sorcery among the Tarahumara is worked by "thinking evil." The sorcerer thinks evil of an enemy and when the latter is asleep goes to him in a dream and seizes his soul. The victim "dies right away."[117]

A medicine man of Laguna Pueblo became blind. His sister attributed his affliction to the ill wishes of other medicine men, who were envious of his many cures.[118] A Cheyenne medicine man, who had dreamed that he possessed a certain power, would put it to the proof "by merely exercising his will." He might take some small object, a hair from his robe, for instance, roll it into a little ball, hold it up toward the sun, and then, "wishing something bad," throw it in the direction of the person whom he desired to injure. The object disappeared, went to the person indicated, got inside him, and made him ill. If a doctor managed to extract the ball this might be returned to the original sender and do him the same kind of injury which he had inflicted.[119] A story current among the Hidatsa tells of a certain medicine man who had lived with very sacred black bears and from them obtained his extraordinary powers. "He helped his people in many ways. When they were hungry, he thought in his mind thus: 'There should be buffalo near the village'; and when he would thus think it, it was so."[120] A Paviotso sorcerer makes no use of spells or other techniques of nefarious magic. He achieves his evil purpose simply by wishing sickness to strike the victim. The latter does not know that this is being done. Discovery of the sorcerer's action comes only when a medicine man is successful in diagnosing the malady of the sufferer.[121] The White Knife Shoshoni believe that *dijibo*, the "power for evil," is acquired through a series of bad dreams, usually those of death, and is frequently manifested by palpitations in the body of its possessor. It can be "thrown" by a sorcerer into a victim by intense concentration of thought often accompanied by some muscular movement.[122] A Maidu sorcerer, who would kill an enemy, merely lets his shadow fall on the man and then bathes in a river and "prays" to his tutelary spirit, saying, "I want So-and-So to die."[123] A Yurok doctor could make people sick in order to earn fees by curing them. All he had to do was to smoke at night and then address his pipe, saying, "So-and-So, I wish you to become ill."[124] A powerful magician of the Takelma Indians could injure a man by merely "wishing" him ill or (mentally) "poisoning" him. This procedure was frequently employed by characters in the tribal myths, such as Coyote, and was indicated in the language by a special verb (*wiyimasi*), meaning "he wished to, poisoned me."[125] Among the Lummi, a Salish tribe, a man familiar with *suin*, the magical art, can employ his knowledge in a very practical way. For example, if he wants a certain boy to win a foot race he stands in a place where he can get a full view of the runners. Then he pronounces the secret name used in magic for "thigh." Concentrating all his powers on the thighs of the best of the rival runners, he deprives that contestant of full bodily support, "and his choice wins the race."[126] Among the Lillooet of British Columbia some medicine men seldom treated sick persons by the usual dancing or singing. Instead, a doctor would lie down beside a patient and sleep with him until he recovered. While doing so the doctor concentrated his thoughts upon the case and seemed oblivious of everything else.[127] The wishes of a Tinne medicine man, "when proffered with a specially intense act of will," are effective to accomplish what he desires. Thus he may cure a patient by directing his familiar spirit to do the job. In this case the medicine man does not attend the patient, but, when consulted, merely sends word to him of his prospective recovery.[128]

Magicians are often distinguished from the laity by a special costume or outfit, a peculiar bearing and manner of life, and the possession of accessories, fantastic or grotesque, that impress the imagination of all beholders.

In the Kolor tribe of Victoria there was a woman known to the English settlers as "White Lady," whom the aborigines so greatly feared that they gave to her whatever she fancied. She had a long staff, painted red, which had been presented to her, so she said, by the spirits. It was carried before her whenever she went on a ceremonial visit and was then hidden at some distance from the camp, "as it was too sacred to be exposed to common inspection." She used to wear a fur boa, really the tail of a lunar kangaroo encountered on one of her visits to the moon, though skeptical white men declared that she had obtained it from them. To support her pretensions she would leave the camp on a moonlight night and return with her bag full of snakes—spirit snakes. No one dared go near them or even look at them.[129] The bag of a Yualayai medicine man holds a miscellaneous collection of magical objects, including a big crystal by means of which he can see anyone at a distance and another stone whose power will knock a person insensible or strike him dead as quickly as a flash of lightning. The magician also carries with him bones to put through the cartilage of his nose when he is in a strange camp, so that he will not inhale the polluting odor of strangers.[130] No one, "for fear of sudden death," ventures to touch the bag of a Kabi doctor in Queensland. It contains a few quartz pebbles, bits of glass, human bones, and a cord or rope made of fur, and perhaps excreta of some person to be injured or killed by black magic.[131]

The outfit of a Mentawei medicine man consists of a hair ornament of chicken feathers worn over the left ear, a breast band of brass spangles, brass armlets, a breechcloth of rattan with bead decorations, and three strings of beads used as headbands. These last serve as "telephone wires" through which he talks to the spirits of the altar. He also has bells attached to his hands for the purpose of summoning the spirits. No medicine man would part with his outfit for any consideration, since by doing so he would lose his ability to practice. It can be inherited from father to son or from brother to brother. If the outfit becomes ruined from age and long usage, the owner must renew it with the aid of another man in the profession, thus renewing his magical power. The same requirement is imposed upon him if he makes a mistake in his work or breaks some taboo which he ought to observe. Under any of these circumstances the spirit would avoid all contact with him and the people would not consult him.[132]

The outfit of a Bathonga magician has been thus described: In his hair were a brass bracelet, some rings, and a necklace with a sixpence attached. All these objects were legacies from his father, who had also been a magician. He hung round his neck a little piece of the skin of a goat, which had been sacrificed upon his father's death; in this way he acquired and kept the latter's occult power. Two panther claws were fixed upon his head, pointing toward each other; they helped him to seize a witch. Two empty goats' bladders swung amidst his crop of curly hair, an unmistakable sign that he had cured patients and received goats as a reward. From his neck hung two crocodile teeth and several horns containing medicines used in exorcisms and in curing bewitched people. Another drug helped him to obtain many wives and have many children. He also wore a cock's spur to give him "courage and weight." On a professional tour throughout the land this exorcist made an impressive appearance in all his attire, wearing big snake skins and carrying the tail of a gnu as a sort of magic wand.[133]

The dress of a Bakongo witch doctor, when engaged in a professional capacity, consists of the skins of wild animals, feathers, dried fibers and leaves, ornaments made from the teeth of leopards, crocodiles, or rats, tinkling bells, rattling seedpods, and anything else that is unusable and wearable. His face and other exposed parts of his person are plastered with chalk and pigments in designs that please his own crude taste. "The effect attained is extremely grotesque, but to the native these things are the proper paraphernalia of a witch doctor and a sign of his power. To inspire the native with awe and fear this get-up is absolutely necessary, for, if a witch doctor arrived at the scene of his operations in the ordinary garb of a native, he would be scouted and turned out of the town."[134]

Practitioners of the occult art among the Wayemba employ a multitude of charms, all supposed to be endowed with magical power. They are ever on the alert to acquire new charms which will impress the simple-minded natives. One of their outfits was found to contain a stick of dynamite, half of which had been used, perhaps to prove that the fortunate owner had command over thunder and lightning.[135]

The insignia and "stock-in-trade" of a Guiana *piai* include a particular kind of bench unlike the ordinary article of furniture found in Indian houses, a rattle, a doll or manikin, certain crystals, and other small objects generally "out of the common." When not in use all these are kept out of harm's way in a special shed which is taboo to common folk. If profaned, they would lose their power and the taboo-breaker would suffer some misfortune.[136]

A Blackfoot medicine man, when engaged in healing practice, had his body entirely covered with the skin of a yellow bear. His head was inside that of the bear, which thus served as a mask, and on his wrists and ankles dangled the animal's huge claws. A yellow bear, being very rare in the Blackfoot country, was esteemed "great medicine." The skins of many other animals, having anomalies or deformities which gave them occult power, were attached to that of the bear.[137]

The dress of Haida shaman differed somewhat in accordance with the kind of spirit speaking through him. He allowed his hair to grow long, never combing or cleaning it, and wore a long bone through his septum. He carried a board, on which he beat time with a baton, and a carved hollow bone through which he blew away disease. An assistant, who thumped a large wooden drum, ably seconded his efforts.[138] While the Haida shaman usually performed without a mask, the Tlingit practitioner had a number of masks. A large figure on each one represented his principal spiritual helper and smaller figures indicated subsidiary spirits which strengthened special faculties of the shaman. Those around his eyes increased his sight and so enabled him to discover hostile spirits; those around his nose helped him to smell better; and those around his jaws kept them firm at all times. Some figures stood for animals, but the favorite device was that of the woodworm, which, because it is such a borer, could well typify keenness of perception. A peculiar hat, a dancing shirt and blanket, and dancing leggings completed the shaman's costume.[139]

Among the Iglulik Eskimo a young man who has become a shaman wears a special belt as a sign of his profession. It is a strip of hide to which fringes of caribou skin are attached by all the people he knows. To the fringes are added carved bone figures, both animal and human. These objects must be presents to the shaman. The people believe that in this way his helping spirits will always be able to recognize them and will never do them any harm.[140]

In everyday life the Siberian shaman is not distinguishable from other people, but when practicing he wears a special dress. Among many tribes this includes a coat, a mask, a cap, and a copper or iron plate on the breast. Of his special instruments the most important is a small drum, or tambourine, by means of which he evokes the spirits and communicates with them. It also has the remarkable power of carrying him through the air to the other world. The spirits will not hear the shaman's voice unless the right dress is worn and the drum beaten. Being sacred, these accessories must not be used by anyone but a shaman; if so used they will not produce any effect on the spirits.[141]

The seances, or public performances, of magicians are to be distinguished from their private practice as healers, diviners, or sorcerers. The medicine man summons his familiar spirits, converses with them, and receives directions from them; or else he seeks them out, perhaps at the end of the world or in another world. The shaman throws himself into a real or simulated trance, in which he speaks and acts as one inspired. All these performances are commonly attended by a good deal of conjuring, especially ventriloquism and prestidigitation. The conjuring is clumsy, as a rule, and only the implicit faith of the audience in the performers saves them from frequent detection. Nevertheless, the feats attributed to these gentry often show much ingenuity, and some of them could with difficulty be duplicated by a Hindu fakir or a professional trickster among ourselves. It is especially curious to discover that feats which have formed the principal stock-in-trade of contemporary mediums are well known to primitive mountebanks, for instance, the magician's freeing himself from a strait jacket, his handling of hot objects with impunity, and his rising and floating through the air—the "miracle" of levitation. In some cases the magician undoubtedly exercises hypnotic powers over his audience. Indeed, his firm belief in himself and the equally firm belief of the spectators in him combine to produce a mental atmosphere most favorable to the suggestions of hypnotism. That these exhibitions impress the multitude with the magician's extraordinary powers and thus confirm and strengthen his hold upon them is obvious. Their recreational aspects are also noteworthy, for they help to dispel ennui and make life interesting in many a lonely community.

The Kurnai of Victoria made a distinction between the ordinary medicine man, or doctor, and the *birraark,* who served as a seer and a bard. The *birraark* foretold future events and composed the songs and dances for social gatherings. His powers were conferred upon him by the ghosts. They met him in the bush, grasped him firmly by the bone peg which every native wears in his septum, and thus conveyed him through the clouds to ghost-land. There he learned new songs and dances, which he afterward taught the people. Having been once introduced to the ghosts he remained on very intimate terms with them. In one seance his voice could be heard shouting to the ghosts, who responded from the tree-tops. Then they jumped down and answered questions put to them by the *birraark.* When morning broke he was found on the ground outside the camp, and round him were ghostly footprints. Another seance took place at night. The camp fires had been allowed to burn low and the people kept a strict silence. At intervals the *birraark* uttered a loud coo-ee, which was answered by the shrill whistlings of the ghosts, first on one side and then on the other. Then a voice was heard in the gloom, inquiring in a strange muffled tone what was wanted. After questions had been asked by the *birraark* and satisfactory replies received, the voice declared, "We are going," and the ghosts made their departure. The next day the *birraark* was found, apparently asleep, on the top of a tall tree to which he had been transported by the ghosts.[142]

An early missionary to New Britain once attended a seance. It was held in an open space in the bush. The surrounding trees cast a deep darkness on the spot, so that he could not see more than a few feet ahead. Two companies of men had assembled, one at each end of the open space. The performers were all dressed in white, "the spirits being supposed to like that color." At the sound of a whistle the two companies marched past each other and changed ends. No noise was made during this weird procession in honor of Ingal, a spirit living in the top of very tall trees. He could be induced to descend to earth and converse with men, but on this occasion the presence of the infidel missionary kept him away. "I was told next day that after I left he came, a sure evidence that I was the hindrance, which added to my security, for if I was stronger than Ingal, I must indeed be strong."[143]

For the purpose of a seance by a Semang *halak*, or shaman, a very small hut is made by sticking palm leaves in a circle of holes. An opening at the base enables the shaman to crawl inside. His performance takes place at night. He starts a chant, each line of which is taken up and repeated by a chorus of men squatting around the hut. A number of chants are thus sung. From time to time the hut is shaken from the inside and then noises are heard as if the shaman was striking the walls of the hut with the flat of his hands. To the auditors, however, they are signs indicating the presence of the shaman's familiar spirit.[144]

The seances of African witch doctors have great interest for the natives, who attend them not only as spectators but also as drummers and singers. On these occasions there will often be much jugglery. Azande witch doctors, according to the account of an eyewitness, placed large hairy caterpillars in a horn and hid this beneath their bark cloth. As they danced the worms emerged from the horn and crawled over their bodies, coming, seemingly, from inside their bellies. Only a few skeptics regarded the performance as a trick and declared that if witchcraft had really put caterpillars inside a man he would not be dancing about happily but would be lying very sick at home. In another performance the magician lay down on his back at full length, and a heavy stone was placed on his chest and pounded with a pestle by a fellow practitioner. The fortitude which the subject of this pseudo ordeal exhibited and his failure to collapse under the weight of the stone were ascribed to the power of his magic. Another common trick of the witch doctor is the production of blood from his mouth. He cuts his tongue quite openly and allows the blood to stream from his lips for all to see. But the wound is supposed to heal in a remarkably short space of time, owing to the medicines which he has eaten after making the incision.[145] Among the Ibibio of southern Nigeria a magician beats a baby to pulp in a mortar and then produces it, alive and well, from the thigh of one of his assistants. In another "play" a man's head is cut off and borne around by the seeming executioner. Meanwhile the trunk is supported by two friends, who fan the neck vigorously; were flies to settle on it the magic would be broken and the man would never return to life. Finally the head is restored to its proper place, and the supposed corpse springs up and rushes about to demonstrate its vitality. In still another exhibition long, sharply pointed palm stems are thrust through a man's body, so that they project on the other side, but after the magician has invoked the ancestral ghosts, they are withdrawn, and the man is apparently unhurt.[146]

Iroquois medicine men, in the old days, were all jugglers. They held annual meetings at which they exhibited the tricks that had come to them, so they declared, in dreams. On one of these occasions each juggler had to perform a new feat or else forfeit his life. Fortunately, nothing very complicated was required of him; even a simple trick answered the purpose if it deceived his brother professionals. Pebbles and knives were swallowed by means of a tube inserted in the throat, and "appearances" were caused in smoke by putting tobacco and perfumes upon the fire. A medicine man had also to be skilled in the interpretation of dreams, and if he failed in this capacity he suffered death.[147]

A conjuring performance found among the Menomini, Ojibwa, Saulteaux, and other Algonquian tribes is the mysterious shaking of a little tent (tipi) constructed for the purpose of the exhibition. The conjuror is tightly trussed up when placed in the tent. Having freed himself from his bonds, he begins to sing, beats his drum, and thus summons the spirits who are his advisers. The spirits obey the call and make their presence known by a violent shaking of the tent and by certain sounds, familiar to those attending the performance but understood only by the conjuror himself. The whole procedure has a definite purpose, usually the healing of a sick person by remedies which the spirits prescribe.[148]

A Pawnee doctor, stripped to the skin and performing within a few feet of watchful spectators, swallows spears and arrows. These are driven down the gullet to the distance of a foot or eighteen inches, sometimes with fatal results to the juggler. He shoots a man with arrows, apparently using the full force of the bow, but instead of penetrating the body they bounce back and fly through the air. He brains a man with an ax, so that blood and gray matter seem to ooze from the wound, yet a few days later the man goes about quite unharmed. He makes corn grow from the seed to the ripened ear within a brief half hour. The same trick is performed with a cedar berry, which, when planted, quickly grows into a good-sized bush.[149] A Ponca medicine man, in an exhibition before about two hundred spectators, seemed to load a revolver. He then handed it to a chief, who fired it at him. The medicine man fell down, as if badly wounded, groaned and coughed incessantly, and after a time spat up the bullet, which was shown in triumph to the crowd. This performance by the Indian juggler showed that he could successfully imitate one of the tricks of his white brother.[150] An Ojibwa magician takes live coals and red-hot stones in his hands and sometimes in his mouth. He asserts that "supernatural power" enables him to perform the feat with impunity, but really he has made the affected parts insensible to fire by the use of certain herbs.[151]

The commonest feat of an Eskimo shaman in the Mackenzie River area is his flight to a neighboring village, a far country, or most often, to the sun, the moon, or the bottom of the sea. This performance usually takes place in the evening and when there is no moonlight. It is announced beforehand, so that an audience may gather in the clubhouse or the nearest available private dwelling. The shaman is first tied and trussed up until he cannot move. When the lights have been extinguished, he begins to chant a magic song in which he describes himself as becoming as light as a feather and as rising like a dry stick in the water. The people hear a curious sound. It is made by a stone or an ax attached to a loose rope which hangs from the shaman's body. He is now flying in circles so fast that the centrifugal force makes the stone or the ax produce a whizzing noise. Were anyone in the audience to open his eyes and try to see what was going on, this object would strike him on the head and kill him instantly. Presently the voice of the shaman is heard announcing his flight above the heads of the people, then near the roof, and then through the window. The voice becomes fainter and fainter and the whizzing noise dies away. The people sit in absolute silence for about half an hour and keep their eyes shut. When at length the shaman is heard announcing his return they open their eyes, light the oil lamps, and untie the celestial navigator, who proceeds to relate his thrilling experiences. Among these Eskimo walking on water and raising the dead are rare performances of the shaman, but his spirit flight often takes place, and its genuineness is universally accepted.[152]

A typical shamanistic performance among the Chukchi is carried on at night in the small sleeping room of a house. When the lights have been put out, the shaman, who is often stripped to the waist, begins to operate. He beats his drum and sings tunes, at first slowly and then more rapidly. Tricks of all kinds break up the monotony of the proceedings, which may last for several hours. The shaman's spirits scratch from outside at the walls of the room. Suddenly, perhaps, a spirit tugs at the skin rug with such violence that things on it fly about in every direction. Because of this mischievous propensity of a spirit the shaman's housemates usually take the precaution of removing kettles and dishes from the room before the performance starts. Sometimes an invisible hand seizes the whole top of the room and shakes it with wonderful strength or lifts it up high from the ground. Other invisible hands toss about lumps of snow, spill cold water and urine, and throw around blocks of wood or stones at the imminent risk of hitting people in the audience. Ventriloquism is skillfully done. The voices of the spirits are heard on all sides of the room, at first faint, as if coming from afar, gradually increasing in volume with a nearer approach, then passing through the room and at length dying away in the distance. Other voices are first heard from above and then from the depths of the earth. The shaman imitates the sounds made by animals, birds, and insects, the howling of a tempest, even an echo. On the whole, the prestidigitation and ventriloquism of the Chukchi shaman compare very favorably with our "parlor magic."[153]

Richard Johnson, of Chancelour's expedition to Muscovy in 1556, witnessed a performance by a Samoyed shaman. The latter took a sword, a cubit and a span long ("I did mete it my selfe"), and stuck it into his belly halfway, but no wound was to be seen. Then the shaman heated the sword, thrust it into the slit of skin at his navel, and continued the movement until the point came out behind his buttocks ("I layde my finger upon it"). Finally, he extracted the sword and sat down.[154] In the district of Kolyma, an anthropologist used to meet a young but very skillful shaman, who performed many difficult tricks. He swallowed a stick, ate red-hot coals and pieces of glass, spat coins out of his mouth, and could even be in different places at the same time. But in spite of these impressive feats he was not considered a first-class shaman, whereas an inspired old woman, whose repertoire of tricks was limited, enjoyed a great reputation.[155]

The rivalry between professional magicians frequently results in competitive exhibitions, sometimes conducted in a fairly amicable spirit but sometimes in grim earnest. We have references to them among such widely separated peoples as the Maori of New Zealand and the Siberian tribes.[156] They are common among the Plains Indians. The Crow describe a contest of this nature between two medicine man as "seizing each other's arms," that is, making an opponent incapable of further feats of magic. These Indians also hold contests in which a number of magicians take part and perform their feats before appreciative audiences.[157] The Creeks and the Osage used to have tribal meetings at which their respective medicine men engaged in contests and endeavored to outdo one another in magical tricks.[158] A Saulteaux magician sometimes summoned to his lodge the soul of a rival magician for a battle royal between them. Each man had the aid of his "dream visitors," or familiar spirits, and each used all the occult power at his command to overcome the other. The lodge bent and shook with their efforts like trees in a storm. Every now and then a thump would be heard; that was when one of the helping spirits had been hit. The struggle continued right before the spectators, until one of the combatants lost strength and could be heard moaning and crying as he realized he could never get back his soul and that death was near.[159] The Yokuts-Mono held a contest between rival doctors. They stood in opposing rows and shot at each other with their "air-shot." Only the doctor who projected a shot into an opponent could remove it. If it were not removed, the victim failed to regain consciousness and died within a few days. It sometimes happened that a chief who wanted a rival chief's doctor put out of the way would hire the magician who could revive him to withhold the cure. In such a case only a pretense at curing would be made.[160] Contests between two rival magicians, to determine who was the more powerful, were common among the Shuswap of British Columbia. One of them would take his charm, blow on it, and throw it at his antagonist. If the latter was the weaker he fell unconscious on his back, with blood flowing from his mouth. The victor would then blow on him and in this way restore him to life.[161] The medicine men of the Tanaina, an Athapascan tribe in Alaska, held public exhibitions at which they performed marvelous feats and advertised their valuable services as healers. These exhibitions had also a competitive character to determine whether newcomers should be admitted within the professional circle or magicians with failing powers should be excluded from it.[162]

Among some of the rudest peoples the magician does not receive any compensation of a material sort. This seems to be usually the case with the tribes of southeastern Australia. We are told, however, that while the doctors received no pay they usually managed to obtain more than their fair share of wives.[163] In northern Queensland a medicine man might have two or three or even four wives.[164] In the Arunta, Ilpirra, and other Central Australian tribes they receive nothing and expect nothing in the way of reward or privilege for their services.[165] Among the Marind of Netherlands New Guinea the magicians do not form a class by themselves and enjoy no particular consideration. They are numerous in each village; indeed, almost every family can boast of at least one practitioner of the magical art.[166] In Mota, one of the Banks Islands, all beneficent magical procedures, such, for instance, as producing sunshine, bringing down rain, promoting the growth of yams, and causing a big surf (this last when some one from another island is on the way to collect debts), are carried out by the experts in these matters without material compensation. They are satisfied merely to add to their reputation as possessors of *mana*.[167] Among the Naron, a Bushman tribe of the Kalahari, medicine men and women dress and live like their fellow tribespeople. For their occasional services they receive a few presents.[168] Yaghan medicine men apparently do not gain much profit from their profession, for like other tribesmen they must procure their own living from day to day.[169]

As a rule, however, a magician is well remunerated by his clients. Among the Murngin of northern Australia he must always be paid for his services.[170] In the western islands of Torres Straits medicine men relied on their reputed powers to obtain special privileges. Presents of food were often made to them.[171] Among the Koita and other tribes of the Papuan Gulf a magician receives large quantities of food, together with tobacco and personal ornaments, to induce him to end a period of long drought, and similar presents are made to him by the friends of a sick man whom he is called upon to cure.[172] It is said that a Kiwai will even give up his wife to discharge his obligations to a sorcerer.[173] In the Trobriands private magic such as sorcery and healing is paid for by the person who benefits from it; public magic for gardens and fishing, is recompensed by the whole community at regular intervals. The compensation varies in amount with the importance of the service rendered. It is sometimes considerable and in other instances it is little more than a formal offering.[174] Magicians among the Manus of the Admiralty Islands are paid in shell money. They are the rich men of their community.[175] In the New Hebrides and Banks Islands anyone who possesses a powerful amulet or stands in an intimate relationship with powerful ghosts or spirits can make a living by the magical art.[176] Sorcerers in Tahiti, who bore the name of "kindlers," because their activity was likened to the kindling of a fire, were well paid.[177]

A Sea Dayak doctor, before undertaking a case, makes sure that his services will be compensated. His fee is paid whether or not the patient recovers. He has only one patient at a time because he lives with the latter while treating him.[178] There are said to be as many as sixteen different ceremonies of healing for which the patient pays a fee, but only four are in common use. If he fails to recover, a *manang* often recommends to him another and more expensive practitioner.[179] Among the Land Dayak the doctor's fee for restoring a man's soul which has left him in sickness is six gallons of uncleaned rice. The same fee is charged for extracting an evil spirit from his body. The value of six gallons of rice is the sixtieth part of the amount which a farm laborer receives for a whole year's labor.[180] In Flores, one of the Lesser Sunda Islands, a doctor's services are often handsomely rewarded.[181] Magicians in Minahassa, a district of Celebes, are frequently the richest and most influential persons in their community.[182]

In the Andaman Islands magicians manage to get the best of everything. They constantly receive substantial gifts. When these are not forthcoming they do not scruple to ask for any article to which they have taken a fancy. Sometimes a magician who does not need a certain article at a particular time will allow the donor to retain it for a while, keeping it in trust for him. Many persons thus possess property which they must relinquish when called for by the magician.[183]

A Matabele doctor and diviner receives one head of cattle for his professional attentions, unless the case is too trifling. Were he treating a child, for instance, he would get only a goat in pay-

ment. He must make a cure to receive any compensation. Sometimes a doctor, having found his own medicines ineffectual, will
obtain a remedy from a colleague. This he pays for out of his
own pocket; he cannot pass on the charge to the patient.[184] With
reference to the Wayao and other tribes in the region of Lake
Nyasa we learn that while a chief derives his revenue largely
from voluntary gifts the magician receives fees, and that these
are rigidly exacted.[185] Successful rain makers among the Nandi
are usually "very well off." They receive large presents of grain
when the crops are harvested, and after a cattle raid they have a
share of the oxen captured.[186] The "fixed rule" of Bateso medicine
men is payment first and treatment afterward.[187] Among the
Shilluk, a Nilotic tribe, a doctor does no charity work.[188] The
nganga of the Lower Congo tribes draws pay from the client who
hires him to blast a thief with illness and from the latter to
remove the evil magic.[189] Liberian medicine men receive an ample
compensation and, in consequence, lead easy lives.[190]

Whatever the magicians of the Abipones wish for "they
extort from the people."[191] The Lengua Indians have a chief for
every clan, but he exerts little authority and seldom grows rich,
since by virtue of his office he must make many presents. It is
the magician who is the rich man, because his services in injuring
the enemies of the tribe and in protecting his own people against
their machinations are so well rewarded. He receives presents
instead of giving them.[192] The Tupinamba magicians, it is said,
took pains to impress upon their native followers that disaster
would inevitably befall those persons who refused them their
daughters or anything else for which they asked.[193] Among the
Uaupés and related Amazonian tribes a native "will give almost
all his wealth to a *page*, when he is threatened with any real or
imagined danger."[194] Guiana Indians dare not refuse the magician
anything; whatever he wants, from some trifle of food to a
man's wife, he demands and gets.[195] A Wapisiana magician,
because of his supposed power to injure and kill at a distance, has
very great influence for good or for evil in the community. The
people obey him implicitly. He always receives compensation for
his services and may extort from those who consult him anything
he desires. Sometimes the exactions of these gentry became so
oppressive that the people in self-defense would kill some of the
worst ones and thus keep the others more or less under control
through fear of meeting the same fate. But an unregarding government has stopped the killings and the people complain, saying,

"Now we have no protection."[196] The Taulipáng magician manages to have the prettiest girls for wives and more wives than anyone else.[197] Tarahumara magicians never render their services gratuitously. The payments which they receive for singing at feasts and treating the sick enable them to live more comfortably than the rest of the people. They get the choicest portions of meat at a barbecue and all the *tesvino* they can hold.[198]

A Pima doctor is promised a fee, perhaps a horse, a cow, a basket, or some wheat, when he is summoned to sing "cure songs" over a patient for the purpose of correctly diagnosing the case. If the contract calls for three nights of singing, with a horse in payment, he will not get the animal should the patient die before the singing has been completed. He will receive some compensation, however, for his musical efforts, even though these prove to be unavailing.[199] Apache medicine men are paid by the patient or by his friends when a consultation takes place.[200] Every effort is made to conciliate a Papago magician, who may use his powers for either good or evil ends. No one would make him an enemy, no one would deny his requests. Consequently he amasses wealth and ranks as the only rich man in his tribe.[201] A Navaho medicine man is always paid, but he never fixes the amount of his fee. This is always supposed to be commensurate with the means and social position of the family offering it. Consequently poor people, as well as the wealthy, feel free to avail themselves of the doctor's services. Whatever his remuneration, he should be satisfied with it. If he went away displeased or angry, his thoughts might harm the patient and thus undo the good effects of the healing rites.[202] In former days among the Blackfoot a man who fell sick and remained so for several weeks or a month usually had to start anew in life upon his recovery. Unless very wealthy all his possessions went as fees to the doctor. Often his last horse and even his lodge, clothing, and extra clothing were parted with by the unfortunate patient.[203] A Karok doctor who loses a case must return his fee. If he receives an offer of a certain sum to attend a person and refuses to give his services he must pay the relatives of the sick man an equivalent amount should the latter die. A Miwok doctor requires that his fee be paid him in advance.[204] Among the Lummi of Washington the medicine man never sets a price upon his services but takes what is offered to him. The payment made is usually a heavy one, for it is feared that, unless treated liberally, he would injure the patient's family.[205] Among the Takulli (Carrier Indians) of

British Columbia the doctor receives a present before treating a sick person. Should the patient die the present must be restored to the relatives of the deceased.[206] The same rule prevails among the Thompson Indians.[207] A medicine man of the Eyak Indians "never works for nothing, and he can ask for anything he wants.[208] The Tanaina medicine man is often a person of wealth and because of his great possessions exercises political functions.[209] Among the Central Eskimo an *angakok* who cures his patient is paid at once and liberally.[210] Among the Labrador Eskimo the doctor always takes his payment in advance; however, if he fails to cure the patient he must return it.[211]

Chukchi shamans try to get as much as possible for their services. It is a common saying of the Chukchi that shamanistic advice or treatment, when given gratuitously, amounts to nothing. However, a Russian anthropologist, who worked among them, never met a shaman who could be said to live solely on the profits of his profession. It was only a source of additional income to him. Yakut shamans are recompensed if their arts are successful, and the same is true of Tungus shamans.[212]

It is evident that, the world over, the profession of a medicine man or a shaman is lucrative and that those who engage in it often contrive to live comfortably at the expense of their fellows. Sorcerers, who are so much feared and whose practice is so often carried on at great personal risk, will be especially well rewarded by their clients. The large incomes which magicians receive and the special privileges which they enjoy tend to raise them above the common herd and thus become a potent factor in the differentiation of social classes within a community.

NOTES TO CHAPTER IX

[1] A. W. Howitt, *The Native Tribes of South-East Australia* (London, 1904), pp. 409 f.

[2] Mrs. K. L. Parker, *More Australian Legendary Tales* (London, 1898), p. xiv.

[3] Sir Baldwin Spencer and F. J. Gillen, *The Native Tribes of Central Australia* (London, 1899), p. 525; *iidem, The Northern Tribes of Central Australia* (London, 1904), pp. 481, 486. According to another account, referring to the Central tribes generally, a medicine man must not eat the flesh of a kangaroo which has fed on new green grass. An infringement of the rule would be followed by the loss of some of his special powers and a consequent drop in the estimation in which he is held by the tribesmen. If he repeated the offense, he would lose all his ability to act as a magician. No one would consult him or pay heed to him henceforth. See Herbert Basedow, *The Australian Aboriginal* (Adelaide, 1923), p. 180.

4 Sir Baldwin Spencer, *Wanderings in Wild Australia* (London, 1928), II, 790.

5 W. L. Warner, *A Black Civilization* (New York, 1937), pp. 210, 217 f.

6 Mrs. Daisy Bates, *The Passing of the Aborigines* (London, 1938), pp. 75 f.

7 F. E. Williams, *Orokaiva Magic* (Oxford, 1928), pp. 9 f., 32 f., 45 f.

8 Stefan Lehner, in R. Neuhauss, *Deutsch Neu-Guinea* (Berlin, 1911), III, 456.

9 Bronislaw Malinowski, *Argonauts of the Western Pacific* (London, 1922), pp. 409 f. The natives say that if a garden magician broke any of the food taboos permanently imposed upon him, his magic would become "blunt" (*idem, Coral Gardens and Their Magic* [London, 1935], I, 107). A Mailu magician, who broke a permanent food taboo, not only lost his power but suffered a serious illness, such as an outbreak of sores over his body (*idem*, in *Transactions of the Royal Society of South Australia*, XXXIX [1915], 656).

10 D. Jenness and A. Ballantyne, *The Northern D'Entrecasteaux* (Oxford, 1920), pp. 123 f.

11 R. F. Fortune, *Sorcerers of Dobu* (London, 1932), p. 132.

12 A. Aufinger, "Wetterzauber auf den Yabob-Inseln in Neuguinea," *Anthropos*, XXXIV (1939), 279, 286.

13 A. B. Deacon, *Malekula, a Vanishing People in the New Hebrides* (London, 1934), p. 685.

14 Elsdon Best, *The Maori as He Was* (Wellington, New Zealand, 1924), p. 83.

15 S. Walleser, "Religiöse Anschauungen und Gebräuche von Jap (deutsche Südsee)," *Anthropos*, VIII (1913), 627, 1061. According to another account the magic workers of Yap are headed by two great magicians, "who support their dignity under very strict conditions indeed." They are only allowed to eat plants and fruits that have been specially grown for them. They may not smoke tobacco, though they may chew the areca nut. When one of them goes abroad the other stays home, for were they to meet on the road some dire calamity would surely follow. See F. W. Christian, *The Caroline Islands* (London, 1899), p. 289.

16 A. W. Hoernlé, in *Harvard African Studies* (Cambridge, Mass., 1918), II, 69. After the initiation ceremonies of the Coast Murring and related tribes of New South Wales the boys who have just been made "men" are forbidden during their period of probation to wash themselves or to go into the water, "lest the influence with which the ceremonies have filled them should be washed off" (A. W. Howitt, *op. cit.*, p. 557).

17 Henry Callaway, *The Religious System of the Amazulu* (London, 1870), p. 387 and note.

18 M. Merker, *Die Masai* (Berlin, 1904), pp. 21 f.

19 A. C. Hollis, *The Nandi* (Oxford, 1909), p. 52.

20 O. F. Raum, *Chaga Childhood* (London, 1940), p. 367.

21 A. Poupon, in *L'Anthropologie*, XXVI (1915), 142 f.

22 S. F. Nadel, "Witchcraft and Anti-Witchcraft in Nupe Society," *Africa*, VIII (1935), 426.

23 Robert Southey, *History of Brazil* (London, 1817–19), II, 37.

24 M. W. Stirling, "Jivaro Shamanism," *Proceedings of the American Philosophical Society*, LXXII (1933), 144; *idem*, "Historical and Ethnographical Material on the Jivaro Indians," *Bulletin of the Bureau of American Ethnology*, No. 117, p. 120.

25 W. H. Brett, *The Indian Tribes of Guiana* (London, 1868), p. 363. These Indians do not like to eat the flesh of such animals as are not indigenous to their country. If there is an utter lack of other food they will sometimes do so, but only after a magician has blown upon the food a number of times and thus dispelled the evil influence (or spirit) in it (Sir E. F. im Thurn, *Among the Indian Tribes of Guiana* [London, 1883], p. 368).

26 Carl Lumholtz, *Unknown Mexico* (London, 1903), II, 236.

27 J. G. Bourke, "The Medicine Men of the Apache," *Ninth Annual Report of the Bureau of Ethnology*, p. 460. A stone with rejuvenating properties, near Kingman, Arizona, used to be visited by medicine men from the pueblos of Laguna and Acoma (*loc. cit.*).

28 M. K. Opler, in Ralph Linton (editor), *Acculturation in Seven American Indian Tribes* (New York, 1940), p. 143. Opler points out that this notion of the destructiveness/attaching to curative power used too long and continuously provides a satisfactory explanation of the deaths of great medicine men.

29 C. D. Forde, in *University of California Publications in American Archaeology and Ethnology*, XXVIII, 198.

30 Isabel T. Kelly, *ibid.*, XXXI, 194. The same belief was entertained by the Pomo of northern California (E. M. Loeb, "Pomo Folkways," *ibid.*, XIX, 307). Among the Baiga, an aboriginal tribe of the Central Provinces of India, a magician not only lost his power but also had sickness and death strike his family because his wife, during her menstrual period, had entered a hut dedicated to his gods (Verrier Elwin, *The Baiga* [London, 1939], p. 358).

31 W. Z. Park, *Shamanism in Western North America* (Evanston, 1938), p. 32. *Northwestern University Studies in the Social Sciences*, No. 2.

32 Isabel T. Kelly, "Chemehuevi Shamanism," in *Essays in Anthropology Presented to A. L. Kroeber* (Berkeley, California, 1936), p. 130.

33 Charles Hill-Tout, in *Journal of the Anthropological Institute*, XXXV (1905), 145.

34 Julius Jetté, "On the Medicine Men of the Ten'a," *ibid.*, XXXVII (1907), 170.

35 Diamond Jenness, *The Life of the Copper Eskimos* (Ottawa, 1922), p. 192. *Report of the Canadian Arctic Expedition, 1913–18*, Vol. XII.

36 W. Bogoras, in *Memoirs of the American Museum of Natural History*, XI, 419.

37 W. Jochelson, *ibid.*, X, 53 f.; Marie A. Czaplicka, *Aboriginal Siberia* (Oxford, 1914), p. 252.

38 D. F. Thomson, "The Hero Cult, Initiation, and Totemism on Cape York," *Journal of the Royal Anthropological Institute*, LXIII (1933), 511; cf. *ibid.*, LXIV (1934), 252. In Lepers' Island, one of the New Hebrides, a person who eats human flesh, something not ordinarily done, will be afraid of nothing. "On this ground men will buy flesh when someone has been killed, that they may get the name of valiant men by eating it" (R. H. Codrington, *The Melanesians* [Oxford, 1891], p. 344). Among the Vedda of Ceylon it was formerly the custom, when a man had been killed, for the slayer to preserve a piece of the liver and carry it about in his pouch. When angry at someone else he would bite off some of the dried liver and chew it, saying to himself, "I have killed this man; why should I not be strong and confident and kill this other one who has insulted me?" (C. G. Seligman and Brenda Z. Seligman, *The Veddas* [Cambridge, 1911], pp. 207 f.).

39 A. C. Haddon and C. G. Seligman, in *Reports of the Cambridge Anthropological Expedition to Torres Straits*, V, 321 f.

[40] F. E. Williams, *Papuans of the Trans-Fly* (Oxford, 1936), p. 342. A case is reported from Papua of sorcerers killing a man and then, when the body had been buried, exhuming it and eating a considerable part of it. See W. N. Beaver, "Some Notes on the Eating of Human Flesh in the Western Division of Papua," *Man*, XIV (1914), 145.

[41] R. H. Codrington, *op. cit.*, pp. 221 f.

[42] A. van Gennep, *Tabou et totémisme à Madagascar* (Paris, 1904), pp. 342 f., on the authority of G. Ferrand. The Antaimorona, neighbors of the Antambahoaka, attribute a "beneficial action" (of purification, it would seem) to sexual intercourse with a cow (p. 343).

[43] H. A. Junod, *The Life of a South African Tribe* (2d ed., London, 1927), II, 68.

[44] Charles Bullock, *The Mashona* (Cape Town and Johannesburg, 1928), p. 316, note 1.

[45] C. M. Doke, "Social Control among the Lambas," *Bantu Studies*, II (1923–26), 41.

[46] Audrey I. Richards, *ibid.*, IX (1935), 250.

[47] E. W. Smith and A. M. Dale, *The Ila-speaking Peoples of Northern Rhodesia* (London, 1920), II, 83; cf. I, 261.

[48] H. S. Stannus, in *Journal of the Royal Anthropological Institute*, XL (1910), 307.

[49] A. G. O. Hodgson, "Rain Making, Witchcraft, and Medicine among the Anyanja," *Man*, XXXI (1931), 267.

[50] Knud Rasmussen, *The Netsilik Eskimos* (Copenhagen, 1931), p. 198. *Report of the Fifth Thule Expedition*, Vol. VIII, Nos. 1–2.

[51] A. W. Howitt, *op. cit.*, pp. 388, 410.

[52] August Kleintitschen, *Die Küstenbewohner der Gazellehalbinsel* (*Neupommern, deutsche Südsee*) (Münster in Westfalen, 1906), p. 350.

[53] W. H. R. Rivers, *The History of Melanesian Society* (Cambridge, 1914), I, 157 f.

[54] Edward Tregear, *The Maori Race* (Wanganui, New Zealand, 1904), p. 499.

[55] A. Erdland, *Die Marshall-Insulaner* (Münster in Westfalen, 1914), p. 332.

[56] S. Walleser, "Religiöse Anschauungen und Gebräuche von Jap (deutsche Südsee)," *Anthropos*, VIII (1913), 1053.

[57] W. W. Skeat, "Malay Spiritualism," *Folk-Lore*, XII (1902), 136. The Mackenzie River Eskimo believe that their shamans can walk on water (Vilhjalmur Stefansson, *My Life with the Eskimo* [New York, 1913], p. 406).

[58] Mrs. Eileen J. Krige and J. D. Krige, *The Realm of a Rain Queen* (London, 1943), pp. 254 f.

[59] H. A. Junod, *op. cit.*, II, 511 f., 524. Magicians are often credited with the ability to cause sickness or death by finger pointing. There are people among the Akamba who, merely by stretching out their index finger toward an objectionable person, can cause his death. This fatal power may even be possessed involuntarily by a man who never resorts to black magic. To avoid its exercise he keeps his hands closed when pointing out anything and uses the knuckle of an index finger as a pointer (Gerhard Lindblom, *The Akamba in British East Africa* [2d ed., Uppsala, 1920], p. 281). A Lango sorcerer, by pointing his bent forefinger at a person, can cause the latter's death (J. H. Driberg, *The Lango* [London, 1923], p. 242). The same belief is found among the Ika, a subtribe of the Ibo, southern Nigeria (P. A. Talbot, *The Peoples of Southern Nigeria* [London, 1926], II,

211). An Iroquois will be recognized as a genuine witch if he can make a person sick or kill him merely by pointing at him (W. M. Beauchamp, "Iroquois Notes," *Journal of American Folk-Lore*, V [1892], 223 f.). A Penobscot magician can injure or kill a person by pointing at him with the forefinger and saying, "You! You will see something before long!" (F. G. Speck, "Penobscot Shamanism," *Memoirs of the American Anthropological Association* (No. 28 [Vol. VI, Pt. 4], p. 262). A Miwok sorcerer, sitting on a mountain top, can kill a man fifty miles away. He does this simply by "filliping poison" from his finger-ends in the direction of the person to be destroyed (Stephen Powers, in *Contributions to North American Ethnology*, III, 354). The Kwakiutl tell of an ancestral hero who perforated the head of an enemy by pointing the index finger at him. Then the enemy retaliated in kind. "Now they knew that they were equally strong, and parted" (Franz Boas, in *Report of the Fifty-ninth Meeting of the British Association for the Advancement of Science* [1889], p. 826).

Because of the association of finger pointing with black magic the gesture is often regarded as very bad form or even as an attempt at sorcery. The Berg-dama of South Africa consider that to point at anybody with the index finger is equivalent to cursing him, and for these Negroes there is nothing worse than a curse (Heinrich Vedder, *Die Bergdama* [Hamburg, 1923], I, 122). Similarly for the Bechuana tribes pointing at a person with the index finger is not merely an insult; it is a curse. They call the index finger the "pointing finger" (W. C. Willoughby, *Nature Worship and Taboo* [Hartford, Conn., 1932], p. 144). For the Ba-ila the simplest act of bewitchery is to point with the index finger in the direction of a person while "thinking or mumbling" a desire for his death. Christian preachers have sometimes got themselves into serious trouble by shaking an index finger in the face of the congregation to emphasize some point in a sermon (E. W. Smith, *The Religion of the Lower Races* [New York, 1923], p. 14). Among the Guiana Indians, while it is permissible to single out a person by nodding your head, to point your finger at him is to offer him as serious an affront as it would be to step over him when he is lying on the ground (W. E. Roth, "An Inquiry into the Animism and Folk-Lore of the Guiana Indians," *Thirtieth Annual Report of the Bureau of American Ethnology*, pp. 239, 271). A magician of the Dakota can paralyze or kill anyone who points a finger at him (S. R. Riggs, in *Contributions to North American Ethnography*, IX, 93). Among the Blackfoot the keepers of the sacred Medicine Pipe must observe a long list of restrictions which, if violated, will result in various misfortunes for themselves and their family. The must-nots include pointing toward anyone with the fingers; the thumb must always be used for this purpose (Walter McClintock, *The Old North Trail* [London, 1910], p. 268).

60 W. S. Routledge and Katherine Routledge, *With a Prehistoric People* (London, 1910), p. 255.

61 A. R. Wallace, *A Narrative of Travels on the Amazon and Rio Negro* (London, 1870), p. 499.

62 Erland Nordenskiöld, "Faiseurs des miracles et voyants chez les Indiens Cuna," *Revista del Instituto de Etnología de la Universidad Nacional de Tucumán*, II (1931–32), 460 ff.

63 Frank Russell, "Myths of the Jicarilla Apaches," *Journal of American Folk-Lore*, XI (1898), 254.

64 Frances Densmore, "Papago Music," *Bulletin of the Bureau of American Ethnology*, No. 90, p. 85.

65 Ruth Benedict, *Zuñi Mythology* (New York, 1935), II, 82.

66 Elsie C. Parsons, in *Forty-seventh Annual Report of the Bureau of American Ethnology*, p. 342.

67 C. G. Leland and J. D. Prince, *Kulóskap the Master, and Other Algonkin*

Poems (New York, 1902), p. 35. The power of an Eskimo *angakok* was sometimes revealed by the fact of his feet sinking in rocky ground "just as in snow" (Henry Rink, *Tales and Traditions of the Eskimo* [Edinburgh, 1875], p. 59).

[68] R. H. Lowie, "The Religion of the Crow Indians," *Anthropological Papers of the American Museum of Natural History*, XXV, 353 f. The Subanun of Mindanao tell stories of their magicians who have died and then have come back to life. See E. B. Christie, *The Subanuns of Sindaħgan Bay* (Manila, 1909), p. 85. *Bureau of Science, Division of Ethnology Publications*, Vol. VI, Pt. I.

[69] R. B. Dixon, in *Bulletin of the American Museum of Natural History*, XVII, 279.

[70] Leslie Spier, in *University of California Publications in American Archaeology and Ethnology*, XXX, 273.

[71] James Teit, in *Memoirs of the American Museum of Natural History*, II, 360.

[72] Diamond Jenness, in *Bulletin of the Bureau of American Ethnology*, No. 133, p. 566.

[73] Kaj Birket-Smith and Frederica De Laguna, *The Eyak Indians of the Copper River Delta, Alaska* (Copenhagen, 1938), p. 209.

[74] Knud Rasmussen, *The Netsilik Eskimos* (Copenhagen, 1931), pp. 299 ff. *Report of the Fifth Thule Expedition*, Vol. VIII, Nos. 1–2.

[75] *Idem, Intellectual Culture of the Hudson Bay Eskimos* (Copenhagen, 1930), pp. 112 f. *Report of the Fifth Thule Expedition*, Vol. VII, No. 1.

[76] Franz Boas, in *Bulletin of the American Museum of Natural History*, XV, 247 f.

[77] Dr. G. B. Kirkland, formerly Government Medical Officer in Southern Rhodesia, describes in a lecture, "My Experiences of Savage Magic," a jackal dance of the natives. After eating "high" meat and drinking large quantities of liquor, they played the part of jackals "with an uncanny realism." The dance was performed under the direction of the witch doctor. See Nandor Fodor, "Lycanthropy as a Psychic Mechanism," *Journal of American Folk-Lore*, LVIII (1945), 310.

[78] Mrs. K. L. Parker, *The Euahlayi Tribe* (London, 1905), pp. 20 f., 23 f., 29 ff.

[79] R. H. Codrington, *op. cit.*, pp. 207 f.

[80] Edward Tregear, *op. cit.*, p. 52.

[81] W. H. Skeat, *Malay Magic* (London, 1900), pp. 160 ff., quoting Hugh Clifford and Sir Frank Swettenham.

[82] W. W. Skeat and C. O. Blagden, *Pagan Races of the Malay Peninsula* (London, 1906), II, 227. See also I. H. N. Evans, *Studies in Religion, Folk-Lore, and Custom in British North Borneo and the Malay Peninsula* (Cambridge, 1923), p. 210 (Sakai).

[83] William Crooke, *Religion and Folk-Lore of Northern India* (London, 1926), p. 425. Among the Naga tribes of Assam, magicians do not practice lycanthropy. The were-tigers and were-leopards are invariably men who make no claim to possess magical powers (J. H. Hutton, "Leopard Men in the Naga Hills," *Journal of the Royal Anthropological Institute*, L [1920], 50). The same would seem to be true, also, of the Taman of Upper Burma. In this tribe a man who wants to turn himself into a tiger urinates, strips himself, and then rolls on the ground which he wetted. As a were-tiger he could kill other tigers and also prey on buffaloes and fowls (R. S. Brown, *ibid.*, XLI [1911], 306).

[84] P. Dehon, in *Memoirs of the Asiatic Society of Bengal*, I (1905–1906), 141.

[85] W. H. I. Bleek, *A Brief Account of Bushman Folk-Lore and Other Texts* (London, 1875), p. 15.

[86] C. M. Doke, *The Lambas of Northern Rhodesia* (London, 1931), p. 303.

[87] J. H. W. Sheane, "Some Aspects of the Awemba Religious and Superstitious Observances," *Journal of the Anthropological Institute,* XXXVI (1906), 155.

[88] F. Bösch, *Les Banyamwezi* (Münster in Westfalen, 1930), pp. 241 f. Cf. Lionel Decle, *Three Years in Savage Africa* (London, 1898), p. 344.

[89] Ernst Marno, *Reisen im Gebiete des blauen und weissen Nil* (Wien, 1874), p. 239.

[90] Mary H. Kingsley, *Travels in West Africa* (London, 1897), p. 468. Many stories are told of people who were carried off by witch crocodiles and kept in places underground for years. As our authority suggests, such stories may have arisen from the well-known habit of the crocodile of burying a body on the bank, sometimes for several days, before eating it (*loc. cit.*).

[91] P. A. Talbot, *In the Shadow of the Bush* (London, 1912), p. 191.

[92] A. G. Leonard, *The Lower Niger and Its Tribes* (London, 1906), p. 491.

[93] Thomas Winterbottom, *An Account of the Native Africans in the Neighbourhood of Sierra Leone* (London, 1803), I, 256, note.

[94] Martin Dobrizhoffer, *An Account of the Abipones* (London, 1822), II, 77.

[95] R. E. Latcham, in *Journal of the Royal Anthropological Institute,* XXXIX (1909), 350. According to an old account sorcerers transform themselves into nocturnal birds, fly through the air, and shoot invisible arrows at their enemies (J. I. Molina, *The Geographical, Natural, and Civil History of Chili* [Middletown, Conn., 1808], II, 78).

[96] Karl von den Steinen, *Unter den Naturvölkern Zentral-Brasiliens* (Berlin, 1894), p. 345.

[97] P. Ehrenreich, *Beiträge zur Völkerkunde Brasiliens* (Berlin, 1891), p. 69.

[98] Curt Nimuendajú, *The Apinayé* (Washington, D.C., 1939), p. 150. *The Catholic University of America, Anthropological Series,* No. 8. Among the Penobscot Indians a white magician could recognize one of the black variety in his disguise as an animal and kill him by killing the creature (F. G. Speck, "Penobscot Shamanism," *Memoirs of the American Anthropological Association,* No. 28 [Vol. VI, Pt. 4], pp. 260 f.).

[99] Thomas Whiffen, *The North-West Amazons* (New York, 1915), p. 182.

[100] Rafael Karsten, *The Head Hunters of Western Amazonas* (Helsingfors, Finland, 1935), p. 387. *Societas Scientiarum Fennica, Commentationes Humanarum Litterarum,* Vol. VII, No. 1.

[101] *Idem, The Civilization of the South American Indians* (London, 1926), p. 501.

[102] Carl Lumholtz, *op. cit.,* I, 325.

[103] William Morgan, *Human Wolves among the Navaho* (New Haven, 1936), p. 3. *Yale University Publications in Anthropology,* No. 11.

[104] F. G. Speck, "Penobscot Shamanism," *Memoirs of the American Anthropological Association,* No. 28 (Vol. VI, Pt. 4), pp. 249 ff.

[105] L. H. Morgan, *League of the Ho-dé-No-Sau-Nee or Iroquois* (edited by H. M. Lloyd) (New York, 1904), I, 156.

[106] W. J. Hoffman, in *Fourteenth Annual Report of the Bureau of Ethnology,* Part I, p. 151. Cf. Peter Jones, *History of the Ojebway Indians* (London, 1861), p. 145.

[107] A. L. Kroeber, *Handbook of the Indians of California* (Washington, D.C., 1925), pp. 854 f.

[108] Diamond Jenness, *op. cit.*, p. 193. Jenness witnessed on Victoria Island a seance in which a female shaman became possessed by her familiar spirit (a wolf), in order to give an oracular utterance. In speaking of this performance some time later "the natives stated as an incontestable fact that Higilak had been transformed into a wolf" (p. 194).

All important seances, declares Jenness, arouse in the spectators a tense emotional excitement. "Usually their minds are keyed up beforehand to the proper pitch by singing and dancing, and especially by the booming notes of the deep-toned drum. The shaman himself is in a condition of hysteria, or of something that nearly resembles it, brought on at the commencement of his seance by the straining of every muscle, the rolling of his eyes, and the ejaculation of cries and strangled gasping sounds. . . . . So intense is the strain that the man nearly faints from exhaustion at the close of the performance. The insertion of the teeth of the animal familiar, or the wearing of garments made from its fur, serve, like stage scenery, to increase the illusion. The shaman is not conscious of acting a part; he becomes in his own mind the animal or the shade of the dead man that is deemed to possess him. To his audience, too, this strange figure, with its wild and frenzied appearance, its ventriloquistic cries, and its unearthly falsetto gabble, with only a broken word here and there of intelligible speech, is no longer a human being, but the thing it personifies. Their minds become receptive to the wildest imaginings, and they see the strangest and most fantastic happenings. If the shaman ejaculates that he is no longer a man but a bear, forthwith it is a bear that they behold, not a human being; if he says that the dance house is full of spirits, they will see them in every corner. It is in this way, apparently, that most of the tales arise of shamans cutting off their limbs, or flying through the air, or changing to bears and wolves" (p. 216).

[109] W. Bogoras, in *Memoirs of the American Museum of Natural History*, XI, 436 f.

[110] A. C. Haddon and C. G. Seligman, in *Reports of the Cambridge Anthropological Expedition to Torres Straits*, V, 322.

[111] H. B. Guppy, *The Solomon Islands and Their Natives* (London, 1887), p. 163.

[112] S. P. Smith, "The 'Tohunga'-Maori," *Transactions and Proceedings of the New Zealand Institute*, XXXII (1899), 262 f. According to Edward Tregear (*op. cit.*, pp. 379 f., 511), the person willed to death was usually a slave, though a relative might be made the object of the experiment. According to Elsdon Best, the magical killing of a near relative really represented the fee paid by a novice to his teacher in the black art. Payment in goods would have been useless, for spells and magical rites so acquired were without power. The victim, *tauira patu*, must be one whose death would bring infinite grief to the slayer; the anguish thus caused him was the teacher's reward for what he had done to him. There were even cases when the teacher offered himself as a *tauira patu* on whom the novice might test the power of his newly acquired magic. See Elsdon Best, "Omens and Superstitious Beliefs of the Maori," *Journal of the Polynesian Society*, VII (1898), 243. See further H. T. Whatahoro, *The Lore of the Whare-Wananaga, or Teachings of the Maori College* (New Plymouth, New Zealand, 1913), p. 102. *Memoirs of the Polynesian Society*, Vol. III.

[113] W. H. R. Rivers, *The Todas* (London, 1906), p. 255.

[114] Sir H. H. Johnston, *The Uganda Protectorate* (2d ed., London, 1904), II, 882.

[115] Erland Nordenskiöld, "Die religiösen Vorstellungen der Itonama-Indianer in Bolivia," *Zeitschrift für Ethnologie*, XLVII (1915), 109.

116 *Idem,* "Cuna Indian Religion," *Proceedings of the Twenty-third International Congress of Americanists* (New York, 1928), p. 673.

117 Herbert Passin, "Sorcery as a Phase of Tarahumara Economic Relations," *Man,* XLII (1942), 13.

118 Elsie C. Parsons, "Witchcraft among the Pueblos: Indian or Spanish?" *ibid.,* XXVII (1927), 107.

119 G. B. Grinnell, *The Cheyenne Indians* (New Haven, 1923), II, 144.

120 G. H. Pepper and G. L. Wilson, "A Hidatsa Shrine and the Beliefs Respecting It," *Memoirs of the American Anthropological Association,* No. 10 (Vol. II, Pt. 4), pp. 309 f.

121 W. Z. Park, *Shamanism in Western North America* (Evanston, 1938), p. 43. *Northwestern University Studies in the Social Sciences,* No. 2. Like the Maori sorcerer a Paviotso magician may also cause illness by touching a person, handing him food, or giving him a pipe to smoke (*loc. cit.*).

122 J. S. Harris, in Ralph Linton (editor), *Acculturation in Seven American Indian Tribes* (New York, 1940), p. 62. The most vicious form of *dijibo* is transferred by a woman to a man by the twitching of her vulva. She may possess this evil power unwillingly and may transfer it without intending to do so. Hence a woman's genitals are always considered dangerous and are kept hidden. Even her husband dares not look at them (*loc. cit.*).

123 R. B. Dixon, in *Bulletin of the American Museum of Natural History,* XVII, 269.

124 A. L. Kroeber, *op. cit.,* p. 67.

125 E. Sapir, "Religious Ideas of the Takelma Indians of Southwestern Oregon," *Journal of American Folk-Lore,* XX (1907), 41, from information supplied by Mrs. Frances Johnson, a full-blooded Takelma.

126 B. J. Stern, *The Lummi Indians of Northwest Washington* (New York, 1934), p. 84.

127 James Teit, in *Memoirs of the American Museum of Natural History,* IV, 287.

128 Julius Jetté, "On the Superstitions of the Ten'a Indians," *Anthropos,* VI (1911), 250; *idem,* "On the Medicine Men of the Ten'a," *Journal of the Royal Anthropological Institute,* XXXVII (1907), 169 f. In the Tinne myth of a great flood the Raven, to cause the reappearance of land, wishes with such concentration of thought that he faints from the effort (*idem,* "On Ten'a Folk-Lore," *ibid.,* XXXVIII [1908], 311, 313).

129 James Dawson, *Australian Aborigines* (Melbourne, 1881), pp. 55 f.

130 Mrs. K. L. Parker, *The Euahlayi Tribe,* pp. 36 f.

131 John Mathew, *Eaglehawk and Crow* (London, 1899), pp. 143 f.

132 E. M. Loeb, "Shaman and Seer," *American Anthropologist* (n.s., 1929), XXXI, 69 f., 79.

133 H. A. Junod, *op. cit.* (2d ed.), II, 520 f. The gnu tail is one of the most common accessories of a Bathonga magician. The natives say that when a mother gnu has given birth, she beats her offspring with her tail and thus gives it the necessary strength to walk and follow her. Hence the magical power of the caudal appendage of a gnu (*loc. cit.*).

134 J. H. Weeks, *Among the Primitive Bakongo* (London, 1914), p. 217. See also W. H. Bentley, *Pioneering on the Congo* (London, 1900), I, 257, who describes the contents of a Bakongo doctor's "charm bundle."

135 M. R. Drennan, "Two Witch Doctor's Outfits from Angola," *Bantu Studies,* VIII (1934), 386.

136 W. E. Roth, "An Inquiry into the Animism and Folk-Lore of the Guiana Indians," *Thirtieth Annual Report of the Bureau of American Ethnology*, pp. 329 f.

137 George Catlin, *Letters and Notes on the Manners, Customs, and Condition of the North American Indians* (2d ed., New York, 1842), Letter No. 6.

138 J. R. Swanton, in *Memoirs of the American Museum of Natural History*, IV, 40.

139 *Idem*, "Social Condition, Beliefs, and Linguistic Relationship of the Tlingit Indians," *Twenty-sixth Annual Report of the Bureau of American Ethnology*, pp. 463 f.

140 Knud Rasmussen, *Intellectual Culture of the Hudson Bay Eskimos* (Copenhagen, 1930), p. 114. *Report of the Fifth Thule Expedition*, Vol. VII, No. 1.

141 Marie A. Czaplicka, *op. cit.*, pp. 203–27. The Yakut say that when a shaman assumes his bird costume he receives the ability to fly anywhere in the world. The Tungus describe the shaman's costume as his "shadow," in which shape his soul flies on its journeys. The Yenisei Ostiak call it and the objects hanging from it his "power." See Uno Holmberg, *The Mythology of All Races* (Vol. IV), *Finno-Ugric, Siberian* (Boston, 1927), p. 519. See also *idem*, "The Shaman Costume and Its Significance," *Annales Universitatis Fennicae Aboensis*, Series B, Vol. I, No. 2, pp. 1–36.

142 A. W. Howitt, *op. cit.*, pp. 389 ff. For an account of a Buandik seance see Mrs. James Smith, *The Booandik Tribe of South Australian Aborigines* (Adelaide, 1880), p. 30.

143 Benjamin Danks, "Some Notes on Savage Life in New Britain," *Report of the Twelfth Meeting of the Australasian Association for the Advancement of Science* (1909), p. 454.

144 I. H. N. Evans, *The Negritos of Malaya* (Cambridge, 1937), pp. 191 f.

145 E. E. Evans-Pritchard, *Witchcraft, Oracles, and Magic among the Azande* (Oxford, 1937), pp. 188 ff. Our authority points out that the children who attend these seances must be profoundly impressed by them, and thus the popular belief in the extraordinary powers of witch doctors is kept alive (p. 154). This is said to be true, also, of the Wachagga of Mount Kilimanjaro (O. F. Raum, *op. cit.*, p. 366, note 2).

146 P. A. Talbot, *The Peoples of Southern Nigeria* (London, 1926), II, 196. Talbot did not witness these performances but relied on information supplied by native informants. For a fuller account of the baby-smashing "play" see *Life in Southern Nigeria* (London, 1923), pp. 72 f., by the same author.

147 J. N. B. Hewitt, as reported in *American Anthropologist* (n.s., 1915), XVII, 622.

148 See W. J. Hoffman, in *Fourteenth Annual Report of the Bureau of American Ethnology*, Part I, pp. 146–49 (Menomini); Frances Densmore, "An Explanation of a Trick Performed by Indian Jugglers," *American Anthropologist* (n.s., 1932), XXXIV, 310–14 (Ojibwa); A. I. Hallowell, *The Role of Conjuring in Saulteaux Society* (Philadelphia, 1942), pp. 35–52. *Publications of the Philadelphia Anthropological Society*, Vol. II. Hallowell calls attention to the "striking analogies" between the conjuring performances of these eastern Indians and the seances of the Semang of the Malay Peninsula (p. 14, note 20).

149 G. B. Grinnell, *Pawnee Hero Stories and Folk-Tales* (New York, 1890), pp. 375 ff., according to accounts by the author's friend, Captain L. H. North.

150 J. O. Dorsey, "A Study of Siouian Cults," *Eleventh Annual Report of the Bureau of Ethnology*, p. 417. This trick was witnessed by Dorsey in 1871.

[151] Edwin James, *Narrative of the Captivity and Adventures of John Tanner* (New York, 1830), p. 135. An Ojibwa magician performs many other tricks which the Indians look upon as "miracles" (p. 370).

[152] V. Stefansson, *op. cit.*, pp. 403 ff. For descriptions of other Eskimo seances see Franz Boas, in *Sixth Annual Report of the Bureau of Ethnology*, pp. 592 ff. (Central Eskimo); Diamond Jenness, *op. cit.*, pp. 194 f. (Copper Eskimo). Rasmussen, who attended a number of seances among the Copper Eskimo, describes these as being extremely naïve and easily exposed if watched at all critically. But we must make allowances for the great faith of the audience in the officiating shaman and in the real presence of the spirits he summons to his aid. And, furthermore, the shaman, though conscious of his trickery, considers that it brings him into touch with the spirits. See Knud Rasmussen, *Intellectual Culture of the Copper Eskimos* (Copenhagen, 1932), pp. 30 f. *Report of the Fifth Thule Expedition*, Vol. IX.

[153] W. Bogoras, in *Memoirs of the American Museum of Natural History*, XI, 433 ff. For an account of a shamanistic performance among the Yakut see W. Jochelson, in *Anthropological Papers of the American Museum of Natural History*, XXXIII, 120 ff., from the description of N. A. Vitashevsky.

[154] Richard Hakluyt, *The Principal Navigations, Voyages, Traffiques, and Discoveries of the English Nation* (Glasgow reprint, 1903–1905), II, 347 f.

[155] Marie A. Czaplicka, *op. cit.*, p. 169, note 2.

[156] See James Cowan, *Fairy Folk-Tales of the Maori* (Wellington, New Zealand, 1925), pp. 109 ff.; Marie A. Czaplicka, *My Siberian Year* (London, 1916), p. 212.

[157] R. H. Lowie, "The Religion of the Crow Indians," *Anthropological Papers of the American Museum of Natural History*, XXV, 344 ff. In a contest between a celebrated medicine man of the Omaha and a Ponca practitioner likewise famous for his occult powers, each secretly sought the other's death by means of magic. The Ponca drew on the ground a picture of the Omaha and struck it with his club (the club being the weapon of the Thunder spirits) and at the same time called on them to strike the original of the picture. The Omaha, who suspected that evil was being prepared against him, sang his magical songs by way of protection. So effective were they that a few days later the Ponca was himself struck by lightning (Alice C. Fletcher and Francis La Flesche, in *Twenty-seventh Annual Report of the Bureau of American Ethnology*, pp. 490 f.).

[158] F. G. Speck, in *Memoirs of the American Anthropological Association*, No. 8 (Vol. II, Pt. 2), p. 133.

[159] A. I. Hallowell, *op. cit.*, pp. 62 f.

[160] Ann H. Gayton, "Yokuts-Mono Chiefs and Shamans," *University of California Publications in American Archaeology and Ethnology*, XXIV, 401.

[161] Franz Boas, in *Report of the Sixtieth Meeting of the British Association for the Advancement of Science* (1890), p. 647.

[162] Cornelius Osgood, *The Ethnography of the Tanaina* (New Haven, 1937), p. 180. *Yale University Publications in Anthropology*, No. 16.

[163] E. M. Curr, *The Australian Race* (Melbourne, 1886), I, 47.

[164] *Tom Petrie's Reminiscences of Early Queensland* (Brisbane, 1904), p. 61.

[165] Spencer and Gillen, *The Native Tribes of Central Australia*, pp. 530 f.; *iidem*, *The Northern Tribes of Central Australia*, p. 480. To the statement in the text there is a curious exception among the Warramunga. In this tribe a particular set of medicine men (the "Snakes") enjoy a license in sexual matters not accorded to ordinary people. The interference of an *urkutu* with another man's wife, though regarded as decidedly reprehensible, is not punishable. The woman

concerned would, however, come in for very severe handling (*Northern Tribes*, pp. 486 f.).

[166] Paul Wirz, *Die Marind-anim von Holländisch-Süd-Neu-Guinea* (Hamburg, 1922–25), Vol. II, Pt. III, p. 67.

[167] W. H. R. Rivers, *The History of Melanesian Society*, I, 157.

[168] Dorothea F. Bleek, *The Naron* (Cambridge, 1928), p. 28.

[169] Wilhelm Koppers, *Unter Feuerland-Indianern* (Stuttgart, 1924), p. 177.

[170] W. L. Warner, *op. cit.*, pp. 193, note 1, 217.

[171] A. C. Haddon, in *Reports of the Cambridge Anthropological Expedition to Torres Straits*, V, 323.

[172] James Chalmers, *Pioneering in New Guinea* (London, 1887), p. 312.

[173] Gunnar Landtman, *The Kiwai Papuans of British New Guinea* (London, 1927), p. 324.

[174] Bronislaw Malinowski, *Argonauts of the Western Pacific*, pp. 426 f. By the Trobrianders the privilege of having more than one wife was granted not only to people of high rank but also to magicians of great renown *(idem, The Sexual Life of Savages in North-West Melanesia* [New York, 1929], p. 130).

[175] R. Parkinson, *Dreissig Jahre in der Südsee* (Stuttgart, 1907), p. 404.

[176] Felix Speiser, *Ethnographische Materialien aus den Neuen Hebriden und den Banks-Inseln* (Berlin, 1923), p. 367.

[177] Teuira Henry, "Ancient Tahiti," *Bernice P. Bishop Museum Bulletin*, No. 48, p. 203.

[178] William Howell and D. J. S. Bailey, *A Sea-Dyak Dictionary* (Singapore, 1900), *s.v. manang;* H. L. Roth, *The Natives of Sarawak and British North Borneo* (London, 1896), I, 266, citing Brooke Low.

[179] E. H. Gomes, *Seventeen Years among the Sea Dyaks of Borneo* (London, 1911), pp. 168 f.

[180] Sir Spenser St. John, *Life in the Forests of the Far East* (2d ed., London, 1863), II, 212.

[181] Paul Arndt, *Mythologie, Religion, und Magie im Sikagebiet (östl. Mittelflores)* (Ende, Flores, 1932), p. 292.

[182] S. J. Hickson, *A Naturalist in North Celebes* (London, 1889), p. 255.

[183] E. H. Man, *On the Aboriginal Inhabitants of the Andaman Islands* (London, 1932), pp. 28 f.; *idem*, in *Journal of the Anthropological Institute*, XII (1883), 96 f.

[184] J. M. Watt and N. J. van Warmelo, "The Medicines and Practice of a Sotho Doctor," *Bantu Studies*, IV (1930), 48.

[185] James Macdonald, "East Central African Customs," *Journal of the Anthropological Institute*, XXII (1893), 105.

[186] A. C. Hollis, *op. cit.*, p. 52.

[187] A. L. Kitching, *On the Backwaters of the Nile* (London, 1912), p. 240.

[188] D. S. Oyler, "The Shilluk's Belief in the Good Medicine Men," *Sudan Notes and Records*, III (1920), 110. When a Shilluk doctor begins to practice he dedicates his first fee to the divine being from whom he received his medical power *(loc. cit.)*.

[189] J. H. Weeks, "The Congo Medicine Man and His Black and White Magic," *Folk-Lore*, XXI (1910), 450 ff.

[190] J. Büttikofer, *Reisebilder aus Liberia* (Leiden, 1890), II, 333.

[191] Martin Dobrizhoffer, *op. cit.*, II, 76.

[192] G. Kurze, "Sitten und Gebräuche der Lengua-Indianer," *Mitteilungen der geographischen Gesellschaft (für Thuringen) zu Jena,* XXIII (1905), 19, 29.

[193] Robert Southey, *History of Brazil,* I (2d ed., London, 1822), 238.

[194] A. R. Wallace, *op. cit.,* p. 500.

[195] Sir E. F. im Thurn, *op. cit.,* pp. 339 f.

[196] W. C. Farabee, *The Central Arawaks* (Philadelphia, 1918), p. 90. *University of Pennsylvania, The University Museum, Anthropological Publications,* Vol. IX.

[197] Theodor Koch-Grünberg, *Vom Roroima zum Orinoco* (Berlin, 1917–28), III, 190.

[198] Carl Lumholtz, *op. cit.,* I, 312.

[199] Frank Russell, in *Twenty-sixth Annual Report of the Bureau of American Ethnology,* pp. 261 f.

[200] J. G. Bourke, "The Medicine Men of the Apache," *Ninth Annual Report of the Bureau of Ethnology,* p. 467.

[201] Ruth M. Underhill, *Singing for Power: the Song Magic of the Papago Indians of Southern Arizona* (Berkeley, 1938), p. 141.

[202] Mrs. F. J. Newcomb, *Navajo Omens and Taboos* (Santa Fe, New Mexico, 1940), p. 70.

[203] G. B. Grinnell, *Blackfoot Lodge Tales* (New York, 1892), p. 284.

[204] Stephen Powers, *Tribes of California* (Washington, D.C., 1877), pp. 26 f., 354. *Contributions to North American Ethnology,* Vol. III.

[205] B. J. Stern, *op. cit.,* p. 75.

[206] D. W. Harmon, *A Journal of Voyages and Travels in the Interiour of North America* (Andover, Mass., 1820), p. 306.

[207] James Teit, in *Memoirs of the American Museum of Natural History,* II, 364.

[208] Kaj Birket-Smith and Frederica De Laguna, *op. cit.,* p. 212.

[209] Cornelius Osgood, *op. cit.,* p. 177.

[210] Franz Boas, in *Sixth Annual Report of the Bureau of Ethnology,* p. 594.

[211] E. W. Hawkes, *The Labrador Eskimo* (Ottawa, 1916), p. 131. *Geological Survey Memoir,* No. 91.

[212] W. Bogoras, in *Memoirs of the American Museum of Natural History,* XI, 432; W. G. Sumner, "The Yakuts. Abridged from the Russian of Sieroshevski," *Journal of the Anthropological Institute,* XXXI (1901), 102; Marie A. Czaplicka, *op. cit.,* p. 177 (Tungus).

Chapter X

THE FUNCTIONS OF MAGICIANS

MAGICIANS form the intelligentsia of primitive society. They live by their wits, and their wits have to be keen if they are to satisfy all the imperious demands laid upon them by their fellows. To natural acuteness they must add some understanding of physical phenomena; an intimate acquaintance with the properties of plants and the habits of animals; familiarity with all the lore and traditions of their community; an insight into human nature and the power of suggestion; cunning and audacity in the practice of deceit; and, not least in importance, some skill in the conjuring arts. The magical profession attracts ambitious and able men, who see in it a sure road to wealth, special privileges, and influence. It is a career open to talents.

It is not surprising, therefore, that magicians should have so often risen to a commanding place in a community. As specialists in the mysterious and uncanny they are often looked upon as sacred persons. Among nearly all primitive peoples they rank next to the chiefs in prestige and authority and sometimes higher than the chiefs. In general, magicians and chiefs appear as allies rather than as rivals and work together in the struggle to secure and preserve control over the multitude.

Medicine men in Australia are frequently invited to attend tribal councils and take part in the deliberations. Their advice is particularly needed when the cause of a death is being investigated or when an explanation is being sought for a prolonged drought or some other adverse climatic condition.[1] In the Fly River area of Papua the magicians, as a body, are politically powerful. Important tribal decisions are usually made in accordance with their advice.[2] In many villages of the Solomon Islands the magicians are held in far greater awe than the chief himself.[3] Thus in the little islands of Owa Raha and Owa Riki, while a chief's authority usually extends over his own clansmen only, that of the magician affects all the clans of a village. He seldom abuses it, we are told. As a rule, he believes sincerely in his pos-

279

session of occult powers and employs them for the welfare of the community.[4] Chiefs and priests in the Fiji Islands realized acutely the necessity for continued co-operation. A chief with whom the gods were angry lost his authority; a priest whose god the chief failed to propitiate fell into disrepute and soon gave way to another.[5] Similarly in Niue, or Savage Island, the priests exerted much political influence and the *toa* ("fighting men") found it to their advantage to keep on good terms with them.[6] In Tahiti, in addition to the regular priests, a superior order of sorcerers was attached to every temple enclosure. They were supposed to destroy by their malefic arts sorcerers of an inferior order, to work black magic upon the private enemies of the king and of the chiefs, and, in time of war, to perform their deadly rites against the foe. It is said that these *tahutahu* exercised a "terrible sway" over all ranks of the people and that they even ventured sometimes to attack the king or the chiefs.[7] The Maori *tohunga* exercised both magical and priestly functions. The degree of respect paid to them depended, not on their birth (as in the case of chiefs), but on their attainments. Being exempt from physical labor, they spent their time in intellectual pursuits and, as a result, engrossed all the learning of the people. Their persons, property, and whatever they touched were sacred.[8] In Ponape, one of the largest of the Caroline Islands, the magicians occupied the principal seats in the council chamber. To them belonged, next to the king's, the best portion of cooked food and kava at the festivals.[9] Among the Batak of Sumatra the priest also practices divination and announces propitious days. The people will not engage in any undertaking, however trifling, or make the smallest alteration in their domestic economy, without first consulting him. He ranks as a most important functionary in every village and often serves as its political head.[10]

A Zulu chief is inducted into his office by the diviners, so that he may be "really a chief," as the natives say, and not one by descent only. In the old days, when a chief had wormed out all the secrets of the diviners, he would often order them to be killed, lest they should use sorcery against himself.[11] Though a witch doctor of the Balamba is regarded as a benefactor to the community, because he ferrets out sorcerers, yet the native attitude toward him is one of fear. He can so easily abuse his enormous power, by accepting bribes to let off a guilty person or to condemn to death an innocent man or woman. "He becomes the instrument of jealousy, envy, hatred, and revenge."[12] A witch doctor of the Angoni can do very much as he likes without fear of punishment. Chiefs will employ him to get rid of persons who have gained their enmity or whose possessions have excited their cupidity. Unjust demands of the chiefs upon the people will also be bolstered up by an appeal to the witch doctor.[13] The role of magicians among the Wanyamwezi of Tanganyika is described as being very great. Their influence affects for weal or woe every aspect of the native life. As long as they are in good humor there is nothing to fear; all will go well. The perpetual occupation of the natives is, therefore, to keep them appeased.[14] The magician of the Barundi is a most important functionary, often with greater power than the royal officials.[15]

The Orkoiyot, the principal magician of the Nandi, has very important duties and responsibilities: he tells the people when to begin planting, obtains rain for them, makes women and cattle fruitful, and acts as a diviner. No war party can expect to meet with success unless he has given his approval to it. His person is sacred. Nobody may approach him with weapons in the hands or speak in his presence unless first addressed. Should anyone touch his most sacred head he would lose his magical powers. Yet one of these great persons was clubbed to death by his own people because, they said, he had brought about various calamities—a famine, an epidemic, and then a raid, which, though sanctioned by him, resulted disastrously. However, it would seem that the Nandi later regretted their action and attributed all the misfortunes which befell them afterward to their having murdered their Orkoiyot.[16] A clever witch doctor is an important personage among the Azande. He can harm or protect, he can kill or cure. He is therefore a man who demands respect and gets it. This is especially true at a seance. No native is absolutely certain of not·being a witch, hence he cannot be sure that his name will not be revealed at the seance, "a condition that undoubtedly enhances a witch doctor's prestige."[17] The profession of witch doctor among the Bakongo is open to any shrewd, artful, and energetic person, either rich or poor, bond or free. It is not confined to either sex. As a rule, this functionary is a lithe and active person, for it is often necessary to dance for hours in order to excite the crowd to the required pitch. "He has restless, sharp eyes that jump from face to face of the spectators; he has an acute knowledge of human nature and knows almost instinctively what will please the surrounding throng of onlookers; but his face becomes after a time ugly, repulsive, and the canvas upon which cruelty, chicanery, hatred, and all devilish passions are portrayed with repellant accuracy. . . . . There is no condition of life that he is unable to affect either for good or evil, and his services must not be despised or some dread catastrophe will follow. Such are the pretensions of the Congo witch doctor, and over the natives he wields tyrannical power."[18] In northern Nigeria the priest is often the supreme judicial authority and, in company with the elders, assesses damages, receives fees, and imposes fines.[19]

There are no chiefs among the Yaghan of Tierra del Fuego, for these rude people do not engage in any communal enterprises. However, their medicine men, because of the fear which they inspire, exert a certain amount of authority.[20] Medicine men of the Patagonian Indians are everywhere received with honor, hospitably entertained, and enriched with presents.[21] The Araucanians of southern Chile consulted magicians on all important occasions. War was never declared or peace made except according to their advice.[22] Among the Indians of Brazil, generally, the magicians act as judges, sureties, and witnesses in private affairs, while in matters of public concern their advice and authority carry very great weight.[23] Magicians in the Ipurina tribe are by far its most influential persons.[24] With respect to the Witoto, Boro, and related tribes of the Upper Amazon we are told that, "other things being equal," a contest between a medicine man and a chief is pretty sure to be decided in favor of the former, because death by poison comes speedily to one who ventures to withstand the magic worker. A weak chief would always be subservient to him. The magician has much influence in tribal affairs, and without his advice warfare is never undertaken. It is his business, also, to warn his tribe of impending hostilities.[25] Magicians among the Kanamari were greatly feared. They enjoyed an authority at least equal to that of the chiefs.[26] The Jivaro of eastern Ecuador have no political organization other than temporary alliances for making war, so that with them the magician (*wishinu*) holds the most important place in his group. He is respected, not only for the power he wields, but also for his wealth, which comes to him from the high fees charged for medical services. Apart from his duties as a healer, he is called upon to determine the action of the tribe in matters of importance, for instance, the choice of a war leader or the admittance of some outsider desirous of joining the tribe. Furthermore, he is on intimate terms with the great nature spirits which produce storms and floods and rule the rivers. In time of war an attacking party always tries to kill the enemy *wishinu* as early in the fight as possible, so as to avoid possible injury by the spirits which he controls.[27] An old writer declares that medicine men among the Guiana Indians were regarded as "the arbiters of life and death." Everything was permitted them; nothing was refused them. No one ever thought of complaining at their exactions.[28] They play an especially important role as guardians of the tribal traditions, which they recount to the people and hand down to their successors in the magical profession.[29] Among the Taulipáng the magician is said to possess much greater power than the chief.[30] The Tarahumara magician, at any rate one of real ability, holds the highest place in his community. Although these democratic Indians defer but slightly to their officials and to the wealthy, they "openly and without shame" pay homage to the magician.[31]

Two classes of Pima magicians, namely, those who treated disease by magical means and those who had power over the weather, the crops, and warfare, were "the true rulers of the tribe, as their influence was much greater than that of the chiefs."[32] Among the Apache the medicine men, as a rule, are closely related to the prominent chiefs.[33] In former times the political influence of the Cherokee medicine men seems to have been very considerable. They accompanied a war party, and its success was held to depend more upon their skill in divination and conjuring than on the prowess and cunning of the fighters. Today, when two settlements are training for the ball game, the medicine man of the one side works to "spoil the strength" of his rival on the other side, and the whole affair has the aspect of a contest in magic between them.[34]

The medicine man of the Sioux or Dakota always served as the war leader, because his services were required to interpret omens when the Indians followed the warpath. He carried on his operations usually at night, so as to be able to predict where the enemy would be next day, what was their strength, and the number of scalps that would be taken during the engagement.[35] Among the eastern Cree the influence of the magician was much greater than that of the chief. Evilly disposed "conjurors" often held an entire community in mental bondage, so that no one dared to deny them anything.[36] Of the Kutchin Indians we are told that "the power of the medicine men is very great, and they use every means they can to increase it by working on the fears and credulity of the people. Their influence exceeds even that of the chiefs."[37] The influence of Paviotso magicians was by no means confined to religious affairs. They were frequently consulted on secular matters and their opinions were respected. In the old days many prominent chiefs also exercised magical functions. The possession of occult power was not necessary to chieftainship, but according to the native account "the power helped."[38]

A chief and a powerful medicine man of the Yokuts and Mono in central California were close friends and associates. Their co-operation was profitable to both parties, for on the one hand it greatly increased the chief's wealth and on the other hand protected the medicine man from attack by the relatives of persons whom he had slain by magic. Sometimes their co-operation went so far that it was possible for the chief to employ medicine men to kill a person in another tribe of whom he was jealous. Perhaps the wealth of the prospective victim had excited the chief's cupidity; perhaps the man's wife was wanted by someone who had bribed the chief to have him put out of the way. Whatever the reason, the man was doomed. The "doctors" could kill him no matter how far off he happened to be.[39] Among the Maidu of northern California the medicine man was, and still is, perhaps the most important personage. His word has great weight, he is regarded with much awe, and as a rule he is more likely to be obeyed than the chief.[40] The medicine man was the outstanding figure in the Klamath tribe of southern Oregon. Before the coming of the whites, which brought about profound changes in the tribal life, he always took precedence of the chief.[41] Among the Haida the life of each clan was guided to a great extent by its respective shaman, who "traded on the superstitious fears of his followers."[42] Among the Tinne of southern Alaska a medicine man enjoyed a high social position. He was consulted and listened to, because of the superior knowledge imparted to him by the spirits; he was feared, because by magic he could injure or kill an enemy; he was rich, because his services were so generously rewarded.[43]

In Labrador the shaman serves as the accredited mediator between the Eskimo and the world of spirits. Without his assistance in dealing with such mighty beings the Eskimo feel that they would be undone. Consequently the shaman, combining in his person the three offices of priest, prophet, and magician, exercises great power over the people.[44] Among the Greenland Eskimo the shaman, being the acknowledged authority on all spiritual matters, necessarily became "a kind of civil magistrate." It was his business to inquire into cases of witchcraft or of any other violation of the customary rules and to denounce the guilty parties.[45]

Almost everywhere in Siberia the shamans occupy a position of exceptional importance. Thus among the Buriat the "white" shamans are universally esteemed, while the "black" ones, though disliked, are greatly feared. At the festivals of the Yakut the shamans have the highest place. Even a prince kneels before a shaman and receives from his hand a cup of kumiss. In everyday life they do not possess special privileges, nor are they in any way distinguished from their fellows. The Tungus, whose territory adjoins that of the Yakut, still have the utmost confidence in their doctors and diviners, and the same is said to be true of the Ostiak.[46]

Magicians famous for good works during life may continue to be reverenced and even to receive worship after death. In the Loyalty Islands people who would succeed a magician contend for the possession of his remains, especially his eyes, fingers, toenails, and bones. Or they will try to have his body buried in their own private grounds, so as to become endowed with his "mystic powers."[47] The oldest and most renowned of Semang shamans, "those who know all the magic of the tribe," as the people say, are buried in tree shelters and provided with a supply of food and water, a jungle knife, and other things needful. By this mode of burial they are enabled to enter a special and no doubt superior paradise, which is not that reserved for their fellow tribesmen.[48] It is believed by the Ho, an aboriginal tribe of Chota Nagpur, that the special qualifications of a deceased magician are usually inherited by his disciples. Should this not be the case the disciples keep watch over the spot where he was cremated, in order to obtain some "mystic power" from his remains.[49] A Bushman magician after death was supposed to possess all the powers which he possessed when alive. A dead rain maker, for instance, might be asked to send rain or a dead game magician to give success in hunting.[50] When the head magician of the Masai dies his corpse is buried and not cast out into the bush to be devoured by wild animals, the regular way in which the Masai dispose of their dead.[51] The Guaraní Indians, when moving about the country, used to carry with them the bones of medicine men. In these, "as in holy preservatives," they placed all their hopes.[52] The funerals of Buriat shamans are celebrated with pomp and circumstance; their burial places are held inviolable; sacrifices are made to them; and prayers are addressed to them. Dead shamans protect their own tribesmen and take particular care of their kinsfolk.[53]

On the other hand, even magicians famous for good works during life may be much feared after death. Thus, the Maler, an aboriginal people of the Rajmahal Hills, Bengal, who regularly bury their dead in the village, deposit the bodies of "priests" in the forest. This is done so that their ghosts may not vex the survivors.[54] The Rautia, a caste of Chota Nagpur, probably of Dravidian origin, believe that women dying in childbirth, persons killed by a tiger, and all exorcists are likely to appear after death as malevolent ghosts and trouble the living. Another exorcist is then called upon to identify the ghost responsible for a visitation and to appease it by gifts. Usually it can be "laid" in a few months, but some very persistent ghosts, who during their lifetime were great exorcists, require an annual sacrifice to induce them to remain quiescent.[55] The Bororó, a Brazilian tribe, suppose that the souls of ordinary people are embodied after death in macaws. But dead medicine men become animals other than macaws. Should these animals be killed purposely or by accident, they avenge themselves by carrying off the living.[56] The Siberian Yakut think that shamans after death become restless ghosts and torment the living, especially their nearest relatives. The corpse of a shaman is buried with great haste at night, and the grave is always carefully avoided.[57]

Sorcerers, whose nefarious activity was so greatly dreaded while they were alive, are often supposed to be even more potent for evil when dead, so that special precautions must be taken to protect the community against them. The Kai of New Guinea, after killing a sorcerer, cut his body into many pieces and strew these around as an example to all who would follow his wicked ways.[58] In Bougainville a sorcerer, when revealed by divination, is bound hand and foot and suspended from a tree. After death his body does not receive burial but is thrown into the forest.[59] In Car Nicobar the body of a sorcerer who has been killed is taken out to sea and sunk with stones, thus making it less likely that his ghost will haunt the community. Sometimes his wife and children are also put to death and disposed of in the same manner.[60] By the Ovambo, a Bantu-speaking tribe of Southwest Africa, the ghost of a dead magician is particularly dreaded, hence his body is dismembered and his tongue cut out. If these precautions are taken immediately after death, his ghost need not be feared; it has been effectually disarmed.[61] The Babemba, after killing a sorcerer, burn his body so that he cannot practice his malefic arts after death. Sometimes he manages to evade even this precaution and continues as an evil ghost to afflict the village. Then they dig up his calcined bones and burn them so completely that no more than a pinch of ashes remains.[62] The Lango, a Nilotic tribe of Uganda, club sorcerers to death and burn their bodies. During this process everyone runs away to escape the malevolence of the ghost. The ashes are collected and buried in a marsh, where the water, it is thought, will effectively nullify any further activity on the part of the ghost.[63] In southern Nigeria the corpses of witches are never buried but are placed on the branches of trees in a place set apart for the purpose.[64] It may happen that through superior cunning or good fortune a witch manages to elude suspicion throughout life and dies lamented by everybody. After death the ghost of such a person cannot conceal its evil nature, however, and comes back to play all sorts of mischievous tricks on the survivors. In such a case the corpse must be dug up and burned, thus securing the family from further molestation.[65] By the Jivaro magicians who were greatly feared while alive are supposed to become evil-minded ghosts after death.[66] Some of the Alaskan Eskimo believe that sorcerers, together with thieves and people who practiced certain forbidden customs, become "uncomfortable" after death and that their shades sometimes return to the land of the living and haunt the vicinity of their burial places.[67]

Among many primitive peoples the public magician is also the headman or chief. Where governmental and magical functions are not combined in the same person, the chief may yet practice some kinds of magic, the better to strengthen his prestige and maintain his authority.

Chieftainship in aboriginal Australia is nonexistent. Such political authority as exists is exercised by the tribal elders, who for the most part seem to be the headmen of their respective local or totemic groups. In the southeastern area they were often magicians, as among the Yuin of New South Wales, whose greatest headman was he who could, as the natives said, "bring the greatest number of things up out of himself" at the initiation ceremonies. On the other hand, among the Wiimbaio, in the same part of Australia, a man might be feared as the possessor of magical powers, but he would not be necessarily a headman.[68] In the central area the headman performs magical ceremonies for the multiplication of totemic plants and animals, but here, again, the *alatunja,* as the Arunta call him, is not necessarily a medicine man or a man who is supposed to have a special power of communicating with the ancestral ghosts (*iruntarinia*) recognized by the tribe. Every totemic group has its headman, but not every group has either a professional magician or a man especially conversant with the spirits.[69]

In New Guinea chieftainship is incipient, rather than developed. With reference to the tribes in Papua we are told that no one has ever been wise enough, bold enough, and strong enough to become the "despot" even of a single district. "The nearest approach to this has been the very distant one of some person becoming a renowned wizard; but that has only resulted in levying a certain amount of blackmail."[70] The chief of the Mawata is able to influence the crops for good or ill. He can also coax the dugong and the turtle to rise up from the depths of the sea and allow themselves to be caught.[71] Among the Girara-speaking tribes, between the Fly and Bamu rivers, a man combining the dual functions of chief and magician would be implicitly obeyed, though in general the chiefs of a village seem to have little authority.[72] In the Motu tribe about Port Moresby the so-called chiefs do not necessarily possess magical powers, but if a person has them he is looked upon as a chief. Thus one man owed his authoritative position to the fact that he ruled the sea, calming it or rousing it to fury at his pleasure. Another man was powerful because of his ability in making rain, producing sunshine, and causing the plantations to be fruitful.[73] At Bartle Bay, among the Southern Massim, there are chiefs with a considerable degree of influence, in addition to "experts" with magical powers as respects rain, fishing, and the crops. While their profession conferred upon these experts no authority to decide matters of war and peace and the larger policies of the people, it appears that they often exercised civil functions. The offices of chief and magician were then combined in the same person.[74] A chief of Kolem, in the former German territory of New Guinea, was a mighty magician; he could raise storms, bring rain or sunshine, and visit his enemies with sickness and death.[75] Among the Yabim the chief is not necessarily a magician also, but very often the two offices are combined in the same person.[76]

In the Marshall Bennett Islands it was the duty of each clan chief to make the gardens of his clan productive by reciting spells over them; in return for this service he had much of his garden work done for him and received presents of food.[77] In the Trobriand Islands the magic of rain and sunshine, so important for a people who live by gardening and fishing, is controlled by the paramount chiefs of Kiriwina. Because these chiefs are credited with the supernatural ability to produce a prolonged drought they hold a whip hand over their subjects and thus "enhance their wholesale power."[78]

There are chiefs in the various Melanesian Islands whose authority rests largely upon their reputation as the possessors of *mana,* derived from the mighty ghosts and spirits with which they hold constant intercourse. Thus in New Britain this *mana* enabled a chief "to bring rain or sunshine, fair winds or foul ones, sickness or health, success or disaster in war, and generally to procure any blessing or curse for which the applicant was willing to pay a sufficient price."[79] In Florida, one of the Solomons, a person believed to hold communication with powerful ghosts (*tindalo*) and to possess that *mana* whereby they could bring the power of the *tindalo* to bear was recognized as a chief. His own character and success enhanced his position, while weakness and failure lost it. "Public opinion supported him in his claim for a general obedience, besides the dread universally felt of the *tindalo* power behind him." In the northern New Hebrides, where the position of a chief is more conspicuous, a son does not inherit the chieftainship. He does inherit, if the father can manage it, what gives him chieftainship, namely, his father's *mana,* charms, magical songs and apparatus, and knowledge of the way to approach spiritual beings. In the Banks Islands, besides those who were really chiefs, there were "great men," with considerable influence in their villages, men of much *mana,* whose spells and magical objects made them valiant in war and successful in all their undertakings.[80] In Pentecost Island (Raga), one of the New Hebrides, "there are men who are regarded as chiefs by Europeans, but their power appears to depend largely on their reputation for *mana,* and especially the *mana* connected with magic."[81]

Throughout Polynesia there formerly existed a class of chiefs with gradations of rank, and sometimes a supreme potentate, ruling over an island group, who may be called a king. They were credited with the possession of marvelous powers and were regarded with the utmost veneration. Among the Maori the offices of chief and *tohunga* were generally united, and the most powerful *tohunga* was the hereditary head (*ariki*) of his tribe.[82]

Among the Subanun of Mindanao a headman may also act

as a magician, but instances of the sort seem to be rare.[83] Among the Sea Dayak of Borneo the *manang* ranks next in importance to the chief. It is by no means unusual for him to be the political head of the village in which he resides. There is nothing to prevent him from assuming this honor if he has gained popularity as an accurate interpreter of dreams and a powerful exorciser of evil spirits.[84]

Among the aboriginal tribes of the Malay Peninsula a successful magician has, ordinarily, the best chance of being chosen a chief. With the Semang the office of leading magician seems to be generally combined with that of chief, but with the Sakai and Jakun these offices are sometimes separated. Though the chief is almost invariably a magician of reputation, he is not necessarily the greatest wonder worker of his tribe any more than the latter is necessarily its political head. The magician's tasks are "to preside as chief medium at all ceremonies, to instruct the youth of the tribe, to ward off as well as to heal all forms of sickness and trouble, to foretell the future (as affecting the results of any act), to avert when necessary the wrath of heaven, and even when re-embodied after death in the shape of a wild beast, to extend a benign protection to his devoted descendants."[85] It sometimes happens among the Andamanese that the leading man of a local group is at the same time a magician, but the two positions are entirely distinct and separate. A man may be a magician without possessing the qualities that are necessary for a chief.[86]

Africa affords the most extensive evidence for the union of governmental with magical functions and, in some parts of the Dark Continent, for the development of the chief out of the magician. With general reference to the Bantu-speaking peoples of South Africa we learn that "in very old days the chief was the great rain maker of the tribe. Some chiefs allowed no one else to compete with them, lest a successful rain maker should be chosen as chief. There was also another reason: the rain maker was sure to become a rich man if he gained a great reputation, and it would manifestly never do for the chief to allow anyone to be too rich. The rain maker exerts tremendous control over the people, and so it would be most important to keep this function connected with royalty. Tradition always places the power of making rain as the fundamental glory of ancient chiefs and heroes, and it seems probable that it may have been the origin of chieftainship. The man who made the rain would naturally become the chief."[87] In more recent times the all-important business of bringing down showers upon the parched earth is usually entrusted to a professional rain maker. He is no mean personage, "possessing an influence over the minds of the people superior even to that of the king, who is likewise compelled to yield to the dictates of this arch-official."[88]

In East Africa the political head of a tribal group is very often the principal magician, skilled not only in rain making but also in divining and the medical art. Among the Masai of Tanganyika the medicine men are often the chiefs, and the supreme chief is nearly always a powerful medicine man.[89] The Nandi of Kenya likewise have a supreme chief, or principal magician (the Orkoiyot), whose overlordship is acknowledged throughout their country. The actual government of each district resides in two men, one of them chosen by the supreme chief as his representative and the other elected by the people but also responsible to him. The elders of each district meet together from time to time for the discussion of affairs of state, and at these gatherings the two governors are present.[90] Among the Bakerewe, who occupy the largest island in Lake Victoria, the king serves as the supreme rain maker, and to him the people address themselves in last resort. If he succeeds in his efforts to bring rain, he enjoys immense popularity; if he fails, he is treated with ignominy and driven from the throne.[91]

In the region of the Upper Nile the medicine men, who possess the ability to make rain, are generally the chiefs.[92] This is true, for instance, of the Lotuko (Latuka), among whom almost all the greater chiefs enjoy a reputation as rain makers. Knowledge of their useful art passes, as a rule, by inheritance from father to son.[93] The influence of Bongo chiefs is said to depend in large measure on the belief in their magical powers.[94] The chief of the Obbo holds authority over his subjects by virtue of his powers as a rain maker and sorcerer. Should there be too little rain or too much at the season for sowing the crops, he calls the people together and tells them how much he regrets that their unseemly conduct has compelled him to afflict them with unfavorable weather. They have been stingy in providing him with food and other necessaries; how then can they expect him to consult their interests. "No goats, no rain, that's our contract, my friends." So the supplies are promptly brought forth, and as a further measure of propitiation the people may present him with their prettiest daughters. An Obbo chief, it is said, has wives in each one of his villages.[95] In the same way, the main source of the authority of an Acholi chief comes from his control of the rain. Every chief has two or three special pots, each containing a number of curiously shaped crystals only found in stream beds. They are heirlooms from the chief's ancestors. When he wishes the rain to fall he smears them with oil and pours water on them. When the rain is to be stopped he puts them in a tree exposed to the sun or in the fireplace. They are so sacred that no private person will touch them or even look at them if he can help it. Possession of these crystals enables a chief to do much as he pleases. If anyone annoys him he can dry up all the crops.[96] The rain maker among the Shilluk and Dinka is a divine ruler, in whom abides the soul of a great and remote ancestor. It is possession by this ghostly power that makes him wiser and more farseeing than ordinary mortals. In theory and no doubt generally in practice his authority is unlimited. The Shilluk rain maker is killed ceremonially when he becomes too old to discharge the heavy responsibilities of his position. The Dinka rain maker perishes in like manner, but only when he himself decides that his enfeebled powers have incapacitated him for the performance of his function.[97]

In Central Africa the magician sometimes exercises governmental functions, as among the Lendu, a tribe to the west of Lake Albert. Here the rain maker either ranks as a chief or almost invariably rises to chieftainship.[98] The Banyoro, a tribe in the same region, ascribe to their king absolute power over the rainfall, but he is accustomed to depute his power to subordinates, so that all parts of the kingdom may enjoy an equal downpour.[99] Among the Bayaka, a tribe in the Kasai district of the Belgian Congo, the chief is the principal magician, as also among the Bayanzi in the same district.[100] In the Congo area, however, it is rare for the functions of chief and magician to be combined in the same person. The village or tribal chief may often have charge of the public cults, but he usually leaves meteorology, medicine, and prophecy to the magician, the *nganga*.[101]

In the Fang or Pangwe tribe of Gabun the chief of a village or of a group of villages is at the same time its magician and its priest.[102] The ruler of the Banjar is described as being both a king and a high priest. His subjects attribute to him the power to bring rain or fine weather just as he pleases. As long as the weather continues to be favorable, they reverence him and load him with gifts of grain and cattle. But should there be a protracted drought or if it rains so steadily that their crops are threatened, they will load him with insults and belabor him until the weather changes.[103] With reference to the tribes of southern Nigeria we learn that the "doctor" is often more powerful than the civil ruler and that in some cases the latter must of necessity be an adept in the knowledge and use of "medicines." Nearly all chiefs, moreover, need some acquaintance with the magical art in order to carry out their public duties, especially as respects the rainfall and the growth of the crops.[104]

As we have seen, the magician among the South American Indians often ranks above the chief in public regard and in influence. Often, also, he is at the same time the chief, as among various Brazilian tribes.[105] There seem to be no instances, however, of his attaining the chieftainship because of his occult powers. Likewise among the North American Indians it does not appear that the magician has ever gained political importance solely by virtue of his office, though in nearly all the tribes he was a personage of great importance.[106]

There have been many roads to leadership. In primitive communities, generally, personal ability is the essential factor making for predominance. Strength of body and strength of will, a persuasive tongue, great energy, initiative, and resourcefulness are the qualities which raise a man above his fellows and constitute the leader. This is not to deny that other grounds for superiority may be often found. In some parts of aboriginal Australia age alone, unless accompanied by mental weakness, suffices to secure a certain measure of predominance. In some of the Melanesian Islands the chiefs seem to be those who rise to the highest degree in the secret societies. Instances are found in Africa and North America where the richest man rules the group. Sometimes, again, the magician has risen to a commanding place. While the chief but seldom appears as the lineal successor of the magician, there can be no doubt that in many a primitive community the man who by hook or crook has gained an authoritative position confirms, strengthens, and to some extent keeps it by his reputed possession of occult powers. Magic often serves as the prop of absolutism, even when it has not been the foundation.

The magician is sometimes a Jack-of-all-trades, combining the offices of healer, exorcist, diviner, seer, prophet, bard, and educator. He may also control the winds, the rain, and the growth of the crops; detect witches and other criminals; impose taboos and conduct purificatory rites to avoid their disastrous consequences when broken; bring down destruction upon the tribal enemies; supply talismans to secure good fortune and amulets to avert all ills to which human flesh is heir; and in war and peace, in the day of plenty or in that of famine, be looked up to as the one person who must be consulted when important business is under way or when things go wrong. The professional magician may also be a sorcerer, whose nefarious activity, though feared and reprobated, is nevertheless socially recognized.

More commonly the regular practitioners of magic have different functions and consequently differ as respects the consideration accorded to them and the remuneration which they receive. This differentiation may go so far that a magician of some sort is available for almost every emergency of life.

Among the tribes of southeastern Australia the medicine man is not always a doctor; he may devote himself to some special form of magic such as rain making, divination, or the composition of spells.[107] In the Melanesian Islands every considerable village "is sure to have someone who can control the weather and the waves, someone who knows how to treat sickness, someone who can work mischief with various charms. There may be one whose skill extends to all these branches; but generally one man knows how to do one thing and one another."[108] Magicians among the Bavenda of the Transvaal include, beside doctors, those who consecrate weapons, make new fire, and bring rain; those who fertilize the crops; those who prepare love potions; and those who deal with cures of delirium and insanity.[109] Of the magical specialists among the neighboring Lovedu one is a rain maker, another has power to change people into animals, another makes witchproof the hedge of the lodge where girls are initiated, another doctors the boys' circumcision lodge, and still another strengthens the rain queen for her official duties. A person who has not inherited the magical profession cannot easily acquire the specialized knowledge required for it; the price is high and the secrets are not readily divulged.[110] Among the Bangala (Boloki) of the Upper Congo there are about eighteen kinds of magicians, while among the Bakongo of the Lower Congo no less than about fifty kinds are found.[111] Among the Fang of Gabun the *nganga* comprises all branches of magic in his own person. Among other tribes of this area each magician has his specialty as physician, rain producer, charm maker, and detector of criminals. Each village contains only one magician as a rule. When the local man is not an expert for a given case, the natives try to find one in a neighboring village.[112] There are some magicians of the Apache, Mohave, and other Southwestern tribes "who enjoy great fame as the bringers of rain, some who claim special power over snakes, and some who profess to consult the spirits only, and do not treat the sick except when no other practitioners are available."[113]

Associations of magicians, often assuming a more or less secret character, are found in some parts of the aboriginal world. In general, the greater the degree of specialization the more marked is the tendency toward organization in guilds or fraternities. These are unknown in Australia, though the medicine men of a tribe regularly co-operate in the initiation and training of aspirants to their profession. When treating a serious case of sickness, several medicine men may be called in for consultation, perhaps even celebrated practitioners from neighboring tribes.[114]

In New Guinea and the Melanesian Islands there are numerous secret societies, often charged with magical duties, but it does not appear that they are limited to magicians. Perhaps the nearest approach to a professional organization is furnished by the Ingiet or Iniat society in the Bismarck Archipelago, to which the majority of men belong. The initiates are believed to possess great powers of magic, and their services are sought after when anyone wishes to injure a personal enemy. Not all members of the society are allowed to practice sorcery, however, but only those who have received a special initiation. The head of each branch of Ingiet is commonly the leading sorcerer of a community.[115] In the Banks Islands, in addition to the widespread Tamate society, which in some respects resembles Ingiet, many minor and local associations are found. A curious example of these is furnished by the *parmal* societies. Each one is specially named after the kind of magic which it employs. The initiates are instructed in this magic, but they may use it only against outsiders. Should a person practice it on a fellow member he would be killed. Not infrequently a man belongs to more than one society in an island and thus secures himself against the sorcery of many people. It is also customary to join societies in other islands, in order to obtain still greater protection.[116]

Among the Bathonga a very successful exorcist starts new rites, discovers more powerful medicines, attracts pupils from all parts, and may become the founder of a school. Great rivalry exists between different schools. Professional hatred is carried so far that they test their colleagues and even steal each other's drugs. Sometimes a disciple will emancipate himself from his master and set up a new society of the exorcised. This proceeding is, of course, extremely obnoxious to the master, for it means lively competition and the loss of the usual fees. So he goes to the altar of his gods and begs them to make the drugs of his rival ineffective. If his prayer is heard, the disciple must seek forgiveness and pay a fine in order to secure success in future cures. "He may perhaps succeed his master, but only when the latter is dead."[117]

Among the Waduruma, a tribal division of the Wanyika of Kenya, societies of medicine men exist in every district. Since a society takes its name from the kind of magic it deals in, there are as many societies as there are kinds of magic. Members of these organizations are engaged to safeguard private property by means of charms suitably treated with a powerful medicine. They also practice medicine extensively. Some of them have been so successful in their treatments that they would feel themselves "slandered" if one were to call them magicians instead of doctors.[118]

Each witch doctor among the Azande has his own practice, collects his own fees, and, generally speaking, is responsible to no one but himself in matters of professional conduct. He does not enter an association in which the members have privileges and obligations in respect to one another. However, communal meals, at which a number of practitioners gather around a fire and eat medicines together, are now a regular feature, and a seance is usually conducted jointly by a number of them. Co-operation of this sort tends to produce a certain degree of group cohesion.[119]

Ewe magicians, though they have no hard-and-fast organization, keep on excellent terms with one another, and if a practitioner gets hold of something new in the magical line he imparts it to his friends.[120] Magicians among the Twi, "all being united to deceive the people," are careful to assist each other and to make known anything that may be generally useful. Sometimes a "fetish priest" will inform an applicant that the god he serves refuses to accord the information or assistance required. The applicant is then recommended to consult another practitioner, to whom, in the meantime, the priest communicates every particular of the case. It is said that the Twi suspect that not all their priests are really inspired but that some are impostors. Hence the people will consult two priests separately and check their statements for possible divergencies. But because of the collusion between them it is rare for the statements of one to disagree with those of another.[121]

Poro (Purrah) among the Kpelle of Liberia presents some resemblance to Ingiet in the Bismarck Archipelago. Like the latter it is a tribal society, initiating every youth at the arrival of puberty, and like the latter, also, only certain pupils are selected to be taught the magical art by the directors. This requires additional fees and a longer period of instruction. After completing a course in the Poro school the newly made magicians become "journeymen" and visit prominent practitioners in neighboring tribes.[122]

Among the tribes of the Gold Coast and the Slave Coast applicants for membership in the priestly orders serve a novitiate for several years. Dancing, prestidigitation, and ventriloquism are important subjects of the course. Some instruction in the healing art is also imparted. The candidates are taught a new language, and after their consecration as priests are given a new name. Generally they must present satisfactory evidence of possession by the god to whom they would devote themselves before being accepted as full members of the priestly order.[123] In this part of West Africa, where there are despotic and hereditary kingships, social classes clearly differentiated, and state cults supporting the civil power, the associated magicians have risen to the dignity of priests.

Secret associations limited to professional magicians seem to be very rare among the South American Indians.[124] They are well developed, however, among the Indians of North America, each one with a ceremony of initiation, degrees of advancement, and a special ritual. Their performances, in part secret and in part public, constitute a rude but often very effective dramatization of the tribal myths and legends. The actors, masked or costumed, represent animals, divine beings, and the ancestors of the tribe. Members of the organizations are accomplished workers in magic for the cure of the sick, the production of rain, the ripening of the crops, and the multiplication of food animals. On certain occasions they perform great "life-giving" ceremonies, which may continue for several days. They also have special medicines, prepared with the utmost secrecy, which are objects of much reverence. In addition to such organizations there exist among some tribes medicine societies composed principally of patients cured of serious ailments and assumed to be able, therefore, to perform healing services for others. These associations are prominent among the Pueblo Indians of the Southwest, where they have largely replaced the medicine man acting in an individual capacity.[125]

In the Eskimo area of North America and in Siberia we hear of no close organization of the shamans. Nor are there hierarchal divisions among them, for such differences in social position and emoluments as exist depend rather upon the special powers of a practitioner and his more or less intimate relations with spirits and gods.

In spite of the mutual understanding among magicians and their common duties, it appears that the guild or fraternal organization is unusual with them. The practice of magic forms, indeed, essentially an individualistic possession, especially the practice of antisocial magic, or sorcery, which a man must engage in at his own risk and carry on as privately as possible. The clearest instances of fraternities, "the first academies," are afforded by the Maori Whare Kura, the priestly orders of West Africa, and those North American societies exercising both magical and priestly functions. In process of time and under favorable conditions such organizations develop into technically trained priesthoods.

NOTES TO CHAPTER X

[1] Herbert Basedow, *The Australian Aboriginal* (Adelaide, 1923), p. 225. Cf. A. P. Elkin, *The Australian Aborigines* (Sydney, 1938), p. 219. It has been said of the Tasmanians, now extinct, that though they were free from the despotism of rulers, "they were swayed by the counsels, governed by the arts, or terrified by the fears, of certain wise men or doctors" (James Bonwick, *Daily Life and Origin of the Tasmanians* [London, 1870], p. 175).

[2] W. N. Beaver, *Unexplored New Guinea* (London, 1920), p. 135.

[3] E. W. Elkington, *The Savage South Seas* (London, 1907), p. 139.

[4] H. A. Bernatzik, *Owa Raha* (Wien, 1936), pp. 250 f.

[5] Sir Basil H. Thomson, *The Fijians* (London, 1908), p. 158.

[6] *Idem*, in *Journal of the Anthropological Institute*, XXXI (1901), 140.

[7] Teuira Henry, "Ancient Tahiti," *Bernice P. Bishop Museum Bulletin*, No. 48, pp. 205 f.

[8] A. S. Thomson, *The Story of New Zealand* (London, 1859), I, 115 f. Thomson's statements apply only to the upper class of *tohunga*. The lower class of *tohunga* were not very important persons in a community. See Elsdon Best, "Maori Religion and Mythology," *Dominion Museum Bulletin*, No. 10, p. 164.

[9] F. W. Christian, *The Caroline Islands* (London, 1899), pp. 325 f.

[10] Burton and Ward, in *Memoirs of the Royal Asiatic Society*, I (1827), 500.

[11] Henry Callaway, *The Religious System of the Amazulu* (London, 1870), p. 340 and note. The despotic Chaka, who founded the power of the Zulu, used to declare that he was the only diviner in that country, for if he allowed rivals

his life would be insecure (Dudley Kidd, *The Essential Kafir* [2d ed., London, 1925], p. 114).

[12] C. M. Doke, *The Lambas of Northern Rhodesia* (London, 1931), p. 320.

[13] W. A. Elmslie, *Among the Wild Ngoni* (Edinburgh, 1899), pp. 60 f.

[14] F. Bösch, *Les Banyamwezi* (Münster in Westfalen, 1930), p. 170.

[15] Hans Meyer, *Die Barundi* (Leipzig, 1916), p. 129.

[16] A. C. Hollis, *The Nandi* (Oxford, 1909), pp. 49 f.

[17] E. E. Evans-Pritchard, *Witchcraft, Oracles, and Magic among the Azande* (Oxford, 1937), p. 251. Magicians, other than witch doctors, have little prestige, partly because most people possess and use medicines for one purpose or another and partly because in the life of the group "political status overshadows all other distinctions" (p. 428).

[18] J. H. Weeks, *Among the Primitive Bakongo* (London, 1914), pp. 216 ff. Among the Bangala of the Upper Congo a witch doctor is never charged with witchcraft and hence does not have to undergo the poison ordeal. If he levels a charge of witchcraft against anyone he does not drink the poison along with the suspected person and pays no damages to the latter for defamation of character if his charge is disproved (*idem, Among Congo Cannibals* [London, 1913], pp. 146, 283). The same rule prevails among the Bambala (E. Torday and T. A. Joyce, in *Journal of the Anthropological Institute*, XXXV [1905], 417).

[19] C. K. Meek, *The Northern Tribes of Nigeria* (London, 1925), II, 43. At Badagry, on the Guinea coast, the "fetish priests" are the sole judges of the people (Richard Lander, *Captain Clapperton's Last Expedition to Africa* [London, 1830], I, 281).

[20] S. K. Lothrop, *The Indians of Tierra del Fuego* (New York, 1928), p. 160.

[21] G. C. Musters, *At Home with the Patagonians* (2d ed., London, 1873), p. 191.

[22] R. E. Latcham, in *Journal of the Royal Anthropological Institute*, XXXIX (1909), 351. The magicians frequently used their great power and influence for purposes of private revenge (E. R. Smith, *The Araucanians* [New York, 1855], p. 237).

[23] C. F. P. von Martius, *Zur Ethnographie Amerikas, zumal Brasiliens* (Liepzig, 1867), p. 76.

[24] P. Ehrenreich, *Beiträge zur Völkerkunde Brasiliens* (Berlin, 1891), p. 33.

[25] Thomas Whiffen, *The North-West Amazons* (New York, 1915), pp. 64, 185.

[26] R. Verneau, in *L'Anthropologie*, XXXI (1921), 266.

[27] M. W. Stirling, "Jivaro Shamanism," *Proceedings of the American Philosophical Society*, LXXII (1933), 137 f., 144 f.; *idem*, "Historical and Ethnographical Material on the Jivaro Indians," *Bulletin of the Bureau of American Ethnology*, No. 117, pp. 115, 120 f.

[28] Pierre Barrère, *Nouvelle relation de la France équinoxiale* (Paris, 1743), p. 210.

[29] Sir E. F. im Thurn, *Among the Indians of Guiana* (London, 1883), p. 335.

[30] Theodor Koch-Grünberg, *Vom Roroima zum Orinoco* (Berlin, 1917–28), III, 190.

[31] W. C. Bennett and R. M. Zingg, *The Tarahumara* (Chicago, 1935), p. 252.

[32] Frank Russell, in *Twenty-sixth Annual Report of the Bureau of American Ethnology*, p. 256.

[33] J. G. Bourke, "The Medicine Men of the Apache," *Ninth Annual Report of the Bureau of Ethnology*, p. 457.

300   MAGIC: A SOCIOLOGICAL STUDY

³⁴ James Mooney and F. M. Olbrechts, "The Swimmer Manuscript. Cherokee Sacred Formulas and Medicinal Prescriptions," *Bulletin of the Bureau of
American Ethnology*, No. 99, pp. 91 f.

³⁵ H. R. Schoolcraft, *Archives of Aboriginal Knowledge*, (Philadelphia,
1860), IV, 495, quoting Captain S. Eastman.

³⁶ Alanson Skinner, in *Anthropological Papers of the American Museum
of Natural History*, IX, 67.

³⁷ W. L. Hardisty, in *Annual Report of the Smithsonian Institution for 1866*,
p. 312.

³⁸ W. Z. Park, *Shamanism in Western North America* (Evanston, 1938),
pp. 66 f., 103. *Northwestern University Studies in the Social Sciences*, No. 2.

³⁹ Ann H. Gayton, "Yokuts-Mono Chiefs and Shamans," *University of California Publications in American Archaeology and Ethnology*, XXIV, 398 f.

⁴⁰ R. B. Dixon, in *Bulletin of the American Museum of Natural History*,
XVII, 267.

⁴¹ Leslie Spier, in *University of California Publications in American Archaeology and Ethnology*, XXX, 94, 107, 275. The Klamath Indians believe that
there will be a heavy storm when a medicine man dies, when his body is cremated, and when his lodge is burned after his death (p. 274). Similarly the
Yakut of Siberia are persuaded that the death of a shaman is followed by
atmospheric disturbances of an extraordinary character. See W. Sieroszewski
(Sieroshevski), "Du chamanisme d'après les croyances des Yakoutes," *Revue de
l'histoire des religions*, XLVI (1902), 211.

⁴² Charles Harrison, *Ancient Warriors of the North Pacific* (London, 1925),
p. 102. The Lillooet avoided letting their shadows fall on magicians. When a
mischance of that sort occurred, the magician passed his hand through the
shadow, thus shoving it back and canceling the evil that might otherwise result.
He performed the same act when his own shadow fell on anybody (James Teit,
in *Memoirs of the American Museum of Natural History*, IV, 288). Tlingit
shamans, both living and dead, were greatly dreaded. Whenever a person came
across a shaman's house in the woods he feared he would fall sick. Only
another shaman could cure him. No one would eat anything near a place where
a shaman's corpse was deposited, lest he become seriously ill and perhaps die.
When a person passed by a canoe in which a shaman's corpse had been laid he
lowered food and tobacco into the sea in front of the canoe, saying, "Give me
luck. Do not let me perish." The eagle claws hung by the urine boxes of living
shamans were asked to keep the petitioner in health (J. R. Swanton, in *Twenty-
sixth Annual Report of the Bureau of American Ethnology*, pp. 466 f.).

⁴³ Julius Jetté, "On the Medicine Men of the Ten'a," *Journal of the Royal
Anthropological Institute*, XXXVII (1907), 163.

⁴⁴ E. M. Hawkes, *The Labrador Eskimo* (Ottawa, 1916), p. 128. *Geological
Survey Memoir*, No. 91.

⁴⁵ Henry Rink, *Tales and Traditions of the Eskimo* (Edinburgh, 1875), pp.
59 ff.; cf. Hans Egede, *A Description of Greenland* (2d ed., London, 1818),
pp. 189, 192. Egede remarks that Eskimo wives thought themselves fortunate
if an *angakok* honored them with his caresses. Some husbands would even pay
him for his sexual services, especially if they themselves could beget no children
(p. 142).

⁴⁶ V. M. Mikhailovskii (Mikhailowski), "Shamanism in Siberia and European Russia," *Journal of the Anthropological Institute*, XXIV (1895), 131 f.

⁴⁷ Emma Hadfield, *Among the Natives of the Loyalty Group* (London,
1920), p. 149.

[48] W. W. Skeat and C. O. Blagden, *Pagan Races of the Malay Peninsula* (London, 1906), II, 226.

[49] D. N. Majumdar, "Bongaism," in *Essays Presented to Rai Bahadur Sarat Chandra Roy* (Lucknow, 1942), p. 70.

[50] I. Schapera, *The Khoisan Peoples of South Africa* (London, 1930), pp. 171 f., 196.

[51] Oscar Baumann, *Durch Massailand zur Nilquelle* (Berlin, 1904), p. 164.

[52] Martin Dobrizhoffer, *An Account of the Abipones* (London, 1822), II, 284.

[53] V. M. Mikhailovskii (Mikhailowski), "Shamanism in Siberia and European Russia," *Journal of the Anthropological Institute*, XXIV (1895), 134. By the Buriat many female shamans of great celebrity are worshiped after death. This practice is also found among other Siberian tribes. See Uno Holmberg, *The Mythology of All Nations* (Vol. IV), *Finno-Ugric, Siberian* (Boston, 1927), p. 499.

[54] E. T. Dalton, *Descriptive Ethnology of Bengal* (Calcutta, 1872), p. 274.

[55] Sir H. H. Risley, *The Tribes and Castes of Bengal* (Calcutta, 1891–92), II, 207.

[56] Karl von den Steinen, *Unter den Naturvölkern Zentral-Brasiliens* (Berlin, 1894), pp. 511 f.

[57] W. G. Sumner, "The Yakuts. Abridged from the Russian of Sieroshevski," *Journal of the Anthropological Institute*, XXXI (1901), 99 ff.

[58] C. Keysser, "Aus dem Leben der Kaileute," in R. Neuhauss, *Deutsch Neu-Guinea* (Berlin, 1911), III, 102.

[59] Richard Thurnwald, *Forschungen auf den Salomo-Inseln und den Bismarck Archipel* (Berlin, 1912), I, 447.

[60] E. H. Man, in *Census of India*, 1901, III, 193.

[61] Hermann Tönjes, *Ovamboland, Land, Leute, Mission* (Berlin, 1911), pp. 193 ff.

[62] Ed. Labrecque, "La sorcellerie chez le Babemba," *Anthropos*, XXXIII (1938), 260 f.

[63] J. H. Driberg, *The Lango* (London, 1923), pp. 209, 241.

[64] A. G. Leonard, *The Lower Niger and Its Tribes* (London, 1906), p. 487.

[65] P. A. Talbot, *Life in Southern Nigeria* (London, 1923), pp. 60 f.

[66] Rafael Karsten, "The Religion of the Jibaro Indians of Eastern Ecuador," *Boletin de la Academia Nacional de Historia*, III (1921), 126.

[67] E. W. Nelson, in *Eighteenth Annual Report of the Bureau of American Ethnology*, Part I, p. 423.

[68] A. W. Howitt, *The Native Tribes of South-East Australia* (London, 1904), p. 301 (Wiimbaio), 314 (Yuin). For other examples of magicians serving also as headmen see pp. 297 ff. (Dieri), 301 f. (Theddora), 302 (Ngarigo and Wolgal), 303 (Wiradjuri), 313 (Yerkla-mining), 317 (Kurnai).

[69] Sir Baldwin Spencer and F. J. Gillen, *The Native Tribes of Central Australia* (London, 1899), pp. 9 f., 15 f.

[70] Sir William MacGregor, *British New Guinea* (London, 1897), p. 41.

[71] E. Beardmore, in *Journal of the Anthropological Institute*, XIX (1890), 464.

[72] W. N. Beaver, *op. cit.*, p. 203.

[73] James Chalmers, in *Journal of the Anthropological Institute*, XXVII (1898), 334.

⁷⁴ C. G. Seligman, *The Melanesians of British New Guinea* (Cambridge, 1910), pp. 455 f.

⁷⁵ M. Krieger, *Neu-Guinea* (Berlin, 1899), p. 334.

⁷⁶ Heinrich Zahn, in R. Neuhauss, *op. cit.*, III, 309.

⁷⁷ C. G. Seligman, *op. cit.*, p. 702.

⁷⁸ Bronislaw Malinowski, *Argonauts of the Western Pacific* (London, 1922), p. 394. At the back of every Trobriand chief's power over the people is the fear of his sorcery, without which "he is little more than a cipher" (C. G. Seligman, *op. cit.*, p. 694, quoting R. L. Bellamy).

⁷⁹ George Brown, *Melanesians and Polynesians* (London, 1910), p. 429. Elsewhere this authority declares that it was "principally the wealth of a man and the number of spells or charms which he possessed that constituted him a chief" (p. 200; cf. 270). In the Shortland Islands magical powers over natural phenomena were claimed by chiefs (Carl Libbe, *Zwei Jahre unter den Kannibalen der Salomo-Inseln* [Dresden, 1903], p. 173). Among the Manus of the Admiralty Islands a chief performs only war magic and leaves other branches of the magical art to his subordinates (R. Parkinson, *Dreissig Jahre in der Südsee* [Stuttgart, 1907], p. 402).

⁸⁰ R. H. Codrington, *The Melanesians* (Oxford, 1891), pp. 51 f., 55.

⁸¹ W. H. R. Rivers, *The History of Melanesian Society* (Cambridge, 1914), II, 99.

⁸² A. S. Thomson, *op. cit.*, I, 114; Edward Tregear, *The Maori Race* (Wanganui, New Zealand, 1904), p. 152; Elsdon Best, *The Maori* (Wellington, New Zealand, 1924), I, 248. *Memoirs of the Polynesian Society*, Vol. V.

⁸³ E. B. Christie, *The Subanuns of Sindangan Bay* (Manila, 1909), p. 84. *Bureau of Science, Division of Ethnology Publications*, Vol. VI, Pt. I.

⁸⁴ H. L. Roth, *The Natives of Sarawak and British North Borneo* (London, 1896), I, 265, quoting Brooke Low.

⁸⁵ W. W. Skeat and C. O. Blagden, *op. cit.*, II, 196 f., 225 f. See also Rudolf Martin, *Die Inlandstämme der malayischen Halbinseln* (Jena, 1905), p. 958 (Semang).

⁸⁶ A. R. Radcliffe-Brown, *The Andaman Islanders* (Cambridge, 1933), p. 48.

⁸⁷ Dudley Kidd, *op. cit.*, p. 114. Cf. S. S. Dornan, "Rain Making in South Africa," *Bantu Studies*, III (1927–29), 185. Among the Zulu each doctor has his own special medicines and treats some special form of disease. When a chief learns that a doctor has been successful in a case which proved to be beyond the powers of the other practitioners, he requires the doctor to surrender the medicine. "Thus the chief becomes the great medicine man of his tribe, and the ultimate reference is to him" (Henry Calloway, *op. cit.*, p. 419, note).

⁸⁸ Robert Moffat, *Missionary Labours and Scenes in Southern Africa* (London, 1842), p. 306.

⁸⁹ Sir H. H. Johnston, *The Uganda Protectorate* (2d ed., London, 1904), II, 830. This supreme chief does not govern directly and has no administrative duties. He has been called the Masai "pope." See M. Merker, *Die Masai* (Berlin, 1904), pp. 18 ff.

⁹⁰ A. C. Hollis, *op. cit.*, pp. 48 f.

⁹¹ Eugène Hurel, "Religion et vie domestique des Bakerewe," *Anthropos*, VI (1911), 84.

⁹² Sir H. H. Johnston, *op. cit.* (2d ed.), II, 779.

⁹³ Franz Stuhlmann, *Mit Emin Pascha ins Herz von Afrika* (Berlin, 1894), pp. 778 f., quoting Emin Pasha.

⁹⁴ Georg Schweinfurth, *The Heart of Africa* (3d ed., London, 1878), I, 145.

95 Sir Samuel Baker, *The Albert N'Yanza* (2d ed., London, 1888), pp. 200 f.

96 E. T. N. Grove, "Customs of the Acholi," *Sudan Notes and Records,* II (1919), 172 f.

97 C. G. Seligman and Brenda Z. Seligman, *Pagan Tribes of the Nilotic Sudan* (London, 1932), pp. 23, 195 ff.

98 Sir H. H. Johnston, *op. cit.,* II, 555.

99 Gaetano Casati, *Ten Years in Equatoria* (London, 1891), II, 57.

100 E. Torday and T. A. Joyce, in *Journal of the Anthropological Institute,* XXXVI (1906), 51; XXXVII (1907), 140.

101 Sir H. H. Johnston, *George Grenfell and the Congo* (London, 1908), II, 658.

102 Oskar Lenz, *Skizzen aus Westafrika* (Berlin, 1878), p. 87.

103 Hyacinthe Hecquard, *Reise an der Küste und in das Innere von West Afrika* (Leipzig, 1854), p. 78.

104 P. A. Talbot, *The Peoples of Southern Nigeria* (London, 1926), II, 155 f.

105 Karl von den Steinen, *op. cit.,* p. 344 (Xingú Indians); Fritz Krause, *In den Wildnissen Brasiliens* (Leipzig, 1911), p. 335 (Karayá). In the Ica tribe of Arhuaco-speaking Indians of Colombia the *mamma* serve not only as doctors but also as judges and governors, "and their power seems singularly unaffected by the group's twenty years' exposure to Christianity" (Elizabeth Knowlton, in *American Anthropologist* [n.s., 1944], XLVI, 264). Among the Jivaro a great chief "is as skilled in witchcraft as a professional sorcerer" (Rafael Karsten, "Blood Revenge, War, and Victory Feasts among the Jibaro Indians of Eastern Ecuador," *Bulletin of the Bureau of American Ethnology,* No. 79, p. 15). On the other hand, among the Chorotí and Ashluslay of the Bolivian Gran Chaco the medicine man seems never to have been a chief (Erland Nordenskiöld, *Indianerleben* [Leipzig, 1913], p. 34).

106 See, in general, Ida Lublinski, "Die Medizinmann bei den Naturvölkern Südamerikas," *Zeitschrift für Ethnologie,* LII–LIII (1920–21), 234–63; J. N. B. Hewitt, "Chiefs," *Handbook of American Indians,* Part I, pp. 263 f.; R. B. Dixon, "Some Aspects of the American Shaman," *Journal of American Folk-Lore,* XXI (1908), 1–12.

107 A. W. Howitt, *op. cit.,* pp. 355 f.

108 R. H. Codrington, *op. cit.,* p. 192. Cf. Friedrich Burger, *Die Küsten-und Bergvölker der Gazellehalbinsel* (Stuttgart, 1913), p. 34 (New Britain); Gerhard Peekel, *Religion und Zauberei auf dem mittleren Neu-Mecklenburg, Bismarck-Archipel, Südsee* (Münster in Westfalen, 1910), p. 83 (New Ireland); Fritz Sarasin, *Ethnologie der Neu-Caledonier und Loyalty-Insulaner* (Munich, 1929), p. 291.

109 H. A. Stayt, *The Bavenda* (London, 1931), pp. 263 f. See also E. Gottschling, in *Journal of the Anthropological Institute,* XXXV (1905), 379.

110 Mrs. Eileen J. Krige and J. D. Krige, *The Realm of a Rain Queen* (London, 1943), p. 224.

111 J. H. Weeks, *Among Congo Cannibals,* p. 215; *idem, Among the Primitive Bakongo,* pp. 214, 230. The different kinds of *nganga* have been enumerated and their functions described by this experienced missionary ("The Congo Medicine Man and His Black and White Magic," *Folk-Lore,* XXI [1910], 452–69). He points out that the *nganga* cults are undoubtedly the product of a long development and also of a free appropriation of magical practices from neighboring tribes. The Congo native is always ready to try something new in the magical line. It is likely, too, that innumerable cults, once enjoying wide popularity, have in process of time fallen into disrepute and been abandoned (pp. 469 f.).

[112] A. L. Cureau, *Les sociétés primitives de l'Afrique équatoriale* (Paris, 1912), p. 364. See also A. Poupon, in *L'Anthropologie*, XXVI (1915), 142 (Baya).

[113] J. G. Bourke, "The Medicine Men of the Apache," *Ninth Annual Report of the Bureau of Ethnology*, p. 454.

[114] Sir Baldwin Spencer and F. J. Gillen, *The Northern Tribes of Central Australia* (London, 1904), p. 516 (Warramunga). In Queensland, while the medicine men of a tribe may be on apparently friendly terms and even consult among themselves when necessary, at heart they do not trust one another. "It is only a common fear which binds them together" (W. E. Roth, *Ethnological Studies among the North-West-Central Queensland Aborigines* [Brisbane, 1897], p. 154 ; idem, *North Queensland Ethnography Bulletin*, No. 5, p. 30). Among the Maori rival *tohunga* were often bitter rivals. They did not hesitate to destroy one another by magic whenever an opportunity offered (W. E. Gudgeon, "The 'Tohunga' Maori," *Journal of the Polynesian Society*, XVI [1907], 69).

[115] George Brown, *op. cit.*, pp. 75 f., quoting the Rev. H. Fellmann. Cf. R. Parkinson, *op. cit.*, pp. 599 f. ; Josef Meier, "Die Zauberei bei den Küstenbewohnern der Gazelle-Halbinsel, Neupommern, Südsee," *Anthropos*, VIII (1913), 288.

[116] W. H. R. Rivers, *op. cit.*, I, 159 ff., with special reference to the island of Mota.

[117] H. A. Junod, *The Life of a South African Tribe* (2d ed., London, 1927), II, 500 ff.

[118] J. B. Griffiths, in *Journal of the Royal Anthropological Institute*, LXV (1935), 287 f. The author is a chief of the Waduruma.

[119] E. E. Evans-Pritchard, *op. cit.*, pp. 202 f. The author also describes a number of associations which have developed in recent years for the performance of magical rites. They have ceremonies of initiation, fees for entrance, grades, an esoteric language, and other features of secret societies. All of them are of foreign origin. At first they were merely closed associations, and only certain rites and medicines were not revealed to outsiders. Nowadays, because of hostility on the part of missionaries and governmental officials, everything is kept as secret as possible (pp. 511, 516).

[120] Jakob Spieth, *Die Religion der Eweer in Süd-Togo* (Göttingen, 1911), p. 257.

[121] Sir A. B. Ellis, *The Tshi-speaking Peoples of the Gold Coast of West Africa* (London, 1887), pp. 126 ff.

[122] Diedrich Westermann, *Die Kpelle* (Göttingen, 1921), p. 211. Poro is found in Liberia, Sierra Leone, and other areas in which Mandingo languages are spoken. See further Braithwaite Wallis, "The Poro of the Mendi," *Journal of the African Society*, No. 14 (1905), pp. 183–89 ; M. H. Watkins, "The West African 'Bush' School," *American Journal of Sociology*, XLVIII (1943), 666–75. On the magical aspects of West African secret societies see, in general, Eugen Hildebrand, *Die Geheimbünde Westafrikas als Problem der Religionswissenschaft* (Leipzig, 1937), pp. 33–41. *Studien zur Religionswissenschaft*. Vol. I. For some illustrations see Adolf Bastian, *Die deutsche Expedition an der Loango-Küste* (Jena, 1874–75), I, 221 ff. (Sindungo) ; Mary H. Kingley, *West African Studies* (1st ed., London, 1899), p. 138 (Kufong of the Mendi of Sierra Leone) ; L. G. Binger, *Du Niger au Golfe de Guinée* (Paris, 1892), I, 379 (Dou or Lou of the Bobo and Bambara).

[123] Sir A. B. Ellis, *Tshi-speaking Peoples*, pp. 119 f. ; idem, *Ewe-speaking Peoples*, pp. 139 f. ; idem, *Yoruba-speaking Peoples*, pp. 97 f.

[124] The absence of such associations has been definitely noticed among the Ona or Selknam of Tierra del Fuego (Martin Gusinde, *Die Feuerland Indianer* [Mödling bei Wien, 1931–37], I, 719) and the Cayapa Indians (S. A. Barrett, *The Cayapa Indians of Ecuador* [New York, 1925], Part II, p. 345).

[125] See, in general, J. R. Swanton, "Secret Societies," *Handbook of American Indians*, Part II, pp. 495–97, and for a summary of the evidence Sir J. G. Frazer, *Totemism and Exogamy* (London, 1910), III, 457–550. See also Leslie A. White, "A Comparative Study of Keresan Medicine Societies," *Proceedings of the Twenty-third International Congress of Americanists* (New York, 1928), pp. 604–19; Clark Wissler (editor), "Societies of the Plains Indians," *Anthropological Papers of the American Museum of Natural History*, Vol. XI, especially pp. 858–76.

CHAPTER XI

PUBLIC MAGIC

Public magic is performed by the social group or by authorized representatives to further those activities which affect all the members of the group and for whose successful outcome all feel responsible. As such it includes the techniques traditionally associated with sorcery or witchcraft, since this may be used against disturbers of the peace, criminals, or a neighboring community, especially in time of war. Indeed, the familiar distinction between magical rites as either "white" or "black" cannot properly be applied to the operations of public magic.

An important department of public magic is concerned with the manipulation and control of physical phenomena. The magician professes an ability to regulate the heavenly bodies, to create sunshine or cloudy weather, to lay a hurricane, to summon thunder and lightning or disperse them, to produce or prevent earthquakes, floods, and other convulsions of nature, and, finally, to bring healing showers or a devastating downpour. Physical phenomena, before which the modern scientist is content to acknowledge impotence, are for the magician subject to his wonder-working power.

It is a general belief of the Queensland aborigines that storms can be raised and dissipated by the agency of their medicine men. When one tribe has a grievance against another, thunder and rain will be made so as to inconvenience the neighboring group as much as possible. Lightning will not be made, however, because the tribesmen, though highly incensed against their enemies, are reluctant to kill them.[1] During a spell of unusually cold weather the Arunta of Central Australia sometimes construct upon a selected ceremonial ground a large colored design representing the sun, from which lines are drawn with red and white vegetable down to represent its rays. These are intersected by a number of concentric circles which stand for the ancestors of the tribe. A stick placed in the center of the design is supposed to be the embodiment of a mythical sun creature. By means of this effigy the

306

natives are able, they believe, to increase the solar heat.[2] A Kaitish medicine man asserted that he had driven away a comet by means of his magical stones. As long as the comet was visible he used to go out every night, draw the stones from his body, and throw them at the celestial visitor. Success finally crowned his efforts, after which the stones returned to his body.[3] Magicians among the Orokaiva, a Papuan tribe, have "specifics," in the shape of certain magical leaves, to bring cold weather.[4] The Kai can delay the setting of the sun by binding it with knots upon which they have whispered the sun's name. They can also hasten its setting by throwing charmed stones at it.[5] The Dobu Islanders regulate their agriculture by the position of the Pleiades in the sky. They clear the bush for the plantations when the constellation has risen in the northeast over the ocean and harvest when, with Orion, it has disappeared below the horizon in the southwest. A magical ritual is employed to ensure that these annual movements of the stars shall take place at the proper time and without fail. For this purpose they sink both the Pleiades and Orion in the southwest by means of a simple ceremony and an equally simple spell, three times repeated.[6] The regular spell for wind in Dobu is exclusively woman's property. The men in their overseas sailing, if they have no true weathermaker with them, must therefore fall back on a makeshift spell. While it is being pronounced, the men do no paddling and the canoe lies motionless on the water. There is complete reliance on the magic to produce the effect desired.[7] A magician in New Britain performs a rite to make the wind blow in any desired direction.[8] In Mala or Malaita, one of the Solomons, there is a rite to cause a mist to envelop a raiding party, thus enabling the warriors to approach their objective without being seen by the enemy.[9] In Malekula, which belongs to the New Hebrides group, a particular clan owns the magic for raising or quelling a wind, and the clan magician performs the appropriate ritual to secure the effect desired. There is, however, a magical art for causing a hurricane, and this is privately owned. Should some enemy be suspected of trying to make a destructive storm the clan magician must repair to the sacred place of his clan and nullify the enemy's base designs by producing a great calm throughout the entire district.[10] A Maori magician, if sufficiently endowed with *mana*, is able to produce a flood or to make a flooded river subside and withdraw to its banks.[11] He can even cause a solar or a lunar halo to appear.[12] The natives of the Marshall Islands, at the first sign of a tidal wave which threatens to sweep over their low-lying atolls, call on their magician to avert by his potent spells the approaching cataclysm. These he recites not far from the beach and in the presence of the anxious multitude.[13]

An important attribute of the Malay magician in former days was his power of controlling the weather by means of spells. He recited these to summon a breeze in a time of calm, when the sails of the boat were flapping uselessly, to change a contrary into a favorable wind, and to moderate a heavy wind into a light one.[14] The Andamanese believe that the weather is under the control of two mythical beings, Biliku, who lives in the northeast and is associated with the northeast monsoon, and Tarai, who dwells in the southwest and is connected with the southwest monsoon. According to another and contradictory belief the weather is controlled by the spirits, particularly those of the sea. The methods followed by magicians to prevent bad weather are, consequently, of two kinds, according as they are directed against Biliku (or Tarai) or against the sea spirits. All are very simple in character. Thus a magician is said to have stopped a violent storm by crushing between two stones part of a certain plant and diving with it into the sea, where he placed it under a rock on the reef. Another magician, for the same purpose and in the same way, successfully used the leaves and bark of a fig tree.[15] In the Nicobar Islands, "if there is a violent storm on the land, and the rain never ceases, and the wind is strong, and palms and other trees are uprooted, and there is much thunder and lightning," the inhabitants will summon the magicians to end these disturbances by using certain leaves and other powerful charms.[16]

Some magicians among the Zulu specialize in defending the villages from hail and lightning. They are known as sky-herds or heaven-herds, because they go forth to control a storm whistling, shouting, and waving sticks much as herdsmen do with their cattle. Thunderbolts, lightning-birds, and bullocks struck by lightning have the power of the heaven in them. By absorbing a medicine made from them the doctor becomes so much in sympathy with the heaven that he knows when there is going to be a storm and can take appropriate measures to counteract it.[17] There are Swazi doctors who can make a place safe from lightning or direct it to another locality.[18]

Medicine men of the Ona, a Fuegian tribe, are supposed to control the powers of nature. One of them, during a great storm, was seen in a defiant attitude, discharging burning arrows into the clouds.[19] A Cherokee magician who would turn aside a storm which threatens to injure the growing corn faces it with out-stretched hand and gently blows toward the quarter to which he wishes it to go. He also waves his hand in the same direction as if he were pushing away the storm.[20] Among the Creek Indians certain men, like their Maori counterparts, claimed the power of causing swollen streams to subside. There were other men who could make dew or prevent its precipitation.[21] A Seminole magician professes an ability to bring down thunder from the heavens and cause it to strike the camp of an enemy. Very powerful "thunder medicine" is required for this purpose, and the person who makes it must first go for four days without eating or drinking. When the medicine has been prepared, the officiant tells the thunder the name of the camp and also the name of the person in it who is to be injured or killed.[22] Blackfoot medicine men were supposed to have power over the weather, and at the time of the Sun Dance they were expected to dissipate all storms.[23] The Chilkotin Indians believed that a solar or lunar eclipse was due to a scab on the face of the sun or the moon. To remove it and at the same time to hasten the reappearance of the luminary they would go outdoors, bend down as though they carried a heavy burden, and strike their right thighs, repeating at the same time in piteous tones, "Come back therefrom." Then they tucked up their clothes, as they did when on their travels, and, leaning on staves, as though heavy-laden, walked in circles until the eclipse was over.[24]

A Chukchi magician, in order to repress the wind, will "catch" it in a big overcoat spread to windward and speedily tie up the garment. The wind thus "tied up" may be quiescent for twenty-four hours, but then it must be let loose. If kept captive longer it would, when finally freed, become a severe and prolonged storm.[25]

To migratory savages, such as the Australian aborigines, who wander over their tribal territories in search of the roots and herbs, insects, and small animals supplying them with food, an unusually dry season spells starvation; to an agricultural people like the Pueblo Indians, living in a semi-arid environment, a pro-tracted drought brings desolation and death for both men and cattle. On the other hand, in tropical regions where the annual rainfall is so heavy as to cause the streams to overflow their banks and the fields to become turbid lakes, its very superabundance militates against human activities. Slight wonder that the man (or woman) who can control the rain ranks as a most important personage and that this function is often entrusted to a special class of magicians.

Rain making is or used to be a common practice in Australia, especially in those parts of the continent subject to frequent periods of drought. Among the Dieri of South Australia the whole tribe joined under the direction of the medicine men in the ceremonies to bring rain. Among the Kurnai of Victoria each clan had men who could produce rain by filling their mouths with water and then squirting it in the direction from which storms usually came; at the same time they sang their special rain songs. These men could also bring thunder, and it was said of them, as of the other magicians, that they obtained their songs in dreams.[26]

Some of the Queensland aborigines use quartz crystals as rain stones. These are crushed and hammered to powder. A straight-stemmed tree is selected and saplings are set up around it, thus forming a sort of shed. In front of this enclosure an artificial water hole is dug. The men dance and sing about it and imitate the movements of ducks, frogs, and other aquatic creatures. Then the men form a long Indian file and gradually encircle the women, over whom they throw the powdered crystals. The women at the same time hold wooden troughs, shields, and pieces of bark above their heads, as though they were protecting themselves from a heavy fall of rain.[27]

In the Arunta tribe a group of people, with water for their totem, possess the secret of rain making. It had been imparted to them in the Alcheringa, the dream time of long ago, by a certain mythical being, who also fixed upon the exact places where the rain ceremonies were to be performed.[28] In the Kaitish tribe the head-man of the water totem, accompanied by the elders of the group, goes to a certain sacred place, where, in the Alcheringa, two old men sat down and drew water out of their whiskers. The latter are now represented by stones, out of which the rainbow arose. The headman first of all smears the stones with red ocher. Then he paints a rainbow on the ground, one or more rainbows on his body, and still another on the shield which he has brought with him. He also decorates the shield with zigzag lines of white pipe-clay to represent lightning. While "singing" the stones he pours water over them and over himself. After this performance the headman returns to camp, taking with him the shield. This may be seen only by men of the same tribal division (moiety) as himself, for if men of the other moiety should see it the rites would be of no avail. The rainbow is regarded as the son of the rain and is supposed to be always wanting to put an end to a downpour; hence the shield with its rainbow decoration is hidden out of sight until a sufficient amount of rain has fallen. Then it is brought forth and the rainbow is rubbed out. While at the camp the headman keeps a vessel containing water at his side. From time to time he throws in all directions small pieces of white down representing clouds. This ritual is considered effective: the rain ought now to come; if it does not, then probably someone must have prevented it by superior magic.[29]

In the western islands of Torres Straits the office of rain maker and wind maker was confined to certain families. In the eastern islands a large number of men could perform rain-making ceremonies, but only a few had any reputation as successful practitioners. The public ceremony as performed on the island of Mer involved the use of *doiom*. These were stone images rudely carved to represent men, but with no indication of sex. All had names. Some *doiom* were more powerful than others; for instance, one could make a very heavy rain with a little thunder and another was exceptionally good at producing lightning accompanied by very loud thunder. The *doiom*, having been specially dressed for the occasion, were suspended on forked sticks stuck in the ground. The officiants, dancers and singers, stood with their backs to these charms. Their first song expressed the idea of a man feeling sick or out-of-sorts after a long drought and beseeching the rain to come and renew his life and strength. The second song asked the rain to fall on certain trees that were parched and drooping. This public ceremony took place regularly at the beginning of the rainy season and doubtless formed the recognized means of securing a full annual supply of rain for the island.[30]

Among the Keraki of southwestern Papua all important weather magic is in the hands of certain hereditary practitioners. Some of them specialize in the making of fine weather and others in the making of rain; occasionally the two professions are combined. Sun magic is openly performed. Rain magic, on the contrary, is always wrapped in secrecy. The rain maker carries on his rites in the depth of the bush, where none but his assistants would dare to go. The reason for secrecy seems to be that rain making has an intimate connection with the mythology of the tribe; it is therefore highly sacrosanct. The rain maker's paraphernalia include stones (rare treasures in what is naturally a stoneless region), crocodile jaws, fragments of turtle shells, and old fish nets. The stones bear the names of various heavenly

bodies. The essential feature of the performance is the transference of the heavenly bodies and the fine weather winds, represented by the stones, from the rack where these ordinarily repose,
high and dry, into a trough. They are then immersed in water
and covered from sight by sheets of bark. The operator thus
symbolically covers the heavens with a blanket of clouds. He
smears his body and the tree trunks nearby with charcoal, the
color of which is appropriate to gloomy weather. By shouting
and beating on the tree trunks he simulates the sound of thunder.
By spouting water from his mouth he simulates the fall of raindrops. He also breaks a coconut with an ax and liberates its
fluid. Besides performing these actions he puts into the water of
the trough the crocodile jaws, turtle shells, and fish nets—all
objects which have an association with water. Finally, to release
the occult power regarded as essential for the success of the
ritual, he makes use of a magical "catalytic," for example, ginger,
which he chews vigorously and spits out in the face of the heavens.
For every detail of these proceedings the rain maker asserts that
he has a mythological justification.[31]

Rain makers and other weather magicians are found everywhere in the Melanesian Islands. Some know one magical procedure and some another, but generally a community has a
sufficient number of these specialists, who, if recompensed for
their services, will provide for all its needs.[32] In New Caledonia
a special class of magicians had charge of rain making. For this
purpose they blackened themselves all over, exhumed a dead body,
brought the bones to a cave, jointed them, and suspended them
over some taro leaves. Water was then poured on the skeleton
so as to run down over the leaves. "They supposed that the soul
of the departed took up the water, made rain of it, and showered
it down again." The magicians had to fast and to remain in the
cave until rain came. If it failed to come within a few days they
sometimes died of starvation. Usually, however, they chose the
showery months of March and April for their performance.
Should there be too much rain they procured fair weather by
kindling a fire under the skeleton and burning it up.[33]

Rain making among the Oraon of Chota Nagpur is a communal
performance, with the village priest and his assistant taking the
principal part. On the occasion of the Sarhul festival they go in
procession through the village, and at each house the women pour
jugfuls of water over their heads. Then everybody is similarly
doused. All that day the people revel in water and daub mud on

one another, so as to present the mud-besmeared appearance of workers sowing seed in the rice fields.[34]

We have seen that in many parts of South Africa and East Africa the chiefs were formerly the great rain makers and that among some tribes rain making is still their most important duty. Procuring rain is normally the business of a Pondo chief. In time of drought the people go to him, tell him how the country suffers from lack of water, and call out the names of his ancestors. "Then it sometimes rains straight away." But if it does not, then the chief sends to a rain maker to perform the necessary magic. Should he be successful the chief presents him with cattle. "And sometimes," say the natives, "if he is not satisfied, he will stop the rain and demand more cattle."[35] The rain maker of the Xosa will not exercise his art for the benefit of any private person. He is a tribal functionary and operates only at the instance of the chief of the tribe.[36] When in response to the call of a chief a Bechuana rain maker arrived at the chief's village, he shut himself up in a hut which had been specially reserved for his operations. He made a fire, heated water, and added to it roots and herbs "of special power to produce rain." As the mixture boiled, he stirred it vigorously so as to make it froth. The rising steam transmitted the virtues of the plants to the clouds and so agitated them that a copious downpour would result.[37]

The king and queen mother of the Swazi have long been famous for their magical power over the heavenly water supply. Rain, if gentle and persistent, is generally attributed to the queen mother; if violent, it has been caused by the king. Should the queen mother herself be unable to bring rain, she will send for her son, and they will work together. If no seasonable rain has fallen the people conclude that the king and his mother are being hard-hearted or that for some reason the tribal ancestors have withheld it. The queen mother can also prevent rain from falling. When she sees clouds approaching she may take a broom, smeared with red clay, and "sweep" the sky, whereupon the clouds will turn red and dissolve.[38]

The queen of the Lovedu, who live in northern Transvaal, is not primarily a civil ruler but a rain maker. Tradition decrees that she must have no physical defect and must not die of old age. She therefore poisons herself at the end of the fourth initiation school held by the tribe. This ritual suicide elevates her to the rank of a divinity. Only by her own act and not because of physical weaknesses did she die. The queen's services are sought whenever they are needed, particularly when the maize has been planted and during the summer months when it might be ruined by a few weeks' drought. She never works alone but always has a rain doctor at hand to discover by divination the causes of a drought and what sorcerers are hindering her occult powers from operation. These powers are not absolute, for she can work only "in agreement with her ancestors." Moreover, certain untoward events cause her rain charms to become weak and even useless unless the proper measures are taken to avoid their evil consequences. Very serious are abortions or miscarriages, the birth of twins, and the death of women in pregnancy or parturition, of babies before cutting their teeth, and of adults struck by lightning. In such cases the dead body must be buried in a wet place near the river or the grave cooled with a special medicine. If the queen herself is thought responsible for the drought, then the people approach her with gifts and hold dances to please her and excite her pity. She must always be kept in good humor, for, if dissatisfied, angry, or sad she cannot work well: her very emotions affect the rain. The queen's rain charms are kept in rough earthen pots. Their chief ingredient is the skin of the deceased queen and the skins of important councillors who were her closest relatives. But the exact nature of the charms, together with the method of their use, is a profound secret which only the queen knows. She does not reveal it to a successor until about to die. Not only does the queen bring rain to her subjects but she can withhold it from their enemies. Because of this fact the Lovedu are better protected against aggression on the part of neighboring tribes than by an army of warriors.[39]

The rain maker does not always work in vain. Sometimes his patient and laborious efforts are abundantly rewarded. A rain maker of the Wotjobaluk, a Victorian tribe, was offered by a white squatter a bag of flour, some tea, and half a bullock, if he would fill a water tank before the evening of the next day. This was in a time of a severe drought. The magician immediately set to work, saying, "All right, we make him plenty rain come." Before twenty-four hours had passed a tremendous thunderstorm filled the tank to overflowing.[40] A female rain maker of the Yualayai of New South Wales was asked to make rain and bound down to a certain day for its appearance. The day dawned, a heavy storm fell just over the parched garden, but within half a mile on each side of the garden the dust was barely laid.[41] While among the Urabunna, Messrs. Spencer and Gillen camped near a hill called in the native language "clouds arising." The fore-fathers of the present Urabunna rain makers arose from the hill in the form of a great cloud. Because these ancestors were able to make rain their descendants likewise possessed that power. The leading rain maker of the tribe performed at this time his weather magic, and within two days there was a downpour, possibly associated, declare our authors, with the fact that the rainy season was then in progress. At any rate the coincidence firmly estab-lished the reputation of the operator as a magician of no mean caliber. "When we next saw him he was brimming over with undisguised, but at the same time dignified, self-satisfaction."[42]

The natives of Ambrym, one of the islands of the New Hebrides, once besought their magician for rain. He consented and placed his rain-making apparatus, a kind of basketwork, in a water hole. The rain came down in torrents and did not cease for two days and nights. It was so heavy that the yams in the plantations were washed out of the ground, and ruin stared the people in the face. They begged him to stop the downpour, but to do so, he explained, was impossible, because his apparatus lay under ten feet of water. Being no diver, he could not get it out. At last in desperation some picked swimmers managed to extricate it, and the rain then ceased immediately. That incident will be talked about for years, and the name of the too-successful rain maker will be handed down to future generations.[43]

In the county of the Kipsigis, one of the Nandi tribes, the rainfall is very heavy. If a man is about to undertake a long journey and does not want to get wet, he sticks in his hair the root of a bamboo, which is very antithetical to rain. When black clouds gather and thunder sounds, he takes the bamboo in his hand and waves it frantically in the direction of the coming storm. No word is spoken by him during the performance. Our authority found this magic to be most efficacious, for whenever he went on his travels, accompanied by a native with the bamboo, he always reached his destination without being soaked. Once while sitting in his tent a storm approached. A friend with the magical root appeared and waved it all around. The clouds burst and the rain descended with tropical violence, but not a drop fell on him and his friend; the rain had stopped one hundred yards away.[44]

A missionary among the Pennsylvania Indians tells how in the summer of 1799 there was a severe drought in the county where he lived. An Indian rain maker failed in his first attempt to break the dry spell, but the second time he was successful. The rain fell on the very day he said it would come and continued for several hours. Yet at the time the sky was perfectly clear, as it had been for almost five weeks continuously.[45]

Weather magic, especially rain making, offers many possibilities of success to a practitioner able to read aright the signs in the heavens. It is very commonly the case that he will operate only at a time when an atmospheric disturbance is most to be expected. Rain generally follows after a corroboree of the Queensland aborigines, but this performance does not take place until the experienced elders of the tribe are pretty certain that a downpour is imminent.[46] A certain rain maker among the Brisbane blacks commenced operations when "it seemed setting in for wet weather." About four days later rain did fall in torrents. The magician was asked to make it stop. He waited until he saw a break in the sky and then started throwing fire-sticks in the air to dry up the rain. Fair weather followed soon afterward. The natives were profoundly impressed by this exhibition, "and he himself evidently believed in his own powers."[47] An old rain maker of the Wonkonguru, South Australia, when asked about producing a downpour in a particularly dry season, replied, "No good make 'em rain this time. Too much dry fella. By and by, cloud come up, me make 'em rain."[48] In the Yeidji or Yeithi tribe of the Kimberley Division, Western Australia, the rain maker performs his ceremonies only during hot weather when rain is expected.[49] The tribes inhabiting the northwestern part of Australia have a rain-making ceremony but it does not take place before favorable signs for rain are manifest, such as clouds skidding swiftly at no great height across the sky, or, better still, when the storm birds come inland in thousands from the marshy coast in order to feed on the flying ants which, after a rain, rise in myriads into the air.[50] In the eastern islands of Torres Straits a rite to make a "big wind" was performed in the season of the southeast monsoon. On being asked whether it was also carried out during the northwest monsoon, the magician replied emphatically, "Can't do it in northwest."[51] Among the Elema tribes of the Papuan Gulf the rain maker and thunder maker does not operate during the dry season, nor does the wind maker attempt to bring on a calm, so that boats can put to sea, at the height of the rainy season.[52] In Eromanga, one of the New Hebrides, a magician employed to raise a great storm, so as to injure the gardens of a village, performed his magic in the hurricane season. On no account could he be induced to work in cool weather, when hurricanes are almost unknown.[53] A Maori magician will not try to bring rain unless there is a great likelihood, from the appearance of the heavens, of an approaching downpour. The natives are skilled weather observers, rarely failing in their prognostications.[54] The Xosa rain makers are well versed in all the signs which indicate the approach of rain, such as the oozing of long-dried springs, the character of the halo around the moon, the chirp of the tree-frog, which heralds a storm, the appearance of clouds, and the changes of the wind.[55] A wise rain maker of the Bechuana never prophesies the coming of rain until he sees atmospheric indications of its near approach.[56] Of the Bari it is said that they have the greatest confidence in the powers of their rain makers during the wet season, "but candidly admit their disbelief in him at any other time."[57] The most noted rain makers among the Mumuye of northern Nigeria live in districts where the rainfall is "abnormally high."[58] Of the Lengua practitioner we are told that "any other Indian could foretell rain were he to observe signs as closely as does the wizard."[59] An authority on the Blackfoot refers to the "extraordinary skill" which the medicine men display in the interpretation of weather signs.[60] The power of an Eskimo magician in Labrador rests to a considerable extent on his skill in interpreting weather signs and on his supposed ability to attract game to the region where he and his friends are hunting. As a matter of fact, he studies with care the habits of deer and other animals so as to be able to anticipate their movements, which are greatly influenced by the weather.[61] A magician of the Baffin Land Eskimo, who is often called upon to subdue the bitter storms which prevent hunters from going out, watches carefully the weather signs and exhibits his magical ability only when the gale has spent itself.[62]

The rain maker may not promise to produce a downpour at any particular date, but continues his efforts until at length the rain does come. Apparently the Keraki rain maker never contracts to get results within a stipulated time, "so that there is no reason to suppose he ever fails or ever will fail."[63] Similarly among the Xosa of South Africa the rain maker does not, as a rule, fix the particular day when rain may be expected.[64] When the Mandan Indians undertake to make rain "they never fail to succeed, for their ceremonies never stop until rain begins to fall."[65]

Notwithstanding the real skill which rain magicians often possess in forecasting the weather and in spite of all the precautions which they take to ensure the success of their predictions, failure must often attend their efforts. When drought and dearth continue to blast the fields or an unseasonable downpour to flood them, people may refuse to accept any excuses for failure, however excellent, condemn the magic worker for culpable negligence or for something worse, and punish him accordingly. A Papuan magician who has made rain but who fails to stop it when too much falls is held responsible for the damage to the gardens.[66] Among the Bechuana an unsuccessful rain maker is sometimes placed in the sun with no shade over his head and is obliged to remain in this position until rain comes.[67] The Bageshu of Mount Elgon, Uganda, entertain great faith in a rain maker. If rain falls after a day or two all is well, but if weeks pass without a welcome shower the people become angry and remonstrate with him for not exerting himself. Should rain still be delayed they attack him, rob him, burn down his house, and roughly handle him.[68] Among the Banyoro or Bakitara of Uganda, the king had a special punishment for a magician who failed to bring rain when wanted. He was compelled to eat a meal of liver cooked with as much salt as possible. Then he had to sit perspiring in the sun and tortured by thirst for several days. If there had been a steady downpour and he failed to stop it the king exposed him to the rain and made him drink huge quantities of rain water. Under these treatments a magician often became ill and sometimes died.[69] The Lotuko (Latuka) of the Anglo-Egyptian Sudan will rob an unsuccessful rain maker of all his possessions and drive him into exile; often they kill him.[70] Death is, or used to be, the penalty for failure to bring rain among other African tribes.[71] A Jesuit informant tells us that among the Natchez Indians "jugglers" were commonly indolent old men who took up magic working as an easy means of livelihood. If they brought rain or fair weather, as desired, their reward was handsome; if they failed, their heads were cut off. The same penalty was exacted in the case of doctors who lost their patients. As the good father remarks, those who engage in this dangerous profession "risk everything to gain everything."[72]

Increase rites for the multiplication of the plants and animals entering into the tribal dietary form another important department of public magic. Few performances of this sort have been recorded among the aborigines of southeastern Australia. The *minkani* of the Dieri and other Lake Eyre tribes was carried out by the initiated men for the purpose of multiplying carpet-snakes and iguanas, and among the Wurunjerri of Victoria certain clansmen had a ceremony to secure a good catch of kangaroos. We also hear of a Queensland tribe in which both men and women, swinging bull-roarers, went through a ritual designed to secure plentiful supplies of fish and honey.[73]

Increase rites are numerous and elaborate among the Arunta, Kaitish, Unmatjera, and Urabunna of Central Australia, where they are associated with the different totemic groups or clans of the tribe. Among the Arunta they go under the general name of *intichiuma*, a term which is also applied to the rain-making ritual. Each totemic group holds its own *intichiuma*, which only initiated clansmen may attend and in whose performance they may take part. The exact time for holding it is fixed by the headman (*ala-tunja*) of the group, but since these rites are connected with the breeding of the animals or the flowering of the plants with which each group is respectively identified, an *intichiuma* will usually be held when there is promise of a good season. The men who have the witchetty grub, emu, honey-ant, and kangaroo for their totems are charged with the duty of multiplying those animals, while the men having the hakea flower and "manna" gum for their totems are responsible for the increase of those plants. After an *intichiuma* has taken place and when, in consequence, the animal or plant concerned has become abundant, men, women, and children of all the totemic groups go out daily and collect large supplies, which they bring into the main camp. They may not eat the food until the headman of the totemic group concerned solemnly eats a little of it and then hands over the remainder to the people of all the other groups, telling them to consume it freely. Unless he did eat a little he could not preside properly over the *intichiuma*. His clan fellows are not absolutely forbidden to eat the food hence-forth, but they must do so sparingly; were they to eat too much they would lose the power of performing the *intichiuma* with success. Thus a particular animal or plant, as the case may be, is almost but not quite taboo to the people who have it as their totem.[74]

The *intichiuma* of the Arunta is secret; it is carried out by the fully initiated men; and it is always held at some place associated with the ancestors of the totemic group in the far-distant past. This place the natives consider highly sacrosanct, as being the home of the spirits of the particular species, animal or plant, whose numbers are to be increased. Thus the purpose of the *intichiuma* is to send the spirits out of the spot where they congregate, so that they may find their way into living witchetty grubs, emus, honey-ants, and kangaroos, and replenish the stock of these totemic animals. The spirits are regarded as amenable to man's control, provided the *intichiuma* is properly performed. The Arunta possess no granaries, but they do have these spirit storehouses to ensure them against starvation.[75]

The increase rites of the Arunta and other Central tribes involve the organized and collective efforts of the various totemic groups, each group assisting the rest in a regular and more or less periodical series of operations, whose net result is supposed to be an abundant supply of food for all. Each group is bound to contribute to the general stock by working magic for the propagation of its particular totemic animal or plant. On no account must this be eaten until it is abundant and fully grown. An infringement of the rule will nullify, it is thought, the effect of the magic and reduce the available supply of food. Australian totemism has thus a definitely economic character as a system of magical co-operation.[76]

The tribes about the Gulf of Carpentaria have no obligatory, regular, or periodical ceremonies corresponding to the *intichiuma*. The men of a particular clan can perform simple rites for the multiplication of their totemic animal or plant, but there is no necessity for them to do so and there is nothing which corresponds to the solemn eating by an Arunta headman of the animal or plant in question. The fact that increase ceremonies are not considered necessary by these tribes seems to find an explanation in their greater assurance of a food supply, because of the more certain rainfall of the coastal area as compared with that of the arid interior. The increase of the different species will take place, it is thought, without man's magical intervention. On the other hand, in many tribes to the west of the Gulf of Carpentaria, the different totemic groups are charged with elaborate ceremonies which furnish a close parallel to those of the Arunta and other Central tribes.[77]

Increase rites associated with particular clans and analogous to the *intichiuma* occur outside the Australian area. In Mabuiag, one of the western islands of the Torres Straits group, two of the seven clans had such rites, those of the Dugong clan to compel the dugong to swim toward the island and be caught and those of the Turtle clan to ensure a supply of turtles. Women and children and members of other clans did not come near the participants in the rites. For the *surlal* ceremony the clansmen painted themselves to represent the turtle, wore headdresses of cassowary feathers, and danced round the animal, whirling bull-roarers. In Mer, one of the eastern islands, the people of different districts held annual masked dances, probably to secure a good harvest. The dance in each case was performed by representatives of a particular group. Spectators from other groups might be present, but they were not permitted to wear the masks or otherwise join in the ceremonies.[78] In Malekula, one of the New Hebrides, each clan has the power, vested in the clan magician, to multiply some article of food or to influence some natural phenomenon such as sunshine and rain. The clans which control the different supplies of food carry out their ceremonies annually for the benefit of the whole district. The clans which influence sunshine and rain will increase these whenever the district especially needs them.[79]

Increase rites may be carried out by a single magician acting in a representative capacity. In the Trobriand Islands every village and at times every subdivision of a village has its own garden magician (*towosi*), who works for the common benefit and receives presents from everybody as compensation for his invaluable services. His office is hereditary and in legal theory coincides with that of the village headman or chief. When its duties weigh too heavily on him, he may sometimes delegate them to a younger brother or son. His position is no sinecure, for, in addition to observing various abstentions and fasts, by no means light or easy, he must exercise a constant supervision of the gardens. If he finds that some people are lagging behind in their work or are neglecting a communal obligation to keep their plots properly fenced, it is incumbent on him to upbraid the culprits and induce them to mend their ways. An excellent gardener, on the other hand, receives his public praise, and this is a great stimulus to the workers. The Trobrianders are convinced that he controls the forces of fertility and that his magic is indispensable to the success of gardening. "The garden magician utters magic by mouth; the magical virtue enters the soil."[80]

Fishing is a very important activity of the Tabar people, who occupy a group of islands off the east coast of New Ireland. A net owner, who happens to be also a magician, can himself perform the necessary rites over his net; in other cases it is usual for him to hire the services of a specialist in this difficult and complicated art. To launch a net without the magic would be as foolish, think the natives, as to go to sea in a canoe without paddles. The launching of a net and the associated magic are a community affair, accompanied by feasts and requiring various payments to be made to the participants. The management of the net at sea likewise involves the co-operative effort of a group of men, and for its success the owner or the magical specialist whom he employs relies on the recital of charms to ensure a good catch.[81]

In the island of Yap, the most westerly of the Caroline archipelago, the magicians of the sacred groves are charged with the duty of working garden magic for the inhabitants. One of them is an expert in fertilizing the taro fields and breadfruit plantations; another knows the proper ritual for sweet potatoes; and another that for coconuts and areca palms. According to native belief the reason for this specialization is found in the fact that formerly a particular article of food was dedicated exclusively to the spirit of a particular sacred grove.[82] Among the Palau (Pelew) Islanders, who combine fishing with various magico-animistic ceremonies, the master fisherman (*koreomel*) owes the authority of his position not only to his knowledge of the piscatorial art, but also and principally to his familiarity with many spells to bind the sea gods. When the natives go out to catch sharks in the open sea, he officiates as the leader and spiritual guide of the expedition. One of these *koreomel* was believed able to calm the stormy seas.[83]

The Sakai are an aboriginal people occupying the center of the Malay Peninsula. Among the Sakai of Perak magical rites in connection with the cultivation of rice are numerous and elaborate. In former days there used to be in every village at least one professional magician who knew the proper spells, but now, as a rule, only the village chief is familiar with them. Before the jungle is cleared a spell must be recited to avoid accidents due to the machinations of evil spirits. The workers are thus protected from being crushed by falling trees, from falls from trees, from wounds inflicted by their choppers and hatchets, from the attacks of wild beasts, and from fever. When the timber has been felled and is ready for burning the recital of another spell will summon the winds to fan the fire. At the sowing of the rice the magician enters the fields, accompanied by all the men, women, and children who are to take part in the operation, and repeats a spell which will make a mere pinch of seed grow a hundredfold, nay, a thousandfold. Finally, before the commencement of reaping, a spell is uttered to bring back the soul of the rice (the "rice baby") to the house, so that it may take up its abode in seven ears of the plant which were the first seven cut at the harvest. Rice grains from these ears will be mixed with the main stock of seed at the next year's planting.[84]

The Talense (Tallensi), a tribe in the Northern Territories of the Gold Coast, engage in communal fishing expeditions. These occur every year and extend over a period of about a month, between the close of the dry season and the commencement of the heavy rains. There must first be a ritual fishing, intended to secure the blessing of the ancestral ghosts; hence the size of the catch counts for very little. On the day appointed for an expedition men and women, boys and girls, and even younger children converge upon some selected pool which is to be swept with nets. But before they enter, a magical specialist calls on his male ancestors by name in ascendant order and, "half entreating, half commanding," exhorts them to drive crocodiles and dangerous fish into their holes or out of the pool so that no one may be injured, to prevent fighting between the fishermen, and to give them a good haul. Then he offers a sacrifice to his ancestors and plants an ax shaft firmly by the water side, thus symbolically pinioning all dangerous creatures. The officiant also provides some of his assistants with medicines and sends them into the pool, where they wade about or swim, squirting water this way and that and crying "Emerge, emerge, vanish, vanish" to expel any dangerous creatures lurking in the water. The efficacy of this rite is never questioned. If someone should be injured by a crocodile or a fish, as occasionally happens, it is understood that he had offended some ancestral ghost who seized an opportunity to punish him.[85]

The *makai* of the Pima Indians of Arizona, who had power over the weather and could bring rain when needed, were also able to procure good crops. For this purpose they gathered the people in the large lodge and had someone bring in an olla (pot) filled with earth. They stirred the earth with a willow stick and then placed the olla before a fire, where it stood all night. At dawn it was emptied and was found to contain wheat instead of earth. Four grains of the wheat were given to each one present to be buried in his field. This magic seems to have been a clever feat of legerdermain by the *makai*.[86]

Public magic finds employment in other economic activities which engage the interest of the entire community.

Papuo-Melanesian (Massim) peoples, who occupy the islands off the southeastern end of New Guinea and the adjacent archipelagoes, including the Louisiades, the D'Entrecasteaux group, and the Trobriands, have a system of inter-tribal exchange of a seemingly unique character—the *kula*. Between the communities of this area articles of two kinds are in constant movement and in a closed circuit. Clockwise move necklaces of red shell; counterclockwise move bracelets of white shell. When they meet an exchange takes place, regulated in accordance with time-honored and traditional rules. Every man who has a place in the *kula* receives a necklace or a bracelet, as the case may be, retains it for not more than a year or two, and then passes it on to one of his partners, from whom he gets an article of the opposite kind. Partners are under a mutual obligation, not only to make the exchanges, but also to provide for each other protection, hospitality, and assistance when needed. A partnership is a lifelong affair—"once in the *kula,* always in the *kula.*" Transactions of this sort occur on a small scale within a village or between contiguous villages, but there are also big periodical expeditions in which the exchange takes place between two communities divided by sea, when as many as a thousand valuables will be passed from hand to hand in the manner described. These overseas expeditions afford an opportunity for a good deal of ordinary trade in useful objects often unprocurable at home, but such trade (conducted by barter) is quite subsidiary to the ceremonial give-and-take of necklaces and bracelets. For the Trobrianders and their neighbors the ritual aspects of the *kula* are by far its most important aspects.

This ceremonial exchange of two articles, intended solely for ornamentation but seldom so used to any extent, has become the basis of a complex institution which binds together thousands of people scattered over an extensive area. To men who engage in the *kula* it forms a vital interest, for temporary ownership of the necklaces and bracelets confers great renown upon their possessors, much as with us the victors in a sporting match treasure trophies as evidence of their superiority. The *kula* as a ritual performance is intimately bound up with magic. Magical rites and the utterance of spells are indispensable for its successful operation, particularly in the case of an overseas expedition. There must be magic addressed to the malignant wood spirits compelling them to leave the trees which are to be made into canoes; magic during the process of building, so that the canoes shall be swift and safe and also lucky in the *kula;* magic at their launching and loading; and magic to avert the dangers of the long sea voyage. There is even magic to affect the minds of the partners in the exchanges to come, so that their gifts shall have surpassing value and bring high honor to the recipients.

Each canoe is constructed by a group of people and is owned and used communally. This magic of the *kula* has, therefore, the same public character as the rites and spells so often employed in the cultivation of gardens, in fishing, and in other economic activities.[87]

For the Kiwai, who occupy a large island off the mouth of the Fly River in southern Papua, the erection of a new house is an undertaking in which the whole population of the village has a part. Everyone lends a helping hand. The old men direct the work, for only they know the many observances which have to be carefully carried out during the various stages of the construction. The erection of a new clubhouse, common to all the men of the village, is an especially important matter, requiring the exercise of much magic to keep away evil influences, not only from the house itself, but from the people as well. If in spite of every precaution sickness should break out, it is attributed to some oversight on the part of the builders. Possessed with this idea, they will proceed to tear down a house only just completed and build a new one. For the success of the undertaking it is essential to secure the services of a very old man and a very old woman to perform the most secret part of the rites and to supervise the work. Their lives are supposed to be forfeited upon its close. The people do not want them to die, but everyone recognizes that they will not long survive the conclusion of the rites. The actual cause of their death is not clear to the natives. There seems to be an idea that the endowment of the house with various magical properties has fatally weakened them and consumed their feeble vitality.[88]

Public magic may be used to set up a closed season for plants and animals and for the protection of community property against intruders and other unlicensed persons. By means of prohibitions (taboos), provided with a magical sanction, camping places, hunting grounds, and fishing streams are kept inviolate and the economic resources of the social group are preserved.

These taboos are sometimes imposed by a secret society or else the society is charged with the duty of enforcing them. In the Mekeo district of Papua the Fuluaari secret society has the responsibility of enforcing a taboo on areca nuts and coconuts, when the supply on the trees is running short. The prohibition is imposed by a special official, the Afu, or taboo chief. When there is a good show of nuts, the chief proclaims that on a certain day the prohibition will be lifted. It has been known to last as long as thirty-two weeks.[89] In the delta of the Purari River occupied by the Namau group of tribes large tracts of land, bearing coconuts, and long waterways were annually put under a taboo. A number of young men, wearing the masks of a secret society, patrolled the river banks and warned passers-by against taking the coconuts or catching the fish in that part of the river that had been marked off. It was "a primitive but effective way of preserving food which was the common right of all their people."[90] In New Britain there are no particular periods during which certain goods may not be eaten except when a taboo is placed upon them by a chief or a secret society. "This is generally done either to increase the quantity by making as it were a closed season, or for monetary reasons."[91] The men's clubs in the Palau (Pelew) Islands proclaim and enforce a taboo laid by the chiefs on pigs, coconuts, the betel palm, and anything else of which there is or may be a scarcity. Formerly death was the penalty for a breach of such a prohibition; now the culprit is confined in the clubhouse until ransomed by the head chief.[92] Purrah or Poro, a secret society of the Mendi of Sierra Leone, places its interdict "upon trees, streams, fishing-pots, fruit trees, oil palms, bamboo palms, growing crops, and in fact upon all and everything that is required to be reserved for any particular use."[93] A piece of rag, a stone, or a few sticks may be the only indication that a taboo has been imposed, but it is effective. "Water is kept uncontaminated; trees laden with fruit are not touched, except by the owner; the entrances of villages and special bush-paths are kept clean; fish are preserved when necessary; and a man's property is absolutely safe."[94] The imposition of such taboos seems to be a common function of the West African secret societies, for we are told that boys undergoing initiation into them learn from their instructors "why there should be closed seasons for certain oil-bearing and fruiting trees, and for certain beasts, birds, and fish."[95]

More commonly the taboos imposing closed seasons are laid down and enforced by the tribal chief or by a magician who acts in behalf of the group. Among the Mailu, a Papuan tribe, if fish become scarce in any particular place on the reef or near it, the old men or the headman of the clan owning rights over the reef erect a taboo sign on the spot. It stands for three or four lunar months. When fish are found to be plentiful again, the sign is removed and fishing is resumed.[96] The natives of the Trobriand Islands put a taboo on both coconut palms and areca nut palms.

It is imposed by a magician, who at the same time recites various spells designed to make the fruit plentiful. During its continuance the people are not allowed to eat or in any way use coconut in the village, though they may do so outside the village precincts. They must also refrain from making a noise, especially by chopping or hammering, and they must be careful not to allow any firelight to be seen in the village. If the coconuts were shocked by either sound or light, they would fall down unripe. The taboo period lasts for two months.[97] In the Loyalty Islands a "big chief" would occasionally taboo all the coconut trees in his district. When the restriction was removed, the nuts were gathered into a huge pile and divided among the people.[98] In the Fiji Islands it was customary for a chief to put coconut groves under an interdict until the nuts ripened. While "fear of the gods" helped to support the regulation, an intending transgressor knew that he might be robbed of his possessions, have his gardens despoiled, or even be killed.[99] In Tikopia the people are arranged in four divisions, each one with a chief and its own district. The chief has the power to taboo any particular locality, in order that the coconut trees on it may reach a certain size before being gathered.[100] In Tonga-tabu, according to the testimony of Captain Cook, the special officer "who presided over the taboo" inspected all the produce of the island, taking care that every man should plant and cultivate his quota and ordering what should be eaten and what not. "By this wise regulation they effectually guard against a famine; a sufficient quantity of ground is employed in raising provisions; and every article thus raised is secured from unnecessary waste."[101] In the Marquesas Islands, should the quantity of breadfruit in a district be seriously diminished, the chief could taboo the trees for as long as twenty months to enable them to recover their vigor. If fish were beginning to get scarce, a taboo might be laid on one part of the bay so that the fish could spawn without being disturbed.[102] In the Mortlock Islands, when the breadfruit becomes ready for eating, the chief taboos coconuts for three or four months so that there may be a sufficient supply of the old nuts. Fishing may also be placed under a general prohibition or be allowed to certain persons only, in order to conserve the supply of fish.[103]

These communal taboos thus have the practical effect of preserving the plants and animals most important in the group economy. Crops are allowed to mature, fruits to ripen, and beasts of the field and fish in the sea to increase and multiply. To the operation of such taboos we may confidently assign no slight influence in restraining individual selfishness for the benefit of the group as a whole and of deepening the sense of social obligation.

Magic is sometimes employed by the community or by a person in its supposed interest to detect and punish people who have violated tribal customs of a stringent character or have otherwise acted in an unsocial manner.

Among the Arunta it is permissible for a husband whose wife has run away and cannot be recovered to punish her by means of sorcery. He and his friends in the local group meet at a secluded spot and there a man skilled in magic marks out on the ground a rude figure which represents the woman lying on her back. While this is being done, the men chant in low tones an exhortation to *arungquiltha* (evil magical power) to enter her body and dry up the fat. They also stick a number of miniature spears, which have been previously "sung," into a piece of green bark representing the spirit part of the woman. The bark with the spears in it is then thrown in the direction in which the woman is supposed to be. Sooner or later her fat dries up, she dies, and her spirit form appears in the sky as a shooting star.[104] In the Northern Territory of Australia a number of people will mete out punishment to a man who has committed incest by "singing" magic against him. The formula used is, of course, traditional. No cure exists for the illness thus produced, first, because this verbal magic does not involve the insertion into the victim of some malefic object which a medicine man can extract, and, second, because very few natives have the strength of mind to resist a social judgment and penalty, especially when expressed through a magical procedure well known and greatly feared.[105]

By the Kwoma, a Papuan tribe, all serious sickness is believed to be caused by sorcery. When, therefore, anyone falls ill, the men of the hamlet repair to the clubhouse and beat an aggressive message on the gongs: "Stop all sorcery. One of our relatives is sick, and anyone who continues to practice sorcery must answer to us, the men of this hamlet." If the sick person does not get well as the result of this action, the men call a special court to establish the identity of the sorcerer.[106]

The natives of Guadalcanal have a spell which is used when a girl is about to become a prostitute. Prostitution, it should be said, is very rare in the island, but a girl is forced to adopt the profession when her actions have already given rise to scandal. The spell states in straightforward language that the girl is already a prostitute. "She seeks men always. . . . . She is without shame." These words are recited over certain objects which are placed on the ground below her bed. The objects include a bundle of leaves, a number of burrs, and strips of bark some with thorns and some white and smooth. The leaves are either very rough in texture or else capable of inflicting a severe sting. They will make the girl walk about and look around for men, instead of staying at home. The burrs and the thorny bark will make desire for men stick in her mind, while the white bark causes her skin to be beautiful. When the operator has finished his recital he spits all over the objects and also runs up and down, imitating the way she will go about in her search for lovers. Finally he places a mat on the top of the leaves. After the girl has slept on it a few nights she will accept without reluctance the prostitute's lot.[107]

In Fiji, if the evidence against a person suspected of wrongdoing was strong, but he refused to confess, the chief sent for a scarf with which "to catch the soul of the rogue." The threat of the rack, it is said, could not be more effectual. At the sight or even the mention of the scarf the culprit generally "came clean" at once. If he did not, the scarf would be waved over his head until his soul was caught in it, when it would be folded up and nailed to the end of the chief's canoe. For want of his soul he would pine away and die.[108]

The Angami Naga sometimes hold "a sort of Commination Service" to curse some member of the community who has given it grave offense. The Kemovo, a village official who directs all public ceremonies, appears before the assembled clansfolk and announces that So-and-So has done such-and-such a deed, whereupon the people answer, "Let him die, let him die!" This is a very powerful curse. To heighten its power a branch of green leaves is put up to represent the culprit, and everyone hurls spears at the object and expresses the wish that he may be killed. The branch dries, the green leaves wither, and the man comes to an untimely end. This performance is also held to be effective even when the name of the culprit is unknown.[109]

It is very commonly the case among the Balamba that when a man dies his relatives make up their minds to fasten the blame for his death upon some one who is a burden to the community owing to old age or who has made himself unpopular. Thus easily and with the acclamation of everybody they rid themselves of the unwanted person.[110]

The Nyakyusa, who comprise an important group of tribes in southern Tanganyika, have elaborated the conception of the "breath of men," this being the public opinion of an entire group, whether a village or a collection of villages under a chief. The "breath of men" acts in an occult manner to bewitch anybody who becomes unpopular by reason of pride or meanness or who offends against the accepted morality. Thus it furnishes a sanction for the fair treatment of wives and for the avoidance of incest. Likewise it ensures the due performance of tribal ceremonies. If, for instance, a man fails to kill cattle and provide beer for a ceremony, when by custom he ought to do so, then the breath of those neighbors who would have eaten the cattle and drunk the beer will make his children or his cattle sick. The popular breath also forms an effective check on the power of a chief. If he abuses it only enough to alienate the inhabitants of a single village, he tries to avoid illness by moving to another village; if, however, all his people are vexed with him, he will surely die. One chief, known to our informant, did not dare to venture a judgment in an altercation between two of his villages because he feared the consequences of the indignant sorcery of the losing side.[111]

Among the Agni of the Ivory Coast those who perish as being witches are most commonly old women, useless for any kind of work, chronic grumblers, refractory, obstinate persons, and poor people without influential friends or relatives. It seems to be true of the Agni, as of other West African peoples, that the witchcraft accusations reflect an unconscious desire to rid the society of those members who for one reason or another have become encumbrances.[112]

A rough-and-ready sort of community justice is sometimes meted out by the Eskimo to people who have made themselves generally obnoxious. A case is reported among the Polar Eskimo of an *angakok* who was a bad comrade, always offending his neighbors in various ways. Especially did he constantly lie to them in regard to the hunting. So the decision was reached to get rid of him. He was killed by two of the best members of the tribe, one of whom married the dead man's wife.[113] An *angakok* of the Hudson Bay Eskimo discovered that a fellow member of the profession had turned sorcerer and had wished a great many people to die. The matter was talked over and the decision was reached to kill him. One day, when he had made a hole in a frozen pond and reached down to remove the broken pieces of ice, he was stabbed in the back by an old man, "who received the thanks of the others for his feat."[114]

Magic enters largely into primitive warfare. The magician's predictions determine whether wars shall be begun, and his advice decides how they shall be waged. His arts defend the tribesfolk against every assault and bring destruction or death upon their enemies. Before the warriors set out on the path which leads to glory or the grave it is often his business to endow them with strength and courage, even, perhaps, to make them invulnerable. In primitive warfare the issue of victory or defeat is often held to depend at least as much on the activity of the magician as on that of the war leader.

The Kiwai Papuans attach much importance to preparing young men for a fight, especially if they have never before taken human life. The ingredients of one of the medicines administered to them consist of small pieces of the eyes, talons, beak, and tongue of a certain large hawk. The eyes help them to find their foe and the bits of the talons and beak to catch him. The tongue symbolizes the fury of fighting, for an animal hangs out its tongue when engaged in a deadly struggle. If an enemy has been killed, the natives sometimes cut off a piece of skin above one eye and require the young man to swallow it. A man's brow is the foremost part of his body when he rushes at the foe and so has much the same symbolic value as the eagle's tongue. It is very desirable for the youthful warrior to eat a portion of the sexual parts of an enemy man and woman, because then he will be able to slay many persons of both sexes. All this war medicine is extremely powerful, and its effects are long-lasting.[115]

Intertribal warfare in the Trobriands is conducted in a quite gentlemanly fashion, for the natives do not go in for nocturnal raids or try to kill their enemies by stealth or treachery. All fighting takes place in a circular arena, which has been cleared for the purpose in the bush. Here the warriors stand, some thirty to fifty meters apart, and hurl their spears at each other, while the women and children watch the course of the fight from positions in the rear. Previous to the engagement an expert war magician recites spells over the shields to give these the power of warding off spears and spits chewed ginger over the bodies of the contestants to make them strong, fierce, and enduring. He will also perform his rites over the fighting arena; if more powerful than the similar rites of the opposing magician their effect is to make the enemy run away. In addition to this official war magic, practiced by a specialist for the benefit of the community, everybody or nearly everybody knows some private spells for use over his own shield and spear. The Trobrianders are persuaded that the employment of magic is absolutely indispensable for victory.[116]

When the warlike Maori were on the march against an enemy's stronghold, they would halt and kindle a fire, over which the *tohunga* recited certain spells. These caused the souls of their adversaries to fall into the flames and perish miserably. But sometimes it happened that the counter spells of the besieged were more potent than those of the besiegers, in which case the latter returned home discomfited.[117] The *tohunga* might resort to other magical devices to overcome the foe. One way of doing so was to take a wallet or basket containing some sacred food, hold it to the fire and then, opening the wallet, point the mouth of it in the direction of the opposing warriors. By the recital of an appropriate spell their souls would be drawn into the wallet, which was then closed to the accompaniment of another spell. When this operation had been performed, it was easy enough for the *tohunga* to destroy their souls by means of a third spell.[118]

Before the Basuto go to war the foreleg of a living bull is cut off, the meat scorched and anointed with medicine, and given to the warriors to eat. They are also sprinkled with the animal's blood. Then the witch doctor proceeds to lance them and to rub into the wounds a powder made from the flesh of the bull. By this threefold operation—eating the flesh, sprinkling the blood, and inoculation—the "strength and courage" of the bull are imparted to the warriors.[119]

In the Baronga group of the Bathonga tribe warriors, before a battle, were sprinkled with medicine by the chief doctor of the army. Every man thus treated was fully convinced that the bullets would be deflected on either side of him or, if they hit him, would be flattened against his body and fall harmless to the ground. The effect of the medicine could only be nullified if he turned his back to the foe; then the bullets might pass through him. Among the Bankuna, one of the clans of the tribe, the sprinkling was done by an old woman who had not engaged in sexual relations for a long time. If she had done so, "the assegais would lose their strength; the masculine weapons would become blind and the feminine weapons alone would see."[120]

In the old days there was a great magician among the Akikuyu who knew how to compound a medicine which would enable them to repel an invasion of the Masai. It is said to have been made from a piece of cloth or an old discarded sandal secretly obtained from an abandoned village of the Masai. The medicine was put in a pot, along with a piece of iron secured from a smith, and was then brought to the path by which the enemy usually came to attack. Another potent charm, used for the same purpose, was a gift to the magician from the high god Ngai.[121] Among the Banyoro of Uganda, when a hostile force drew near, the medicine man maimed or killed a blind cow or sheep and a dog and left the animals on the road by which the army was approaching. The enemy would then be struck with blindness and could be easily overcome.[122] An important chief among the Dinka of the Anglo-Egyptian Sudan does not practice magic as a rule, for the high god of the tribe is usually amenable to his requests. When a raid is in preparation, however, he will take a stone and revolve it in his hands, a procedure which confuses the enemy's sense of direction. The stone is then buried in the ground; this procedure keeps the enemy at home.[123]

The war dance of the Jivaro fills the participants with strength, courage, and confidence for the coming fight and preserves them from wounds or death. At the same time it lulls the enemy into a false sense of security and so makes a surprise attack possible. Without the dance no war expedition would have a favorable outcome. The Jivaro also have a special song which, when sung by the warriors before they start out, will ensure their victory.[124]

Certain songs, composed by Omaha women and sung by them exclusively, were supposed to transmit courage and increased fighting power to an absent warrior. When a party had gone out on the warpath women, particularly of the poorer class, would stand before his tent and sing one or more of these songs. In return for their services his wife gave them presents. This custom also prevailed among the Ponca and the Osage.[125]

The medicine arrows and sacred hat of the Cheyenne, which came to them long, long ago, brought by their culture heroes, were strong magic in war. When some grave injury had been received from another tribe the whole camp, men, women, and children, moved out against the aggressor, taking with them the arrows and the hat. These were never carried on small war parties. Just before the fight started, the keeper of the arrows put in his mouth a bit of the root which was always tied up with the arrows, chewed it fine, and then blew it toward the enemy, in order to make them blind. Then, holding the arrows in his hand, he pointed them

toward the (collective) enemy's foot, next against his leg from
ankle to thigh, next against his heart, and finally against his head.
After this demonstration two warriors, one who wore the sacred
hat and the other who carried the arrows, rushed toward the
foe on swift horses and executed movements intended to confuse
and frighten their adversaries. The neglect to perform these
ceremonies with the arrows took from them their protective
power and involved the failure of the campaign.[126]

Among the many duties of the head medicine man of a Maidu
village in northern California was the infliction of disease and
death on a hostile village. For this purpose he took certain roots
and his sacred cape and repaired to the vicinity of the enemy.
Having selected a spot where the wind blew toward the village,
he put hot coals under the roots and produced a fire. As the smoke
arose, he blew it toward the doomed village, saying, meanwhile,
"Over there, over there, not here! To the other place! Do not
come back this way. We are good. Make these people sick. Kill
them, they are bad people." Then he returned to the dance house,
fasted for several days, and implored the spirits to bring sickness
and death to the other village but to protect his own.[127] The Hupa
of northern California, who largely resorted to magic in warfare
as in all other serious undertakings, had certain songs which
put the enemy into a sound slumber when a night attack was to
be made.[128] Among the Haida of Queen Charlotte Islands a
shaman accompanied every war party. It was his duty to find
a propitious time for launching the attack and, still more important,
to fight with and kill the souls of the enemy. The Haida were
persuaded that once a man's soul had been killed the death of his
body was a foregone conclusion.[129]

The magician in his official capacity often has charge of
aversive rites to ward off demonic assaults, witchcraft, or epidemic
sickness from the community. For these purposes the Bamang-
wato, a Bechuana tribe, rely on potent medicines which are con-
cocted by "the united wisdom" of the chief doctor and all his assistants. The medicines are conveyed outside the town and placed on
all the paths leading to it. Every year they must be renewed.[130] A
village of the Bathonga is surrounded by a fence, not as a protection against human enemies, for in the case of an attack the
natives' only resource is instant flight, but to guard against
witches, the dreaded *baloyi*. The fence, the main entrance, and
the threshold of the headman's hut were all treated with magical
drugs when first built, and from time to time a magician "revives"

the drugs by burning a powder on the road which enters the village. The smoke keeps witches away. It acts wonderfully, for if one of them should get inside a hut he (or she) would suddenly be seen there quite naked, apparently dreaming, seeing nothing, knowing nothing. Then the witch flies home.[131] When the cattle of the Bahima, a tribe of Uganda, were suffering from an epidemic, it was customary, by means of a ceremony, to transfer the disease to one member of the herd. The magician then killed it and sprinkled its blood over the other animals. The people belonging to the kraal were likewise lustrated. At the conclusion of the ceremony each person jumped over the carcase and all the animals were driven over it.[132] The Bullom and Timne of Sierra Leone make use of simple charms called "greegrees" to protect their settlements. A few rags attached to a pole and floating in the wind, an ax fixed in the trunk of a tree, an old pot placed on a stake, or an old pewter dish laid on the ground are effective to prevent the incursions of evil spirits or witches. It is a serious offense to remove or even touch one of these objects.[133] When an epidemic rages near a village of the Sherente, a Brazilian tribe, a medicine man can keep it away by tying together two wooden staves and placing these across all the paths which lead to the village. A good doctor is also able to take the disease in his hands and carry it off to the west, or he may cover it with a gourd bowl, or he may make it harmless by blowing on it.[134] During an epidemic in a Papago village the medicine man, holding a branch of cholla, walks all around the houses, and the men sing as he moves about. After being carried into every part of the village it is taken to the north, the direction of evil, and burned. The cholla is the thorniest cactus known to the Papago, hence they believe that a branch of it will surely catch and hold any evil influence in their neighborhood.[135] Sometimes among the Wisconsin Ojibwa a man believed to possess important powers through his fasting dream is warned by his tutelary spirit in a dream that a plague is about to descend upon the community. He then assembles the people, tells them of his experience, and dedicates to the spirits food and tobacco which the people have brought with them. Meanwhile a small human figure has been made in straw or hay and dressed in a minature man's costume. At the dreamer's signal the men proceed to shoot at it with their guns and then the women and children rush up to club it, cut it, and chop it to bits. The remains are collected, placed on a pile, and burned.[136]

The field of public magic thus includes all rites to manipulate and control natural forces for the common benefit; those which provide for the basic economic needs; those for the conservation of communal property and resources; those which deal with the internal and external enemies of the community; and, finally, those intended for its protection against the powers of evil. In primitive society the crises of individual life—birth, puberty, marriage, and death—also often call for the performance of magical rites in which the social group or its authorized representative takes part.

NOTES TO CHAPTER XI

[1] W. E. Roth, *North Queensland Ethnography Bulletin*, No. 5, pp. 8 f. Similarly, the Valman people about Berlinhafen, in what was formerly German New Guinea, believe that an excessive rain, which ruins their plantations, has been made by neighboring tribes with hostile intent (C. Schleiermacher, in *Globus*, LXXVIII [1900], 6). The natives of Bilibili Island are reputed to make wind by blowing with their mouths. In stormy weather the Bogadjim on the mainland say, "There are the Bilibili folk again blowing lustily" (Bernhard Hagen, *Unter den Papua's* [Wiesbaden, 1899], p. 269).

[2] Herbert Basedow, *The Australian Aboriginal* (Adelaide, 1923), p. 265.

[3] Sir Baldwin Spencer and F. J. Gillen, *Across Australia* (2d ed., London, 1912), II, 327.

[4] F. E. Williams, *Orokaiva Magic* (Oxford, 1928), p. 201.

[5] C. Keysser, "Aus dem Leben der Kaileute," in R. Neuhauss, *Deutsch Neu-Guinea* (Berlin, 1911), III, 159. In San Cristoval, one of the Solomon Islands, it is said that a famous ancestor of the Mwara clan, belated on his journey, caught the sun in a noose, "and now not only Mwara clan men but others may do the same (may keep the sun from setting) by tying a knot with a *tea* leaf round a tree by the roadside" (C. E. Fox, *The Threshold of the Pacific* [London, 1924], p. 263). If the sun is about to set, a belated traveler in Fiji makes a sign to the luminary as if beckoning him, takes a reed, knots it, and holds it firmly until he reaches his destination. The daylight will continue as long as he grasps the knotted reed; when he throws it away the night falls (A. M. Hocart, "Pierres magiques au Lau, Fiji," *Anthropos*, VI [1911], 726). For other instances of the widespread practice of sun retardation see R. B. Smyth, *The Aborigines of Victoria* (Melbourne, 1878), II, 334 (Bangerang); James Chalmers, *Pioneering in New Guinea* (London, 1887), p. 172 (Motu); E. Gottschling, in *Journal of the Anthropological Institute*, XXV (1905), 381 (Bavenda of the Transvaal); D. S. Fox, *ibid.*, LX (1930), 461 (Masai); A. G. O. Hodgson, *ibid.*, LXIII (1933), 162 (Achewa of Nyasaland); E. E. Evans-Pritchard, *Witchcraft, Oracles, and Magic among the Azande* (Oxford, 1937), pp. 468 f.; C. G. Seligman and Brenda Z. Seligman, *Pagan Tribes of the Nilotic Sudan* (London, 1932), p. 195 (Dinka); Lopez de Cogolludo, *Historia de Yucatán* (Madrid, 1688), Bk. IV, chap. iv.

[6] R. F. Fortune, *Sorcerers of Dobu* (London, 1932), p. 127.

[7] *Ibid.*, p. 213.

[8] Wilfred Powell, *Wanderings in a Wild Country* (London, 1883), p. 169.

[9] H. I. Hogbin, in *Oceania*, VI (1935–36), 262 f.

[10] A. B. Deacon, *Malekula, a Vanishing People in the New Hebrides* (London, 1934), p. 665. The clan magician has also the ability to produce a drought or a famine, but he will exercise his powers for harm only when his own group is warring with another clan (*loc. cit.*).

[11] Elsdon Best, "Maori Magic," *Transactions and Proceedings of the New Zealand Institute,* XXXIV (1901), 89.

[12] *Idem,* "Maori Religion and Mythology," *Dominion Museum Bulletin,* No. 10, p. 168.

[13] August Erdland, *Die Marshall-Insulaner* (Münster in Westfalen, 1914), pp. 320 f.

[14] W. W. Skeat, *Malay Magic* (London, 1900), pp. 107 f. (Selangor).

[15] A. R. Radcliffe-Brown, *The Andaman Islanders* (Cambridge, 1933), pp. 147, 178 f.

[16] George Whitehead, *In the Nicobar Islands* (London, 1924), p. 160.

[17] Henry Callaway, *The Religious System of the Amazulu* (London, 1870), pp. 375 ff.

[18] B. A. Marwick, *The Swazi* (Cambridge, 1940), p. 241.

[19] S. K. Lothrop, *The Indians of Tierra del Fuego* (New York, 1928), p. 97.

[20] James Mooney, "Sacred Formulas of the Cherokees," *Seventh Annual Report of the Bureau of Ethnology,* pp. 387 f.

[21] J. R. Swanton, "Religious Beliefs and Medical Practices of the Creek Indians," *Forty-second Annual Report of the Bureau of American Ethnology,* p. 631.

[22] R. F. Greenlee, "Medicine and Curing Practices of the Modern Florida Seminoles," *American Anthropologist,* XLVI (n.s., 1944), 325.

[23] Walter McClintock, *The Old North Trail* (London, 1910), p. 320.

[24] A. G. Morice, in *Proceedings of the Canadian Institute* (3d series, 1888–89), VII, 154.

[25] W. Bogoras, in *Memoirs of the American Museum of Natural History,* XI, 475.

[26] A. W. Howitt, *The Native Tribes of South-East Australia* (London, 1904), pp. 394 ff.

[27] W. E. Roth, *North Queensland Ethnography Bulletin,* No. 5, p. 10.

[28] Sir Baldwin Spencer and F. J. Gillen, *The Native Tribes of Central Australia* (London, 1899), p. 89.

[29] *Iidem, The Northern Tribes of Central Australia* (London, 1904), pp. 294 ff.

[30] A. C. Haddon, in *Reports of the Cambridge Anthropological Expedition to Torres Straits,* V, 350; VI, 194 ff. Not only were the *doiom* powerful in bringing rain but so also were the incantations which accompanied their use. During Haddon's visit to Mer in 1898 a very celebrated rain maker on the island started to recite to Mr. John Bruce some of these potent formulas. No sooner had he begun to do so than a short shower fell, though it was a clear night. "The next morning every one on the island knew why that shower had fallen" (VI, 201).

[31] F. E. Williams, *Papuans of the Trans-Fly* (Oxford, 1936), pp. 320 ff. For an earlier account by the same authority see "Rain Making on the River Morehead," *Journal of the Royal Anthropological Institute,* LIX (1929), 387 ff.

[32] R. H. Codrington, *The Melanesians* (Oxford, 1891), p. 200.

[33] George Turner, *Samoa* (London, 1884), pp. 344 f.

[34] S. C. Roy, "Magic and Witchcraft on the Chota-Nagpur Plateau," *Journal of the Royal Anthropological Institute*, XLIV (1914), 330. Cf. E. T. Dalton, *Descriptive Ethnology of Bengal* (Calcutta, 1872), p. 261.

[35] Monica Hunter, *Reaction to Conquest* (London, 1936), pp. 79 ff.

[36] J. H. Soga, *The Ama-Xosa: Life and Customs* (Lovedale, South Africa, 1931), p. 175.

[37] S. S. Dornan, "Rain Making in South Africa," *Bantu Studies,* III (1927–29), 186 f. The Bechuana believed that the ancestral ghosts were withholding rain because the chief or his subjects had failed to make the customary sacrifices or in other ways to accord them due honor. It was necessary, therefore, to force them by magical means to send rain. Lest they become aware of coercion being practiced on them, the rain maker was summoned stealthily and by night (*loc. cit.*).

[38] B. A. Marwick, *op. cit.,* pp. 218 ff.

[39] Mrs. E. J. Krige and J. D. Krige, *The Realm of a Rain Queen* (London, 1943), pp. 165 ff., 270 ff.

[40] A. W. Howitt, *op. cit.,* p. 398.

[41] Mrs. K. L. Parker, *The Euahlayi Tribe* (London, 1905), p. 48. On another occasion there came to the station an aboriginal of a tribe which had almost a monopoly of wind making. He wanted to marry a native girl there, but she refused him and told him to go home. He went, threatening to send a storm to wreck the station. "The storm came; the house escaped, but stable, store, and cellar were unroofed. I told my Black-but-Comely to kindly avoid such vehemently revengeful lovers for the future" (p. 82).

[42] Sir Baldwin Spencer and F. J. Gillen, *Across Australia* (2d ed.), I, 14 f. How among the Warramunga a weather magician shouted down the wind and produced at least a temporary calm is told elsewhere (II, 366).

An anthropologist from Adelaide University has described the rain-making ceremonies of the little-known Pitjendadjara tribe occupying the Mann Range on the border between South Australia and Central Australia. The ceremonies, which are forbidden to women and uninitiated youths, center around the *ringili,* a fragment of oval pearl shells found on the northwest coast of Australia and passed from tribe to tribe across the entire continent. The aborigines believe that the *ringili* contains the "essence" of water, and the rituals and songs which they employ are designed to release that essence, project it into the sky and cause it to form large clouds and finally rain. The rain-making ceremony witnessed by our authority was staged in August, in the middle of a long drought and about three months before the beginning of the normal rainy season in late November. The officiating magician predicted a downpour three to five days after his performance. "Him rain all right. Me been mak' em rain; him always come." It did come—on the fourth day and enough to leave water in the rock holes. See C. P. Mountford, in *National Geographic Magazine,* LXXXIX (1946), 101.

[43] E. W. Elkinton, *The Savage South Seas* (London, 1907), pp. 169 ff.

[44] J. G. Peristiany, *The Social Institutions of the Kipsigis* (London, 1939), p. 229.

[45] John Heckewelder, *History, Manners, and Customs of the Indian Nations Who Once Inhabited Pennsylvania and the Neighbouring States* (new ed., Philadelphia, 1876), pp. 236 ff. *Memoirs of the Historical Society of Pennsylvania,* Vol. XII.

[46] W. E. Roth, *Ethnological Studies among the North-West-Central Queens-*

land Aborigines (Brisbane, 1897), p. 168; idem, North Queensland Ethnography Bulletin, No. 5, p. 10.

[47] Tom Petrie's Reminiscences of Early Queensland (Brisbane, 1904), pp. 201 f.

[48] G. Horne and G. Aiston, Savage Life in Central Australia (London, 1924), p. 117.

[49] A. P. Elkin, "Totemism in North-Western Australia," Oceania, III (1932–33), 479.

[50] E. Clement, in Internationales Archiv für Ethnographie, XVI (1904), 6.

[51] A. C. Haddon, in Reports of the Cambridge Anthropological Expedition to Torres Straits, VI, 201 f.

[52] F. E. Williams, in Oceania, III (1932–33), 146 f.

[53] C. B. Humphreys, The Southern New Hebrides (Cambridge, 1926), p. 167.

[54] William Yate, An Account of New Zealand (London, 1835), p. 147.

[55] J. H. Soga, op. cit., p. 176.

[56] J. Tom Brown, Among the Bantu Nomads (London, 1926), p. 129.

[57] F. Spire, "Rain Making in Equatorial Africa," Journal of the African Society, No. 17 (1905), 18 f. Bari chiefs, who are the principal rain makers, always build their villages on the slopes of a fairly high hill. No doubt they know that hills attract clouds. If besought to make rain for a village the chief selects a day when clouds are visible and the wind is favorable (W. E. R. Cole, in Man, X [1910], 91).

[58] C. K. Meek, The Northern Tribes of Nigeria (London, 1925), II, 68.

[59] W. B. Grubb, An Unknown People in an Unknown Land (4th ed., London, 1914), p. 147.

[60] Walter McClintock, op. cit., p. 320.

[61] L. M. Turner, in Eleventh Annual Report of the Bureau of Ethnology, p. 196.

[62] J. W. Bilby, Among Unknown Eskimo (London, 1923), p. 204.

[63] F. E. Williams, "Rain Making on the River Morehead," Journal of the Royal Anthropological Institute, LIX (1929), 388.

[64] J. H. Soga, op. cit., p. 176.

[65] George Catlin, Letters and Notes on the Manners, Customs, and Condition of the North American Indians (2d ed., New York, 1842), Letter No. 19.

[66] M. Krieger, New Guinea (Berlin, 1899), p. 185.

[67] J. Tom Brown, op. cit., p. 132.

[68] John Roscoe, The Northern Bantu (Cambridge, 1915), p. 182.

[69] Idem, The Bakitara or Banyoro (Cambridge, 1923), p. 33.

[70] Franz Stuhlmann, Mit Emin Pascha ins Herz von Afrika (Berlin, 1894), p. 779, quoting Emin Pasha. After one such unsuccessful rain maker had been driven into exile it happened, a few days later, that rain fell in torrents. So the people recalled him and restored him to honor (Gaetano Casati, Ten Years in Equatorial Africa [London, 1891], I, 133).

[71] Henry Callaway, op. cit., pp. 391 f. (Zulu) ; K. R. Dundas, in Journal of the Royal Anthropological Institute, XLIII (1913), 48 f. (Wawanga of Kenya) ; F. Spire, "Rain Making in Equatorial Africa," Journal of the African Society, No. 17 (1905), 19 (Bari); C. K. Meek, Tribal Studies in Northern Nigeria (London, 1931), I, 315 (Sukur). According to Father Zuure an unsuccessful rain maker of the Barundi will sometimes voluntarily resign his office. He presents the chief, the judges, and the young people with pots of beer to in-

demnify them for the failure of his efforts and swears a solemn oath never to have anything more to do with the rain. It is believed that if he did so he would be struck by lightning (Bernard Zuure, *Croyances et pratiques religieuses des Barundi* [Brussels-Elizabethville, 1929], p. 150).

[72] Le Petit, in *The Jesuit Relations and Allied Documents* (Cleveland, 1896–1901), LXVIII, 153, 155.

[73] A. W. Howitt, *op. cit.*, pp. 154, 399 f., 798.

[74] Spencer and Gillen, *The Native Tribes of Central Australia*, pp. 167–211.

[75] The *intichiuma* rites, it has been pointed out, rest on a belief in the "pre-existence of spirits." Unless the rites are performed and the sacred places maintained as homes of the spirits, man and nature are separated, and neither man nor nature has any assurance of life in the future. See A. P. Elkin, "The Secret Life of the Australian Aborigines," *Oceania,* III (1932–33), pp. 130 ff. Among the Arunta these rites are also performed by the sun, evening star, and stone totemic groups and among the Unmatjera by those who have darkness (*quinnia*) for their totem. Flies and mosquitoes are also magically multiplied by means of the *intichiuma* in some of the Central tribes (Spencer and Gillen, *The Northern Tribes of Central Australia*, pp. 160 f.). Among the tribes in the Kimberley Division of Western Australia not only flies and mosquitoes, but also lice and snakes are multiplied. Some of the aborigines assert that these pests can be used against their enemies. When inedible and dangerous species of plants and animals thus come in for attention, perhaps the reason is to be found in the desire to perpetuate the existence of natural phenomena in the environment of the native "as he knows it." See Phyllis M. Kaberry, *Aboriginal Woman, Sacred and Profane* (London, 1939), pp. 204 f. See further *idem, in Oceania,* V (1934–35), 433 f. On the other hand, in the Waduman tribe of Northern Territory, when mosquitoes become very troublesome, the men of the mosquito totem have a ceremony to drive them away. Each performer wears two imitation mosquitoes, one fixed in his belt in front and the other behind. He dances about, clenches his fists, and moves his arms up and down, meanwhile singing loudly. The performance is supposed to kill the insects. See Sir Baldwin Spencer, *The Native Tribes of the Northern Territory of Australia* (London, 1914), pp. 324 f.

[76] See Bronislaw Malinowski, "The Economic Aspect of the 'Intichiuma' Ceremonies," in *Festkrift Tillägnad Edvard Westermarck* (Helsingfors, 1912), pp. 81–108.

[77] Spencer and Gillen, *The Northern Tribes of Central Australia,* pp. 283–319; Spencer, *The Native Tribes of the Northern Territory of Australia,* pp. 18 ff., 179, 197 ff. Among the Kimberley tribes women often attended the increase ceremonies for fish, wild honey, yams, fruits, and, in fact, for most of the foods for which they forage. In other tribes in this part of Western Australia women were responsible for the performance of the ceremonies (Phyllis M. Kaberry, *op. cit.*, p. 104).

[78] A. C. Haddon, in *Reports of the Cambridge Anthropological Expedition to Torres Straits,* V, 182 ff.; VI, 209 f.

[79] A. B. Deacon, *op. cit.*, p. 665.

[80] Bronislaw Malinowski, *Coral Gardens and Their Magic* (London, 1935), I, 62 ff. The Trobrianders also have private garden magic, consisting of certain formulas individually owned. These are used either by the owner or by an expert on the payment of a fee. It would seem, however, that such magic is relatively unimportant and inconspicuous, because of the feeling that the public formulas accomplish about all that can be expected of them. Moreover, in a community where gardening is such an extremely important activity, it would be dangerous for anyone to claim that his private magical activity could secure

for him results far surpassing those attained by his neighbors generally (I, 153, 472).

81 W. C. Groves, "Fishing Rites at Tabar," *Oceania,* IV (1933–34), 432–57.

82 S. Walleser, "Religiöse Anschauungen und Gebräuche von Jap (deutsche Südsee)," *Anthropos,* VIII (1913), 1055.

83 J. S. Kubary, *Ethnologische Beiträge zur Kenntnis der Karolinischen Archipels* (Leiden, 1895), pp. 127 f.

84 W. W. Skeat and C. O. Blagden, *Pagan Races of the Malay Peninsula* (London, 1906), I, 345 ff. For the ritual of the rice field as found among the Malays of Perak see Sir R. O. Winstedt, *Shaman, Saiva, and Sufi* (London, 1925), pp. 75–95. He points out that the magic controlling the growth of rice is often performed, not by a man but by a woman, "fitting midwife for the rice baby" (pp. 75 f.).

85 M. Fortes, "Communal Fishing and Fishing Magic in the Northern Territories of the Gold Coast," *Journal of the Royal Anthropological Institute,* LXVII (1937), 131–42.

86 Frank Russell, in *Twenty-sixth Annual Report of the Bureau of American Ethnology,* pp. 256 ff.

87 See Bronislaw Malinowski, " 'Kula'; the Circulating Exchange of Valuables in the Archipelagoes of Eastern New Guinea," *Man,* XX (1920), 97–105; *idem, Argonauts of the Western Pacific* (London, 1922), especially pp. 81–104, 509–18. See also R. F. Fortune, *op. cit.,* pp. 200–34. The magical ritual of the *kula,* as found in Dobu, differs markedly from that in the Trobriands (p. 209).

88 Gunnar Landtman, "Papuan Magic in the Building of Houses," *Acta Academiæ Aboënsis, Humaniora,* I, 5 (1920), 1–28. After the clubhouse has been completed various objects are placed under the great center post. These include the eyebrows, fingernails, and tongues of slain enemies. When the men are on the warpath the eyebrows will reveal to them the foe; the fingernails will help them to seize hold of the foe; and the tongues have reference to the shrieks of the dying foe (*idem, The Kiwai Papuans of British New Guinea* [London, 1927], p. 13).

89 A. C. Haddon, *Head-Hunters, Black, White, and Brown* (London, 1901), pp. 270 ff.

90 J. H. Holmes, *In Primitive New Guinea* (London, 1924), pp. 235 f.

91 George Brown, *Melanesians and Polynesians* (London, 1910), p. 126.

92 J. [S.] Kubary, *Ethnographische Beiträge zur Kenntniss der Karolinichen Inselgruppe und Nachbarschaft,* Heft I, *Die socialen Einrichtungen der Pelauer* (Berlin, 1895), pp. 85 f.

93 T. J. Alldridge, *The Sherbro and Its Hinterland* (London, 1901), p. 133.

94 Dorothy Cator, *Everyday Life among the Head-Hunters and Other Experiences from East to West* (London, 1905), p. 192. See also B. Wallis, "The 'Poro' Society of the Mendi," *Journal of the African Society,* No. 14 (1905), 188.

95 F. W. Butt-Thompson, *West African Secret Societies* (London, 1929), p. 141.

96 Bronislaw Malinowski, in *Transactions of the Royal Society of Australia,* XXXIX (1915), 586.

97 *Idem, Coral Gardens and Their Magic,* I, 301 ff. The Trobrianders have also a protective taboo to prevent the theft of ripening fruits or nuts so far from the village that they cannot be watched. A small parcel of medicated substance is placed on a stick, near or on the tree, and a spell is recited by the magician. Anyone who touched the fruit would be stricken with a disease. Sometimes a

wood spirit is also invited to reside on the stick and substance and to guard the fruit. This is the only form of Trobriand magic in which personal agency is ever invoked *(idem, Argonauts of the Western Pacific*, pp. 425 f.).

⁹⁸ Emma Hadfield, *Among the Natives of the Loyalty Group* (London, 1920), pp. 65 f.

⁹⁹ Thomas Williams, *Fiji and the Fijians* (3d ed., London, 1870), pp. 198 f.

¹⁰⁰ W. H. R. Rivers, *The History of Melanesian Society* (Cambridge, 1914), I, 388 f.

¹⁰¹ James Cook and James King, *A Voyage to the Pacific Ocean* (London, 1784), I, 410 f.

¹⁰² Eyriaud des Vergnes, in *Revue maritime et coloniale*, LII (1877), 730. The Marquesans had a regular closed season for the bonito (J. A. Moerenhout, *Voyages aux îles du grand océan* [Paris, 1837], I, 531).

¹⁰³ Otto Finsch, *Ethnologische Erfahrungen und Belegstücke aus der Südsee* (Wien, 1893), pp. 305 f. *Separat Abgedrukt aus den Annalen des K. K. Natur-historischen Hofsmuseums in Wien*, Band III.

¹⁰⁴ Sir Baldwin Spencer and F. J. Gillen, *The Native Tribes of Central Australia*, pp. 449 f.

¹⁰⁵ A. P. Elkin, *The Australian Aborigines* (Sydney, 1938), pp. 210 f.

¹⁰⁶ J. W. M. Whiting, "The Frustration Complex in Kwoma Society," *Man*, XLIV (1944), 142.

¹⁰⁷ H. I. Hogbin, "Mana," *Oceania*, VI (1935–36), 252 f.

¹⁰⁸ Thomas Williams, *op. cit.*, p. 210.

¹⁰⁹ J. H. Hutton, *The Angami Nagas* (London, 1921), p. 241. Sometimes these Naga also observe a communal rite *(kenna* or *penna)* which has the power of making the person named as its subject grievously ill or even of bringing about his death (pp. 193, 241).

¹¹⁰ C. M. Doke, *The Lambas of Northern Rhodesia* (London, 1931), pp. 314 f.

¹¹¹ Godfrey Wilson, "An African Morality," *Afrika*, IX (1936), 85 ff.; *idem*, "An Introduction to Nyakyusa Society," *Bantu Studies*, X (1936), 277, 286 f.

¹¹² Louis Tauxier, *Religion, mœurs, et coutumes des Agnis de la Côte-d'I-voire* (Paris, 1932), pp. 83, 87.

¹¹³ H. P. Steensby, in *Meddelelser om Grønland*, XXXIV (1910), 366 f.

¹¹⁴ Franz Boas, in *Bulletin of the American Museum of Natural History*, XV, 117 f.

¹¹⁵ Gunnar Landtman, "The Magic of the Kiwai Papuans in Warfare," *Journal of the Royal Anthropological Institute*, XLVI (1916), 322–33.

¹¹⁶ Bronislaw Malinowski, "War and Weapons among the Natives of the Trobriand Islands," *Man*, XX (1920), 10–12.

¹¹⁷ Elsdon Best, "Spiritual Concepts of the Maori," *Journal of the Polynesian Society*, IX (1900), 181.

¹¹⁸ *Idem*, "Notes on the Art of War as Conducted by the Maori of New Zealand," *Journal of the Polynesian Society*, XII (1903), 72.

¹¹⁹ H. E. Mabille, in *Journal of the African Society*, No. 20 (1906), 352.

¹²⁰ H. A. Junod, *The Life of a South African Tribe* (2d ed., London, 1927), I, 464 ff.

¹²¹ C. W. Hobley, *Bantu Beliefs and Magic* (London, 1922), p. 186.

¹²² John Roscoe, *The Soul of Central Africa* (London, 1922), pp. 217 f.

¹²³ C. G. Seligman and Brenda Z. Seligman, *Pagan Tribes of the Nilotic Sudan* (London, 1932), p. 195.

[124] Rafael Karsten, "Blood Revenge, War, and Victory Feasts among the Jibaro Indians of Eastern Ecuador," *Bulletin of the Bureau of American Ethnology*, No. 79, pp. 22 f.

[125] Alice C. Fletcher and Francis La Flesche, in *Twenty-seventh Annual Report of the Bureau of American Ethnology*, pp. 421 ff.

[126] G. B. Grinnell, "The Great Mysteries of the Cheyenne," *American Anthropologist* (n.s., 1910), XII, 570 ff.

[127] R. B. Dixon, in *Bulletin of the American Museum of Natural History*, XVII, 331.

[128] P. E. Goddard, in *University of California Publications in American Archaeology and Ethnology*, I, 63.

[129] J. R. Swanton, in *Memoirs of the American Museum of Natural History*, VIII, 40.

[130] John Mackenzie, *Ten Years North of the Orange River* (Edinburgh, 1871), pp. 383 f.

[131] H. A. Junod, *op. cit.* (2d ed.), I, 311; II, 522.

[132] John Roscoe, in *Journal of the Royal Anthropological Institute*, XXXVII (1907), 111.

[133] Thomas Winterbottom, *An Account of the Native Africans in the Neighbourhood of Sierra Leone* (London, 1803), I, 258 f.

[134] Curt Nimuendajú, *The Serente* (Los Angeles, 1942), p. 90.

[135] Ruth M. Underhill, *Singing for Power; the Song Magic of the Papago Indians of Southern Arizona* (Berkeley, 1938), p. 146.

[136] Robert Ritzenthaler, "The Ceremonial Destruction of Sickness by the Wisconsin Chippewa," *American Anthropologist* (n.s., 1945), XLVII, 320–22.

CHAPTER XII

PRIVATE MAGIC

Private magic may be undertaken by anyone who knows the proper procedures and techniques, but with the development of professional practitioners ever greater reliance will be placed upon them to do what the ordinary person comes to regard as being beyond his powers. While public magic is often the inalienable property of a clan, secret society, or some other subdivision of a community, private magic is frequently owned by individuals, who cherish it as their most valuable possession, bequeath it to their descendants, or dispose of it (usually for an ample consideration) to outsiders.

The field embraced by private magic is very extensive, for the occasions are few when man does not seek its aid to promote his welfare, gratify his passions, or avert the ills, real and imaginary, which invest him. All the basic activities of the food quest—hunting, fishing, herding, farming—have their magical accompaniment. The great crises of human life, which come with birth, puberty, marriage, and death, are magic ridden. There is private magic for inspiring or alienating affection, for the protection of property, for success in warfare, for controlling the phenomena of nature, for the cure of sickness and disease, for counteracting the malicious designs of sorcerers, and for the exorcism of evil spirits.

Erotic magic is practiced by most primitive peoples. Among some Queensland tribes a man who would attract a woman paints himself with red clay. He also smears over the front of his body a preparation made of the inner bark of a certain tree mixed with charcoal. The peculiar scent which he thus acquires is supposed to be quite overpowering when the woman in question sees and smells him. A man will also employ the bull-roarer (a magical instrument of many uses) as a love charm. He goes out at night, some distance from the camp, and swings it at intervals. The curious sounds thus produced are sure to arouse passion in the object of his affections.[1] The Central Australian tribes have certain well-recognized methods of obtaining a wife by magic. In all cases, however, the woman must belong to the proper class into which the man may lawfully marry. If his magic proves successful, he and his friends will still have to fight the man whose wife he has stolen, together with *his* friends. Use of this magic is consequently a fruitful source of quarrels within the local group. The woman, too, runs a good deal of risk, for if caught in the act of elopement she will be severely punished if not killed by her outraged spouse. In view of the extremely cruel treatment which she then receives it is really a matter of wonder, declare our authorities, that she ever consents to an elopement. Sometimes the cases are reversed, and it is the woman who seeks by magical arts to win the affection of the man.[2] The women of some of the Kimberley tribes (Western Australia) have love songs which they sing while their husbands are absent on a journey and also during menstruation and pregnancy, when sexual relations are forbidden. The songs are believed to induce continence on the husband's part. From time to time the women hold secret corroborees in which the songs and dances represent or symbolize the whole procedure of courtship, culminating in that of coitus. The actors are young women, while the older ones serve as assistants and provide the vocal accompaniment. The effect of the performance is to turn the men to amatory thoughts, arousing sexual desire in husbands and initiating or perpetuating love affairs on the part of bachelors. The men know that such a corroboree is being held but may not witness it. Should they do so they would fall ill. Moreover, their presence would prejudice, if not nullify, its magical efficacy.[3]

The eastern islanders of Torres Straits relied in their love charms on the subtle associations of scent. A young man, having dried and burnt certain plants, prepared a paste by mixing the ashes with charcoal and anointed himself with it. At the same time he thought as intently as possible about the girl, saying to himself, "You come! You come!" Another charm was a piece of black lava carved in the form of a penis. This would be rubbed with the paste of ashes and oil and then wrapped in the shredded leaves of the sago palm. The leaves of the sago were considered to be very efficacious, for from them women made their petticoats. To make success doubly certain he would spread the paste on each temple, think intently about the girl, and recite an appropriate spell whenever he saw her. She was now bound to go to him.[4]

Among the Kiwai, a Papuan tribe, parents provide their children with love medicines. These are especially necessary for boys. Girls, being much sought after, have no difficulty in getting married. A son begins to be doctored immediately after his birth. When he grows up and engages in public dances the parents help him to impress the girls by placing medicines in the ornaments he wears, especially in the long feather stuck in his headdress. It sways to and fro with his movements and beckons the girls to come to him.[5] An Orokaiva man knows how to punish the girl who has turned him down in favor of a rival. The story is told of a revengeful lover who found in the bush certain blue berries which always grow two by two together. These he crushed and mixed with lime and then smeared the pigment thus produced on his face—a strip on each cheek. He now made it his business to encounter the girl (who by this time had been married to the other party). All unsuspecting she looked at him and saw the two tell-tale streaks. The young man immediately retired to the seclusion of the bush, scraped off the paint, wrapped a leaf about it, and stuffed it into a hole in one of the large bulging nests of a certain species of ant. His revenge was now certain. He knew that when the girl became pregnant her figure would swell tremendously even as the ant nest, and that when her time came she would be delivered of twins to her intense chagrin but to his untold gratification.[6]

In Dobu Island there are many forms of erotic magic, both spells and charms. According to the native theory, desire for the opposite sex would not exist were these not employed to arouse and stimulate it. Men and women mate only because they are constantly exerting occult power over each other. All the magic they use has a close association with animistic beliefs, for the operator's soul is exhorted to go forth in the night and influence that of his beloved. A man tries out his magic at first on a disengaged maiden; if successful with her, he experiments further by attempting to seduce another man's wife.[7] In Goodenough Island the simplest way of gaining a girl's affection is to acquire her grass skirt. If the youth manages to steal it he binds it about his waist, goes into the water to bathe, and sings a magical song. Then he returns the skirt to the girl's hut. When she puts it on and wears it she will feel her heart go out to her enchanter. Both the boy and the girl resort to magic to ensure the abiding affection of the loved one. The boy will privately sing over the tobacco he gives his fiancée to smoke or the betel nut they chew together, and the girl will do the same. Both know, of course, that these objects have been infused with occult power. Such knowledge would seem to be essential to the success of the procedure.[8]

For the Trobrianders, as for neighboring Melanesian peoples, erotic magic is the only successful means of wooing. If properly executed and not counteracted it cannot fail. The man or woman who is its object may not yield to the first few rites or spells but must do so when all of them have been put into operation consecutively. Their cumulative effect is irresistible. The lover gathers and prepares certain leaves full of virtue for his purpose, rubs them over his body, and, having recited a spell, throws them into the sea. This performance will induce sweet dreams about him in the girl's mind. The natives say, "As the leaves will be tossed by the waves, and as they move with the sea up and down, so the inside (the belly) of the girl will heave." If she does not surrender readily, stronger magic is employed. A little food or a betel nut or some tobacco is magically treated and given to her. She will not refuse the gift, even though she suspects the motive of the giver. She eats this *douceur,* the magic enters into her "inside," and moves her mind in the desired direction. But if still obdurate, she can be worked upon through the senses of touch and smell, by smearing aromatic oil upon her body or by putting the oil on a piece of cigarette paper (in the olden days on a flower), so that the smoke or scent may enter her nostrils. The all-powerful mint plant, the symbol of charm and seduction, the herb which plays a central part in the myth of the origins of love, can also be used in the same way to make her cognizant that magic is being wrought upon her and to overcome her final scruples. The recital of appropriate spells accompanies all these proceedings. For the magic to alienate affection the Trobrianders have a special name, *bulubwalata,* a black art which can be used with equal efficacy to send away an enemy's pigs into the bush. It will be employed by a man with a grudge against a girl or, more often, against her paramour or her husband. If of the mild variety, the girl leaves her lover or husband and returns to her own village. But if it is strong magic, administered in large amounts, with minute accuracy in spell and rite, and with scrupulous observance of the necessary taboos on the part of the operator, the girl will run away to the bush, lose her way, and perhaps disappear forever. The evil thus wrought cannot be undone by the victim. Should the evildoer repent of his action, he can resort to the "fetching back" formula which, when recited toward the various points of the compass, so that its occult power may reach the girl wherever she may be in the bush, has the result of restoring her to husband or lover and bringing happiness to a broken household.[9]

In New Ireland a man finds most use for erotic magic in his extramarital affairs. It is also customary for him to direct it toward a newly acquired wife just before consummation of the marriage. Underlying this magic is the theory that passion and all emotion reside in the belly. The love spell, when recited, first causes a woman's belly to become agitated and then her whole body, so that she feels an overpowering desire for the man. She may be miles away, but that night she dreams fondly of him. Next morning she sits in a kind of lethargy; refuses to eat, smoke, talk or work; and believes she will die unless she can go to her lover. Finally, unable to stand it any longer, she seeks him out. A lover may employ spells and charms to revenge himself upon a mistress who has jilted him. They will cause the death of her child, if she is pregnant, and sometimes her own death as well. Women, who use erotic magic far less than men, also rely on spells, but these are not concerned with the belly, the seat of love. A girl will recite a spell over her straw apron or over a banana which she then gives to the loved one to eat, in the hope of drawing him to her side. Sometimes she merely expresses a wish that her dancing may be powerful enough to attract him.[10] Erotic magic as practiced in the New Hebrides seems to be notably effective, presumably because the woman, toward whom it is directed, almost always knows that she is its object. Some impulsive gesture on the man's part is enough to convince her that he desires her.[11]

The Maori armory of *karakia* included spells which a man used to make a girl accede to his proposal of marriage and to win back a wife who had left him. Women resorted to similar spells. When two people loved each other very much but might not marry, because of parental objections, the man might seek out a *tohunga*, skilled in the magical art, and undergo a rite which would "soften the pain of separation" and "withdraw the love from the heart."[12]

The Bornean peoples, with the exception of the Kayan and the Kenyah, have frequent recourse to erotic magic. The charms employed are in most cases odorous substances. Thus a Sea Dayak will string together a necklace of certain strongly scented seeds and carry it about with him. When his fancy falls on a girl he puts it under her pillow or tries to persuade her to wear it. If she consents, he reckons her half won. A Klemantan makes much use of a scented oil with which he secretly anoints the girl's garments or her other belongings.[13] In Alor, one of the Lesser Sunda Islands, a woman feels sure of keeping her husband's love if she puts into the bottom of the food pot shreds of her loin-cloth, some of her pubic or axillary hair, or clippings from her nails.[14]

Malay books of magic contain innumerable spells for success in love, for securing conjugal fidelity, for beautifying the person, and even for restoring one's lost youth. Some of these spells clearly belong to the realm of the black art, for they attempt to abduct or in some way "get at" another person's soul, in order to influence it in the operator's favor, or, on the other hand, to inflict some harm on the victim. A recipe for sowing dissension between husband and wife directs you to make two wax figures resembling the persons and to hold them face to face, meanwhile repeating three times a formula which describes the woman as a goat and the man as a tiger. "If Fatimah is face to face with Muhammad, she will be as a goat facing a tiger." Next, lay the figures on the ground on each side of you but back to back, burn incense, and repeat the formula twenty-two times over the man and twenty-two times over the woman. Then put the figures together back to back, wrap them in seven thicknesses of certain leaves, tie them up with thread of seven colors wound about them seven times, repeat the formula once more, and bury them. After seven days dig on the spot. If you find them your magic has failed; if they have disappeared the couple will surely be divorced.[15]

Among the Baiga, an aboriginal tribe of the Central Provinces of India, magic forms an essential part of love-making. A girl is delighted when a man resorts to a love charm; it proves the seriousness of his attentions. Its effect is to make her restless as "parched grain in the pan," uneasy as "a fish stranded in a dried-up stream," wretched as "wood being devoured by white ants." But erotic magic, as indeed all dealing with occult power, is highly dangerous. Disastrous consequences are likely to follow mistakes in the ritual or failure to remove a love charm after it has been successfully used. There are love charms so powerful that if left too long on a woman they may drive her to eat her own children.[16]

Many varieties of love medicines are found among the Bakgatla of the Bechuanaland Protectorate. Adolescents still fresh in their amorous career consider them to be very effective. A girl will sometimes obtain from a professional magician a medicine to retain her lover. Some of it she burns in a potsherd, letting the smoke bathe her face and calling, meanwhile, on the boy by name; the rest she smears on her face whenever he visits her or puts into the food she gives him. The doctors also have medicines by whose use a wife with an unfaithful husband can bewitch her rival or bring back the erring spouse to her side. He in turn can procure medicines which will not only pacify his wife but can make her friendly with his concubine. Polygamists with relatively peaceful households are almost always supposed to possess medicines of this potent character. We are told of a doctor who used his own medicines so effectively that whenever he scolded one wife the other always took her part.[17]

A jealous Yoruba wife puts a medicine in her husband's food so that he will no longer care for another woman. It is "one hundred per cent" effective. He dreads it greatly, for sickness and even death may follow its administration. Sometimes, again, she gives a medicine to a wife whom he favors more than herself. This causes the "other woman" to lose her attractiveness.[18]

In Morocco (Mogador) a woman who has lost her husband's love by failing to give him a child goes outdoors some night when the moon is shining, dishevels her hair, takes off her clothes, and sits down upon them by the side of a trough filled with water. Then she says, "O Moon! If you are in love and I am nice-looking, come to me." By this invocation she hopes to induce the moon to impart to the water occult power, and this power she will use in a fertility rite.[19]

Among the Guiana Indians the women all have their *bina* (charms) for managing the opposite sex. An Arawak girl will take a plant, usually a caladium, bathe with a leaf of it or carry it about with her, and then, without being seen, rub it over her lover's hammock. Or she may rub her own hands with it and then touch his. If this procedure is carried out properly and the man remains in ignorance of what has been done, he will never have any desire to transfer his affections elsewhere. The male Arawak brushes his leaf charm over his girl's face or shoulders to prevent her from showing a partiality for other men. The Caribs have similar practices. Charms which use the parts of animals are also found among these tribes. Thus when a woman wants another's husband she puts wasp eggs into his drink, a device which will make him leave his wife and go off with her. In great demand are the skin and feathers of a certain bird, which the Indians think fascinates its comrades and leads them a weary dance through the bush. The happy possessor of such relics will be sure to have a train of lovers and followers.[20]

The Cherokee Indians employ a number of spells affecting almost every aspect of their sexual life. So powerful are these spells that a man who has them at his disposal need never be long without a wife. Having gained her by magic he keeps her by magic. If she is attractive and likely to be won over by the spells of male rivals, he recites over her at night, while she sleeps, a formula which affirms the solidarity existing between them, and at the same time he anoints her breast with his spittle. To be effective this must be done for four nights in succession. But sometimes, in spite of the husband's efforts, she will be drawn away from him by a rival's superior magic. Some spells for this purpose are intended to separate husband and wife. Each is likened to a noxious animal and a repulsion is thus set up between the conjugal pair. The wife will then leave her husband, unless he resorts successfully to counter magic. When a rejected suitor's love turns to hatred he will use magic making her lonesome and repulsive to all men. Or he may continue to ply her with spells and finally succeed in having her fall head over heels in love with him and go through many undignified acts to show her passion. Thus he gets his revenge. Cherokee beauty magic is illustrated by the spells to enhance a person's physical charms. Ugly men often resort to them in order to get a wife.[21]

Among the Omaha, Ponca, and other Siouan tribes sorcerers will pay a high price for a small quantity of the catamenial discharge of a virgin. This is mixed with a love potion. If administered to a man, "he cannot help courting the woman, even when he knows that he does not love her."[22]

A Haida lover fasts, collects a certain kind of medicine, rubs it upon his palms, and then puts it on the person or the clothing of the loved one. For this procedure to be effective he has to undertake an elaborate series of observances. After fasting for several days he goes to a creek, doffs his clothes, and looks for spruce cones. If he finds two old cones lying near each other, he takes one in each hand, pronounces his own name and that of the woman, and declares whether he merely loves her or would marry her. This statement must be repeated four times in an increasingly loud tone of voice. He then enters the creek until the water comes up to his heart, puts the cones upstream some distance, and lets them float toward him, again takes them in his hands, and again utters aloud what he wants. After three repetitions of this act he goes into the woods, makes a pillow, places the cones on it, and covers them with leaves, meanwhile mentioning his wish four times more. All this done, he returns home, breaks his fast, and waits for the woman's message of love.[23]

This constant reliance on erotic magic will seem astonishing to those who think of primitive peoples as incapable of real passion and insensible to the attractions of the opposite sex. Such magic obviously belongs to the white variety, when expected and welcomed by its object, whether man or woman; just as obviously it is black if the contrary holds true. Not less dark in shade, because ministering to disreputable ends, is the magic employed by a jilted lover to revenge himself upon his inamorata or, again, to cause dissension between husband and wife and break up a happy family. On the whole, erotic magic seems to have a predominantly nefarious character.

Just as magic is frequently employed to enforce certain prohibitions (taboos) on community property, so it finds constant use to safeguard goods and chattels, domestic animals, growing crops, fruit trees, and other personal possessions. These taboos may be imposed directly by the owner, or else a chief, a secret society, or a professional magician may be called upon to establish them. Their existence is usually indicated by some simple sign which is readily understood by the passer-by. They operate automatically; sooner or later the threatened evil descends on the hapless offender; he and his suffer sharp and condign punishment.

The simplest form of these prohibitions involves the use for protective purposes of something identified with a man's personality. On the principle of *pars pro toto,* whatever is so used has all the occult power of its owner. When a Queensland native is about to go away from the camp, leaving there his food and weapons, he sometimes urinates near these possessions. No one will touch them and he can be sure of finding them intact on his return.[24] Spittle is used in the same way. In the D'Entrecasteaux Islands a man expectorates on his fruit trees, making his saliva red by chewing betel nut; then bloody postules will form on the head and body of a thief and he may even die.[25] When the Barotse, a South African tribe, "do not want a thing touched they spit on straws and stick them all about the object."[26] Among the Bakongo "if a person is called away from his meal, he will pretend to spit on it, and no one will dare to touch the food while he is away."[27]

Charms of various sorts are often used alone for the protection of private property. Some of the Queensland aborigines hang up a bull-roarer over anything they wish to secure from molestation. A baby's navel-string can also be employed to place a taboo on yams and other objects, because the natives think that anything brought to the spot where a newly born child is lying or which it is allowed to touch becomes affected with its occult power.[28] By the eastern islanders of Torres Straits a reddish powder called *kamer*, found in rotten driftwood, was believed to be very potent in magic, especially as a means of protecting gardens from thieves. When bananas or other foodstuffs were ripe, the owner of a garden would secretly prepare *kamer* and doctor one of his trees. "As the thief was not certain which tree had been poisoned, he was afraid to risk it and so left the food alone."[29] In New Georgia, one of the Solomon Islands, the preventive against all trespass and robbery is the erection of property signs called *hope*. At the entrance to his coconut plantation the owner will set up a single stick, three or four feet in length, with its top cleft for a short distance. In the opening are placed a bunch of dead leaves, a piece of fern root, and a wisp of grass. Sometimes the stick will be crowned with a skull, part of an ant's nest, or a large shell. The would-be thief, gazing on this complicated structure, has a picture of the fate in store for him: according to the emblem of sanctity exhibited will he wither away like the grass, become as hopelessly moribund as the original owner of the skull, or perish like the ants which once lived in the nest or the fish which once occupied the shell.[30] The Samoans made extensive use of property signs to prevent stealing from plantations and fruit trees. Any sort of stick suspended horizontally from a tree indicated the owner's wish that a thief who touched the tree might have a disease running right across his body and remaining there until he died. A few pieces of clam shell buried in the ground and surmounted by some reeds tied together at the top warned a prospective thief that he would be afflicted with ulcerous sores. Another object of terror was the white shark sign, made by plaiting a coconut leaf in the form of a shark. When suspended from a tree this was tantamount to an expressed imprecation that the culprit might be devoured by a white shark the next time he went fishing.[31]

Spells are often used in association with charms. Where the belief in the potency of spells is emphasized, their simple recital may be held to be adequate for protective purposes. Among some of the Massim tribes of southeastern New Guinea taboos of private property are indicated by a particular kind of sign. This has been smeared with a certain medicine and set up by an old man who knows the correct formulas to recite at the time. Anyone who stole an object so marked would become sick. The owner himself would suffer as severely as a stranger. He would not think of taking any fruit from a coconut tree thus protected until the taboo had been lifted by the man who imposed it.[32] Among the Mailu, when an owner of a coconut tree suspects that his nuts will be stolen, he utters a spell and binds the nuts together with some of their own fiber. A man who steals them or intends to do so gets boils and swellings all over his body and eventually dies. Banana trees and taro patches are similarly safeguarded.[33]

In some parts of the Melanesian area all or nearly all the diseases recognized by the natives are supposed to be caused by the violation of taboos, with which spells of great power and virulence are associated. There is a special spell for each disease. In Dobu Island every man and woman knows at least one; sometimes as many as five will be known to a single person. Taboos, reinforced by such spells, are commonly used to protect fruit trees situated away from the village. It would be quite out of the question to taboo a tree in the village, for everyone would contract a disease by mere propinquity to the tabooed object. Before a man dares take the fruit from his own private tree he must first nullify the effect of the spell, thus removing the taboo.[34] Similarly in Wogeo, one of the Schouten Islands, most diseases are ascribed to violation of taboos laid on fruit trees. If a man knows what particular kind of spell has been used in imposing the taboo, as in most cases he does, he can tell precisely what disease will afflict him if he violates the taboo.[35] In Eddystone Island, one of the Solomons, there is the same definite connection of disease with the infraction of a taboo (*kenjo*) on the fruit of certain trees. Many varieties of *kenjo* are recognized, each one with special rites for its imposition and removal. The rites, as a rule, can be performed only by the man or the small group of men owning the variety of *kenjo* in question. He and his fellows are consequently the only people who are able to treat the disease produced by the infraction of that particular taboo.[36]

Among the Maori the first step in the imposition of a property taboo was to set up a post on the edge of the forest or the bank of the stream to be safeguarded. A lock of hair or a bunch of grass was attached to the post. The officiating magician then recited a spell "to sharpen the teeth" of the sign (*rahui*), "that it might destroy man." A taboo without a spell could be imposed by a chief only, and its observance was a tribute to his prestige. A chief would set up a post and hang an old garment on it as a sign of the prohibition; sometimes this was proclaimed simply by word of mouth.[37] An early authority on the Maori enumerates among the things which might be made taboo, articles left in a house not occupied by its owner, a house containing seeds, a canoe lying on the beach, a tree selected for future working up into a canoe, and a sweet potato (*kumara*) plantation.[38]

Similar prohibitions are commonly imposed in the East Indies, and there is an extensive reliance upon them in Africa. Slaves from West Africa seem to have carried the private property taboo to the New World, where it is still found among the Negroes of Surinam. It was not unknown, also, to some of the aboriginal Indian tribes. Thus over a large part of the aboriginal world beliefs and practices of a magical nature have often been used with success to buttress a system of individual ownership.

By the primitive man health is presumed to be his normal state. He would live indefinitely, in complete possession of his faculties, were it not for hostile influences and agencies which beset him from the cradle to the grave. It is true that some Australian aborigines can understand a death caused by an accident that they can see or by physical violence as in a fight, and that ordinary aches and pains, such as colds, sore eyes, headaches, and festering wounds, are endured by them without inquiring into their origin. By the Melanesians common complaints, fever and ague, for instance, are accepted as coming in the course of nature. The natives of South Africa consider some minor forms of sickness to be "only sickness and nothing more," for which an explanation may or may not be forthcoming. An American Indian views quite rationally some ailments accompanied by pain, debility, loss of appetite, or fever, if the cause of these symptoms has been observed in certain natural conditions such as extremes of cold and heat, and if no complications arise. But in the lower culture, generally, any serious and protracted illness, especially if of a rare or mysterious sort; any accident not obviously due to the patient's carelessness or stupidity; and any death, save that of a very young child or a very old person, will be attributed to human or non-human agency. By some primitive peoples every kind of illness, every accident, and all deaths are so regarded.[39]

The explanations offered under such circumstances are various. Sorcery may have been practiced, sometimes unintentionally but more often with malice prepense. A spiritual being may have been responsible for the visitation. A dread taboo, carrying with it an automatic penalty, may have been violated. One's soul may have been lost, perhaps by reason of its natural propensity for wandering away from the body. Still another widespread theory is that of demoniacal possession, especially for acute mental disorders. Disease and death, again, are sometimes vaguely conceived as a sort of miasma or atmospheric poison, spreading a fatal influence far and wide, so that when one person has been struck down other persons are likely to suffer the same fate. If sorcery is regarded as the responsible agency, any one of these explanations is likely to be advanced. For the sorcerer, in addition to following the usual procedures and techniques of black magic, may cause a man to break a taboo, or steal his soul, or summon an evil spirit to lodge in his body, or send a pestilence which brings low an entire community. There are no limits to the sorcerer's capacity for wickedness.[40]

The primary task of the doctor, if a professional magician, will be to discover the cause of the complaint, sometimes by observation of its symptoms, but more commonly by an inquiry into the patient's deeds and misdeeds and supplemented, in the more difficult cases, by recourse to divination. If magic has been practiced, counter magic must be employed to nullify it. An angered spiritual being must in some way be appeased. When a taboo has been broken, the violator must undergo a rite of purification. An errant soul must be sought for, recovered, and replaced. Should the patient be possessed, resort must be had to exorcism. The doctor either works alone or with the help of the spirits under his control. He engages in what is regarded as a contest between his own occult power, aided perhaps by that of his spirits, and the power of the opposing magician, who may also rely on spiritual assistance. In some parts of North America, as among the Navaho Indians, there is a marked development of healing ceremonials, often conducted by several doctors, who rely on songs, dances, and other rituals of a most elaborate character. In such cases a ceremonial is supposed to cure by virtue of its inherent power or through the help of the spirits and gods. Not only the patient but also other members of the community may have a share in a "life-giving" performance of this character and partake of its benefits.

Sometimes a doctor, conscious of his powerlessness over certain ailments, will not treat them. Among the tribes of southern Queensland a doctor would not try to suck out the crystals which had supposedly been inserted in a man's body by some enemy if he considered the case to be hopeless.[41] Arunta medicine men "waste no antics" on senile decay.[42] A Sea Dayak *manang* refuses to treat cholera or smallpox.[43] Doctors among the Jivaro and Canelos Indians of Ecuador believe themselves to be completely powerless against smallpox, scarlet fever, dysentery, and venereal infections. All these diseases have been introduced by contact with white men.[44] Navaho doctors have often tried, but without success, to make new magical songs for the white man's tuberculosis, measles, influenza, and syphilis.[45] A Cherokee medicine man readily admits that he cannot possibly cure diseases of an infectious and contagious nature. These are reputed to be imported by the white people and "more specifically" caused by the white doctors.[46] Shamans among the Tungus do not intervene in cases that cannot be cured by suggestion, such as typhoid fever, pneumonia, and smallpox.[47] Yakut shamans do not treat scarlet fever, measles, smallpox, syphilis, scrofula, or leprosy. They are especially afraid of smallpox and will not perform their rites in a house where a case of it has recently occurred.[48] In the case of an infectious disease the doctor's fear of acquiring it is doubtless largely responsible for his refusal to deal with it.

Disease is always conceived of materialistically. Some tangible object possessing a malefic quality has been introduced invisibly into the patient's body, or some substance possessed by an evil spirit has entered him. Between the quality and the "spirit" there is often no essential difference; the doctor may deal with the one by the same procedures which he employs with the other. This is very commonly the case even when specific diseases, especially serious ones, are personified and endowed with occult power. The evil spirits to whose agency the Sakai of the Malay Peninsula attribute physical discomfort and sickness are those responsible, respectively, for fatigue, headache, stomach-ache, mosquitoes, and a group of ailments including fever, elephantiasis, ulcers, and rheumatism.[49] Among the Thado Kuki of Assam, as an experienced observer points out, the terms "evil spirits" and "bacteria" are in effect synonymous. "To the Thado all sickness is caused by spirits, and when I asked an exceptionally intelligent interpreter why, in that case, quinine should cure malaria, he replied in some surprise that it was surely obvious; Europeans had discovered with greater exactitude than Kukis what precise smell each variety of evil spirit disliked most, and hence used quinine for fever, chlorodyne for a flux, and castor oil for a pain in the stomach."[50]

Quite recently smallpox has entered the pantheon of the Ho of Chota Nagpur as the deity Mata and as Angar Mata among the Korwa.[51] By the Bathonga smallpox is "more or less personified" and with the name Nyedzana is looked on as a real and terrible visitor coming at intervals to search for sinners among the people. The great sin which he especially wishes to discover is murder by witchcraft.[52] The Bahima evil spirits, a numerous company, are mostly identified with the various maladies such as neuralgia, fever, bubonic plague, and smallpox, from which the natives suffer.[53] A similar identification is made by the Bangala of the Upper Congo, among whom the names of serious illnesses are also the names of the spirits responsible for sending them.[54] The Jivaro Indians recognize the existence of as many as six disease spirits, all with names and associated with various animals. Each spirit is responsible for a particular set of ailments. Chingi causes stomach troubles; Morovi, all localized aches and pains in various parts of the body other than in the stomach; Tunchi, rashes, itches, and skin eruptions—and so forth.[55] By some Siberian tribes smallpox is regarded as an evil spirit introduced among them by the Russians.[56]

Disease being "materialized impurity," the doctor adopts appropriate measures for its treatment. He often operates by rubbing or sucking various parts of the patient's body, perhaps reciting, meanwhile, potent spells or utilizing potent charms. At length he produces some small article—a pebble, a stick, a leaf, a thorn, a fragment of bone, a worm, or an insect—which is the visible form of the disease. This practice has almost a world-wide distribution.

A middle-aged Warramunga man fell very ill, the natural consequence of his having deliberately eaten food which the elders reserved to themselves. No one, therefore, was the least surprised at what happened to him. "Amongst the men in camp there were five doctors, and as the case was evidently a serious one, they were all called into consultation. One of them was a celebrated medicine man from the neighboring Worgaia tribe, and after solemn deliberation he gave it as his opinion that the bone of a dead man, attracted by the campfire, had entered the patient's body and was causing all the trouble. The others agreed with this opinion but, not to be outdone by a stranger, the oldest among the Warramunga doctors decided that, in addition to the bone, an *arabillia* or wart of a gum tree had somehow got inside the man's body. The three less experienced men looked very grave, but said nothing beyond the fact that they fully concurred in the diagnosis of their elder colleagues. At all events it was decided that both the bone and the wart must be removed, and, under cover of darkness, they were in part removed after much sucking and rubbing of the patient's body." The man died soon afterward—of dysentery.[57]

In Borneo a Kayan doctor resorts to the sucking cure more particularly when localized pain is a prominent feature of the disorder. After inquiring of the patient where the pain is felt, he holds up the polished blade of a sword, gazes at it intently, "as one seeing visions," and sings several verses, half a spell, half an invocation, addressed to Bali Dayong, that is, to Holy Dayong. Men and women sitting around him, join in the refrain. Gradually the doctor seems to become more and more oblivious to his surroundings, acts strangely, and makes curious clucking sounds. Then he produces a short tube, presses the end of it upon the affected spot, sucks strongly, and at length blows out of the tube a small black pellet, which moves mysteriously upon his hand as he exhibits it to the patient and the audience. If the patient feels pain in several places the operation is repeated. "The whole procedure is very well adapted to secure therapeutic effects by suggestion. The singing and the atmosphere of awe engendered by the *dayong's* reputation and his uncanny behavior prepare the patient, the suction applied through the tube gives him the impression that something is being drawn through his skin, and the skillful production of the mysterious black pellet completes the suggestive process."[58]

The element of trickery in such performances is so manifest that one may wonder why it should not be more often discovered. We must remember, however, that the doctor is sometimes called upon to deal with a real splinter, stone, or bone which has become imbedded in the patient's flesh, and that his success in removing it would justify confidence in his operative skill when the presence of the extraneous object is not apparent to the senses. If in such cases the doctor resorts to his expulsive treatment there is usually little or no disposition to question its effectiveness. With reference to the Xosa of South Africa we are told that the onlookers, fearful of being bewitched, dare not look carefully at what is being produced; they merely give it a frightened glance and turn their eyes away. As for the patient, he never asks to see the wound or cut through which the offending substance has been drawn out. "He is content to accept the practitioner's word at its face value. A miracle has been performed, and surely that's enough for anyone."[59] Among the Azande of the Anglo-Egyptian Sudan a more skeptical attitude prevails, and a doctor must be well trained in prestidigitation to avoid exposure. Should he be found out he can always assert that the pretended extraction of spiders and black beetles is not what cures his patient, but the medicine which he administers internally and externally at the same time. His surgery may be questionable; his physic, at any rate, is successful.[60]

Widespread, also, is the practice of exorcism. All maladies are sometimes attributed to demoniacal possession, but more often they are limited to idiocy and to such deep-seated afflictions as hysteria, delirium, epilepsy, and mania. To compel the hasty exit of the occupying spirit the patient is pricked with needles, as in Hawaii, or sprinkled with pungent spices, as in the Malay Islands, or thoroughly beaten, as in West Africa. The more unpleasant the treatment the more efficacious it is deemed to be.

The procedure followed in Fiji for the exorcism of a disease spirit has been described by a Christianized native. The doctor "passed his hands over the patient's body till he detected the spirit by a peculiar fluttering sensation in his finger ends. He then endeavored to bring it down to one of the extremities, a foot or a hand. Much patience and care were required, because these spirits are very cunning, and will double back and hide themselves in the trunk of the body if you give them a chance. 'And even,' he said, 'when you have got the demon into a leg or an arm which you can grasp with your fingers, you must take care or he will escape you. He will lodge in the joints, and hide himself among the bones. Hard indeed it is to get him out of a joint! But when you have drawn him down to a finger or a toe, you must pull him out with a sudden jerk, and throw him far away and blow after him lest he should return.' "[61]

An English authority describes an exorcism among the Macusi, an Arawak tribe of British Guiana. Our Englishman, suffering from headache and a slight fever, submitted to treatment at the hands of a *peai*. The patient spent the night in the dark hut of the magician, who, having imbibed freely of tobacco juice, worked himself up apparently into a state of frenzy and for six hours conducted an incessant ventriloquial conversation with the spirits responsible for the illness. Their shouts and roars filled the hut, shaking its walls and roof. The rustling of their wings and the thuds, as each one alighted on the floor, could be plainly heard. These noises were caused by shaking leafy boughs and then dashing them suddenly on the ground. In the morning the *peai* produced a caterpillar which he had extracted from the patient while asleep. It was the bodily form of the spirit that had caused all the trouble.[62]

With reference to the Indians of Cumaná, Venezuela, an old writer tells how the medicine men "said the patient was possessed with spirits, stroked all the body over, used words of enchantment, licked some joints, and sucked, saying they drew out spirits; took a twig of a certain tree, the virtue whereof none but the physicians knew, tickled their own throats with it till they vomited and bled, sighed, roared, quaked, stamped, made a thousand faces, sweated for two hours, and at last brought up a sort of thick phlegm, with a little hard black ball in the middle of it, which those that belonged to the sick person carried into the field, saying, 'Go thy way, Devil; Devil, go thy way.' "[63]

There are many instances where the exorcist must first become himself possessed, in order to discover what evil spirit was responsible for the disease in question or to secure the aid of a good spirit able to deal effectively with the devilish adversary.

Temporary possession induced by a magician for curative purposes has been described among the Papuans of Geelvink Bay, in Netherlands New Guinea. If a person has fallen sick one of the members of his family is stupefied by the fumes of incense, or by some other method of producing a trance-like condition. An image of a deceased ancestor is then placed on the medium's lap, in order to cause the ancestral ghost to pass out of the image into his body. When that happens, the ghost speaks through the medium's mouth and tells how a cure of the patient may be effected. The medium, upon returning to his normal state, professes to know nothing of what he said during the trance.[64] In Niue or Savage Island the so-called "priests" are now possessed by ghosts, though in the old heathen days the possession was by gods; hence their name, taula-atua ("anchor of the gods"). Besides his employment for weather making, bewitching, and prophesying, a taula-atua cures by going into a trance or fit and thus establishes contact with the ghostly powers. When these appear he usually becomes unconscious, but sometimes he sees them without losing his senses. They tell him whether the patient is likely or not to recover and also how to compound his medicines. If he makes a mistake they come back and rectify it. In addition to medicine he relies on massage to expel an evil spirit from a patient, and for the same purpose makes bad smells by pounding certain leaves, or beats and cuts the sufferer to relieve him of his unpleasant spiritual parasite. The evil spirit comes out in human form.[65] Among Indonesian peoples possession of this sort seems to be common. In Poso, a district of central Celebes, when the priestess of a god is consulted in a case of disease she becomes possessed by the god, who speaks through her mouth and through her hands draws forth from the patient the alien substance—it may be a piece of tobacco or a stick—inserted by a sorcerer into the sufferer's body.[66] The Malanau, a division of the Klemantan of Sarawak, have an elaborate ceremony to induce a "big spirit" to enter a female doctor, so that she may cure a sick person. When it comes into her she feels its presence like a flash, but does not see its form. She asks for food and drink, which she consumes to gratify the spirit within her, though she is not aware that she is eating and drinking. The doctor, or, rather, her possessing spirit, then summons forth the demon afflicting the patient and causes it to enter a basket prepared for its reception.[67]

A Malay magician, called upon to treat a sick man, goes through a ceremony whereby he becomes possessed by the spirit of a tiger. He thus obtains its assistance in expelling a rival spirit of less power. The performance is carried out realistically. Once the tiger spirit has entered the *pawang* he goes down upon his hands and feet, growls like the dreaded "lord of the forest," indulges in cat-like leaps, and licks over, as a tigress would lick its cub, the all but naked body of the patient. Then the *pawang*, rising to his feet, engages in a fierce hand-to-hand combat with the invisible foe which he had been summoned to exorcise from the sick man.[68]

The relation of possession to the cure of sickness is further illustrated by the *bori* cult of the Hausa, a Negroid people of the Sudan. The *bori* are disease spirits, some of Mohammedan origin and some purely heathen. Each spirit has its own name and its own mode of manifestation. It is summoned by its special song, accompanied by drumming and incense burning. Members of the cult hold great ceremonial dances in which the performers, both men and women, are "mounted" by the spirits, possession being imagined as a ride on horseback. When so possessed by a spirit, a *bori* doctor is able to cure the disease which it has caused, by a sort of "transcendental inoculation."[69]

Among the Arecuna of Venezuela a doctor drinks tobacco juice in order to send out his soul and enlist the ghosts of former medicine men for help in curing his patient. A ghost, when brought back from the other world, enters the doctor's body, speaks through him (but in a voice quite unlike the doctor's), answers questions, and offers advice as to the proper treatment of the case. If the doctor, after drinking tobacco juice, cannot succeed in securing ghostly aid of this sort, his patient dies.[70]

Every doctor among the Yuma Indians has his familiar spirit. In most cases of illness it merely directs him to undertake the treatment of a sick person and gives him strength to effect a cure. But in the practice of sorcery and in the procedure to avert the effects of sorcery the spirit is supposed to enter the doctor, so that true possession then takes place. When the patient is at the point of death, the doctor also tries by singing to induce the spirit to enter his own body, whence it will pass into that of the sick man and bring back the latter's soul, about to flee away forever. In these cases the doctor will speak as if he were the spirit; indeed it is the spirit speaking, but using the doctor's voice because it has no voice of its own.[71]

True possession for curative purposes also occurs among the Haida and Tlingit. With these northwestern tribes the shaman, when treating a patient or otherwise performing, was supposed to be possessed by a spiritual being. He bore its name, imitated its dress, and spoke with its voice. The spirit showed him the cause of the sickness, which he then removed by blowing upon the affected part of the patient's body, sucking at it, or rubbing a charm on it. If the patient's soul had wandered, he captured and restored it. If the patient had been bewitched, he revealed the name of the sorcerer and told how the man should be dealt with. All these things he accomplished by means of the possessing spirit.[72]

A disease that has been removed by the sucking process or a disease spirit that has been driven out by exorcism is often transmitted through bodily contact or in some other way to an inanimate object, an animal, or a human being. A Malay magician makes little dough images of all kinds of animals and sets them on a tray, together with betel leaves and cigarettes. He then repeats a spell, inviting the evil spirit, or "mischief," to leave the body of the patient and enter into the choice collection of objects lying on the tray.[73] The Baganda medicine man, having made an image of his patient in clay, would cause this object to be rubbed over the latter's body. At nightfall the image was buried in the road or hidden in the grass nearby. The first person who stepped over it or passed by it got the disease. A plantain flower, tied up in the semblance of the patient, might be used in the same way. Such procedures, though doubtless efficacious, were attended with some danger, for a person caught thus seeking the death of another would himself be killed.[74] The Lobi of French West Africa try to transfer a man's illness to a big tree. He is first anointed with a special medicine and made to lean against the trunk. The attendant priest then "catches the tree's breath" and passes it into the patient's body. At the same time the latter's breath is passed into the tree. If the tree withers and dies, the sick man is certain of recovery; if, however, it continues to be vigorous and full of life, he is doomed to death.[75] The Creek Indians believe that "in the beginning" the animals or animal spirits made all diseases. Accordingly, after a medicine man has expelled a disease from his patient, he throws it into an animal spirit, though not the one which caused it.[76] A Yakut shaman, called upon to treat a sick person, tries to drive away the spirit by frightening it or by sucking it out from the painful place. He also resorts to spitting and blowing as expulsive measures. Sometimes, however, the sickness is transferred to the cattle, which are then sacrificed.[77]

The procedures of disease transmission are not in themselves magical. They involve nothing more than the familiar notion that the qualities of objects are both material and transmissible. They may be employed and often are employed by laymen or by healers who make no pretensions to proficiency in magical arts. When, however, the patient suffers from a long and serious ailment a recognized practitioner of magic is likely to be called in, not only to expel it but to get rid of it permanently by transferring it to some "scapegoat," animate or inanimate. He alone has the occult power to make the transfer really effective.

If a disease has been caused by the abstraction from a person of his soul or of some part of his body (often identified with his soul), the doctor tries to recover the missing object or substance so that he may replace it in his patient. Sometimes he devises a trap for it or ensnares it. In the Banks Islands, if the doctor decides that the soul of the sick man has been stolen by a spirit, he proceeds to brew a potion of leaves and drinks it before going to sleep. In his sleep he has dreams, and these are taken as an indication that his own soul has gone away to seek out that of the patient. The latter is hard to find, for it may have been hidden on the branch of a tree or in the cleft of a rock; moreover, the spirit-kidnaper tries his best to keep it by raising a barrier of stones or some other obstacle to balk the pursuing soul. Sometimes, indeed, the doctor's efforts are in vain; if so, he will announce his failure upon waking up in the morning.[78] The professional soul-catcher among the Kayan falls into a trance in order to send his own soul in pursuit of that of his patient and induce it to return. If successful, he comes out of his trance, "with the air of one who is suddenly transported from distant scenes," and exhibits some small animal, perhaps only a grain of rice, a pebble, or a bit of wood, in which the captured soul is confined. This object he places on the top of the patient's head and drives it in by rubbing.[79]

The Buriat shaman makes a diagnosis in order to decide whether the patient's soul has been lost or whether it has been stolen and is now languishing in the gloomy realm of Erlik, lord of the underworld. In the former case the shaman seeks the soul, which may be near at hand or perhaps far away in the deep wood, on the steppes, or at the bottom of the sea. If it cannot be found on earth, then the shaman must go to Erlik. This requires a toilsome and expensive journey, and the patient must first offer heavy sacrifices. Sometimes Erlik will not give up the soul without receiving in exchange another soul, so the shaman must ensnare that of the sufferer's dearest friend and hand it over to Erlik. The sick man recovers, but only for a limited period, at the most, nine years; his friend becomes ill and dies.[80]

The doctor, as well as his professional brother, the rain maker, must sometimes pay the penalty for a failure of his operations. Among the Bangerang, a tribe of Victoria, a doctor who had lost a patient might have to undergo the ordeal of spears.[81] The natives of Zambales, one of the Philippines, evince a natural disinclination to enter the medical profession for, while it is lucrative, a practitioner whose patient dies may himself be killed.[82] The Nicobarese occasionally put to death a doctor who failed to cure the sick.[83] The Puelche of Patagonia frequently punish with death an unsuccessful doctor.[84] The same practice is reported among the Payaguá of Paraguay.[85] The Jivaro reason that a medicine man who has undertaken to cure a sick person and does not do so must have used his occult power to kill him. The relatives of the deceased consider it their duty to take revenge upon the supposed sorcerer, who is promptly murdered, unless able to escape by flight.[86]

Among the Indians of the southwestern United States unsuccessful medicine men are or were often killed. A doctor unable to cure a child would be readily excused, and even a single failure with an adult might be passed over, on the ground, for example, that the patient's bad heart was responsible for his demise. But should a doctor lose a number of cases successively he is believed to have lost his curing powers or even to have become a sorcerer; hence he is killed to prevent his doing further harm. To avoid the sole responsibility for treating a hopeless case, the doctor will sometimes call upon other practitioners for assistance or will refer the patient to a specialist for his particular ailment.[87]

The Indians of southern and central California almost universally believed that the medicine man who could cause a disease was also the one who could cure it. Whether he killed a man or healed him was entirely a matter of his inclination. If, then, he failed to effect a cure, his failure must obviously be due to malevolence, for which he deserved to be, and often was, killed. In northern California medicine men were much less frequently murdered and then not as sorcerers but rather for their refusal to attend a sick person or for unwillingness to return their fee after an unsuccessful treatment.[88]

Among the tribes of British Columbia a doctor who failed to effect a cure was always liable to be put to death, on the assumption that he did not wish his patient to recover.[89] On the other hand, a Tinne doctor who tried with the aid of his familiar spirit to dislodge a disease spirit from a patient, incurred no odium for a failure. Obviously, thought these Indians, the doctor's spirit was less powerful than the intruder's.[90]

Magico-medical practice among some primitive peoples reaches a high degree of specialization. Among the Elema tribes of the Papuan Gulf the specialists in magic who deal exclusively with disease may limit themselves to its diagnosis or else engage only in practice. Sometimes they combine their activities; sometimes the two kinds of doctors work in partnership.[91] Among the Tami on the northeastern coast of New Guinea there is a specialist for a pain in the chest, a second for a pain in the abdomen, a third for rheumatism, and a fourth for catarrh. One specialist may treat only internal ailments by reciting spells over the patient's food; another takes leaves, roots, or feathers, which have been similarly made magically potent, and rubs them over the patient's body.[92] In Eddystone Island, which belongs to the Solomons group, such ailments as rheumatism, fever, epilepsy, and insanity are treated by different practitioners.[93] The *nganga* of the Bavenda of the Transvaal is the medicine man proper, and his principal function is the cure of disease. There are also many specialists. While familiar with the general principles of the magico-medical art, they treat only certain diseases. They often inherit their knowledge from a long line of ancestors who were themselves specialists. The doctor's profession is, indeed, nearly as complicated among the Bavenda as among ourselves.[94] In the case of certain ailments the Navaho believe that besides an obvious cause, such as an accident resulting in broken bones, some unknown and baneful influence may be at work to prevent the patient's recovery. Therefore, in addition to the regular doctor, who treats the symptoms that can be recognized, a diagnostician must be called in to learn by divination what this baneful influence really is and then to recommend another medicine man who will be able to deal with it.[95] Throughout northern California a distinction is likewise made between the man who is a diagnostician only, singing, dancing, or smoking before the patient in order to become clairvoyant and "see" the cause of the disease, and the doctor who performs the actual cure by sucking it out of the patient. The sucking doctor seems to be rated higher than the diagnostician. This distinction has been found among the Hupa, Pomo, Maidu, and other tribes.[96]

In some primitive communities it is not usual to seek the aid of a doctor for minor complaints. Thus among the tribes of Queensland, where knowledge of the therapeutic value of certain herbs, of massage, and other simple treatments is common to everybody, the sick man cares for himself or a wife for her husband or a mother for her child.[97] Many communities, not so primitive, support a class of healers who claim no special relation to ancestral ghosts or spirits and exercise no functions of a magical character. These "leeches," as they have been called, treat minor ailments by the use of a few well-known drugs which they dispense without ceremony; they may also practice a rudimentary surgery. Only when their measures prove to be unavailing will professional medicine men be consulted. It is significant that while leeches work along more or less scientific lines and may often help their patients, they never enjoy the high esteem paid to the practitioners of magic.

NOTES TO CHAPTER XII

[1] W. E. Roth, *Ethnological Studies among the North-West-Central Queensland Aborigines* (Brisbane, 1897), p. 182; idem, *North Queensland Ethnography Bulletin*, No. 5, pp. 23 f.

[2] Sir Baldwin Spencer and F. J. Gillen, *The Native Tribes of Central Australia* (London, 1899), pp. 541 ff.; *iidem, The Northern Tribes of Central Australia* (London, 1904), pp. 472 ff.

[3] Phyllis M. Kaberry, *Aboriginal Woman, Sacred and Profane* (London,

1939), pp. 239, 253–68. The authoress witnessed six corroborees. According to her informants, they are never followed by sexual license between men and women. They are thus distinguished from certain ceremonial dances (*Itata*) found among the Arunta and Luritja tribes. For those who take part in them the *Itata* mean "romance and public life, legalized license and adventure." See G. Róheim, "Women and Their Life in Central Australia," *Journal of the Royal Anthropological Institute,* LXIII (1933), 209 ff.

[4] A. C. Haddon, in *Reports of the Cambridge Anthropological Expedition to Torres Straits,* VI, 220 f. For the erotic magic of the western islanders see *ibid.,* V, 327 f.

[5] Gunnar Landtman, *The Kiwai Papuans of British New Guinea* (London, 1927), p. 241.

[6] F. E. Williams, *Orokaiva Magic* (Oxford, 1928), pp. 188 f.

[7] R. F. Fortune, *Sorcerers of Dobu* (London, 1932), pp. 235 ff.

[8] D. Jenness and A. Ballantyne, *The Northern D'Entrecasteaux* (Oxford, 1920), pp. 98, 135.

[9] Bronislaw Malinowski, *The Sexual Life of Savages in North-Western Melanesia* (New York, 1929), pp. 344–83.

[10] Hortense Powdermaker, *Life in Lesu* (New York, 1933), pp. 232 ff.

[11] A. B. Deacon, *Malekula, a Vanishing People in the New Hebrides* (London, 1934), p. 674.

[12] *The Old-Time Maori* by Makereti (London, 1938), pp. 83 f. Edited by T. K. Penniman.

[13] Charles Hose and William McDougall, *The Pagan Tribes of Borneo* (London, 1910), II, 127. See also W. Howell and R. Shelford, "A Sea Dyak Love Philtre," *Journal of the Anthropological Institute,* XXXIV (1904), 207–10.

[14] Cora DuBois, *The People of Alor* (Minneapolis, 1944), p. 110.

[15] W. W. Skeat, *Malay Magic* (London, 1900), pp. 361 ff., 566 ff., 573.

[16] Verrier Elwin, *The Baiga* (London, 1939), pp. 344 f., 357.

[17] I. Schapera, *Married Life in a South African Tribe* (London, 1941), pp. 53, 208.

[18] Edward Ward, *The Yoruba Husband-Wife Code* (Washington, D.C., 1938), pp. 158 f. *Catholic University of America, Anthropological Series,* No. 6.

[19] Edward Westermarck, *Ritual and Belief in Morocco* (London, 1926), I, 126 f.

[20] W. E. Roth, "An Inquiry into the Animism and Folk-Lore of the Guiana Indians," *Thirtieth Annual Report of the Bureau of American Ethnology,* pp. 285 ff.

[21] James Mooney, "Sacred Formulas of the Cherokees," *Seventh Annual Report of the Bureau of Ethnology,* pp. 380 f.; W. H. Gilbert, Jr., "The Eastern Cherokees," *Bulletin of the Bureau of American Ethnology,* No. 133, pp. 289 ff.

[22] J. O. Dorsey, "A Study of Siouan Cults," *Eleventh Annual Report of the Bureau of Ethnology,* p. 416. Among the Atxuabo of Angola women often use menstrual blood as a charm, either to protect themselves or to injure men in many ways (M. Schulien, in *Anthropos,* XVIII–XIX [1923–24], 78).

[23] J. R. Swanton, in *Memoirs of the American Museum of Natural History,* VIII, 45.

[24] W. E. Roth, *North Queensland Ethnography Bulletin,* No. 11 (*Records of the Australian Museum,* Vol. VII, No. 2, pp. 75 ff.).

[25] D. Jenness and A. Ballantyne, *op. cit.,* p. 74.

PRIVATE MAGIC 369

²⁶ Lionel Decle, *Three Years in Savage Africa* (London, 1900), p. 77.

²⁷ J. H. Weeks, *Among the Primitive Bakongo* (London, 1914), p. 239.

²⁸ W. E. Roth, *loc. cit.*

²⁹ A. C. Haddon, in *Reports of the Cambridge Anthropological Expedition to Torres Straits,* VI, 226.

³⁰ B. T. Somerville, in *Journal of the Anthropological Institute,* XXVI (1897), 404 f. In Mala or Malaita the areas under cultivation are at a considerable distance, often as much as two miles, from the homesteads. In this island sorcery finds one of its most important uses to protect orchards and gardens from thieves. Nowadays far more thefts occur among Christianized natives, who depend simply on "No-Trespassing" signs for protection, than among the heathen natives, who are still fearful of black magic (H. I. Hogbin, "Sorcery and Administration," *Oceania,* VI [1935-36], 20).

³¹ George Turner, *Samoa* (London, 1884), pp. 185 ff.

³² C. G. Seligman, *The Melanesians of British New Guinea* (Cambridge, 1910), pp. 574 ff.

³³ Bronislaw Malinowski, in *Transactions of the Royal Society of South Australia,* XXXIX (1915), 586 f.

³⁴ R. F. Fortune, *op. cit.,* pp. 138 ff.

³⁵ H. I. Hogbin, "Sorcery and Administration," *Oceania,* VI (1935-36), 4.

³⁶ W. H. R. Rivers, *Medicine, Magic, and Religion* (London, 1924), pp. 32 ff. Rivers and A. M. Hocart found in Eddystone Island about one hundred examples of such conjoined processes of taboo and medicine.

³⁷ Elsdon Best, "Notes on the Custom of 'Rahui'," *Journal of the Polynesian Society,* XIII (1904), 83-88.

³⁸ Ernest Dieffenbach, *Travels in New Zealand* (London, 1843), II, 100 f.

³⁹ With reference to the tribes of southeastern Australia it is said that "death by accident they can imagine, although the results of what we should call accident they mostly attribute to the effects of some evil magic. They are well acquainted with death by violence, but even in this they believe . . . . that a warrior who happens to be speared in one of the ceremonial fights has lost his skill in warding off or evading a spear through the evil magic of someone belonging to his own tribe" (A. W. Howitt, *The Native Tribes of South-East Australia* [London, 1904], p. 357). By the Arunta and other Central tribes "all ailments of every kind, from the simplest to the most serious, are without exception attributed to the malign influence of an enemy in either human or spirit shape" (Spencer and Gillen, *The Native Tribes of Central Australia,* p. 530). The Mountain Arapesh believe that a man cannot be killed in a fight or die of a wound received when fighting unless previously some portion of his personality was sent to a sorcerer to be worked on magically. You thrust a spear through him and he fell dead, but your spear was merely the agent of the sorcerer's magic (Margaret Mead, in *Anthropological Papers of the American Museum of Natural History,* XXXVII, 353 f.). Among the Iatmul, another Papuan people, the relatives of a man killed in a raid always suspect that a sorcerer in the village sold the soul of the victim to the enemy *before* the raid took place (Gregory Bateson, *Naven* [Cambridge, 1936], p. 64, note 1). In the New Hebrides it is always assumed that no misfortune suffered by a man could be completely destructive without the aid of magic. The native knows that the blow of a club may kill him, but he also believes that the hand which struck the blow must have been magically guided (Felix Speiser, *Ethnographische Materialien aus den Neuen Hebriden und den Banks-Inseln* [Berlin, 1923], pp. 300 f.). For the Baiga, an aboriginal tribe in the Central Provinces of India, life is heavily overshadowed by the "dark cloud" of witchcraft. Although many diseases and dis-

asters are attributed to evil spirits, yet witches seem to be held chiefly responsible for human ills. When a man has been killed by a tiger or bitten by a poisonous snake, when a woman cannot be delivered of her child, when the crops have been destroyed by a storm, witches have brought about these untoward events and made them happen to the particular persons involved (Verrier Elwin, *op. cit.*, p. 370; cf. p. 289). The Bakongo, declares a missionary authority, believe that no one can be hurt or killed or die a "natural" death unless the bullet, the crocodile, or the complaint has some witchcraft in it. "What the natives fear above all things is witchcraft, and in that fear they live and move and pass their existence" (J. H. Weeks, *op. cit.*, p. 266). Such testimonies might be multiplied.

40 By some North American Indians dreams are regarded, not only as predictive of sickness, but as directly responsible for it. Such dreams are usually those of death or of ghosts. This belief has been found among the Pima (Frank Russell, in *Twenty-sixth Annual Report of the Bureau of American Ethnology*, p. 253), the Yuma (C. D. Forde, in *University of California Publications in American Archaeology and Ethnology*, XXVIII, 187 ff.), and the Navaho (William Morgan, "Navaho Treatment of Disease: Diagnosticians," *American Anthropologist* [n.s., 1931], XXXIII, 400 f.). Among the Paviotso often the dreamer does not suffer the ill effects of his dream but a relative or a member of his household suffers them. In some instances sickness can be prevented by counteractive measures taken in time, for instance, if the dreamer, upon awakening and recalling his unpleasant experience, addresses the Sun and prays for good health. But should he be unable to remember what he dreamed the sickness follows. It can only be cured if a medicine man forces the patient to recall the content of the dream and the time of the occurrence. The Paviotso, we are told, seem to regard dreams as the "chief cause" of all illness. See W. Z. Park, *Shamanism in Western North America* (Evanston, 1938), pp. 38 f. *Northwestern University Studies in the Social Sciences*, No. 2.

41 *Tom Petrie's Reminiscences of Early Queensland* (Brisbane, 1904), p. 64.

42 Spencer and Gillen, *The Northern Tribes of Central Australia*, p. 532.

43 E. H. Gomes, *Seventeen Years among the Sea Dyaks of Borneo* (London, 1911), pp. 177, 191.

44 Rafael Karsten, *The Head Hunters of Western Amazonas* (Helsingfors, 1935), pp. 395 f. *Societas Scientiarum Fennica, Commentationes Humanarum Litterarum*, Vol. VII, No. 1.

45 Gladys A. Reichard, *Social Life of the Navajo Indians* (New York, 1928), pp. 147, 154.

46 James Mooney and F. M. Olbrechts, "The Swimmer Manuscript. Cherokee Sacred Formulas and Medicinal Prescriptions," *Bulletin of the Bureau of American Ethnology*, No. 99, p. 108.

47 S. M. Shirokogoroff, "What Is Shamanism?" *China Journal of Science and Arts*, II (1924), 369.

48 W. G. Sumner, "The Yakuts. Abridged from the Russian of Sieroshevski," *Journal of the Anthropological Institute*, XXXI (1900), 104 f.

49 W. W. Skeat and C. O. Blagden, *Pagan Races of the Malay Peninsula* (London, 1906), II, 183.

50 J. H. Hutton, in *Man*, XXXIV (1934), 76.

51 D. N. Majumdar, "Bongaism," in *Essays Presented to Rai Bahadur Sarat Chandra Roy* (Lucknow, 1942), p. 72.

52 H. A. Junod, *The Life of a South African Tribe* (2d ed., London, 1927), II, 465.

53 Sir H. H. Johnston, *The Uganda Protectorate* (2d ed., London, 1904), II, 631.

[54] J. H. Weeks, in *Journal of the Royal Anthropological Institute*, XL (1910), 377.

[55] M. W. Stirling, "Jivaro Shamanism," *Proceedings of the American Philosophical Society*, LXXII (1933), 141 ff.; *idem*, "Historical and Ethnographical Material on the Jivaro Indians," *Bulletin of the Bureau of American Ethnology*, No. 117, pp. 118 ff.

[56] J. Stadling, "Shamanism," *Contemporary Review*, LXXIX (1901), 94, note.

[57] Spencer and Gillen, *The Northern Tribes of Central Australia*, pp. 515 f. Among some of the Arunta a medicine man, in addition to the magical stones by means of which he removes extraneous objects from a patient, has in his body a particular kind of lizard, and this remarkable creature endows him with great suctorial power, such as the natives attribute to the lizard itself (*iidem, The Native Tribes of Central Australia*, p. 531).

[58] Charles Hose and William McDougall, *op. cit.*, II, 120 ff.

[59] J. H. Soga, *The Ama-Xosa: Life and Customs* (Lovedale, South Africa, 1931), p. 168.

[60] E. E. Evans-Pritchard, *Witchcraft, Oracles, and Magic among the Azande* (Oxford, 1937), pp. 231 f.

[61] R. H. Codrington, *The Melanesians* (Oxford, 1891), p. 198, note 1, on the authority of the Rev. Lorimer Fison.

[62] Sir E. F. im Thurn, *Among the Indians of Guiana* (London, 1883), pp. 335–38.

[63] Antonio de Herrera, *The General History of the Vast Continent and Islands Called America* (London, 1725–26), III, 310.

[64] F. S. A. de Clerq, in *Tijdschrift van het koninklijke Nederlandsch Aardrijkskundig Genootschap* (2d series, 1893), X, 631.

[65] E. M. Loeb, "The Shaman of Niue," *American Anthropologist* (n.s., 1924), XXVI, 393 ff. On the similar curing functions of the Samoan *taula-aitu* see J. B. Stair, *Old Samoa* (London, 1897), pp. 70, 224 f.

[66] A. C. Kruijt, in *Mededeelingen van wege het Nederlandsche Zendelinggenootschap*, XXXVI (1892), 399 f.

[67] Charles Hose and William McDougall, *op. cit.*, II, 131 ff.

[68] W. W. Skeat, *op. cit.*, pp. 436 ff., with reference to the Malays of Selangor.

[69] A. J. N. Tremearne, *Hausa Superstitions and Customs* (London, 1913), pp. 145–51; *idem, The Ban of the Bori* (London, 1914). See further *idem*, "Bori Beliefs and Ceremonies," *Journal of the Royal Anthropological Institute*, XLV (1915), 23–68.

[70] Theodor Koch-Grünberg, *Vom Roroima zum Orinoco* (Berlin, 1917–28), III, 196 f.

[71] C. D. Forde, in *University of California Publications in American Archaeology and Ethnology*, XXVIII, 184.

[72] J. R. Swanton, in *Memoirs of the American Museum of Natural History*, VIII, 38 (Haida); *idem*, "Social Condition, Beliefs, and Linguistic Relationship of the Tlingit Indians," *Twenty-sixth Annual Report of the Bureau of American Ethnology*, pp. 463 f.

[73] W. W. Skeat, *op. cit.*, pp. 432 f.

[74] John Roscoe, *The Baganda* (London, 1911), p. 344.

[75] Henri Labouret, *Les tribus du rameau Lobi* (Paris, 1931), p. 318.

[76] F. G. Speck, *Ethnology of the Yuchi Indians* (Philadelphia, 1909), p. 133; *idem*, in *Memoirs of the American Anthropological Association*, No. 8 (Vol. II, Pt. 2), p. 121.

77 Marie A. Czaplica, *Aboriginal Siberia* (Oxford, 1914), pp. 237 f.

78 W. H. R. Rivers, *The History of Melanesian Society* (Cambridge, 1914), I, 165 f.

79 Charles Hose and William McDougall, *op. cit.*, II, 29 ff.

80 V. M. Mikhailovskii (Mikhailowski), "Shamanism in Siberia and European Russia," *Journal of the Anthropological Institute*, XXIV (1895), 69 f., citing G. N. Pontanin.

81 E. M. Curr, *The Australian Race* (Melbourne, 1886), I, 47.

82 W. A. Reed, *Negritos of Zambales* (Manila, 1904), p. 66. *Department of the Interior, Ethnological Survey Publications*, Vol. II, Pt. I.

83 E. H. Man, *The Nicobar Islands and Their People* (London, 1932), p. 165.

84 G. C. Musters, *At Home with the Patagonians* (2d ed., London, 1873), p. 191.

85 Martin Dobrizhoffer, *An Account of the Abipones* (London, 1822), II, 252.

86 Rafael Karsten, "Blood Revenge, War, and Victory Feasts among the Jibaro Indians of Eastern Ecuador," *Bulletin of the Bureau of American Ethnology*, No. 79, p. 9.

87 Aleš Hrdlička, "Physiological and Medical Observances among the Indians of Southwestern United States and Northern Mexico," *Bulletin of the Bureau of American Ethnology*, No. 34, pp. 223 f. See further J. G. Bourke, in *Ninth Annual Report of the Bureau of Ethnology*, p. 454 (Mohave), 466 (Apache) ; Frank Russell, in *Twenty-sixth Annual Report*, p. 256 (Pima) ; Leslie Spier, in *Anthropological Papers of the American Museum of Natural History*, XXIX, 253, 281, 289 (Havasupai). The Maricopa did not kill an unsuccessful doctor who had tried his best, it was believed, to effect a cure (*idem, Yuman Tribes of the Gila River* [Chicago, 1933], p. 285).

88 A. L. Kroeber, *Handbook of the Indians of California* (Washington, D.C., 1925), p. 853.

89 R. C. Mayne, *Four Years in British Columbia and Vancouver Island* (London, 1862), pp. 260 f.

90 Julius Jetté, "On the Medicine Men of the Ten'a," *Journal of the Royal Anthropological Institute*, XXXVII (1907), 164.

91 F. E. Williams, *Drama of Orokolo* (Oxford, 1940), p. 102. Among Elema specialists are the bloodsuckers, who remove surplus blood from a patient, in order to relieve his pains ; the phlegm experts, who suck the affected parts and spit out mouthfuls of phlegm supposed to be drawn from him ; and the extractors, so-called, who remove crocodile teeth, fragments of glass, three-inch nails, and other objects which sorcerers have lodged in the patient's body (*loc. cit.*).

92 G. Bamler, in R. Neuhauss, *Deutsch Neu-Guinea* (Berlin, 1911), III, 516.

93 W. H. R. Rivers, *Medicine, Magic, and Religion*, p. 46.

94 H. A. Stayt, *The Bavenda* (London, 1931), pp. 263 f. See also E. Gottschling, in *Journal of the Anthropological Institute*, XXXV (1905), 379.

95 L. C. Wyman, "Navaho Diagnosticians," *American Anthropologist* (n.s., 1936), XXXVIII, 238.

96 A. L. Kroeber, *op. cit.*, p. 855. On the other hand, among the Papago Indians the medicine man confines himself to diagnosis. Having done so, some humble "dreamer" is called in to effect a cure. He has little prestige and for his services receives no payment except food. See Ruth M. Underhill, *Singing for Power: the Song Magic of the Papago Indians of Southern Arizona* (Berkeley, 1938), p. 142.

97 W. E. Roth, *North Queensland Ethnology Bulletin*, No. 5, p. 29.

CHAPTER XIII

SORCERY

THE special procedures and techniques traditionally associated with sorcery or witchcraft, as we have seen, may sometimes be employed for public ends, when directed against unsocial members of a community or against a hostile clan or tribe. But black magic is essentially an individualistic affair. It finds regular and constant use by men and women who work deliberately, by means of the spells they utter, the charms they manipulate, and the rites they perform, to bring misfortunes upon their fellows. So used it may be licit, reputable, and even praiseworthy, for instance, if the same magical arts that have slain a man are resorted to by an avenger of blood against the slayer. As a rule, however, sorcery is carried on more or less secretly, in defiance of public opinion, and those who practice it are objects of constant suspicion, fear, and enmity.

Almost if not universally homebred sorcery is presumed to be far less effective than that of a remote and unknown group. An aura of mystery invests sorcery (as it does all magic), and the more mysterious it is the more powerfully it acts. Distance lends terror to the view.[1]

In Central Australia all distant tribes are supposed to be especially devoted to magic and skilled in its practice.[2] Among the Kaitish, Warramunga, and other northern tribes a very potent form of evil magic, called *mauia*, is associated with certain little stones. These are endowed with their power only by members of the Worgaia and Gnanji tribes, but they are traded away to the south as far as the Kaitish, who use them occasionally to injure the Arunta. Another instance of magic associated with a distant region is afforded by the knout, which men of the Arunta, Kaitish, and Ilpirra tribes carry about with them concealed in their wallets. It is very useful in securing a wife's prompt obedience to her husband. "The very sight of the knout is enough to bring her to a sense of what is right and proper, whilst a blow from it is supposed to have most serious and usually fatal results. Even

373

a distant woman can be injured by cracking the knout in her direction, the evil magic which it contains flying off from it through the air." Precisely the same object is worn by men of the Warramunga and Tjingilli tribes as an ordinary waistbelt devoid of malefic properties. But after a knout has been "sung" by a native it will be traded southward to the Arunta and other tribes and acquire a special value as containing the magic of a remote and unknown group of people.[3] The natives of the Murray Islands, Torres Straits, believe foreign sorcery to be so effective that it can be deadly when the black magician and his victim are a hundred miles apart.[4] The Kiwai Papuans hold their neighbors to be accomplished sorcerers. For the more delicate and difficult operations of black magic they prefer the services of an outsider to those of their own local practitioner.[5] By the Keraki the imputation of sorcery is almost invariably leveled at persons living at some distance and not members of the local group. However, a comparatively close neighbor or even a member of the local group itself can procure a "foreign" professional sorcerer to do what he cannot do himself. Consequently among the Keraki one takes due care not to offend one's fellows, because of the risk of such retaliation by the injured party.[6] Those Arapesh who live on the beach or in the mountains know no nefarious magic. All misfortunes suffered by them, all accidents, illnesses, and deaths, they attribute to the sorcery of the Plains Arapesh, who live beyond the mountains. Because of the evil power possessed by a Plainsman he can walk safely through the country of the Mountain people.[7] The Trobrianders, "frightened enough" by sorcery at home, are terribly fearful of that supposed to be practiced on the island of Dobu.[8] The Tonga Islanders are said to fear especially Fijian sorcery.[9] The Malays of the Peninsula regard themselves as inferior in the practice of the black art to the magicians of the Semang and other aboriginal tribes.[10] The Toda dread the death-dealing sorcery of the Kurumba far more than that of their own magicians; the domestic variety can be remedied, but for the foreign variety there is no remedy. When a Kurumba has made a Toda ill, the only thing to be done is to kill the malefactor. On the other hand, the Toda magicians are so greatly feared by the Badaga that the latter pay tribute to them.[11] Aryan Hindus, settled in Chota Nagpur, ascribe great powers of witchcraft to the Munda, an aboriginal tribe of this region.[12] The Balamba, a Rhodesian people, credit the Bakaonde with a general superiority in witchcraft, while holding that in certain branches of the black art the Babemba excel.[13] The Akamba fear the magic of the Atharaka.[14] The Azande are persuaded that the arts of foreign magicians are far superior to their own. When one of the fraternity visits another country and acquires there new medicines and magical procedures, he is regarded by colleagues and laymen alike as a practitioner quite out of the ordinary.[15] The Dinka, who adjoin the Bongo, say that the latter are dreadful fellows, with an ability in black magic far exceeding their own.[16] In Ashanti superior powers of black magic are invariably attributed to wilder and more distant tribes rather than to those nearer home. The farther away the district from which a man hails the more likely he is to be "full of medicine."[17] The Navaho resort to the Pueblo Indians to be cured of witchcraft. They also fear these Indians as being themselves witches.[18]

In some communities sorcery is said to be nonexistent. Natives will declare that they have only white magicians. People who practice the black art belong to a tribe so far away that it is unknown and strange or to another and hostile tribe. When the group is acknowledged to contain sorcerers it is assumed that their nefarious practices will never be employed against its members.

Among the southern clans of the Murngin of Northern Territory, Australia, a black magician is not looked upon by his fellows as fearsome, because they regularly seek his aid in repaying a wrong done to them by another group. He would never be asked to kill by black magic anyone belonging to his own clan or to another clan with which friendly relations exist; his business is to destroy outsiders, who are regarded as enemies and whose hostile feelings are well known.[19]

With regard to the Mailu, a Papuan tribe, we are told that the magician of a clan is always believed to work for its interests, being charged with the duty of making ineffective the pernicious influence of the magician in another clan. For his own people he is a *vara egi* (a white magician); to outsiders he appears as a *barau egi*, a sorcerer.[20] Apparently a Mafulu sorcerer never exercises his powers against any member of the village, or of the clan, or even, as a rule, of the larger tribal group to which he belongs. Hence he is not shunned or feared by his own people.[21] Sorcerers of the Mekeo tribes are not supposed to work against members of their own clan. A sorcerer guilty of "such a breach of professional decorum" would be driven out of the local clan settlement.[22] Among the Roro-speaking tribes, while sorcerers

who presume on their powers to interfere in the domestic concerns of their comrades will sometimes be driven out of the
community or killed, the general attitude toward them is one of
perfect good fellowship. "Indeed a sorcerer may have great
influence in his own village, and not only may not be feared but
may be regarded generally as a real protection, for besides being
able to thwart the acts of sorcerers of other villages, the latter
will, it is supposed, refrain from hostile magic in order not to
provoke reprisals."[23]

Among the Naga tribes of Manipur every village has its doctor,
who is an independent private practitioner of medicine and magic.
Bad magicians, who cause illness, are likewise found, but always
"in the next village, or a day's journey away, or over the next
range of hills."[24] The Lakher of Assam say that while there are
no black magicians among them there are many among their
neighbors, the Lushai and Chakma. Hence when traveling in the
territory of these tribes they are very circumspect as to their
behavior. In the same way the Lushai, while denying that they
have any sorcerers, believe that the Thado Kuki possess them in
abundance.[25]

In the Bechuana tribes, when sorcerers confine themselves to
working magic against their own hated rivals, their activities
are regarded with great respect, as being beneficial to the community.[26] Among the Nuer, a Nilotic people of the Anglo-Egyptian Sudan, the sorcerer does not try to injure anyone in his own
village. When he works magic against a person in another village
he enjoys the support of his fellow villagers, who regard his
activity as being advantageous to themselves.[27]

It is the duty of a Lengua magician to send ill luck and plagues
upon the enemies of his people and protect them from the machinations of foreign sorcerers.[28] All bad magicians among the tribes
along the Xingú (central Brazil) live, or are supposed to live, in
the villages of outsiders.[29] The Witoto of eastern Peru account for
every fatality among them as due to the pernicious activity of a
medicine man, but they never hold their local practitioner responsible for bringing about a death.[30] Similarly among the Yagua, in
the same part of Peru, no medicine man is believed to practice
black magic against people of his own clan. He operates exclusively against other clans and consequently is much feared (as
well as respected) by their members.[31]

However, sorcerers generally show little or no reluctance to
employ their nefarious arts, not only against individual members

of their own group, but often, also, against the group itself. Among the Motu of the Papuan Gulf the weather magician can make heavy seas so that fishermen are unable to go out in their canoes; if well paid, however, he will still the winds and produce a calm.[32] The Kuni once accused the local sorcerer of not making rain in order to dry up their gardens and starve them to death.[33] A Kiwai sorcerer sometimes works harm against men of his own community who are at sea harpooning dugong.[34] In the Loyalty Islands certain persons could control the sun, but they were not very popular because the natives suffered so much from excessive heat and often laid the blame for it upon the solar magicians. It was even insinuated that one of them would sometimes send down so much heat as to burn up the plantations and cause a famine, so that many people died of hunger, thus providing more human flesh for food. It was a privilege of this functionary to proclaim a cannibal feast whenever he felt inclined to do so.[35] Among the Bakitara or Banyoro of Uganda every district has its rain makers. Because of their valuable services they are allowed to levy certain taxes. If the people do not pay their assessment, a magician will threaten to destroy their crops by sending a heavy rain, wind, or hail.[36] Among the Lango, when the magical ceremonies to bring rain are unsuccessful, the old men suspect that one of their number has obtained a "rain spear" and has used it maliciously to "tie up" the rain and cause a drought. Should they discover the guilty party they beat him severely, make him pay a fine of goats and sheep, which they eat themselves, and require him to undo his evil magic. If the culprit cannot be found, the elders are suspected of shielding him. Then the unmarried young men give them a good beating to induce them to deliver him up.[37] A magician among the Apinayé, a Brazilian tribe, may use black magic against an entire community and cause an epidemic sickness. One method of accomplishing this end is to bury pieces of a giant armadillo's armor on both sides of the road leading to the source of the village water supply.[38] Pima medicine men, if not accorded proper respect by their fellows, are likely to cause heavy rains and floods in the rivers. The annals of these Indians refer to several occasions when medicine men, suspected of producing plagues, were executed. As the result of this salutary action "nobody was sick any more."[39] The Zuñi have a story of a husband whose wife left him for another man. He goes to a priest who could cause earthquakes and epidemics and begs for power to make everyone as unhappy as himself. He gets the power and uses it to send a terrible epidemic which caused many deaths. But he fails to pay the priest for services rendered and so the latter kills him by magic.[40]

The activities of the white magician and of the black magician are necessarily connected, for the one seeks to nullify the work of the other. Both make use of occult power, and victory in the contest between them goes to him who wields the stronger power. The "good" practitioner must therefore be familiar with the methods of his rival, the sorcerer, in order to cope with him successfully, and vice versa. Many primitive peoples distinguish between the man who employs his talents for the public benefit, practicing openly and by daylight to cure diseases, foretell the future, and prevent every sort of misfortune, and the man who seeks to injure the community or its members, executing his projects by secret means and often in the obscurity of night. The one upholds the social order, the other would subvert it. This distinction between the two is often indicated by the names applied to them. Thus the Ba-ila contrast the *munganga*, the doctor, skilled in all kinds of medicines, with the *mulozhi*, a trafficker in forbidden forces, always with a bad purpose. The two come into association, however, when the sorcerer secures from a doctor the powerful drugs with which he or she works. A doctor may also practice black magic, but that is not part of his profession.[41] By the Balamba the doctor (*umulaye*), who uses occult power in a way beneficial to society, is contrasted with the witch (*imfwiti*), who can also tap the hidden resources of nature and devote them to nefarious ends.[42] The Baganda distinguish between "prophets" (*basamizi*), whose knowledge and occult power come to them as the result of inspiration by the ancestral ghosts, and sorcerers (*balongo*). The latter learn their evil secrets "heaven knows how," and their identity rarely becomes known, so cunning are they at casting spells over great distances. Nevertheless the recognized and reputable practitioners engage in nefarious magic for ends which are regarded as socially justifiable.[43] The Bakairí, Kulisehu, and other Brazilian tribes distinguish the good medicine man (*piaje*) from the sorcerer (*omeoto*), the "poison possessor," but they sometimes use these expressions indiscriminately.[44] The Ojibwa contrast the *mide* with the *jessakkid*. Sometimes a *jessakkid* tries to injure a *mide*, but the latter, aided by his superior spirits, becomes aware of the magic employed against him and averts it.[45] While the Paviotso often designate the sorcerer by the term in use for the good medicine man, he is also known as the "eater of people."[46] By the Greenland Eskimo the *angakot* are contrasted with witches (*illiseersut*), the latter being very often decrepit old women.[47]

Among other primitive peoples the functions of the white magician and of the black are exercised by the same practitioner, acting now in the one capacity and now in the other. This seems to be universally true of the Australian aborigines, whose medicine men are by no means averse to indulging, at times, in sorcery.[48] It is also true, though perhaps not universally, of the Papuan tribes.[49] In the Melanesian Islands the magicians who cure diseases may be the same men who cause them, but it often happens that the "darker secrets" of the magical art are known only to people who have a special power of doing harm.[50] The Maori *tohunga* were skilled in every variety of magic, though the highest class of these functionaries, who acted as priests, did not concern themselves with "low-class" jugglery and sorcery.[51] In Flores, one of the Lesser Sunda Islands, the *busung* is a doctor who can also make people sick and kill them. In fact, he practices all kinds of magic, both white and black.[52]

Among the Tanala of Madagascar nearly all *ombiasy* know how to make charms for black magic and will sell these to clients, with directions for using them. A transaction of this sort is kept secret, but even if discovered the *ombiasy* is seldom punished. "It is considered part of his legitimate business."[53] The Hottentot magician who cures can also kill.[54] In the Bechuana tribes the services of a magician may be secured either for good or for evil purposes, by the payment of a fee.[55] Among the Wabena of Tanganyika, while the legitimate medicine men are the avowed enemies of sorcerers, there are cases when they also practice both the white and the black arts, the first openly and the second in secret.[56] Nearly all the *nganga* of the Lower Congo employ both white and black magic. Indeed, the more maleficent a magician is, the more powerful he is presumed to be for curing diseases and removing curses.[57]

Among the Indians of northeastern Peru it is usually the case that the tribal medicine man upon occasion engages in sorcery.[58] A Jivaro magician, since he controls the various spirits responsible for different ailments, can send a sickness into people as well as call it forth. Because of this power he is "the most feared and most respected member of his tribe."[59] It sometimes happens that in the opinion of his colleagues a Tarahumara magician has turned his power for good to evil purposes, has become, in fact, a sorcerer. So they hold a consultation regarding a suspect and perhaps decide that the light of his heart has failed him and that he must be excluded from their ranks. "From that time on, good people avoid him; they no longer give him food, and do not tolerate him about their homes; they are afraid of him, and the better a shaman he was before, the more terrible a sorcerer he is now supposed to have become. Soon every accident that happens in the locality is laid at the accused man's door."[60]

A Cherokee magician attains the "summit of occult power" when he can kill a man by reciting a spell against him. He does so, as a rule, only when hired for the purpose by the victim's enemies. Spells of this fatal character will not be taught a candidate during the first few years of training, and they will never be revealed to quarrelsome or irascible persons, who would be likely to use them even if insulted only once. More considerate sorcerers always endure several insults, perhaps as many as four, before setting their magic at work against a man to kill him.[61]

Among the tribes of central and southern California the magical power of a medicine man can be used for beneficent or maleficent ends. How he uses it is merely a matter of his inclination. Sorcery and healing are therefore indissolubly bound together. In northwestern California this intertwining of the two aspects of magical power is less pronounced. Here the white magician (almost invariably a woman) is seldom suspected of engaging in outright witchcraft.[62]

In Greenland the Eskimo *angakot* sometimes practice witchcraft, though their doing so is condemned by public opinion as an evil abnormality.[63]

In Siberia the division of shamans into white and black seems to be the general rule, as with the Yakut and the Buriat. With the Samoyeds and Lapps, however, shamans serve for both good and bad ends, as occasion arises.[64]

Sorcery finds employment from time to time to satisfy a man's feelings of envy or jealousy toward a neighbor or as an effective means of revenge against some personal enemy. Why does he engage in sorcery as a regular profession? No less than the white magician he expects to be paid for services rendered, and we have already seen that in many instances his compensation is on a liberal scale. If clients are few and business is slow, he can always resort to blackmail. It is not only among ourselves that the crafty, unscrupulous sharper is able to enjoy a comfortable living at the expense of his more credulous fellows. In Eddystone Island, if the sorcerer sees a man of substance, he begs for food or some article of value, and, if refused casts a spell upon him. Chiefs are especially exposed to magic of this character.[65] Among the Maori envy of eminent persons in other families and the desire to supplant the ruling chiefs led constantly to the use of black magic against them.[66] A Toda sorcerer may ask a rich man for a buffalo or for money. Should the request be met by a point-blank refusal, the sorcerer does not proceed further in the matter. But if the rich man promises a gift and does not make it, or if he procrastinates and puts off a decision from day to day then the sorcerer resorts to occult measures. He ties together five small stones by means of some human hair, wraps them up in a piece of cloth, and, holding them in his hand, recites a spell: "May his calves perish; as birds fly away may his buffaloes go when the calves come to suck; as I drink water, may he have nothing but water to drink; as I am thirsty, may he also be thirsty; as I am hungry, may he also be hungry; as my children cry, so may his children cry; as my wife wears only a ragged cloth, so may his wife wear only a ragged cloth." Having uttered this terrible imprecation, the sorcerer takes the hair and stones to the victim's village and hides them secretly in the thatch of the roof of his hut. This magical practice would seem to be regarded as quite proper when the sorcerer, as indicated in the spell which he recites, is a poor man.[67]

While the hope of easy though unlawful gains doubtless accounts in large measure for the adoption of sorcery as a profession, it is also true that men will take up its practice out of sheer perverseness and depravity. There are those in every community whose delight in causing human suffering amounts to a passion, almost to a homicidal neurosis, and who experience a ghoulish glee in the performance of rites secret, dangerous, obscene, and horrible. Theirs is the "motiveless malignity" of an Iago.

The procedures followed and the techniques employed by the black magician, whether amateur or professional, are often those of the practitioner of white magic. To produce accidents, sickness, disease, and death the sorcerer makes use of manual acts, spells, and charms, either separately or in combination; sometimes, as has been shown, he relies on will power alone to secure the results desired. He often practices exuvial magic, believing that if a person's name, some portion of his body, some item of his clothing, some remnant of his food, in fact, anything connected or associated with him, can be obtained, it will be possible to work upon him nefariously. Likewise characteristic of the sorcerer's methods, though by no means confined to them, is iconic magic, whereby the image or effigy of the victim is treated as if it were the victim himself.

Resort is also had to soul abduction. Witches in West Africa set traps to catch the soul that wanders from the body when its owner lies asleep. "This is merely a regular line of business, and not an affair of individual hate or revenge. The witch does not care whose dream soul gets into the trap, and will restore it on payment." Also there are witch doctors, "men of unblemished professional reputation," who keep asylums for lost souls, that is, souls that have wandered afar and have found on their return to their owners that their place has been taken by other "low-class" souls (*sisa*) seeking a human embodiment. These witch doctors keep souls and administer them to patients "who are short of the article." But there are also people who from pure wickedness or because they are hired to do evil will set and bait a trap to catch a man's soul. Concealed in the bait at the bottom of the trap are knives and hooks which tear and rend the soul, either killing it outright or so mauling it that if it escapes and returns to the owner he will become ill.[68] Baluba sorcerers assert that they can steal away a man's personality and leave his body a mere mindless automaton, "an empty ear of corn."[69]

Much less common, though occasionally found, is sorcery to cause a man to break taboos, with all the dire consequences that follow their infraction. Among the Maori, whose taboos were so numerous and so strictly observed, it was not an uncommon practice to get a man to violate a *tapu* unknowingly, with the express purpose of causing his illness or death.[70] This practice was a recognized branch of sorcery. A person who resorted to it was usually in an inferior position or one who did not dare show animosity openly. The sick man would consult a diviner, who might be able to point out the culprit and also to nullify the evil effects of the broken *tapu*.[71] Among the Loango Negroes every person has a food taboo (*tschina*) which he observes with scrupulous care. If he can be caused to break it unwittingly and then is told that he has done so he dies of fright.[72]

Of specialized devices for the practice of black magic perhaps the best known are the pointing bones and sticks of the Australian aborigines. Under various forms they seem to have been in universal use.[73] In the Tongaranka tribe and related tribes of New

South Wales the fibula of a dead man, scraped, polished, and ornamented with red ocher, serves as a pointing bone. To it is attached a cord made of the dead man's hair. Any person toward whom the bone is pointed will surely die, so the natives believe, and a man supposed to possess one is feared accordingly. A magician of the Wiradjuri takes some hair of a dead man, adds some of the man's fat and that of a lizard, rolls the mixture into a ball, and fastens it to a stick. When he wants to make a person sick or cause his death, he takes the stick from its wrappings and lays it before a fire, pointing in the direction of the intended victim. "It is believed that the spirit of the dead man whose fat has been used will help the charm to act."[74] A Queensland native who finds a pointing bone destroys it at once in order to prevent its use against him. If a woman came upon a bone and touched it, or even looked at it, she would fall sick immediately.[75] The Dieri of South Australia suppose that the bone can kill at a distance of from fifty to one hundred miles.[76] Among the Wonkonguru male children are taught the use of the bone "almost as soon as they understand anything," but boys rarely use it until they have been initiated into the tribe and made men. Girls, however, very often direct it against a man who has spurned their advances. They will boast of having done so, in the hope that he may be frightened and come to them.[77] The Arunta attribute the great majority of deaths among them to the use of these bones or sticks. Hence the performance of pointing must be conducted in great secrecy. Were anyone caught in the act he would be most severely punished and very likely be killed.[78]

A special form of the pointing apparatus, made and used by some of the Arunta, consists of a long string of human hair. To one end five small bones are attached and to the other end another bone and a pair of eagle-hawk claws. Two men operate the apparatus, pointing and jerking it in the direction of the intended victim. This device is said to cause great pain because the eagle-hawk claws grip a man's internal organs, squeeze them, and lacerate them. An Unmatjera sorcerer points with a stick and at the same time utters a mystic formula, consisting, apparently, of meaningless words. The stick, after being used, is secretly placed at night on the ground close to the intended victim's camp. If next morning the point is seen to be broken, the sorcerer knows that it has gone inside him. A common form of the stick among the Kaitish has at one end a lump of resin covered with blood drawn from the man who is to operate it. He keeps it for some time in his camp, carefully wrapped up in bark. When ready to use it, he goes to his enemy's camp under cover of darkness. If he finds the intended victim asleep, he turns around, holds the stick between his legs, and jerks it toward the unconscious object. Then he quietly returns to his own camp and places the stick in a hollow log somewhere out in the bush. Should anyone find it there it would be left severely alone. Among all these Central tribes pointing bones and sticks are used exclusively by men.[79]

A short, hard, sharp stick is used by a magician among the Murngin of Northern Territory, Australia, to puncture the heart of a victim. It has great power, principally because the latter's ghost remains in or on the stick. The more people a magician kills the more ghosts cluster about the point of the stick and the greater its capacity for evil. Actually the ghosts are looked upon as one, and it is not so much an individual ghost "as a kind of diffused power, or *mana*." Such a stick is always kept covered with paper bark, just as though it were a ceremonial object, and, like the latter, it must not be seen by women or uninitiated men.[80] The Karadjeri, a tribe in the Kimberley Division of Western Australia, believe that any man who comes near the camp of an intended victim is able to kill him by pointing the bone at him. But death from a great distance can only be achieved when a professional magician points the bone.[81]

In the western islands of Torres Straits the sorcerer takes a crocodile tooth, paints it red, fills it with various plants, and finally anoints it with fat from a decaying human corpse. Then he places the tooth in the fork of a tree, bends the tree back by means of a rope fastened to it, releases the rope, and the recoil shoots the tooth forward for a considerable distance into the bush. The man whom this missile is supposed to hit is also supposed to die at once.[82] In the eastern islands of Torres Straits the sorcerer who would kill a man first carved from wood the image of a crocodile and placed in the snout a crocodile's tooth. The tooth was anointed with a supposedly poisonous substance found on coral reefs. Then he pointed the image and a spear in the direction of the victim, meanwhile uttering an incantation. In order to make this potent it was necessary for him at the same time to "earnestly think" of the man's name. The sorcerer now returned home and hid the crocodile charm in the thatch of his dwelling.[83]

A sorcerer of the Kiwai Papuans, to hit an enemy at a distance, makes use of a small stone obtained in a dream from some ghost. The stone is fixed into a shaft like that of a harpoon, and both are smeared with a magical grease from a decaying human body. The sorcerer then throws the stone in the direction of the enemy, at the same time mentioning his name and saying, "You go kill him that man. What place you find him, you kill him. You come back." The missile flies away with a whizzing sound, finds the man wherever and how far away he may be, and inflicts an invisible wound from which he dies at once. When first hurled the stone is quite small, but when it strikes the man it has become very large. Having done its work, the stone returns to the sender and resumes its original size.[84]

A very potent instrument of black magic is the "ghost-shooter," found in the Banks Islands and elsewhere in the Melanesian area. This is a piece of bamboo stuffed with leaves, a dead man's bone, and other ingredients. Over it the "proper *mana* song" must be chanted. Fasting on the part of the prospective user adds to its effectiveness. A "ghost-shooter" is very easily operated. All you need do is to keep the open end of the bamboo covered with the thumb until your enemy appears, then you let out the magical influence and hit him. Once a Mota man, waiting with his instrument in his hand for the man he meant to shoot, let fly too soon, just as a woman with a child on her hip stepped across the road. "It was his sister's child, his nearest of kin, and he was sure he had hit it full. To save it he put the contents of the bamboo into water, to prevent inflammation of the invisible wound, and the child took no hurt."[85] Quite similar to the "ghost-shooter" is the bamboo tube, filled with certain pulverized leaves, which a Tongan sorcerer carries under the belt, ready for use. He sits beside an intended victim, laughing and smoking in apparent friendliness, but when opportunity offers, secretly points it at him. The victim dies in a day or so unless the sorcerer is induced to save him. This can be done by exposing the tube to the sun or by changing its contents.[86]

Among the Semang, a Negrito people of the Malay Peninsula, the sorcerer takes a sliver of bamboo about two inches long, lays it upon the palm of his hand, and commands it to go and kill an enemy. Thereupon it flies through the air, reaches the appointed victim, who may be as much as two days' journey distant, and pierces him to the heart. A bamboo with a nick in it is especially deadly, for it can "twist itself round his heartstrings." The Malays of the Peninsula are in great fear of the *tuju,* as this appliance is called by them. Its use, they declare, has almost always fatal consequences.[87]

The Naron, a Bushman tribe, make miniature arrows having only one sharp point, which is struck into a bunch of grass. A miniature bow goes with these "grass arrows." Bow and arrows are kept in a tiny leather quiver easily hidden in the owner's clothes or bag. A magician who has a grudge against a fellow member of the magical profession and would destroy him comes up close and shoots one of the arrows at him, blunt end foremost. The missile falls harmlessly to the ground, but the victim dies.[88]

Valenge sorcerers in Portuguese East Africa create *shigono* simply by an effort of will. These "thought entities" can be made to assume animal or human shape as their master desires. He may send an animal *shigono* to join a herd of cattle and bewitch them. Or a woman may put several *shigono* in a pot or bin, and then anyone who goes to that pot or bin will be bewitched and perhaps killed by the creatures.[89] Among the Bondei of Tanganyika cobs of Indian corn, when dressed by the sorcerer to resemble dolls. and properly "charmed," are supposed to become animated. They are then sent out against a designated victim, whose blood they suck. He sickens and dies.[90] Akamba sorcerers have a medicine powder so powerful that it will kill at a distance of a mile or two. It is put in the palm of the hand and blown toward the intended victim. A milder form of the medicine is used by a thief at night. He blows it in the direction of the inmates of a hut, who then become stupefied, thus enabling him to steal with impunity.[91]

A sorcerer among the Ipurina of western Brazil can kill an absent person by means of the magical stones which he takes out of his mouth. These he throws in the direction of the victim, who, upon being hit, feels a sharp sting "like that of a wasp," say the natives, and dies at once.[92] The Karayá of eastern Brazil have an apparatus called by them *kuoluni*. It is shaped like a fish. Red feathers are stuck on it and pieces of mother-of-pearl are inserted to serve as eyes. The operator grasps it by the rear end and holds it against the index finger of his left hand. Anyone against whom it is aimed must die, unless immediately treated by a doctor.[93] The Akawai of British Guiana are said to rub a very potent poison called *wassi* on a thin stick, which is then pointed at someone whom they desire to injure. The person so indicated must come to the sorcerer holding the stick, and as he walks along he falls down in a kind of fainting fit.[94]

The Jivaro Indians of eastern Ecuador make a definite distinction between ailments caused by sorcery (*tunchi*) and those due to disease (*sungura*). Headache, rheumatic pains, suppurating wounds, colic accompanied by swelling of the stomach, painful affections of the heart and liver—all these are attributed to sorcery. On the other hand, feverish ailments are generally referred to the category *sungura*. The word *tunchi* properly signifies "arrows," referring to the small objects which sorcerers are supposed to throw against their enemies. A bewitching arrow is sometimes like the thin stick of palm wood used as a projectile in the blow gun, but more often it resembles a chonta thorn, a small stone, a worm, the sting of a wasp, or the tooth of an animal. The sorcerer keeps it in his body and withdraws it for use as a projectile. It is sent from the mouth and also, if the operator is thoroughly experienced in the black art, from the eyes. Our authority comments on the close parallelism between the poisoned arrow of a Jivaro hunter, which kills by inflicting an insignificant wound, and the sorcerer's magic arrow, which causes mysterious pains and results in a speedy death. It should be noticed that according to the belief of these Indians the *tunchi* has no effect on white men.[95]

A Papago sorcerer, by diffusing poison in the air, causes sickness and death throughout the village. For this purpose he uses a contrivance "resembling a bomb with a time fuse." It is a piece of jointed straw closed at one and and with a plug inserted in the other end. After a certain number of days (the sorcerer knows how many), the poison in the straw "begins to work," pushes out the plug, and is thus liberated. Only another medicine man can detect the presence of a poison tube. If found before it has exploded, it is burned and the poison then reacts on the sorcerer, generally killing him in a few months. A poison tube is so deadly that a medicine man seldom takes hold of it alone; usually a group of men act together in wrapping it in a cloth and throwing it into the flames. When burned it makes a slight explosive noise like a cork popping out. The poison in such a tube is so powerful that it would kill all the villagers, beginning with the old people.[96]

The Shasta of northern California have elaborated the conception of "pains," these being small, needle-like objects, about three inches in length and in appearance like ice. The magician obtains a pain from a familiar spirit, an Axeki. He is supposed to keep it in his own body much of the time, but when angry at anyone he throws it at him and makes him ill. A magician may have many such pains, because he may meet a number of spirits at different times and secure a pain from each one. When the magician dies all his pains fly back to the spirits from whom he received them. The man who can thus send disease-causing objects into people's bodies may also be called upon to extract them when they have been sent in spite by another doctor. He does this, not by means of the sucking process, but by seizing them in the hand and pulling them out. He then dispatches the pains to the original sender, with orders to kill him.[97] The Northern Maidu describe pains as tiny things like bits of sharpened bone or ice, but sometimes like little lizards, frogs, or mice. They are alive. If one of them is thrown at a person it must be sucked out by a doctor. When extracted it talks to him and calls him "father." The doctor then makes it disappear by rubbing it between his hands or else he buries it. Pains are obtained from spirits whom a doctor meets when far away in the mountains; they also come to him in dreams. He keeps them very carefully and usually hides them in a hollow log far from the village.[98]

Among the Lillooet of British Columbia a magician, to bewitch an enemy, would sharpen a feather, stick, or stone and fasten on it some hair taken from the head of the intended victim. To it he also tied some hair or feathers from the animal that was his tutelary spirit. The missile was then shot into the enemy's body. Though it left no mark, the man became ill immediately. He was sure to die, unless the services of another magician could be promptly secured to discover and extract the fatal bolt.[99]

An *angakok* among the Polar Eskimo puts bones of various animals together, covers them with turf and clots of blood, and then, by means of special magical song, conjures life into the object. Such a *tupilak* is usually a seal. It will appear to anyone against whom the *angakok* bears a grudge. Sometimes it capsizes the victim's skin canoe without letting itself be harpooned and killed; sometimes it lets this happen, but the person who captures it soon loses all strength of body and becomes a helpless cripple. To meet a *tupilak* is perilous indeed.[100] We are further told that if the *tupilak* fails to bring ruin and death to the person against whom it has been sent it turns against the sender and destroys him.[101]

Sorcerers are often supposed to have certain animals under their control, and these they can send out upon occasion to annoy or hurt their enemies. A Kurnai medicine man in Victoria dreamed several times that he had become a lace lizard and in its shape had assisted at a corroboree of the lizards. Thus he acquired power over these reptiles. As proof of possessing it he exhibited a tame lizard in his camp. The creature accompanied him wherever he went, perched on his shoulders or his head. It warned him of danger, assisted him in tracking his enemies or young couples who had eloped, and visited the camps at night in order to injure people while they slept. In short, the man and the lizard were "like the same person." Another Kurnai magician had a tame brown snake, which he fed on frogs. The natives were very much afraid of him, because they thought that he sent out the snake at night to do them harm.[102]

Among the Roro-speaking tribes of Papua, snakes and sometimes crocodiles are sent by a sorcerer on man-killing missions. A fragment of the intended victim's clothing, or some object believed to retain his body odor, is placed in a pot with a snake; the pot is heated and the snake, annoyed by the heat, strikes at the fragment. Then the snake is let loose in the bush near a spot which the victim is to pass. It recognizes his smell, follows him, and bites him.[103]

A Malay sorcerer employs a caterpillar as an emissary. The creature is carefully reared and fed on rice. When sent against a person it enters his body invisibly, leaving, however, a livid spot, devours his vitals, and eventually causes his death.[104]

Zulu sorcerers are credited with the power of sending dogs, cattle, and snakes on a "message of malice" to injure people whom they hate.[105] Matabele sorcerers, it is believed, dig up newly buried corpses, restore them to life, and transform them into wolves. The animals are then sent to destroy gardens and kill cattle and human beings. If a wounded wolf escapes into a kraal, the Matabele think that its master must live there.[106] A witch among the Bathonga can send a crocodile or a lion or more often a snake to the place where an enemy is about to pass, for the purpose of wounding or killing him.[107] A Batoka magician keeps a snake in his wallet and sends it out to bite people.[108] The Bechuana believe that a sorcerer can "give over" someone who has gone hunting to a buffalo, elephant, or other dangerous animal. If the hunter is killed, his friends will remark, "It is the work of enemies; he was 'given' to the wild beast."[109] Witches in Nyasaland are supposed to possess tame hyenas and owls. They keep the animals in caves and feed them on human flesh every day. When a pupil has finished a course of instruction in the black art, his teacher presents him with a hyena and an owl.[110] The Wakonde think that sorcerers, in order to destroy their enemies, are able to enlist the services of man-eating lions and crocodiles. When a crocodile secures a human victim it considerately leaves a part of the body for its "father," the sorcerer.[111] Among the Bari of the Anglo-Egyptian Sudan there are sorcerers renowned for their power over wild animals. A lion-caller, for example, by whistling shrilly can summon lions from the wilderness and send the man-eaters against a neighboring village. If his own people have angered him, he will instruct the lions to destroy them. However, if the sorcerer has been appeased, it is incumbent on him to place a stick across every entrance to the village so that the lions will know that "the matter is now closed."[112] Among the Lower Congo tribes a sorcerer can order a leopard or a crocodile to go out and destroy people. He obtains this power by means of a medicine rubbed into his eyes. The animal then becomes visible to him and he knows that it is at his service.[113] In the Cameroons a man selects as a friend and helper some animal which is either very powerful or can easily conceal itself, for example, an elephant, hippopotamus, crocodile, or gorilla. The animal chosen is expected to harm the man's enemies by stealth.[114] On the Slave Coast the sorcerer has at his disposal an owl, the bird of night. It goes to the house of the person to be killed and devours his heart in the darkness. But if the bird can be seized and its claws and wings broken then the sorcerer will suffer the same injury in his limbs.[115]

A sorcerer among the Lengua Indians of Paraguay, by striking his head, could produce live slugs, caterpillars, beetles, and other creeping things. He caused them to enter persons whom he wished to destroy.[116] Tarahumara sorcerers send snakes, scorpions, toads, centipedes, and even small bears into a man's body. They eat his heart so that he dies.[117] Sorcerers among the Mazatec, a tribe in the Mexican state of Oaxaca, make use of an "invocation and spell" which causes a piece of rope or vine to become a serpent. When thrown in the enemy's direction, it goes to him and kills him.[118]

Pueblo Indian sorcerers send caterpillars and grasshoppers to destroy crops. They can also insert centipedes and other insects into the body of a human victim.[119] A sorcerer among the Yokuts-Mono would often frighten a person and bring about a self-induced illness by sending some animal against him. Thus an owl might be sent to hoot outside his house at night or a dove might be sent to a group of people sitting outdoors. The dove would fall down and die near someone, and that person was doomed. A malicious doctor was certainly responsible for the bird's behavior, for no ordinary bird would do such a thing of its own accord.[120] The Twana Indians of Washington explain sickness as produced by an evil animal sent by a sorcerer to eat away the patient's life.[121]

For their nefarious practices sorcerers are sometimes able to secure the help of spiritual beings associated with them. While the Roro-speaking tribes of Papua account for disease and death as produced by sorcery, they suppose that certain spirits are also capable of causing sickness and bodily hurts. These two etiological factors are not ordinarily confused by the natives, but there are some cases in which a real, though undefined, belief exists that malevolent spiritual agencies are controlled by a sorcerer.[122]

The belief in ghostly familiars, of a malignant character, who acted as the agents of sorcerers, was found throughout the Polynesian area, being especially elaborated in Tahiti. Here the sorcerers (of both sexes) communicated with their familiars by means of little images, the *ti'i* ("fetchers"), whose occult power came to them from Ti'i, the first man. The images, hewn out of stone, coral, or wood, had the form of human beings. The sorcerer dressed them as little men and women, gave each one a name, and invoked the malignant ghost after whom it was named to enter it. The images were kept on shelves in a special enclosure. Beneath them was the sorcerer's bed, where he slept with them either in person or in effigy. From time to time he bathed, sunned, and anointed them; he also fed them with the spiritual essence of the food which he himself consumed in its gross material form. If he neglected these attentions, the images tumbled him out of the image house during his sleep. Thus the sorcerer recruited a family of evil-minded ghosts; he was their father and they were his sons and daughters. Obedient to his orders, they attacked in spirit form an enemy whose exuviae had first been obtained and laid before them. Their entrance into the victim's body produced terrible pain: the stone imps weighed him down; the rough coral imps lacerated his intestines; and the wood imps pierced him through and through. If this torture was not speedily checked by remedial measures, the sufferer usually died in a day or so.[123]

In the Marquesas Islands a would-be sorcerer gained magical power by killing his or her father, mother, or sister (whether by a spell or by physical means is unknown). Offerings and prayers were made by him to the ghost of the victim, which became there-after his familiar.[124] The Hawaiian sorcerer secured a familiar by persistent addresses and gifts to an unattached ghost. The familiar took up residence in an image, a bundle of bones, or some other object. It required constant attention in the way of offerings, and if these were not made, it refused to work for its keeper and wreaked vengeance on him for the neglect. A sor-cerer might acquire several familiars, so that if one felt indisposed and unable to go on an errand another one might be sent out for the work of evil.[125] The Maori sorcerer's familiar was the ghost of a defunct relative. It obeyed its keeper's commands and took pos-session of a victim whose exuviae had been subjected to magical treatment, thus producing disease and death. Only one familiar was considered necessary for each sorcerer.[126]

There seems to be good reason to believe that a sorcerer some-times administers various poisons, but in the nature of the case trustworthy evidence of their use is difficult to procure. In Australia, which has very few poisonous plants, vegetable poisons are apparently unknown to the aborigines. We hear of blood-poisoning, however, as practiced by the Narrinyeri of South Australia. They prick an enemy while asleep with a sharp-pointed bone which has been stuck in the fleshy part of a putrid corpse and kept there for several weeks. The natives are terribly afraid of *neilyeri,* "poison revenge." It is said that the "mere pointing" of the *neilyeri* bone at them makes them feel ill. They attribute to it a "deadly energy."[127]

In New Guinea there are quite a number of poisonous plants, and some of these are recognized as poisons by the natives. But as one authority points out (with reference to the Orokaiva), when we consider how many plants are thought to possess deadly properties and as a matter of fact are harmless, and when we consider, further, that the so-called "poisons" are seldom admin-istered through the mouth or in any other way that might make them effective, "we may be justified in regarding the imputed use of poisons in native sorcery with the greatest skepticism."[128] Among the Roro-speaking tribes sorcerers have no knowledge of vegetable or mineral poisons.[129]

The Dobuans use a certain plant as a fish poison that is effective, another plant as an abortifacient probably effective, and the sap of still another plant as a poison in feuds. No magical spells accompany these practices. The attitude of the Dobuan "is no whit different from a European scorning the idea of praying

for relief from stomach-ache at the same time that he takes salts."
There are many other plants believed to be poisonous and used
in sorcery.[130]

In the Melanesian Islands the natives are said to have been
unacquainted with the use of any substance which, when taken
with food or drink, would be injurious by its natural properties,
until they learnt the use of arsenic from Queensland. Sorcerers, to
be sure, had "poisons" and mixed them with food, but the effect
of these was believed to be due to the powerful magic with which
they were endued.[131]

Outside the Australian and Melanesian areas the evidence for
actual poisoning by sorcerers is more conclusive. In Niue shamans
who find it difficult to work "merely by the power of mental suggestion" employ poisons imported by them from Tonga or Fiji.[132]
Christianized natives in Tahiti have confessed that when they
used to practice sorcery and found it of no avail they sometimes
secretly administered poison to their victims.[133]

Poisoning is practiced at times by the Bakgatla of the Bechuanaland Protectorate. They regard it as a form of sorcery.[134]
Many medicine men of the Akikuyu are said to be skilled and
unscrupulous poisoners. Those with whom our authority became
acquainted always begged him to give them antidotes to the
poisons of rival practitioners, though never admitting that they
themselves ever used anything poisonous in their art.[135] A sorcerer among the Bari in theory "and perhaps in practice" is a
poisoner. It is doubtful, however, if the people have any real
knowledge of poisons apart from snake venom.[136] Sorcerers in
southern Nigeria have knowledge of many poisons as yet unknown to science. The Ibibio are described as being "perhaps the
most expert poisoners on earth."[137] Among the Twi of the Gold
Coast priests (if well paid) will tell an applicant how to procure
by magical means the death of an enemy. If no harm ensues to
the intended victim the priest, to maintain his reputation or,
rather, that of his god, will cause some vegetable poison to be
secretly administered to the man. The priest does not let the
applicant know that this has been done; consequently the latter
attributes the death of his enemy to the magic that has been set
in operation.[138]

Medicine men among the tribes of the Upper Amazon are
acquainted with various poisons and their effects. A doctor who
declares that he has exhausted all his skill in treating a patient
and that the sufferer must die, makes sure that he does die by

secretly administering to him a dose of poison. For the doctor it is more important to have a death verdict confirmed than risk the chance of the man's recovery, thus falsifying the prognostication that has been made.[139] The art of poisoning was practiced by the Yokuts-Mono and other tribes of south-central California. When known to have caused deaths, poisoners were killed just as were sorcerers. Doctors were not called in to treat cases of poisoning unless other methods failed.[140] Among the Tinne sorcerers seem to have no knowledge of poisons or any way of preparing them.[141]

NOTES TO CHAPTER XIII

[1] It is quite in accordance with these notions that white men in a primitive community are regarded as impervious to sorcery. They cannot be harmed by it because of the superior counter magic which the strangers wield. For some illustrations see Samuel Gason, in George Taplin (editor), *The Folklore, Manners, Customs, and Languages of the South Australian Aborigines* (Adelaide, 1879), p. 71 (Dieri); R. Parkinson, *Dreissig Jahre in der Südsee* (Stuttgart, 1907), p. 121 (Gazelle Peninsula); S. M. Lambert, *A Yankee Doctor in Paradise* (Boston, 1941), pp. 150, 154 (Fiji); Siméon Delmas, *La religion ou le paganisme des Marquisiens* (Paris, 1927), p. 79; Diedrich Westermann, *Die Kpelle* (Göttingen, 1921), p. 209.

[2] Sir Baldwin Spencer and F. J. Gillen, *The Native Tribes of Central Australia* (London, 1899), p. 541; *iidem, Across Australia* (2d ed., London, 1912), II, 350. The aborigines of the Northern Territory will often fix upon some person, living fifty or one hundred miles away, as the sorcerer who caused the death of a member of their own group (Sir Baldwin Spencer, *Native Tribes of the Northern Territory of Australia* [London, 1914], p. 38).

[3] Sir Baldwin Spencer and F. J. Gillen, *The Northern Tribes of Central Australia* (London, 1904), pp. 467 ff., 685 f.

[4] A. C. Haddon, in *Reports of the Cambridge Anthropological Expedition to Torres Straits*, VI, 225.

[5] Gunnar Landtman, *The Kiwai Papuans of British New Guinea* (London, 1927), p. 326.

[6] F. E. Williams, *Papuans of the Trans-Fly* (Oxford, 1936), pp. 252, 355 f.

[7] Margaret Mead, *Sex and Temperament in Three Primitive Societies* (New York, 1935), pp. 12 f.; *idem*, in *Anthropological Papers of the American Museum of Natural History*, XXXVII, 353 f.

[8] Bronislaw Malinowski, in R. F. Fortune, *Sorcerers of Dobu* (London, 1932), p. xviii.

[9] A. M. Hocart, in *Bernice P. Bishop Museum Bulletin*, No. 62, p. 176.

[10] W. W. Skeat and C. O. Blagden, *Pagan Races of the Malay Peninsula* (London, 1906), II, 539.

[11] W. H. R. Rivers, *The Todas* (London, 1906), pp. 261 ff. A Badaga, it is said, will not meet a Kurumba alone, but flees from his approach as from a wild beast (J. Shortt, in *Transactions of the Ethnological Society of London* [n.s., 1869], VII, 277).

[12] E. T. Dalton, *ibid.*, (n.s., 1868), VI, 6.

13 C. M. Doke, *The Lambas of Northern Rhodesia* (London, 1931), pp. 303, 315.

14 Gerhard Lindblom, *The Akamba in British East Africa* (2d ed., Uppsala, 1920), p. 279.

15 E. E. Evans-Pritchard, *Witchcraft, Oracles, and Magic among the Azande* (Oxford, 1937), p. 201.

16 M. G. Richards, "Bongo Magic," *Sudan Notes and Records,* XVIII (1935), 144.

17 A. W. Cardinall, *In Ashanti and Beyond* (London, 1927), p. 212. See also Margaret J. Field, *Religion and Medicine of the Ga People* (Oxford, 1937), p. 124.

18 Clyde Kluckhohn, *Navaho Witchcraft* (Cambridge, Mass., 1944), p. 35. *Papers of the Peabody Museum of American Archaeology and Ethnology,* Vol. XXII, No. 2.

19 W. L. Warner, *A Black Civilization* (New York, 1937), pp. 193, 243.

20 W. J. V. Saville, *In Unknown New Guinea* (London, 1926), p. 267.

21 R. W. Williamson, *The Mafulu Mountain People of British New Guinea* (London, 1912), pp. 276 f.; *idem, The Ways of the South Sea Savage* (London, 1914), p. 284.

22 G. H. Lane-Fox Pitt-Rivers, *The Clash of Cultures and the Contact of Races* (London, 1927), p. 203.

23 C. G. Seligman, *The Melanesians of British New Guinea* (London, 1910), p. 279.

24 T. C. Hodson, *The Naga Tribes of Manipur* (London, 1911), p. 142.

25 N. E. Parry, *The Lakhers* (London, 1932), pp. 464 f.

26 I. Schapera, *A Handbook of Tswana Law and Custom* (London, 1938), p. 276.

27 E. E. Evans-Pritchard, *The Nuer* (Oxford, 1940), p. 167.

28 G. Kurze, "Sitten und Gebräuche der Lengua-Indianer," *Mitteilungen der geographischen Gesellschaft (für Thüringen) zu Jena,* XXIII (1905), 19.

29 Karl von den Steinen, *Unter den Naturvölkern Zentral-Brasiliens* (Berlin, 1894), p. 344.

30 W. C. Farabee, *Indian Tribes of Eastern Peru* (Cambridge, Mass., 1922), p. 144. *Papers of the Peabody Museum of American Archaeology and Ethnology,* Vol. X.

31 Paul Fejos, *Ethnography of the Yagua* (New York, 1943), p. 91. *Viking Fund Publications in Anthropology,* No. 1.

32 James Chalmers, in *Journal of the Anthropological Institute,* XXVII (1898), 333.

33 W. M. Strong, *ibid.,* XLIX (1919), 307.

34 Gunnar Landtman, *op. cit.,* p. 137.

35 Emma Hadfield, *Among the Natives of the Loyalty Group* (London, 1920), p. 112.

36 John Roscoe, *The Bakitara or Banyoro* (Cambridge, 1923), p. 28.

37 J. H. Driberg, *The Lango* (London, 1923), pp. 249, 261.

38 Curt Nimuendajú, *The Apinayé* (Washington, D.C., 1939), pp. 147 f. *Catholic University of America, Anthropological Series,* No. 8.

39 Frank Russell, in *Twenty-sixth Annual Report of the Bureau of American Ethnology,* pp. 38, 48, 59.

40 Ruth Bunzel, *Zuñi Mythology* (New York, 1935), II, 78–85, 276.

[41] E. W. Smith and A. M. Dale, *The Ila-speaking Peoples of Northern Rhodesia* (London, 1920), II, 94 f.

[42] C. M. Doke, *op. cit.*, pp. 290 f., 302.

[43] Lucy P. Mair, *An African People in the Twentieth Century* (London, 1934), pp. 243 f.

[44] Karl von den Steinen, *op. cit.*, p. 344.

[45] W. J. Hoffman, "The Midewiwin of the Ojibwa," *Seventh Annual Report of the Bureau of Ethnology*, p. 157.

[46] W. Z. Park, *Shamanism in Western North America* (Evanston, 1938), p. 42. *Northwestern University Studies in the Social Sciences*, No. 2.

[47] Hans Egede, *A Description of Greenland* (2d ed., London, 1818), pp. 192 f. It is a fact suggestive of the primitive attitude toward sorcery that some peoples who have no general term for white magic do have one for the black variety or for its practitioners. Thus among the Orokaiva, a Papuan tribe, the words *kai* and *inja* denote magical substances used nefariously by a sorcerer; he himself is known as a *kaiembo* or *injambo* (F. E. Williams, *Orokaiva Magic* [London, 1928], pp. 203, 209). The Trobriander has the word *megwa*, which in the broadest sense means "magic." If, however, he would emphasize the evil character of a magical rite or a spell, he uses the name *bulubwalata*, verbal form *bulati* (Bronislaw Malinowski, *Coral Gardens and Their Magic* [London, 1935], II, 145 f.). The Maori call witchcraft *makutu* (Edward Tregear, *The Maori-Polynesian Comparative Dictionary* [Wellington, New Zealand, 1891], *s.v.*). Among the Twi *abonsum*, the general term for a very malignant spirit, also means "witchcraft" (Sir A. B. Ellis, *The Tshi-speaking Peoples of the Gold Coast of West Africa* [London, 1887], p. 19).

[48] A. P. Elkin, *The Australian Aborigines* (Sydney, 1938), p. 215.

[49] R. F. Fortune, *op. cit.*, p. 289.

[50] R. H. Codrington, *The Melanesians* (Oxford, 1891), pp. 202 f. Cf. H. B. Guppy, *The Solomon Islands and Their Natives* (London, 1887), pp. 55, 163.

[51] Elsdon Best, *The Maori* (Wellington, New Zealand, 1924), I, 244. *Memoirs of the Polynesian Society*, Vol. V. The *tohunga* of the highest class were concerned with the cult of Io. This Supreme God had no dealings with sorcery or with anything else that was evil. Such true prayers as the Maori used were addressed to Io (I, 235, 262).

[52] Paul Arndt, *Mythologie, Religion, und Magie im Sikagebiet (östl. Mitteflores)* (Ende, Flores, 1932), pp. 290 f.

[53] Ralph Linton, *The Tanala* (Chicago, 1933), p. 227. *Field Museum of Natural History, Anthropological Series*, Vol. XXII. There is little competition among *ombiasy*, since usually a village has but one practitioner and never more than two. Each one, it is said, guards his own secrets (pp. 202 f.).

[54] I. Schapera, *The Khoisan Peoples of South Africa* (London, 1930), p. 390.

[55] J. Tom Brown, *Among the Bantu Nomads* (London, 1926), p. 133.

[56] A. T. Culwick and G. M. Culwick, *Ubena of the Rivers* (London, 1935), pp. 116 f.

[57] J. H. Weeks, "The Congo Medicine Man and His Black and White Magic," *Folk-Lore*, XXI (1910), pp. 447, 452, 471.

[58] Günter Tessmann, *Die Indianer Nordost-Perus* (Hamburg, 1930), pp. 589, 600.

[59] M. W. Stirling, "Jivaro Shamanism," *Proceedings of the American Philosophical Society*, LXXII (1933), 140; *idem*, "Historical and Ethnographical Material on the Jivaro Indians," *Bulletin of the Bureau of American Ethnology*, No. 117, p. 117.

60 Carl Lumholtz, *Unknown Mexico* (London, 1903), I, 322 f.

61 James Mooney and F. M. Olbrechts, "The Swimmer Manuscript. Cherokee Sacred Formulas and Medicinal Prescriptions," *Bulletin of the Bureau of American Ethnology*, No. 99, pp. 87, 93, 100.

62 A. L. Kroeber, *Handbook of the Indians of California* (Washington, D.C., 1925), p. 853.

63 Henry Rink, *Tales and Traditions of the Eskimo* (Edinburgh, 1875), pp. 53 f.; Fridtjof Nansen, *Eskimo Life* (2d ed., London, 1894), p. 240.

64 Mary A. Czaplicka, *Aboriginal Siberia* (Oxford, 1914), pp. 194, 200 f.

65 A. M. Hocart, "Medicine and Witchcraft in Eddystone of the Solomons," *Journal of the Royal Anthropological Institute*, LV (1925), 230.

66 P. H. Buck, *Regional Diversity in the Elaboration of Sorcery in Polynesia* (New Haven, 1936), p. 3. *Yale University Publications in Anthropology*, No. 2.

67 W. H. R. Rivers, *op. cit.*, pp. 257 f.

68 Mary H. Kingsley, *Travels in West Africa* (London, 1897), pp. 461 f., 517 f.

69 Sir H. H. Johnston, *George Grenfell and the Congo* (London, 1908), II, 660. For other instances of soul abduction by sorcerers see W. W. Gill, *Myths and Songs from the South Pacific* (London, 1876), p. 191 (Danger Island); W. W. Skeat, *Malay Magic* (London, 1900), pp. 374–79; W. H. Bentley, *Life on the Congo* (London, 1887), p. 71; L. J. B. Bérenger-Féraud, *Les peuplades de la Sénégambie* (Paris, 1879), p. 277 (Serer); A. I. Hallowell, *The Role of Conjuring in Saulteaux Society* (Philadelphia, 1942), pp. 59 ff. *Publications of the Philadelphia Anthropological Society*, Vol. II; E. W. Nelson, in *Eighteenth Annual Report of the Bureau of American Ethnology*, Part I, p. 422 (Eskimo of Bering Strait).

70 Edward Shortland, *Traditions and Superstitions of the New Zealanders* (2d ed., London, 1856), pp. 114 ff.

71 Edward Tregear, *The Maori Race* (Wanganui, New Zealand, 1904), pp. 201 f.

72 E. Pechuël-Loesche, *Volkskunde von Loango* (Stuttgart, 1907), pp. 338 f.

73 See Geza Róheim, "The Pointing Bone," *Journal of the Royal Anthropological Institute*, LV (1925), 90–112.

74 A. W. Howitt, *The Native Tribes of South-East Australia* (London, 1904), pp. 360 f.

75 W. E. Roth, *Ethnological Studies among the North-West-Central Queensland Aborigines* (Brisbane, 1897), p. 152; *idem, North Queensland Ethnography Bulletin*, No. 5, p. 34.

76 Samuel Gason, in J. D. Woods (editor), *The Native Tribes of South Australia* (Adelaide, 1879), p. 276. A Dieri legend recounts how one of the Mura-Mura (predecessors and prototypes of the natives), when out hunting in a time of great drought, was shown where game was to be found by a clever boy whom he met. Afterward the boy was killed by other Mura-Mura, who were angry with him for having drunk out of their water-bag and forgetting to shut it up again. Then the man who had been helped came upon his friend, lying cold in death. He proceeded to separate the flesh from the bones and used these as pointers to kill the murderers. Such was the origin of the pointing bone in use among the Dieri. In another version of the legend two Mura-Mura avenged the boy's death. It is for this reason that two persons almost always act together in manipulating the bone. See Mary E. B. Howitt, "Some Native Legends from Central Australia," *Folk-Lore*, XIII (1902), pp. 405 f.

[77] G. Horne and G. Aiston, *Savage Life in Central Australia* (London, 1924), p. 151.

[78] Spencer and Gillen, *The Native Tribes of Central Australia*, p. 536.

[79] *Iidem, The Northern Tribes of Central Australia*, pp. 459 ff. In the Kaitish tribe the headman of the water totemic group must not use or even touch a pointing bone or stick. Should he do so, the water would stink and "go bad" (p. 463).

[80] W. L. Warner, *op. cit.*, pp. 238 f.

[81] S. D. Porteus, *The Psychology of a Primitive People* (London, 1931), p. 49.

[82] A. C. Haddon, in *Reports of the Cambridge Anthropological Expedition to Torres Straits*, V, 326.

[83] *Idem*, in *Reports of the Cambridge Anthropological Expedition to Torres Straits*, VI, 228 f. In Torres Straits "the power of words and the projection of the will were also greatly believed in by the natives" (VI, 220).

[84] Gunnar Landtman, *op. cit.*, pp. 322 f.

[85] R. H. Codrington, *op. cit.*, p. 205. For another instance of the deadly use of the "ghost-shooter" see pp. 205 f. According to W. H. R. Rivers it can kill "a powerful and healthy man" in a couple of days (*Medicine, Magic, and Religion* [London, 1924], p. 13).

[86] E. W. Gifford, "Tongan Society," *Bernice P. Bishop Museum Bulletin*, No. 61, pp. 339 f.

[87] W. W. Skeat and C. O. Blagden, *op. cit.*, II, 199, 233 f., 539.

[88] Dorothea F. Bleek, *The Naron* (Cambridge, 1928), p. 28. On this "Bushman revolver" see also F. Seiner, in *Mitteilungen der anthropologischen Gesellschaft in Wien*, XLIII (1913), 322 f.

[89] E. Dora Earthy, *Valenge Women* (London, 1933), p. 218.

[90] Godfrey Dale, in *Journal of the Anthropological Institute*, XXV (1896), 223.

[91] C. W. Hobley, *Ethnology of A-Kamba and Other East African Tribes* (Cambridge, 1910), p. 95.

[92] P. Ehrenreich, *Beiträge zur Völkerkunde Brasiliens* (Berlin, 1891), p. 69.

[93] Fritz Krause, *In den Wildnissen Brasiliens* (Leipzig, 1911), pp. 334 f.

[94] W. E. Roth, "An Inquiry into the Animism and Folk-Lore of the Guiana Indians," *Thirtieth Annual Report of the Bureau of American Ethnology,* pp. 358 f.

[95] Rafael Karsten, *The Head Hunters of Western Amazonas* (Helsingfors, 1935), pp. 394, 403, 409 f. *Societas Scientiarum Fennica, Commentationes Humanarum Litterarum*, Vol. VII, No. 1. A bewitching arrow is used by Karayá sorcerers. It bears on the tip two teeth of a snake and when it enters the victim produces an incurable malady (P. Ehrenreich, *op. cit.*, p. 33).

[96] Frances Densmore, "Papago Music," *Bulletin of the Bureau of American Ethnology*, No. 90, pp. 84 ff.

[97] R. B. Dixon, "Some Shamans of Northern California," *Journal of American Folk-Lore*, XVII (1904), 23 f.

[98] *Ibid.*, p. 26.

[99] James Teit, in *Memoirs of the American Museum of Natural History*, IV, 287.

[100] Knud Rasmussen, *The People of the Polar North* (London, 1908), pp. 155 f.

[101] Fridtjof Nansen, *op. cit.*, p. 285. As Nansen points out, the whole con-

ception of the *tupilak* seems to be a borrowing by the Greenland Eskimo of Norwegian and Icelandic beliefs in *gand,* or "messengers." See also Henry Rink, *op. cit.,* pp. 53, 151 f., 201, 461 f.

[102] A. W. Howitt, *op. cit.,* pp. 387 f.

[103] C. G. Seligman, *op. cit.,* pp. 282 ff.

[104] W. W. Skeat, "Malay Spiritualism," *Folk-Lore,* XIII (1902), 147, 157.

[105] Henry Callaway, *The Religious System of the Amazulu* (London, 1870), p. 348. An owl, buzzard, turkey, or red-breasted eagle settling on the roof of a house is regarded by the Zulu as a harbinger of evil. The omen has been sent, they think, by a malignant person who is a witch (James Macdonald, in *Journal of the Anthropological Institute,* XX [1891], 115).

[106] T. M. Thomas, *Eleven Years in Central South Africa* (London, 1872), pp. 293 f.

[107] H. A. Junod, *The Life of a South African Tribe* (2d ed., London, 1927), II, 512.

[108] J. Torrend, *A Comparative Grammar of the South-African Bantu Languages* (London, 1891), p. 292.

[109] John Mackenzie, *Ten Years North of the Orange River* (Edinburgh, 1871), pp. 390 f.

[110] W. H. Garbutt, "Witchcraft in Nyasa," *Journal of the Royal Anthropological Institute,* XLI (1911), 301, according to an account by a native.

[111] D. R. MacKenzie, *The Spirit-ridden Konde* (London, 1925), p. 263.

[112] A. N. Tucker, "Witchcraft Applied to Animals," *Sudan Notes and Records,* XIV (1931), 191 ff.

[113] R. E. Dennett, in *Folk-Lore,* XVI (1905), 391 ff.

[114] Charles Partridge, *Cross River Natives* (London, 1905), pp. 225 f.

[115] Baudin, in *Les missions Catholiques,* XVI (1884), 249.

[116] W. B. Grubb, *An Unknown People in an Unknown Land* (4th ed., London, 1914), pp. 151, 155 f.

[117] Carl Lumholtz, *op. cit.,* I, 315.

[118] J. B. Johnson, *The Elements of Mazatec Witchcraft* (Göteborg, Sweden, 1939), p. 133. *Ethnological Studies,* No. 9.

[119] Elsie C. Parsons, "Witchcraft among the Pueblos: Indian or Spanish?" *Man,* XXVII (1927), 107. A witch may also call on the ghost of some member of a family he is persecuting and, having thus summoned it, require it to draw away to the realm of the dead its living relative. "I want him to go," says the witch (*loc. cit.*).

[120] Ann H. Gayton, "Yokuts-Mono Chiefs and Shamans," *University of California Publications in American Archaeology and Ethnology,* XXIV, 391.

[121] Myron Eells, *Ten Years of Mission Work among the Indians* (Boston, 1886), p. 43.

[122] C. G. Seligman, *op. cit.,* pp. 291, 303 f.

[123] Teuira Henry, "Ancient Tahiti," *Bernice P. Bishop Museum Bulletin,* No. 48, pp. 203 ff.

[124] E. S. C. Handy, "The Native Culture in the Marquesas," *ibid.,* No. 9, p. 273 (Hiva Oa).

[125] David Malo, *Hawaiian Antiquities* (Honolulu, 1903), pp. 116, 158. On these "fetchers" see also Martha Beckwith, *Hawaiian Mythology* (New Haven, 1940), pp. 105 ff. When the bones of a dead member of a family were preserved

and regularly provided with offerings the ghost became the protector of the family. Not everyone who thus kept an *aumakua* used it for sorcery (*loc. cit.*)

126 P. H. Buck, *op. cit.*, p. 5. See also W. H. Goldie, "Maori Medical Lore," *Transactions and Proceedings of the New Zealand Institute*, XXXVII (1904), 31.

127 George Taplin (editor), *The Folk-Lore, Manners, Customs, and Languages of the South Australian Aborigines* (Adelaide, 1879), pp. 36 f. Cf. A. L. P. Cameron, in *Journal of the Anthropological Institute*, XIV (1885), 362. A. W. Howitt was of the opinion that in some of the southeastern tribes (Yuin, Kamilaroi) "actual poison" was used (*op. cit.*, pp. 561 f.).

128 F. E. Williams, *Orokaiva Magic*, pp. 213 f. However, W. N. Beaver, formerly a British magistrate in Papua, knew actual cases where "something" presumably poisonous was administered by Orokaiva sorcerers. "There is one substance which is applied to the lips of the victim during sleep and which has the effect of rendering them dry, so that on wakening he licks his lips and swallows, with consequent death in a few days. There is another substance which is also placed in the open mouth during sleep, and the involuntary motion of swallowing absorbs the poison" (*Unexplored New Guinea* [2d ed., London, 1920], p. 134).

129 C. G. Seligman, *op. cit.*, p. 289.

130 R. F. Fortune, *op. cit.*, p. 299.

131 R. H. Codrington, *op. cit.*, pp. 213 f. With reference to the New Hebrides it is said that by far the greater number of "poisonings" are simply cases of black magic working by suggestive processes (E. A. C. Corlette, in *Oceania*, V [1934–35], 484).

132 E. M. Loeb, "The Shaman of Niue," *American Anthropologist* (n.s., 1924), XXVI, 395.

133 Teuira Henry, "Ancient Tahiti," *Bernice P. Bishop Museum Bulletin*, No. 48, p. 212. Cf. William Ellis, *Polynesian Researches* (2d ed., London, 1827), I, 367 f.

134 I. Schapera, *Married Life in an African Tribe* (London, 1940), p. 35.

135 W. S. Routledge and Katherine Routledge, *With a Prehistoric People* (London, 1910), pp. 272 f. Canon Roscoe, during many years of research among the Baganda and other East African tribes, never found any evidence of poisons being administered in food or drink. "Every case was genuine magic-working, often with grave effect, upon the mind" (John Roscoe, "Magic and Its Power," *Folk-Lore*, XXXIV [1923], 30).

136 C. G. Seligman and Brenda Z. Seligman, in *Journal of the Royal Anthropological Institute*, LVIII (1928), 437.

137 P. A. Talbot, *The Peoples of Southern Nigeria* (London, 1926), II, 162.

138 Sir A. B. Ellis, *The Tshi-speaking Peoples of the Gold Coast of West Africa* (London, 1887), pp. 142 ff.

139 Thomas Whiffen, *The North-West Amazons* (New York, 1915), pp. 168 f.

140 Ann H. Gayton, "Yokuts-Mono Chiefs and Shamans," *University of California Publications in American Archaeology and Ethnology*, XXIV, 390, 402 f. The authoress describes at length the case of a Tachi chief who used poisons from sheer maliciousness as well as to make money. This chief was also credited with the possession of some "supernatural power" (pp. 403 ff.)

141 Julius Jetté, "On the Medicine Men of the Ten'a," *Journal of the Royal Anthropological Institute*, XXXVII (1907), 168.

CHAPTER XIV

IMAGINARY SORCERY

THE sorcerers whom we have considered thus far are mostly creatures of flesh and blood, real men and women. They may be amateurs or professionals; they may be known or unknown; and their activities may be licit or illicit according to circumstances. There are also imaginary sorcerers, men and women whose nefarious potency is most often considered to be innate, though it may also be secured by a formal rite of initiation, by training, and in still other ways. Their possession of this potency is some- times obvious to their fellows, as in the familiar cases of twins and people with the evil eye; in other cases they cannot be recognized except by the misfortunes they cause. In still other cases the sorcerer is himself ignorant that he is endowed by nature with the ability to injure or kill his unsuspecting neigh- bors. If he knew it he might be the first to deplore it. Some primitive peoples do not discriminate between the two kinds of sorcerers. Others, while so discriminating, call them by the same name. But still others clearly distinguish by different names the "day witches," as the Lovedu of the Transvaal describe professional sorcerers, using spells and charms, and the "night witches," creatures who work evil consciously or unconsciously, because their nature is evil. But whether they know or do not know what they do the community holds them all equally respon- sible for their actions.

The belief in imaginary sorcery has been described among some tribes of Australia. In the western part of the continent the aborigines are said to evince great fear of "boylyas." These witches can transport themselves through the air at pleasure and can make themselves invisible to everyone except other "boylyas." If they dislike a man, they kill him by coming upon him at night and consuming his flesh. They eat many people "as fire would"; they move stealthily, "you sleep and they steal on you"; they "come moving along in the sky"; they cannot be seen.[1]

Some Massim tribes occupying the southeastern extremity of

Papua suppose that any woman who has borne children can project from her body a shadow-like form known at Bartle Bay as a *parauma* or *labuni*. It exists in or is derived from an organ in her body called *ipona*, literally meaning "egg" or "eggs." The *labuni* emerges from the woman while she seems to be asleep and afterward re-enters her through the rectum. It causes sickness by means of a sliver of bone or a fragment of stone or coral, which is thrown at the victim from a distance of about sixty yards and lodges in his body. The sickness is often, though not always, fatal. Because of the fear of meeting a *labuni* people are afraid to go outdoors at night. Should anyone see it, the creature turns into a snake or some other animal and then again resumes its human form. A *labuni* rarely enters a house. It is frightened away by the howling of dogs, who are able to see it. After the woman's death the *labuni* may pass to her daughter or with her soul depart to the other world.[2]

The natives of the Trobriand Islands are firmly persuaded that certain women pass a secret existence as "flying witches" (*yoyova*). Their power for evil is inherited from mother to daughter, but an early initiation into the black art is also necessary for its practice. Some of them are said to have sexual relations with nonhuman and very malignant beings, from whom they receive further instruction in matters occult and evil. The witch goes out at night in the form of an "invisible double" and flies through the air. She can assume at will the shape of a firefly, of a night bird, or of a flying fox; she can hear and smell at enormous distances; she feeds on corpses. The disease which a *yoyova* causes is seldom curable even if the victim resorts at once to counteraction by another witch. It is rapid in action, and death ensues as a rule immediately after the witch has removed the victim's insides, which she then consumes. A *yoyova* employs neither spells nor rites of sorcery such as are actually practiced by a male sorcerer, or *bwagau*. Though she lives "merely in legend and fiction" and engages in purely imaginary witchcraft, a woman thus credited with malign occult power is an object of terror to her neighbors. This she knows very well and will often play up to her supposed role, in order to batten on the fears of the people. The Trobrianders distinguish between a *yoyova* and a *bwagau*. The latter, indeed, is credited with the ability to vanish at will, emit a shining glow from his person, and employ accomplices among the nocturnal birds—but this is about the extent of his occult power. He never partakes of his victim's flesh. Moreover, the best he can hope for from his black magic is to inflict a lingering disease which may result fatally after months or years of steady labor with his spells and rites. Even then another sorcerer can be found to counteract his efforts and restore the patient to health. It is to be noticed, also, that while a native will often own up to the fact that he practices sorcery and will refer to it quite openly in conversation, a woman never directly confesses to being a flying witch, not even to her husband.[3]

The natives of the Banks Islands consider that it is possible for one's soul to go out and eat the soul or lingering life of a person who has just died. A woman who made no secret of her depraved tastes once announced on the death of a neighbor that she would go in the night and consume his body. So the friends of the deceased kept watch in the house where he lay, and during the night they heard a scratching at the door and then a rustling noise close by the corpse. One of them threw a stone and seemed to hit the unseen thing. Next morning the woman had a bruise on her arm where the missle had struck her. "Such a woman would feel a morbid delight in the dread which she inspired, and would also be secretly rewarded by some whose secret spite she gratified."[4]

The Sea Dayak suppose that certain people—the *tau tepang*— have the power to inflict all sorts of disasters on their neighbors or the crops. It is only the head of a *tau tepang* that can do harm. At night the head departs secretly and, after accomplishing the work of evil, returns to the body in the early morning. This nefarious power cannot be acquired; it is always passed on to a child of a *tau tepang* family by the mother, who touches the cut edge of the child's tongue with her spittle. One who has it is an object of dread, everyone shuns him, and he leads the life of a leper. In the old days he had to dwell apart from the village. He can seldom get a wife unless he marries a woman who herself belongs to a *tau tepang* family. He is destined, the natives believe, to "supernatural" punishment.[5]

The people of Alor, one of the Lesser Sundas, think that both men and women can be witches. A female witch most frequently gains power over a victim by inviting him to have sexual intercourse. Then, while he sleeps, she steps over his body and urinates on him; thereafter she is able to feast on his liver at leisure. Witches can transform themselves into civet cats or streaks of light that are seen at night. They can even detach their heads and send them rolling about after dark. They eat small children.[6]

A witch in Cambodia is always a woman. She may be recognized by her wild, staring eyes. At night she wanders about, with her head on her shoulders, and feasts on unclean food, even food in the entrails of sleeping people. She does not need to employ charms or spells to injure anyone who displeases her; a simple act of will suffices for bewitchment. Some of these creatures inherit their dangerous powers and remain unaware of possessing them, but others acquire them by special exercises. If discovered, they may be put to death without mercy.[7]

The Oraon, an aboriginal people of Chota Nagpur, entertain a lively belief in the witch whose soul can leave the body at will and go forth, usually by night, in the form of a black cat or a human dwarf no higher than a man's thumb. Entering a dormitory, the witch licks up the saliva which trickles from the corners of a sleeper's mouth, or nibbles at the dead skin on the soles of his feet, or bites off a portion of the hair (of a sleeping woman). Not long afterward the person so attacked falls seriously ill and perhaps may die. With the help of a powerful spell a witch can also extract unperceived the liver of an intended victim. By the Oraon the liver is considered to be the seat of the vital principle. The extracted organ is carefully preserved and watched by the witch for the following twenty-four hours. In the meantime, if the victim summons the help of a magician and if the latter, by means of counter spells, succeeds in keeping the ants from touching the liver during the twenty-four hours then it must be restored to its owner, who recovers from his illness. But should the ants get at it within the fatal period he becomes worse and worse, and finally, when the witch eats up the liver, the patient forthwith expires.[8] The Oraon believe that witches from several neighboring villages are wont to hold secret conclaves, especially on a night when there is a new moon. They assemble under a tree in some secluded spot, strip themselves, sacrifice a black chicken, and dance by the light of lamps burning in tigers' skulls. It is on such occasions that novices learn the spells and other techniques of the black art.[9]

There are witches (*mpamosavy*) among the Tanala, a hill tribe of Madagascar, who follow their diabolical art for the mere pleasure to be got out of it. The witches are of both sexes. They work at night, naked except for a turban, visit graves, and engage in dances which strengthen their power of causing deaths in the village. They also rob graves and from corpses make charms. When someone is ill they congregate outside his house and mourn for him as if he were already dead. Soon he dies. They scratch at doors and windows, terrifying the inmates though never breaking in. They ride cattle until the poor animals sink down exhausted, break fences, and do as much wanton damage as possible. They are powerless against people who confront them openly and boldly. A person may become an unconscious *mpamosavy* as the result of some evil charm directed against him. He goes to bed at night like anyone else, then rises and steals away to do his wicked deeds in a somnambulistic state. One man did not know that he was a witch until told by his wife that he rose every night after they had gone to bed, went out, and returned hours later with his body icy cold and his feet wet with dew. In view of these prevalent conceptions it is not hard to understand why persons accused of witchcraft often doubt their own innocence.[10]

By the Pondo of Pondoland the vast majority of deaths are attributed to witchcraft. This is actually practiced in secret, but in most cases it is purely imaginary. Certain men and women are thought to have familiars, who may appear in human form, with whom they enjoy sexual relations, and by means of whom they can destroy property and life. Sometimes the familiars are hereditary. Of these creatures the most widely believed in is Thikolose, a dwarf so small that he reaches only to a man's knee. Hair covers all his face and comes out of his ears; his face is squashed like a baboon's; his penis is so long that he carries it over a shoulder; he has only one buttock. By means of a charm he makes himself invisible, and he is only seen by adults who possess him and by some children. A witch who has such a familiar as Thikolose or his female counterpart is able to send evil omens which portend misfortune in the village where they occur and also to raise the dead and enslave them, though this can be done only before the bodies have decayed in the grave. Formerly witches went about naked at night while engaged in their wicked practices. "Some, while people are asleep, go to the skies. They climb up on ropes like spider webs." No society of witches is recognized, though it is said that "they meet together by night and joke together." The Pondo believe that no one can practice witchcraft unconsciously. Witches always know what they do and want to do it.[11]

The Bavenda of the Transvaal designate by the term *vhaloi* (singular, *muloi*) those people who use magic to destroy property, inflict disease and misfortune on their neighbors, or cause their death—often entirely without provocation. They may be of either sex, but women predominate among them. Some *vhaloi* act unconsciously and do not realize that they possess this evil power; some are deliberate malefactors. The nefarious activity of unconscious witches is at night, when they may travel long distances on the back of a hyena or some other animal. During these nocturnal prowlings their place at home is taken by hideous monsters, which cannot be seen by ordinary persons, though powerful magicians sometimes recognize them. One of these witches appears as a shadowy human form, always stark naked, since she left her clothes behind in the hut to cover her metamorphosed body. Her eyes are bright and shine like burning lumps of coal. Sometimes she meets with several associates, and together they feast on human flesh. When not intent on murder the *vhaloi* play mischievous tricks on the natives, such as sending a stoat to suck the cows dry. Or they may act as vampires, sucking the blood of enemies and causing them to become emaciated and anemic. Indeed there is very little that is horrible and revolting which these creatures do not at some time accomplish.[12]

Witches (*baloyi*), both male and female, are numerous among the Bathonga. Their power is hereditary, being transmitted by the mother and not by the father. It is sucked in at the mother's breast, but it must be strengthened by special medicines to become really efficient. A son to whom they are not given will be free from this dread power. A mother sometimes refrains from administering the medicines to a child so that later, should one of her offspring be accused of killing by witchcraft and be required to undergo the trial by ordeal, she can send the immune child to swallow the poison draught. It will have no effect on the substitute and so the true witch will escape. The *baloyi,* who form a kind of secret society, meet at night in their spirit bodies to eat human flesh and discuss what they shall do to injure property and destroy life. The nocturnal activity of these dreadful creatures is unknown to them when they have returned to their daily vocations. However, those who have been long at their trade seem to be aware of and even proud of what they do and therefore are more or less conscious of the double lives they lead. Some renounce their wicked ways and use the knowledge acquired by them to baffle the enchantments of their former associates in evil-doing. Fortunately, when a case of serious illness occurs and witchcraft is believed to have caused it, the Bathonga know ways of detecting the culprit. A man who quarrels with another and says in his anger, "I shall see you," is surely a witch. The same conclusion will be drawn if he pointed to another person with the index finger. A woman who loses many children must have eaten them by witchcraft. The mere fact that one belongs to a family of *baloyi* suffices as an indication of guilt. But before punitive action can be taken against a suspect the relatives of the patient must consult a diviner, who can determine whether or not the illness is due to witchcraft.[13]

Witchcraft beliefs, essentially the same as those which have been described among the Pondo, Bavenda, and Bathonga, are found among other South African tribes such as the Basuto, the Lovedu of the Transvaal, and the Balamba of Northern Rhodesia. In the case of the Lovedu it is noteworthy that while witches are believed to feel a certain compulsion to do evil—"their fingers burn to bewitch"—they are never unconscious of their wicked powers and deeds, as is sometimes held to be true of the Bavenda and Bathonga practitioners of the black art. Furthermore, their knowledge of witchcraft does not inevitably involve its practice. The child of a witch may refuse to kill people and use her powers instead to increase the crops and perform other beneficent actions.[14]

Among the Anyanja of Nyasaland the power of witchcraft (*afiti*) is confined to members of a certain clan. They are able to keep this power only by eating human flesh and hence are supposed to kill people for cannibal feasts. A person sometimes acquires the dread *afiti* without realizing what its possession involves for him. It can be expelled by a professional witch finder, who is generally a woman. By the application of medicines she causes the patient to vomit and in this way rids him of his affliction.[15] According to the belief of the Wakonde, if either a father or a mother is a witch, the children will inherit the witchcraft power. An expectant mother, who knows that her husband is a witch, will take care to have her child born at a distance so that it may be free of the hereditary taint. Witchcraft derived from the mother is of peculiar virulence. If it comes from the father it may lie quiescent and do no harm.[16] The Nyakyusa of Tanganyika likewise think that witchcraft power can be inherited from either parent. A child playing with an older child who is a witch may acquire it merely by contact or proximity with such a person. The power in children is dormant, becoming active only in adult life.[17] The Kipsigis, a branch of the Nandi-speaking peoples, also consider witchcraft power to be inheritable. A father transmits it to all his sons and a mother to all her daughters. Witches are usually people of a jealous disposition. They cannot see their neighbors healthy and prosperous without at once wanting to bring them low by the practice of malefic arts.[18]

Among the Lango, a Nilotic tribe of Uganda, a woman who, though fertile, bears only weakling children that do not live long, is believed to have in her body some "magic property" causing their death. She may bring this about either intentionally or un-intentionally. In such a case she will be divorced and returned to her family. Our authority tells of a woman married to three husbands in succession and divorced by each one as ill-omened because all her children died soon after birth. Though not harshly treated, she brooded over her terrible situation and finally com-mitted suicide.[19]

The Azande of the Anglo-Egyptian Sudan consider that witch-craft power is transmitted by unilinear descent from parent to child. A person whose body contains the power does not neces-sarily use it, however; it may remain inoperative, "cool," as the natives say, throughout his lifetime. Practically, therefore, it is regarded as an individual trait and is treated as such, in spite of its association with kinship. To bridge over the distance be-tween the witch and the victim the Azande imagine that it is not the witch in person who engages in malefic arts but the power or "soul" of witchcraft. This may quit its corporeal home at any time, but it does so generally by night when the victim is asleep. It sails through the air, emitting a bright light like the gleam of firefly beetles, only much larger and brighter than they. While the witch remains quietly at home, the witchcraft soul removes the psychical part of the victim's organs, "the soul of his flesh," which will be devoured by the evil one and his (or her) fellows. Unlike some African peoples, the Azande do not admit that a person can engage in witchcraft unconsciously and therefore without volition. They think that witches lead a secret life and share confidences, laughing about their misdeeds and boasting of their exploits against those whom they hate. At the same time, when accused of witchcraft, they will plead innocence of inten-tion—an inconsistency both understandable and pardonable.[20]

The Baluba of the Belgian Congo believe that people can be witches and act as witches unawares in their sleep. When a charge of witchcraft is laid the accused will answer, with the best faith in the world, "You have said so, but I know nothing about it; I am not to blame, I was asleep."[21] A Baluba mother, whose children die one after another at an early age, may have the horrible suspicion that she is an unconscious witch. Without telling anyone she procures some of the poison used in the witchcraft ordeal and administers it secretly to herself. If it takes effect and she feels herself about to die, she calls in the neighbors, expresses her joy that she is soon to relieve them of the danger of harboring a witch, and declares that all her wicked deeds were done unknowingly.[22]

The witchcraft power (*kindoki*) recognized by the Bakongo may be either congenital or else gradually acquired. In the former case the person who is born a witch works evil unconsciously or without any deliberate effort to do so. He acts according to his nature. In the latter case a person goes to the school of a witch and secures his services as instructor by handing over to him a close relative as payment. The student is then taught how to manipulate various charms and by means of them to turn himself into some animal, large or small, for the purpose of stealthily approaching and mercilessly killing a victim. Our missionary authority declares that practically all Bakongo are supposed to die from the assaults of witches. If a person is mortally ill of pneumonia the Bakongo say that "they" have attacked him with a snake; and if he has fallen from a tree that "they" have made him fall. Envy, for the Bakongo, is the prime cause of *kindoki*, at least that of the conscious sort.[23]

Among the Mambila of the British Cameroons the power of witchcraft may be acquired by heredity, by purchase, or by accident. It is inherited only in the female line. The children of a woman who is a witch obtain their evil power (the "witch soul") by imbibing her milk. Before practicing, however, they must first partake of a medicine prepared by the mother or, more usually, by an elder sister, in order to make them conscious of the possession of the power. While witchcraft is not transmitted through the father he may, if a practitioner of the black art, reveal it to a son. This is accomplished by procuring the soul of one of his maternal relatives, cooking it in the right magical way, and giving a piece of the liver to his son, together with part of a slippery fish or a secret medicine. Or a man may purchase witchcraft from a witch who is not related to him by presenting her with the soul of one of his maternal relatives. The souls of paternal relatives are not given to witches because such relatives are not regarded as one's kith and kin.[24]

In southern Nigeria, where witchcraft beliefs are rife, a witch is usually aware of his or her possession of occult powers for evil and glories in them. Some persons do not know, however, that they are witches and engage in the black art perhaps for years, until their true character is revealed to their associates. Such witchcraft is purely imaginary, being supposed to occur while the practitioners are apparently lying asleep or in a trance-like state induced by the use of medicines. There is no doubt, however, that people regarded as witches do often meet secretly and plan wickedness against those of whom they are envious or with whom they are at enmity. It is commonly believed that they attend these meetings completely naked and in the guise of lame, blind, or otherwise deformed persons.[25]

Among various tribes of the Northern Territories of the Gold Coast the inheritance of witchcraft is in the female line only, hence a male cannot transmit the witchcraft taint acquired from his mother. When an attempt is made to discover a witch by means of the ordeal, this test is applied only to her female descendants.[26] A Timne witch in Sierra Leone is said to be born, not made. She derives her power from her mother, who eats a person and transmits to the unborn child "some of the cannibal feast." She kills with her eyes only.[27]

Among the Ga of the Gold Coast a witch's *kla* (life essence) remains with her body on her bed, so that she seems to be asleep, but her *susuma* (personality) goes forth to meet her associates. Sometimes she proceeds along an invisible cobweb which stretches from her house to the meeting place, but usually she travels on the back of a snake or some other animal. She may also "fly." Her flight is accompanied by a ball of fire about the size of a man's hand and shooting out sparks. At a convocation of witches they devour other people's *kla*. While invisible, this has arms, legs, and organs corresponding to those of the visible body. The witches cut it up and share it. Once completely eaten, the owner dies.[28]

The *subach*, or cannibalistic witches of the Bambara and other Sudanese, have charms to acquire the souls of people and change them into eatable animals. This dread power can be exercised only over people with whom they are related by birth or marriage. Each *subach* brings a soul to the meeting of witches. There it is transformed into an animal and killed. The witches eat only the body, leaving the head for a future feast. When the head is consumed the man whose soul has been abducted and transformed and who has passed a miserable existence ever since, finally dies.[29]

Throughout a wide area of Central Africa (the Congo basin and Upper Guinea), the custom prevails of opening a corpse immediately after death or after a provisional burial and of examining it for any indications of the presence of something supposed to contain the witchcraft power. By various African peoples this power is called *likundu,* and under other names it is known elsewhere.[30] As to what may be disclosed by an autopsy there is a wide range of opinion. Thus the Fang or Pangwe of Gabun think of the witchcraft power as animal-like, even providing it with mouth and teeth. Though usually localized in the abdomen, it can wander thence into other parts of a person's body and cause severe illness; if it gets into a man's head, he dies and if into a woman's vulva, she cannot cohabit. The Fang also believe that while as a rule a witch has only one of these creatures in his or her body, very powerful magicians may have as many as ten.[31] The witchcraft power is often supposed to be represented by some concrete object such as a certain kind of pebble. Or, again, it is identified with some organic abnormality revealed by the dissection. Animistic notions combine with the belief in witch substance, which can readily be thought of as the embodiment of an evil spirit. It seems evident that all these ideas are only to be understood by reference to the more general conception of occult power in its evil aspect.

We are told of a young couple among the Wasafwa (in Tanganyika) who lost a baby and shortly thereafter another child that had just begun to walk. They opened the body of this child and discovered that the urinary bladder was missing, a sure sign that it had been bewitched. The suspicion that either husband or wife might have been the unconscious witch led them to drink the ordeal poison; fortunately both vomited the poison and thus cleared themselves of the terrible fear oppressing them. "Then we had faith in each other once more."[32]

Among the tribes of the Upper Ogowe River, in Gabun, an autopsy is very rarely undertaken to discover the kind of illness which carried off a person. Its purpose, rather, is to inform the survivors what *endjanga* has "eaten" him. This *endjanga* is variously conceived as a little insect, as a vampire-like creature sucking human blood, as a cardiac nerve or an intestinal polypus inhabited by a spirit; sometimes, again, as the soul of the witch, which can go forth at night in the form of a ball of fire and harm people. A native authority assures us that a person kindly by nature will seldom be suspected of possessing the witch power to do evil. It is rather a person who is envious and jealous of his neighbors who comes under suspicion.[33]

Among the Cameroons tribes in doubtful cases of death, that is, in all cases not arising from actual violence, when blood appears on the victim, it is customary to make post-mortem examinations. The body is cut open to find in the entrails some sign of the path of the injected witch. Most commonly it is the lung that is supposed to be witch-eaten. Or the autopsy may be thought to disclose the witch power itself, thus demonstrating that the deceased was himself or herself a witch. An instance is told of a woman who dropped dead on the beach. The natives could not understand what had happened. The post-mortem showed a ruptured aneurism of the aorta, but the local verdict was "She done witch herself," in other words, she was a witch eaten by her own familiar. Great were the rejoicings, therefore, over her demise.[34] In southern Nigeria, when a suspected witch has undergone the poison ordeal and died, the body will be opened and the "witchcraft" extracted, usually in the form of a bat or a bird or occasionally as a black butterfly. If this were not done the dead witch would become a vampire.[35]

The practice of autopsy, obviously, is not without social value. If no indication of witchcraft is discovered in the body of the deceased, the survivors will be relieved to learn that it does not run in the family; furthermore, when the outcome of the investigation is purely negative, there can be no ground for complaints and possible revengeful actions against the survivors on the part of people who suspected that they had been bewitched.[36]

The Maya tribes of Guatemala and Yucatán entertain a firm belief in the existence of witches called *zahoris* (a Spanish word of Arabic origin). They can forecast the future, take on an animal form, make themselves invisible, fascinate animals and human beings by their steady gaze, and call up spirits. The Indians in the state of Vera Cruz and elsewhere in southern Mexico call these mysterious personages *padrinos*, "godfathers." They are supposed to cause sickness and domestic calamities. By the Indians they are looked upon with a mixture of fear and respect.[37]

In Laguna Pueblo, as in the other Indian pueblos, witchcraft beliefs are prevalent and strongly held. Witches inherit their power. "If a woman is not right, her children get it." They appear as lights in the night, jumping from place to place and assembling in a cave several miles from the village. At their meetings they wear the skins of animals and birds. They can remain abroad until cockcrow, then their time is up. Witches injure and kill people. If bewitched, you may offer a relative in your place; thus a husband once offered his wife and she was drowned in a flood. Should you meet a witch the thing to do is to hit him in the chest four times, then "the bad goes back into him." Persons reputed to be witches are feared. In former days when one was caught he would be placed in a squatting position and kept in it until he toppled over and died.[38]

Hopi witches may be of either sex. Their occult power comes to them from an animal familiar and varies in amount according to the nature of the associated animal. Little black ants provide it most abundantly, but coyotes, wolves, owls, crows, bull snakes, cats, and dogs are also important sources. In keeping with this belief witches are described as being "two-hearted," that is, possessed of an animal heart as well as a human one. All witches are dedicated to the taking of human life, in order to prolong their own, but their murderous ability is restricted to relatives. Every year a witch must bring about the death of someone thus near to him; if he repents and refuses to fulfill the obligation his own death will soon follow. Since he is most likely to kill a person whom he dislikes and since, further, no one can tell which one of his relatives may be a *poaka,* the Hopi live in perpetual fear of black magic. There are said to be more witches than normal people in each of their villages.[39]

Navaho witchcraft presents the same general pattern as that of the Pueblo Indians. Both men and women bewitch; men are the more numerous practitioners. Female witches are generally old and often, if not always, childless. Witchcraft is usually learned from a parent, a grandparent, or a spouse, but a spouse may remain ignorant that the partner engages in it. People become witches in order to satisfy vengeful feelings, to acquire wealth, or simply to injure wantonly those who excite their envy. Killing a near relation is a prerequisite for admission into the black art. Witches are active chiefly at night, when they roam about rapidly in the form of wolves, coyotes, and other animals. They hold nocturnal convocations in caves. They are all naked, save for masks and jewelry. The proceedings are directed by a chief witch, "for whom the others just work." Songs are sung and dry paintings, often described as of "colored ashes," are made. At these sabbaths, witches initiate new members, have intercourse with dead women, commit incest, feed on corpses, and kill people at a distance by the use of exuviae, personal leavings, images ("dolls"), and projectiles ("arrows"). Spells are recited, these often setting the number of days after which the victim is to die. Saying "good prayers backwards" is described as a technique. For some spells it is of great advantage to know the personal and secret name of the person to be injured or killed. Witchcraft is also carried out against animals, crops, and other property; even an automobile may be bewitched. Against these diabolic arts a very common prophylactic is "gall medicine," which conservative Indians carry about with them when in a crowd or away from their home country. Drinking a liquid made from certain herbs and anointing the body with it also afford protection. In general, the Navaho feel that the possession of ceremonial objects and ceremonials—"good songs and prayers and stories"—provides the best insurance against being bewitched.[40]

The Cherokee make a distinction between "man-killers," who are sorcerers able to dispose of their victims by inflicting them with disease or by shooting invisible arrowheads into them, and witches properly so called. Man-killers, say the Cherokee, "work against us" because we have offended them in some way; usually we have only ourselves to blame if they try to harm us. They only take revenge for some uncalled-for offense, whereas witches do harm simply because of their wicked nature. Although, as a rule, such persons must be "brought up" by their parents for the profession, it is possible to enter upon it by drinking a certain magical potion and fasting for four days. By prolonging the treatment for seven days the power of animal metamorphosis is acquired. Witches indulge in their nefarious activities only at night, when they can be seen traveling through the air as a purple flame or a reddish-blue spark. Whatever they can steal of the life and therefore of the "power" of their victims they add to their own. It is for this reason that they are always hovering invisibly about feeble, sick, or moribund people. The most satisfactory way of dealing with these fearsome creatures is to shoot them with a gun. In order to do so, however, a person must be able to see them in their regular human form. One acquires this ability by fasting until sunset for seven days and drinking an infusion of the same root to which they owe their power.[41]

Witchcraft among the Choctaw was practiced by many persons, both men and women. Old people were most often suspected of exerting this evil power. A witch could remove at night his viscera, thus reducing his weight and enabling him to fly easily through the air. He was always accompanied on a nocturnal excursion by several spirits resembling men, but no larger than a man's thumb. On reaching the person against whom black magic was to be employed the witch would stop and point toward him, whereupon one of the little spirits would go noiselessly and touch him. Then the witch would fly back to the village and resume his natural form.[42]

By the Hupa of northern California witches were greatly feared because of their possession of certain objects which gave them power to bring disease and death upon the people. One of these objects was a bow made of a human rib and provided with a bowstring from the sinews of a human wrist. After repeating the necessary spell the manipulator shot a "mystic" arrow causing death to whomever it hit. One who was provided with this bow could run at great speed by pressing it to his breast; by means of it he could turn himself into a bear or a wolf and so remain unknown. A witch engaged in nefarious activity at night. After killing a person he went to the grave of the victim and stole the clothing and utensils heaped upon it. He thus got back the power which he lost by committing the murder.[43]

The essential features of this imaginary sorcery or witchcraft are thus repeated in one primitive society after another, ranging from Australia to North America. The witches belong to both sexes. They practice metamorphosis, usually into some animal form. They work secretly and under cover of darkness. They feed on human corpses so as to acquire the special powers possessed by ghosts. They fly through the air and assemble for dances and orgiastic ceremonies. Sometimes they have regular guilds or societies. All that they do of wickedness results from their envious, jealous, or unsocial disposition, which in many cases is not acquired but is inherited from either parent. In some instances witchcraft is practiced unconsciously; frequently, however, the witch knows what he or she does and enjoys doing it. By some African peoples the occult power of witchcraft is further imagined as resident in a tangible object within the witch while alive and discoverable by an inspection or dissection of the witch's body after death.

To separate truth from fancy in these accounts seems to be as difficult as it was in the witchcraft trials of Europe a few centuries ago. The difficulty is increased by the fact that real sorcerers and persons who pose as witches so often work together, help each other, and use each other's procedures and techniques.

It cannot be doubted that the so-called witches sometimes form societies, hold meetings, or "sabbaths," and observe a variety of secret and obscene rites. While not all witches are human flesh eaters, some certainly rob graves and engage in necrophagous practices. There is evidence, also, that at least occasionally a candidate for admission to the witch order must first try to bewitch someone to death, usually a member of his or her household, as a sacrifice of what is nearest and dearest to the neophyte. All these features were reproduced in the witchcraft of the later Middle Ages. What we learn of witchcraft, whether as practiced by existing primitives or by our ancestors, indicates that witches are often mentally unbalanced and convinced that it lies in their power to harm others by thinking harm of them. In short, they may be "compulsion neurotics." But in a community where witchcraft beliefs are rife any normal person, if only he is envious and spiteful enough, can be looked upon as a witch. The people know, or think that they know, that ill will affects its recipients in a way that is physically detrimental, and the consciousness of this fact becomes for them also an obsession.

A peculiar form of imaginary sorcery or witchcraft is found widely in Australia and the Melanesian area, where it may have been diffused from some center as yet unidentified. It has also been reported, sporadically, from Indonesia, Africa, and America. Its characteristic features include an attack on the victim when alone in the bush, an operation on him usually involving the removal of his internal organs and resulting in his death, and then his magical revival but in such a demented state that he can seldom or never remember what happened to him or recognize his assailants. He seems to be unharmed by the terrible experience, but shortly thereafter he really sickens and dies. The details of this bewitchment afford ample scope for the imagination and hence vary endlessly from one community to another.

The Wiimbaio of Victoria say that medicine men of a hostile tribe will sneak into a camp by night, strangle a man with a rope, drag him forth, cut up his abdomen, take out the kidney and caul fat, and then stuff a handful of grass and sand into the wound. It would seem that this operation is actually performed, for the victim generally dies within twenty-four hours. But the Wiimbaio also say that in the night the medicine men can knock a man down with a club and remove his fat without leaving a sign of the operation. The Wotjobaluk, another Victorian tribe, practice this imaginary fat-taking to a great extent. "The victim is laid on his back and the medicine man sits astride of his chest, cuts him open on the right side below the ribs, and abstracts the fat. Then bringing the edges together and singing his spell, he bites them together to make them join without a visible scar. Then he retires to a distance, leaving the man lying on his back. The medicine man then sings a song with the following effect. At the first singing the victim lifts one leg, at the second the other, at the third he turns over, at the fourth a little whirlwind comes, and, blowing under his back, lifts him up. At the same time a star falls from the sky . . . . with the man's heart. He thereupon rises and staggers about, wondering how he came to be sleeping there."[44]

For the Herbert River aborigines of northern Queensland the witchcraft called *kobi* is the most dreadful thing imaginable. A man subjected to it by a magician of another tribe has his entrails extracted and replaced with grass. Usually he dies soon after this operation, but prompt recourse to a friendly magician may lead to his recovery.[45]

The dread of the sorcery called *millin* is universal among the Narrinyeri of South Australia. For its operation the sorcerer disguises himself by marking face and body with white streaks. He generally takes a companion with him. The two then prowl about the hunting grounds of the tribe to which their intended victim belongs. Finding him alone they steal noiselessly upon him, fell him with a heavy blow on the head, and then, as he lies insensible, hit different parts of his body, but not hard enough to break his bones. Finally, they pull his ears until they crack, so that he will be unable to tell who attacked him. It is now all up with the victim. If he takes part in a fight he will receive a fatal wound; if he walks in the bush he will tread on a dangerous snake; if he does not meet his end in one of these ways he will succumb to some disease.[46]

Among the Arunta and other Central Australian tribes a *kur-daitcha* is a man who has been formally chosen by the council of elders to lead a band of avengers and kill a person accused of having injured someone by magic, or else he is a man who on his own initiative goes out as an avenger. The *kurdaitcha* wears shoes consisting of a thick pad of emu feathers matted together with human blood, and having on the upper surface a network of human hair string. The shoes are sacrosanct; no woman or child may see them, and when not in use they are placed for safety in the storehouse of the social group, along with the *churinga,* the sacred sticks and

stones. Before a man may wear the shoes he has to submit to a
very painful ordeal. One of his little toes is dislocated. It does
not matter, apparently, which foot is subjected to this treatment.
The *kurdaitcha* whose mission has been sanctioned by the elders
is always accompanied by a medicine man. The latter must himself
have previously served as the leader of an avenging party and be
qualified by having a little toe dislocated. Before setting out,
both men are rubbed with charcoal (black in the Arunta tribe
being the color associated with magic) and are decorated with
bands of white down. Both carry shields and spears, and also
one or more *churinga,* which impart to them strength, courage,
accuracy of aim, and invulnerability. Followed by the medicine
man, the *kurdaitcha* takes the lead until the enemy is in sight,
then creeps stealthily forward, and, suddenly rising up, hurls a
spear at him before he is aware of the action. The spear cannot
fail to strike home, for both the *kurdaitcha* and the medicine man
have put the sacred *churinga* between their teeth. The *kurdaitcha*
now retires from the scene of operations and the medicine man
proceeds by means of his magical power to heal the victim and
remove all external traces of the wound. The victim becomes alive
again, though completely ignorant of what has been done to him
and unaware of the fact that he is now full of evil magic. He returns to his camp, soon falls sick, and dies. His death is attributed
to a *kurdaitcha,* but no one can trace the avenger's tracks. In the
other and more favored form of this custom the avenger goes
out alone, spears the enemy, restores him to life again, and, by
means of a charmed bone which is pressed under his tongue, causes
him to lose all recollection of what has taken place. Before very
long the victim becomes ill and dies for good. Our authorities met
several *kurdaitcha* men who asserted that they had killed their
victims in the manner just described, and many men who were
perfectly certain that they had seen these avengers. Every native
is firmly convinced, in fact, that people do actually engage in the
practice and is quite prepared to let others think that he himself
does; he will even suffer the pain of having a toe dislocated in
order to prove that he has "gone *kurdaitcha.*"[47]

Among the Murngin of Arnhem Land, Northern Territory,
the sorcerer, having determined to kill a tribesman, makes a long
rope and hides it near the camp. During the night he and an
accomplice sneak up to the intended victim, who lies asleep. One of
them takes the rope, loops it, and slides it over the victim's head
and around his neck. The man holding the other end of the rope

then twists it until the sleeper begins choking. The two pick him up and carry him to a safe place in the jungle. The first man returns to the victim's camp and lies down beside his wife, with whom he is supposed to copulate. The second man opens the left side of the victim, while he lies in a dead faint, pulls two ribs back, and pierces his heart with a sharpened stick. When the heart stops beating, the soul, which for native thinking resides in the heart, has been let out. A further and rather elaborate operation restores the man to life. He sits up and looks very much as he did before being magically killed. The operator now hits him on the head and tells him that he will not remember what has happened to him. He is also told that in three days he will die. The man who has lost his soul feels extremely weak. His wife asks him if he has had his soul stolen but he answers, "Oh, no, I have had dysentery and I am very sick from it." On the third day the man dies. When a woman is magically killed the operation is considerably different, but its results are the same: the woman dies.[48]

The Murray Islanders, in the eastern group of the Torres Straits Islands, have a form of black magic known as *maid*. The operator, having found his adversary alone in the bush, picks up a chance stone, spits on it once or twice, meanwhile whispering to himself a spell, and throws the missile with great force at the back of the victim, who falls senseless. The assailant and his helpers proceed to belabor the man with clubs "until he half dead." Next they rub the body with a mixture of herbs and oil to remove all traces of the blows. Finally, while the man is still unconscious ("he know nothing"), they tell him that he is to climb a coconut tree and fall down, breaking a leg, or that someday he will be bitten by a centipede, swell up all over, and die. They now make off, and the man slowly returns to life and consciousness. Panic-stricken he runs home, calls for coconuts to drink to assuage his intense thirst, but refuses all food. Then he lies down to die, telling his friends that the *maid le* had attacked him. His death occurs in a few days.[49]

The Marind, a tribe of Netherlands New Guinea (near Merauke) have a myth relating how a famous hero was killed by means of death magic (*kambara*). One of five sorcerers first rubbed his body with coconut oil and then the others so belabored him that he fell down unconscious. While in this state they cut his body from the inside, under the skin, without leaving any trace of the operation. Upon recovering from his swoon the hero did not realize what had been done to him and went quietly home. But that evening he felt very ill indeed, complained of head pains, and could not eat; by next morning he was dead.[50]

The Kiwai Papuans of the Fly River estuary attribute to the bush tribes in their neighborhood the practice of *mauamo* sorcery. Several sorcerers, it is said, generally act together. They prepare themselves by eating some kangaroo meat (otherwise a forbidden food), together with flesh from a human body dug up from a grave, and thus reduce themselves to a state of frenzy or ecstacy. Having approached their victim without anyone seeing them ("all same mosquito he come"), they make him unconscious by throwing some "devil-thing" at him or touching him with it. Then they shoot him dead with arrows, open the body, take out the intestines, and place them in a kangaroo; those of the latter are placed in the victim. They also dismember his body and put it together again, interchanging, however, the legs with the arms and the head with the genitalia. By means of a certain medicine both the man and the kangaroo are restored to life. The man has no recollection of what has happened to him and for a short time goes about as usual. But the next night he feels ill, his stomach swells, his mouth turns black, and he froths at the lips and nose. When an effort is made to bleed him and relieve the fever, no blood will flow. It is known then that *mauamo* has been practiced upon him, for all the blood was emptied from his body when it was dismembered. Toward morning he dies. The kangaroo also dies at the same time.[51]

The Koita of the Central Division of the Territory of Papua practice *vada* sorcery. The sorcerer follows an intended victim into his garden or into the bush, spears and clubs him to death, and cuts him in pieces. One end of a length of rope is then looped around the dead man's head or knee, while the opposite end is steeped in a certain medicine. This "go along rope make man get up," that is, the power of the medicine, passing along the rope to the defunct, restores him to life. Upon his revival he is dazed, "he mad," and knows not where he is or what has befallen him. He is told that he will die shortly, but does not remember the prediction upon returning to the village. His friends notice, however, his feeble, silly condition and know what has happened to him.[52]

According to another account of *vada* sorcery among Papuans of the Central Division the magician, after knocking down the victim with a club and making him unconscious, rams certain poisonous plants down his throat, sings magical formulas over him, and gradually brings him back to consciousness again. The magician may leave him before he has returned to his senses, or wait and later tell him to go home to his village, where he will die shortly. Natives assert that although a man thus attacked may have seen his assailant he would not recognize him again even a short time after the assault has been committed. The official post-mortem on one of these assumed victims of *vada* sorcery resulted in a verdict of "Death from a broken spleen."[53]

The tribes in the neighborhood of Hood Point and Hood Bay do not recognize, it is said, the possibility of a natural death. This is always caused by a *wara,* a sorcerer who wanders at night through the gardens and plantations of neighboring villages until he finds some man asleep. With a bamboo knife he decapitates and dismembers the victim, then replaces the head in its natural position on the shoulders, and rubs the wounds with an ointment which removes all traces of mutilation. Before quitting the scene of these nocturnal labors he also rubs on the instep of the victim another ointment which attracts venomous snakes and causes them to bite the spot anointed. The victim sleeps on and awakes in the morning apparently unhurt. But one day a snake attacks him and he dies. The relatives assemble and examine the body for marks of the *wara's* work. These are plainly to be seen, for in death by snakebite there is much discoloration. One man, pointing to a mark on the neck, will say, "Look! here is where his head was cut off," or "Here is where he was speared," or "Here is where he was dismembered."[54]

The Mailu of Toulon Island in Orangerie Bay have elaborated the conception of a *barau,* a living man endowed with the ability of working evil magic. When he leaves his abode at night to go on a nefarious errand, his place in the house is empty. By smearing his body with magical herbs and muttering certain spells, he becomes invisible. Some people say, however, that he is invisible from his front only and that he can be seen from behind. When therefore, they see mysterious shadows moving about in the dark, they have met a *barau.* He can travel great distances, going like the wind. His victim, when found asleep at home, is killed and then brought to life again. Sometimes, when two or three men are out fishing or working in their gardens, he fells them with blows of a club, but they never know that they have been assaulted by a *barau.* The Mailu consider that all deaths among them are due to his activity. They never suspect anyone in their own or a friendly village of being a *barau;* he always belongs to a hostile community.[55]

Sorcery by magically cutting open a man's body, abstracting his vital organs, closing up the body, and then restoring him to life but in a state of daze and forgetfulness, has been described in Dobu Island. It is called *wawari,* from the sorcerer's shout as he springs upon his victim; it is also the term for the yells by means of which Dobuans scare away the spirits of witches believed to be approaching a village.[56]

In Rossel Island, one of the Louisiade group, there are various methods of killing people by sorcery. *Ngwivi* sorcery is most feared. In order to practice it a man fasts for ten days (often eating, however, a certain centipede which smells strongly of prussic acid), drinks salt water, and mutters certain spells. He thus becomes invisible or able to take on the appearance of some animal such as a dog. The sorcerer generally works at night and tackles his victim when asleep, disarranging or breaking his upper ribs. The latter realizes next morning what has happened to him and soon dies.[57]

The inhabitants of Wogeo, one of the Schouten Islands off the northern coast of New Guinea, know of a deadly form of sorcery called *yabon.* The sorcerer, having found out where an enemy is likely to be alone, gets ready the necessary magical paraphernalia and enlists the aid of two friends. They fall upon the man, overpower him, and recite a spell to make him unconscious. He is then stripped and his joints and ribs are thoroughly pummeled. The magician pierces his heart with a dagger and into the wound pours the sap of a tree known only to sorcerers. This has the property of piercing the victim's bowels. A cut under his tongue and a spear thrust in the left flank complete the operation. Next a magical leaf is laid on the wounds, which immediately heal without leaving a trace. Another leaf, laid on his mouth, makes him forget entirely what has happened to him, or, some say, prevents him from speaking about it. The assistants now retire and the sorcerer restores him to consciousness. He goes home, soon falls sick, and within ten days is dead. The Wogeo people account for all sudden deaths as the result of this kind of sorcery.[58]

The Sulka of New Britain suppose that all people come to their end as the result of sorcery, except little children, persons who fall in battle or meet some other violent end, and those who die of sores or of old age. Death-dealing sorcery of this sort (called *pur-mea*) is very greatly feared. Only certain persons know how to practice it. The victim, who must be alone at the time, is suddenly attacked in the bush, knocked on the head, choked or otherwise manhandled, and finally killed. He is then restored to life by being sprinkled with earth over which various spells have been recited. He returns home, falls sick and declares that he has been bewitched, but no marks of evil magic are discoverable on his body. Death follows sooner or later unless another sorcerer, familiar with *pur-mea,* can be found to treat him. If the victim is a sorcerer who knows this black art he can sometimes cure himself.[59]

Vele sorcery in the Solomon Islands is so called from the native word meaning "to pinch," with reference to the pinched or tingling feeling in the arms that warns protected persons of the proximity of a practitioner of this black art. The magical power which he exercises resides in a small globe of fiber, the *vasa,* which contains various articles taken from the place inhabited by his ancestral ghost. Or they may be articles which belonged to the ghost in life and, being impregnated with his *nanama* (*mana*), are dangerous and powerful. One standard ingredient the *vasa* must have, namely, sacred earth from a certain island in the Russell group. The *vasa* is "made alive" by the recital of spells and is then ready for its deadly work. The sorcerer proceeds to hide by the side of a road and waits for the approach of the victim. When the latter draws near the sorcerer makes a sharp noise to attract the man's attention. He turns and sees the *vasa* suspended from a finger. Immediately he collapses, usually in an unconscious condition, whereupon the sorcerer forces bits of rubbish down his throat and touches with the *vasa* various parts of his body. These become crushed internally without leaving any mark on the skin. Sometimes the *vele* operator carries, in addition to the *vasa,* the tail of a sting ray and a dead man's bone, and with these the victim is pricked all over. The man is then revived by placing ginger plant or some other potent object under his nose, is told the sorcerer's name, and is ordered to go home. He suffers, apparently from an attack of fever, but never mentions what has occurred. At length he dies, usually within three days. Some men enjoy such protection from their ancestral ghosts that the *vele* cannot prevail against them. It is also possible, by putting certain sacred leaves or grass in one's armbands, to obtain warning of the proximity of a *vele* and so escape him by taking another road. The *vele's* power is lost as the result of contact with anything sexual; even the sight of a woman's genitals is fatal to it. It is a common belief that if a woman, attacked by a *vele* man, throws off her grass skirt and exhibits her genitals, she will escape should he laugh at the sight or even think of having intercourse with her. When a man falls sick, the doctor first determines whether the patient really does suffer from *vele* sorcery. If so he will get well if he can be made to vomit up blood, earth, undigested vegetable matter, and a worm. After the third day he is out of danger.[60]

A form of black magic, known as *nembike*, has been reported from Malekula in the New Hebrides. The victim is first stunned by a blow of a stone and a mask is put over his face. The magician rubs his body with leaves, operates upon him, and then brings him back to life. When the victim reaches home people notice that his ideas are perverted; for instance, if asked where the ground is he will point to the sky and if asked where the sky is he will point to the ground. He proceeds to roast and eat a small piece of his own flesh, which was taken out of his body by the sorcerer. Upon consuming this food he becomes very sick and soon draws his last breath.[61]

The Toradya of central Celebes believe that while a man lies asleep his "inside" (*lamboyo*) can go forth from him as a deer, pig, buffalo, or some other animal. In this form the *lamboyo* approaches a victim, who at once feels so sleepy that he can put up no resistance and soon becomes unconscious. The *lamboyo* then resumes the human form (though his real body lies at home), hacks the victim in many pieces, takes out the liver, and eats it. Finally he joins together the dissevered parts so that the victim seems to be completely restored. When the latter returns to consciousness, he is entirely unaware of what has happened to him and that his liver has been extracted from him. Soon after the victim awakes he dies.[62]

The Wahadimu, who are supposed to have been the original inhabitants of Zanzibar before the coming of the Arabs, entertain a lively faith in witches. These creatures require human victims for their cannibal feasts. They will bring a man out of his house into the forest (how no one knows), and while he is still asleep belabor him with sandbags or with their witch bags. They will also prick his tongue with a needle. He is then taken back to his house. When he wakes up in the morning he feels very ill, for his whole body is swollen and his tongue is so sore that he cannot speak or eat. Soon he dies and is buried. That same night a witch causes the corpse to rise from the grave, binds it on her back, and dances with it. Then all the assembled members of the witch guild feast on the remains.[63]

Among the mysterious and evil powers with which the Bathonga credit witches, or *baloyi,* is that of opening all things—the power of *mpfulo.* A witch can come into a village at night and throw all the inhabitants into a deep sleep. Then, waving a hyena's tail daubed with medicines, he opens the kraal, lets the cattle out, and leads the stolen animals to his own kraal. He can open a hut, remove the sleeping husband without waking him, and have intercourse with his wife. But the great *mpfulo* consists in opening a man. We are not told how this is done without his being aware of the operation, but its effect is to wear out the victim, making him a mere shadow of himself and resulting in his death a few days later.[64]

By the Indians of Guiana the term *kanaima* (*kenaima*) is applied to a man who has devoted himself to slaying someone as a deed of vengeance, but it is likewise the name of the murderous spirit "under whose influence he acts, and which is supposed to possess him."[65] There is also a purely imaginary *kanaima,* who works invisibly by sending out his soul to injure or kill an enemy. Or he may put his soul into the body of a jaguar, snake, sting ray, or some other creature and in this guise approach his victim. By these Indians the activity of a *kanaima* is considered to be the cause of almost every misfortune occurring among them. Against such an evil being their only means of protection is the counter magic of the *piai,* or medicine man. The imaginary *kanaima* is naturally thought of as belonging to a tribe different from that of his victim, and thus the feelings of suspicion and hatred with which one tribe regards its neighbors are perpetuated and intensified.[66]

Some features of this belief in *kanaima,* as found among the Barama River Caribs, are identical with the *kurdaitcha, vada,* and *vele* sorcery already described. According to these Indians the *kanaima* throws a victim into a trance-like state, leaps upon him, twists his joints, and stretches his tendons. A black powder put in his mouth makes him cough and sneeze and get a cold. If it is swallowed, his viscera decay. A person who has been mal- treated in this manner usually does not remember enough about it to tell his relatives and friends, but to prevent any possibility of betrayal the *kanaima* may pierce his tongue with a snake's fang. After regaining consciousness the victim goes home, de- velops fever and "boneache," and speedily dies. His relatives and friends, seeing the blue marks left on his body by the man-handling he received, know that he was killed by a *kanaima*.[67]

Among the Taulipáng, another Carib group, a *kanaima* is supposed to go about at night and hit people with a short, heavy, four-edge club, this being the old-time war club still carried on the shoulder at a dance. The victim does not die at once as the result of the blow, but goes home, falls into a fever, and after four or five days succumbs. A *kanaima* attacks only one person in this way, never several persons at the same time. The Indians believe that all members of a hostile tribe can be *kanaima*.[68]

The Cherokee have a tale of a cannibal ogress whose food was human livers. She could assume any shape she desired. In her ordinary form, however, she looked like an old person except that her whole body was covered with skin as hard as stone and that her right hand had a long forefinger of bone, like an awl or spear-head. With this forefinger she stabbed everyone to whom she could get close enough. When she had stabbed a person she would take out the liver, without leaving a wound or causing pain, so that the victim remained unconscious of what had been done to him and for a time went about his affairs apparently unharmed. But all at once he felt weak and gradually pined away. He was sure to die.[69]

It is scarcely possible to dismiss this sorcery as always a pure hoax, existing only in the excited fancy of its victim and the megalomania of its supposed practitioner. In some instances, at least, the sorcery must be described as genuine, though violence need not have been done to the victim or poisons or other lethal matter injected into him. He may be so paralyzed with fear that he becomes entirely receptive to the sorcerer's will and under a mental compulsion to think and act as ordered by his enemy. He broods over his impending fate until his mind becomes over-wrought and all the dreadful consequences of the sorcerer's vengeance are believed to be real and about to happen to him. When actual sorcery of this sort had been occasionally practiced in a community it would readily come to be regarded as a normal procedure, not only of living sorcerers, but also of those imaginary authors of human ills, the witches.[70]

NOTES TO CHAPTER XIV

[1] Sir George Grey, *Journals of Two Expeditions of Discovery in North-West and Western Australia* (London, 1841), II, 337 ff. "The 'boylyas' are persons who have the power of *boylya*" (II, 338), that is, possess evil occult power.

² C. G. Seligman, *The Melanesians of British New Guinea* (Cambridge, 1910), pp. 640 ff. In the Maisin tribe of Collingwood Bay the noxious emanation from a woman is called *farum* and is like a limbless old crone. It turns into a mosquito and sucks human blood, resuming the human form at dawn. Old men also have within them and can expel from their bodies something called a *baravu*, essentially similar to a *labuni*. The sender of a *baravu* need not have children (*lot. cit.*).

³ Bronislaw Malinowski, *Argonauts of the Western Pacific* (London, 1922), pp. 237 ff.; *idem*, *The Sexual Life of Savages in North-Western Melanesia* (New York, 1929), pp. 45 ff. On the flying witches of Dobu, one of the D'Entrecasteaux Islands, see R. F. Fortune, *Sorcerers of Dobu* (London, 1932), pp. 150 ff. In these islands witches, seated in a half-coconut husk, can fly to Port Moresby in Papua, three hundred miles away, and there exercise their malign influence on people who have incurred their displeasure (J. H. P. Murray, in *Territory of Papua, Annual Report for the Year 1930–1931*, p. 15). Some of the tribes of southern Nigeria believe that the shell of a ground nut is the "boat" of witches and that in it they travel through the air and over the water (P. A. Talbot, *The Peoples of Southern Nigeria* [London, 1926], II, 202).

⁴ R. H. Codrington, *The Melanesians* (Oxford, 1891), p. 222.

⁵ W. Howell, in *Sarawak Museum Journal*, I (1911–13), 153 ff.

⁶ Cora DuBois, *The People of Alor* (Minneapolis, 1944), pp. 169 f. In Flores witches also eat human flesh and have the power of turning themselves into animals. Their souls go forth at night and ride through the air, while their bodies remain asleep at home. They have only one eye, which shines like fire. See Paul Arndt, *Mythologie, Religion, und Magie im Sikagebiet (östl. Mittelflores)* (Ende, Flores, 1932), pp. 294 ff.

⁷ Étienne Aymonier, "Notes sur les coutumes et croyances superstitieuses des Cambodgiens," *Cochinchine Française. Excursions et Reconnaissances* (Saigon, 1883), No. 16, pp. 181 f.

⁸ S. C. Roy, "Magic and Witchcraft on the Chota-Nagpur Plateau," *Journal of the Royal Anthropological Institute*, XLIV (1914), 325, 338, 341 f.

⁹ *Idem, Oraon Religion and Customs* (Ranchi, India, 1928), pp. 257 f.

¹⁰ Ralph Linton, *The Tanala* (Chicago, 1933), pp. 227 ff. *Field Museum of Natural History, Anthropological Series*, Vol. XXII.

¹¹ Monica Hunter, *Reaction to Conquest* (London, 1936), pp. 275 ff.

¹² H. A. Stayt, *The Bavenda* (Oxford, 1931), pp. 273 ff.

¹³ H. A. Junod, *The Life of a South African Tribe* (2d ed., London, 1927), II, 504 ff., 524 ff.

¹⁴ See E. H. Ashton, "Medicine, Magic, and Sorcery among the Southern Sotho," *University of Cape Town. Communications from the School of African Studies* (n.s., 1943), No. 10, pp. 8 f. (Basuto) ; Mrs. E. J. Krige and J. D. Krige, *The Realm of a Rain Queen* (London, 1943), pp. 250 ff. (Lovedu) ; C. M. Doke, *The Lambas of Northern Rhodesia* (London, 1931), pp. 302 ff.

¹⁵ A. Hetherwick, "Nyanjas," Hastings' *Encyclopaedia of Religion and Ethics*, IX, 421. The Wayao and other tribes of Nyasaland also have the conception of the witch human-flesh eater (H. S. Stannus, in *Harvard African Studies*, III [Cambridge, Mass., 1922], pp. 293 ff.). In many districts the fear of cannibalism by witches is so pronounced that the dead are not buried until putrefaction sets in, and a grave will be watched for a considerable time after an interment (James Macdonald, "East Central African Customs," *Journal of the Anthropological Institute*, XXII [1893], 107). Among these tribes an instructor in sorcery requires his pupil to eat the roasted liver and heart of a

newly buried child (W. H. Garbutt, "Witchcraft in Nyasa," *ibid.*, XLI [1911], 301).

[16] D. R. MacKenzie, *The Spirit-ridden Konde* (London, 1925), p. 252.

[17] Godfrey Wilson, "An African Morality," *Africa*, IX (1936), 86.

[18] J. G. Peristiany, *The Social Institutions of the Kipsigis* (London, 1939), p. 226.

[19] J. H. Driberg, *The Lango* (London, 1923), pp. 164 f. Among the Bathonga a man who loses a child by death often concludes that his wife is a witch and has "eaten" it. Such an accusation is almost certain to result in a divorce (H. A. Junod, *op. cit.* [2d ed.], I, 193, 199). Among the Kpando of Togo a man whose wife dies during her pregnancy or a man who has lost several previous wives is suspected of harboring an "evil spirit" within him, and it is very difficult for him to marry again (E. Breitkopf, in *Anthropos*, XXII [1927], 498).

[20] E. E. Evans-Pritchard, *Witchcraft, Oracles, and Magic among the Azande* (Oxford, 1927), pp. 21 ff., 34 ff., 119 ff. By the Azande a bad dream, for example, a nightmare, is regarded as an actual experience of witchcraft. In waking life a man knows that he has been bewitched by meeting with a subsequent misfortune or by an oracular revelation, but in dreams he actually sees witches and may even converse with them. "We may say that Azande see witchcraft in a dream rather than that they dream of witchcraft" (pp. 134 ff.). For an earlier account of Azande witchcraft (improperly described as the power of the evil eye), see C. R. Lagae, *Les Azande ou Niam-Niam* (Brussels, 1926), pp. 97, 106 ff.

[21] Pierre Collé, *Les Baluba* (*Congo Belge*) (Brussels, 1913), p. 424.

[22] Edmond Verhulpen, *Baluba et Balubaïsés du Katanga* (Antwerp, 1936), p. 162.

[23] J. Van Wing, "Bakongo Magic," *Journal of the Royal Anthropological Institute*, LXXI (1941), 94 f. By the Bakongo a serious accident, such as a fall from a palm tree, drowning, or the death of a chief, is considered to be the work of several witches—one alone could not accomplish such a deed. A missionary reports a case where six men died when their canoe was upset in the rapids and three witches were killed for each man (W. H. Bentley, *Life on the Congo* [London, 1887], pp. 68 f.). On witchcraft beliefs among other peoples of the Belgian Congo see Joseph Halkin and Ernest Viaene, *Les Ababua* (*Congo Belge*) (Brussels, 1911), p. 341, quoting Dr. Védy; Bernard Zuure, *Croyances et pratiques religieuses des Barundi* (Brussels-Elizabethville, 1929), pp. 127–42.

[24] C. K. Meek, *Tribal Studies in Northern Nigeria* (London, 1931), I, 550.

[25] P. A. Talbot, *The Peoples of Southern Nigeria* (London, 1926), II, 200 ff., with a map showing the prevalence of witchcraft beliefs and the extent to which they are held. See also C. K. Meek, *Law and Authority in a Nigerian Tribe* (London, 1937), pp. 79–84 (Ibo).

[26] R. S. Rattray, *The Tribes of the Ashanti Hinterland* (Oxford, 1932), I, 233, 240 f. (Nankanse); II, 345 (Talense); II, 375 (Kusase).

[27] N. W. Thomas, *Anthropological Report on Sierra Leone*, Part I (London, 1916), p. 46.

[28] Margaret J. Field, *Religion and Medicine of the Ga People* (Oxford, 1937), pp. 95, 142 ff.

[29] Louis Tauxier, *La religion Bambara* (Paris, 1927), pp. 45 f. See also Leo Frobenius, *Kulturtypen aus dem West-Sudan* (Gotha, 1910), pp. 76 ff. *Petermanns Mitteilungen, Ergänzungsheft* No. 166. The *subach* who fails to bring a yearly sacrifice of a soul to the witch meeting is beaten to death by his associates (p. 78). Among the Wahadimu of Zanzibar those who belong to the guild

of witches must be ready to sacrifice any of their relatives. If they refuse to do so, they will be killed (Dora H. Abdy, "Witchcraft among the Wahadimu," *Journal of the African Society*, No. 63 [1917], 234).

30 See Hermann Baumann, " 'Likundu.' Die Sektion der Zauberkraft," *Zeitschrift für Ethnologie*, LX (1928), 73–85; Willy Schilde, " 'Likundu'," *ibid.*, LXX (1938), 254–62. Baumann enumerated forty-two tribes and peoples among whom the existence of witchcraft is determined by an autopsy. Schilde added eighty-two more to the list. In some instances, however, the evidence for the custom lacks conclusiveness. See their maps and references.

Autopsies for witchcraft are also practiced by the Pygmies. They say that if a person dies suddenly, without having been previously sick, he has been killed by *oudah*. The next-of-kin at once cuts the corpse clean in two and exhibits "to any doubting ones" some abnormality indicating that the defunct perished by reason of the possession of *oudah* (James J. Harrison, *Life among the Pygmies of the Ituri Forest, Congo Free State* [London, 1905], p. 20).

31 Günter Tessmann, *Die Pangwe* (Berlin, 1913), II, 129 f. The dried and pulverized "witchcraft," after extraction, is used as a medicine (A. L. Bennett, in *Journal of the Anthropological Institute*, XXIX [1899], 91).

32 Elise Kootz-Kretschmer, *Die Safwa* (Berlin, 1926–29), II, 268 f.

33 A. Walker, in *Bulletin de la société de recherches Congolaises*, No. 8 (1928), 136 f. The abbé Walker is a converted native of Gabun.

34 Mary H. Kingsley, *Travels in West Africa* (London, 1897), pp. 467 f. Dr. Nassau knew of a case whereat the fimbriated extremities of the fallopian tubes in a woman were held up as proof of her having been a witch. The ciliary movements of these fimbriae were regarded as the efforts of her familiar to eat her (R. H. Nassau, *Fetichism in West Africa* [New York, 1904], p. 122, note 1). Another missionary, referring to the tribes of Upper Guinea, declares that they suppose the power or instrument of witchcraft to be a material substance, "and I have known native priests, after a post-mortem examination, to bring forth a portion of the aorta, or some other internal organ which the people would not be likely to recognize as belonging to the body, as proof that they had secured the veritable witch" (J. L. Wilson, *Western Africa* [London, 1856], p. 228).

35 P. A. Talbot, *op. cit.*, II, 207.

36 Examination of the body of a dead man, to discover the existence of sorcery and the identity of the sorcerer, has been found outside of central Africa. The Trobrianders, after a man's death by supposed sorcery, try to find out why he was killed and on whose behalf the sorcerer killed him. This is achieved by the correct interpretation of certain marks or symptoms to be seen on his corpse. It is exhumed on the day following the preliminary burial and carefully examined for the signs which may indicate, for instance, that he had been only too successful in his love affairs, to the annoyance of some influential man; or that he had indulged in too ambitious decorations of his hut and thus aroused the chief's resentment; or that he had not paid a sufficient tribute of his taro to the chief; or, again, that he had dealt dishonestly with the pigs which the chief had entrusted to his stewardship. A sick man always thinks that he knows who is the sorcerer guilty of making him ill and for whom the sorcerer is acting. If he dies, the survivors are pretty certain as to what signs on his body they may expect to find. The proceedings, in fact, have all the characteristics of a formal verification of what is already known (Bronislaw Malinowski, *Crime and Custom in Savage Society* [London, 1926], pp. 87 ff.; *idem, The Sexual Life of Savages in North-Western Melanesia*, p. 155). After a death among the Araucanians of Chile the body is dissected and examined by a medicine man. Should he find the liver in a healthy condition, the death is attributed to natural causes;

430   MAGIC: A SOCIOLOGICAL STUDY

if the liver is inflamed, sorcery has been practiced. In the latter case the medicine man must now discover how the mortal disease was produced. He takes out the gall, puts it in a pot and cooks it; if after this process a stone is found in the bottom of the pot the victim was certainly killed by the stone. Then the medicine man, having thrown himself into a trance, is able to discover the guilty person who cast the stone (E. R. Smith, *The Araucanians* [London, 1855], pp. 236 f.). In British Guiana, when a medicine man has been called in after a death, he must first determine whether the deceased fell a victim to an evil spirit or to a sorcerer. If he decides for the latter explanation, the corpse is closely examined. Should it have a blue mark anywhere, that is the place where the sorcerer's invisible pointed arrow entered the man. The next step is to find the culprit. A pot containing a magical decoction is set on the fire. When the pot begins to boil over, the side on which the scum first falls is the quarter where the supposed murderer must be looked for (J. H. Bernau, *Missionary Labours in British Guiana* [London, 1847], pp. 56 ff.). With these practices may be compared a custom of the Tonga Islanders. It was a firm belief with them that if a man broke a taboo or committed any other sacrilege his liver or some other internal organ would become enlarged and indurated. The bodies of the dead were therefore often opened to discover whether or not they had been sacrilegious during their lifetime (John Martin, *An Account of the Natives of the Tongo Islands . . . . from the Extensive Communications of Mr. William Mariner* [3d ed., Edinburgh, 1827], I, 172, note).

³⁷ D. G. Brinton, "Nagualism. A Study in Native American Folk-Lore and History," *Proceedings of the American Philosophical Society*, XXXIII (1894), 34.

³⁸ Elsie C. Parsons, in *Forty-seventh Annual Report of the Bureau of American Ethnology*, pp. 242 ff. "The prime difference between asking a witch or asking a medicine man to help you in any undertaking is that after you succeed the medicine man removes from you the 'power' he has imparted to you, whereas the witch does not, and the 'power' may abide with you for life in punishment for having resorted to it, something like the affliction of King Midas" (p. 243). On witchcraft beliefs in the Keresan pueblos generally see L. A. White, in *Proceedings of the Twenty-third International Congress of Americanists* [New York, 1928], pp. 608 ff.

³⁹ Mischa Titiev, "Notes on Hopi Witchcraft," *Papers of the Michigan Academy of Science, Arts, and Letters*, XXVIII (1942), pp. 549 ff.

⁴⁰ Clyde Kluckhohn, *Navaho Witchcraft* (Cambridge, Mass., 1944), pp. 14–35. *Papers of the Peabody Museum of American Archaeology and Ethnology*, Vol. XXII, No. 2. See also William Morgan, *Human Wolves among the Navaho* (New Haven, 1936). *Yale University Publications in Anthropology*, No. 11.

⁴¹ James Mooney and F. M. Olbrechts, "The Swimmer Manuscript. Cherokee Sacred Formulas and Medicinal Prescriptions," *Bulletin of the Bureau of American Ethnology*, No. 99, pp. 29 ff.

⁴² D. I. Bushnell, *ibid.*, No. 48, p. 29.

⁴³ P. E. Goddard, "Life and Culture of the Hupa," *University of California Publications in American Archaeology and Ethnology*, I, 64 f.

⁴⁴ A. W. Howitt, *The Native Tribes of South-East Australia* (London, 1904), pp. 367 ff.

⁴⁵ Carl Lumholtz, *Among Cannibals* (New York, 1889), pp. 280 f. What is supposed to happen to a victim of *kobi* varies in different localities of northern Queensland. In the Boulia District he is deprived of blood, this being replaced by a bone or a pebble; on the Pennefeather River his blood is made "bad"; on the Tully River a rope is inserted in his chest; at Cape Grafton he is choked

when asleep, his tongue and blood removed, and a splinter of bone inserted in his head; at Cape Bedford he is hit with a stick, his head severed from the body and then replaced, his neck twisted, or his hamstrings cut (W. E. Roth, *North Queensland Ethnography Bulletin*, No. 5, pp. 28, 32 ff.).

[46] George Taplin, in J. D. Woods (editor), *The Native Tribes of South Australia* (Adelaide, 1879), pp. 26 ff.

[47] Sir Baldwin Spencer and F. J. Gillen, *The Native Tribes of Central Australia* (London, 1899), pp. 476 ff. It is said to be possible to recover from a *kurdaitcha* attack, but only with the aid of a medicine man particularly strong in magic (*iidem, Across Australia* [2d ed., London, 1912], II, 355).

[48] W. L. Warner, *A Black Civilization* (New York, 1937), pp. 194 ff. See also pp. 223 ff. for other accounts. *Mipurama* sorcery of a type similar to that found among the Murngin has also been described in the Northern Territory, but without an indication of the special area or tribe where it is practiced. See W. E. H. Stanner, in *Mankind*, II (1936–40), 21.

[49] C. S. Myers, in *Reports of the Cambridge Anthropological Expedition to Torres Straits*, VI, 222 ff. John Bruce, who knew the natives intimately, was familiar with many cases of *maid*. Under its influence the victim usually died within two or three days. His friends would never ask Europeans for medicine for him, "as that would be going against *maid*." Our informant adds that he never saw on the bodies of the victims any marks of injury such as would be caused by blows of a stone or a club. He reported a case in which the man who was supposed to have caused a certain person's death by means of *maid* was one hundred miles distant at the time.

[50] Paul Wirz, *Die Marind-anim von Holländsch-Süd-Neu-Guinea* (Hamburg, 1922–25), Vol. I, Pt. II, 67 ff.

[51] Gunnar Landtman, *The Kiwai Papuans of British New Guinea* (London, 1927), p. 323.

[52] C. G. Seligman, *op. cit.*, pp. 170 f., 187 f., from an account by Ahuia, a clan chief, village constable, and official interpreter.

[53] R. L. Turner, "Malignant Witchcraft in Papua and the Use of Poisons Therein," *Man*, XXIV (1924), 117–19.

[54] R. E. Guise, in *Journal of the Anthropological Institute*, XXVIII (1899), 216 f.

[55] Bronislaw Malinowski, in *Transactions of the Royal Society of South Australia*, XXXIX (1915), 648 ff. One of Malinowski's informants added the important detail that the *barau*, after killing his victim, opens the body, takes something out of it, and puts something into it.

[56] R. F. Fortune, *op. cit.*, pp. 161 ff., 284 ff., from an account by a native informant, supposedly an eyewitness of *wawari* sorcery.

[57] W. E. Armstrong, *Rossel Island* (Cambridge, 1928), pp. 170, 173, note 1. According to our authority it is certain that people were sometimes smothered at night and had their ribs broken, a "diabolical reality" difficult to disentangle from the imaginary *ngwivi* sorcery (p. 170, note 1).

[58] H. I. Hogbin, "Sorcery and Administration," *Oceania*, VI (1935–36), 11 ff.

[59] M. Rascher, in *Archiv für Anthropologie*, XXIX (1904), 221 f. R. Parkinson (*Dreissig Jahre in der Südsee* [Stuttgart, 1907], p. 200) follows Father Rascher's account of *pur-mea*.

[60] L. W. S. Wright, "The 'Vele' Magic of the South Solomons," *Journal of the Royal Anthropological Institute*, LXX (1940), 203–209. See also R. H. Codrington, *op. cit.*, pp. 206 f.; W. G. Ivens, *Melanesians of the South-East Solomon Islands* (London, 1927), pp. 292 f.; S. G. C. Knibbs, *The Savage Solomons as They Were and Are* (London, 1929), pp. 39 f. According to Wright

vele sorcery is confined to Guadacanal, the small island of Savo, and the adjacent Russell Islands. Codrington says, however, that it is "known" (though not necessarily practiced) at Florida and Mala or Malaita.

[61] Felix Speiser, *Ethnographische Materialien aus den Neuen Hebriden und den Banks-Inseln* (Berlin, 1923), p. 370, quoting Boyd, in "Quarterly Jottings from the New Hebrides," April 1911. Codrington (*op. cit.*, p. 207) describes the *vequa* of Lepers' Island in the New Hebrides as very much resembling the *vele* of the Solomons.

[62] A. C. Kruijt, "De weerwolf bij de Toradja's van Midden-Celebes," *Tijdschrift voor Indische Taal-Land-en Volkenkunde*, XLI (1899), 551 ff.; N. Adriani and A. C. Kruijt, *Die Bare'e-sprekende Toradja's van Midden-Celebes* (Batavia, 1912–14), I, 255 ff.

[63] Dora M. Abdy, "Witchcraft among the Wahadimu," *Journal of the African Society*, No. 63 (1917), 235.

[64] H. A. Junod, *op. cit.*, (2d ed.), II, 513 f.

[65] W. H. Brett, *The Indian Tribes of Guiana* (London, 1868), pp. 373 f.

[66] Sir E. F. im Thurn, *Among the Indians of Guiana* (London, 1883), pp. 329 ff. See also W. E. Roth, "An Inquiry into the Animism and Folk-Lore of the Guiana Indians," *Thirtieth Annual Report of the Bureau of American Ethnology*, pp. 354–62.

[67] John Gillin, *The Barama River Caribs of British Guiana* (Cambridge, Mass., 1936), pp. 340 ff. *Papers of the Peabody Museum of American Archaeology and Ethnology*, Vol. XIV, No. 2.

[68] Theodor Koch-Grünberg, *Vom Roroima zum Orinoco* (Berlin, 1917–28), III, 216 ff.

[69] James Mooney, "Myths of the Cherokees," *Nineteenth Annual Report of the Bureau of American Ethnology*, pp. 316 ff.

[70] With reference to this type of sorcery it is worthy of notice that only in Australia is the victim supposed to be deprived of his "kidney fat" (really the caul fat from the omentum). By the aborigines human fat is greatly prized, for they believe that the prowess and virtues of a dead man will pass to those who eat it, anoint their bodies with it, or carry some of it about as a charm for success in hunting and fighting (A. W. Howitt, *op. cit.*, pp. 367, 411). Among the Toradya of Celebes and the Cherokee Indians it is the victim's liver which is taken out and eaten. This form of cannibalism is obviously connected with the corpse-eating so often attributed to sorcerers, both real and imaginary.

CHAPTER XV

SAFEGUARDS AGAINST SORCERY

Primitive man, whose capacity for conjuring up the evils of sorcery seems limitless, is equally ingenious in devising means of nullifying them by aversive rites or by defensive techniques and devices. Since the success of the black art depends entirely upon the fear which it inspires in its victims, counter magic, divination, and exorcism, by appealing even more strongly to the imagination, may be effective safeguards against the sorcerer and all his extraordinary works.

In Samoa, when a man was ill there was a special inquiry made of his sister, and also of her children, "as to whether any of them had cursed him and thus caused his illness, and in all such cases the sister would take some coconut water into her mouth and eject it towards or even over the body of the sufferer, by which action she expressed her own innocence, and also removed any other supposed spell. This was done on account of the fear which was always felt of the effects of a sister's curse."[1] A Maori *tohunga,* by dipping a young man in a purificatory stream and reciting the appropriate formulas, protected the youth's "life principle" and rendered him immune from magical attacks. This practice, from the confidence which it inspired, was of the greatest psychological value.[2] In the Lower Congo area a native can procure a charm to protect him from an enemy's magic. Its effect is to compel the latter always to put off until "tomorrow" the commission of the dreaded act; thus it never takes place, for tomorrow never comes.[3] The Yagua Indians of northeastern Peru consider that a magician can succeed in practicing sorcery against another magician only if the latter does not know of the attempt. If he becomes aware of his colleague's dastardly efforts, he can make himself immune simply by drinking tobacco juice. He may even kill his opponent by the use of stronger magic.[4] Among the Thompson Indians of British Columbia an enemy who gained possession of a man's weapons could bewitch him, take away his luck, and kill him. But if the owner of the weapons was stronger in magic than his would-be persecutor, it was often the latter who sickened and died.[5] If two Shuswap magicians, with equally powerful tutelary spirits, tried to bewitch each other, both died at the same time or one shortly after the other.[6]

Fear of the black magic that can be wrought by using the separable parts (exuviae) or personal leavings of an individual results in practices whose effect is hygienic and sanitary. Clearly enough, cleanliness in itself was not their original purpose, but rather the desire to put out of the way anything that might be serviceable to an ill-wisher.

Of the aborigines of Victoria we are told that nothing offensive is ever to be seen in the neighborhood of their camps. All ordure belonging to adults and half-grown children is buried at a distance from their habitations.[7] The Narrinyeri of South Australia are careful to burn the bones of the animals they eat, so as to prevent their enemies from getting hold of them.[8] Among the Kakadu of Northern Territory several men, with the assistance of a woman, try to catch an enemy's "spirit part" and thus deprive him of a protector to warn him of danger or guide him in the search for food. For this purpose some of the enemy's excrement must be secured, ground up, put in wax spheres, and burned in an earthen oven, along with a stick which represents the protecting spirit. Such magic is most effective, hence everyone takes care to cover and hide from view all fecal matter, with the result that the Kakadu camps are cleaner than those of many other tribes.[9]

Similar precautions in respect to excrement are observed by Papuan tribes. Among the Mafulu they apply only in the case of an infant or quite young child. Adults feel no necessity to observe them. On the other hand Mafulu men and women never carelessly throw aside remnants of their food. These are preserved until it is possible to cast them into a river and thus render them harmless. But no such precautions are taken with the food leavings of very young children.[10] The Arapesh classify things associated with a man that can be used in sorcery against him into two groups, each with a special designation. These are, first, personal leavings such as bits of food, half-smoked cigarettes, and butts of sucked sugar cane, and second, excreta, including perspiration, saliva, scabs, semen, vaginal secretion, urine, and feces. But the excreta of adults are not potent for magical purposes, only those of infants.[11] Among the Mountain Arapesh, children of seven or eight years are provided with tiny net bags in which they must hide all gnawed bones, uneaten food, bandages from sores, broken pieces of their g-strings or aprons, and any bit of rubbish which may contain some part of their personality. All these are guarded carefully and secretly buried.[12] Among the Kwoma a child is first warned, while still being weaned, not to eat food given to him by anyone except a near relative, lest there be "poison" in it. Nor ought he to eat away from home, lest he carelessly spill fragments of his food. In later years other warnings are added. He must be careful, for instance, not to spill his blood if he cuts himself lest it be found by a sorcerer. When adolescent he must avoid sexual intercourse with a girl likely to give his semen to a sorcerer.[13]

In the Melanesian Islands the common practice of retiring into the sea or a river no doubt originated in the belief that water washes away that portion of the personality which clings to fecal matter.[14] In Fiji, until Christianity undermined the belief in exuvial magic of the black variety, every man was his own scavenger, and the villages were kept clean. "From birth to old age a man was governed by this one fear; he went into the sea, the graveyard, or the depths of the forest to satisfy his natural wants; he burned his cast-off *malo;* he gave every fragment left over from his food to the pigs; he concealed even the clippings of his hair in the thatch of his house."[15]

All persons of high rank in Tahiti provided themselves with attendants whose duty it was to dispose of objects which could be used in black magic. Anything of this sort was burned, buried, sunk in the sea, or deposited in the refuse heap of a sacred enclosure, where it was safe from interference.[16] These attendants in Hawaii included a wardrobe keeper, who kept an eye on all the clothing and ornaments worn by a chief and prevented their abstraction for purposes of sorcery; a spittoon bearer, who had to be constantly on hand to anticipate the chief's desire to expectorate (any neglect on the former's part being visited with capital punishment); and a private servant, who cared for the disposal of the chief's urine and feces. These were buried secretly at night or were cast into the sea.[17] In New Zealand the food, clothing, and personal possessions of the privileged classes were safeguarded by stringent taboos, which no commoner dared violate; consequently they had no need of special attendants to prevent the collection of "bait" objects by would-be sorcerers.[18]

The victim of sorcery or his associates may sometimes be able to induce the sorcerer to undo the fatal work.[19] In the Wotjobaluk tribe of New South Wales a man suspected of having "pointed the bone" at another would be asked by the latter's friends to place the bone in water, so as to neutralize the evil effects of this magical act. Should the victim die his friends would try to kill the offender by the same means or by direct violence.[20] Among the Murngin of Arnhem Land, Northern Territory, some men know certain songs which are regarded as the most deadly forms of black magic. One of these is the whitefish song. It makes the victim's breath come rapidly and very hard, as the fish proceeds to eat out his insides. When the tide comes in he gets worse and worse; at full tide he dies. Should the sorcerer experience a change of heart and decide to save the victim all he needs to do is to swim out into the water at daybreak, wash himself, return to the shore, and paint his body with red ocher.[21] If a Bukaua man becomes seriously sick, his kinsmen seek out the sorcerer supposed to be responsible for the visitation and pay him to desist from his fell work. He readily agrees to do so, provided the payment is adequate and he has not been hired by persons of greater importance in the community. If his counter magic proves ineffective and the patient continues to be ill, another sorcerer is held responsible. Should *his* counter magic fail to produce satisfactory results then an explanation is sought in the activity of evil spirits.[22] Black magic practiced over a person's feces is common in Rossel Island, which belongs to the Louisiade Archipelago. The victim suffers at first from diarrhea, but the case need not be fatal until the sorcerer carries the operation further. If he wants the man to die he puts the feces, together with various plant and animal products, including a poisonous eel, over a fire. The man becomes feverish and soon dies. But should the sorcerer relent at the last moment he places what remains of the mixture in cold water, and the man recovers.[23] In New Britain, when a Sulka sorcerer has been discovered, the people promise him gifts to induce him to withdraw the appurtenances of the victim from the fire or water in which they have been placed. If he does so, the victim recovers; if not, death follows inevitably.[24] A victim of sorcery in the Tonga Islands could be cured only by the man who worked it. The victim's relatives would beg him to do so and pay him for his services.[25] A Marquesan sorcerer was also paid to remove his spell.[26] Magicians among the Achinese of northwestern Sumatra make much use of certain kinds of toadstools, especially those which grow near each other in pairs. Of each pair one is the "prince" and the other is the "princess." The former, which works evil, is given by a sorcerer to his customers for destruction of their enemies; the latter, which provides an antidote to the poison, he keeps hidden. But for a handsome fee he will often hand over the princess toadstool to an intended victim, who is thus able to nullify the black magic of his adversary.[27]

Counter magic may be worked by a rival practitioner against the sorcerer. This is invariably the case in the Trobriand Islands, where for every spell there is an opposing spell. The contest between the two magical forces, evil and good, black and white, takes place almost openly.[28] In Eddystone Island sorcerers have their opponents. These men, by the aid of the spirits which they control, can discover a practitioner of the black art and cure the malady which he has caused.[29] In Ontong Java, the counter sorcerer waves oiled coconut leaflets over the sufferer's head, reciting meanwhile a spell in which sea slugs and other unpleasant things are mentioned, and then calls upon certain of his ancestors to remove the slugs which the sorcerer's ancestral ghosts had placed in the man's belly. If this simple treatment is successful, splendid presents are made to the operator. It seems that he would be unwilling thus to undo the work of another unless he had the backing of public opinion, which supported a man who had been unjustly bewitched.[30]

In defense against sorcerers the Tahitians had a healing god of high rank in the native pantheon. The relatives of a person suffering from the effects of black magic presented gifts to the god in the person of the attendant priest, and the latter then undertook the cure of the patient. It was necessary, however, for the sick man, or his relatives for him, first to confess any sins which might have been responsible for the affliction. The priest took in one hand a banana shoot to represent the sorcerer and in the other hand some kava root representing his own god. By means of a healing "prayer" he transferred the evil to the banana shoot and so to the sorcerer for whom it stood. At the same time he asked the god to forgive any sins confessed and conjured the patient to throw off the evil spirits vexing him. If the priest had full control of the case, the demonic powers entered the sorcerer's body and destroyed both him and his family.[31]

In East Africa good magicians discover and destroy sorcerers, both real and imaginary. Thus among the Anyanja of Nyasaland the "throat-cutter" and "he of the hammer," by means of their more powerful medicine, compel sorcerers to reveal themselves and then attack them, the one with his knife and the other with his hammer.[32] Among the Shilluk a sorcerer makes a mud image of his intended victim, sticks nails in its ears, and puts it in the fire. The man will either go crazy or die. But a good magician, if appealed to for help by the man, makes another representation of him and puts it into water, thus neutralizing the heat of the original image.[33]

A sorcerer of the Barama River Caribs, having been duly commissioned by a man to injure someone, first gets in touch with his spirits by drinking pepper water, a potion which produces a violent reaction resembling fits, approaches the intended victim and, without being noticed, picks up some small object, blows tobacco smoke upon it, and throws it at him. The consequences of this action depend upon the kind of object which is thrown: a piece of offal will cause him to rot away; a piece of wood will make him stiff. Or the sorcerer may merely blow tobacco smoke upon him, making a wish at the same time, and if the smoke touches the victim, the wish will be fulfilled. Men have even been turned into monkeys by this simple procedure. The tobacco smoke seems to be the "embodiment" of the sorcerer's power. The victim consults another sorcerer, who, with the help of pepper water, interviews his spirits in the night, for he can see in a dark room as if it were lighted up. In the morning he tells his client who has done the mischief and why, and requires him to observe certain food taboos to neutralize the machinations of the rival practitioner. But should the client, in his ignorance, have consulted the sorcerer who had been originally hired, this fact is concealed by the latter, who proceeds to inflict still more harm on the unfortunate man.[34]

Among the Takelma of Oregon, besides the regular medicine man (goyo), who was able both to inflict and cure disease, there was another functionary whose activities were entirely confined to curing. He was frequently hired to counteract the evil activity of a goyo. The two practitioners appealed to entirely different spirits and had different medicine songs.[35] When the goyo, who "eats up people," had too recklessly indulged in murderous practices, the good medicine man could drive out his tutelary spirits visibly from his bound body and thus reduce him to impotence.[36]

Black magic may be made to bounce back upon its operator, perhaps with fatal results. The tragic tale is told of a celebrated sorcerer in Malekula who was tricked into performing rites and reciting spells over his own excrement instead of that of his enemy. A month or so later he learned of the deception. By that time it was too late to overcome the effects of the magic; "his blood was no good." Ulcers and paralysis confined him, a helpless invalid, to his bed.[37] One variety of Maori magic was intended, not only to ward off and nullify a sorcerer's spells, but also to send them back upon him and destroy him. Counter spells of this sort would always be successful provided the *tohunga* using them possessed a greater store of *mana* than his rival. If the patient recovered, the latter, of course, died.[38] Among the Bavenda of the Transvaal perhaps the most popular form of black magic utilizes sand from an enemy's footprint. The sand, when combined with poisonous herbs, forms an exceedingly potent charm. But there is a prophylactic for it. A man about to go through a district where an enemy lives obtains from a magician a certain powder mixed with fat and rubs the ointment on the soles of his feet, sometimes for good measure on his entire body. The ointment forms a magical barrier between the traveler's feet and the ground, thus preventing the escape of his "essence" or personality. Moreover, the powder of the magician from whom they were obtained, will, in turn, infect the ground. If this power is greater than that wielded by the enemy, the traveler can proceed on his way unharmed, while the enemy will suffer the fate which he prepared for the other fellow.[39] The most destructive form of magic among the Azande is *bagbuduma,* magic of vengeance. When a man dies his kinsman consider that he was a sorcerer's victim, and they use this magic to slay the slayer. They say that it is both a judge and an executioner, that it "settles cases as judiciously as princes." Were a man to use *bagbuduma* to kill out of spite an innocent person, it would not only prove ineffectual but it would turn against the operator and destroy him. Before resorting to it, therefore, the Azande seek assurance by divination that their kinsman died from sorcery and not as the result of his own misdeeds.[40] The Ga people of the Gold Coast consider it very necessary that a pregnant woman should protect herself against witches, who are wont to prey on the spirits of unborn children. So she proceeds to wash herself in water containing a powerful herb and small pinches of every kind of food which anyone can suggest, whether the eatables are of native or of foreign origin. The idea is that, however catholic in her eating, the witch will discover that her own food has been included in the decoction. The food with which the woman bathed then protects her by saying to the witch, "I am your own food. You cannot hurt me without hurting yourself."[41] When a Cherokee is dangerously ill, witches from far and near gather invisibly about his house after nightfall and do their best to trouble him and thus hasten his demise. Should the patient succumb, the years that he might otherwise have lived are added to those of the attacking witches, who will thus live to a green old age. The Indians have a potent counter spell against one of these "night goers." It not only drives the witch away but also kills him, for according to the general belief the counteracting of a deadly spell always results in the death of its author.[42] The Netsilik Eskimo believe that a formula of "wicked words" must kill if there is any power in it. If it does not destroy the person against whom it is directed, it turns against the maker and reciter; should he not succumb then one of his nearest relatives will die. Spells may thus have a boomerang effect. Stories are told of just such misadventures.[43]

A death occurs in a primitive community. Was it the result of something for which the victim could be held responsible, perhaps a broken taboo, perhaps some fault of omission or commission calling for his just punishment by the spiritual powers? Or was it due to black magic practiced on him by someone at home or abroad? Resort will often be had to divination to determine the cause of the death, and if sorcery is held responsible then to discover the sorcerer.

The Watchandi of Western Australia carefully clear the ground around the grave of a man who has recently died and visit it every day to discover whether any living thing has passed over it. In course of time the tracks of some animal, for instance, a beetle, are sure to be seen. The direction taken by the creature indicates the whereabouts of the guilty sorcerer. Then the nearest of kin sets off in pursuit of him, though he may be hundreds of miles away.[44] The tribes of Victoria have several ways of ascertaining the direction in which the avengers must go to find a sorcerer who killed a man. One method is to heap a mound over his grave and coat it smoothly with wet clay. The fierce sun overhead soon cracks the clay, and the direction of the first main fissure in it points out the path which the avenging party should take.[45]

The Orokaiva, a Papuan tribe, set up a burning brand on the outskirts of a village where a man has recently died. His relatives observe it carefully and when it proceeds to fly away, carried by the ghost of the deceased, they try to follow it until it comes to rest on the house veranda of the guilty party. This procedure, to be sure, easily leads to the victimizing of an innocent person who happens to be in the bad books of the diviners. A dead brand or a bit of charcoal is a common object on a man's veranda, so that almost anyone can be accused of the murder.[46] In New Britain, after a death, the villagers assemble. One of them takes a pearl shell in his hand and lies down by the corpse. Another man then calls out, one by one, the names of all the men in the village, and then, if nothing happens, the names of men in neighboring villages, until a rapping is heard in the shell. This is done by a spirit to whom an appeal has been made for information. The man whose name was being uttered when the rapping was heard is adjudged the guilty party. Nothing will convince the people that he is innocent. He is usually a person who owed the deceased a grudge during the latter's lifetime, "and there is plenty of room for all kinds of personal revenge on the part of those engaged in the test."[47]

In the Tanga Islands, a group off the eastern coast of New Ireland, it used to be the custom to "fish for the ghost" of a person supposed to have come to his end by sorcery. For this purpose the men took a bamboo pole and at one end tied a bunch of highly perfumed leaves. Within the leaves were three vertebrae covered with succulent flesh from one of the pigs eaten at the mortuary feast. When all was ready the men placed the rod on their shoulders and marched away, being very careful to place the "bait" in their rear so as to avoid catching sight of the ghost. As they walked about the bush they tried to attract its attention by whistling to it and invited it to come and smell the fragrant leaves and taste the juicy morsels of meat. The pole in time grew heavy on their shoulders, an indication that they had ensnared the ghost. Then it was questioned: "Who has made this evil sorcery against you?" Several names might be mentioned as those of possibly guilty persons. If the pole did not move, the questioning would be continued until at length, when a certain name had been called out, the pole began to vibrate so violently that the strength of twenty men was required to prevent it from moving away. Since all this action took place in the dark, it seems quite probable that a majority of the performers, by moving the pole, could give expression to their own private opinion as to who killed the person in question. But the natives themselves were emphatic that no trickery was employed and that the procedure they followed was an infallible means of obtaining evidence against a sorcerer.[48]

Among the Baiga, a tribe of the Central Provinces of India,

every funeral is accompanied by divination to discover the cause of death. One method of doing so is to examine the level of the grave when this has been filled up. If it is even with the surrounding ground, then the death was due to the Creator god, who brings forth life and ends life; if it sinks below, then the deceased was punished for having broken a tribal taboo; but if it rises above, he had been a victim of black magic.[49]

By the Tanala of Madagascar a person who dies suddenly is believed to have been bewitched. In such a case a diviner is called in to discover the guilty man. After consulting his oracle he wraps up some grains of black sand, places them on the head of the corpse, and says, "He who is caught carrying his cloth (i.e., his dress) within a month is mine." The Tanala think that the black sand will cause the sorcerer to go about naked. If anyone is seen doing so within the allotted period he is promptly killed.[50]

Among the Bechuana tribes, when a man fell sick or some other misfortune happened to him, a diviner would be called in to find out why he had been afflicted. If satisfied that a sorcerer was responsible, the diviner never named the offender, but stated his sex, totem, and other details that might enable the people to identify him. They would hold an inquiry to obtain further evidence in the matter and could report the result to the chief. The alleged wrongdoer was then formally tried. If held guilty, the chief ordered him to cure the patient and, if necessary, tortured him until he consented to do so. The sorcerer was released if the patient recovered, but if the latter died he was put to death.[51] A witch doctor of the Babemba performs various tests to find the person who is exerting an evil influence in the community. For instance, he takes a large seed, about the size of a pigeon's egg, places it on a mat, and puts a gourd over it. Then he waves the gourd to and fro over the seed, making a rattling sound, and at the same time mentions the names of suspected persons. On coming to the name which the witch doctor has decided to identify as that of the culprit, the seed stops rattling and, by some sleight-of-hand on the part of the operator, attaches itself to the side of the gourd. Although the witch doctor is obviously open to bribery or other improper influence, his procedure is so implicitly trusted that an innocent man, when so named, will believe himself guilty.[52] A witch doctor of the Benga in Gabun goes the round of a village ringing a small bell. It stops ringing outside the hut of a guilty sorcerer. Among the Fiote (Fjort) a witch doctor will take on and off the lid of a small basket, while he repeats the names of all the people in the village. When the lid fails to come off at someone's name, that person is doomed. Another inquisitor will rub the flattened palms of his hands together. When his palms fail to meet at a name and his hands fly about wildly, he has got his man.[53]

When a Haida Indian falls sick or dies, three men are selected to discover the man who has bewitched him. They prepare themselves for this difficult business by drinking a mixture of sea water and pulverized dried frog. The vomiting produced by the potion cleanses their systems, clears their minds, and makes them able to pass an infallible judgment on the matter. The next thing is to catch a wood mouse and put it in a little cage on a platform before the judges. Then they begin naming over suspected persons, and presently the mouse nods its head. The sorcerer, thus revealed, must pay money or blankets as compensation for his evil deed.[54]

Divination is also practiced by means of the body of a person supposedly the victim of sorcery. In the Tharumba tribe of New South Wales a corpse is rubbed all over with a mixture of burnt bark and grease. A number of such applications produces an ashy layer. Some of this powder, together with the exudations from the corpse, is burned by the elders. If the smoke ascends straight up for some distance before it disperses, the meaning is that the murderer lives quite a way off. But if the smoke goes up only a little way and bends to one side, then the man they seek must be near them. In either case the direction in which the smoke bends shows the direction of his camp. This powder from the corpse has the further remarkable property of guiding the avengers right into the camp of the guilty party, where they can work magic on him.[55] Among some Victorian tribes the corpse is carried on a bier to various places where the deceased had lived. Meanwhile a man under the bier converses with the corpse and asks who bewitched him to death. If the answer implicates someone present, the bier moves round by itself and touches the guilty sorcerer.[56] The Warramunga, in common with other tribes of Central Australia, place their dead on platforms in trees. After a corpse has been deposited and has decayed, a careful examination is made of the fluid trickling down. The direction which this takes indicates the region from which the murderous sorcerer came. If the stream flows only a little way he must be near at hand, but if it flows for a long distance he must have come from a remote group. In the latter case they follow the stream to its end and usually—so they say—find there a little beetle supposed to resemble a man. They kill the creature, believing that they thus cause the death of the culprit.[57]

Among some Papuan tribes about Hood Peninsula certain portions of the corpse are allotted to certain relatives, and then, after decomposition has sufficiently advanced, the epidermis is stripped off it by a friend of the deceased. If this fails to peel from some part of the body, the relative to whom that part has been assigned is held to have caused his death.[58]

In New Britain, on the night following a man's death, his friends would ask the deceased to designate the enemy who had bewitched him. If no answer was received, the magician called out the names of suspected persons, one after another, until a sound, like that made by tapping the fingers on a board or mat, was heard in the house or on a pearl shell held in the questioner's hand. Such an answer was taken as "conclusive evidence" that the guilty party had been found.[59]

In some parts of Sierra Leone the practice prevailed of hoisting a corpse upon the heads of six bearers and then of questioning it as to the cause of its death. The corpse answered either by impelling the bearers forward, which signified "Yes," or by moving to the side, which signified "No." When the cross-examination reached the point at which the offending sorcerer was to be denounced, the corpse moved forward and bumped against a green bough held by a relative or friend of the deceased. To make the identification quite certain, this bumping was repeated several times.[60]

In order to track down a sorcerer some of the Guiana tribes cut off the fingers and toes of his victim and boil them in a pot. The side of the pot where the first finger or toe is cast over the rim by the bubbling water is the side where the sorcerer is to be looked for.[61] The Djuka (Bush Negroes of Dutch Guiana) leave a corpse unburied for a number of days. In the humid heat the flesh undergoes partial liquefaction. The putrescent fluid is then collected in a calabash and carried from door to door in the village. Every person must put the gourd to his lips and go through the motion of swallowing some of its contents. Should anyone refuse to do so he has shown himself to be the murderer.[62]

While suspected sorcerers are sometimes made to confess by torture or the threat of torture, they often freely acknowledge their misdeeds. Among the Moi of French Indo-China the accused, far from trying to prove himself innocent, openly exults at his success as a practitioner of the black art and takes delight in explaining his mode of operations.[63] An anthropologist working among the Pondo of Pondoland herself heard three confessions of witchcraft, and other recent cases were reported to her. These were not extracted by torture, though formerly torture was in common use for the purpose. Many confessions made before a diviner and in the presence of a crowd of people are afterward recanted. It seems likely, thinks our informant, that they are often the result of hypnotic influence.[64] Among the Mashona of Southern Rhodesia there are people, more especially women, who will confess themselves to be witches.[65] Among the Bakaonde of Northern Rhodesia a full and free confession seems to be the general rule, and when once it is made the supposed witch faces death bravely.[66] An accused person among the Wanyamwezi and other tribes of Tanganyika not only confesses but boasts of his criminality: "Verily I slew such a one! I brought about the disease of such another!"[67] Yoruba old women, after admitting their guilt, will charge themselves with the deaths that have recently occurred in the community.[68] It is said to be exceedingly common for Timne witches to confess to spoiling farms, killing people, and other wicked deeds.[69] In Northwest America nearly all Indians accused of sorcery make a "surprising admission of guilt," even in face of the death penalty which its practice carries.[70] It is clear from these instances that a powerful group suggestion of guilt can often overcome the defendant's belief in his own innocence and result in the otherwise inexplicable phenomenon of self-accusation. On the other hand, to reveal oneself as a successful worker of sorcery, that most difficult and dangerous of all arts, satisfies a man's sense of importance, affords him an almost paranoiac thrill, and supports him under torture and in the pangs of death.

Many primitive peoples, with the noteworthy exception of the American Indians, rely on some form of the ordeal for the detection of sorcerers. In Africa, the area of its most extensive use, it generally consists in the administration of poison to a suspect. The accused (sometimes the accuser as well) swallows a poisonous draught or eats some poisonous substance; if it nauseates him and he vomits it, he is pronounced innocent; if he retains it or evacuates it, he is declared guilty. His death from the effect of the poison is regarded as infallible evidence of guilt, for the poison is supposed to have "almost sentience," following like a policeman the evil substance or evil spirit in the culprit's body, detecting it, and destroying it. When nothing evil is found the poison does not act. Frequently the spectators at an ordeal, impressed by a person's inability to eject the poison in the approved manner or by the vertigo and dizziness which it produces in him, take matters into their own hands and dispatch him with every refinement of cruelty.[71]

That a good deal of trickery and downright fraud often surrounds these proceedings is obvious. Among the Babemba the accused would, if possible, take an emetic just before swallowing the deadly potion, or the witch doctor might be induced by secret gifts to mix an emetic with the poison so as to cause instant vomiting.[72] A witch doctor of the Lower Congo tribes is sometimes bribed to prepare a mild dose of the poison and of such a character as will ensure vomiting. On the other hand, in some districts the witch doctor loses his fee if the accused vomits, indeed may be severely punished for having made a false charge of witchcraft. Hence there is good reason for him to be thorough in his preparations and not to tamper with the deadly draught.[73] Among the Ovimbundu of Angola the person accused of sorcery and his accuser undergo the ordeal together, and both beforehand make handsome presents to the witch doctor. He has one kind of medicine in a bag and another kind in a smaller receptacle within it. One of the substances is harmless and the other is poisonous. He mixes the drink, saying, "You can all see that I am taking the medicine for both from the same bag." But the man who is to be proved innocent gets the harmless mixture and the other gets the poisoned draught. The doctor's procedure evidently does not command universal confidence, for there is a native proverb, "What is seen by the eye is superior to the poison test."[74] The witch doctor of Gabun frequently practices blackmail. When he condemns a person to undergo the ordeal he expects that the latter's family will secretly bring him presents to induce him to mix so little poison in the drink that the accused will be none the worse for it.[75] The Ekoi of southern Nigeria use for the poison ordeal the *esere* bean, ground and mixed with water. But if the bean is boiled beforehand, drinking the potion will result only in intense pain followed by vomiting. This is a secret jealously guarded by the witch doctors. Some natives assert that the virulence of the poison varies according to the quantity administered and that an underdose or an overdose will not be fatal. The exact amount that should be administered is known only to initiates.[76] The Balante of Senegal generally commission an old woman to brew and administer the poison. Before doing so she visits the village where the suspects live, and if well paid by them or their friends agrees to provide them with a powerful antidote, probably something to produce vomiting.[77]

Nevertheless, the popular attitude toward the ordeal is usually one of complete faith in its efficacy. Those who take it are almost always convinced of their innocence and sure, therefore, of its harmlessness to them. For this reason they undergo it readily and even clamor for the opportunity of clearing themselves from the charge of sorcery. In rare cases, when the accused person denies his guilt but refuses to submit to the ordeal, he will be tortured until he confesses and names his accomplices.[78]

As a result of witchcraft accusations many natives lose their lives by the ordeal or by lynch law. It is calculated that in Pondoland, before that district was annexed to Cape Colony, at least one person was put to death every day, on an average, as a suspected witch.[79] Among the Bechuana tribes it has been asserted that 30 percent of the population used to suffer death for sorcery.[80] The fear of sorcery results in more deaths among the Anyanja of Nyasaland "than all the diseases of the climate put together."[81] With reference to West Africa, generally, an experienced missionary estimates that "for every natural death at least one, and often ten or more, have been executed under witchcraft accusation."[82] Another competent authority declares that the belief in witchcraft "has killed and still kills more men and women than the slave trade."[83] A tribe of the Cameroons was reduced by prosecutions for witchcraft and judicial murders from about ten thousand in 1845 to about two thousand in 1885.[84] A small tribe of Calabar became almost extinct by the constant use of the poison ordeal. On one occasion the whole population took the poison; about half of those who did so perished.[85] In southern Nigeria, where resort to the poison ordeal is still common, the immense number of people who die in this way every year is "almost unbelievable."[86]

The African witch doctor, besides administering the ordeal for sorcery, is often called upon to "smell out" the sorcerer by inquisitorial methods. This procedure, as found among the Xosa tribes of South Africa, has been described at length by a native informant. The case was that of a sick child, believed by the relatives and friends to be a victim of the black art. So they approached the doctor, seeking information as to the identity of the supposed culprit.

"He begins by guessing, though his guesses are thrown out in the form of statements. 'You have come about a horse,' he says. The company reply 'We agree,' and accompany their assent with clapping of their hands. From the indifferent manner of their assent and clapping he knows that he is not yet on the right track. He then remarks, 'I am playing with you' or 'I'm telling a lie.' He then essays another guess—'It's a woman.' Still no interest is manifested by his clients, though they give the usual 'We agree' and an impartial clapping of hands. He tries again. 'It is someone who is ill.' The response to this venture is more marked, the assent and clapping become more accentuated. The clients, now satisfied that the diviner has got on the track, add 'Throw behind,' which is equivalent to saying 'You have scored a point.' So it goes on, guess after guess, assent after assent, from the nature of which the diviner knows when he is off or on the correct line of their suspicions. Ultimately, with the help of this guidance, he says, 'It is a sick child.' The clapping and assent become vigorous and unmistakable. That point, then, is fixed. The next step is to discover who the sorcerer is. The same process of question and agreement proceeds. During the whole course of the seance, the diviner dances and gesticulates in so violent a manner that perspiration pours from his body, but he is accustomed to it and it is calculated to impress his audience. Step by step he worms out of his clients the whole circumstances connected with their suspicions, and the personality of the suspected individual, also his or her relationship to the sick child or quarrel with its family. At length, if the 'culprit' be one of those present, he suddenly dances up to the individual and shouts out, 'This is the one who is destroying the home.' 'This is the sorcerer.' "[87]

In East Central Africa the witch doctor (a woman) travels about the country on her official business of detecting cases of sorcery. "She goes accompanied by a strong guard, and when she orders a meeting of a clan or tribe, attendance is compulsory on pain of confessed guilt. When all are assembled, our friend, who is clad in a scanty loin cloth of leopard skin, and literally covered from head to foot with rattles and fantasies, rushes about among the crowd. She shouts and rants and raves in the most frantic manner, after which, assuming a calm, judicial aspect, she goes from one to another, touching each person's hand. As she touches the hand of the bewitcher, she starts back with a loud shriek and yells, 'This is he, the murderer; blood is in his hand.' . . . . But the accuser is not content with simply discovering the culprit. She proves his guilt. This she does by 'smelling out'—finding— the 'horns' he used in the prosecution of the unlawful art. . . . . The prophetess smells out the horns by going along the bank of a stream, carrying a water vessel and an ordinary hoe. At intervals she lifts water from the stream, which she pours upon the ground and then stops to listen. She hears subterranean voices directing her to the wizard's hiding place, at which, when she arrives, she begins to dig with the hoe, muttering incantations the while, and there she finds the horns deposited near the stream to poison the water drunk by the person to be bewitched. As they are dug out of the ground, should anyone not a magician touch them, even accidentally, the result would be instant death. Now how does the witch detective find the horns? By what devil's art does she hit upon the spot where they are concealed? The explanation is very simple. Wherever she is employed she must spend a night in the village before commencing operations. She does not retire to rest like the other villagers, but wanders about the livelong night listening to spirit voices. If she sees a poor wight outside his house after the usual hour for retiring, she brings that up against him the next day as evidence of guilty intention, and that, either on his own account, or on account of his friend, the wizard, he meant to steal away and dig up the horns. The threat of such dire consequences keeps the villagers within doors, leaving the sorceress the whole night to arrange for the tableau of the following day."[88]

On the whole, the African witch doctor, a sort of public prosecutor, seems to do more good than harm. He does not himself resort to sorcery as a regular occupation, though occasionally he may indulge in it or (for an ample compensation) provide a would-be practitioner with the materials for it. Particularly in West Africa sorcery involves the use of actual poisons; "even in that common true Negro form of killing by witchcraft, putting medicine in the path, there is a poisoned spike as well as charm stuff." There can be no doubt "that the witch doctor's methods of finding out who has poisoned a person are effective and that the knowledge in the public mind of this detective power keeps down poisoning to a great extent."[89]

For most primitive peoples sorcery, whether practiced against the social group or against its individual members, ranks among the worst of offenses. In the one case it is an act of treason; in the other case it is murder or attempted murder. Death by community action or at the hands of the outraged relatives and friends of the victim is the black magician's usual fate. In some instances sorcery alone is capital.[90] Occasionally, however, the popular rage against a convicted sorcerer is satisfied less drastically, perhaps by his expulsion from the community and the loss of all his property. A sorcerer among the Mashona of Southern Rhodesia might lose his ears and suffer banishment. Beggared and homeless, his lot was pitiable, for no one who knew of his infamy would harbor him.[91] Bathonga sorcerers were generally impaled or drowned, but when their crime was not considered so heinous they might be let off with a flogging and expulsion from the community. In the Khosa clan they "roamed about the country, sleeping in the ruins, mocked at and insulted by the children."[92] Among the Embu and other tribes of Kenya, when sorcerers have reached the point of terrorizing the community, the tolerance of the people breaks down. Concerted action is then taken to put a stop to their depredations by driving away the offenders or even drowning them.[93] Among the Banyankole of Uganda the sorcerer was left in abject poverty. No one would employ him in the honorable service of a herdsman. Either he quitted the country or else, if he remained at home, he sank to the level of a serf and agriculturist.[94] A traveler in the Belgian Congo met some children who had been driven from home by their parents as being suspected sorcerers. No one dares to give food or shelter to these waifs. Even when they are taken in at the mission stations, cared for, and educated, they continue to be outlawed for the rest of their lives by their own people.[95] The Bangala require both accuser (unless a witch doctor) and accused to undergo the poison ordeal. If the test results in the latter's favor, he claims and receives damages. If it goes against him, he pays the damages should he be rich enough to do so. A poor man must sell himself as a slave; a slave's master must pay for him. But no one lightly accuses another of witchcraft, since the compensation assessed for an unjust charge is very heavy.[96] Among the Navaho, as also among the Zuñi and other Pueblo Indians, a suspected witch is first questioned and given a chance to confess. If he proves to be recalcitrant, he is tied down and not allowed to eat, drink, or relieve himself until he admits his guilt. Confession is believed to produce a cure for witchcraft unless the victim is obviously about to die. A witch who refuses to confess is (or used to be) often killed, though in some cases he was allowed to escape if he left the community for good.[97] The Tlingit of southern Alaska tied up a sorcerer and deprived him of food and drink for as long as ten days, unless he made confession and promised to find the medicine he had used. When this was produced he waded into the sea and scattered it. The sorcerer who refused to confess was set free at the end of the period mentioned, though not unfrequently he died before being liberated.[98]

The sorcerer does not always suffer the extreme penalty or even severe punishment for his supposed misdeeds. While throughout Australia he knows that sooner or later he will be pointed out as the murderer of a fellow tribesman and will be exposed to retaliation, in the neighboring islands of Torres Straits he seems to go on his way unscathed, being neither robbed nor killed.[99] Not much is done by the Orokaiva, a Papuan tribe, to punish sorcerers. Conciliation of them, by the giving of presents, is a common practice; sometimes, also, retaliatory magic is worked against them. But sorcerers, or at least those supposed to be such, constitute a large class of the population. Any old man of character and parts is likely to be regarded as at least an occasional practitioner of the black art. If innocent of the charge he may deny it or he may accept it and play up to it. "In any event his power and reputation are enhanced, and he probably lives on undisturbed, fearing nothing more than a magical reprisal."[100] It is said that in New Caledonia, when a sorcerer is believed to have caused a general famine, by using a certain piece of polished jade known as the "stone of famine," the people, instead of killing him, make many gifts to him so that he will undo his evil work and restore plenty to the land.[101] Sea Dayak sorcerers are disliked and shunned, but are not killed, as they would be among the Kayan and Kenyah tribes.[102] The Andaman Islanders sometimes conspire to kill a magician when a disaster, which the people think was in his power to avert, occurred, but apparently they never have the hardihood to carry out their designs.[103] The Toda seem to tolerate the existence of sorcerers among them. When a man has been subjected to black magic in the form of a spell, he pays the magician to remove it.[104] Known practitioners of sorcery among the Azande of the Anglo-Egyptian Sudan do not suffer social ostracism nor can they be prosecuted for their actions except when proved to be murderers. A man has a right to ask a sorcerer to leave him in peace, but he must not insult or injure the sorcerer, for the latter is also a member of the tribe, and so long as he does not kill anybody he must be allowed to go on his way without molestation. On the other hand, if a sorcerer refuses to comply with the request made to him, he will lose standing in the community; moreover, he will run the grave risk of bringing death upon his victim and eventual retribution upon himself.[105] Of the Mbali, an Angola tribe, it is said that an influential and courageous man is little likely to be pointed out as a sorcerer and if he should be thus singled out, nothing would be done to punish him. But a man of slight importance must often leave the country to escape persecution on a charge of sorcery.[106] If we are to believe an old writer, an Araucanian medicine man—one of whose functions was the inquisition of sorcery—never accused the principal families of this crime.[107] Of the Zuñi Indians it is reported that despite their intense fear of sorcery, only poor and unfortunate members of the community are ever condemned to death for its practice. Seldom are other people even brought to trial as being alleged sorcerers.[108] The Penobscot Indians of today have no remembrance of a black magician having been slain for vengeance by the friends of his victims or of his having been attacked on account of his maleficence. "This seems a little extraordinary since nearly every mishap and evil consequence in the little native community was in the early times attributed to the action of a shaman whose identity, if not actually known, was, we are told, at least generally suspected."[109] In spite of the general dread of sorcery by the Omaha, no one who practiced it was persecuted or punished for his acts; he might be avoided, but he would remain unmolested.[110]

It is manifest that the belief in sorcery, when strongly held, nourishes the sentiments of fear, hatred, and vengefulness separating village from village, clan from clan, and tribe from tribe. With regard to the aborigines of Australia, generally, we are told that "sorcery makes them fear and hate every man not of their own coterie, suspicious of every man not of their tribe; it tends to keep them in small communities, and is the great bar to social progress."[111] Among the Arunta and other Central Australian tribes there is "an undercurrent of anxious feeling which, though it may be stilled and, indeed, forgotten for a time, is yet always present. In his natural state the native is often thinking that some enemy is attempting to harm him by means of evil magic, and, on the other hand, he never knows when a medicine man in some distant group may not point him out as guilty of killing someone else by magic."[112]

For the tribes of the Elema and Namau groups in Papua "sorcery was the terror by night, the pestilence that walked in darkness. It dogged their lives from birth to death."[113] For the Fly River tribes it was "the biggest curse of native life."[114] The indirect evil effects of sorcery, as found among the Orokaiva, are "very considerable. The harm is wrought upon the body through the mind. It follows that in the main it is not the practice of sorcery which does the harm, but rather the belief in it, and especially the fear of it."[115] The Monumbo, a tribe of Potsdam Harbor, exhibit great dread of black magic. Behind every tree, in every corner, they think there lurks a sorcerer who can injure them with his pointed stick.[116] The production and infliction of disease and death upon near neighbors is one of the customary occupations of the Dobuan people. "Underneath the surface of native life there is a constant silent war, a small circle of kindred alone placing trust in one another. The whole life of the people is strongly colored by a thorough absence of trust in neighbors and the practice of treachery beneath a show of friendliness. Every person goes in fear of the secret war, and on frequent occasions the fear breaks through the surface."[117]

With reference to the Solomon Islanders we are told that "all the positive side of magical procedure, with its associated ideas, seems to work for the good of native society . . . . but, on the other hand, there seems no room for doubt that the fear of black magic casts a great shadow over the existence of each and every individual."[118] In Fiji "professed practicers of witchcraft are dreaded by all classes, and, by destroying mutual confidence, shake the security and comfort of society."[119] In New Zealand "during every action, whether eating, drinking, sleeping, or taking his walks abroad, whether among friends or foes, if no enemy were within a hundred miles, yet death ever attended the Maori and walked side by side with him, awaiting the opportunity to strike him down and dispatch his spirit to the gloomy underworld."[120]

Witchcraft, among the Bathonga, "has a deadly effect on native life. It is a continual source of trouble, fear, quarrels, sorrow. Strange to say, it has been on the increase in recent years. It ruins the villages. 'Formerly,' say my informants, 'you could see villages of ten or twenty huts. Now the accusations of witchcraft have broken them up. Each man builds his own hut apart, from fear of being bewitched, or because he is suspected of being a *noyi*.' "[121] Among the Jaluo, a Nilotic tribe of Uganda, it is easy for an unscrupulous person to obtain a neighbor's property on a charge that the latter had killed one of his relatives by witchcraft. Such is the dread of this crime by the Jaluo that the accuser, however baseless his charge, is sure to have the sympathy and support of the community.[122] With reference particularly to the Bakongo of northern Angola we are told that witchcraft is their greatest curse. "Mothers will forsake their children on account of it. Dearest friends become bitterest foes through it. No Congo Negro has any use for a witch, be it son, daughter, neighbor, or stranger. They are either exiled, ostracized, or killed. Proofs of confederacy with it or guilt of it may be anything which others lack and covet, or which may markedly differentiate one person from another. A peculiarity, an extraordinary phenomenon, an unusual trait, an omen, a dream, a good harvest, an accident, wealth, wisdom, skill, prosperity, and so forth, are among the 'proofs' that one is a *ndoki.*"[123] The fear of witchcraft is intense among nearly all the Nigerian tribes. It colors their entire existence and exercises "an almost paralyzing effect" on human activities. Witchcraft, declared an Ibibio chief, a Christian and a government official, is "a very deep thing. Among our people there is nothing else so deep, and the dread of it darkens multitudes of lives."[124]

When among the Jivaro a man falls ill with one of the diseases which these Indians ascribe to sorcery, he or the head of his family is most likely to attribute it to the malicious arts of a neighbor with whom his family has quarreled—and the Jivaro are by nature impulsive and choleric. If the patient dies, recourse is had to divination to discover the guilty person, and the latter is usually the neighbor upon whom suspicion had fallen. The family's sense of justice and its duty to the deceased require that revenge for the death shall be exacted, so the supposed sorcerer or a substitute for him is assassinated. Such action calls for revenge on the part of the family thus outraged. The blood feud thus started may last a long time and even tend to become permanent, in spite of the fact that the Jivaro are generally satisfied when only one life is taken in retaliation. This is because in cases of supposed sorcery the accused person often does not admit his guilt but asserts that he and his family are innocently persecuted by the relatives of the deceased. If, then, he or a member of his family is murdered, his relatives seek revenge, instead of regarding the murder as justified under the circumstances. Sorcery likewise plays a great part in producing the destructive wars which rage interminably between the different Jivaro tribes or between them and their neighbors. If in a tribe, and especially within the family of a chief, cases of disease, death, or fatal accident occur frequently, these are generally set down to the machinations of sorcerers in a neighboring tribe. A war which starts in this way is waged à outrance, ending in the extermination of the defeated tribe.[125]

Fear of sorcery was "easily the chief source of intra-tribal strife and violence" among the Paviotso. The most frequent cause of murder was a charge of sorcery; even the mere suspicion of practicing it might be enough to endanger a man's life.[126]

The belief in sorcery, when an obsession, destroys individual initiative and numbs the desire for self-advancement, thus becoming a potent cause of the stagnation of culture. In the Trobriand Islands "any prominence, any excess of qualities or possessions not warranted by social position, any outstanding personal achievement or virtue not associated with rank or power," is resented by rich and influential people. Great success of a man in love making, unusual personal beauty, exceptional skill as a dancer, inordinate desire for wealth, recklessness in the display and enjoyment of worldly goods—these arouse resentment and lead to punishment by the chief. He does not use violence to enforce the golden mean of mediocrity, but resorts to a sorcerer (paying the latter out of his private purse) for spells and charms which will bring the culprit low. Sorcery thus forms a support of vested interests; it is always a conservative force.[127] The people of Dobu feel great resentment toward any conspicuously successful person. They use the black art against a man whose garden yields too abundantly, because he is believed to have stolen other people's yams from their gardens by magic; against rivals who interfere with one's own success in trading ventures overseas; even against the owner of too many pigs. In short, the Dobuans rely on sorcery to "cast down the mighty from their seat."[128]

In the Mentawei Islands it is usually a person of superior ability and abundant means who is "poisoned" by sorcery. "If a man is more successful in the hunt or in fishing than his neighbors, if he is more diligent and acquires more possessions . . . . he bears the onus of the group suspicion and envy. It is not by natural means, argue the natives, that So-and-So is long-lived or is rich in possessions. If he were not possessed of magical powers, if he were not in league with the evil ghosts, he could not have been so successful." Thus the superior type of individual is eliminated by sorcery and the Mentawei ideal of communism and equality is preserved.[129]

Among the South African tribes, generally, "many people purposely refrain from undue cultivation of their land, lest others should accuse them of using magical practices to increase the fertility of the soil. . . . . There is little hope for the elevation of these tribes until the fear of the accusation of witchcraft is removed."[130] Among the Pondo in former times any persons who excited the jealousy of their neighbors or of the chief by becoming well-to-do were in danger of death. Today those who use improved methods of agriculture are often accused of harming their neighbors' crops, because fertilizer is a medicine causing neighboring fields to rot.[131] Of the Bavenda of the Transvaal it is said that any person may be suspected of sorcery, "especially if someone of high rank has a spite against him, or if he is a wealthy man."[132] Among the Lovedu successful people—those who reap better crops than others, bring home more game from the hunt, or enjoy the special favor of European masters—are most likely to be bewitched by envious neighbors. On the other hand, their success is also likely to be attributed to the exercise of witchcraft.[133] If a Basuto does anything a little better than another or a little different than another, he "may expect trouble," that is, a charge of witchcraft. "To build a large house, to have unusually fertile fields, to have a fine herd of cattle are most certain ways of attracting the jealousy of others."[134] The victims of witchcraft among the Bechuana "were usually old women, men of property, persons of eccentric habits, or individuals obnoxious to the chief. Any person in advance of his fellows was specially liable to suspicion, so that progress of any kind towards what we should term higher civilization was made exceedingly difficult by this belief."[135] Among the Ba-ila "a person who should labor hard to increase his crops above those of his fellows, or who should be sparing and not waste his grain, would expose himself to a charge of witchcraft. . . . . So a man dare not be too prosperous, and the ambition, if he feels it, to rise above his fellows is very rudely checked."[136]

The Angoni, who live north of the Zambesi River, are fervent believers in witchcraft. "It is a slavery from which there has been found no release. It pervades and influences every human relationship, and acts as a complete barrier to all advancement wherever it is found to operate. . . . . The reason for his [a native's] apparent laziness is the fear that, if he became possessed of goods, his circumstances will excite jealousy and bring on him accusations of witchcraft and death as a result. It is productive of unrest, cruel treatment, and great loss of property and life."[137] The Wakonde take it as good evidence that a man is a witch if his livestock increase rapidly or if in other ways his affairs are exceptionally prosperous.[138] Among the Hehe of Tanganyika a man must not seek to gain wealth or social superiority by methods which involve too great a departure from the traditional tribal life; if he does so, a witch will kill him. The belief in witchcraft thus represses the desire for individual advancement and accentuates the natural conservatism of Hehe society.[139] While the Azande do not associate unusual intelligence or skill in technological pursuits with the possession of witchcraft, they suspect it if a person claims the power to do extraordinary things. Thus, for example, people believe that witch doctors can perform the "miracles" attributed to them only if at the same time they are witches.[140]

With reference to the Bangala (Boloki) of the Upper Congo, we learn from an experienced missionary that the native "has a wonderful power of imitation, but he lacks invention and initiative; but this lack is undoubtedly due to suppression of the inventive faculty. For generations it has been the custom to charge with witchcraft anyone who has commenced a new industry or discovered a new article of barter. The making of anything out of the ordinary has brought on the maker a charge of witchcraft that again and again has resulted in death by the ordeal. To know more than others, to be more skillful than others, more energetic, more acute in business, more smart in dress, has often caused a charge of witchcraft and death. Therefore the native, to save his life and live in peace, has smothered his inventive faculty, and all spirit of enterprise has been driven out of him."[141] The same stultifying effects of the witchcraft belief are found among the widespread tribes of the Lower Congo. Their witch doctors are "largely responsible for crushing any inventive genius the people have shown by putting public calamities, such as an epidemic of sickness, to the account of any inventor who might be known at the time, and they have hindered all progress by charging with witchcraft anyone who was more skillful in work, or more energetic and shrewd in trading, than his neighbors. The fear of being charged with witchcraft has been so great and continuous that it has hampered and destroyed every attempt at advancement."[142]

The Tarahumara Indians of Mexico feel strongly an obligation to share their goods with relatives and neighbors. If they fail to do so they are fearful of being bewitched and probably killed. Yet, human nature being what it is, many people try to evade the obligation by becoming as secretive as possible about their possessions. A man has his hidden storehouses, very difficult to find; he does not boast about the size of his harvest; he goes and returns to market in the dead of night; often, when not precisely poor, he will wear old and tattered clothes, live in a tumble-down house, and in other ways conceal his affluence. Under these circumstances fear and mistrust is generated against persons who may have been affronted by a refusal to share goods and from whom, in consequence, sorcery is expected by the *beati possidentes*. Sorcery, with the Tarahumara, does not result in overt physical strife, but it produces the feeling that one's relatives and neighbors are likely to be evildoers and enemies.[143]

It is commonly believed by the Navaho that poor people, without many sheep or much jewelry, are seldom victims of witchcraft. They do not arouse the envious feelings of their neighbors.[144]

Among the Pueblo Indians the most abusive and serious charge which can be brought against anyone is that of being a witch. Grounds for this suspicion are many, one of them being reckless speech directed toward others—"not caring what you say." Another ground is dishonesty in regard to property or, still more, the possession of wealth from sources unknown. Thus a certain member of the council at Taos was reputed to be a witch because, though not a worker, he wore good clothes.[145] With particular reference to the Hopi we are told that they tend to distrust anyone who shows unusual capacity or whose behavior singles him out among the multitude. A village chief may be accused of being "two-hearted" by reason of his unconventional ways. One chief was denounced as a witch because he had begun to earn a livelihood by the manufacture and sale of *katcina* dolls, instead of farming in company with his neighbors. Since the chief no longer had any personal need of rain, the people argued that he had been using his evil power to drive off the clouds. This all-pervading fear of witchcraft has had a marked effect on the character of the Hopi. "They quickly learn to avoid all appearance of having exceptional ability and to emphasize moderation in all things."[146]

The belief in sorcery, however repressive its effect on industry, economy, and inventiveness, does operate to a certain extent as an agency of social control. In rude communities without a police force, a prison system, or a powerful leadership to maintain order, it provides a means of legal redress for wrongs otherwise unpunishable, secures obedience to the established moral rules, and preserves family and social relationships in accordance with traditional usage. And, as we have already learned, the headman or chief is himself often a sorcerer; when this is not the case he often has a sorcerer at his right hand to enforce obedience to his will.

In the Dieri tribe of South Australia "as no person is supposed, from whatever cause, to die a natural death, but is conjectured to have been killed, either by one of a neighboring tribe or by one of his own, men, women, and children are in constant terror of having offended someone who may therefore bear them enmity." The natives, therefore, avoid exciting the ill-will of their fellows.[147] Of the Narrinyeri, another South Australian tribe, it is said that the belief in sorcery makes them less bloodthirsty than they would otherwise be. Instead of exacting sanguinary vengeance for any injury, they are generally content to use black magic against an offender.[148]

In the Murray Islands of Torres Straits the belief in sorcery acted as a deterrent against adultery. An adulterer was always fearful of being killed by the secret black magic known as *maid*, which the wronged husband or the latter's friends could employ against him. *Maid*, when used to punish an adulterer, was recognized as justifiable.[149]

Among most Papuan tribes sorcery can be practiced by one member of the local group against another. Consequently dread of a retaliation in kind by a neighbor or by the latter's relatives tends to keep a man from acting wrongly toward him.[150] In the Trobriands a professional sorcerer, though ready to obey the orders of chiefs and people of rank and wealth, would not lend himself to unjust or fantastic requests by lesser men. "When a real injustice or a thoroughly unlawful act is to be punished, on the other hand, the sorcerer feels the weight of public opinion with him, and he is ready to champion a good cause and to receive his full fee." In such cases the culprit, having learned that a sorcerer is at work against him, is likely to make amends or come to an equitable arrangement with the person whom he has wronged.[151] Sorcery in Wogeo, one of the Schouten Islands, is used in innumerable ways: to produce disease, make taro shrivel up and die, cause garden fences to rot quickly so that wild pigs can break through and eat the crop, send village pigs running into the hills, drive away fish from a canoe, and so forth. In short, every real or fancied grievance, whether it is that of a lover who has stolen a man's wife or of debtor who has failed to meet his obligations, will be thus requited. Knowledge that sorcery can be thus employed certainly acts in some measure to prevent interference with a person's property or rights.[152]

In Mala or Malaita (Solomon Islands) black magic acts as a safety valve for anger which is considered justifiable. In practically all minor offenses, such as failure to pay debts or to furnish assistance in gardening or other work, theft of produce, lying, and slander, the injured party makes no further move than to practice sorcery against the offender. This mode of retaliation is secret, and the victim does not learn about it. Thus a man can relieve his feelings without causing the slightest inconvenience to anyone.[153]

Sorcery in the island of Ontong Java was often the means by which vengeance was wreaked, for instance, against a thief or a man who seduced another man's wife. Like the "unwritten law" of justifiable homicide, it had the passive approval of society. On the other hand, a sorcerer who used his powers out of pure malice and for antisocial ends, was avoided by everybody and was sometimes killed by the victim's relatives.[154] In Hawaii sorcery exerted a very powerful influence in shaping the lives and character of the people. This fact was recognized by Kamehameha I, who united the Hawaiian group under his sway. He took especial pains, therefore, to secure for himself all the strong sorcery gods worshiped by the ruling chiefs in the various islands and to set up "god houses" for their tendance.[155] Among the Maori the belief in *makutu*, or sorcery, fostered hospitality and politeness and tended to repress evildoers. "Men knew that if they sought to injure a fellow tribesman in any way, the shafts of magic might be leveled against them."[156] In particular, sorcery often provided a weapon for slaves and commoners who had no other means of obtaining redress against the high and mighty. There is no doubt, we are told, that fear of its use acted as a restraining influence in a society where no law but that of force generally prevailed.[157]

The Pondo of South Africa recognize various cases where black magic directed against a fellow tribesman is considered legitimate. As with other African peoples, it may be resorted to as a means of punishing thieves. The thief who loses his teeth through eating stolen mealies treated with medicine has only himself to blame. An erring wife may be treated so that a lover who comes to her will get a disease. Magic to influence the judgment in a case or to "tie up the tongue" of a witness does not arouse disapprobation. Its employment to secure payment of bills seems also to be regarded as a proper procedure. On the other hand, it is never legal to use black magic destructively except to defend one's property against intrusion. Even to use it against reputed witches is illegal, though protective measures which may harm them are allowable. A chief has no right to work magic against his subjects.[158] The implicit belief of the Bavenda of the Transvaal in the power of their magicians to detect and punish evildoers keeps the people fairly law-abiding. Especially does their fear of being pointed out by him as witches serve as a check on the criminally intentioned. This fear is also a powerful influence in fostering the courtesy and spirit of fair dealing so noticeable among the Bavenda.[159] Among the Tumbuka-Kamanga of Nyasaland a man with a grievance against a neighbor proceeds to pluck a number of twigs and place them around the latter's grain crop in the field or, if the crop has been reaped, then in his barn. No one now will enter the field or take grain from the barn until a public inquiry has revealed the person who imposed the embargo. He himself comes before the council of elders, tells what he has done, and states his grievance. The council, if satisfied that he has been wronged, orders the defendant to pay damages and the plaintiff to remove the twigs so that the people can use the grain.[160] A witch doctor of the Anyanja generally levels an accusation of witchcraft against a man who has quarreled with the chief and adduces his grievance as the reason why he avenged himself by stopping the rain.[161] Of the Hehe of Tanganyika it is said that the fear of sorcery tends to reinforce obedience to the tribal authorities. Many headmen and chiefs accumulate medicines for the express purpose of causing loss or death to rebellious subjects. On the other hand, a powerful and wealthy commoner may sometimes buy the services or the medicines of sorcerers and use these to overthrow a chief and usurp his place.[162]

By the Baganda it is taken as a matter of course that a person with a legitimate grievance for which he can get no other redress will resort to black magic. He procures it openly from a reputable magician and with the tacit approval of his neighbors. Sorcery of this sort is employed, for instance, against a suspected thief who cannot be induced to confess. It has even acquired a special value as a recourse against what the people regard as injustices brought about by the white man's innovations. Thus a native who loses a case in the High Court will sometimes fall back on sorcery to relieve his injured feelings.[163] Similarly the Azande make a clear distinction between the use of black magic as a defensive weapon and its use for aggression. The former practice does not excite public reprobation.[164] Since the Azande do not know who are and who are not witches they are careful to avoid offending anybody without good cause. Any show of spleen or meanness or unjustified hostility may bring serious consequences if the offended person should turn out to be a witch. This notion works in two ways. A jealous man is likely to be suspected of witch-craft by those of whom he is jealous; hence he will seek to avoid suspicion by curbing or concealing his real sentiments. On the other hand, people of whom he is jealous may be witches and may try to injure him in return for his enmity, and so again he has a powerful motive for not giving himself away.[165] Among the Kwotto, a Nigerian tribe, a man will secretly patronize a sorcerer, in order to be revenged on some person who has injured him. But he would not set black magic in operation against innocent people.[166]

A professional sorcerer among the Barama River Caribs of Guiana may be enlisted to obtain satisfaction for a person who feels himself to have been unjustly treated.[167] In the West Indies a Negro robbed of some domestic animal applies at once to a magician (obeah man or woman) to set obi on the culprit, and the fact that this has been done is then made known to everybody. The thief may perhaps resort to some more eminent practitioner of magic to counteract the operations of the other, but if such an ally cannot be found, he is certain to anticipate all sorts of impending calamities. Under their pressure he enters on a slow decline of all his faculties and sinks gradually into the grave.[168]

Among the Navaho the intense belief in witchcraft accounts for their practice of always giving hospitality to an aged person, no matter how unpleasant he may be. Fear of refusing a request four times repeated seems to have the same explanation. Willing-ness to aid a sick kinsman is strengthened by the realization that his death without such care might result in a charge of witchcraft against the survivor. In general, anyone who "acts mean" in a Navaho community is likely to be considered a witch.[169] The Pueblo Indians consider that bewitching is very often the result of a grievance, since a witch who feels injured will retaliate. "As you never know who is a witch, you are always careful not to give offense—unless you are yourself a witch." Thus the pronounced social timidities of these Indians are closely connected with their belief in black magic.[170] By what means, it is asked, did the Yokuts-Mono of California maintain public order? Largely by the fear of sorcery. "A man dared not cheat another at gambling or trading, commit adultery, or neglect any civil or ceremonial duty toward his neighbor, lest the offended person visit sickness or death upon him or some member of his family, either by his own power or that of a shaman hired for the purpose. On the other hand, a man could not take offense for no reason and retaliate by this means unless completely justified, for the matter would eventually be aired before the chief."[171]

The belief in the activity of sorcerers or witches, both real and imaginary, provides for primitive thought a general explanation of all human ills, even that greatest of ills, death itself. If animistic conceptions are strongly held, a belief in the agency of evil spirits may assume equal or greater prominence, but from the nature of the case spiritual beings cannot be dealt with so successfully as the professors of the black art. Sickness, accidents, and death produce for the individual concerned and for the group to which he belongs a profound disturbance of equilibrium, and this can only be restored when the sorcerer has been uncovered, held responsible, and, as in most cases, put out of the way by exile or execution. Such measures are more than punishments, more than reprisals, for all the wickedness that has been unearthed; they are also intended to clear the air of noxious influences and ensure that life henceforth shall be untroubled. The community can now go forward, with renewed strength and confidence, to the tasks which lie before it.

Some primitive peoples and other peoples not so primitive are described as having very little to do with sorcery. The northern clans of the Murngin believe in the existence of black magic but have no practitioners of that art, though these flourish in the southern part of the tribal area.[172] By various Papuan tribes sorcery is supposed to occur "many times more often" than it is ever really practiced.[173] The Manus of the Admiralty Islands, northeast of New Guinea, attribute the ills of unweaned infants and generally those of women in connection with childbearing to black magic. But all other ills which afflict them are attributed to offended ghosts. Propitiation of spiritual beings, rather than rites of exorcism, is thus the normal procedure among the Manus.[174] In the island of Alor, one of the Lesser Sundas, black magic is regarded as only a minor cause of illness and death.[175] Among the Negritos of Malaya sorcery is little used, though it exists.[176] The Jur of the Anglo-Egyptian Sudan are said to have no faith in witchcraft.[177] The Bambute Pygmies seemingly make little use of sorcery. What knowledge they have of it comes to them chiefly from their Negro neighbors.[178] In Zuñi Pueblo the techniques of witchcraft are neither owned nor taught, though it is greatly feared.[179] Among the Omaha certain magical practices causing disease and death were almost wholly confined to members of the Shell and Pebble societies. In this tribe witchcraft had nothing like the importance which it assumed among other Plains Indians.[180] Black magic finds little use among the Netsilik Eskimo of Arctic America.[181] On the whole, it seems probable that the fear of sorcery is often out of all proportion to its actual practice; in other words that it is often an "anxiety neurosis" rather than a vital cult.

NOTES TO CHAPTER XV

[1] George Brown, *Melanesians and Polynesians* (London, 1910), p. 224.

[2] P. H. Buck, *Regional Diversity in the Elaboration of Sorcery in Polynesia* (New Haven, 1936), p. 13. *Yale University Publications in Anthropology*, No. 2. A rite of immunization, called *kopu ehu*, was also practiced in the Marquesas Islands (E. S. C. Handy, "The Native Culture in the Marquesas," *Bernice P. Bishop Museum Bulletin*, No. 9, p. 278).

[3] J. H. Weeks, "The Congo Medicine Man and His Black and White Magic," *Folk-Lore*, XXI (1910), 465.

[4] Paul Fejos, *Ethnography of the Yagua* (New York, 1943), p. 91. *Viking Fund Publications in Anthropology*, No. 1.

[5] James Teit, in *Memoirs of the American Museum of Natural History*, II, 360.

[6] James Teit, *ibid.*, IV, 613.

[7] James Dawson, *Australian Aborigines* (Melbourne, 1881), p. 12.

[8] George Taplin, in J. D. Woods (editor), *The Native Tribes of South Australia* (Adelaide, 1879), pp. 24 ff. Often a native who has obtained a bone from some animal eaten by another man goes to him and says, "I have your *ngadhungi;* what will you give me for it?" Perhaps the man answers that he has the *ngadhungi* of the questioner. In that case they make an exchange and each destroys the dangerous object. Otherwise the man tries to secure the *ngadhungi* by offering nets, spears, or other objects to his potential enemy (*loc. cit.*).

[9] Sir Baldwin Spencer, *Native Tribes of the Northern Territory of Australia* (London, 1914), pp. 257 ff.

[10] R. W. Williamson, *The Mafulu Mountain People of British New Guinea* (London, 1912), pp. 280 f.

[11] Margaret Mead, *Sex and Temperament in Three Primitive Societies* (New York, 1935), p. 12, note 1.

[12] *Idem*, in *Anthropological Papers of the American Museum of Natural History*, XXXVII, 445.

[13] J. W. M. Whiting, *Becoming a Kwoma* (New Haven, 1941), p. 205. Among the Banyankole of Uganda, if you wished to injure a man one way of doing so was to get your sister to make love to him and lure him to her couch. She would thus obtain some of his semen which, in your possession, could be used in a magical rite to make him impotent (John Roscoe, *The Northern Bantu* [Cambridge, 1915], p. 135).

[14] R. H. Codrington, *The Melanesians* (Oxford, 1891), p. 203, note 1. In Tanna, one of the New Hebrides, everybody carries a small basket into which is put banana skins, coconut husks, and bits of uneaten food. Then the basket is taken across a stream, a procedure which prevents its contents being used magically against you. It is said that a man who has got hold of something of this sort belonging to an enemy will walk miles to avoid crossing flowing water, lest the occult power thus acquired be lost (B. T. Somerville, in *Journal of the Anthropological Institute*, XXIII [1894], 20).

[15] Sir B. H. Thomson, *The Fijians* (London, 1908), p. 166.

[16] Teuira Henry, "Ancient Tahiti," *Bernice P. Bishop Museum Bulletin*, No. 48, p. 204.

[17] P. H. Buck, *op. cit.*, pp. 16 f.

[18] *Idem*, p. 14. In New Zealand personal instruction as to the disposal of "bait" was given to children at an early age. Buck was taught by his Maori mother never to spit on the ground and never, in the presence of strangers, to walk about while eating. His mother, he adds, always concealed her hair combings, "perhaps more from habit than from any immediate danger." Members of his own tribe, when passing through a district notorious for its sorcerers, always timed their march along a beach route to coincide with the coming in of the tide. They walked in single file and close to the water, so that the rising tide would quickly obliterate their footprints (pp. 13 f.).

[19] In the Narrang-ga tribe of South Australia a medicine man could not remove the evil which he had inflicted. It could be successfully treated only by another practitioner (A. W. Howitt, *The Native Tribes of South-East Australia* [London, 1904], p. 405). Similarly the Anula, a tribe on the Gulf of Carpentaria, do not endow a medicine man with curative powers. He can impart but cannot withdraw "evil magic" (Sir Baldwin Spencer and F. J. Gillen, *The Northern Tribes of Central Australia* [London, 1904], p. 502 and note 1). It is probably significant that the Anula furnish the only known instance among these tribes of an appeal addressed to a spiritual being to help a sick person. In a case of illness the medicine man, will "sing" to a certain friendly spirit to come and make the patient well (*loc. cit.*). The Jivaro Indians think that a magician who has sent a disease spirit into a man lacks the power to cure him. The spirit in question would be annoyed and refuse to act were it called upon to undo something that it had been previously directed to do (M. W. Sterling, "Jivaro Shamanism," *Proceedings of the American Philosophical Society*, LXXII [1933], 143; *idem*, "Historical and Ethnographical Material on the Jivaro Indians," *Bulletin of the Bureau of American Ethnology*, No. 117, p. 120). Among the Chemehuevi of southern California, while most sorcerers were sometimes able to cure, this was not true of a "follow-doctor," who had the power of following a person in his travels and of bewitching him from afar. The intended victim could never escape, for the doctor was able to follow him "mentally" and kill him (Isabel T. Kelly, "Chemehuevi Shamanism," in *Essays in Anthropology Presented to A. L. Kroeber* [Berkeley, 1936], pp. 133 f.).

[20] A. W. Howitt, *op. cit.*, p. 361. Among the Dieri steeping a bone in water was the approved method of depriving it of occult power (Samuel Gason, in J. D. Woods [editor], *The Native Tribes of South Australia*, p. 275).

[21] W. L. Warner, *A Black Civilization* (New York, 1937), pp. 207 f.

[22] Stefan Lehner, in R. Neuhauss, *Deutsch Neu-Guinea* (Berlin, 1911), III, 464.

[23] W. E. Armstrong, *Rossel Island* (Cambridge, 1928), p. 172.

[24] M. Rascher, in *Archiv für Anthropologie*, XXIX (1904), 220.

[25] E. W. Gifford, "Tongan Society," *Bernice P. Bishop Museum Bulletin*, No. 61, p. 340.

[26] E. S. C. Handy, "The Native Culture in the Marquesas," *ibid.*, No. 9, p. 277.

[27] C. S. Hurgronje, *The Achehnese* (Leiden, 1906), I, 414 f.

[28] Bronislaw Malinowski, in R. F. Fortune, *Sorcerers of Dobu* (London, 1932), pp. xviii f.

[29] A. M. Hocart, "Medicine and Witchcraft in Eddystone of the Solomons," *Journal of the Royal Anthropological Institute*, LV (1925), 229.

[30] H. I. Hogbin, *Law and Order in Polynesia* (London, 1934), pp. 219 f.

[31] Teuira Henry, "Ancient Tahiti," *Bernice P. Bishop Museum Bulletin*, No. 48, pp. 209 ff.

[32] A. Hetherwick, "Nyanjas," Hastings' *Encyclopaedia of Religion and Ethics*, IX, 421.

[33] D. S. Oyler, "The Shilluk's Belief in the Evil Eye. The Evil Medicine Men," *Sudan Notes and Records*, II (1919), 133.

[34] John Gillin, *The Barama River Caribs of British Guiana* (Cambridge, Mass., 1936), pp. 147 f. *Papers of the Peabody Museum of American Archaeology and Ethnology*, Vol. XIV, No. 2.

[35] Edward Sapir, "The Religious Ideas of the Takelma Indians of Southwestern Oregon," *Journal of American Folk-Lore*, XX (1907), 44 f.

[36] *Idem, Takelma Texts* (Philadelphia, 1909), pp. 183 f. *University of Pennsylvania, Anthropological Publications of the University Museum*, Vol. II, No. 1.

[37] A. B. Deacon, *Malekula, a Vanishing People in the New Hebrides* (London, 1934), pp. 666 f.

[38] Elsdon Best, "Maori Magic," *Transactions and Proceedings of the New Zealand Institute*, XXXIV (1901), 69, 75. This counter magic was known as *whakahokitu* (Edward Shortland, *Maori Religion and Mythology* [London, 1882], p. 35). In the Chatham Islands (Moriori) the ghost of a person killed by sorcery returned from the shades and in its turn killed the sorcerer—a circumstance which, nevertheless, did not appear to deter the natives from the practice of the black art (Alexander Shand, in *Memoirs of the Polynesian Society*, II [1911], 15).

[39] H. A. Stayt, *The Bavenda* (London, 1931), p. 277.

[40] E. E. Evans-Pritchard, *Witchcraft, Oracles, and Magic among the Azande* (Oxford, 1937), pp. 388 f.

[41] Margaret J. Field, *Religion and Medicine of the Ga People* (Oxford, 1937), p. 164.

[42] James Mooney, "Sacred Formulas of the Cherokees," *Seventh Annual Report of the Bureau of Ethnology*, pp. 384 f.

[43] Knud Rasmussen, *The Netsilik Eskimos* (Copenhagen, 1931), p. 201. *Report of the Fifth Thule Expedition*, Vol. VIII, Nos. 1–2.

[44] Augustus Oldfield, in *Transactions of the Ethnological Society of London* (n.s., 1865), III, 246.

[45] R. B. Smyth, *The Aborigines of Victoria* (Melbourne, 1878), I, 110.

[46] F. E. Williams, *Orokaiva Magic* (London, 1928), pp. 219 f.

[47] Benjamin Danks, "Burial Customs of New Britain," *Journal of the Anthropological Institute*, XXI (1892), 350.

[48] F. L. S. Bell, "The Divination of Sorcery in Melanesia," *Man*, XXXV (1935), 84 ff.

[49] Verrier Elwin, *The Baiga* (London, 1939), p. 291.

[50] James Sibree, *The Great African Island* (London, 1880), pp. 291 f.

[51] I. Schapera, *A Handbook of Tswana Law and Custom* (London, 1938), p. 276.

[52] J. C. C. Coxhead (editor), *The Native Tribes of North-Eastern Rhodesia: Their Laws and Customs* (London, 1914), pp. 17 f. *Occasional Papers of the Royal Anthropological Institute*, No. 5.

[53] Mary H. Kingsley, *Travels in West Africa* (London, 1897), p. 464.

[54] A. P. Niblack, in *Report of the U.S. National Museum for 1888*, p. 348, quoting J. G. Swan.

[55] R. H. Mathews, *Ethnological Notes on the Aboriginal Tribes of New South Wales and Victoria* (Sydney, 1905), pp. 72 ff.

[56] E. J. Eyre, *Journals of Expeditions of Discovery into Central Australia* (London, 1845), II, 344.

[57] Spencer and Gillen, *The Northern Tribes of Central Australia*, pp. 538 f.

[58] R. E. Guise, in *Journal of the Anthropological Institute*, XXVIII (1899), 211.

[59] George Brown, *op. cit.*, pp. 385 f.

[60] John Matthews, *A Voyage to the River Sierra-Leone* (London, 1791), pp. 121 ff.

[61] Sir Richard Schomburgk, *Reisen in Britisch-Guiana* (Leipzig, 1847–48), I, 325.

[62] M. C. Kahn, *Djuka* (New York, 1931), pp. 133 f.

[63] Jules Canivey, "Notice sur les mœurs et coutumes des Moi de la region de Dalat," *Revue d'ethnographie et de sociologie*, IV (1913), 22.

[64] Monica Hunter, *Reaction to Conquest* (London, 1936), p. 309.

[65] Charles Bullock, *The Mashona* (Capetown and Johannesburg, 1928), p. 160. Among the Balamba, however, it is said that a confession will be often made because the accused realizes that all protestations of innocence are useless. By confessing it is always possible to implicate someone else against whom the accused bears a grudge (C. M. Doke, *The Lambas of Northern Rhodesia* [London, 1931], p. 313).

[66] F. H. Melland, *In Witchbound Africa* (London, 1923), p. 194.

[67] Sir R. F. Burton, *The Lake Regions of Central Africa* (London, 1860), II, 347.

[68] Sir A. B. Ellis, *The Yoruba-speaking Peoples of the Slave Coast of West Africa* (London, 1894), p. 117.

[69] N. W. Thomas, *Anthropological Report on Sierra Leone*, Part I (London, 1916), p. 47. Cf. Thomas Winterbottom, *An Account of the Native Africans in the Neighbourhood of Sierra-Leone* (London, 1803), I, 238 note.

[70] A. P. Niblack, in *Report of the U.S. National Museum for 1888*, p. 348.

[71] On the poison ordeal in Africa and Madagascar see Sir J. G. Frazer, *Folk-Lore in the Old Testament* (London, 1919), III, 307–405. See also A. H. Post, *Afrikanische Jurisprudenz* (Oldenburg, 1887), II, 110–20.

The African explorer, Paul B. Du Chaillu, describes realistically a poison ordeal witnessed by him in 1858 among the Camma or Commi of Gabun. Three suspects swallowed the drink. They were women. One of them had asked for some salt from a relative, Mpono, but upon being refused, for salt was scarce, had spoken unpleasant words to him. Another, a niece of the "king," was barren, and she envied Mpono, who had a child. The third, a slave woman with six children, had asked Mpono for a looking glass, and he had refused her. They all failed to overcome the effects of the poison and were quickly dispatched (*Explorations and Adventures in Equatorial Africa* [New York, 1861], pp. 441–47). In 1865 Du Chaillu was present at a witchcraft trial among the Otando. On this occasion three nephews of the "king," being suspected of bewitching him and his family, drank the poison, but recovered from its effects and were acquitted. To close the proceedings the witch doctor himself took an enormous draught of the poisoned liquor. Under its influence he announced, to everybody's joy, that the sorcerers responsible were not the king's own subjects. Du Chaillu considered that the witch doctor's immunity to the poison, fatal to so many, largely explains his power and influence over the people (*A Journey to Ashango-Land* [New York, 1871], pp. 172–77).

⁷² Cullen Gouldsbury and Hubert Sheane, *The Great Plateau of Northern Rhodesia* (London, 1911), p. 62.

⁷³ W. H. Bentley, *Pioneering on the Congo* (London, 1900), p. 277; cf. idem, *Life on the Congo* (London, 1887), p. 68.

⁷⁴ Mrs. L. S. Tucker, "The Divining Basket of the Ovimbundu," *Journal of the Royal Anthropological Institute,* LXX (1940), 198 f.

⁷⁵ Albert Schweitzer, *African Notebook* (New York, 1939), pp. 79 f.

⁷⁶ P. A. Talbot, *In the Shadow of the Bush* (London, 1912), p. 165.

⁷⁷ L. J. B. Bérenger-Féraud, *Les peuplades de la Sénégambie* (Paris, 1879), pp. 305 f.

⁷⁸ In the Lower Congo area passing the ordeal for witchcraft is one way of setting up as a witch doctor. A missionary met a man who had been accused four times of being a witch but each time had vomited after the poison drink and so had proved his innocence. After the fourth ordeal he informed his friends that he would henceforth practice as a witch doctor. His services were in much request, and he never again had to face an accusation of witchcraft (J. H. Weeks, "The Congo Medicine Man and His Black and White Magic," *Folk-Lore,* XXI [1910], 448 and note 1).

⁷⁹ Dudley Kidd, *The Essential Kafir* (2d ed., London, 1925), p. 176.

⁸⁰ S. S. Dornan, *Pygmies and Bushmen of the Kalahari* (London, 1925), pp. 295 f. Our authority thinks this estimate "far too high."

⁸¹ A. Hetherwick, "Nyanjas," Hastings' *Encyclopaedia of Religion and Ethics,* IX, 421.

⁸² R. H. Nassau, *Fetichism in West Africa* (New York, 1904), pp. 241 ff.

⁸³ Mary H. Kingsley, *op. cit.,* pp. 462 f. In the Calabar district there is a sanctuary where people accused of witchcraft and other crimes are safe if they reach it. "But an attempt at flight is a confession of guilt; no one is quite certain but the accusation will fall on him, or her, and hopes for the best until it is generally too late. Moreover, fleeing anywhere beyond a day's march, is difficult work in West Africa" (p. 466).

⁸⁴ Sir H. H. Johnston, *George Grenfell and the Congo* (London, 1908), II, 663, note 1.

⁸⁵ Hugh Goldie, *Calabar and Its Mission* (new ed., London, 1901), pp. 37 f.

⁸⁶ P. A. Talbot, *The Peoples of Southern Nigeria* (London, 1926), II, 215, 219. See also A. G. Leonard, *The Lower Niger and Its Tribes* (London, 1906), p. 480.

[87] J. H. Soga, *The Ama-Xosa: Life and Customs* (Lovedale, South Africa, 1931), p. 171.

[88] James Macdonald, "East Central African Customs," *Journal of the Anthropological Institute,* XXII (1893), 106 f. The performance of a female witch doctor among the Bakongo of northern Angola is vividly described by an eyewitness, G. C. Claridge (*Wild Bush Tribes of Tropical Africa* [London, 1932], pp. 135 ff.).

[89] Mary H. Kingsley, *West African Studies* (1st ed., London, 1899), pp. 218 f. W. H. Bentley, a missionary, describes the witch doctor as "a cunning rogue." He employs agents to discover whether anyone is in special disfavor with his fellows or whom it will be safe to accuse as a sorcerer (*Dictionary and Grammar of the Kongo Language* [London, 1887–95], I, 504), with special reference to Loango.

[90] The inquisition and execution of suspected sorcerers is sometimes a function of secret societies. The members of these organizations act in the role of "vigilantes" for the prompt and swift disposal of people considered inimical to the community. See W. H. Bentley, *Pioneering on the Congo,* I, 283 (Nkimba among the Bakongo) ; W. R. Bascom, "The Sociological Role of the Yoruba Cult Group," *Memoirs of the American Anthropological Association,* No. 63, pp. 66 f. (Egungun and Oro) ; Mrs. M. C. Stevenson, in C. S. Wake (editor), *Memoirs of the International Congress of Anthropology* (Chicago, 1894), p. 314 (Zuñi Priesthood of the Bow) ; B. J. Stern, *The Lummi Indians of Northwest Washington* (New York, 1934), p. 86 (the Xunxanital fraternity). It is said of Egungun and Oro among the Yoruba that they were chosen as executioners because their "supernatural powers" were so great that even sorcerers were afraid of them (Bascom, *loc. cit.*).

[91] Charles Bullock, *op. cit.,* p. 302.

[92] H. A. Junod, *The Life of a South African Tribe* (2d ed., London, 1927), II, 534.

[93] G. St. J. Orde Browne, *The Vanishing Tribes of Kenya* (London, 1925). p. 184.

[94] John Roscoe. *The Northern Bantu* (Cambridge, 1915), p. 135.

[95] Paul Schebesta, *My Pygmy and Negro Hosts* (London, 1936), pp. 112 f. Among the Kaska, a seminomadic group of tribes in British Columbia, it has been quite common to account for a serious illness as the result of bewitchment. and to fix upon some child of either sex as the guilty party. Sometimes the suspect, not understanding the accusation, would acknowledge its truth; if he refused to admit his guilt, he was tortured to obtain a confession. Then he might be killed or starved to death. A mature person often sought to escape a charge of witchcraft by leveling suspicion on a child. See J. J. Honigmann, "Witch-Fear in Post-Contact Kaska Society," *American Anthropologist* (n.s., 1947). XLIX, 225 ff.

[96] J. H. Weeks, *Among Congo Cannibals* (London, 1913), p. 189 and note 1.

[97] Clyde Kluckhohn, *Navaho Witchcraft* (Cambridge, Mass., 1944), p. 28. *Papers of the Peabody Museum of American Archaeology and Ethnology,* Vol. XXII, No. 2.

[98] J. R. Swanton, "Social Condition, Beliefs, and Linguistic Relationship of the Tlingit Indians," *Twenty-sixth Annual Report of the Bureau of American Ethnology,* pp. 469 f. The Tsimshian of British Columbia also tied up a supposed sorcerer and starved him until he confessed his crime. But if he proved obdurate, he was either left to die of starvation or was placed on the beach at low tide until the rising water drowned him (Franz Boas, in *Report of the Fifty-ninth Meeting of the British Association for the Advancement of Science* [1889], p. 855).

⁹⁹ A. C. Haddon and C. G. Seligman, in *Reports of the Cambridge Anthropological Expedition to Torres Straits*, V, 323 (western islands).

¹⁰⁰ F. E. Williams, *Orokaiva Magic*, pp. 209 f., 223.

¹⁰¹ Lambert, *Mœurs et superstitions des Néo-Calédoniens* (Nouméa, 1900), pp. 292 f.

¹⁰² Charles Hose and William McDougall, *The Pagan Tribes of Borneo* (London, 1912), II, 116 f.

¹⁰³ E. H. Man, *On the Aboriginal Inhabitants of the Andaman Islands* (London, 1932), p. 29; *idem*, in *Journal of the Anthropological Institute*, XII (1883), 97. According to A. R. Radcliffe-Brown a man practicing evil magic might be liable to the vengeance of those who thought themselves injured by him, "but it does not seem that the society ever acted as a whole to punish a man suspected of it" (*The Andaman Islanders* [Cambridge, 1933], p. 51).

¹⁰⁴ W. H. R. Rivers, *The Todas* (London, 1906), p. 252.

¹⁰⁵ E. E. Evans-Pritchard, *op. cit.*, pp. 86 f., 114 ff. Rich and powerful persons are immune, as a rule, from accusations of sorcery. All children are likewise free from suspicion of practicing it (p. 33).

¹⁰⁶ C. Estermann, "Coutumes des Mbali du Sud d'Angola," *Africa*, XII (1939), 81.

¹⁰⁷ J. I. Molina, *The Geographical, Natural, and Civil History of Chili* (Middleton, Conn., 1808), II, 93.

¹⁰⁸ Mrs. M. C. Stevenson, in *Twenty-third Annual Report of the Bureau of American Ethnology*, p. 393.

¹⁰⁹ F. G. Speck, "Penobscot Shamanism," *Memoirs of the American Anthropological Association*, No. 28 (Vol. VI, Pt. 4), p. 244.

¹¹⁰ Alice C. Fletcher and Francis La Flesche, in *Twenty-seventh Annual Report of the Bureau of American Ethnology*, p. 602.

¹¹¹ E. M. Curr, *The Australian Race* (Melbourne, 1886), I, 50.

¹¹² Sir Baldwin Spencer and F. J. Gillen, *The Native Tribes of Central Australia* (London, 1899), pp. 53 f. Cf. Sir Baldwin Spencer, *Native Tribes of the Northern Territory of Australia* (London, 1914), p. 38.

¹¹³ J. H. Holmes, *In Primitive New Guinea* (London, 1924), p. 199.

¹¹⁴ W. N. Beaver, *Unknown New Guinea* (London, 1920), p. 133.

¹¹⁵ F. E. Williams, *op. cit.*, p. 215.

¹¹⁶ Franz Vormann, "Zur Psychologie, Religion, Soziologie, und Geschichte der Monumbo-Papua, Deutsch Neu-Guinea," *Anthropos*, V (1910), 410. Women and children, even in broad daylight, almost never go alone for any considerable distance, and after dark men will not venture, unaccompanied, to proceed from one village to another (*loc. cit.*).

¹¹⁷ R. F. Fortune, *op. cit.*, p. 137. Cf. W. E. Bromilow, "Dobuan (Papua) Beliefs and Folk-Lore," *Report of the Thirteenth Meeting of the Australasian Association for the Advancement of Science* (1911), p. 417; *idem, Twenty Years among Primitive Papuans* (London, 1929), p. 90. Since sorcery is performed in secret, the best precaution against it is never to go out alone. There ought always to be an escort, if only a child, for a man as well as for a woman. Even at home it is rare for anyone to be alone (Fortune, *op. cit.*, pp. 77, 152 f.)

¹¹⁸ Beatrice Blackwood, *Both Sides of Buka Passage* (Oxford, 1935), p. 481 (Bougainville and Buka).

¹¹⁹ Thomas Williams, *Fiji and the Fijians* (3d ed., London, 1870), p. 209.

¹²⁰ Elsdon Best, "Maori Magic," *Transactions and Proceedings of the New Zealand Institute*, XXXIV (1901), 70.

121 H. A. Junod, *op. cit.* (2d ed.), II, 535. The Azande, who believe that a witch can injure the more severely the nearer he is to his victim, interpose a wide stretch of bush and cultivated land between the separate homesteads (E. E. Evans-Pritchard, *op. cit.*, p. 37). The feeling on the part of the Tarahumara (a Mexican tribe) that all one's neighbors are enemies and evildoers, likely to indulge in sorcery, prevents them from clustering in adjoining households and villages. A family lives as far apart from other families as possible and often moves its habitation (Herbert Passin, "Sorcery as a Phase of Tarahumara Economic Relations," *Man*, XLII [1942], 14).

122 G. A. S. Northcote, in *Journal of the Royal Anthropological Institute*, XXXVII (1907), 63.

123 G. C. Claridge, *op. cit.*, p. 173.

124 P. A. Talbot, *The Peoples of Southern Nigeria*, II, 200; *idem, Life in Southern Nigeria* (London, 1923), p. 57. With this condemnation of witchcraft by an Ibibio chief may be compared the statement of Two-Hearts, a Hopi chief, that witches "cause most of the trouble in the world" (L. W. Simmons [editor], *Sun Chief. The Autobiography of a Hopi Indian* [New Haven, 1942], p. 257). Two-Hearts loved his mother "more than anything else," but some of her dreams made him wonder whether she was not, perchance, a witch (pp. 325 ff.).

125 Rafael Karsten, "Blood Revenge, War, and Victory Feasts among the Jibaro Indians of Eastern Ecuador," *Bulletin of the Bureau of American Ethnology*, No. 79, pp. 8 ff.

126 W. Z. Park, *Shamanism in Western North America* (Evanston, 1938), p. 44. *Northwestern University Studies in the Social Sciences*, No. 2.

127 Bronislaw Malinowski, *Crime and Custom in Savage Society* (London, 1926), pp. 91 ff.

128 R. F. Fortune, *op. cit.*, p. 176.

129 E. M. Loeb, "Shaman and Seer,"*American Anthropologist* (n.s., 1929), XXXI, 83.

130 Dudley Kidd, *op. cit.*, p. 147.

131 Monica Hunter, *op. cit.*, p. 317.

132 E. Gottschling, in *Journal of the Anthropological Institute*, XXV (1905), 375.

133 Mrs. E. J. Krige and J. D. Krige, *The Realm of a Rain Queen* (London, 1943), p. 269.

134 E. A. T. Dutton, *The Basuto of Basutoland* (London, 1923), pp. 85 f.

135 G. McCall Theal, *Ethnography and Condition of South Africa before A. D. 1505* (London, 1919), p. 245. The Bechuana witch doctor, "is often bribed to smell out a certain individual, generally one with large herds or flocks, or against whom the chief has a grudge" (S. S. Dornan, *op. cit.*, p. 296).

136 E. W. Smith and A. M. Dale, *The Ila-speaking Peoples of Northern Rhodesia* (London, 1920), II, 97.

137 W. A. Elmslie, *Among the Wild Ngoni* (London, 1899), pp. 59 f.

138 D. R. MacKenzie, *The Spirit-ridden Konde* (London, 1925), p. 255.

139 G. G. Brown and A. McD. Bruce Hutt, *Anthropology in Action* (London, 1935), p. 182.

140 E. E. Evans-Pritchard, *op. cit.*, p. 51.

141 J. H. Weeks, *Among Congo Cannibals*, pp. 177 f. Cf. *idem*, "Stories and Other Notes from the Upper Congo," *Folk-Lore*, XII (1901), 186. "Some years ago," writes Weeks, "I knew a native medicine woman who was success-

ful in treating certain native diseases, and as she became wealthy, the natives accused her of giving the sickness by witchcraft, in order to cure it and be paid for it; for they said, 'How can she cure it so easily unless she first gave it to them?' She had to abandon her practice or she would have been killed as a witch. The introduction of a new article of trade has always brought on the introducer a charge of witchcraft; and there is a legend that the man who discovered the way to tap palm trees for palm wine was charged as a witch and paid the penalty with his life" (*Journal of the Royal Anthropological Institute*, XXXIX [1909], 108).

[142] *Idem, Among the Primitive Bakongo*, p. 231; cf. *idem*, "Notes on Some Customs of the Lower Congo People," *Folk-Lore*, XX (1909), 51 f. For further evidence see W. H. Bentley, *Pioneering on the Congo*, I, 273; G. C. Claridge, *op. cit.*, p. 173; J. J. Monteiro, *Angola and the River Congo* (London, 1875), I, 280 f.

[143] Herbert Passin, "Sorcery as a Phase of Tarahumara Economic Relations," *Man*, XLII (1942), 12 ff.

[144] William Morgan, *Human Wolves among the Navaho* (New Haven, 1936), pp. 39 f. *Yale University Publications in Anthropology*, No. 11.

[145] Elsie C. Parsons, "Witchcraft among the Pueblos: Indian or Spanish?" *Man*, XXVII (1927), 108.

[146] Mischa Titiev, "Notes on Hopi Witchcraft," *Papers of the Michigan Academy of Science, Arts, and Letters*, XXVIII (1942), 553, 556.

[147] Samuel Gason, in J. D. Woods (editor), *The Native Tribes of South Australia*, p. 275

[148] George Taplin, *ibid.*, p. 29.

[149] C. S. Myers, in *Reports of the Cambridge Anthropological Expedition to Torres Straits*, VI, 222, 225, on the authority of John Bruce.

[150] F. E. Williams, *Papuans of the Trans-Fly* (Oxford, 1936), pp. 252, 355 f. (Keraki); *idem*, in *Oceania*, XI (1941), 383 (Kutubu); J. W. M. Whiting, *op. cit.*, p. 219 (Kwoma).

[151] Bronislaw Malinowski, *op. cit.*, p. 86.

[152] H. I. Hogbin, "Sorcery and Administration," *Oceania*, VI (1935–36), 9 f.

[153] *Idem, Experiments in Civilization* (London, 1939), pp. 83, 87.

[154] *Idem, Law and Order in Polynesia* (London, 1934), pp. 220 ff.

[155] Martha Beckwith, *Hawaiian Mythology* (New Haven, 1940), p. 105.

[156] Elsdon Best, *The Maori* (Wellington, New Zealand, 1924), I, 327. *Memoirs of the Polynesian Society*, Vol. V.

[157] Edward Shortland, *Traditions and Superstitions of the New Zealanders* (2d ed., London, 1856), p. 116; *idem, Maori Religion and Mythology*, pp. 33 f. In West Africa masters hesitate to chastise slaves severely or inflict unmerited punishment on them from fear of their black magic, in which they are supposed to be particularly skillful. As a result, slaves are comparatively well treated. See J. L. Wilson, *Western Africa* (London, 1856), pp. 179, 271; Paul B. Du Chaillu, *Explorations and Adventures in Equatorial Africa*, p. 379.

[158] Monica Hunter, *op. cit.*, p. 311.

[159] H. A. Stayt, *op. cit.*, pp. 300 f.

[160] T. C. Young, *Notes on the Customs and Folk-Lore of the Tumbuka-Kamanga Peoples* (Livingstonia, South Africa, 1931), pp. 118 f.

[161] A. G. O. Hodgson, "Rain Making, Witchcraft, and Medicine among the Anyanja," *Man*, XXXI (1931), 268.

[162] G. G. Brown and A. McD. Bruce Hutt, *op. cit.*, p. 183.

163 Lucy P. Mair, *An African People in the Twentieth Century* (London, 1934), pp. 252 f.

164 C. R. Lagae, *Les Azande ou Niam-Niam* (Brussels, 1926), p. 105.

165 E. E. Evans-Pritchard, *op. cit.*, p. 117.

166 J. R. Wilson-Heffenden, *The Red Men of Nigeria* (London, 1930), p. 198.

167 John Gillin, *op. cit.*, p. 147.

168 Bryan Edwards, *History, Civil and Commercial, of the British West Indies* (5th ed., London, 1819), II, 107 ff.

169 Clyde Kluckhohn, *Navaho Witchcraft*, pp. 31 f., 64 f. *Papers of the Peabody Museum of American Archaeology and Ethnology*, Vol. XXII, No. 2.

170 Elsie C. Parsons, "Witchcraft among the Pueblos: Indian or Spanish?" *Man*, XXVII (1927), 107. "Why are the Pueblo Indians so pacific? Why do they not try even to defend themselves in quarrels? Because from their youth their elders have taught them that nobody can know the hearts of men. There are witches everywhere, and woe to him who has trouble with them" (Noël Dumarest, in *Memoirs of the American Anthropological Association*, No. 27 [Vol. VI, Pt. 3], p. 162).

171 Ann H. Gayton, "Yokuts-Mono Chiefs and Shamans," *University of California Publications in American Archaeology and Ethnology*, XXIV, 409.

172 W. L. Warner, *op. cit.*, p. 223.

173 F. E. Williams, *Orokaiva Magic*, p. 222; idem, *Papuans of the Trans-Fly*, p. 337 (Keraki).

174 R. F. Fortune, "Manus Religion," *Memoirs of the American Philosophical Society*, III (1935), 11. A magical, not animistic, diagnosis and treatment are also prescribed in cases of illness due to stealing from tabooed palm trees (p. 70).

175 Cora DuBois, *The People of Alor* (Minneapolis, 1944), p. 172.

176 I. H. N. Evans, *The Negritos of Malaya* (Cambridge, 1937), p. 209.

177 Georg Schweinfurth, *The Heart of Africa* (3d ed., London, 1878), I, 307.

178 Paul Schebesta, *Among Congo Pygmies* (London, 1933), pp. 163 f.; idem, *Revisiting My Pygmy Hosts* (London, 1936), pp. 196, 199.

179 Ruth Benedict, *Zuñi Mythology* (New York, 1935), I, xv, xvi. See also II, 110–63, "Tales of Conflicts with Witches."

180 Alice C. Fletcher and Francis La Flesche, in *Twenty-seventh Annual Report of the Bureau of American Ethnology*, pp. 583, 602.

181 Knud Rasmussen, *The Netsilik Eskimos* (Copenhagen, 1931), p. 299. *Report of the Fifth Thule Expedition*, Vol. VIII, Nos. 1–2.

Chapter XVI

THE BELIEF IN MAGIC

Almost everywhere primitive peoples hold firmly to the belief in magic and repose an implicit confidence in the occult powers of their magicians, both white and black. Of the southeastern tribes of Australia we are told that magic "mingles so intimately with the daily life of the aborigines that no one, not even those who practice deceit themselves, doubts the power of other medicine men, or that if men fail to effect their magical purposes the failure is due to error in the practice or to the superior skill or power of some adverse practitioner."[1] An Arunta "will often tell you that he can and does do something magical, whilst all the time he is perfectly well aware that he cannot and yet firmly believes that some other man can really do it. In order that his fellows may not be considered in this respect as superior to himself he is obliged to resort to what is really a fraud, but in course of time he may even come to lose sight of the fact that it is a fraud which he is practicing upon himself and his fellows."[2] A native of New Ireland sucks in the belief in magic with his mother's milk and only loses it with his last breath.[3] The "one subject" upon which all the Bantu-speaking peoples of South Africa are agreed is the reality of magic. No one "in his senses" dreams of doubting its tremendous power.[4] The Bakongo, declares an experienced missionary, move in a world where their thoughts and sentiments, words and actions, all have a magical background. One cannot disabuse their minds of magic, for with them it has taken on the appearance of a science, "in which contradictions and gaps are blurred to such an extent that they present nothing other than more or less obscure portions of a system. To this system they cling tenaciously as though in calm possession of the truth."[5]

As between white and black magic, it seems to be true that greater confidence is often placed in the latter than in the former. The Azande of the Anglo-Egyptian Sudan are never sure that their medicines for healing or to promote the growth of the crops will achieve the results aimed at, whereas those used against murderers and thieves are supposed to be very successful. They point out that people constantly die because of having been be-witched, that always magical efforts are made to avenge their deaths, and that it is very rare for such efforts to fail. When black magic is directed against a thief, the people can give instance after instance of stolen property being returned after the per-formance of the rite. They say that it is very foolish to steal and run the risk of dying from sorcery. When asked what proof can be adduced that thieves are so punished, they will reply, "There have been many thefts this year. There have also been many deaths from dysentery. It would seem that many debts have been settled through dysentery."⁶ A Navaho Indian is not inclined to scoff at black magic because the phenomena with which it is con-cerned are outside the realm of personal knowledge or experience. "There is always the fear that such things are true, and then the scoffers would be punished with sickness or ill luck."⁷

Occasional cases reveal a skeptical attitude toward the alleged power of the magician, and these are not always to be explained as the result of contact with unbelieving Europeans. In Victoria some aborigines "refuse to become doctors and disbelieve alto-gether the pretensions of those persons."⁸ A missionary in New Guinea often asked the natives, "Do you really believe the sor-cerer extracts stones and sticks from the body?" "No," they would answer, "but he says he does. The man (patient) is dying, and we don't know what to do."⁹ In the Nicobar Islands there is a very considerable amount of skepticism as to the professed powers of the magicians and a general unwillingness to join their ranks, in spite of the privileges which they enjoy. "Some who have been initiated refuse to practice, and will among their closest friends call it tomfoolery."¹⁰

In Africa skepticism seems to be most prevalent among chiefs and men of rank, who feel themselves comparatively exempt from the delusions of the multitude. A missionary reports the speech of a Basuto chief, who held forth in his presence as follows: "Sorcery only exists in the mouths of those who speak of it. It is no more in the power of man to kill his fellow by the mere effect of his will than it would be to raise him from the dead. This is my opinion. Nevertheless, you sorcerers who hear me speak, use moderation."¹¹ The celebrated Zulu ruler, Chaka or Tshaka, who early in the nineteenth century imposed an iron military rule over much of South Africa, put the witch doctors to a practical test. Secretly and by night he smeared blood over the ground in front of the royal hut—an act regarded with horror if committed by any member of the tribe. Next morning a great uproar arose, and all the witch doctors were summoned to discover the perpetrator of the outrage. One person after another was pointed out by them as the guilty party. But one doctor exclaimed that a greater power had done it, a statement which pleased Chaka and which he interpreted to mean himself. This doctor was not put to death. All the others were slain by their would-be victims on the king's orders. Ever after he would not have a man executed because of having been "smelled out" as a witch.[12] How King Nyadwai of the Shilluk (Anglo-Egyptian Sudan) unmasked the witch doctors is another instructive tale. He had a hole dug, wood put into it, and the wood set afire. The excavation was filled up with earth. He then ordered a quantity of beans to be cooked in his presence. Having assembled the witch doctors he said to them, "You children of chiefs, I do not know what this humming in the earth is" (meaning, however, the noise caused by the boiling beans). Then one of the magicians listened and declared that something was bewitching the village. Another listened and reached the same sage conclusion. Other doctors agreed with them. But finally a doctor discovered the cause of the humming and said, "Well, bring water." So the king gave orders to spare him but to kill all his colleagues.[13]

Many Azande will declare that the great majority of witch doctors are liars, solely concerned with getting rich. They say that what the doctors tell their audience is just "supposition," something put forward as a likely guess but not derived from the medicines eaten by them. This skepticism is not socially repressed. Though prevalent and increasing since the European conquest of the Sudan, it only accounts for the failures of particular doctors and leaves unimpaired the belief that some of them have wonderful powers as healers and diviners.[14] Before missionaries came to the Bangala of the Upper Congo many people had no faith in their magicians, but dared not oppose them for fear of being charged with witchcraft.[15] Among the Bakongo a man may believe or disbelieve in the powers of particular witch doctors; he may snub one of them and talk slightingly of his spells and charms; he may pass one by to call in a distant practitioner and suffer no inconvenience from his attitude. But he must profess a belief in witches or else his life will be made wretched by accusations that he is himself a witch.[16]

Some Chukchi are certainly aware of the deceit practiced by

shamans. Several people declared to a Russian investigator that the performances they had witnessed were mere trickery, made possible only by the operator's ability to produce illusions on the part of the spectators.[17]

If skepticism is rare among the laity, it is scarcely less rare among professionals. The magician may sometimes be doubtful as to his own powers; he seldom questions those attributed to other practitioners. To assume the contrary is to make of every medicine man or shaman a rationalistic freethinker far in advance of his age. We are often told that when a doctor is ill he will call in another doctor to treat him and that he will likewise employ the services of a colleague to treat a sick member of his family.[18] It is also significant that doctors sometimes treat themselves when sick and also perform their rites over sick members of their family.[19]

The general good faith of the medicine man and of the shaman would seem to be beyond question. His initiatory training for the practice of the magical art, with its privations, tortures, and mysterious, awe-inspiring experiences, tends in many cases to produce an indelible impression on his mind. He regards himself, henceforth, as more than a normal person, as one now really possessed of superhuman powers. This attitude will naturally be most pronounced when, as so often, the magician is of an excitable, nervous, more or less unbalanced disposition, verging, perhaps upon insanity. His hallucinations in a condition of ecstasy, whether spontaneous or induced, appear to him real; he sees spirits, converses with them, perhaps feels himself to be possessed by them. How easily, then, will he impose upon himself and afterward upon his fellows. The belief, already referred to, that his ability to operate as a magician will be lost if he proves to be unworthy of his calling or violates any taboos or other restrictions laid upon him affords the best evidence of the essential sincerity of his attitude.

The aborigines of southeastern Australia are firmly convinced that when asleep they can see and talk with the ancestral ghosts. This power is most frequently exercised by the magicians, who have "visions that are to them realities."[20] Magicians in the Solomon Islands apparently "believe without question" in the efficacy of the charms, formulas, and techniques which they have inherited and have been taught to use.[21]

The Subanun of Mindanao live in a world tenanted by spirits, with whom there is always the possibility of intercourse. This belief is constantly reinforced by dreams, ominous occurrences, and the strange shapes seen and strange sounds heard in the depths of the primeval forest. So a man comes easily to suppose that he has been selected by a spirit as a medium of communication, that he is, indeed, its authentic mouthpiece.[22] Magicians among the Orang Kubu of Sumatra receive their inspiration through dreams. Are they deceivers, it is asked. No, for these men are so simple-minded, so accustomed to ascribe occult qualities and powers to what they do not understand, that for them an extra-ordinary dream may be decisive of their call to the magical pro-fession.[23]

In Korea a *mutang,* or magician, is always a woman. She enters upon her office as the result of demoniacal possession. The spirit may seize any woman, maid or wife, rich or poor, patrician or plebeian, and compel her to serve it. Upon receiving the call she will leave home and family, breaking every tie that had united her to her fellows. Henceforth she becomes a social outcast and is not even allowed to live within city walls. Her services are in constant demand, however, and for them she receives an ample compensation.[24]

The *ajoka,* or shaman of the Lango, a Nilotic tribe of Uganda, is persuaded that his gifts of clairvoyance, hypnotism, and ven-triloquism are evidence of the interest which Jok, the high god, takes in him. Jok has thus marked him out from other men, and in exercising his gifts he is fulfilling the intention of the god. "That his ends are not selfish the modesty of his remuneration proves, but desiring eminence in his profession and a more than local reputation he enhances his natural gifts by a species of magi-cal symbolism, the bizarre mysticism of which tends not only to attract attention, but offers a safe retreat should his inspiration prove to have been at fault. His aim is not to deceive—for with but rare exceptions deceit would profit him nothing—but he sincerely believes that his pronouncements are the veritable words of Jok."[25]

West African witch doctors, declares Miss Kingsley, "believe in themselves, or perhaps it would be safer to say they believe in the theory they work by, for of that there can be very little doubt, I do not fancy they ever claim invincible power over disease; they do their best according to their lights. It would be difficult to see why they should doubt their own methods, because, remember, all their patients do not die; the majority recover."[26]

We should do an injustice to the Brazilian magicians if we

regarded them simply as impostors. They deceive themselves, as well as others.[27]

Among the Yuma Indians the spirit which a would-be doctor encounters in his dream remains faithful to him throughout life, advises him when to accept a patient, and gives him strength to effect a cure. When the doctor's mind is optimistic and vigorous, he knows that he has the right power; when his mind is reluctant and apathetic, he knows that he cannot succeed. It is said that he makes no use of sleight-of-hand or of other manipulatory actions, nor does he resort to conjuring of any sort. "The doctor has received a divine essence which flows into him from his guardian spirit and ultimately from the Creator himself. His duty is to transfer this power to the patient or use it to bring back his soul; any jugglery or physical demonstration is superfluous and inappropriate."[28] Of the Lillooet doctor in British Columbia it is said that his belief in the efficacy of his practices and in the power of his tutelary spirit to effect the cures which he undertakes "is as sincere as the belief of his more sophisticated brother in his trained professional skill and in his powerful drugs."[29]

Most shamans among the Central Eskimo believe in their performance, "as by continued shouting and invoking they fall into an ecstasy and really imagine they accomplish the flights and see the spirits."[30] It is probable that shamans of the Greenland Eskimo "partly believed in their own arts, and were even convinced that they sometimes received actual revelations."[31]

The evidence for the dissociated condition of Siberian shamans during their mantic rites seems to be incontrovertible. With those of the northern and central tribes it is brought about naturally by singing, dancing, and drumming and is characterized by a strong hysterical attack which ends with a cataleptic collapse. Further south, while young shamans often become dissociated in a natural way, there is more reliance on attaining this state by means of narcotics; again, it may be simply imitated in a realistic manner.[32]

The magician is, then, not a mere impostor, an arrant fraud. Imposture forms, nevertheless, a constant feature of his art. Trickery and deceit, the production of bizarre and astonishing effects by means of ventriloquism, prestidigitation, and conjuring in all its branches characterize the magical art everywhere. No doubt charlatanism grows by what it feeds on. The aspiring youth who started out with a profound respect for his vocation, believing himself in touch with unseen powers, their confidant and agent, haply may end as a disillusioned old veteran who knows his magic to be fraudulent but continues to practice it as an easy means of livelihood. No doubt, also, the more intelligent the magician the greater charlatan he will be. Sooner than his dumb-witted associates he will realize how easy it is to impose on the fears of the vulgar and cater to their appetite for marvels. "Indeed," said a missionary who labored for many years among the Paraguay Indians, "it is no difficult matter to cheat ignorant and credulous savages, who account every new thing which they have never seen before a prodigy, and immediately attribute it to magic art."[33]

Instances of conscious deceit are innumerable. A Papuan prophet announced, as the result of a communication from a spirit, that during the next full moon an earthquake, an eruption, and a tidal wave would destroy the coastal villages. This terrible upheaval was to be followed, apparently, by a millennial period when the people would have all the food they wanted without working for it. As a result of the prediction they killed and ate their pigs, together with all their available garden produce.[34] A number of Orokaiva villages (in Papua) once combined for a surprise attack on a distant settlement. The weather turned unusually cold, a circumstance which called for some discussion by the warriors. An explanation was soon forthcoming, however. One of the raiders declared that he had himself brought about the frigidity, with the idea of making the hostile villagers lie abed in the morning so that the surprise of the attack would be complete. As it turned out, the weather was so severe as seriously to diminish the enthusiasm of the attackers; nevertheless, this fact did not impair their belief in the efficacy of "cold magic."[35] At a Malay seance a shaman supposed to be possessed by a spirit while in a trance remembered court etiquette sufficiently to bow to members of the royal family; a toothless shaman asked why the betel nut had not been pounded, since the spirit inside him was stricken in years; another shaman, whose possessing spirit was of the female sex, arranged his costume to suit the part—to the amusement of the spectators.[36] We are told of a doctor among the Ao Naga who, on going into a trance as a part of his procedure to heal a patient, unfortunately selected a secluded corner of the house where fleas were swarming. Flesh and blood could not withstand the torment of their bites; the doctor simply had to interrupt his trance and scratch vigorously; and the seance came to an abrupt end.[37] In South Africa a female doctor of the

Fingo was once called upon to treat a man with a pain in his side. She sucked at the sore spot and produced some grains of Indian corn. Inspection of her mouth showed nothing there, but when she sucked again and again more grains of corn appeared. Finally, she spat out a piece of tobacco leaf, rolled up. The trick was now explained. She had swallowed the tobacco first, to produce nausea, and then a quantity of corn. By the help of a rope round her waist she could keep such a control over her stomach as only to bring up a few grains of corn at a time.[38] A missionary among the Lengua Indians of Paraguay was frequently asked by a magician to secure for him several packets of the smallest needles obtainable. "He was an ingenious fellow to have invented this new line of business, but our suspicions were aroused. What possible use could an Indian have for very small needles? These suspicions were strengthened when, shortly afterwards, a new epidemic, as it were, broke out among the people. 'Needles' became the fashionable disease. But we determined to stamp it out. The supply of needles was cut off, and as no more were obtainable the malady ceased, and the wizard's lucrative occupation with it."[39]

There was once a shaman among the Eskimo of Alaska who gathered the people together and told them that he wished to be burned alive. By submitting himself to this painful mode of death, he declared, he would be able to return in another form and be of still greater service to them. Accordingly, under the shaman's directions, a crib of drift logs was built waist high, with an open space in the center where he could stand. His hands and feet were bound and a large mask, covering both face and body, was put on him. He was then placed inside the crib, which his two assistants set afire. The smoke and flames made the interior of the crib somewhat indistinct, but the people could see the mask with the shaman apparently within it. They were then told to return to their homes and remain indoors until the next morning. After they had gone away, the assistants unbound the shaman and substituted for him a log of wood behind the mask. Next morning the shaman, who had hidden himself from everybody, suddenly made his appearance. Taking a couple of firebrands from the pyre he mounted the roof of the assembly house and sat down by the smoke hole. Over its cover he waved his firebrands, scattering sparks everywhere and at the same time moving his feet now here and now there. "He is walking in the air over the window," said the spectators. When the shaman felt satisfied that he had created a sensation he descended and returned to the people, who ever afterward held him to be a very great shaman indeed.[40]

The ingenious magician can usually offer a good excuse for the failure of his operations and his clients are usually ready to accept it. A doctor whose patient obstinately refuses to get better under his treatment may assert that he was called in too late, after the ailment had become impossible to cure. Or he may express profound regret that the patient did not consult some other doctor, since his own specialty did not include the ailment in question. Nothing is easier than to throw the blame for a miscarriage on the superior counter magic of a rival practitioner or on the intervention of a hostile spirit or god. Perhaps the magician may confess to a mistake in his performance, a slip of memory or the omission of some significant act, which has invalidated the whole proceedings. Perhaps he may assert that his client has neglected to observe a taboo or some other regulation imposed upon him. Almost always there is a sort of "saving clause," expressed or implied, to the effect that no witchcraft must be made, no persons ritually unclean must be near, and no other malefic influences must be present if his operations are to be crowned with success.

A missionary in northern Queensland once promised, in the presence of the whole camp of natives, to give their magician a bag of flour if he could make rain fall during the next twenty-four hours. It did not fall, however, and the magician explained that his failure was due to the missionary's presence at the performance. On other occasions failures were accounted for by the intrusion of natives on the forbidden spot where rain making rites were in progress.[41] Among the Wonkonguru of the Lake Eyre district the presence of the white man's cinematograph accounted for the failure of rain magic." "All time turn 'em handle too much wind, *pudney* rain."[42] An Orokaiva doctor who has attended a patient without success is likely to throw up the case, explaining that the sickness must have been caused by sorcery and hence incapable of being cured by the ordinary healing methods.[43] A Malay magician, who had the reputation of being able to raise a sandbank in the sea at will, was asked by a skeptical European to perform this feat. But our wonder worker explained that it could not be done for the sake of mere ostentation; he did it only in time of war when he was hard pressed by an enemy's boat.[44] When the Pondo go to a magician to make rain and it does not come, he tells them that it has been prevented from falling because of a broken taboo. Someone has not shown respect to the rain. Or

someone has hit a member of the rain maker's family. Or someone has shaken the rain off his clothing. Or someone has covered
his head when it rained. Then the taboo breaker must be fined by
the chief, and once the fine has been paid the rain will surely
come.[45] Among the Bechuana tribes a rain maker would send out
his clients to hunt and capture an animal of a certain color, usually
rather uncommon. He knew very well that they would be a long
time securing it and that he would thus have ample leisure to think
up a good excuse if meanwhile rain did not come after his rites.
When the people finally brought the animal to the rain maker, he
might reject it as being of the wrong color or defective in some
way. So the hunters would go off again in search of another
animal and the magician gained still more leeway for his efforts.[46]
The private diviner of the Basuto ruler once proposed to a missionary to make common cause with him. "He saw no end to the
advantages which would result, to both himself and me, from this
alliance. 'I cannot lie,' I answered, 'and lying is your trade.' 'We
do not lie,' he replied, 'but we are mistaken. When my predictions
are not realized, I say that all days are not alike, and they believe
me again.' "[47] Some of the Lower Congo people attributed a
drought to the fact that the missionaries wore a certain kind of
cap during religious services. "The missionaries showed the native princes their garden, that their cultivation was being ruined
for want of water, and asked if it was probable that they would
spoil their own crops. The natives remained unconvinced, and only
when the rains at length fell plentifully did the excitement subside."[48] A rain maker in northern Nigeria is rarely deposed, for
he can always assert that someone has committed sacrilege or
engaged in witchcraft, thus nullifying his efforts. An accusation
of this sort requires a lengthy investigation and atoning sacrifices.
The rain maker gets a week or a fortnight's grace, which is generally sufficient for the rains to occur.[49] In Ashanti a man who
procured from a magician a charm to secure invulnerability hast-
ened to put it to the proof, but received a gunshot wound in the
arm. The magician explained that the charm failed to work
because the man had had intercourse with his wife on a forbidden
day. He acknowledged that this was true and accepted the
explanation.[50]

By the primitive-minded, whether savage or civilized, a chronological sequence is regularly interpreted as a causal sequence;
hence the importance of coincidences in upholding and fostering
the belief in magic. Any rite, spell, or charm, the use of which

happens to be followed by success, will be considered the means of that success. A simple instance of the sort arrests the attention, is magnified with telling and retelling, and is enough to satisfy the credulous. But many instances to the contrary are often not enough to justify the skeptical.

While coincidences occur most frequently in the realm of physical phenomena, especially the production of rain, they are common enough elsewhere, and we can be sure that the magician makes full use of them to bolster his pretensions as a wonder worker. A missionary in Papua obtained from a famous Koita magician a parcel of crystals and also a large piece of clear quartz. The latter was a "death stone" upon which no one could look and live. A few weeks later the missionary suffered a very bad attack of fever, which, of course, all the natives ascribed to his possession of these dangerous objects.[51] A former governor of Papua once knew an exceptionally intelligent native who was supposed to have power "to cause death at will." Perhaps he really believed himself possessed of this power. At any rate he made good use of his reputation for deadliness. He would sit outside his house, and when anyone passed by, bearing food, money, or other valuables, he would say to that person, "You had better give me some." And this was always done, for fear of exciting the man's ill will. It happened one day that an old friend of the governor's came along and, being asked to give up money, refused point blank to do so. What happened? That very night his child died. Said he to the governor afterward, "You white people are quite right in thinking that there is a lot of nonsense about sorcery. But there is a kind of sorcery that is quite real and about which white people know nothing; it does not affect you, and you think that it does not exist, but it does, and we know it."[52]

In the island of Mala or Malaita, one of the Solomons, the people suffer from many tropical diseases as well as from diseases introduced by Europeans. These are not usually fatal, but a native is fortunate if he goes through the year without being confined to his bed for several weeks. For none of the ailments is there any known means of cure except by magic. It results, therefore, that curative magical rites are commonly followed, sooner or later, by the recovery of the patient, so that his restoration to health is assumed to be the direct consequence of their performance.[53]

The regalia of Malay sovereigns are highly sacrosanct. Great danger is supposed to be incurred by one who meddles with these insignia of royalty. Among the regalia of a Sultan of Selangor were two drums and a long silver trumpet. They were kept in a small, galvanized iron cupboard, which stood on posts in the lawn of His Highness' garden residence. They had previously been kept in the house, but their very uncanny behavior indoors was a source of much annoyance and anxiety to the inmates. Once one Raja Baka accidentally trod upon the wooden barrel of the drums and died in consequence of his inadvertence. A hornet's nest having been found inside one of these drums, a Chinese was ordered to remove it, since no Malay would do so. The Chinese, after a few days' interval, "swelled up and died." These happenings were related to our informant, Mr. Skeat, by the Sultan himself. Mr. Skeat, upon expressing a wish to examine the trumpet and drums, was begged not to do so. "No one could say what would happen." Nevertheless, he did see and even handle them in the presence of the Crown Prince. "I thought nothing more of the matter at the time, but, what was really a very curious coincidence, within a few days' time of the occurrence I was seized with a sharp attack of malarial influenza, the result of which was that I was obliged to leave the district, and go into hospital at headquarters." The news of what had happened much impressed the Malays.[54]

In the country of the Bongo, Anglo-Egyptian Sudan, the decayed and worm-eaten branch of a giant fig tree fell to the ground, narrowly missing a hut near by. The natives attributed its fall to the evil eye directed against it by a passing soldier. He had pointed to the bough and said that it was rotten and likely to topple any time on people's heads. No sooner said than done. Hardly were the words out of his mouth than, creaking and cracking, it tumbled down.[55]

An anthropologist, working among the Navaho, mentions several coincidences which strengthen the belief, even of sophisticated Indians, in magical causation. It is thought, for instance, that mistakes made in learning the Night Chant cause the learner to become paralyzed. A native who suffered from paralysis was popularly supposed to have paid the penalty for his failure as a memorizer of the ritual words. For the Navaho, eclipses portend bad luck. An eclipse of the sun in 1918 was followed by the worst epidemic of influenza that the people had ever experienced, and after the eclipse in 1925 there came a very severe winter during which much illness occurred and many cattle perished.[56]

At a dance of some Alaskan Eskimo a native gave two fox skins to a shaman, in return for the latter's promise that he would capture two whales the following whaling season. The man did get the two whales, just as the shaman had promised. This coincidence "somewhat strengthened at Point Barrow the general opinion that while Christian prayers are very good in ordinary things, the old-fashioned whaling charms are much more effective when it comes to catching whales."[57]

In curative rites and in the practice of the black art, suggestion on the part of the operator and faith on the part of the subject play the leading and sometimes the only role. His methods may be utter hocus-pocus, but they do actually produce the results aimed at—whether curing or killing. The doctor heals without the use of medicaments; the sorcerer causes a man's death without a resort to poison. In either case success depends on the antecedent belief of both operator and subject in the reality and effectiveness of magic, provided the right conditions obtain. Of magicians, generally, it may be said with truth, *Possunt quia posse videntur.*

Death madness, or thanatomania, as it has been called, is a phenomenon quite common in the lower culture. A man, tired of living, announces that he intends to die, lies down, refuses nourishment or medicines, and soon passes away quietly and easily. A man may die because he has violated some dread taboo or thinks that he has fallen into the clutch of malignant spirits, from whom death is the only escape. A doctor may pronounce him doomed, perhaps because his soul has gone away and cannot be recovered. The patient accepts the inevitable and proceeds to die without delay. Seldom need he apologize, as did the Merry Monarch, for taking an "unconscionable time" to do so.[58]

In a community where sorcery is held responsible for most accidents and misfortunes, a man is likely to die if he believes himself bewitched, especially when the practitioner of black magic is unknown, or, if known, refuses to relent and undo the evil work. The man may be strong and healthy; nevertheless he falls into a decline and soon expires. He does not consciously will himself to death, but, being profoundly convinced of the sorcerer's unlimited powers, he makes no effort to oppose the latter's authoritative will. There are many well-authenticated instances of thanatomania of this sort, instances for which no evidence exists of death being due to natural causes or to the administration of poison.[59]

In Queensland Mr. W. E. Roth knew personally of several cases where a sick man, believing that someone had pointed the bone at him, gave up hope and died. Roth's native servant, a mere layman, ventured to attack a doctor in this way; the man died about a fortnight later.[60] There is no doubt whatever, declare Messrs. Spencer and Gillen, that an aboriginal of Central Australia will die after the infliction of even the most superficial wound if only he believes that the weapon causing it has been "sung" and thus endued with *arunquiltha*, or evil occult power. Our authorities mention three cases of thanatomania which came under their observation.[61]

It is very easy for a Papuan to die. Let a sorcerer tell a man that he is doomed and he goes off into the bush, and soon expires.[62] A Kiwai sorcerer, if angry at a man, may say to him: "This is your last day; you will not see the sun rise tomorrow." The condemned man is sure to sicken and die unless some effective counter magic can be performed for him in time.[63] A Solomon Islander, lying sick, may get a message: "So-and-So has bewitched you; you will die in three days." And die he does.[64] A certain white settler in Fiji, being much incensed against a native, wished him dead in very emphatic language and added that he would die within the next twelve months. The poor fellow fretted so much that he died before the allotted time had passed.[65] In the Hawaiian Islands the "less enlightened people" think that no one dies a natural death. Every instance of mortality is ascribed to black magic or secret poisoning. A man who learns that he has fallen under a sorcerer's displeasure and that he has been "prayed to death" is almost certain to die.[66]

The effectiveness of Maori *makutu*, or sorcery, is (or was) very great. Let a native once be told that someone has bewitched him, and the suggestion, falling on ground already well prepared for it, will rapidly effect its object of killing him, unless another magician can interpose a counter suggestion.[67] "I once was at the deathbed of an old chief, who was supposed to be dying of typhoid, but the real cause of his death was fear. In some way he had offended another chief, and that man had him cursed by a *tohunga*, or priest. I was unable to ascertain exactly what he had done, but the result of it was that an image made of clay, which was supposed to represent him, was placed in a creek, and as the water washed away the figure, so the chief gradually sank; and when the last particle was softened by the slowly trickling water and vanished down the stream, so that moment the soul of the old chief passed over the border."[68]

A significant case of thanatomania is reported among the Ba-ila of Northern Rhodesia. "We remember a man—a big stalwart fellow, who never appeared to us of a cowardly nature—being greatly concerned because after returning home he found a string of beads, with a small black mass attached, hanging in his hut. Nobody could tell him who had put it there. It seemed to have sprung up out of the earth. The strangeness of it preyed on the man's mind. He had of course from childhood been accustomed to hearing about warlocks and their doings, and had never for a moment doubted their power. Now what was to him the awful truth took possession of his mind: somebody had put this in his hut to bewitch him. He was changed at once from a bright, laughing, cheerful being into a miserable creature. You could see him getting ill, and we believe that if we had not taken him in hand he would have died."[69] Canon Roscoe, long a missionary in British East Africa, tells how three men were once brought to him to have their wounds dressed. Two of them had been badly clawed by a leopard, but the third bore only a scratch on the neck. "I attended to him last and after dressing his wound I said, 'There is not much the matter with you; you will soon be well.' To my surprise he said, 'I am dying.' Thinking he had got an exaggerated idea of his wound, I talked to him for a few mòments and dismissed them all, telling them to come again in the morning. Next morning two of the men came, but the third with the scratch on his neck was missing, and when I asked for him I was told that he was dead. He had gone home and, saying that he had been killed by magic, died in a short time. So far as it was possible to discover, no complications had arisen, but he was convinced that the animal had been caused by magic to attack him and the power of his imagination had done the rest."[70] Major Leonard declares, "I have seen more than one hardened old Hausa soldier dying steadily and by inches, because he believed himself to be bewitched; so that no nourishment or medicines that were given to him had the slightest effect either to check the mischief or to improve his condition in any way, and nothing was able to divert him from a fate which he considered inevitable. In the same way, and under very similar conditions, I have seen Kru-men and others die, in spite of every effort made to save them."[71]

It is not too much to say of the Eskimo magicians in Baffin Land that through the "paramount psychic influence" which they exert they hold everybody's life in their hands. There was once a fully qualified practitioner, well known as being a sensual, self-indulgent man, who cast longing eyes on the attractive, half-breed wife of a certain hunter; the latter, however, refused to give her up. Now the hunter was somewhat unpopular in the village, for though amply provided with this world's goods he did not squander them on his lazy neighbors and also kept more or less to himself. It happened that a long season of bad weather set in, bringing the usual accompaniment of sickness and semistarvation. The magician could not remedy the situation by his arts, but excused himself on the ground that the spirits were incensed by the stingy, unsociable practices of the hunter. Only his death would satisfy the spirits and end the famine. The majority of the villagers agreed with this statement, whereupon the magician boldly faced the hunter and said, "I command you to die." The man was strong and healthy and in the prime of life. "But so ingrained was his belief in the conjuror, in his power to get into communication with the spirit world, that this command was virtually fatal." He gave up his occupations, withdrew to his tent, ate and drank very little, and within four days died. Friends had indeed visited him before the end, argued with him, laughed at him, tried in every way to disabuse his mind of its obsession, but all in vain. His sole response was, "I am commanded to die." The magician, of course, proceeded to acquire the victim's wife without delay.[72]

Thus the belief in magic, far from appearing unreasonable and illogical to those who hold it, seems to be confirmed over and over again by the experiences of daily life. The avowed objective of the magician is so often attained: he brings rain, quells a storm, cures the sick, or kills an enemy by performing his rites; at any rate, these results often follow their performance. How the results are secured does not interest the primitive-minded. Not for them a meticulous inquiry into the laws of chance, the power of the human imagination, and the psychology of suggestion. Let it be remembered, also, that the magician rarely attempts the impossible, such as rain making in the dry season; that he often relies on his practical knowledge and skill in cases where magic alone would be fruitless (e.g., he may be a good weather forecaster or a competent leech); that he is a master of trickery and deceit; and that if he fails he has a whole armory of excellent excuses to explain his failure. Let it be remembered, finally, that magic always enjoys the sanction of a hoary antiquity. It comes down from the remote past, the dream time, the Alcheringa, when the mythical ancestors of the tribe employed it and bequeathed it as their most precious legacy to the men of today. Magic has, therefore, the full support of tradition, and its acceptance by the individual is as natural and inevitable as that of any other ready-made pattern imposed upon the members of the social group.[73]

NOTES TO CHAPTER XVI

[1] A. W. Howitt, *The Native Tribes of South-East Australia* (London, 1904), p. 356. Cf. Lorimer Fison and A. W. Howitt, *Kamilaroi and Kurnai* (Melbourne, 1880), p. 251.

[2] Sir Baldwin Spencer and F. J. Gillen, *The Native Tribes of Central Australia* (London, 1899), p. 130. It takes a good deal, declare our authorities, to astonish an Australian aboriginal. "He is brought up on magic, and things that strike us with astonishment he regards as simply the exhibition of magic of greater power than any possessed by himself" (*iidem, Across Australia* [2d ed., London, 1912], I, 51 f.). The Eskimo are not usually impressed by the white man's ingenious devices and inventions. "The wonders of our science and the wildest tales of our own mythologies pale beside the marvels which the Eskimo suppose to be happening all around them every day at the behest of their magicians" (Vilhjalmur Stefansson, *My Life with the Eskimo* [New York, 1913], p. 184).

[3] Gerhard Peekel, *Religion und Zauberei auf dem mittleren Neu-Mecklenburg, Bismarck-Archipel, Südsee* (Münster in Westfalen, 1910), p. 1.

[4] Dudley Kidd, *The Essential Kafir* (2d ed., London, 1925), p. 139.

[5] J. Van Wing, "Bakongo Magic," *Journal of the Royal Anthropological Institute*, LXXI (1941), 96.

[6] E. E. Evans-Pritchard, *Witchcraft, Oracles and Magic among the Azande* (Oxford, 1937), pp. 466 f.

[7] Mrs. F. J. Newcomb, *Navajo Omens and Taboos* (Santa Fe, New Mexico, 1940), pp. 14 f.

[8] W. E. Stanbridge, in *Transactions of the Ethnological Society of London* (n.s., 1861), I, 300. The author lived for eighteen years in Victoria.

[9] C. W Abel, *Savage Life in New Guinea* (London, 1901), p. 100. "Sorcerer" in this quotation refers to a practicing doctor.

[10] George Whitehead, *In the Nicobar Islands* (London, 1924), pp. 147 f.

[11] E. Casalis, *The Basutos* (London, 1861), p. 275. Another Basuto chief, when paying the diviners for their services, did not hesitate to tell them that in his opinion they were "the biggest impostors" in the world (*idem, My Life in Basuto Land* [London, 1889], p. 185).

[12] W. H. Garbutt, "Native Witchcraft and Superstition in South Africa," *Journal of the Royal Anthropological Institute*, XXXIX (1909), 536.

[13] Diedrich Westermann, *The Shilluk People* (Philadelphia, 1912), pp. 175 f.

[14] E. E. Evans-Pritchard, *op. cit.*, pp. 183 ff., 193 f.

[15] J. H. Weeks, *Among Congo Cannibals* (London, 1913), p. 293.

[16] *Idem, Among the Primitive Bakongo* (London, 1914), pp. 284 f. "The village witch doctor is seldom, if ever, engaged by the natives of the village in which he lives. They know too much about him to waste their money on him. They see him repairing his charms and fetishes from the depredations of rats, cockroaches, and white ants; they know his fetish power and his charms are unable to keep him, his wives, his children, or even his goats, pigs, and dogs in good health; so they flout him and send for the medicine man of another village

of whom they know little or nothing. Therefore a faith in all witch doctors is not a necessary part of their creed" (loc cit.).

17 W. Bogoras, in Memoirs of the American Museum of Natural History, XI, 429.

18 See E. M. Curr, The Australian Race (Melbourne, 1886), I, 48 (Bangerang); Samuel Gason, in George Taplin (editor), The Folklore, Manners, Customs, and Languages of the South Australian Aborigines (Adelaide, 1879), p. 79 (Dieri); E. M. Loeb, "The Shaman of Niue," American Anthropologist, (n.s., 1924), XXVI, 395; E. H. Gomes, Seventeen Years among the Sea Dyaks of Borneo (London, 1911), p. 175; D. S. Oyler, "The Shilluk's Belief in the Good Medicine Men," Sudan Notes and Records, III (1920), 112; J. Van Wing, "Bakongo Magic," Journal of the Royal Anthropological Institute, LXXI (1941), 95; Theodor Koch-Grünberg, Vom Roroima zum Orinoco (Berlin, 1917–28), II, 199 and note 4 (Taulipáng and other Carib tribes); V. M. Mikhailovskii (Mikhailowski), "Shamanism in Siberia and European Russia," Journal of the Anthropological Institute, XXIV (1895), 139 (Buriat).

19 See Godfrey Dale, ibid., XXV (1896), 216 (Bondei of Tanganyika); E. E. Evans-Pritchard op. cit., p. 234 (Azande); W. H. Brett, The Indian Tribes of Guiana (London, 1868), p. 366; Leslie Spier, in Anthropological Papers of the American Museum of Natural History, XXIX, 280 (Havasupai); James Mooney and F. M. Olbrechts, "The Swimmer Manuscript. Cherokee Sacred Formulas and Medicinal Prescriptions," Bulletin of the Bureau of American Ethnology, No. 99, p. 93; Knud Rasmussen, The People of the Polar North (London, 1908), p. 156.

20 A. W. Howitt, op. cit., p. 89. Among the Arunta children born with their eyes open are believed to be able to converse with the ancestral ghosts (iruntarinia) upon arriving at maturity, provided always that they grow up modest and sedate in bearing. The iruntarinia do not reveal themselves to scoffers, the frivolous-minded, and chatterers. Children born with their eyes closed never acquire this power when they grow up unless they become medicine men (Spencer and Gillen, The Native Tribes of Central Australia, pp. 515 f.).

21 A. I. Hopkins, In the Isles of King Solomon (London, 1928), p. 206. The author lived for twenty-five years in the Solomons.

22 E. B. Christie, The Subanuns of Sindangan Bay (Manila, 1909), p. 72. Bureau of Science, Division of Ethnology Publications, Vol. VI, Pt. I.

23 Bernhard Hagen, Die Orang Kubu auf Sumatra (Frankfurt am Main, 1908), pp. 147 f., quoting A. G. Valette.

24 I. M. Casanowicz, "Paraphernalia of a Korean Sorceress in the United States National Museum," Proceedings of the U.S. National Museum, LI, 593.

25 J. H. Driberg, The Lango (London, 1923), p. 236.

26 Mary H. Kingsley, West African Studies (1st ed., London, 1899), pp. 217 f. The typical Yoruba diviner, we are told, believes in the art which he practices. He himself resorts to other diviners for advice and makes the sacrifices which they prescribe for him (W. R. Bascom, "The Sanctions of Ifa Divination," Journal of the Royal Anthropological Institute, LXXI [1941], 52). On the other hand, it is said of mediums among the Ga of the Gold Coast that their "fits" are a curious mixture of unrestraint and self-conscious behavior. There are few mediums unable to produce a convincing imitation fit if their audience demands it (Margaret J. Field, Religion and Medicine of the Ga People [Oxford, 1937], p. 103).

27 C. F. Ph. von Martius, Von dem Rechtszustande unter den Ureinwohnern Brasiliens (Munich, 1832), p. 30.

[28] C. D. Forde, in *University of California Publications in American Archaeology and Ethnology*, XXVIII, 182 f., 199.

[29] Charles Hill-Tout, in *Journal of the Anthropological Institute*, XXXV (1905), 144.

[30] Franz Boas, in *Sixth Annual Report of the Bureau of Ethnology*, p. 594. Rasmussen knew a young Iglulik of highly nervous temperament. When out alone on hunting expeditions he had many weird visions. His imagination peopled the whole world with spirit forms which appeared to him as soon as he lay down to sleep or while wandering, tired and hungry, in search of caribou. Though not averse to the use of trickery in order to convince others of the reality of his experiences, he seemed to believe sincerely in his shamanistic powers when he was worked up into an ecstatic condition. Thus we can understand, declares this excellent authority, how a shaman who habitually deceives his fellows may nevertheless continue to think of himself as being really honest with them. His trickery, in short, is only incidental to the practice of his profession. See Knud Rasmussen, *Intellectual Culture of the Hudson Bay Eskimos* (Copenhagen, 1930), pp. 42 ff. *Report of the Fifth Thule Expedition*, Vol. VII, No. 1.

[31] Fridtjof Nansen, *Eskimo Life* (2d ed., London, 1894), p. 282.

[32] Some Yakut shamans are "as passionately devoted to their calling as drunkards to drink." There was a shaman who several times had been condemned to punishment for practicing his art. His professional dress and drum had been burned, his hair had been cut off, and he had been compelled to make a number of obeisances and to fast. He said to a Polish investigator, "We do not carry on this calling without paying for it. Our masters [the spirits] keep a zealous watch over us, and woe betide us afterwards if we do not satisfy them! But we cannot quit it; we cannot cease to practice shaman rites. Yet we do no evil." (W. G. Sumner, "The Yakuts. Abridged from the Russian of Sieroshevski," *Journal of the Anthropological Institute*, XXXI [1901], 100). On the Lower Lena Stadling was told of a "good shaman" who struggled hard for three days and nights to expel the *ospa* (smallpox) from his people. He swooned away several times and finally died in the attempt. See J. Stadling, "Shamanism," *Contemporary Review*, LXXIX (1901), 94 and note.

[33] Martin Dobrizhoffer, *An Account of the Abipones* (London, 1822), II, 68.

[34] C. W. Abel, *op. cit.*, pp. 104 ff. Another instance of a magician's disastrous prediction is recorded for South Africa about 1857. It was announced that if the confederated tribes slaughtered their cattle, destroyed all their stored grain, and left the ground untilled the ancestors would return, drive the English settlers into the sea, and then provide every man with as many cattle and as much grain as he could want. The sign given for these great events was that on the morning succeeding the full moon the sun would rise double. The deluded people made a clean sweep of all their food supplies and passed the time in feasting and dancing, in expectation of the millennium (James Macdonald, "Manners, Customs, Superstitions, and Religions of South African Tribes," *Journal of the Anthropological Institute*, XIX [1890], 280 ff.)

[35] F. E. Williams, *Orokaiva Magic* (London, 1928), p. 197.

[36] Sir R. O. Winstedt, *Shaman, Saiva, and Sufi* (London, 1925), pp. 105 f.

[37] J. P. Mills, *The Ao Nagas* (London, 1926), p. 245.

[38] James Backhouse, *A Narrative of a Visit to the Mauritius and South Africa* (London, 1844), pp. 284 f.

[39] W. B. Grubb, *An Unknown People in an Unknown Land* (4th ed., London, 1914), pp. 153 f.

[40] E. W. Nelson, in *Eighteenth Annual Report of the Bureau of American Ethnology*, Part I, p. 434. Sometimes magicians acknowledge their duplicity, especially those who have become Christians. In the D'Entrecasteaux Islands a converted magician abandoned his doctoring and of his own accord stood up one Sunday in church and described his methods of healing. Some of the natives were very angry when they learned of the deceit which he had practiced upon them, "but it hardly shook their faith in the doctors who remained" (D. Jenness and A. Ballantyne, *The Northern D'Entrecasteaux* [Oxford, 1920], p. 140). A young woman in the Banks Islands had a reputation for healing toothache by means of a charm which had been taught her by an aged relative then deceased. She would lay a certain leaf upon the inflamed tooth and at the same time would mutter a spell. When in course of time the pain subsided, she would take out the leaf, unfold it, and show within it the little white maggot that had caused the trouble. "When Christian teaching began in the islands she made no difficulty about disclosing the secret, and all laughed over it together" (R. H. Codrington, *The Melanesians* [Oxford, 1891], p. 193). A Barolong rain maker, who had derived some benefit from a missionary's medicines and consequently regarded him as a magician and one of his own fraternity, said to him, "It is only wise men who can be rain makers, for it requires very great wisdom to deceive so many." And he added, "You and I know that" (Robert Moffat, *Missionary Labours and Scenes in Southern Africa* [London, 1842], p 314). The hereditary chief rain maker of the Bari confessed to an English officer that neither he nor any of his assistants really believed that they could make rain. But their fathers before them were supposed to possess this magical power and the people ascribed it also to them. "What, therefore, were they to do?" (F. Spire, "Rain Making in Equatorial Africa," *Journal of the African Society*, No. 17 [1905], 20). A Bangala sorcerer drove a spirit, or rather, an animal possessed by a spirit, into the corner of a hut, stabbed it there, and showed the blood upon his spear. His son afterward confessed to a missionary that the blood had been produced by the sorcerer's scratching his own gums. The semidarkness of a native hut makes it easy to carry out a trick of this kind (J. H. Weeks, *Among Congo Cannibals*, pp. 284 f.). A missionary among the Bakongo baptized a chief who had once been a vendor of charms and who for several years had vigorously pushed the sale of a new charm advertised as a wonderful protection against witchcraft. It won him quite a modest fortune, but, as he afterward acknowledged, he did not himself believe at all in its power. Nevertheless, in his unconverted state, he always carried about his person other charms to protect himself against the *ndoki*, the dreaded witches (J. Van Wing, "Bakongo Magic," *Journal of the Royal Anthropological Institute*, LXXI [1941], 95). Two Tinne medicine men who were held in great repute and who undoubtedly were intelligent men confessed on their deathbeds to a Catholic priest that they had never believed in their magical power and had long been anxious to get out of their awkward situation. They persevered in it, however. because of the fear of universal reproof had they given it up. "People, they alleged, would have considered them as mean and stingy fellows who refused to help the sufferers when they had the means to do so" (Julius Jetté, "On the Medicine Men of the Ten'a," *Journal of the Royal Anthropological Institute*, XXXVII [1907], 176 f.). Among the Copper Eskimo Rasmussen met a very intelligent young woman who had once practiced as a shaman but had given up the profession. As she frankly admitted, she "could not lie well enough." The other shamans had sought in vain to dissuade her, saying, "Once you start trying and people are listening, you can almost always hit upon something" (Knud Rasmussen, *Intellectual Culture of the Copper Eskimos* [Copenhagen, 1932], p. 30). *Report of the Fifth Thule Expedition*, Vol. IX. "There are many liars in our calling," declared a Chukchi shaman to a Russian investigator (W. Bogoras, in *Memoirs of the American Museum of Natural History*, XI, 429).

494   MAGIC: A SOCIOLOGICAL STUDY

W. E. Roth, *North Queensland Ethnography Bulletin*, No. 5, p. 9.
42 G. Horne and G. Aiston, *Savage Life in Central Australia* (London, 1924), p. 121.
43 F. E. Williams, *Orokaiva Society* (Oxford, 1930), pp. 293 f.
44 W. W. Skeat, *Malay Magic* (London, 1900), p. 60.
45 Monica Hunter, *Reaction to Conquest* (London, 1936), p. 82.
46 S. S. Dornan, "Rain Making in South Africa," *Bantu Studies*, III (1927–29), 189.
47 E. Casalis, *The Basutos*, p. 284.
48 R. C. Phillips, "The Lower Congo: a Sociological Study," *Journal of the Anthropological Institute*, XVII (1888), 220.
49 C. K. Meek, *The Northern Tribes of Nigeria* (Oxford, 1925), II, 68.
50 T. E. Bowdich, *Mission from Cape Coast Castle to Ashantee* (London. 1819), p. 439.
51 James Chalmers, *Pioneering in New Guinea* (2d ed., London, 1887), pp. 310, 317 f.
52 Sir J. H. P. (Hubert) Murray, *Papua of To-day* (London, 1925), pp. 69 f.
53 H. I. Hogbin, *Experiments in Civilization* (London, 1939), p. 87.
54 W. W. Skeat, *op. cit.,* pp. 41 f.

55 Georg Schweinwurth, *The Heart of Africa* (3d ed., London, 1878), II, 250.

56 Gladys A. Reichard, *Social Life of the Navajo Indians* (New York, 1928), pp. 152 ff.

57 Vilhjalmur Stefansson, *op. cit.,* pp. 88 f.

58 The Bakongo believe so implicitly in their witch doctor that when he declares a case of illness to be incurable and that the patient will die, this "invariably" happens. His friends begin at once to prepare for the funeral, dig a grave, and summon his relatives to the obsequies. See J. H. Weeks, *Among the Primitive Bakongo*, p. 217. For other instances of the doctor's fatal pronouncements see Charles Chewings, *Back in the Stone Age. The Natives of Central Australia* (Sydney, 1936), p. 68; J. Sieber, *Die Wute* (Berlin, 1925), p. 81 (Cameroons); G. Bolinder, *Die Indianer der tropischen Schneegebirge* (Stuttgart, 1925), p. 139 (Arhuaco-speaking Indians of Colombia).

59 Expressed in medical language, a persistent and profound emotional state, the result of uncontrollable fear on the part of the subject, is followed by a disastrous fall of blood pressure, ending in death. Lack of food and drink collaborates with the damaging emotional effects to induce the fatal outcome. See W. B. Cannon " 'Voodoo' Death," *American Anthropologist* (n.s., 1942), XLIV, 169–81.

60 W. E. Roth, *Ethnological Studies among the North-West-Central Queensland Aborigines* (Brisbane, 1897), p. 154; idem, *North Queensland Ethnography Bulletin*, No. 5, p. 28.

61 Spencer and Gillen, *The Native Tribes of Central Australia*, p. 537. Cf. F. J. Gillen, "Magic amongst the Natives of Central Australia," *Report of the Eighth Meeting of the Australasian Association for the Advancement of Science* (1900), p. 115. The case was reported by Professor E. C. Stirling of a robust man who was wounded in the fleshy part of the thigh by a spear that had been "sung." He died without the intervention of any surgical complication that could be detected. In another case, reported Dr. Gorrie, the post-mortem of a man who had died after bone pointing revealed no macrosocopic lesions in any organ. See J. B. Cleland, "Disease amongst the Australian Aborigines," *Journal*

of *Tropical Medicine and Hygiene*, XXXI (1928), 233 f. Herbert Basedow (*The Australian Aboriginal* [Adelaide, 1925], pp. 178 f.) describes vividly the pitiable state of a native who discovers that he is being or has been boned.

62 C. W. Abel, *op. cit.*, p. 101, referring to the tribes of southeastern Papua.

63 E. B. Riley, *Among Papuan Headhunters* (London, 1925), p. 280.

64 A. I. Hopkins, *op. cit.*, p. 208. Court proceedings against a sorcerer living in a village not far from Rabaul, New Britain, revealed a case of thanatomania as the result of a spell cast by him. See Caroline Mytinger, *Headhunting in the Solomon Islands around the Coral Sea* (New York, 1942), pp. 359–61.

65 Berthold Seemann, *Viti* (Cambridge, 1862), p. 190. According to the missionary, Thomas Williams, a Fijian who learns that black magic has been worked against him will lie down on his mat and die through fear (*Fiji and the Fijians* [3d ed., London, 1870], p. 210).

66 C. S. Stewart, *Journal of a Residence in the Sandwich Islands during the Years 1823, 1824, and 1825* (London, 1828), pp. 264 f.

67 S. P. Smith, "The 'Tohunga'-Maori," *Transactions and Proceedings of the New Zealand Institute*, XXXII (1899), 264. See also W. H. Goldie, "Maori Medical Lore," *ibid.*, XXXVII (1904), 77 ff.

68 E. W. Elkington, *The Savage South Seas* (London, 1907), pp. 49 f.

69 E. W. Smith and A. M. Dale, *The Ila-speaking Peoples of Northern Rhodesia* (London, 1920), II, 97 f.

70 John Roscoe, "Magic and Its Power," *Folk-Lore*, XXXIV (1923), 32 f. Roscoe also reports on excellent authority the case of a Sudanese soldier on Lake Albert who believed himself to be dying from a bone which another soldier had placed by magic in his throat. After the man's death no trace of anything in his throat could be found (*loc. cit.*).

71 A. G. Leonard, *The Lower Niger and Its Tribes* (London, 1906), p. 257. Leonard records in some detail the case of a young Ibo who lost two children, presumably by sorcery, and then himself died under the belief that he had been bewitched (p. 258).

72 J. W. Bilby, *Among Unknown Eskimo* (London, 1923), pp. 228 ff.

73 Hypnotism, which is suggestion raised to the *n*th degree, seems to be practiced at least occasionally by magicians. When successful in producing such phenomena as anesthesia and catalepsy it would undoubtedly confirm the belief in magic. But the evidence for it is both scanty and unsatisfactory in character. The Maori *tohunga* "certainly seem to have had the ability to make people believe that they had seen things which as a matter of fact did not exist. I have heard of numerous instances of this strange power, mesmerism or hypnotic suggestion or whatever it may be, and it has not yet been quite lost to the race" (James Cowan, *The Maoris of New Zealand* [Christchurch, New Zealand, 1910], p. 120. According to another authority the Maori were acquainted with "some form of hypnotism and telepathy." See S. P. Smith, "The Evils of 'Makutu' or Witchcraft," *Journal of the Polynesian Society*, XXX [1921], 172). Bavenda magicians possess "undoubted" hypnotic ability, "fostered by the ease with which the will of the hypnotist is imposed on the weaker minds of his hypercredulous clients" (H. A. Stayt, *The Bavenda* [London, 1931], p. 300). The Congo sorcerer, it is said, has often great powers of hypnotism over himself as well as other people. "He deludes himself quite as much as his fellow man or woman" (Sir H. H. Johnston, *George Grenfell and the Congo* [London, 1908], II, 659). In the Niger Delta many magicians are credited with the exercise of hypnotism, especially those of Fernando Po (P. A. Talbot, *Tribes of the Niger Delta* [London, 1932], pp. 138 f.). An American anthropologist, attending a Wichita dance, noticed a subject who offered unusual resistance to the magician's

efforts to hypnotize her. He waved a black handkerchief before her eyes and then an eagle's wing. After a struggle which lasted half an hour, during which time she trembled as if in agony and tried to brace herself to avoid falling, the woman finally collapsed in a rigid state, as other dancers had done (James Mooney, as reported in *American Anthropologist* [n.s., 1915], XVII, 623). This authority believed that an entire audience of Indians might be hypnotized during such a performance as the Ghost Dance, when the subjects became hysterical. At the Ghost Dance as found among the Arapaho and Cheyenne in 1890 he noticed that young women were usually first to be affected, then older women, and finally men. About three women to one man proved to be susceptible subjects. They seemed to be usually as strong and healthy as average members of the tribe. Not every leader in the Ghost Dance could put people in the hypnotic sleep, but anyone might try to do so if he felt that he possessed the necessary power. See James Mooney, "The Ghost Dance Religion," *Fourteenth Annual Report of the Bureau of American Ethnology*, Part II, pp. 923 ff.

Chapter XVII

THE ROLE OF MAGIC

Magic, both white and black, both beneficent and maleficent, presents itself as an inchoate, unorganized mass of beliefs and practices, traditional in character and uncontrolled by experience. Its only logic is that of assumed possibilities, and these are forever incapable of verification. The results of a magical operation, when not accounted for by mere coincidence, can always be explained as due to the effects of suggestion, aided by whatever real knowledge the magician happens to possess. Magic is necessarily barren, and as such it is for us a pseudo science. This note of futility it shares with all other erroneous beliefs and practices which wider knowledge of causation has at length dispelled.

As a pseudo science magic belongs to a realm where what happens often seems to be the result of pure chance or accident and where man's practical measures—his technical devices and processes—are never certain of fruition. Magic offers him a way of dealing with forces and phenomena that otherwise appear incapable of control or are believed to contain an element of mystic danger that must be removed or nullified. Thus the economic activities with which magic is chiefly concerned include hunting, fishing, gardening ("hoe cultivation"), cattle breeding, and the art of sailing, whereas such homely occupations as food collecting, fire making, the manufacture of utensils, and house building, whose outcome is regarded as completely within human capacity, are seldom attended by magical rites. A system of magic may be very extensive and woven into the fabric of society, but it is always no more than supplementary to the routines of everyday life.

Women of the Kimberley tribes in Western Australia use no magic, either in their foraging activities or in their ordinary domestic concerns.[1] In the Trobriands the most reliable method of fishing—that by the use of poison—has no magic whatever, whereas fishing with seine nets on the lagoon (a fitful pursuit) and the dangerous fishing for shark in the open sea are both associated with magical rites, in the latter case those of a public character. Again, the small canoes used for transport in the lagoon and the estuaries of creeks require no magic to be performed over them, but the larger boats employed in overseas expeditions must be made safe and speedy by magical rites. The processes of industrial manufacture are likewise unaided by magic, though it is sometimes resorted to for inspiration in artistic carving.[2] In Dobu Island, where success in life is success in magic, the spells used to produce pregnancy are "the one isolated instance" of magic being used to secure an effect which it is recognized may also occur naturally.[3] The Azande of the Anglo-Egyptian Sudan have no medicines to promote the growth of a large number of plants; about any of these plants they say "its medicine is in the earth alone." They also lack medicines associated with various crafts, such as the making of shields, baskets, pots, and drums, as well as hut building and thatching.[4]

The social utility of white magic seems to be, within limits, real and considerable. The magic worker acquires confidence in the happy issue of his undertakings, and confidence is a most excellent thing provided it leads to no slackening of one's efforts but rather intensifies them. In an unfavorable environment such as that of the island of Mala (Malaita) in the Solomons, where timber rots quickly in the hot, damp climate and where bad weather and insect pests so often combine to spoil the crops, the belief that by magical rites these obstacles can be overcome helps to put things right and supplies driving power for a people notoriously lazy and unthrifty.[5] When among the Bakgatla of the Bechuanaland Protectorate, a pastoral as well as an agricultural tribe, a persistent drought kills off the cattle from lack of water or forage, or when an epidemic breaks out and destroys the herds, the native falls back on magic to reinforce his efforts to cope with the calamity and restore him to hopefulness and equanimity.[6] So also with the evils, no less awful because so often imaginary, which for primitive thought invest the world. If these are not distinctly envisaged, one can learn about them by a resort to divination in its many varied forms and then take the proper measures to avoid or nullify them. If, on the other hand, they are known, "medicines" may be available as safeguards against them. In many ways the Vai magician (in Liberia), "calms the troubled soul and gives peace to him who is besieged on every hand by wicked, invisible, and malignant spirits."[7] "It is almost impossible," declares an observer of the Guiana tribes, "to overestimate the dreadful sense of constant and unavoidable danger in which the Indian would live, were it not for his trust in the protecting power of the 'peaiman'."[8]

White magic also serves in no slight degree as an integrating and organizing factor in primitive society. We have already seen how the "good" medicine man or shaman, in addition to his strictly magical functions and his activity in combating the machinations of sorcerers, often leads his group in the pursuits of both peace and war. When he is not the titular leader, he is usually at the right hand of the chief and not seldom the power behind the throne. In general, he is the trusted custodian of social regulations and taboos, the champion of everything old and therefore tried and tested, the sturdy upholder of the traditional ways. It is natural to find him the strongest opponent of missionary effort and the newfangled ideas and practices introduced by intercourse with Europeans. The witch doctor of the Bomvana (in Cape Colony) works to preserve the tribal customs. To him belongs the dread power of accusing of witchcraft those who flaunt them, and an accusation is usually followed by a verdict of guilty. Sometimes for good reason he sanctions a departure from time-honored observances. What he then orders to be done the people accept as necessary and beneficial, such is his influence over them.[9] The magician of the Bari tribes of the Anglo-Egyptian Sudan is undoubtedly a power making for social cohesion. Many of the ceremonies in which he takes a prominent part not only inspire confidence but help to maintain the unity of the family and of larger social groups.[10] The Bakongo magician is largely responsible for maintaining the continuity of native life. When baffled in curing a person he often ascribes his failure to a broken taboo or a slighted "country custom."[11]

The belief in black magic, we have already learned, may exert some influence in repressing antisocial attitudes and activities. The extensive use of sorcery to protect both communal and private property affords a further instance of a practice, harmful to those affected by it, but directed toward ends that can only be described as socially beneficent.

Magicians comprise the only leisure class in the lower culture, as well as a class distinguished by superior intellectual attainments. They are able, therefore, to devote time and ingenuity to inquiries whose practical outcome has sometimes been the increase of knowledge. The weather magician becomes something of a meteorologist; another magician studies the changing aspects of the heavens and forms the earliest calendars; another acquires a special familiarity with the ways of wild animals; still another learns about the properties of drugs and minerals. Their primary purpose is the acquisition of more magic to satisfy importunate clients, but real discoveries are made by them as a sort of by-product of their magical activities.

This development may be most clearly noted in the art of healing. Some primitive doctors are reported to possess a large stock of plants with undoubted medicinal properties. It seems highly probable that such plants or many of them were originally selected in accordance with the time-honored doctrine of "signatures," a fancied connection between their shape, color, or other characteristics and particular ailments being taken to indicate their value as medicines.[12] Their haphazard application would in time lead to the discovery that some of them really helped the patient; these would come into more and more use and at length take a recognized place in the pharmacopoeia.[13] Primitive medicine, however, is always deeply involved in magic. Azande doctors, for instance, know and use more than a thousand drugs derived from plants, but in treating sickness and disease they do not differentiate between drugs with a real therapeutic value and those without it; in other words, their leechcraft confounds techniques which we call empirical with those which we call magical. They themselves do not recognize any qualitative difference between the two categories.[14]

Where the belief in sorcery is rampant, this tends to impede or even prevent any advance in medical knowledge. Thus among the Congo tribes, by whom all sickness, or at least all serious sickness, is attributed to sorcery, it follows as a natural consequence that there is practically no knowledge of medicinal plants.[15] Similarly among the natives of South Africa "their universal belief in witchcraft has led to the almost entire neglect of the art of healing by medicines."[16]

It is well known that some therapeutic measures employed by primitive peoples afford real help to nature in her cures. Massage, cupping, blistering and cauterizing, fomentation, the vapor bath, emetics, and purges all find occasional use. They represent scientific procedures, real discoveries which have been hit upon, more or less accidentally, by the doctor in the course of his treatment. Here, again, magic is mingled with common sense. Some of the Queensland tribes, for example, treat snakebite by suction of the wound, cauterization, and ligatures "to stop the blood come up," but the magical services of a doctor are also required to make sure of the patient's recovery.[17]

The medicine man and the shaman were the first to discover the role which mental factors play in the treatment of various ailments. The doctor impresses his personality upon the very susceptible patient by his outlandish trappings, grotesque gestures, unintelligible utterances, and a "bedside manner" which radiates calm confidence in his ability to relieve or cure. As for the patient, he co-operates at every step with the doctor, confessing freely and at length any sins which may have been responsible for the visitation, submitting without a murmur to the treatment, however unpleasant or painful, and accepting cheerfully any burdensome restrictions laid upon him. In this connection the fact should be recalled that frequently the doctor will not treat a case which to his more or less experienced eyes appears hopeless or one for which the ordinary suggestive measures are inapplicable. No doubt conscious use of suggestion must be excluded from the doctor's treatment. In his own eyes, as in those of the patient, his success is entirely attributable to his occult power.[18]

There is good reason to believe that magic has had a not inconsiderable part in the early development of the fine arts. Engravings, paintings, and sculptures are often employed for magical purposes. This practice goes back to the cave men of the Stone Age, who sought through pictorial representations to gain control over the animals they hunted. The more realistic such representations the more occult power would be attributed to them. Curiously enough, a magical element is almost wholly lacking from the decorative art of the American Indians. The Latin word *carmen,* a spell and then a song, bears witness to the magic of sung or chanted speech. To describe something in words as accurately as possible is to influence it magically. With words the magician summons rabbits out of empty hats and spirits from the vasty deep. Rhythm, assonance, and rhyme, as these develop, reinforce the magical character of words. The constant use by medicine man and shaman of those primitive instruments, the drum and the rattle, testifies to the early association of music with magic. Dance and dramatic spectacle often represent wished-for events in nature and in human life, but it is difficult, if not impossible, to distinguish the occult potency ascribed to them from their purely secular use as an organized pastime. In various parts of the world games are played, especially by agricultural peoples, to promote the growth of the crops. However, the magical character of a performance can seldom be separated from its recreative aspects.[19]

More certainty attaches to the magical origin of many ornaments of both men and women in primitive communities. These seem to have been often worn for adornment only after having served as amulets against illness, sorcery, or other misfortunes or as talismans to bring good luck. It has been pointed out in the case of amulets how frequently they are worn at or near the various openings of the body, through which evil influences or evil spirits might enter or the soul escape or be drawn forth. Magical properties are still ascribed to various ornaments such as coral, amber, mother-of-pearl, and especially gems, whose medicinal and other virtues have been attributed to them in accordance with the doctrine of signatures.

The importance which the beliefs and practices of magic assume varies greatly from one cultural area to another. They are seldom completely absent anywhere, but some peoples are more "unsophisticated in superstition" than others. Thus divination as a developed art is far from universal. The Australian aborigines, for instance, know little about it and use it rarely. Its forms are also much less complicated and elaborate in America than in the Old World. We have already learned that black magic or sorcery is sometimes resorted to only occasionally, and the same holds true of white magic (other than divination) in more than one community.

The Murngin and surrounding tribes of Arnhem Land, Northern Territory, have a profound belief in magic as a power that can benefit and cure or harm and destroy. However, the northern clans of the Murngin lack magicians of any kind. Hence members of these clans must travel to the south or west for treatment by practitioners of white magic, though such visits are comparatively rare. When the clansmen believe that they have been bewitched by outsiders, there is no sorcerer among them to whom they can appeal for punitive measures against the offenders. "It is analogous to knowing the effects of heavy artillery but not possessing it."[20] The Mountain Arapesh, a Papuan tribe, make some use of spells and magical herbs, but these are so little regarded that fathers do not always trouble to teach their sons the magic which they know. Also, there is always present with the Arapesh the "comfortable belief" that a person without magic can probably get on just as well as a person with it.[21] The Sentani of Netherlands New Guinea are described as being poor in magical rites.[22] In Tikopia, an island included within the Melanesian area but an outpost of Polynesian culture, magic is completely absent. If it existed there formerly, the isolation of the island may have allowed it to become extinct.[23] Among the Kayan, Kenyah, Punan, and Sea Dayak (Iban) of Borneo magic is in a neglected and backward state, as also among some of the Klemantan tribes of the interior. However, some of the coastal Klemantan cultivate it assiduously.[24] Among the Semang of the Malay Peninsula, magic has nothing like the importance which it assumes among their non-Malay neighbors, the Sakai and Jakun.[25] The Chenchus, an aboriginal jungle people of Hyderabad, know no magical means to bring success in hunting or in collecting wild fruits and nuts, although these occupations have always been their chief reliance for a livelihood. Nor do they employ magic in connection with cattle breeding or with their sporadic efforts at raising millet and maize. Sorcery is only occasionally practiced, probably as the result of contacts with neighboring Hindus and Moslems, and divination is likewise but little used. In short, magic seems to have a very inconspicuous place in the cultural life of the Chenchus.[26] Magic plays a small part in the life of the Vedda. Among those natives who have not been much exposed to Singhalese influence it seems to be almost entirely lacking.[27] Apparently there is little that can properly be called magic among the Dinka of the Anglo-Egyptian Sudan.[28] Neither white magic nor black magic is prominent among the Bambute Pygmies of the Congo.[29] The Bachwa Pygmies are said to have adopted some magical beliefs and practices from the neighboring Nkundu Negroes, but only in a tentative way. They wear various kinds of charms around their wrists to bring good luck in hunting and to avert the spells of sorcerers.[30] Other scattered Pygmy groups in Africa are described as either unfamiliar with the use of charms or as using them sparingly.[31] Among the Polar Eskimo the magical art is not so highly developed as among the Eskimo on the east coast of Greenland, where the struggle for existence is bitter and never-ending. The Polar Eskimo, by contrast, are comparatively prosperous. Sea and land provide them with food in abundance and with reasonable certainty, so that periods of famine or semistarvation are unusual. They do not need, therefore, to resort constantly to magic or appeal to spiritual powers for alleviation of their lot.[32]

It is of interest to point out that among the primitive peoples little concerned with magic are some who rank very low in the scale of culture, including the Negritos of the Malay Peninsula

(Semang), the Vedda of Ceylon, the Chenchus of India, and the Pygmies of Africa. In New Guinea some tribes are described as being by no means magic-ridden. In aboriginal Australia, on the other hand, both white and black magic finds universal acceptance.

Magical beliefs and practices disappear but slowly under the impact of European culture introduced by missionaries, traders, and government officials. The aborigines of Queensland have still a firm faith in the efficacy of magic. "Even Christianized blacks cannot shake it off."[33] In spite of the fact that the islanders of Torres Straits have long since accepted Christian teaching, they perform occasionally their rain-making ceremonies.[34] In Dobu Island, where for forty years the missionaries have stoutly opposed the idea that without certain spells and rites no garden will bear, nevertheless these rites are deemed necessary and are never omitted.[35] In the Solomon Islands sorcery seems to be almost impossible of eradication. "The white man thinks it is rubbish," say the natives, "but we know it is true."[36] Of all the beliefs of the Fijians witchcraft exerts the strongest influence on their minds. "Men who laugh at the pretensions of the priest tremble at the power of the wizard; and those who become Christians lose this fear last of all the relics of their heathenism."[37] By the pre-European Maori few occupations could be properly undertaken without a magical accompaniment. Agriculture and fishing, in particular, were embedded in a setting of magic. Now that several generations have passed since the old beliefs were first challenged these have largely fallen into desuetude. Yet even now there are districts where much fishing magic is still practiced.[38] Among the Bechuana tribes, generally, sorcery continues to be dreaded and, in spite of education and other civilizing influences, to rank as an important factor in the life of the people.[39] Thus in the Bakgatla tribe "many a man who has long abandoned ancestor worship in favor of the Gospels, or perhaps never even known the old tribal cult, yet feels it necessary to have himself and his family, his huts, his cattle, and his fields, regularly 'doctored' to ensure good health and prosperity. The belief in sorcery is also vigorous."[40] After twenty-five years of evangelization among the Babemba of Northern Rhodesia the Christianized native still manifests an extraordinary fear of sorcerers and attributes most cases of sickness and death to their activity.[41] It was the considered opinion of a missionary authority that were the restraints against witchcraft introduced by European governments in West Africa to be removed the witch doctors, who are rarely converted to Christianity, would promptly re-establish themselves, along with the poison ordeal and execution of suspected witches.[42] By the Iroquois Indians magic is even yet accepted as something real and powerful. A very intelligent Indian, the "best Christian" whom our authority ever met among them, told her soberly of marvels he himself had wrought. "He had stayed the flames of a burning church by holding forth his right hand. He had lamed for life a man who was stealing cherries by pointing his finger at him. Few bad Indians came into his presence without begging him not to 'bewitch' them."[43] The Bellacoola of British Columbia, it is said, have not relinquished their belief in magic after a century of contact with white men.[44]

Religious and moral teaching, together with instruction in elementary science, may be counted upon, slowly but surely, to get rid of much white magic among primitive peoples, or to reduce it, as among ourselves, to pale and inconsequential survivals. Even the weapon of ridicule may be usefully employed to undermine faith in the efficacy of magic for rain making, garden growing, fishing, and the like. In Central Australia, for instance, the aborigines often have their magical notions shattered as the result of the contemptuous attitude toward them displayed by white settlers.[45]

To deal reasonably and justly with black magic in such areas as New Guinea, Melanesia, and Negro Africa, where to the natives it is a potent and dreadful reality, presents many difficulties for the European administrator. These are, indeed, a part of the much larger problem of the relations of the "higher" races to the "lower" throughout much of the world. In former days a person suspected of witchcraft was usually put to death by the outraged neighbors or by direction of the chief; now the white man's law punishes the slayers, who, according to native thought, have only performed their necessary and obvious duty. It is even made a penal offense to impute the practice of sorcery against anyone. From the native point of view the law, instead of repressing the black art, actually encourages it by removing all fear of punishment on the part of witches, who, consequently, tend to multiply their nefarious activities. Usually the more respectable and serious-minded members of a community have the greatest detestation of witches. They feel most deeply, therefore, the dilemma in which they are placed by the arrival of the European with his regulations which do not recognize the existence of witchcraft and punish murder only when there is the evidence of material facts to prove it. Furthermore, the witch doctor, who formerly performed his duty of "smelling out" witches openly and with popular sanction, is now driven to carry on his operations secretly or in holes and corners. To the native he is a public benefactor; in the eye of the law he is a criminal. The situation which thus arises was well stated in the complaint of a prominent magician of the Roro-speaking tribes to a governor of Papua: "If a man falls sick, his family come to me and ask me to make him well. If I don't do something for him they say, 'Tata Ko, the sorcerer, desires to kill our brother,' and they are angry and will perhaps try to kill me. If I do give them something they insist on paying me well for it; should I refuse to take their presents they would not understand it, and they would think I was trying to kill their friend, but when I do take what they give me, you arrest me on a charge of sorcery or blackmail."[46] So among the Pondo of South Africa the old men speak bitterly of how witches now work their will with impunity and bring much sickness to the land. In the good old days they were in terror of the law and consequently restrained themselves. "If the Government did not interfere there would be few people using familiars. The Government is not troubled itself, so does not care."[47]

It has been suggested that if the present penal laws relating to witchcraft are retained there should be coupled with them the provision of reservations to which people who have been duly "convicted," by their fellows, of practicing the black art could be exiled and allowed to live undisturbed. No doubt the "witches" themselves would welcome such an arrangement.[48] But before the sorcerer can be reduced to comparative impotence and with him the witch doctor, who under present conditions is really an indispensable functionary, it will be necessary to educate the belief in sorcery out of the people by giving them some insight into the real causes of sickness, death, and natural calamities.

Magic must rank among the greatest of man's delusions. In the presence of the unknown and the disconcerting the magician does not investigate critically, but is content with an explanation that appeals to his imagination. He builds an airy fabric of fancy and discovers in the external world sequences of cause and effect which are nonexistent. He thinks that he understands them and, self-reliant and imperturbable, would turn them to his own benefit. Thus an element of the capricious and the incalculable enters into all his activities. Considered in the large, magical beliefs and practices have operated to discourage intellectual acquisitiveness, to nourish vain hopes that can never be realized, and to substitute unreal for real achievement in the natural world. Between the methods of magic and the methods of science how impressive the contrast! The choice of one or the other has long confronted humanity.

NOTES TO CHAPTER XVII

[1] Phyllis M. Kaberry, *Aboriginal Woman, Sacred and Profane* (London, 1939), p. 17.

[2] Bronislaw Malinowski, *Coral Gardens and Their Magic* (London, 1935), I, 435, 444.

[3] R. F. Fortune, *Sorcerers of Dobu* (London, 1932), p. 241.

[4] E. E. Evans-Pritchard, *Witchcraft, Oracles, and Magic among the Azande* (Oxford, 1937), pp. 437 f.

[5] H. I. Hogbin, *Experiments in Civilization* (London, 1939), p. 87.

[6] I. Schapera, "Herding Rites of the Bechuanaland Bakxatla," *American Anthropologist* (n.s., 1934), XXXVI, 564 f.

[7] G. W. Ellis, *Negro Culture in West Africa* (New York, 1914), p. 122.

[8] Sir E. F. im Thurn, *Among the Indians of Guiana* (London, 1883), pp. 333 f.

[9] P. W. A. Cook, *Social Organization and Ceremonial Institutions of the Bomvana* (Cape Town and Johannesburg, 1931), p. 139.

[10] C. G. Seligman and Brenda Z. Seligman, *Pagan Tribes of the Nilotic Sudan* (London, 1932), p. 251.

[11] J. H. Weeks, *Among the Primitive Bakongo* (London, 1914), p. 231.

[12] The analogical element is very prominent in the materia medica of some primitive peoples. To cure spasms and twitching of the flesh, the Zulu make a medicine from a small beetle which curls up when handled and from plants which when touched fold their leaves. The medicine is swallowed and is also rubbed into the body through holes in the skin. To cure an effusion of blood through the nose or mouth, they take the bark of trees whose juice resembles blood and parts of an animal which has much blood or bleeds easily, mix these together, burn them into a powder, and then administer the remedy both internally and externally (Mrs. E. J. Krige, *The Social System of the Zulus* [London, 1936], p. 334). The Azande say, "We use such-and-such a plant because it is like such-and-such a thing." The ripe fruit of the *varuma,* round, velvety, and full of milky sap, has a resemblance to the breast of a woman who has just borne a child; hence its root is given to her in an infusion if she lacks an adequate supply of milk. The fruit of the *danga* resembles the human scrotum; it is therefore burnt so that its ashes may provide a cure for scrotal hernia and elephantiasis. The reddish patches conspicuous on the trunk of the *kunga* tree resemble the patches that appear in cutaneous leprosy; consequently the tree furnishes a remedy against this disease (E. E. Evans-Pritchard, *op. cit.,* pp. 449 f.).

[13] An anthropologist who worked among the Queensland aborigines found them using more than forty plants, some of which had undoubted remedial virtue (W. E. Roth, *North Queensland Ethnography Bulletin,* No. 5, pp. 38 ff.). A comparison between the Cherokee pharmacopoeia and the United States Dispensatory revealed that of twenty remedies investigated five had pronounced therapeutic value, while three more were possibly valuable (James Mooney, "Sacred Formu-

las of the Cherokees," *Seventh Annual Report of the Bureau of Ethnology*, pp. 323 ff.). It has been pointed out that Indian medicine men first discovered the virtues of coca, sarsaparilla, jalop, cinchona, and guiacum (J. G. Bourke, "The Medicine Men of the Apache," *Ninth Annual Report*, p. 471).

[14] E. E. Evans-Pritchard, *op. cit.*, pp. 482, 492, 504.

[15] W. H. Bentley, *Pioneering on the Congo* (London, 1900), I, 264.

[16] John Maclean, *A Compendium of Kafir Laws and Customs* (Mount Coke, South Africa, 1858), p. 88.

[17] W. E. Roth, *Ethnological Studies among the North-West-Central Queensland Aborigines* (Brisbane, 1897), p. 161; *idem, North Queensland Ethnography Bulletin*, No. 5, p. 42.

[18] A very competent medical authority describes a case of suggestion which came under his observation while in Nigeria. It concerned a Cross River man who had been treated for three weeks at the Native Hospital in Old Calabar. The crisis had long passed, the physical signs of illness were clearing up, and by ordinary rules the man should have improved daily. On the contrary, he got worse, and his death seemed inevitable. At the last moment our authority sent for the patient's own doctor, who arrived when the man seemed moribund. The two recognized each other, however. The doctor then carried out his ritual, burned an evil-smelling "incense," and sang a low chant to which the patient now and again made a feeble response. Gradually his pulse, from an intermittent flicker, steadied to a regular beat; he got better rapidly, and by the end of the day he was out of danger. The doctor, declining a fee, then took his way homeward (R. A. Bennett, *"Suggestion" and Common Sense* [London, 1922], pp. 31 f.).

The Chickasaw Indians sometimes use group suggestion for curative purposes. A fire is lighted before the main doorway of the patient's house (the doorway being always toward the good-luck direction) and little canes, adorned with ribbons, images, and other objects properly conjured by the doctor, are stuck in the ground near the fire. Then the sick man's friends and acquaintances assemble and dance between the fire and the house, while he himself sits in the doorway and watches the proceedings. The vigorous actions of the dancers are supposed to energize him and "drive away" his malady (J. R. Swanton, "The Subjective Element in Magic," *Journal of the Washington Academy of Sciences*, XVI [1926], 197).

[19] On the magical aspect of games see Gunnar Landtman, *The Kiwai Papuans of British New Guinea* (London, 1927), pp. 78 f.; C. Keysser, in R. Neuhauss, *Deutsch Neu-Guinea* (Berlin, 1911), III, 125 f. (Kai); N. Adriani and A. C. Kruijt, *De Bare'e-sprekende Toradja's van Midden-Celebes* (Batavia, 1912–14), II, 248 f.; A. W. Nieuwenhuis, *Quer durch Borneo* (Leiden, 1904–1907), I, 167 ff., 322 ff. (Kayan); J. H. Hutton, *The Sema Nagas* (London, 1921), 106; P. A. Talbot, *The Peoples of Southern Nigeria* (London, 1926), III, 816; Franz Boas, in *Bulletin of the American Museum of Natural History*, XV (1901), 151, 161 (Eskimo). See also Stewart Culin, "Games of the North American Indians," *Twenty-fourth Annual Report of the Bureau of American Ethnology*, p. 809.

[20] W. L. Warner, *A Black Civilization* (New York, 1937), pp. 193, 223.

[21] Margaret Mead, in *Anthropological Papers of the American Museum of Natural History*, XXXVII, 343, 448.

[22] Paul Wirz, in *Tijdschrift voor Indische Taal-Land-en Volkenkunde*, LXIII (1923), 38.

[23] W. H. R. Rivers, *The History of Melanesian Society* (Cambridge, 1914), II, 407, 420.

24 Charles Hose and William McDougall, *The Pagan Tribes of Borneo* (London, 1912), II, 114; Charles Hose, *Natural Man* (London, 1926), p. 249.

25 W. W. Skeat and C. O. Blagden, *Pagan Races of the Malay Peninsula* (London, 1906), I, 340; II, 120 f.

26 Christoph von Fürer-Haimendorf, *T̞he Chenchus* (London, 1943), pp. 198 ff.

27 C. G. Seligman and Brenda Z. Seligman, *The Veddas* (Cambridge, 1911), p. 190.

28 *Iidem, Pagan Tribes of the Nilotic Sudan*, p. 194.

29 Paul Schebesta, *Among Congo Pygmies* (London, 1933), pp. 163 f. However, in a later work Father Schebesta declares that the Bambute are more addicted to "superstition and magic" than he had formerly supposed (*Revisiting My Pygmy Hosts* [London, 1936], p. 187).

30 *Idem, My Pygmy and Negro Hosts* (London, 1936), pp. 236, 240.

31 Alexandre Le Roy, *Les pygmées* (Paris, 1928), pp. 180 f. (Bonis, Kenya); 184, 187 (Beku and Ajongo, Gabun); 188 (San, South Africa).

32 Knud Rasmussen, *The People of the Polar North* (London, 1908), pp. 156 f.

33 John Mathew, *Two Representative Tribes of Queensland* (London, 1910), p. 173.

34 A. C. Haddon, in *Reports of the Cambridge Anthropological Expedition to Torres Straits*, VI, 200 f. (eastern islands).

35 R. F. Fortune, *op. cit.*, p. 106.

36 Beatrice Blackwood, *Both Sides of Buka Passage* (Oxford, 1935), p. 482 (Bougainville and Buka). However, in the island of Mala or Malaita the precautions against sorcery are now being given up by young people who have become Christians. They do not take the slightest care to dispose of their food leavings, even when in the presence of heathen folk who are strangers to them. Acceptance of Christianity, they believe, renders a person invulnerable to sorcery (H. I. Hogbin, *op. cit.*, p. 217).

37 Thomas Williams, *Fiji and the Fijians* (3d ed., London, 1870), p. 209. Cf. Sir B. H. Thomson, *The Fijians* (London, 1908), p. 164.

38 H. B. Hawthorn, "The Maori: a Study in Acculturation," *Memoirs of the American Anthropological Association*, No. 64, pp. 58, 65, 70, 82. The belief in the power of *makutu* (witchcraft) is likewise by no means extinct. A collector of Maori tales and traditions once had a charge of *makutu* laid against him, "and things were very warm for a while." This was in 1895. See Herries Beattie, *Tikao Talks* (Dunedin, New Zealand, 1939), p. 93.

39 I. Schapera, *A Handbook of Tswana Law and Custom* (London, 1938), pp. 275 f.

40 *Idem, Married Life in an African Tribe* (London, 1941), p. 35. Cf. *idem,* "Cattle Magic and Medicines of the Bechuanaland Bakxatla," *South African Journal of Science*, XXVII (1930), 557.

41 Ed. Labrecque, "La sorcellerie chez les Babemba," *Anthropos*, XXXIII (1938), 265.

42 R. H. Nassau, *Fetichism in West Africa* (New York, 1904), pp. 124, 133, 241.

43 Mrs. Erminnie A. Smith, "Myths of the Iroquois," *Second Annual Report of the Bureau of Ethnology*, p. 68.

44 H. I. Smith, "Sympathetic Magic and Witchcraft among the Bellacoola," *American Anthropologist* (n.s., 1925), XXVII, 116.

[45] Charles Chewings, *Back in the Stone Age. The Natives of Central Australia* (Sydney, 1936), p. 151.

[46] C. G. Seligman, *The Melanesians of British New Guinea* (Cambridge, 1910), p. 280. Some Arapesh village officials, resident near Wiwiak, actually indicted certain murderous sorcerers before an Australian magistrate. The culprits, though convicted, received only brief terms of imprisonment. See R. F. Fortune, "Law and Force in Papuan Societies," *American Anthropologist,* XLIX (n.s., 1947), 250 ff.

[47] Monica Hunter, *Reaction to Conquest* (London, 1936), p. 275.

[48] F. H. Melland, *In Witch-bound Africa* (London, 1923), p. 198.

INDEX

Ababua of the Belgian Congo, 17
Abipones of Paraguay and Argentina, 190, 248, 264
Abyssinia, 118, 161
Achinese of Sumatra, 27, 436, 437
Acholi of Uganda, 292
Achomawi of California, 23, 159
Acoma Pueblo, Indians of, 268
Admiralty Islands, Manus of, 216, 263, 302, 463, 473
Agaria of central India, 177
Agni of French West Africa, 330
Ainu of Japan, 9, 178
Ajok, high god of the Lotuko, 31, 32
Akamba of Kenya, 15, 31, 94, 107, 108, 131, 144, 154, 157, 158, 173, 183, 185, 189, 217, 269, 375, 386
Akawai of British Guiana, 386
Akikuyu of Kenya, 15, 31, 52, 76, 88, 89, 108, 135, 138, 144, 146, 154, 156, 157, 164, 166, 175, 183, 205, 245, 332, 333, 393
Alcheringa, remote legendary era of Central Australians, 39, 222, 310, 489
Aleuts of the Aleutian Islands, 191
Alfuro of Celebes and the Moluccas, 152, 153
Alor, island of, 349, 403, 404, 464
Amboina, island of, 153
Ambryn, island of, 152, 215
Amhara of Abyssinia, 118
Ammassilik Eskimo, 99, 100
Amulets, 121
Andaman Islands, 11, 126, 147, 158, 169, 173, 185, 189, 204, 230, 263, 290, 308, 451, 470
angakok, Eskimo magician, 191, 213, 214, 227, 231, 232, 246, 266, 271, 284, 285, 300, 330, 331, 379, 380, 388
Angas of Nigeria, 52, 53
Anglo-Egyptian Sudan, *see* Anuak, Azande, Bari, Bongo, Dinka, Jur, Lotuko, Nuer, Obbo, Shilluk
Angola, *see* Atxuabo, Mbali, Ovimbundu
Angoni of Nyasaland and Northern Rhodesia, 280, 281, 456, 457

Animals, "helpers" and "familiars" of magicians, 215; transformation of magicians into, 246–50, 271, 272, 273, 402, 403, 409, 412, 413, 414, 415, 425, 427; magically multiplied, 318–21, 340; controlled by sorcerers and become agents of evil, 388–91
Animism and magic, 38, 39, 53–55
Annam, 10, 11
Antaimorona of Madagascar, 269
Antambahoaka of Madagascar, 243
Anuak of the Anglo-Egyptian Sudan, 108, 109
Anula of the Northern Territory of Australia, 160, 174, 465
Anyanja of Nyasaland, 14, 244, 407, 437, 438, 447, 461
Apache Indians, 23, 141, 147, 159, 174, 183, 186, 190, 206, 218, 230, 245, 265, 283, 295
Apinayé of Brazil, 185, 190, 205, 206, 230, 377
Arabia, Rwala Bedouin of, 155
Arapaho Indians, 68, 136, 186, 193, 197, 207, 208, 220, 496
Arapesh of Northeast New Guinea, 98, 116, 178, 369, 374, 434, 435, 502, 510
Araucanians of Chile, 155, 159, 185, 190, 192, 248, 272, 282, 299, 429, 430, 452
Arawak of Guiana, 43, 350, 360, 361
Arecuna of Venezuela, 43, 362, 363
Argentina, *see* Abipones, Chané
Arhuaco-speaking Indians of Colombia, 190, 303, 494
arungquiltha, conception of, among the Arunta and other Central Australian tribes, 3, 4, 26, 27, 328, 487
Arunta of the Northern Territory of Australia, 3, 4, 73, 74, 96, 123, 124, 126, 132, 133, 141, 160, 180, 184, 187, 203, 204, 222, 237, 262, 288, 306, 307, 310, 319, 320, 328, 340, 357, 368, 369, 371, 373, 383, 417, 418, 431, 452, 474, 491
Ashanti, 375, 483
Ashluslay of Bolivia, 303

511